Ruined by a gambling [...]
New Orleans, Laurel [...]
Rafe King's offer o[...]
accompanies him to h[...] where
she is to care for his troublesome daughter.

Once there, Laurel begins to untangle the secrets of
Rafe's past—including his mysterious dead wife,
Hélène. And as she does so, she falls in love with
the enigmatic master of Moonrise, even though it
becomes increasingly apparent that he will never be
able to love her . . .

Master of Moonrise
Hazel Smith

MILLS & BOON LIMITED
15–16 BROOK'S MEWS
LONDON W1A 1DR

First published in Great Britain 1984
by Mills & Boon Limited

© Hazel Smith 1984

Australian copyright 1984
Philippine copyright 1984
This edition 1984

ISBN 0 263 74882 0

Set in 11 on 12 pt Linotron Times
04–1084–52,000

Photoset by Rowland Phototypesetting Ltd
Bury St Edmunds, Suffolk
Made and printed in Great Britain by
Cox and Wyman Ltd, Reading

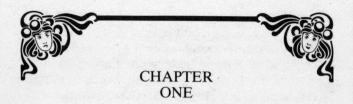

CHAPTER ONE

THERE was a taut expectancy in the room as the tall, white-haired man glanced at the last upcard dealt him; it showed the King of Hearts. Slender white fingers touched the short moustache as he hesitated a second, then murmured, 'And two.'

A narrow smile curved the lips of the third man at the table, echoing the murmur that went around the room. There were no chips on the green baize, no currency of any kind, yet each person in that cigar-clouded room knew that a bet had been made of a further two hundred dollars, raising the pot to almost five thousand.

The man from Texas folded. 'Too rich for me,' he confessed ruefully and rose to pour himself a generous three fingers of Bourbon from one of the bottles on the well-stocked table against the far wall.

'And so we are alone again,' smiled the swarthy young man in the midnight blue lounge jacket. 'I'll see you, of course.' His cool professionalism was apparent in the calm, still features and the steady fingers clasped loosely on the table before him.

His opponent returned the smile. 'Of course . . . but I believe that this time it is my game, M'sieu Castille,' and there was an undeniable note of triumph in his voice as he revealed his ace-in-the-hole, an Ace of Diamonds that joined the three showing. 'Four of a kind.'

The young Creole rose with fluid grace and gave a short bow. 'Your game indeed, M'sieu Faversham. You are a more than worthy opponent and may I say one of the best poker-players it has been my fortune . . . or in this case *mis*-fortune, to meet. May I look forward to a return game tomorrow?'

Wallace Faversham accepted his winnings, and took a glass of brandy from a silver tray offered by a lovely octoroon girl. 'The least I can do, sir.'

'And perhaps we may again have the honour of your daughter's company?'

Attention focused, not for the first time that afternoon, on the slender flaxen-haired girl in the pale blue gown of ottoman silk who had sat, as if carved from ivory, on the chaise-longue. The incredible woodsmoke eyes seemed to eclipse her fine-drawn features, and during the whole game they had not left her father's face. Now they swung to the aristocratic Creole, and she gave a slight nod. 'I always accompany my father.'

Her voice was low and slightly husky, and Philippe Castille felt his pulse beat a fraction faster—as it had almost every afternoon for the past month when the couple had arrived in New Orleans from London. The Creole was accustomed to beautiful women about him; indeed the octoroons of New Orleans were world-famous for their beauty, but not one had the obvious breeding and unconscious grace of the ethereal Laurel Faversham. She lifted the fur-tipped pelisse, and the Texan leapt forward to settle it about her shoulders with a clumsy 'Allow me, ma'am.'

'Thank you, Mr Ellis. I am so sorry you had to lose.'

He blushed at the small compliment of her re-membering his name, pulling at his collar with range-roughened fingers. 'Shucks, ain't nuthin', ma'am . . . a few head of beef, is all.'

Philippe Castille appeared at her side, lifting her fingers to his lips in farewell. '*A demain*, Mam'selle Faversham.'

'Until tomorrow, M'sieu Castille,' she echoed, with a coolness in her tone that had been absent in her words to the man from Texas.

'Do I not warrant your sympathy as a loser?'

The wide grey eyes regarded him speculatively and he felt a churning hunger in his stomach. What would he not give for a few hours alone with her! He would melt that ice and awaken the dormant volcano that he was sure lay beneath. Very quietly she said, 'I have no sympathy for professional gamblers, m'sieu. They ride an unbroken horse down a mountain and disdain the reins. It is an exhilarating ride, but the end is quite inevitable, is it not?' Then, turning deliberately away from him, she took her father's arm. 'Will you take me to see the paddle-wheelers come in before we return to the hotel—there may be someone from England?'

The room forgotten, and conversing lightly, they left.

'*La personnification de la fragilité et de la beauté*,' murmured the Creole. '*Mais quel sang-froid!*'

Had he seen her later that evening, however, he might have revised some of his ideas about her fragility and icy composure, but the heart, which many said he lacked, would undoubtedly have beaten faster.

Laurel faced her father, the long-lashed eyes flashing fire, the ivory cheeks rose-tinted as she hurled a pearly necklace to the floor, followed by a garnet brooch, diamond pendant and silver bracelet. 'Take them! Take them!' she cried, her voice low, yet quivering with fury as she emptied the contents of the silver jewel-box at his feet. 'You will lose them tomorrow—or the next day—so take them now.'

'Laurel, my dear . . .' he placated, raising his hand in a simple gesture.

'I'm *not* your dear: I'm your chaperon, even your jailer, am I not? I'm the conscience you don't have and the banker you sorely need.'

'Did I not win this afternoon?'

'Yes; you recovered almost five thousand of the fifteen thousand we have lost since we arrived. Papa, you're a fool!'

His frown was belied by the twinkle in his eyes as he confronted her anger with a knowledge born of long experience. 'Laurel Faversham, whatever your thoughts on the matter, a good daughter does not call her father a fool. Only your mother when she was alive could call me a fool—and then only because she loved me enough to not mean it!'

'Oh, Papa!' Laurel choked, mid-way between laughter and tears, and quite unable to sustain her anger for long. 'I love you too; but this endless travelling, this endless succession of gaming-rooms and ridottos in every capital in Europe and now here . . . it has no future, no stability. Only last year we played through Her beloved Majesty's Diamond Jubilee, and I would so loved to have seen the splendid uniforms of the Indian cavalry that escorted the royal landau. We went to none of the firework displays—unless you count those that I could see from Lord Duckham's window! We saw the bunting along Oxford Street only because that ancient cab-driver lost his way. Then what of the year before? Paris—the greatest couture shops in Europe—Worth and Doucet along the Rue de la Paix. When Amélie Guillo asked me to drive there with her, as everyone does between four and five before taking tea, you remarked that you had a game arranged for then and I was to go ahead and enjoy myself . . . as if I could have! We've been to Madrid and not attended a single bullfight, Athens and barely glimpsed the Acropolis and . . . and I haven't even learned tennis or ridden in a horseless carriage!'

He came to her then, treading carefully over the scattered jewellery, to gather her mutinously rigid frame into his arms. 'Laurel! Laurel! Come, my White Rose; don't hide your sweetness behind those thorns.'

She attempted to pull away, but the insidious masculine scent of bay-rum hair-dressing and Havana cigars, and the gentle fingers stroking her hair, worked a magic that rendered her helpless. 'Oh, Papa . . . you're a fool!' but there was only a hopeless, chiding love in her voice, and he smiled.

'Now *that*'s how your mother used to say it! Fret not, child, I know things will be well with us. I know Philippe Castille's play now. He is good, very good, but I am better. I can take him, I know I can. A few more games and I'll exchange your garnets for diamonds, I promise you. We'll return home then; you'd like that, I know. Frascati's for champagne and strawberries, a black-painted phaeton with two matched greys stepping out in Rotten Row . . . Laurel, can you see it?'

His fingers were tight on her arm, crushing the gigot sleeves, willing her to believe, but her eyes were still unhappy. 'Yes, I see all that. I also see the clubs of St James's . . . Brooks's or Boodle's, where I can't even accompany you. London in June doesn't mean the same to you and to me, Papa, and since your illness it has become even more distant.'

'Nonsense! It's nothing—less than nothing—an occasional shortness of breath—a small palpitation of the heart. You fuss like a mother hen.'

'The last one was *not* small,' she repudiated, 'and not an isolated case. The doctor told you to relax, not to become too excited.'

'The good doctor is a well-meaning bumbler,' he broke in. 'Excitement is the very stuff of life. It has been months since I have been inconvenienced by my so-called illness. Forget it, Princess; I have. Tomorrow I play Philippe Castille and win.'

Laurel turned away with a sigh, well aware that nothing she could say or do would change her father's belief in his eventual fortune. 'All right, Papa. At least M'sieu Castille has the manners of a gentleman whether he wins or loses, and is always willing for a return game. He is as true a professional as you yourself, but what if that awful Mr King is there? He is an even better player than the other and yet doesn't even pretend to enjoy the game. I don't know why he plays.'

The grey eyes, so like his daughter's, darkened. 'Yes, Rafe King is another matter entirely. There is an enmity between those two that I'd give my right arm to fathom. In spite of their surface politeness, I've never known them to play in the same game; whenever one arrives, the other either leaves, or watches like some predatory animal awaiting the other's fall. I've heard that King is one of the old Virginia King family, and since his parents first came south he has made and lost more fortunes than Castille will ever see, yet he plays with an intensity that even I, in my worst moments, have not surrendered to. It's almost as if he's trying to prove something.'

'That he is a better player than M'sieu Castille, perhaps . . . or a better man? I have heard that they both ride and fence as if possessed and that Mr King's stallion nearly killed M'sieu Castille's mare in a local race through the bayous last year. I also heard that when Mr King's wife died of the yellow fever two years ago Mr Castille stayed drunk for a week and saw no one!'

'Laurel, that's enough! Gossip doesn't suit you!'

'But I don't gossip . . . only to you,' she protested. 'And then only because I worry about your finding yourself between two sworn enemies, and the target of both. You know how servants talk, and even if much of it is speculation, there is more than a grain of truth in all the rumours, I'll be bound. Oh, Father, I'm sure we should never have come to New Orleans.'

Evading his outstretched arm, she moved to the dressing-table, taking the combs from her hair with a weariness that had nothing to do with long days and sleepless nights, and allowing the cascade to tumble down her back in all its glory.

'How is it,' her father murmured, lifting it in loving fingers, 'that such fragile shoulders can take more than half my burdens and still have room for your own?'

'I have no burdens but yours,' she smiled and the gentle irony was not lost on him. He took up the silver-backed brush and began smoothing it rhythmically through her hair, as he had done since his wife's death. 'Do you have to play tomorrow?' she pursued, for once unpacified by the loving ritual.

With a sigh Wallace put down the brush and turned her to face him, taking the trembling chin between thumb and forefinger, forcing her anxious eyes to meet his. 'Come now, my White Rose, you must trust me. I have a friend in Lady Luck—a fickle lady, to be sure, but smiling on me just now, I'll warrant. Now forget green baize and think blue silk. We have an invitation to attend Mrs Franklin on Esplanade. She married well, so I'm told, in spite of being an English parson's daughter.'

'Now that *is* gossiping!' Laurel reprimanded with a smile, allowing him to believe he had deflected her. For love of him she would make conversation with the insipid Mrs Franklin and politely fend off the clumsy advances of her heavy-set, heavy-handed husband . . . and worry all the while what the morrow would bring. If only she could have known . . .

When they arrived at the gaming-room on Rampart Street, Laurel knew that it would take more than a smile from Lady Luck to tip the scales in her father's favour. Rafe King rose with the other men at her entrance, his broad shoulders filling the black evening suit as though he had been poured into it, the muscular thighs accentuated by the knife-edge pleats in the slim-fitting trousers. He barely glanced at her, but for that instant when their eyes met she felt that he had probed her very soul. She had not yet made up her mind whether his eyes were grey or green, but they were, she was certain, as cold as the Atlantic and just as merciless.

This was their fourth meeting, and she still remembered the first one with ambivalent feelings. Anti-Spanish sentiment was running high in the city since well before the battle of Manila Bay on 1 May. The victory, accomplished in only seven hours after that powerful 5.40 a.m. broadside, had raked the Spanish line from end to end, and had created a jubilation in New Orleans that surpassed even the Mardi Gras. Drink flowed freely and the roistering Americans were in no condition to differentiate between octoroon or Creole. Their dislike of the aristocratic indolence of the latter and the calculated social climbing of the former boiled over, so that anyone of vaguely dusky hue was considered a 'spik' and treated accordingly.

Laurel's fair hair protected her from most of the harassment, but she was nevertheless accosted by one inebriate who insisted that she must be wearing a wig, ''cos no real hair is that colour'. Laurel had concealed her fear behind a haughty reply, whereupon the man had seized her upper arm in thick fingers and pulled her to within inches of his glowering features. 'Don' you come high-'n-mighty with me, li'l lady,' he had threatened, just as a tall stranger laid a deceptively gentle hand on his shoulder.

'I suggest you seek other amusement, friend,' a well-modulated voice had urged.

'What the . . .' the other ejaculated, but then, glaring up into the eyes as glacial as mountain peaks, he sobered fast. 'Jus' a bit o' fun,' he slurred, shaking loose. 'Can' a fella have a bit o' fun?'

'Elsewhere,' came the icy rejoinder.

Muttering to himself, he released Laurel and lurched unsteadily on his way. Gratefully she turned to thank her rescuer, but found his eyes scornful. 'I don't want thanks for saving a fool from herself,' he snapped. 'You walk alone in a town that is full of men with too many drinks and too few women and expect to emerge unscathed? Unless, like some women, you prefer the dubious excitement of a brush with danger, I offer you safe conduct to your hotel.' His tone manifested no pleasure at the prospect, and Laurel would have refused such a contemptuously-phrased offer had she not at that moment seen another young woman similarly accosted on the far corner.

'Thank you, sir,' she replied icily and with difficulty. 'As both a foreigner and a stranger to New Orleans I am unacquainted with your . . . customs.'

Surprisingly, her insult brought a smile to the mocking lips. 'As I am with yours, ma'am. Perhaps we could remedy that? My carriage is but a few steps from here.'

'Do you propose to educate me in the correct behaviour of a Southern lady during the few minutes it will take us to reach the St Louis Hotel? Is it such an easy lesson to learn, then?'

The smile stiffened a little and the grey-green eyes became glacial. 'I would not presume, ma'am. As with your English gentlewomen, a Southern lady is the product of generations, not of minutes. Your servant, ma'am.'

They had reached the glossy black carriage and with punctilious formality he had handed her in. Little had been said on the short drive to the hotel: Laurel kept her peace in the knowledge that she had behaved abominably, and Rafe King, she assumed, had reached the same conclusion. At the hotel he had helped her from the light phaeton, and the chiselled features had given her no encouragement to apologise for her ingratitude, yet she felt the need to do so and touched her hand lightly to his arm. 'I am in your debt, sir.'

For a moment the mobile lips had twitched in humour. 'I shall take that IOU,' he said, holding her eyes.'

Confused, she had turned away and hurried into the safe luxury of the hotel.

*　　　*　　　*

Now, facing him across the room lit by both gas-light and candles for atmosphere, she again felt the same magnetism of the man.

'Mr Castille sends his apologies . . . apparently some business transaction up-State. I trust you will allow me to take his place?'

'My pleasure, Mr King,' agreed Wallace Faver-sham with as much warmth as he could muster, and was introduced to the other players.

'Mr Butler from Virginia, a plantation-owner like myself, but preferring cotton to sugar, Mr Stewart from San Francisco; hotels, isn't it, Mr Stewart? Elliot Cord from New York'—his voice was a subtle degree cooler as he introduced the Northerner, giving him neither background nor title—'and of course Mr Ellis, whom you have already met.'

'And beaten,' the Texan grinned affably. 'But then I only came to see the li'l lady again. Howdy, ma'am.'

Laurel smiled warmly at him, not at all offended by the bluff and clumsy compliment. 'I would wish you better luck this evening if my father had not been playing,' she said, taking her customary place on the chaise-longue; a little too close to Rafe King's table position for comfort, but able to watch her father's every expression.

He seemed strangely excited tonight and his normally pale skin, accentuated by too many hours in gas-lit rooms and too few walks in the sunshine, held twin patches of colour high in his cheeks. As the game progressed, he glanced her way once or twice and his eyes glittered in the subdued lighting.

The game was a long one and, with the inbuilt tension between the Northerner and the others, Laurel felt that her nerves were stretched to breaking-point. 'The war has been over for thirty-three years!' she wanted to cry out. 'Why can't you forget?' She knew that each player was affected by it as the stakes rocketed. The Texan folded first, then the man from San Francisco. Laurel knew that her father was betting more heavily than he had ever done, so it was with a swiftly indrawn breath that she heard the New Yorker challenge, 'What say we separate the men from the boys and lift the limit? All right with you, King?' Laurel noted the reciprocation of address and was not surprised to hear the affirmative answer.

Wallace Faversham mopped his brow, as he had done twice before in the game, and carefully replaced the snowy linen handkerchief in his pocket before replying, 'Sky's the limit as far as I'm concerned.' They were playing Five Card Stud with deuces wild, and his upcards showed three Aces and a two of Hearts.

'It can't be,' muttered the Virginian and shook his head, no longer able to believe in the supremacy of his own four Queens and a Jack. 'No,' he said. 'No, not for me.'

A thinly triumphant smile curved the challenger's lips as he again won his war. 'Then I'll bet the pot.'

Laurel came to her feet in horror, spilling the contents of her reticule. The pot stood at thirty thousand dollars. 'I'm sorry,' she apologised, knowing how her father resented any reaction from her, but he was smiling as he replaced the handkerchief that he had again used.

'That's all right, my dear; I'm sure we all appreciate your surprise. I shall, of course, call Mr Cord and raise another thousand.'

The Northerner's pale eyes narrowed in disbelief as Rafe King equalised the bet, and he felt obliged to raise it another five thousand. He had been quite sure that his challenge would have eliminated all his opponents. Even thirty-three years after the war the South was only just regaining its former prosperity, and thirty thousand dollars was the total worth of many plantations. However, the game continued and, to Cord's chagrin, the pot stood at over a hundred thousand at the final showdown. With sinking heart he saw his straight beaten by Rafe King's Royal Flush, then, incredibly, the Englishman had risen with a high-pitched laugh. 'I have you! I did it, Laurel! We're rich!'

With a sob of relief Laurel saw his downcard revealed as a second deuce, giving him an unbeatable five of a kind, but suddenly Wallace Faversham's eyes lost their jubilation as he swayed, then staggered, reaching for the chairback. His disbelieving gaze locked on to Laurel's with dawning horror as he fought for breath, clutching at his chest as the pain seared through him. A scream rang out as he gave a choke, crumpling to the floor.

Laurel fell to her knees beside him, cradling the snowy head in her arms and sobbing out his name. Dazed, pain-filled eyes met smoky grey, and

Wallace gave a bare shake of his head, fighting for speech. 'Best way . . . Promise . . .'

'Oh, Papa, anything!'

'Remember good times and . . . and . . .' His body arched, but still he fought for, and found, a smile.

'Yes? Yes?'

'No black . . . Doesn't suit you . . .' He gave a parody of a wink. 'Fooled them, my White Rose . . . I fooled them all.' His features stiffened in a final agony, then relaxed completely . . . and for ever.

For a moment the stunned silence of the room was broken only by the sobbing of the flaxen-haired girl in the ivory silk dress, kneeling, regardless of the dusty floor, clinging to the body of the man she tried to recall to life by her grief-stricken pleas. Then there was a disconcerted movement towards her, halted by the cool voice of Rafe King.

'One moment.' He went down on one knee and took hold of the girl's upper arms, raising her a little. 'Miss Faversham, I am deeply sorry to have to do this, but had I spoken later I would not have been believed, and there is a great deal of money at stake.' Swiftly he took the handkerchief from Wallace Faversham's pocket and, before their disbelieving eyes, revealed a five of Clubs. 'This, I'm afraid, was part of his original hand. The switch was well done, but not all of us were distracted by your carefully dropped reticule, Miss Faversham.' His eyes were as cold as the Arctic, but something moved there as he saw the genuine shock as his words hit her with an almost physical blow.

Her lips parted, but no words came until the outburst of incredulity from the others fell about her. 'So you didn't know,' he mused—an instant before her palm cracked against his cheek.

'I hate you! Hate you!' and the tear-bright eyes filled afresh. 'Get out! Just get out and take your money with you. Get out, all of you! Oh please . . . for pity's sake . . . leave us alone!' Bending again to the fallen man, she sobbed as if her heart would break.

The shuffling and muttering died away, telling her that the men had filed out, embarrassed, still disbelieving. Her sobs subsided into choking gasps; a shudder ran through her frame and she murmured brokenly, 'You fool! Oh you beloved, wonderful fool!'

'That's better,' came a quiet voice, and she spun round.

'You!'

Rafe King rose from the chair in which he had waited in watchful silence. Laurel stared at him in pain and anger as he said, 'I apologise again for adding to your grief. I shall take you back to your hotel and make arrangements for your father. There is a woman I know who will stay with you; you should not be left alone at a time like this, and I doubt that you'll want my company.' His well-modulated voice was almost gentle, but Laurel saw him only as the instrument of her father's downfall.

'I want nothing from you.'

'I can understand that, but you need *someone* at the moment, and wanting has little to do with it.'

He crossed to stand over her, then effortlessly lifted her to her feet.

'Don't touch me!'

'Then please accompany me quietly. I shall send someone for your father. You don't have to like me, Miss Faversham.'

'Like you? I hate you! I'll always hate you.'

He gave her a long look, then went to take the antimacassar from the couch at the other end of the room and draped it over the fallen man, covering the patrician head. The finality of it brought the full horror of her situation home to her as nothing had before. Her head swam and the room seemed to tilt crazily as shock and despair united against her. A low moan was torn from her as she swayed and, just before losing consciousness, felt herself swung up into arms of steel.

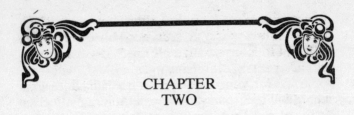

CHAPTER
TWO

FOR ALL of the week that followed Laurel lived in a
tormented nightmare world, drugged by barbitu-
rates at night and racked with sobs by day. She
came out of it briefly to attend her father's funeral,
for in the heat of the Mississippi June it was necessary to carry out burials without delay. Supported
on the arm of the plump, matronly quadroon whom
Rafe King had sent, she was unaware of the mul-
tiple vaults behind the tombs of the St Louis Cemetery No. 1 which allowed the older bones to be
pushed down shafts as the new were interred. She,
and the woman who had introduced herself simply
as 'Tante Honoré', were the only mourners at the
mercifully brief ceremony, though once Laurel
thought she saw a familiar wide-shouldered figure
in the shadows of the camphor trees. Strangely, the
sight brought her comfort, but she did not see him
again until a week later.

The sedatives had been discontinued and the
tortured days had eased into desolate reality.
Looking about her room, she realised for the first
time that she had been moved from the sumptuous
St Louis Hotel, with its exquisitely frescoed rotun-
da, to a more modest apartment. She learned from
Tante Honoré that these cool, airy rooms were on

Royal Street near the world-famous gambling-house known simply as 'Number Thirteen Royal'.

'Did Mr King arrange all this?' she asked her, already guessing at the answer.

'And everything else. Mr King usually does what he wants.' There was nothing but tolerant affection in the other's tones, but Laurel felt a small irritation at the remark.

'Perhaps something should be done about that,' she snapped, regretting her tone and apologising instantly, all too aware of the woman's kindness over the past days.

Unperturbed, the quadroon smiled. 'Plenty have tried, but now I come to think on it, I can't think of any one time when Mr King changed his mind one little bit once it was made up. Either way, he said that when you started chafing at the bit he'd be obliged if you would see him. Will you let me call him?'

'No . . . Yes . . . I don't know . . . Oh, Tante Honoré, I don't known whether I'm ready to see anyone yet, least of all Rafe King.' She did not add, considering this woman's obvious affection for him, that she still considered King to be the trigger that had produced her father's final attack. Some-how reason told her that she should not hate him; indeed, she had much to be grateful for in the way he had handled her affairs without once intrud-ing on her grief, yet reason has no place in the heart, and her heart was too badly bruised for logic.

'That Mr Castille has been round twice,' Tante Honoré continued. 'He got back into town the day after . . . well just about a week ago, but Mr King told me quite firmly that you weren't to see anyone until you had seen him.'

Laurel went to the gilt-edged mirror on the dressing-table and stared at the stranger there. Gone were the sweet curves of cheek and chin: in seven days she had lost over twelve pounds in weight, and the ivory skin was drawn like parchment over the fine bones. Always a slender girl, she was now almost skeletal. Gone the soft, bright cascade of waves, for her hair needed washing and had been drawn back into a severe chignon. Only the eyes remained, those glorious woodsmoke eyes that now seemed to fill her mirror-image to the exclusion of all else.

'See him, child,' the woman urged. 'See him and start living again.'

When King did arrive, however, his massive frame filling the doorway, the memory of that fateful evening twisted within her like a knife. She had to turn away from the searching gaze, murmuring, 'Tante Honoré said that you wished to see me.'

'Only when you were well enough to discuss your future.'

The lace-edged handkerchief that she had been twisting between her fingers tore, and the sharp sound restored a little equilibrium. She was finally able to face him, and he felt his heart lurch at the lost vulnerability in those huge eyes. 'Mr King, I'm deeply aware of the considerable debt I owe you . . . this hotel and the other arrangements. I have a little money and . . . some jewellery. I'll repay you as far as I can. I must trust you to tell me the correct figure, since I know the price of nothing. I wouldn't wish for charity . . . Not from you.'

'But you'd accept it from someone else?' he challenged sharply, ignoring all but her last words.

Laurel turned away with a sigh, glad that Tante Honoré had discreetly withdrawn. 'If I have enough for my passage home . . . I believe that the steerage fare is quite inexpensive . . . I shall go to my Aunt Sophie in Bath. That might be termed charity, since she hardly knows me.' Intent on shredding the unfortunate cambric, she did not see his eyes narrow.

'Have you ever travelled steerage? Do you know what it is like to travel like cattle with the stench of jostling, unwashed bodies in your nostrils, and the coarse language of the lowest orders in your ears, not to mention the unwanted attentions accorded to a young woman travelling alone? And who is this Aunt Sophie whose charity you are willing to accept?'

An involuntary shudder went through her as the image of Sophia Fortesque-Lyons came sharply to mind. Dressed in eternal black bombazine over hoops of a bygone age; mourning, as did the queen she revered above all, a long-dead husband, she ruled the bleak house and its meagre staff with iron discipline. The pianoforte remained covered and silent, the heavy red velvet curtains drawn. The servants spoke in whispers and a rare burst of laughter was frowned upon. Yet Laurel knew that she would be made welcome there, after a fashion, for the older woman was not deliberately cruel, only unfeeling, all love buried in a pinewood box, all emotion concealed beneath the rigidly corseted frame. Laurel would read to her in the evenings and embroider during the long, solitary days. She would attend church on Sundays and take the waters once a month, but there would be no soirées, no afternoon teas and never again the excitement of a ridotto or the gaiety of a party. Her looks would fade within those candle-lit rooms and her spirit break beneath the emotionless order of the house.

'And who *is* this Aunt Sophie?' Rafe King reiterated, and was shocked at the tear-washed despair, quickly veiled by long lashes, as she turned back to him.

'She . . . she is my late mother's sister. Uncle William died shortly after I was born. They were very close, having no children, and . . . well, she has almost closed the house down since he died. There is of course no company, but . . .' a sigh and her inveterate optimism lit a small flame, 'we may perhaps bring each other comfort and, in time, when she . . . well . . . there may be a position in a milliner's shop or as a governess.'

'I presume your own home was sold when you began travelling?'

She gave a ghost of a smile, but there were traces of bitterness in her tone as she said. 'The house never was ours, we only lived there. When my grandfather died he willed the estate to the younger brother, my Uncle Hayward. Even in those days my father was not considered stable enough to run Greenacres without using it as a table stake! Uncle

Hayward's Stock Exchange dealings kept him in the City—he always said that he had an abacus for a brain and a gold nugget for a heart—so he never married and was quite happy to allow us to stay there and to use the profits of the land to live on. The last I heard he was considering selling, but I don't know whether he has yet done so . . . we rather lost touch, you see. Whatever the outcome, it is no longer my home, even though Uncle Hayward and I were fond of each other. He must, and would, put profit before a White Elephant that he has no intention of using. There really is no alternative, you see. It has to be Aunt Sophie.' It was a frightening future for a spirited twenty-two-year-old, but Laurel was determined to face it bravely, if not eagerly and her chin lifted a fraction.

Rafe saw the conflicting emotions in the lovely face and the courage in that last lift of the head, and a strange tightness enclosed his heart, the like of which he had never known. 'There is an alternative,' he suggested, keeping his voice deliberately cool, his emotions hidden. 'I have a plantation called Moonrise, and my twelve-year-old daughter lives there with me. Her mother died two years ago and we have hired and lost seven governesses in that time. She is a difficult child who needs someone with the strength to discipline her and the patience to do it slowly; someone who will love her without spoiling her and be a stable part of her future . . . in short, a mother. A concept we have both rejected totally . . . until now.'

Stunned, Laurel searched his face for humour. 'Is this some kind of a joke, sir?'

One devilish eyebrow twitched upward. 'I believe it is called a proposal of marriage.'

'But . . . but you know nothing of me . . . nor I of you.'

The grey-green eyes flickered over her with a regard that brought a flush to her cheeks. 'Since it would be merely a marriage of convenience for both of us, in which I gain a mother for Marie-Louise and you lose a life with Aunt Sophie, I fail to see that mutual soul-baring is at all necessary. You are well bred, quite beautiful and highly intelligent . . .'

'So is a thoroughbred mare!' Laurel burst out, unable to contain her anger and incredulity any longer, but he merely nodded, his face a mask. 'And spirited. Your analogy is most apt. Well? Will you accept, or are you going to offer the vacillations of your sex and demand time to think? Would you even be courted, madam?'

Characteristically, Laurel's anger had evaporated with her outburst and in its place was an agony of despair. Gone were the rolling Sussex hills and a firm-muscled horse beneath her. Gone the tenderness of her father's love and the laughter in his ever-youthful eyes. No more the bustle of packing and unpacking, the excitement of gambling-halls and the flirtatious repartee of sophisticated strangers. The choice was crystal clear; she could become the unpaid companion of a harsh, grieving matriarch or she could enter virtual bondage as a compromise between wife and governess to this coldly arrogant plantation-owner. But then she thought of the child she had never seen; a child so lonely, so unhappy, that she had to lash out at anyone who came near. 'I'll accept your offer, Mr King,' she decided, though her voice came out barely above a whisper, 'and carry out all my duties to the best of my ability.'

'I'm sure you will, Miss Faversham,' he answered gravely, and Laurel felt that she must have imagined the hint of laughter in his tone, for this was surely a man who would not know the meaning of the word.

'I shall need time . . . a dress . . .'

'I shall make the necessary arrangements and send a woman to you. Shall we say a week from today?'

'A week!' Laurel had been thinking of at least a month in which to prepare herself both physically and mentally for this loveless marriage. It was true that the idea of an arranged marriage would have caused her no loss of sleep had it been through her father or Aunt Sophie. It was to be expected that her family would choose a husband for her, a man of their own class and background who would provide adequately for her, and on those counts Rafe King could not be faulted. However, her father at least would have chosen a younger man— Rafe must be . . . well . . . almost forty—and most certainly a gentle and loving husband would have been of prime importance, a man who would nurture and care for her until love grew naturally between them with friendship and trust. On this last count no one could be more unacceptable than this granite-featured Southerner with the eyes of ice. Yet, Laurel reflected with innate honesty, this was the man who had carried her from her father's body into a waiting carriage, had sent her the motherly Tante Honoré, had paid her bills, given her time alone for the shock and grief to subside— then given her the chance of respect and a future, however bleak. She raised her eyes to his, nervousness making her tongue flick over her top lip, unaware of how sensuous that movement was. 'A week it is, Mr King. I shall be ready.'

He noted the rigidity of her spine and the unconscious lift of that chin, and respect muted the flame of desire that she had already and quite unknowingly ignited within him almost a month ago. He gave a brief bow. 'I have preparations of my own . . . If you will excuse me?'

'Of course.' Then, as his hand went to open the door, 'Mr King . . .' and halted him. 'I . . . I am exceedingly grateful to you for what . . . for all you have done.' And was shocked at the sudden anger in his eyes.

In three strides he crossed the room and had taken her arms in fingers of steel. 'I don't want your gratitude, dammit!' He gave her a shake; the eyes, all green now, green fire, bored into hers. 'I ask you again; will you be my wife, Laurel Faversham?'

The magnetism, the very predator in him, drew from her a response which shook her to her very foundations. 'Oh, yes . . .' A whisper from her lips as, helpless, she watched his features darken and a muscle leap in his jaw—but then, almost violently, he put her from him.

'Very well. It is not charity I'm offering, nor sympathy. I want neither in return.' And he was gone, closing the door with ominous quietness behind him.

Tante Honoré put in an anxious head. 'You all right, Miss Laurel?'

'Yes . . . yes, thank you.' A high-pitched laugh broke from her, coloured with more than a trace of hysteria. 'Oh, yes, I'm all right now! Mr King has asked me to marry him.'

The brown velvet eyes softened in intuitive understanding. This was no time for formality. Crossing the room, she gathered the ashen-faced, wide-eyed girl into her arms and let her sob out her fears on the ample bosom.

Night fell. 'I think you should take one of your tablets, child.' And day came and went. 'Come now, Laurel, honey, let me wash that hair.' And the next night and day, until, 'There's Mr Castille below. You want to see him?'

Laurel, mentally and physically exhausted, seized upon the one light in her tormented existance. 'Yes . . . yes, send him up . . . No . . . wait . . . help me change . . . My hair . . .'

'Don't you fret none, child. Mr Castille is a man who can wait.' 'Like the spider for the fly,' she added beneath her breath, selecting a pale pink morning dress for the girl she had come to love. The waist-length hair was swept up into a shining coronet and adorned with a string of pearls.

Then he was there, faultless elegance in dark grey suit and the new willow-pattern waistcoat, a malacca stick, more ornament than use, under one arm, his grey kid gloves and matching hat already handed to the disapproving Honoré.

'Laurel . . . Forgive me for using the name I have always used in my thoughts. I am sorry, so very sorry.' The deep velvet of his eyes registered all the gentle concern that Rafe King's had lacked, and she found herself responding with a feminine helplessness that no one else had evoked.

'Mr Castille . . . Philippe . . . I . . .'

'No, don't speak! I know it's presumptuous of me, quite indelicate, almost scandalous, to appear when you are unchaperoned. Forgive me, but an avenging angel could not have kept me away . . . even though she tried!'

A modicum of her inveterate rationality returned as he took her hands in a surprisingly firm grip for a supplicant. Gently she withdrew the captives, taking a step backwards. 'Mr Castille, it was most kind of you to come to offer your condolences. I regret having been . . . shall we say *hors de combat* . . . during your previous calls, but I am quite recovered now. May I offer you some of Tante Honoré's excellent mint julep, or perhaps something stronger?'

He accepted the change in her voice and replied in like vein. 'A Bourbon, if you have it. Some ice? Perfect. Laurel . . . Please allow me to use your given name? Have you thought—though I do not suppose that you have thought at all during these terrible days—of your future?'

She had moved to the damask-covered couch and he joined her there, too close for comfort, yet far enough away so that only a prude could object. 'I have, as you so intuitively guessed, given it little thought, but others have considered it. In fact,' she rose to her feet, leaving him there, 'Mr King—you are acquainted with him, of course—Mr King has done me the honour of asking me to be his wife.'

'No!' Incredulity, then a bark of disbelieving laughter, that died as he read the truth in her face. 'But you can't! You cannot possibly incarcerate yourself in that place! It isn't a mansion, it's a mausoleum—a tomb—for a woman who died two years ago!'

Laurel felt the blood drain from her face as even the vision of gentle evenings around the piano and a laughing, loving child faded into the icy mists of the grave. 'He must have loved her very much.'

'Loved her?' He shook the raven head, laughing cynically now. 'One did not *love* La Belle Hélène any more than one could love a slumbering tigress or an exotic orchid. Yes, that's what she was—an orchid, so beautiful that it made your heart ache just to look at her.'

'I don't want to hear any more!'

He gave her a long, searching look. 'But an orchid is a parasite, *ma petite*. It feeds off whatever it clings to . . . and it is not too particular to what it clings. Hélène was a hunger in the dreams of every man who met her, but only Rafe King . . . and perhaps one other . . . could satisfy her own brand of hunger. Sometimes I think they hated each other. They burned each other up and fed on the flames they created. Without her he is a shell, a cold, ruthless shell, who lives only for the plantation . . . her plantation; not even the child whom he appears to ignore. But that is all servants' gossip, and already I can see that I have said too much. I am no saint, *ma chèrie*, but I am here to offer you a far warmer, gayer, life than your Mr King is capable of. Come with me . . . courtesan, croupier, in my bed, or as my untouched queen of the gambling-hall. I can give you life! You are the daughter of a gambling man. I have watched you; it is in your blood! Come, Laurel, it is not too late.'

For a moment she was tempted, and he read her indecision, moving from the couch to her side. 'Laurel.' His voice was deep and vibrant, promising her independence, laughter . . . and much more. His eyes glittered as his long fingers took hold of her shoulders from behind, drawing her back to melt into the lean muscular length of him.

'No!' Pulling away, she released herself and, contrite, faced him. 'Mr Castille . . . Philippe . . . I do not profess to understand myself, so how can I ask you to? He has offered me nothing and I have accepted his offer. To refuse you is against all reason—yet I must. There is no logic to it; it simply . . . is so.' Those wide grey eyes begged him, and he knew that he was, for the moment, bested.

'So, it begins again,' he murmured enigmatically. 'Very well, Laurel, I shall respect your decision, but remember this; if you ever need someone to turn to—a friend who will ask no questions and nothing more from you than you are prepared to give—then come to me. I own the Coq d'Or on Rampart Street, and one or two others. Go there, and I will join you, wherever I am; remember that.' Lean fingers came up to capture her face and Laurel found herself a little afraid before the strange light in his dark eyes. 'Remember . . . and remember this.' His lips came down gently, moving with calculated expertise over hers until she pulled free with a gasp, her eyes brilliant, her breathing erratic.

'You go too far!' But he smiled, experience having confirmed the passion in her that he had already suspected and of which she was totally unaware.

'Forgive me,' he apologised, with no hint of apology in his tone. 'I must leave before I forget myself further. You are far too lovely, *ma belle*, to marry Rafe King. One day you will know that I speak the truth, but until then . . .' He spread his hands in an expressively Latin gesture. 'I am a patient man, Laurel Faversham.' He gave a deep bow, totally negated by a wicked wink, and left her, her emotions in tatters, her control in carefully held shreds.

Her fingers rose to touch the lips that, quite against her will, had parted beneath his, and the colour rose in her cheeks. 'What kind of person am I?' she whispered, aghast. 'Oh, this is awful!' Quickly she took some cologne from her dressing-bag and splashed it on wrists and neck. 'Foolish child! Pull yourself together!' she remonstrated to the mirror-image. 'Men have kissed you before.'

But the bumbling, half-respectful, half-fearful kisses of the boys she had known bore no resemblance whatever to the slow fire that Philippe Castille had ignited, and Laurel was not one to lie to herself. 'You are upset, off balance and far too vulnerable,' she scolded. 'You are engaged to be

married—which is a far more respectable state than
Philippe was offering.' Yet the kiss that Rafe King
had *not* given her, as his fierce mouth had hovered
inches above hers, had seared her mind with more
fire, she knew, than the Creole's cunning skills ever
could.

'Glad *he*'s gone,' stated Tante Honoré, bustling
into her reverie.

'What? Oh, yes . . . perhaps.' Then she smiled.
'Papa always said that fine feathers do not neces-
sarily make a fine bird, but you must confess that
M'sieu Castille possesses exceedingly fine feathers.' She read the relief in the other woman's eyes,
and was comforted. It was the first time since his
death, that she had been able to speak aloud of her
father, and, although the thought brought pain, it
was a deep, burning, yet controllable pain, and she
knew that she was once more ready to face life.
'Will Mr King send a seamstress, do you think, or
will he choose something of . . . something he
already has?'

The quadroon gave a disgusted snort. 'As if you
could ask such a thing! 'Course he will send a girl
round—and if I know Mr King—and I do know Mr
King—she will be the best in New Orleans.'

'For someone he hardly knows?'

'For his future wife! *Tais-toi*, child! You must
think of other things.'

'But will he love me?' she dared.

'How could he help it? 'Course, he'll probably
love you more with a little extra flesh on those arms
and a better colour in those cheeks. I'll send out for
some special sweetmeats. If'n you're goin' to eat

like a bird, it's gotta be fattening-up food.'

Laurel smiled at her fussing, and relaxed a little. Even if the cold stranger that was her future husband was still in mourning for his dead wife, surely he could be softened a little by a woman's care. Perhaps, in time, even love of a kind would come.

The following days sped by in a whirl of fittings with the tiny French dressmaker, and breathtaking tours around shoe-shops, milliners and florists. She had thought that, with so little notice, the wedding would be a quiet affair, so was shocked to learn that over a hundred people would attend. 'But I'll know no one!' she cried. 'How could he have done this to me!'

'It's a question of honour, child,' the other stated with some surprise. 'Mr King would have you accepted by all who know him. He has little family of his own, but he is a well-known figure in Louisiana and respected even by those who might find him a little stand-offish. They admire and envy him, and it's only fitting that they should do the same honour to his wife.'

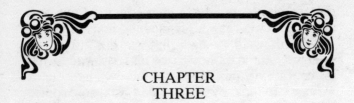

CHAPTER
THREE

'His wife! Yes, that's what I am now,' thought
Laurel, stealing a look at the unreadable, carved-
granite features beside her, then at the strong
hands guiding the horses that drew them westwards
to Moonrise. 'Last week must surely have happened to another person, or I would remember
more of it.' Yet the fawning deference of seamstress and florist, of hair-stylist and jeweller could
not have spoken more volubly of her husband's
influence—and affluence.

The creation of white satin overlaid with old
Brussels lace that had been slipped over her head
only that morning had momentarily brought her
situation out of a dream and into reality. She had
turned, then, suddenly fearful, to a hovering Tante
Honoré and cried, 'I don't know him!'

Again she found that intuitive understanding she
had experienced since the woman's first appearance, as, dismissing the bustling and giggling
dressers and attendants, the quadroom had taken
hold of the trembling frame and held it firmly until
the shuddering spasm had passed. 'Sit there,' the
woman ordered gently, then poured a generous
measure of brandy into the delicate crystal goblet

that had appeared on a silver tray earlier that morning. 'Drink.'

'But I don't!'

'Drink! Mr King sent it up and said to tell you that it was only medicine.'

How had he known? Why had he cared that his bride might consider herself a lamb for the slaughter and need such 'medicine' to calm her fears? Obediently Laurel swallowed the fiery liquid, choking as it burned through her veins. Clucking, Tante Honoré took the pins from the ornately piled, tightly drawn and curled hair and let it fall, then gently gathered it into a loose coil at the nape of the slender neck, easing Laurel's splitting headache instantly. 'But I still don't know this man I'm marrying,' Laurel whispered, her voice calmer, but the hysteria only a breath away.

'It is not necessary, *ma petite*,' Tante Honoré soothed. 'For a man and wife it is a lifelong study. For the moment it is enough to know that you are beautiful and you are needed. The rest will follow.'

'But will it?' Laurel reflected, as the bays effortlessly ate up the miles, drawing them past the big square two-storey white frame houses of the River Road. Not by a word or gesture had Rafe King indicated that this was any more than a marriage of convenience, though the grey-green eyes had leaped into flame as she had appeared in the glory of silk and lace and drifted down the aisle towards him. He had again shown some emotion—his tall frame stiffening once as she faltered in her replies, but now no trace of weakness showed in the man by her side, and she wondered whether she had imagined it.

'Tired?' he asked, his eyes on the road.

'A little.'

'A few miles more.' And that had been the monosyllabic quality of their conversation since the beginning of the journey. They turned north-west, following the River Road, then, without warning, into a pair of wide gates. A long *allée* stretched before them, bordered by moss-festooned oaks and, further on, azaleas, some still dotted with late blooms.

As lovely as the setting was, there was yet something missing, something indefinable. An air of gloom pervaded the place, an aura of neglect, as though the thing which had given it light had ceased to exist . . . had died. A shudder ran through her as Laurel recalled Philippe's words, and then she saw the house and her worst fears were confirmed.

The fluted columns surrounding the structure and raising it well above ground-level were choked with vines, the insidious tendrils pushing into the cracks. Vines, too, and a rampant wisteria clung to the central staircase that led from ground-level to the main floor, creeping persistently along the balcony above. It was not only the ugliest, but also the most neglected, house that Laurel had ever seen.

Something of her consternation must have shown in her face, for Rafe said matter-of-factly, 'Hideous, isn't it? They call the style Steamboat Gothic. My father won it from an old steamboat captain. Many of them retired, yet couldn't leave the river, so they built these monstrosities to resemble as closely as possible the only homes they had known. Hélène liked it, though,' and he drove on as if that said it all.

'Perhaps she did,' thought Laurel a little rebelliously, 'but for better or worse I am mistress here now and it can surely do no harm to clean things up a little.'

They had reached the end of their journey and an ebony-skinned boy appeared as if by magic to take the horses' heads. Laurel thought she detected a movement at one of the high dormer windows, a pale face appearing for a moment from the shadows, but could not be sure. Could this be the 'difficult' child who, according to Tante Honoré's sources, had thrown such a tantrum at receiving the news of her father's wedding that it had been heard clearly in the garden? She had apparently used such language in her refusal to attend the ceremony that Rafe had ordered her to be confined to her room for the whole week. A harsh sentence, thought Laurel privately, and hardly one to endear her to her future mother. However, she had little time for conjecture as Rafe leapt down to help her from the carriage, strong hands encircling her waist.

His fingers sank into the yielding flesh, and he raised surprised eyes to her rose-tinted face.

'It was . . . was too warm for stays,' she faltered, regretting her abandonment of the constricting whalebone and all too aware of the heat from those lean fingers through the light silk travelling-dress.

Without a word he lifted her to the ground, but did not release her, and his fingertips touched at her spine as his thumbs met at the front. 'I have never met a woman with a true hand-span waist,' he observed with a smile. 'Why, I believe it's even smaller than *with* that infernal creation of the devil. Why do you wear the things?'

'It's . . . it's the fashion.'

'Would you put the caprice of some Parisian corsetière before the preferences of your husband?' Again there was that trace of laughter in his voice.

'Why no, but . . .'

'Then I would take it as a great compliment, Mrs King, if you did not wear those things again.'

Cheeks flaming, she avoided the eyes so near her own. 'Very well, if that's your wish.' She was not at all sure she should have acquiesced so quickly, but it was so comfortable without them! Almost reluctantly his hands slid from her and she took a small step backwards. Inexplicably her breath was coming faster than it would had she worn 'that infernal creation of the devil'. Was it obvious to him, she wondered? A sliding glance caught his eyes upon her, but the fire in them was quickly quenched as, formally, he offered his arm.

'Welcome to your home, madam. May I introduce you?'

As they mounted the long staircase, the main door opened and a tall, slender coloured woman in black crêpe de Chine appeared, her high cheekbones and thin, slightly hooked, nose denoting North African blood. 'Welcome home, Mr King, Mrs King.' Her tone was polite and her look expressionless, yet Laurel was aware of a cold dislike as their eyes met.

'This is Leona, my . . . our housekeeper. She runs the house totally—has done for the past fifteen years—so there will be nothing for you to do on that score.'

Laurel nodded with a smile that was not returned, and felt the almost black eyes on her back as they went into the long hall that bisected the house.

Rafe turned to the housekeeper. 'Take Mrs King upstairs, then bring Miss Marie-Louise down to the drawing-room. When Mrs King has refreshed herself, you will serve a cordial there before dinner. Our luggage has, of course, arrived?'

'Yes, Mr King, and been taken up. This way, please, Mrs King.'

Laurel opened her mouth to speak, but already Rafe had turned and was crossing to one of the large panelled doors that flanked the hall. Feeling inexplicably rejected, she followed the tall figure up the stairs to a large square room in the east wing. Throwing open the door, the housekeeper stood aside to allow Laurel to pass, and Laurel caught the feline, musky scent of her and felt the predator there. Determined to ignore the antagonism that she sensed, she walked into the room and her heart sank. The huge canopied bed belonged to another era, as did the heavily ornate furniture. The oppressive combination of maroon velvet curtains and almost black mahogany furniture gave the room a funereal air.

'Your bags and your maid will be sent up, Mrs King,' Leona stated flatly, and turned to leave, but Laurel forestalled her.

'Leona, was this the previous Mrs King's room?'

Only a slight thinning of the lips betrayed the woman as she replied, 'This is the main guest-room. No one has used the mistress's room since her death. Nothing has been moved, and the door is kept locked.' She jangled the large bunch of keys at her waist. 'Only *I* attend to that room.' Before Laurel could give vent to her rising anger, the other had turned and gone, shutting the door firmly behind her.

Frustrated, Laurel went over to the hand-painted jug and wash-bowl and felt, with reluctant approval, the fresh, cool water. A knock heralded the arrival of an elderly negro, bringing her dressing-bag, followed by a diminutive, dusky-skinned girl barely in her teens. Her light colouring and straight black hair were highlighted by light brown eyes, quickly veiled now by gold-tipped lashes. 'Welcome, mistress,' she murmured, bobbing an awkward curtsy, and Laurel's heart went out to her.

'What is your name?'

'Vashti, missis, though I think I am called Pansy or Posy . . . I keep forgetting . . . but my Ma says I must never forget my old name.'

'Your mother is quite right, so I shall call you Vashti. But where do you . . . did you come from? Do you remember, or did your mother tell you that too?'

The almond-shaped eyes were raised in bewilderment. 'I have always been here. My Pa was a white man . . . but my Ma she tell me tales of a place, far away, called Algérie, where there ain't no plantations and no green bayous nor cotton or sugar like this here. She say it even further than the end of the Mississippi. Can you imagine that!'

'Oh, yes,' Laurel breathed, 'I can imagine that only too well, but . . .' and here she was interrupted by Rafe's icy voice from the corridor outside.

'You did *what*?' Her door was flung wide as he stood ominously in the opening. Beyond, Laurel could see Leona and, if revenge was sweet, then the terror in the housekeeper's face was all that Laurel could have asked for, but she was given no time for reflection as her husband bowed formally before her. 'My apologies, madam; I should have instructed Leona more fully as to your exact status.' Laurel's gasp went unnoticed as he turned his steely look back to the woman, who remained motionless before his fury. 'If Mrs King's clothes are in this wardrobe, remove them. If there is anything of Mrs King's in this room, you will attend to its removal personally . . . or I shall attend to yours. I shall speak with you later. Come, Laurel.' And he strode out, leaving her to follow.

As Laurel passed before the rigid frame of the housekeeper, their eyes met for the second time, and she was shaken by the hatred she saw there. Rafe led the scurrying entourage to the far side of the house and turned before a panelled door with a look of white heat at the woman, who, fumbling with her keys, opened it with shaking hands. 'My wife's room,' he stated, bowing Laurel inside. 'My apologies, madam. Your dresses will be with you instantly. I trust that when you have changed you will join Marie and me in the drawing-room.'

Just before the door closed, a breathless Vashti slid around it, flattening herself in the shadows of a large chest, so that only she saw the new mistress sink to her knees and bury her face in trembling hands. Great dry sobs racked the taut frame and only she, with the empathy of a child, recognised the loneliness and frustrated fury behind the heaving shoulders.

When Laurel had regained a modicum of control, she raised her head and saw the girl cowering in the corner. Instantly she was contrite. 'Oh, Vashti, did we alarm you? No one is going to hurt you, least of all I. Come now, as a lady's maid, aren't you supposed to attend me? Come, little one . . . attend, then.' Gradually the trapped wariness melted beneath the half-bantering tone and she relinquished her position, sidling cautiously closer and reminding Laurel of a time in Paris and a filthy scrap of feline woefulness she had coaxed from an alleyway there. 'Come,' she repeated gently. 'I need to be unhooked if I am to change.' With something definite to accomplish, the frightened creature darted forward and began undoing the back of the dusty travelling-dress, her thick straight brows locked in concentration.

Laurel drew in a deep shuddering breath and looked about her at the room she had inherited from La Belle Hélène . . . Philippe's orchid. To have called this room opulent would have been to use an understatement of the first magnitude. A huge *lit de ciel* dominated the room, its blue satin canopy echoing the colour of the walls, on which gilt-framed miniatures hung from velvet ribbons that flanked large mirrors. The deeper blue chaise-longue was covered in white velvet cushions, large and soft; some, incredibly, still bore the imprint of a reclining body. White, too, were the curtains that hung from ceiling to floor, a colour almost unknown for furnishings in England, where Victorian practicality ruled. The deep pile of the Aubusson carpet, in muted pinks and blues, was reflected in the display of silk flowers in one corner. A delicate armoire matched the two corner what-nots which were crowded with silver and lovely white Parian statuary. On an inlaid walnut chest stood a mother-of-pearl envelope-box and writing materials, all lovingly dusted and replaced in their exact positions as though awaiting their owner's return.

It was a room designed for sensualism, for indulging the langourous beauty who had slept there, not a room for a *mariage de convenance*, and Laurel reacted with characteristic courage. 'It is not going to change *me* into a Southern Belle,' she stated emphatically. 'Vashti, there is a deep blue shot silk dress in that other room. Since they are taking an inordinately long time to effect the transfer, perhaps you could find it for me? There are some slippers to match, and a fan.'

The girl darted away, returning a little later with the required dress over one arm. Eager to please, she went to slip it over her mistress's head, and Laurel laughed aloud for the first time in over a month. 'No, silly, *this* one I step into. Oh, what a pair of hen-witted ninnies we both are! Now, my tiny Algerian princess, I wonder if you can dress hair?'

'Hair, yes,' the girl stated with a firmness that allowed her to seat her mistress on the chair before the dressing-table and to hold her motionless while she removed the pins, allowing the flaxen mane to cascade down Laurel's back. Vashti uttered a cry of wonder. 'Oh, missis!' Then, deftly, with many murmurs of delight, she tended the almost white cloud, brushing and coiling with a totally instinctive skill. Only when she had finished did two pair of eyes meet in complete understanding.

'Thank you, Vashti.'

'You mo' than welcome, mistress. I am pleasured to serve you, and I hope you stay for all time—long as you don't never cut that hair!' And as they shared smiles, a bond was formed for life.

Slowly, holding tight to her new-found confidence, Laurel descended the staircase; the silk dress shot with sparks of blue, green and gold was a new material from Paris and one that she knew accentuated the fairness of her hair. Guided by a youthful voice raised in anger, she reached the door of the drawing-room, then froze with her fingers on the handle.

'I hate her!' cried an unseen child. 'I don't care what she's like! I hate her and I'll never, never, call her mother!' Laurel felt a tremor run through her, but lifted her chin and pushed open the door.

In the great square room father and daughter faced each other in unyielding confrontation; the man, fists clenched, broad shoulders rigid in anger, the girl poised behind the brocaded sofa, tear-washed eyes and the deepening red mark on her cheek testifying to the fury of the argument. At first Rafe did not see the horrified newcomer, but the abrupt change in his daughter's expression brought him about. In spite of his anger he was softened by the vulnerability of the woman who was only ten years older than his own daughter, but whose lovely smoky eyes held all the loneliness and heart-break of a month in which each day had equalled a year.

Before he could speak, however, Marie-Louise walked forward with the stiff-legged gait of an angry combatant. 'I have been instructed to make you welcome, so welcome, ma'am.'

'Marie!' and there was steel in Rafe's voice, but swiftly Laurel intervened, going forward to meet the child half-way.

'Thank you, Marie-Louise; I know what an effort that cost you.' She saw a willow-slender girl with hair the colour of mahogany and eyes of a rare tawny gold. Her skin was creamy white, and a sprinkling of freckles covered the retroussé nose, extending to her high cheeks. 'It is difficult for me,' she continued, aware of Rafe's eyes on her, 'to come as an intruder and wish to be a friend. Perhaps, therefore, we could allow a little formality for the moment. Later, when we become friends—and I am sure that we shall—you may prefer to call me Laurel,' turning to him, 'with your permission, of course, Rafe.'

She thought she detected relief, and possibly a trace of respect, in the deep-set eyes, but it was gone in an instant as that habitual cold barrier fell. 'You are too lenient with her, but I shall bow to your wishes . . . for the moment. Marie, you may leave us; I have things to discuss with your mother.' There was no gainsaying the warning emphasis he put on those last two words. With a defiant toss of the severe plait dropping down the centre of that stiff back, Marie-Louise stalked wordlessly from the room, closing the door behind her a little more firmly than was warranted.

For a long moment Laurel deliberately avoided Rafe's eyes, staring blankly at the walls, the curtains, the fireplace, then upward—to be riveted by the oil-painting that dominated the room. Only then did she spin round to face him, her shattered pride reflected in her eyes . . . For Hélène looked down upon them, the full lips curved in a half-smile, heavy-lidded eyes promising the artist a paradise on earth which the extreme *décolleté* of the black lace dress corroborated. The fire of the red-gold hair was brought into sharp relief by the white backdrop—white velvet—the velvet curtains of her bedroom. The implication would be lost on anyone who had not seen that sensuously decadent room, but the momentary bleakness in Rafe's eyes betrayed him.

'Rafe . . .' she faltered, and the barriers descended.

'My late wife. Do you think you can compete?'

The sheer cruelty of the question brought the colour flooding to her face and a gasp from her lips. Instantly he regretted his words, but saw that familiar raising of her head as she held back the threatening tears. 'No, Rafe. But then I don't have to, do I? Now, I believe you had something to discuss with me.'

'Of course. I shall be as succinct as possible and I apologise for my last remark; it was quite unnecessary. I am aware of your feelings towards me . . . or should I say lack of them . . . and I am aware that for both of us this is to be a marriage of convenience. However, it is a marriage none the less, and no one, least of all the child, must be allowed to entertain any doubts as to its stability. I saw you, loved you and swept you off your feet all in the space of a month. For you, too, it was love at first sight, and only your duty towards your ailing father kept you from expressing your feelings until after his death. Do you understand? Anything less than that will fail to make you mistress of this house and frustrate any efforts you may make to overcome Marie's dislike and distrust.'

His tone was unemotional, and Laurel wondered how he could expect her to act such a part when his very coldness negated communication, much less affection. 'What of your housekeeper's dislike of me? Will that melt before this great love we are supposed to share? If I am to be mistress of this house, I need her support before even that of Marie-Louise.'

The grey-green eyes were sombre. 'Leona is a different case altogether. She comes from a fierce branch of the desert Berbers whose men, not women, go veiled at all times. She came here when she became separated from her mother on one of the many migrations north; when the freed slaves thought that their liberty entitled them to the same food and shelter they had always earned, but without the need to work for it. Some turned to crime, some starved, some—especially the younger women—found that they could earn money for that which had already been taken by force on many plantations. Leona, like the rest of her people, was very beautiful, but fiercely proud. When a certain plantation overseer offered her money, she threw it at him . . . with predictable results. The mistress of the house found her, half-dead, took her in and cared for her. In contravention of all tradition the overseer was flogged, then dismissed. Leona stayed on at the house until long after her daughter, Vashti, was born. Her whole life revolved round the woman who had saved her from degradation and probably the loss of her child.'

Laurel found the whole jigsaw falling into place as he continued, 'So, you see, to change Leona's allegiance . . . even to a ghost . . . would be like trying to change a leopard's spots. If you can earn her respect, it must be considered a victory.'

'And shall I have your help in that, too?' Laurel ventured.

'Have I not already given it?'

'You demanded the obedience from her that is your right and, I assume, reprimanded her on the matter of the rooms, but . . .' Dare she, she wondered?—'perhaps a little softening of discipline in matters that . . . well . . . concern me?'

'Would you have preferred the guest-room?' And there was undoubted scorn in his tone as his gaze raked her from head to toe.

'Of course not, but . . .'

'Then allow me to be the best judge of Leona's treatment and, until you are more experienced, in the treatment of everyone on Moonrise.' The warning was clear, but Laurel's rising anger was interrupted by the dinner-gong, and Rafe turned to his wife with a sardonic bow, presenting his arm. 'Your public await . . . my love.'

'Let them!' she thought mutinously, but she caught the close regard and, controlling the tremor that went through her at the ripple of muscles beneath her fingers, allowed him to lead her into the dining-room. 'I *will* succeed! I *will*!' she vowed silently. 'It is better than being Aunt Sophie's companion, and no worse than any other marriage that she might have arranged for me.' She firmly put aside a treacherous cobweb of a thought that involved the handsome Creole, Philippe Castille, and concentrated on the task in hand.

Marie-Louise looked up with a scowl, then deliberately down at her plate as Laurel was seated; through the Creole gumbo and the pompano en papillote to the mouth-watering crêpes, evading every attempt that Laurel made to draw her into conversation. Even when her father spoke, she answered in monosyllables bordering on rudeness. Finally, Rafe could stand it no longer.

'You are excused, Marie-Louise,' he said firmly. 'You are obviously tired. I trust that we shall hear more from you over breakfast.' Those tawny eyes flashed him an agonised look, but he had turned to Laurel, covering her hand with his, and effectively shut the child out as he asked, 'Do you wish coffee, my dear?'

With a choked sob Marie fled from the room, and the clatter of her feet echoed through the house.

'Betrayed,' Rafe stated softly. 'She will recover in time.'

'Should I go to her?'

A thin smile touched his lips, but his gaze was inflexible as he shook his head. 'She must learn that her tantrums will not be tolerated.' Then, as if aware for the first time that his hand still covered hers, he turned it over to reveal her fingers tightly clenched. 'Yes, you are a fighter, Laurel, that is why I chose you rather than . . .' But he rose abruptly before another name passed his lips, leaving her with yet another riddle to solve, another, this time anonymous, enemy to overcome.

'When will it end?' her heart cried. 'Oh, Papa, why did you leave me?' 'It has been a tiring day,' she said with a gulp. 'With your permission, I shall retire.'

A flame kindled in the eyes that raked over her. 'Of course. I shall not be long myself.'

The implication was obvious, and Laurel found herself flushing, a feeling of panic rising within her as she excused herself and almost ran from the room. Was this not, after all, to be a simple business arrangement? No comfort was to be granted by that room designed for sensual pleasures. The too-wide bed with its turned-down sheets and the diaphanous nightdress laid out seemed to mock her. 'Not that one, Vashti. The other nightdress, the cambric one in the drawer there.'

The girl's chatter was quelled by the trapped look

on her mistress's face, and in silence she helped her into the enveloping garment. Sadly she left, puzzlement clouding her eyes. Was it not a wonderful thing to have someone like the master to love you? She had seen the bright eyes and heard the laughter that the dance of love had induced in her other mistress. Why not this one? She could not know that Laurel was asking herself much the same question, and reprimanding herself for being all kinds of a fool and coward.

When the adjoining door opened, however, and she saw him standing there, her heart leapt sickeningly to her throat. She was still seated at the dressing-table, as if carved from stone, quite unable to complete the ritual of unpinning her hair. She felt cold to the very core of her being and her mind churned with excuses, apologies . . . anything to escape from the loveless union that he must expect. The very sight of this broad-shouldered stranger, resplendent in a dark green silk dressing-gown that revealed his tanned chest, was enough to turn her limbs to water; yet when he crossed to stand before her, those grey-green eyes looking into her very soul, it was all she could do to keep from screaming.

A mirthless smile touched his mouth as he saw the colour drain from her face, then return again to crimson her cheeks as his eyes took in the high-necked and much ruffled gown. 'I did not force you into this marriage, madam. You had more than one choice.'

So he knew of Philippe's offer. Her eyes grew dark with pain. 'I sold myself, and chose to do it legally instead of going to Philippe Castille or to some ageing English squire.'

His eyes narrowed. 'Is that what you think of your position—a legalised prostitute?'

A shock went through her at the word, but she held her ground, hands tightly clenched in her lap. 'There is no love between us . . . we hardly know one another. You bought me as you would a plantation slave; an ornament for your house, a governess for your daughter.'

'A rather expensive slave.' But there was no humour in the words.

'A slave none the less, and with not even a place to go when the day is done!' Her eyes were wide and bright with unshed tears, and a muscle leapt in his jaw.

'You made a contract of marriage.'

'And I shall keep it. I shall honour it to the letter. But it will be only a shell you will own, Rafe, unless . . .'

'Unless?'

She dropped her gaze then, for an instant closing her eyes tightly. 'Unless you give me time . . . some little time at least, to come to know you.' She could not look at him. The silence seemed endless; then she thought she heard a sigh.

'I have never had to force my way into a woman's bed. Quite the contrary. However, you are my wife, Laurel, and my patience is not infinite.' He turned away and re-crossed the room with that long tigerish stride. 'Sleep well, my Victorian virgin.'

'Where . . . where are you going?'

'Do you care?'

'Yes,' and she bit her lip, regretting the word as soon as it was uttered, but, inexplicably, she did care.

In an instant he was before her, his strong hands on her arms, lifting her to her feet, forcing her to look up at him. 'Why, Laurel? Why do you care? God, if I thought there was fire beneath that ice . . .' She trembled before the flame in his eyes, and closed her own a heartbeat before his mouth descended, pillaging hers mercilessly, forcing her lips apart and savouring the inner moistness with his tongue. The earth rocked as one hand moved to cup her breast beneath the enveloping material, and she heard a harsh sound in his throat. But then he put her away so roughly that she fell back against the hard wood. 'I shall keep my promise, but you must make one, too. Until you are my wife in *every* way, you will not question my movements, or any action I take. You do not have the right. Well?'

Senses still reeling, lips swollen and bruised from that punishing kiss, yet achingly, wondrously so . . . 'I promise,' she whispered huskily—and felt the flame that his touch had kindled die within her.

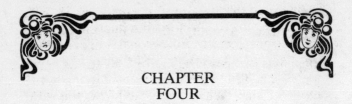

CHAPTER
FOUR

AFTER THE rigours of the day, Laurel slept with the
deep exhaustion of an overtaxed child, yet still
awakened early and surprisingly refreshed.
Summoning Vashti, she dressed in a pastel blue
chiffon blouse and fawn silk skirt, knowing that the
sleek hipline would accentuate her tiny waist. The
girl coiled her hair high on her head, setting a velvet
ribbon it to match the chocolate brown of the belt.
Laurel added a touch of lip-salve, eschewing the
newly fashionable colouring sticks, pinched her
cheeks, and went downstairs to where the aroma of
coffee and chicory wafted from the dining-room.

Predictably, Rafe was awaiting her and rose at
her entrance, his eyes commenting favourably on
her appearance.

'Is Marie-Louise not joining us?' she asked,
forestalling any ambiguous question as to how well
she had slept.

'She has contrived to get a headache,' he commented dryly. 'I suspect that it will continue
through luncheon, but disappear miraculously for
Mr Jordan's arrival this afternoon.' At her questioning eyebrow, he explained, 'Steven Jordan is a
new-off-the-boat French émigré, a self-confessed
libertine of almost sixty and, in his heyday, a

Corinthian of the first order. He is a Parisian, with more deaths to account for from duels in the Bois de Vincennes than any professional soldier . . . and more broken hearts swept aside than Don Juan could have dreamed of. However, he was also educated at the Sorbonne, speaks five languages fluently, writes creditable Latin, and can make the driest figures and heaviest prose pulse with life. In short, he is Marie's tutor and has taught her far more in the nine months he has been with us than anyone else could in the previous five years. You have at least one thing in common—he plays piquet and bézique, but considers poker a game for fools. May I recommend the omelette? It is a concoction of Lucille's—our Creole-nigra cook—and contains crab-meat and a trace of finely chopped oyster.'

When the omelette had been served—puffed, brown and as light as a meringue—Rafe continued, 'I thought you might wish to see the remainder of Moonrise. It is not large, only just over a thousand acres—half that of Magnolia to the south, which, incidentally, is also one of the biggest producers in the State. Only four hundred and fifty acres are turned to sugar—we grow a small amount of tobacco as a parallel crop. The rest is broken up between the tenants. However, it warrants a horse, since not all the roads are passable by carriage. I assume that you ride?'

He wondered at the sudden animation in her face, and the sparkle in those usually sombre eyes, until she answered, 'Since I was seven years old. Papa bought me a chunky Welsh pony for my birthday. It had a scarlet harness and ribbons in its mane. After that, in my teens, there was a bay mare called Pippa. Oh, what a jumper she was! She took the low hedgerows around the estate as if she were one of Phaethon's horses.' For a moment Laurel's eyes clouded over. 'She jumped once too often and once too high. She was startled by a poacher's gun, and bolted. I tried to rein her in, but I was too young and far too weak. She attempted a stone wall surrounding one of the cottages.' Her voice caught for a moment, and she was unable to speak. 'She . . . she somersaulted, throwing me into a bush which broke my fall . . . She broke her neck.' Rafe watched, as he had done before, the indrawn breath and lifting of that courageous chin. 'When I had recovered I was given a dapple gelding; a pretty animal, but not Pippa.' She came back to the present with a rueful smile. 'It was just as well, considering that she was lost to a pair of Kings six months later! It was shortly after that time that Mama died and we began our own Grand Tour . . . a little like gipsies, but without the fortitude . . . But I fear I'm boring you. I'm sorry. Of course I'd love to see the estate.'

A glint of humour flickered in those unfathomable eyes. 'Not your English country estate . . . you betray your origins, but a plantation, which I think you will find quite different. Do you have riding clothes? If not, I'm sure we can find you something.'

Laurel thought of the dark green velvet costume, five years old but still becoming, and nodded. 'I shall change.' '*Nothing*,' she thought, 'nothing shall force me to wear something of *hers*!'

With wary optimism she changed, then went outside to where Rafe stood between two horses. The mare was an exquisite Arabian, the delicately curved ears and large liquid eyes turning to Laurel's approach even before the velvety muzzle reached for her hand. 'Oh, you beauty!' Laurel breathed, caressing the silky neck. A snort and an irritable tattoo of hooves brought her attention to the other, a magnificent Arab-thoroughbred with fiery eyes and flattened ears. Restlessly he chewed at the bit, earning a mild slap from the man at his side.

'Meet Serena and Saladin,' Rafe introduced. 'It should be unnecessary for me to warn you against attempting to pet *this* one . . . or, for that matter, even to approach too closely. He has already savaged two blacks, not to mention a self-opinionated Yankee who swore he could ride anything on four legs. I regretted the loss of the boys.' He came to swing Laurel effortlessly into the high-pommelled saddle before leaping into his own. Two of a kind, Laurel thought, with reluctant admiration.

They rode in silence towards the fields in which the young cane, which had sprouted in April from the joints of the old stalks laid down, was already waist high. Suddenly a loud cry rang out, startling Saladin who cavorted and bucked; then, pleased with his progress, he reared high on powerful hind-quarters. Rafe laughed aloud—the first time Laurel had heard him do so—and brought the stallion down with the ease of a master, the muscular thighs iron hard beneath the tight fawn trousers. Laurel froze, communicating her fear to the mare, who trembled violently but then quietened almost immediately.

The cry grew in volume, rising and falling in strange cadence, and Laurel threw a questioning look of surprise at the smiling man on the still restive black. 'That's just Ben starting a holler. Saladin never will get used to it.'

'A . . . holler?'

'Listen.' As he spoke, other voices took up the weird rhythmic. 'Ha-oo-la-ya-oo' sound, giving it their own variation and tone until the field rang with the work-song of men who had no need to see each other, yet who could work together, hoeing in unison. 'Hollers have been echoing in these and other fields since even before the slave days,' he explained. 'Sometimes they turn into real songs—cotton-field songs, tobacco-picking songs, even love-songs like "Row After Row" about a man who is hoeing and thinking about the woman he wants, even though some say she's neither pretty nor sweet-tempered. For the most part, however, it's this wordless cry. You wait until cutting-time at the beginning of November, when we hire casual labour from the fishing and trapping families in the bayous. Then you will hear some real music.' He gave a mirthless chuckle. 'Devil's music, some call it, which seeks to enslave a man's mind as well as his body. You see, Laurel, freeing the slaves didn't change the attitudes and ingrained beliefs of their owners one jot—or make the blacks more free. They simply exchanged one form of slavery for another.'

'But at least they now have a choice of where they work, and they are paid for it,' Laurel objected. 'The South can't possibly go back to what it was.'

He gave her a brief, half-pitying look. 'Of course the South will never be the same. We were the roosters on the dunghill—by freeing the slaves they removed the dunghill. Oh, we can still crow—and sip our mint juleps if we grow hoarse—but if the dunghill is gone, what in God's name are we crowing about? We lost the war to people with the same misconceptions as you have. Slavery? Freedom? Who were the slaves and who the freemen? Most of the South were dirt farmers who never owned slaves. As for the others . . . Well, most of the old people you will see today were in these fields in my father's time, and their fathers simply changed masters, not homes. When the Declaration ordered their freedom, should my father have turned them out of the only home they knew to face an unknown road north or west? A lot did, but we gave ours the choice—such as it was. Of course we couldn't afford to feed or house them; many blacks and poor whites were richer than the planters who survived the war and were then crippled by taxes. Some planters even moved into the warmth and charity of their ex-slaves' quarters while they rebuilt the plantations together. Of course hundreds of slaves left, and many are still wandering in a hopeless, bewildered quest for the freedom they were promised. Our people stayed, and we recovered the faster. I've watched my father working the fields in overwashed denim pants and homespun cotton shirts. My mother cooked over open fires in faded calico, mending the tears with hands more accustomed to delicate embroidery. Pork was the staple diet and sometimes we had cornbread and raw greens . . . but we were a "family" of around fifty, and when others fell, we rose. It was a time when God closed his eyes for a moment, but when he opened them we were still there . . . and on our feet, not our knees. We divided the land, since we had no money to give them, and they work it now as tenant farmers. We provide their homes and they give back a percentage of their crop. They work my fields and are paid a percentage of *my* crop. The harder they work, the greater the yield . . . yet it was only last year that we once again reached our yield of 1860 . . . Next year it will be even better. In the meantime . . . and you must forgive me if my protracted speech-making has bored you . . . allow me to show you the so-called slave quarters.'

When Laurel saw the neat whitewashed huts, some with flowering shrubs before the doors, some with gay ribbon tying back the crisp white curtains, her preconceived ideas of run-down wooden shacks housing abject tenants completely disappeared. A girl came from one and approached, smiling. 'Welcome, Marse King. Is a bright and beautiful day.' Her black hair fell straight to her shoulders and the creamy skin was only a shade darker than Laurel's own.

Answering Laurel's puzzled glance, Rafe stated. 'Minna is an octoroon. Her father was white, her mother a quadroon. She was another of

Castille's would-be neophytes to whom I gave an alternative.'

Laurel was shocked. 'But she's only a child!'

'She is fifteen now; quite old enough to work in the fields or bear children, and she has been with us for just over two years.' Bending gracefully, he put a lean hand on the girl's shoulder, speaking low in French patois.

The liquid black eyes swung to Laurel and she gave a slight frown, her good humour dissolved. 'Welcome . . . mistress,' she said as if forced into it by convention and her master's reminder, then, shaking off Rafe's hand, she stalked back into the hut.

Rafe's words of the previous night echoed in Laurel's heart. 'You will not question my movements or any action I take. You do not have the right.' Suddenly the day seemed oppressively hot. She was quite, quite certain now with whom he had spent his wedding night, and her heart cracked just a little. 'I think I would like to go back now . . . the heat . . .'

He gave her a strange look, but nodded. 'Can you find your own way? I have to check on the workers.'

'Of course,' Laurel agreed, thinking that she would have to find her own way down more than one path from now on.

Pensively she handed the mare to the waiting negro and walked slowly into the house. So much of her life, so many of her beliefs, had taken a beating of late that it was only her indomitable spirit which kept her head high. If marriage was not an institution founded on love and affection, at least it could last on mutual respect. If the daughter she had always wanted did not love and revere her, then perhaps even her jealousy could be turned to acceptance and, in time, friendship. If the ex-slaves about her were treated more like the beloved family retainers she had known as part of her childhood's 'extended family', then possibly, in time, she could earn their regard and even affection.

Crossing the great hall, she hesitated as a voice from the drawing-room brought her to that door. 'She won't fit, Mama; she never will.' Laurel eased open the door silently, revealing a lost and lonely figure confronting the huge portrait. 'I'd run away, Mama, truly I would—no one wants me here—but he'd just send the pattyrollers after me like he did you. Oh, Mama, you never talked to me much when you was living. Can't you just give me some small idea of what I should do now you have more time? He can't love her, Mama, not after you—He just can't!'

Tears streaming down her cheeks, Laurel fled to her room, flinging herself down on the bed—*her* bed—letting the great dry sobs tear through her.

'Rafe . . . what is a pattyroller?' she asked over luncheon.

He hesitated, a forkful of broiled and spiced redfish half-way to his lips, and the eyes, all grey now, narrowing. 'Why?' Ice touched the air about them.

'Oh, just a word that came to mind . . . perhaps something I heard while in New Orleans and never enquired into.'

There was no mistaking the relief in his eyes. 'The word is patter-roller, an old slave term that you may have heard in a corruption of some old plantation song such as "Run, Nigger, Run". A law was passed that no negro should be off his plantation at night without a special permit. There were patrols posted along the roads to catch those who disobeyed the order; the slaves called them patter-rollers. The old ballads of how the slaves eluded those patrols—or were caught by them—have been handed down over the years—and will probably be handed down for a few generations more. That's all there is to it.'

Laurel forced a smile, turning her attention to the delicately spiced fish on her plate, tasting nothing. Why should Marie-Louise say such a thing? Why would a man—any man—send patrols after his wife . . . and why would the lovely Hélène ever run away from a husband who had always, and still, loved her?

After the meal Rafe rose with the air of one who wishes to be alone. 'There is a matter I must attend to in the fields,' he stated abruptly. 'Quarrels break out and I must play Solomon. I doubt that I shall be in before dinner: I trust you will be able to occupy yourself. Plantation life can be lonely for a woman accustomed to the endless whirl of the town.'

Laurel was unable to restrain a smile. 'I'm from a Sussex family, even though after my mother died we went on a seemingly endless tour of Europe.

There is really little to choose between the mandatory pursuits of the land-owner's well-brought-up daughter, who sees the London season only during May and June, and the plantation-owner's wife. You ride the fields, my father rode to the hounds; you shoot wild animals, he shot pheasant and grouse . . . I was too young for shooting or archery until it was too late. Then I followed him around Europe, watching him trying to replace my mother with the cards . . . or anything else that would stop him thinking. One hotel room, one gambling-hall, is much the same as another. I read well, Rafe, as I have grown accustomed to doing, while waiting . . . so have no fear that I will become bored by waiting for you instead of for him. As for loneliness, it's an old friend, so don't let me detain you.'

With a relieved nod he strode out, calling for Saladin, his orders ringing up through the open windows.

'Shall I clear, missis?' Laurel looked up, startled from her reverie by the little black housemaid in starched black cotton and white apron.

'Yes . . . yes, of course.' The girl began stacking the china, watched by Leona, who had appeared silently in the doorway. She made no move to step aside at Laurel's approach and, feeling the anger start within her, Laurel demanded, 'Did you want me, Leona?'

The black eyes betrayed nothing as she finally moved out of Laurel's path. 'No, Mrs King . . . I didn't want you.' 'Nor ever will,' her tone implied.

'I shall be in the library. I should like a word with

Mr Jordan immediately he arrives—immediately, do you understand?'

'Yes, Mrs King. Will you see him there or in the drawing-room with a cordial?'

'The drawing-room. A cordial and some biscuits.' The 'please' refused to come, but, glad of having made use of the woman, Laurel turned to the library, as conscious as before of that malevolent stare boring into her back. She knew that her tone had been too sharp and resolved to improve it, but there was something about the woman that made politeness difficult and anything warmer quite out of the question.

The library was to the right of the front door and from its large square window one could see the long drive. It was a warmly inviting room, yet both practical and totally masculine. The large oak desk near the window was covered with assorted ledgers and papers relevant to the running of the plantation, yet the chair behind it was almost an armchair; a vast high-backed piece in dark brown leather—a full seventy years before its time. Unusually, there were no curtains, only heavily hinged shutters which allowed an unobstructed view of the azaleas by day and closed out the chill air by night.

Laurel wandered across to one of the bookshelves, touching Shakespeare and Wordsworth, Plato and his disciple Aristotle, and works by authors she did not know in French and Spanish. All had been read and re-read and she wondered at the complexity of the cold man she had married. The education of the Southern gentlemen even at that time was more a matter of chance than choice, and the handling of horses and women infinitely more preferable to the handling of a set of books. Here was a man who appeared to do all three, and yet still had time to read for pleasure. There were reference works, complete shelves covering history and geography, mathematics and law, and, un-surprisingly, all aspects of growing sugar, tobacco and cotton. Laurel browsed, fascinated, and it seemed that but a moment had passed before Steven Jordan was announced.

As Laurel opened the drawing-room door her smile of welcome froze as her breath caught in her throat, her mind screaming repudiation. The same spare frame, the same shock of white hair . . . but then the man turned from his contemplation of the portrait, and the face was that of a stranger. The lined patrician features registered concern as he saw the slender figure sway, her hand going to the heavy door-frame for support as her face drained of colour. In an instant he was beside her, pale blue eyes searching hers, surprisingly firm hands beneath her elbows.

'Madame, what is it? Come, sit down.'

Shaken, Laurel allowed him to lead her to the sofa and pour a glass of cordial. For several seconds she was unable to speak, but eventually raised those wide, mist-grey eyes to his, taking his breath away. 'Mr Jordan, what must you think of me? I do apologise . . .'

'*Au contraire*, madame, it is I who should apologise, since it was obviously the sight of me that caused you such distress.'

'No . . . no, not you . . . It was . . . I thought . . .

Oh, you will think me the most hen-witted ninny in the world, but I have recently lost my father and for that instant . . . the hair, the same figure . . .'

'Please, madame, do not distress yourself further. I quite understand. My deepest condolences on your loss.'

Thanking him, quite recovered now, she gave a brief smile. 'What a disastrous introduction!'

'Not at all,' he differed, returning her smile, the blue eyes twinkling. 'Had it been any other way, we might have spent our first meeting in politely restrained small talk. As it is, we have dispensed with formalities and are already friends, no?'

'I hope so,' she agreed in that husky voice that made him wish for half his years and twice his fortune. 'I shall be honest and admit to the need for a friend. We had been in New Orleans only a month before my father died of a heart-attack, so there was little time to socialise . . . My father was a gambling man, you see.'

His soft 'Aah!' held a wealth of understanding, for which she was grateful.

'But enough of myself. My husband said that you were Parisian, but your name . . . Steven Jordan?'

Again that twinkle that belied his years. 'It is a corruption—anglicised to help these Americans who appear to have some difficulty in pronouncing Étienne Jourdan. Since he told you of me, it is also likely that you know more about me than just my name . . . My profligate past, for instance?' His tone conveyed no regrets; indeed a trace of pride showed through, which Laurel found quite irresistible.

'I was given the distinct impression,' she said, 'that not only should I insist on a chaperon when in your company, but that my husband risked instant death should he object.'

A bark of laughter greeted her sally. 'And yet you came. Bravo, madame!' Her fingers were carried swiftly to his lips in appreciation. 'There has been little humour in this house since I came. You are a ray of light in an otherwise dull existence . . . not that I wish to imply that the young mam'selle is dull . . .'

Laurel rose on cue, terminating their brief conversation and bringing him to his feet beside her. 'And, talking of Marie-Louise, I have kept you too long already. She is finding the transition difficult enough without the needless worry of sharing even the smallest part of your friendship with a mother she neither likes nor wants.'

'Surely not!' But Laurel's eyes, bright with pain, confirmed her remark, and his aristocratic features took on a new determination as her stark loneliness fired his protective instincts. 'I shall say nothing, *chère* madame, but be assured that I shall do all in my power to advance your case. Children can be difficult over any change, but I have no doubts at all that she will soon come to love you. How could she not?' And the kindly blue eyes held hers in warm reassurance as his lips again brushed her fingers. At the door, he turned with a smile. 'Madame King . . . My youth was blessed with a number of ladies . . . some beautiful, some high born, all unforgettable. I never dreamed that the winter of my years would be blessed by one who is all three.

Humbly I offer my friendship and whatever small part of my battered old heart you might choose to accept.'

Smiling, Laurel swept him a low court curtsy. 'I would be honoured to accept both, sir . . . if I might be permitted to address you as Étienne and if you would call me Laurel.'

'You do me honour . . . Laurel,' and he made music of her name, accentuating the last syllable rather than the first.

His going left an emptiness in the room, yet it also left a hope in Laurel's heart and more comfort than she had known since her arrival, for she knew that she had at least one ally in this house of strangers. Somehow she *would* win the love of this child only ten years her junior. 'I *must* find a way!' Unconsciously she paced the room, arms folded defensively before her, her emotions taut as a spring. It was not just Marie-Louise, it was Leona and Rafe too who had to be wooed and won . . . and all the unknown shadows lurking in the halls of memory and waiting to leap out and destroy her present. Her throat felt dry, and agitatedly she poured some more cordial into her glass. It spilled over her shaking fingers and she returned her glass to the tray. 'I won't give in! I won't! I have help now.' But the day was warm, far too warm, when already her skin felt aflame. 'Leona!'

Almost instantly—like a spider awaiting the fly— 'Yes, Mrs King?'

'A bath in my room. I'd like to take a cool bath.'

'Yes, Mrs King.' No argument there; no wonder

at the mistress taking a bath half-way through the afternoon.

Laurel took a deep breath as the woman disappeared on silent feet. 'You won't beat me!' she said to the smiling portrait. 'You have stacked the cards against me, but I shall beat you yet, because I am the here and the now.' Imagination painted a shade of scorn on that perfect mouth, and Laurel swept from the room before her determination faltered.

She did not have long to wait before she was soaking in the scented water, yet even that failed to ease her tormented, searching mind. After drying herself with the luxuriously fluffy towel, she slipped into a peignoir of the palest blue silk before calling for the tub to be emptied. Ritualistically she brushed out the unruly mass of flaxen waves, knowing them too long for fashion yet not having the heart to allow them to be cut, remembering how her father had loved them so. Thanks to the style set by the popular Lily Langtry, her hair could be set in a large chignon low on the nape of her neck, but at times it seemed unbearably heavy and at times . . . a time like this . . . She let it fall in a veiling cloak about her face as she buried her head in her arms.

Beside the brush was a deck of cards which she had taken from her dressing-bag, and the mere sight of it brought her some small comfort. Now, as she raised tear-blurred eyes, she saw it as a tangible part of her past, and her fingers closed over it spasmodically, bringing it to her cheek as if the very touch could bring him back. She thought of the

number of times she had awakened to the slap-slap
of cards on the table as he dealt endless hands, even
when there was no game to play. The number of
times she had dreamed and awakened on some
couch to the staccato rattle of roulette wheels in
casinos from Paris to Rome, the clink of chips and
the dealer's clear call of *'Faites vos jeux'*. No more!

She had risen and taken the deck to the small
walnut table by the chaise-longue where, almost
absent-mindedly, she began to shuffle; the years
of practice spent trying to please that beloved
gambling man taking over. Waterfalls cascaded
between flying fingers, fans and ripples rolled over
the table before her as faster and faster she dealt,
cut, spread and re-gathered until with a low moan
she swept the cards to the floor, falling forward
across the table with arms outstretched before her
in an agony of despair.

She did not hear him enter, only the sudden,
sharp intake of breath, but when she surged upright
in shock, his expression was masked. Instinctively
her hands went up to gather her tumbled curls into
some semblance of order. 'Rafe! I . . . I thought
you were out!'

'Obviously.' He gave a short bow. 'I did not
mean to disturb you, Laurel.' His all-encompassing
look took in the star-washed eyes and the trembling, rose-tinted lips, parted with the same agitation
that caused her breasts to rise and fall rapidly
beneath the clinging folds of the peignoir. But it
was her hair, the like of which he had never seen
loosened in such abundance, that held his gaze. Yet
the granite features never betrayed the turmoil

within him, never betrayed the longing to sweep
her into his arms and bury his lips in that flaxen
harvest. 'I apologise for startling you. I shall be in
the library, should you need me; there are some
papers I have to attend to.' With another almost
formal bow, as one stranger to another, he left her.

'Why does he despise me so?' she wondered
aloud—never dreaming that his very coldness
might cloak emotions so white hot that he dared not
unleash them for fear of losing her for ever.

CHAPTER
FIVE

THAT VERY coldness drew Laurel inevitably closer
to the Frenchman, who proved to be quite the
contrary of Rafe in every respect. He entertained
her with tales that held more fantasy than fact,
boasting with laughing, grandiose gestures while
sipping juleps or strolling with her in the overgrown
garden. Yet there was nothing but warmth in the
pale blue eyes that often appraised her, and nothing but support and affection in the occasional
touch of his hand, and more and more she found
herself confiding in him.

'I feel that I have made no progress at all,' she
confessed after a particularly trying day. 'I know
that it hasn't been long, but each hour I have been
here seems like a day and each day an eternity.'

Only that morning, she remembered, Marie-
Louise had caught her gazing at the portrait of
Hélène, and remarked, 'She was very beautiful,
wasn't she?'

'Yes, very,' Laurel had reflected, not choosing
her words with as much care as she might have
used. 'The painter may have idealised her a little,
accentuated certain points as artists undoubtedly
do, but, yes, she was quite beautiful.'

'*Quite* beautiful!' the child had cried, tawny eyes flashing. 'My mother was the most beautiful lady in Louisiana . . . and probably in the whole of America. You aren't like her at all!'

'You're right, Marie.' And at Rafe's voice from the doorway, they both turned to face him. He had come in from the fields, and the mane of honey-blond hair was shiny with perspiration and ruffled by the wind and careless fingers. His eyes flickered over the two, and a half-smile touched his mouth as he delayed for an instant before going upstairs. 'Quite right,' he continued. 'Laurel is no more like your mother than the moon is like the sun, but after the heat of the day, how cool the night . . .' and he was gone, the click of his heels echoing across the hall.

'You heard him,' jeered Marie-Louise triumphantly. 'He said you were just like the pale old moon and my mother bright and beautiful like the sun.' Laughing cruelly, she ran off into the garden.

'Yes . . . I heard him,' Laurel mused softly, 'but perhaps it was my imagination that heard it differently' . . . 'or my vain hopes and storm-tossed dreams,' her mind challenged.

'Give her time, Laurel,' the Frenchman soothed, sipping fresh lemonade during their precious half-hour together at the end of the afternoon. 'She is softening; even talks of you during her lessons. Just a chance remark here and there.'

'At your instigation, no doubt?'

He smiled. 'You are too suspicious. I do, at times, mention a certain colour that you have worn which might suit her . . . She is very conscious of her appearance just now, the cygnet slowly emerging as a swan, and she feels that I am the only ally she has. That tea-gown you wore yesterday, the one with the silver buckles . . . Did you not notice a similarity in her dress today? She would die rather than admit it, but she knows in her heart that the brilliant plumage I am told Hélène wore would smother Marie herself, so you are the obvious choice. Children have to emulate someone, having neither the wisdom nor the experience themselves. Then, too, there is a certain . . . *je ne sais quoi* about you, a certain *tristesse* that appeals to her own loneliness.'

'I *have* caught her watching me on occasion, but . . . Oh, Étienne, if only she would take just one step forward. It has been a whole week now . . .'

'It has been only a week, *ma chère* . . . forgive me . . . Laurel. Only a week in a lifetime of weeks.'

Impulsively she covered his hand with hers, bringing its coolness to her cheek.

'Very pretty!' drawled Rafe from the doorway, springing them apart.

The Frenchman's eyes were suddenly icy as he rose to face the sardonic Virginian. 'I was reassuring your wife that her unceasing efforts to win your daughter's love were not totally in vain. Perhaps, m'sieu, if you would leave your library more often you could do a far better job than I.'

'Has my wife complained of neglect, Mr Jordan?' There was a trace of steel underlying the apparently mild tone.

'Your wife has not spoken of you at all, Mr King
. . . which makes its own point, I believe.'

'Oh, stop it, both of you!' Laurel cried, leaping to
her feet, heavy-lashed eyes wide in distress. 'If my
husband and the only friend I have in the world are
going to quarrel over me, whom do I have left?
Whom do I turn to without offending the other?
Oh, I wish I had never *seen* New Orleans!' She ran
blindly, pushing past Rafe and fleeing to the garden
and into the trees, pushing through the tangled
undergrowth and whipping branches until she came
to a panting halt beneath a giant oak.

Unaware of time, she slowly regained control of
her shattered emotions, only then feeling the stinging of a dozen tiny scratches on her face and hands.
Her fingers went to her tumbled hair and removed
the twigs and leaves caught there before winding it
into a loose knot. Suddenly she froze at the sound
of cracking branches and the low blowing of a
horse.

'Laurel? . . . Laurel!'

Defeated, she leaned back against the rough
bark. 'I'm here, Rafe. Over here.'

Within seconds he was beside her, sliding from
Saladin's bare back and taking hold of her arms in
iron-hard fingers, his eyes angry, yet with a flicker
of something else in their stormy depths. 'Don't
ever do that again!' he growled, giving her a little
shake that brought a gasp of pain to her lips.
Immediately he released her as he became aware
of the source of her indrawn breath, a deep scratch
on her arm, already oozing blood.

His cool fingers slid through the jagged rent in

her sleeve, exploring the skin, burning it as if by fire. She flinched sharply, earning a murmured apology. 'It must be thoroughly cleansed,' he instructed, his voice tight with suppressed emotion.

Their eyes met and the earth seemed to tilt beneath her feet. With an effort, she brought her errant thoughts under control. He was not concerned for her, only for the defacing of his property. He was not worried about her, only angry at the embarrassment she had caused him. 'It's nothing . . . a scratch.' Her slightly husky voice conveyed some kind of fear, a rejection of her own feelings that found a reflection in his eyes.

His lips tightened, but his voice was surprisingly gentle as he stated, 'You are no doctor, madam. Until you are, you will allow me to know what is best for you. It is time I took you back.' Easily he lifted her to Saladin's broad back, leaping up behind her before the stallion could rear at the unaccustomed weight. Strong arms came about her, one to gather the reins, the other encircling her waist, holding her against him. Laurel caught the male scent of him, felt the heat of his body through the thin dress, and stiffened. 'Don't fight me, Laurel,' he murmured, his lips against her ear. 'You are bound to lose.'

There was no answer she could make, but as the giant Arab-Thoroughbred picked its way delicately back to the house she found her body relaxing into the curve of the arm about her, her head finding the hollow of his shoulder. Within sight of the unkempt structure that was her home—for better or worse—she asked, 'What of Étienne . . . Mr Jordan?'

A slight stiffening of his frame was all that betrayed him, and his tone was light as he answered, 'I would be a fool to dismiss so excellent a tutor over such an incident.'

Breathing more easily, Laurel ventured, 'And may I see him again?'

'It would seem unavoidable,' he commented dryly, and was rewarded by those incredible eyes turned up to his in gratitude. 'Thank you!' she breathed. 'Oh, thank you, Rafe!'

Her lips were only inches from his own and he knew that, in her present mood, should he bend and claim them, they would part in response. He also knew that, once the mood had passed, she would regret her weakness. 'We are here,' he stated unnecessarily, and slipped to the ground to lift her down.

Looking up, he saw that slender frame bent towards him, awaiting his attention, and his throat became dry. His strong hands curved about her waist and effortlessly he lifted her from Saladin's gleaming back, but then drew her towards him so that her body slid slowly, so slowly, down his. Her cheeks were crimson as her feet touched the ground, and she felt her heart pounding against the thin fabric of her gown. The finely chiselled features bent towards her. His breath fanned her cheek and the eyes—all green again, as jade as that ever-warm stone—narrowed with desire. A moment out of time. A heartbeat when she felt her whole being sway towards him, then . . . 'We must tend that wound,' and she was released.

She had been so sure that he had been about to

kiss her, and her mouth ached with the neglect . . . as her heart ached with yet another example of his rejection. Part of her longed to feel again those strong arms about her and the touch of his lips against her skin. Yet there was another part of her, conditioned by a society for whom passion was the prerequisite of whores, that shrank from the very maleness of him. 'He is too much man!' her timid heart cried, yet, as his hand curved beneath her elbow to escort her into the house, her body gave her heart the lie.

'I shall instruct Leona to put some healing herbs in a bath for you,' he said, holding open the front door. 'I am going to the library.'

'Of course.' The words slipped out before she could stop them, and Laurel bit her lips as his eyes darkened.

'I have a plantation to run, madam; Moonrise is what feeds and clothes you . . . and buys you friends such as Steven Jordan!' The previous intimacy between them vanished as though it had never been.

'I'm sorry, Rafe, I didn't mean . . .' but already he had turned away.

Miserably Laurel went to her room and within minutes was soaking in deep, scented water. 'Oh why does it always end this way?' she agonised. 'Each time we meet I offend, or am offended; reject, or am rejected. He still loves Hélène, that is obvious. Does he think of her *every* time he looks at me? Wish his arms were about her voluptuousness instead of my skinny frame?' Laurel soaped the 'skinny frame' without seeing the bloom on the ivory skin, and totally unaware of the beauty of those willow-slender curves, too conditioned to Rubens to appreciate Gainsborough. 'He will never stop loving her, but if only, for once, he would see me as a wife instead of a governess for Marie-Louise . . . or if Marie would, just once, see me as a friend and not as a rival of a woman long dead. If only for one brief moment out of each day they would let me into their lives . . .' With a sigh at the apparent impossibility of her dream, she bathed the stinging scratches as well as she could, and washed her tangled hair.

Afterwards, sitting wrapped in two large soft towels, she surveyed herself in the cheval mirror, touching the ugly scratches on her face with trembling fingers. 'You are a mess!' she remonstrated aloud; then, aware of another presence, turned to find the housekeeper behind her.

'Yes, Leona?' she queried more sharply than intended, then, forcing a more reasonable tone, 'What is it?'

The woman held out a pottery jar containing a yellowish-white cream. 'This will take away the pain and prevent scars.'

Surprised, Laurel took the jar and sniffed at it warily. At once she wrinkled her nose with an expression of disgust. 'Whatever it is, it smells awful!'

The trace of a smile lifted the housekeeper's lips and then was gone, but the usual harsh expression had disappeared from the black eyes. 'It is not attar of roses,' she admitted, 'but you may wipe it off before dinner.' Firmly she took hold of Laurel's gashed arm, dipped two fingers into the malodorous cream and smoothed it thickly over the wound.

Flinching at first, Laurel soon found a strange coolness pervading the whole area that had been burning and bleeding freely after her bath. Before she could speak, however, Leona had pulled back the hair from the girl's face, wrapping it in a large piece of cotton which she tucked under, turban fashion, and then proceeded to cover the whole of her face with the balm. Her fingers were as light and cool as the ointment, and Laurel relaxed under her ministrations—until she opened her eyes and saw her reflection in the mirror.

A bubble of laughter rose and burst forth at the sight of the apparition before her. 'Oh, merciful heavens, what a sight! I look as if I have been dragged through the bayou and out through the Mississippi mud!' Her eyes met those of the housekeeper and found, incredibly, an echo of her own mirth. 'Oh, Leona, thank you—it feels much better already—but I'll never forgive you if you let anyone see me like this . . . anyone!'

Again came that flicker of a smile. 'It is a rare woman who could find laughter in this,' Leona said softly. 'I shall keep them away, don't worry . . . mistress.' She was gone before the full import of that last word registered, and then Laurel let out her breath in a slow exhalation of disbelief.

'I've won!' she said aloud. 'Whatever happened . . . she no longer hates me!' and she hugged herself, the pain quite forgotten.

*　　*　　*

During dinner, however, her new-found optimism was overshadowed by Marie-Louise's veiled yet constant insolence. 'You never did tell us just why you came to America,' she queried over the fresh peach sorbet. The tawny eyes were wide and ingenuous, but Laurel felt the hair prickle at the nape of her neck.

'Why, it seemed the next place to visit,' she answered with a forced smile. 'My father and I had travelled a fair way through Europe and could not have missed the chance to see America . . . Now, of course, I'm very glad we did.'

'Are you? Are you really?'

'Why yes, Marie; had we not done so, I would never have met you and your father.'

'Would that have been such a loss?'

'Marie!'

'But, Papa, I only meant . . .'

Arctic grey eyes met tawny gold, and it was the latter that dropped. She gave a mutinous pout. 'Laurel knows I mean nothing. *She* hasn't said anything.'

'Laurel is a lady, so she refuses to rise to your bait . . . a bait, my girl, that is barbed with ignorance and tipped with malice. It betrays your age as well as your blood. Now you may retire.'

'I haven't finished my sorbet . . . I am always having to leave meals because of her!'

His voice was quiet, yet crackled with pure ice. 'And will continue to do so, Marie-Louise, until your venomous tongue is starved of its poison. Now leave . . . at once!'

With a glare at her embarrassed stepmother she

ran from the room, not daring to slam the door, but leaving it wide in equal protest.

'I apologise for her,' Rafe offered. 'She will come round . . . She will have to.' The steel was still there and, Laurel realised with a small start of surprise, genuine dislike beneath the threat.

'But she is his daughter!' she wondered. 'How can he not be saddened by her behaviour and regretful of his own?' Sensing something there that she did not understand, she quickly changed the subject and saw his rigid frame relax. By the time they had finished coffee his mood had changed and she breathed more easily.

Finally, he revealed, 'I have more then Hélène's brat on my mind just now. Her mother, too, is coiling herself to strike. Madame Vautour advises me that she will be honouring us with a visit the day after tomorrow. She is a martinet to rival even your Aunt Sophie! If I could prevent her from coming, I would do so, but it has taken many abortive attempts to teach me otherwise. She will stay over-night only, much preferring the glitter of town and the fawning obsequiousness she receives at the St Louis Hotel. While here she will not be the easiest of company.'

Laurel studied her cup. So . . . Hélène's mother was coming to assess her.

Rafe saw her fingers go unconsciously to the scratches on her face and felt a wave of sympathy. 'They will be almost healed by then.'

She shot him a look of bitter self-knowledge. 'It will hardly matter, will it? Were I Sarah Bernhardt herself, she would still find me wanting.'

* * *

She had spoken with remarkable foresight. From the moment the iron-grey head nodded a frosty greeting and the sharp golden eyes—Marie-Louise's eyes—had raked her from elegantly coiffeured head to satin-slippered toe, missing nothing, the cards, as Wallace Faversham would have said, were on the table. 'So you are the girl Rafe married in such haste. I regret not being able to attend the wedding, but forty-eight hours' notice was a little short, even for me. I understand you knew each other little longer than that, anyway. Why, you must be almost strangers.'

Laurel held Madame Vautour's gaze levelly. 'Love sometimes happens that way, madame. After all, we have a lifetime of discovery ahead. Will you not come and have a sherry before dinner? Leona will show you to your room; you must be fatigued after your journey.'

Imagining the vulture-like woman with her sombre grey plumage in that sombre guest-room gave Laurel inestimable satisfaction, and she mentally remonstrated with herself for her lack of charity. During the next few hours, however, her charity, as well as her patience, was stretched to the limit. Over dinner, the stuffed crab was 'do you think . . . a trifle over-spiced?' and the wine 'a little over-chilled . . . even for white?' The crêpes soufflées, 'Quite delicious, but you really must try ours—our cook is a French émigrée, of course.' Rafe looked 'tired' and Marie-Louise 'peaky', and 'Don't worry about all those enchanting freckles, my dear; I'm sure you will grow out of them . . . one day.' To Laurel she addressed hardly a word.

After the tense meal Marie-Louise retired, for once with alacrity, and the adults repaired to the drawing-room, where Madame Vautour's sharp eyes went immediately to the fireplace. 'Aah!' she breathed in triumph. 'I see that you have retained *dear* Hélène's portrait, Rafe. I'm so glad.'

He glanced upward as if noticing the fact for the first time. 'That's right. I have had nothing with which to replace it . . . so far.'

'Her continued presence must be a little disconcerting for your . . . wife.'

'Not at all,' Laurel intervened. 'I find her quite lovely, and I am always interested in Rafe's past.'

Her slight emphasis on the last word did not escape madame's notice, and the tawny eyes narrowed a fraction. 'For Rafe, of course, there are other reminders very much in the present,' and, addressing him, 'Aurora is here, too.' Returning to Laurel, 'Hélène's younger sister. She was born just as dawn broke, so it just had to be Aurora.'

'But you didn't bring her here with you?'

'No, she went direct to the hotel. Unlike myself, she was unsure of her reception here. I am always certain of exactly the kind of welcome I shall receive, am I not, Rafe?'

'Always,' he agreed, equally ambiguously.

In an attempt to soften her, Laurel enquired, 'She and Hélène were alike, were they not?'

'Almost twins, even though there was a year between them. In fact Rafe would tease them about it unmercifully when he first came to call; pretending not to know the one from the other.'

Laurel could not imagine the granite-featured man by her side being so light-hearted as to tease anyone about anything—but it must have been, after all, fourteen or fifteen years ago. 'Then I really think I should meet her, don't you, Rafe?'

Before he could reply, Madame Vautour had stated, 'I shall telephone her first thing in the morning. I was going direct to town, but in this way she could be here for dinner and it will be . . . almost . . . like old times. I am sure you look forward to meeting her again, Rafe, close as you once were.'

'It will be my pleasure,' he agreed dryly, and some undercurrent passed between them that quite eluded the watching Laurel, making her wonder what hand she had dealt herself this time.

'But now I really must retire,' said the older woman, gathering her fringed shawl about her. 'Will you walk with me to my room?'

'Of course,' Laurel agreed, a little amused by the fact that not once since her arrival had this martinet addressed her by name.

'Goodnight, Rafe, dear. Thank you so much for the warmth of your hospitality.'

'It was no more than you deserve. Sleep well.'

Little was said until they reached the heavily panelled door of the guest-room, when those heavily-lidded eyes turned directly to Laurel's in open challenge. 'I make no apologies for my hopes that Rafe would, some day, re-marry into my family, as he could have done since there is no blood tie between him and Aurora, and Louisiana is still under Napoleonic Law. We both have land, breeding, money . . . and ambition. Rafe is an exceedingly handsome man; strong, arrogant and sometimes cruel—so are we. He will swamp you, my dear, and I shall do all I can to help him. Love is a fire; it needs fuel.'

Laurel felt her lips tight against her teeth as she forced a smile. 'I appreciate your honesty, madame, and I am sure you mean to intimidate me by it. However, you have told me nothing about either my husband or your daughters of which I was unaware. You will forgive me if I find nothing in your words to disconcert me in the slightest: on the contrary, we English are known for both our patience and our stubbornness.'

'You will need both. You are *only* married to him, and as you may have appreciated by now, it takes more than a rather ostentatious circle of gold to hold Rafe King.'

Laurel looked down at the wide wedding-ring that, together with the breathtaking square-cut emerald engagement-ring that Rafe had insisted on, reached the first joint of her finger. 'I entirely agree,' she said, 'but I have also found that it takes more than rather ostentatious plumage to divert him.' The simple cotton dress and liquid black eyes of the octoroon, Minna, came sharply to mind, but her pain was not to be shared and her eyes were steady. She opened the door with unmistakable deliberation. 'I regret the dated décor . . . I have heard of a much lighter fashion, that is taking young Parisians by storm, called 'Art Nouveau'. I thought of introducing a little of it here—just as a start to the many changes I plan. Sleep well, madame.'

The iron-grey head inclined in acknowledgment of the retrieved gauntlet. 'I always do, my dear.'

'She had to have the last word!' Laurel seethed, returning to the drawing-room where Rafe sprawled on the sofa, a glass of brandy held between negligent fingers. He gave one of his rare smiles at the set features.

'Did you receive the impression that the deck was stacked against you this evening?'

'And with marked cards,' Laurel agreed, returning the smile gladly. 'But it takes more than one game to break a run. I'm not afraid to play again tomorrow.'

Setting down his brandy, he rose and came to stand before her, the deep-set eyes more green than grey and with an expression she had not seen before. Gently he tilted up her chin with one finger and she drowned in those fathomless depths. 'My fearless fighter,' he murmured. She closed her eyes as his lips touched hers with a kiss so light that, as she was released, and the door closed behind him, she wondered if it had ever been. Her fingers went to the place, reassuring her. It had been a kiss with neither passion nor yet love, not the kiss of a husband, nor quite that of a friend . . . yet somehow an intangible combination of all. Bemused, she wandered up to her own room, lying awake long into the night, watching the moon's patterns on the ceiling and wondering how she would fare in her coming confrontation with Aurora . . . goddess of the dawn.

Yet, when the 'goddess' appeared, it was as though all Laurel's doubts had been groundless. Aurora was as charming as she was lovely, and from the first 'Laurel, how kind of you to invite me,' she appeared to make a special effort towards friendship. Not difficult, Laurel thought a trifle enviously, when your hair was the colour of the sunset and your eyes the azure blue of the Mediterranean; when your skin was the pink-white of camellia blossoms and your mouth a musk rose. The crépon and silk gown was of the palest grey, with the wide, embroidered, blue lawn cape setting off the gently sloping shoulders. The blue silk of the bodice was echoed in the silk let into each seam of the skirt and in the silk cuffs; the total effect being one of sweet femininity. Although she was Laurel's senior by almost nine years, those years melted away before the spell cast by her slightly breathless voice wearing Deep South on its tongue, and her wide eyes.

'How beautiful you've grown!' she exclaimed on seeing the hesitant Marie-Louise, sweeping the child to her in a hug that Laurel would never have dared. 'And Rafe, more handsome than ever! Laurel, I should hate you for possessing such a perfect family, but how can I when you are so lovely yourself? Oh *do* let me see if things have changed. You don't mind, do you? Of course you couldn't. Why, this was almost my second home.'

Madame Vautour's eyes met those of Laurel, and a mocking smile curved the thin lips. 'Look well, my dear. Laurel informs me that there are sweeping changes to be made.'

'Not to my room,' Marie-Louise growled mutinously.

'Nor to mine, I hope,' smiled Rafe more gently, but Aurora again eased the situation.

'You mustn't be stuffy, Rafe, darling. I am sure Laurel has excellent taste.' Laurel threw her a look of gratitude and received a conspiratorial wink in return. 'Now, I'm famished. What delicacies are you going to offer me for dinner?' She linked her arm into Rafe's with old familiarity and together they strolled towards the dining-room, conversing in low tones.

Laurel felt a flicker of envy, wishing with all her heart for that bright insouciance, but covered it with a smile as she caught the twin looks of Madame Vautour and the child, so similar, so triumphant, even though years apart. 'Well, shall we follow them?'

The meal was undoubtedly the most pleasant that she had taken in that dismal house, with Aurora complimenting everything and everyone and flirting so outrageously with Rafe that no offence could possibly be taken. His lips seemed set in a vague smile, and once he actually laughed outright at one of her sallies, calling her a wicked minx. Her azure eyes widened with such feigned innocence that they all joined his laughter. Marie-

Louise was allowed to stay up until well past eleven and encouraged to chatter like a magpie, and by midnight Laurel was regretting the close of the day.

As though reading her thoughts, Aurora said, 'Why don't you come back with us after breakfast, Laurel? I could introduce you to a miracle of a seamstress that Hélène always used—no woman can have too many dresses, don't you agree, Rafe, honey? Of course you do. Then we could take coffee and beignets at the Café du Monde, visit old friends and exchange life-stories. You have had such an exciting life in comparison with little old me . . . all over Europe . . . Paris gowns . . . I must hear all. Your carriage could bring you back well in time for dinner—or you could even stay overnight at the hotel. Please say you will come? You will let her, Rafe, won't you? Please?'

Turning to Rafe for his sanction, Laurel caught a look of puzzlement in his eyes. 'I don't know . . .'

'For my sake?' Aurora wheedled with that melting charm against which harder men had proved defenceless.

He gave a frown. 'I'll consider it,' and that rosebud mouth curved into a deliciously dimpled smile of triumph.

'Go on . . . Say it . . . You know you will.'

Finally defeated, he nodded. 'Why not? You will enjoy the chance of female chatter, Laurel. Heaven knows you get little enough here.'

To her surprise, the matriarch at her side offered no comment, but Laurel wondered at the slight smile that seemed to play about the normally harsh mouth. Dismissing the icy premonitions as unwarranted, she allowed the others to finalise arrangement for the following day.

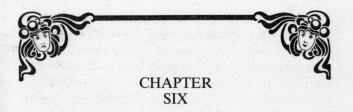

CHAPTER
SIX

THE FOLLOWING morning Rafe watched interested-
ly as the two younger women strolled in the garden
before leaving: Aurora lifting her skirt clear of a
large patch of mud by means of the ornate 'page'
attached to the waist-chain, Laurel dipping, grace
and aristocratic blue blood apparent in every movement, to sweep up the trained skirt in lace-gloved
fingers. The breath stopped in the watcher's throat
as flaxen head bent towards red in light conversation, then was thrown back in a burst of gurgling
merriment that he had thought never to hear.

Laurel was quite unaware of his presence at the
library window, and he could drink his fill. Surely
he had not needed the detectives that he had employed the second time he had seen her. Her ancestry could be traced back to the Saxon invaders of
England; her blood was that of ancient war-lords,
golden-haired kings and the icy blue-eyed maidens
they had bedded, wedded and finally loved.

Something of his intense gaze must have communicated itself to her and she turned, her eyes
going unerringly to where he stood. She gave a
little start and, although she could not see his eyes
nor he hers, a spark of electricity flashed between
them, and it was almost as if he had touched her.

Aurora spoke in laughing remonstrance and Laurel turned to her, breaking the spell, allowing herself to be led away. Only then did Rafe realise that he had almost stopped breathing.

Laurel was enchanted by the carriage-ride, which was in every way the opposite of her ride *to* Moonrise. Even the frosty Madame Vautour—Madam Vulture as Laurel had re-christened her—appeared more friendly, even using her name on one occasion! Aurora pointed out birds and plants that Laurel would not have seen, educating her and diverting her with amusing anecdotes of local people and customs. A bull 'gator roared in the swamp and Aurora told how the Indian boys sometimes proved their manhood by wrestling the great reptiles. 'Though I can think of other ways far more pleasurable,' she laughed.

They left the older woman at the hotel and continued on to Aurora's seamstress, a tiny plump quadroon with a permanent smile that revealed two gold front teeth. Rhapsodising over Laurel's tiny waist and full, yet uptilted, breasts revealed by the fine camisole, she swathed her in yard upon yard of material, draping it in folds about shoulder and waist. With a laugh Aurora remarked, 'I can see you'll be here another hour at least. Would you mind terribly if I took the carriage and met you at the Café du Monde? I can see an old friend in the meantime, and then we can window-shop afterwards, or even watch the boats come in.'

'Of course I don't mind,' Laurel exclaimed. 'You

have been most kind already. I am sure I can find my way to the French Market, and the walk will do me good.'

'Well, if you are going to walk, you'd best take the shortest route. Now, let me see . . . Yes . . . Three blocks from here, across North Rampart and right along Burgundy, then left down Dumaine.'

'But, madame!' gasped the seamstress. 'She can't . . .'

'Be quiet!' Aurora snapped, eyes flashing. 'Of course she can. I have been by that route plenty of times.'

The velvet eyes became veiled. 'Yes'm, *you* probably have,' she muttered.

'Now don't you go pretending it's a long walk. I'm sure Mrs King is quite able to walk that far.'

'Of course I am,' Laurel smiled, a little disconcerted by the incident, but unable to comment since she knew nothing of the area of which they spoke.

'Well then, I shall meet you in an hour or so. Take your time, Laurel. 'Bye now.' Aurora whisked out of the shop in a cloud of French perfume and rustling silk.

The seamstress remained ill at ease throughout the next hour, torn between losing an affluent and influential client in the Mississippian and thereby most of her other trade, and telling this lovely innocent that the area she was about to walk through held some of the toughest mixed-colour houses in the whole red light district. Her valued customer obviously had a purpose, but what it was eluded her, and caused her to ask anxiously, 'Won't you let me call you a carriage, Miz King?'

'That's the third time you have asked, and I *still* don't want one. Now . . . you know where to send those dresses, don't you?'

'Yes'm—I sewed plenty for th'other Miz King.' Laurel did not feel obliged to pursue that line of discussion, so said her farewells and left.

Within minutes she realised her mistake . . . or was it Aurora's? Surely the other had accidentally confused two street names. The houses became seedier and so did the people. A negress in crimson satin lounged in a doorway and made some remark in gumbo French as she passed, and another of lighter skin eyed her up and down with studied insolence, muttering something about the wrong beat. Confused and a little frightened now, Laurel quickened her pace, seeing with relief a white man in an elegant cut-away morning coat alight from a carriage. 'Excuse me, sir, could you . . . ?' She faltered to a halt at the wide, gold-toothed smile and the look in his eyes as they swept her from head to toe.

'I sure could, little lady. Never thought to see the likes of you off Lafayette Street.'

'I . . . I'm afraid I don't . . .'

'You like it straight, eh? New to the game? Well that's all right with me, sweet thing. Well? Where do you bunk?'

To her horror his arm came over her shoulders and the large be-ringed hand closed firmly over one breast. Realisation dawned! With a cry she broke free and ran, hearing his angry shout mingling with the laughter of the two women. Panic-stricken, she turned the wrong way, finding herself in St Louis

Street and among a conglomeration of filthy one-room shanties, some with doors ajar revealing a single bed—nearly always occupied. Unknowingly, she had stumbled into the worst street in Storyville, where for twenty-five cents you could buy almost any perversion of your choice in the lowest cribs in New Orleans.

As she turned back blindly, a scream was torn from her as a black brougham drew alongside and a tall figure leapt out and seized her in strong arms. 'Laurel! Laurel!' Half-fainting, she raised terror-filled eyes—then collapsed sobbing against Philippe Castille's chest. Murmuring soothing endearments, he lifted her into the carriage and the driver took them away from that nightmare place to a coolly shuttered house in Royal Street.

Still half-supporting her, he led the trembling girl into a large square room with tapestries on the stuccoed walls and brass lamps which threw a gentle glow over rich satinwood furniture.

'I . . . I'm all right now,' she said, more for her own assurance than his, stepping away from him and smoothing back her hair. 'I don't know what I would have done had you not appeared. I was quite lost and . . . Oh, Philippe, I was so scared! What a terrible place . . . and those people . . . the women . . . even children in those awful huts. Without you finding me . . .' She turned to him, eyes brimming with gratitude, then found her heart beating a little faster as she really saw him for the first time.

The lightly macassared hair gleamed in the lamplight and the olive skin took on a deeper hue.

He looked, Laurel thought, like one of Jean Lafitte's pirates and the resemblance did not end there, for he was wearing a full-sleeved shirt of fine white silk open almost to the waist, and black trousers that appeared to have been poured on.

He read the dual emotions in her eyes and smiled—with devastating effect. Philippe Castille was a past master in the art of seduction—especially in cases such as this, when there was an ulterior motive to the simple bedding of a lovely woman—and his voice was vibrant with emotion, not entirely contrived, as he said, 'My dear Laurel, I am so very glad that I found you. What a shock you have had! I saw you as my carriage was taking a fast route through Burgundy Street. You were running as if all the fiends in Hell were after you, so I followed with all haste. Then you turned into St Louis Street, and I knew that you must be totally lost. I reached you as fast as I could. Whatever were you doing in such an area? No, don't answer just yet. Allow me to take your coat and offer you a glass of orange wine to soothe your nerves?'

He could feel the tremors that still ran through her, and the velvet eyes flashed fire when he thought of the fate which must have befallen her had Aurora had her way. God! how the Mississippian must hate her! He could see those eyes now, glittering like azure as she taunted him.

'So you too fell under the spell of that whey-faced miss! Well, let me tell you, my fine Creole friend, after today *no* one will want her . . . if she survives.'

His face had paled and, seizing her arms, he had

shaken her violently. 'What do you mean? What have you done? Mon Dieu, I believe you're quite as evil as your sister!'

'More so,' she had laughed, 'because I can make people trust me. Hélène looked the whore she was, but no one could possibly believe ill of me. Oh, you should have seen your Victorian miss—all eyes ashine and tail awag for friendship! She has precious little in *that* house, and it shows.'

'I repeat . . . What have you done?'

'I may tell you—if you are nice to me—or I may not.' She smiled up at him sweetly, sure of her position, but then paled before the gaze in those dark eyes, a look she had never seen in any man. 'You really did want her, didn't you? she realised, her voice barely above a whisper.

'Yes, I wanted her. I would have had her, too. She would have come to me in time just as your sister did—to escape the boredom and the loneliness of that mausoleum.' His voice was ominously low, and the fingers that dug into her arms brought a gasp of pain to her lips. 'Now . . . you will tell me everything.'

'He should have married me! He *will* marry me!' she cried, but the fingers tightened, bringing tears to the lovely eyes.

'You *will* tell me, Aurora, or I shall beat you to within an inch of your miserable life. I shall scar you so badly that not even your mother will be able to look at you without being sick to her stomach . . . Now talk!' And, looking into those implacable eyes, she did.

*　　*　　*

'It's so good of you, Philippe, but I mustn't intrude on your hospitality any longer. I must get home later today, so I have to find Aurora and the carriage. She would not have waited this long at the café and I'm a little embarrassed to telephone the hotel—they are at the St Louis—lest I bring her mother's ire down on her. You just can't imagine how heavy that might be unless you have met the mother! I'm sure she meant no harm when she directed me to the French Market. I must have misheard her directions.'

Philippe revealed even white teeth in another perfect smile. 'I quite understand, and of course you must take *my* carriage.' Then, at her concerned look, 'Do not worry, *ma belle*, it is a new one, and Rafe will not recognise it. However, you will surely not desert me yet, will you? Another small glass of wine . . .'

Laurel allowed herself to be persuaded, feeling the warmth seep through her. Already it was mid-afternoon and she had eaten nothing since breakfast.

Philippe watched and waited, amusing her with anecdotes that finally brought the sparkle back into those bayou-mist eyes; entertaining her with light conversation which, interspersed as it was with subtle questioning, revealed more about her relationship with Rafe than even she was aware of.

When he offered the third glass, their fingers touched, and fire shot up her arm. 'I really must go.'

Instantly he sensed her panic and, man of the world that he was, the reason for it. Smoothly he rose from her side, his voice liquid gold. 'I shall call your carriage,' he soothed, inwardly smiling at her instant relief, 'but why waste good wine? I'll instruct the driver to await you outside, so that you may leave whenever you wish.'

Laurel sipped the wine, a subtle blend of Napoleon brandy and mandarin oranges, feeling the tongues of flame spread through her and her body relaxing against the cushions. A bubble of merriment rose within her and she gave a husky chuckle. 'I fear that if I finish this, you will have to carry me down to the carriage, and wouldn't that be terrible?'

'Terrible,' he agreed with mock solemnity. 'Terribly sinful, terribly decadent and terribly, terribly, pleasurable.'

'You must not tease so.'

'But of course I must, because it makes you smile just the way you're smiling now, and when your lips part just so what can a man do but . . . this?' And before she could object, his mouth descended, moving over hers with such sensual expertise that the hands she had brought up to push him away slid of their own volition about his neck.

'Philippe, no!' she protested weakly, and at once he released her, smiling down into eyes that revealed more than she knew. Yes, he could wait.

'Forgive me, *chérie!* I was bewitched . . . but what sweet enchantment! However, I am truly mortal and if I do not send you home immediately I may offend you further . . . if one could call such an offence.'

A dimple appeared at the side of her mouth as

Laurel returned his smile, even while trying not to. 'You didn't offend me, Philippe,' she confessed with complete honesty. 'In fact I must confess that I found it quite enjoyable . . .'

'*Chérie* . . .'

'No . . . it mustn't happen again . . . ever.'

'You leave me bereft.'

She laughed then, regaining her equilibrium. 'Oh, I doubt that . . . but leave I must.'

Bowing gracefully before defeat, quite certain now that it was only temporary, Philippe went to call the carriage, and within minutes Laurel was being helped into the deeply sprung brougham. 'My gentle knight,' she teased, taking his hand between both of hers. '*Sans peur et sans reproche*. How shall I ever thank you?'

'You have done so,' he answered gallantly. 'And, in spite of what you say, *mon chou*, you *shall* feel my lips repeating that perfect offence one day. Until then . . . a man may dream. *Au revoir*, Laurel.'

The driver slapped at the reins and the well-muscled chestnut set off at a fast trot. Once out of town, the animal settled into a smooth gaited stride and Laurel settled back with her thoughts. She knew that she would be too late for dinner and worried a little at Rafe's reaction. Not in her worst conjectures, however, could she have guessed at the storm which broke over her the moment she appeared.

'So you have deigned to return, madam!' he said icily, flinging open the front door, obviously having seen her arrival from the library window.

'I am sorry I am late. I was delayed.'

The grey-green eyes flashed fire and his lip curled. 'Is that what they call it now . . . a delay?' And gripping her by the arm he dragged her into the library, slamming the door behind them.

'Rafe . . . please . . . you're hurting me!'

'Hurt you . . . I should beat you. Delay, indeed! I was advised by my triumphant ex-sister-in-law just who "delayed" you. Visiting old friends, Laurel? She said that she waited an hour and a half at the Café du Monde, though I doubt that, knowing her. She said that she then went to Philippe Castille's house, since you had mentioned his name as that of an acquaintance. Apparently she arrived just in time to see you both alighting from his carriage. She was pleased to tell me that his arm was about you, your head on his shoulder. You and Philippe! I thought you so pure, so innocent! You're no different from . . . You're all the same!'

'Stop it, Rafe!' she cried, his words searing her very soul. 'I'm *not* like her . . . I'm not! There was nothing—*is* nothing—between Philippe and me. I found myself lost in the most terrible part of town you could imagine.'

'And he just happened to be there, "in the most terrible part of town", to find you. Do you take me for a complete fool? Is he the kind of man you want? A man who breaks hearts and sweeps them aside like so much chaff? A man who treats women like toys?' He swung her to face him, his fingers cruel on her shoulders. 'Is *this* what you want?'

Brutally he pulled back her head with hard fingers in her hair, while with the other hand he crushed her against him as his lips descended, ravaging her mouth with kisses so harsh that she tasted blood. A moan was torn from her throat as she fought the tide of passion that surged up from within her even in her pain and humiliation. At the sound, a shudder ran through him and abruptly he released her, his face grey, his eyes revealing the fires of purgatory. One icy look, and then he thrust her aside and walked out, not deigning to close the door after him, or turning to see whether she had fallen. Shaking uncontrollably, she heard the clatter of hooves and a scream of equine rage as a whip descended on Saladin's flank, sending the stallion careering suicidally along the track towards the River Road . . . towards New Orleans.

Rafe did not return the next day, nor the day after, until the evening, when he went directly to his room, refusing dinner and any communication. Laurel ate little and even Marie-Louise was subdued, sensing something beyond her ken and realising that this was not the time or place to question. He came to the drawing-room after the child had been put to bed and the house was still. Pouring a large brandy, he met wary grey eyes and silently offered a cordial. She nodded acceptance. Then he cleared his throat. 'Laurel . . .' and at his husky tone she knew that her fears were unfounded and the hours of torment, wondering whether he would kill Castille, her, himself or the stallion had been but wasted emotion. Something small died within her and she met his tormented eyes levelly now, and unafraid.

Carefully he set her glass down on the small coffee-table before her and she was aware that, had he handed it to her, their fingers would have touched, and that he was aware of it too. Neither of them was ready for any contact at all yet . . . not yet. He went to sit opposite her, leaning back against the cool damask of the deep armchair, and her senses vibrated beneath the intensity of his gaze, but still she held those brooding eyes. At last he spoke. 'I saw Philippe Castille.'

'Yes.'

He rose, sat down again, then rose and came to stand over her. A hesitation, then he lowered himself to the couch beside her, a foot away, yet it was as though they touched. 'He told me every-thing . . . Aurora . . . everything.' His voice was ragged with the horror that he concealed from her, the knuckles of those lean hands white as they clenched on his knees.

But even before he had spoken, her heart had quickened its beat and her mouth felt suddenly dry. 'Aurora? I don't understand.'

He coughed, bringing his voice under control. 'I never could reconcile myself to her sudden over-tures of friendship towards you. I knew that she and her mother had entertained quite different plans for my future. They should have hated you . . . Merciful heaven, I never realised how much!' He covered his face with his hands; for that instant his imagination was running riot and an awful sus-picion closed Laurel's heart in a vice.

'Tell me, Rafe.'

And he did so, sparing her nothing, castigating himself for his jealous fury and his belief that she, like Hélène, had turned to the more experienced lover. 'I had to know,' he finished. '*This* time I had to be sure. It is not easy for a man such as I to ask for forgiveness, yet I do so. I misjudged you harshly and punished you even more harshly.' His eyes were on her lips, to which her fingers had automatically flown at his words. 'I do apologise, Laurel, deeply and sincerely. Will you accept it?'

Her lashes were golden at the tips, he noticed, as they fluttered downwards; her hands twisted nervously on her lap and she clasped them together tightly to still them. 'I don't know, Rafe,' she answered, her voice even huskier than usual with her emotion. 'Philippe likened Hélène to an orchid. My father used to call me his White Rose. The orchid and the rose . . . and you will always compare us in your heart. I can fight Aurora's hatred . . . even, in time perhaps, forgive her for the terrible thing she did. But I can't compete with a ghost.' He made to speak, but she stopped him with a gesture. 'Oh, I know you never offered me love, nor did I expect it. It was for Marie-Louise that you married me, and for her sake I came, and I seem to have failed there, too.' Her voice grew even lower so that he had to strain forward to hear. 'Our marriage has never been . . . complete . . . If you wish to say that I have denied you your . . . rights . . . a divorce should cause you no trouble. The scandal, if there is one, which I doubt in this enlightened time, will not touch you . . . nothing touches you that you cannot brush aside. Please don't answer now . . . I don't think I could take it. But when you have thought on it . . . on my failure, not yours, perhaps we could talk again.'

Rising swiftly, unable to look at him now, she hurried out and up to her room, too heart-sick even to cry. Tossing restlessly on the bed she heard his footsteps in the corridor: they stopped outside her door, then continued to his own. She heard him moving about and saw the thin wafer of light beneath the adjoining door. Then it went out and there was silence. 'What have I done? What have I said?' she whispered brokenly in the moonlit room. 'Divorce? Did I really use that word?' She had been badly hurt by this last betrayal, yet not as hurt as by his distrust of her. She had been angry at first, then, as the hours passed, despairing, certain that some terrible event had taken place. Finally, and it had seemed the worst feeling of all, she had become indifferent to her fate and empty inside . . . until a few moments ago, when it had been all she could do to restrain herself from flying through that door and into his arms.

Restlessly she tossed and turned, but sleep eluded her. The moon was brilliant through her window and she rose to draw the curtains more closely. Below, a white rose clung with despairing tenacity to the ruins of a pergola; its petals trembled in the breeze, reminding her of home. Unthinking, she slipped out of her nightdress and pulled on a loose flowing muslin gown in the newly revived Empire style. Knowing that no one would be abroad at this late hour, she did not bother to pin in the lace fichu that covered the décolleté, but ran downstairs and into the garden, seeking the wild rose.

As restless as she, Rafe heard her movements in the adjoining room and sat up, instantly alert. At the sound of her slippered feet running down the stairs, a tremor ran through him as harsh memory seared his mind. 'Not again!' he agonised aloud, re-living his worry and fear when Hélène had first vanished. He had sent the patrols looking for her, visions of that voluptuous body afloat in the bayous driving him to distraction. They had brought her back before dawn—together with a trunk full of lace-trimmed underthings and satin and silk dresses that he had never seen before. She had not spoken to him for a week and had never once mentioned the name of that other man, to whom she had been running . . . Later, there was no need.

Stopping only to pull on his trousers and boots, he followed Laurel outside—saw her—and grew very still. She stood before the climbing rose, bathed in brilliant moonlight, her skin the same white, faintly flushed with pink, of the blossoms, the pale hair shimmering silver-white. The camellia pink of her dress made a fey thing of her, an ethereal, transient being that must surely vanish with the next breath of wind. Rafe's breath caught in his throat and his heart-beat became a drum-roll in his chest.

Lost in her private world, she picked one of the double blossoms, brushed it with her lips and slipped it behind one ear, and a fierce, volcanic hunger rose within him that he had thought long dead. He took an involuntary step forward.

A twig cracked underfoot and she spun round with a cry; then relief chased the fear from her eyes as she recognised him and came forward. 'Couldn't you sleep either?' She indicated the snowy flowers. 'Aren't they lovely?' The breeze caught a wisp of moonlit hair, swirling it across her mouth and, reaching out one finger, he brushed it away, letting his touch move up over her cheek.

'Quite, quite lovely,' he agreed, his voice low and vibrant.

Laurel could not read the expression in the night-shadowed eyes, but his tone quickened her breath as if the anger of that punishing kiss had never been. Eyes wide on his, she swayed towards him, nerves tingling, a pulse throbbing uncontrollably in her throat. She was unable to look away as he reached out and drew her towards him. Her heart was pounding, breathing was difficult, and her lips parted. She could not know how she looked—the fear, the wanting, the uncertainty and the yet unawakened passion starkly revealed in her gaze. Desire flared deep in the eyes so near her own and the steely fingers tightened on her shoulders as the curve of her breasts taunted him.

Suddenly he stopped, drawing a deep, shuddering breath. His forehead was damp with perspiration and his eyes burning as he put her from him. 'Christ . . . I must be out of my mind . . .' he groaned, his voice thickening. 'Go back to bed, Laurel,' and his hands clenched at his sides. Her eyes widened in hurt incomprehension, tearing at his warring emotions still further. 'Go!' he reiterated harshly. 'You would not want to be with the man I become just by looking at you.'

'I . . . I still don't understand,' she implored, feeling herself on the edge of some unseen precipice, afraid of falling, yet unable to withdraw. 'Tell me, Rafe . . . Show me . . . please . . .'

'Show you?' And some evil within him, the Mr Hyde that is in every man, sent powerful fingers to close on the flimsy material encasing her breasts and with one rending movement to expose them. Shock paralysed both of them for one heart-stopping moment when the moonlight bathed those rose-tipped globes with wondrous clarity. Then, with a cry, she ran, sobbing in fear and disbelief, to the sanctuary of her room. Rafe watched her go, unable to follow, the shame deep within him . . . and yet . . . Before his eyes swam the incomparable beauty that he had just witnessed, and his fingers burned with the touch. Slowly, as if sleep-walking, his footsteps followed hers. His wife—and yet not his . . . He knew that it would be a difficult day on the morrow.

CHAPTER
SEVEN

HAVING DECIDED to remain in her room for breakfast, more afraid of her own tumultuous thoughts than of facing Rafe, Laurel sent Vashti to the kitchen for a glass of milk and some freshly baked croissants. She had barely started to eat, however, when raised voices from the hall downstairs brought her out of bed. Throwing a fawn silk peignoir across her shoulders, she went to the top of the stairs.

A thick-set, raven-haired stranger was talking to Rafe in the almost incomprehensible Gumbo-French of the Cajuns, gesticulating with short, chopping movements and moving restlessly about the floor. Marie-Louise was hanging on every word, having come from the breakfast table at the visitor's entrance. Not wanting a stranger to see her *en déshabillé*, Laurel ran back to her room and quickly donned a light lounge gown, returning in time to hear the child cry out. 'No! No, he can't be!'

'What is it?' Laurel called, her heart constricting as she hastened down the staircase.

'It's Jordan,' Rafe explained shortly. 'A 'gator had him. They're bringing him in now.'

'A . . . 'gator? I don't understand . . .'

But Rafe was already shouting orders on his way to meet the light wagon that bore the wounded Frenchman, and it was left to Marie-Louise to explain with rising hysteria, 'Mr Jordan hunts. All the men hunt. They hunt 'coons and . . . and deer . . . and ducks and things. But no . . . that's too tame for a man who fought duels in the Bois de Vincennes. Mr Jordan hunts alligators . . . by lamp, at night . . . in some silly little pirogue in the bayou,' and, torn by hiccuping sobs, she raced to her room.

Pushing down the faintness that threatened to overwhelm her, and torn between following Rafe and going to Marie-Louise, Laurel chose the latter. As she hastened upstairs she could hear the child's frightened, heart-rending crying. She tried the door, and for once it was unlocked. In an agony of indecision conditioned by rejection, her fingers froze on the handle, but then, as pity and a strange kind of love welled up in her, she entered. She crossed swiftly to the heaving, racked form lying across the bed like some broken doll, uncaring of the stiffening, the too fragile, too thin body in her arms. 'Hush, oh, hush, my sweet. It will be all right.'

'No, it won't!' came the ragged voice. 'He's gonna die . . . just like Mama died . . . just like everybody dies on me,' and, with a child's sense of injustice, 'I hate God! He's not fair!'

Ignoring the blasphemy, Laurel soothed her. 'I know how it hurts, little one, I know.'

'You can't!' the muffled voice repudiated. 'You're grown up!' But the body nestled against her, soaking the thin cashmere overdress, did not pull away.

Swallowing her own pain, Laurel remembered, 'I was just two years older than you are now when a terrible 'flu epidemic hit London. Mama was never one to take heed, and when it spread to the country she went to all our neighbours and the village families, soothing them with herb drinks, cooling the fever with water-soaked cloths. Within two weeks she too contracted what they called "Russian 'flu", but hers turned to pneumonia, and she died within a month.' Her throat constricted and she could not speak for a while; when she regained control it was to meet tear-reddened eyes searching her own.

'I thought you didn't care about anything or anyone,' the child whispered.

Laurel took a deep, calming breath, and Marie-Louise saw for the first time that slight lift of the chin that her father knew so well. 'It isn't seemly for a lady to show her true feelings, but between the two of us . . . and I trust you to keep my secret . . . I care far more than I should about almost everyone and everything.'

A frown creased the smooth brow beneath the tumbled mahogany locks, and a tentative finger came up to touch Laurel's cheek where, unbidden, two tears had brimmed over and spilled down. 'Does Papa know?'

'He knows that my parents are dead, of course, for he was there when my . . . my father died.'

'No, I didn't mean that.' Laurel saw compassion in the eyes that had always been so cold or full of hate. 'About *your* hurt.'

'No, Marie-Louise, I don't think your father knows about our kind of hurting. Men are different, and their pain is more easily drowned in drink or work . . . or both. We do not have these remedies, so we must nurse our hurt, like our children, until time takes both away.'

'But I do miss Mama still, and it has been two years.'

'I know, sweetheart. I miss my mother after eight years, but it will fade, I promise you. Come now; I think I hear the men below.'

Suddenly afraid of the unknown, Marie-Louise hung back. 'I don't want to see.'

Understanding her fear, Laurel smoothed back the rich brown hair. 'I'll go down, and when everything is under control I'll send for you. In the meantime Vashti can be with you for companionship. Did you know that she comes from a tribe in Africa where the men go veiled all the time? You must have something about them in one of your school-books. How pleased Mr Jordan would be if you could learn something that he hadn't taught you, and surprise him with it at your next lesson.'

Momentarily diverted, Marie-Louise made a scramble for the other room, for once eager to read.

With dread in her heart, Laurel descended once more to where the muscular Cajun and a tall negro had just set down a rough litter, and on it, barely conscious and with no colour but that oozing from the jagged, torn horror below his knee, the Frenchman. A belt, forming a rough tourniquet, brutally cut into his thigh, but even that could not entirely stem the flow. 'Étienne!' They turned at her choked cry, but she did not see them. She saw no one but the man on the litter, and threw herself down beside him, enveloping him in a cloud of warm cashmere and heady perfume. 'Oh, you fool!' she cried. 'You beloved, wonderful fool!'

No sooner had the words left her lips than the one watcher saw her stiffen before those great grey eyes flew to his, totally naked, totally vulnerable, in searing self-knowledge. 'It's going to be all right, Laurel,' Rafe said in sudden understanding. 'We won't let this one die.' His voice was low and with a tenderness that she must surely have imagined. Then, as on that other terrible occasion, he lifted her to her feet. 'The doctor will be here soon, but we must act now.'

Laurel nodded. 'Forgive my weakness,' and earned a smile.

'Women are meant to be so.'

'Then I *will* be . . . *later*.' Her voice hardened and up came that determined chin. 'Can he be taken to the kitchen?'

His eyebrows shot up, but then he understood and there was respect in his eyes. 'Leona!' The ever-present shadow stepped forward. 'Direct these men to the kitchen. The table must be scrubbed.'

'Done already, Mr King.' Her eyes met Laurel's in complete empathy as the girl enquired. 'White linen?'

'All waiting, mistress,' and Rafe felt himself as

excluded as hundreds of other men had in those historic years when once-fragile Southern flowers manned hospitals and tilled fields.

They carried the Frenchman to the kitchen, and as they set him down, he groaned and writhed. 'Laudanum,' ordered Rafe, using a fine-honed kitchen knife to cut away the trouser-leg.

Fighting down nausea, Laurel forced herself to look at that terrible wound. The improvised tourniquet had probably saved his life, but he still might die of the poison from those filthy jaws that fed on putrid carcasses rotting in the lair beneath the bank. 'We must loosen that tourniquet for a moment,' she ordered, remembering one of the harvesters who had gashed his leg on a scythe. The belt was loosened and she again controlled the faintness that threatened to overwhelm her. 'So much blood! Oh, God, why doesn't the doctor come? We must clean it: we can't wait.' And clean it she did; tears streaming down her face, fawn cashmere in ruins, hands bloodied, and no one dared approach until Rafe said, 'The doctor's here, Laurel.'

Then the soothing competence of his voice, 'I'll take over now, ma'am.'

She stepped away, looked into those calm, reassuring eyes and stated quite firmly, 'He will not die!' before the world tipped crazily about her and, as once before, Rafe caught her in strong arms.

During the week that followed, in which Steven Jordan hovered between life and death, sometimes screaming as he re-lived the nightmare, at other times lying grey and silent, it was said in the servants' quarters that Laurel never left his side. She did. Once. It was after eleven o'clock one night, just at the time when she knew Rafe would be retiring. Slowly, yet deliberately, she left Jordan in the guest-room and walked along the corridor to his room, pushed open the door and entered. She walked to the centre of the large, square room, turned, and looked about her. It was the first time she had seen what was beyond any doubt the master's bedroom.

The bed had been hand made; it was almost square, uncanopied and of solid oak, its four corners intricately carved and buffed to a deep patina. It was covered by a huge spread that fell to the floor on both sides and was fashioned from a variety of furs—wolf predominating. A visiting Russian count had presented it to Rafe, but Laurel was not to know that. The rest of the room, she found, was almost as barbaric. No wall-coverings, but a Spanish-effect stucco between black vertical beams. A floor-to-ceiling bookcase in the same blackened oak held well-thumbed volumes of French, Spanish and American authors, together with some in Greek, German and Latin. One of the two dark oak panelled wardrobes stood open to reveal a number of suits in the latest mode, and Laurel wondered at the elegant European fashions not yet seen in the United States. It was, she found, a disquieting room, a room out of its time and, like the man who slept there, an enigma. Then she considered the purpose of her visit, and the room seemed even more threatening. For a moment her heart almost failed her and she took a step towards the door, then froze as a footfall sounded outside.

It seemed that an eternity passed in the second it took for the door to open, but then he was standing there, the broad shoulders almost filling the frame. 'What the . . . ? Laurel . . . is it Steven? No, you would have come down. Then why?' His concerned voice trailed off before the look on her face, the tortured, half-fearful, half-hypnotised gaze of the bird before the snake, and his tone challenged, 'Why are you here, Laurel?'

With difficulty she swallowed. 'I came . . . to ask . . . to beg . . .' Then, as if gaining courage from his silence, she blurted out, 'I want Étienne to stay here . . . to live here with us . . . I'll do anything . . .' She faltered before the incredulity in his eyes, continuing almost in a whisper, 'Anything, Rafe, if you'll let him stay.'

The silence dragged interminably as he turned and slowly walked to the window, one fist clenched within the other. Afraid of leaving, terrified of staying, she followed him. Involuntarily her hand moved to the tanned smoothness of his arm, revealed by the rolled-up shirt-sleeve. He started at her touch as if burned by fire, his muscles contracting; the leonine head jerked downward, and he stared unseeingly at her fingers before his eyes lifted to her face. Too late the mask covered his features, for in that instant she had seen the storm of desire within. Nervelessly her hand dropped to her side. Only inches separated them, yet neither could span that gap, separated by an insurmountable barrier of what had been, what might have been and what, surely, never could be. Thickly he ordered, 'Get out!' and though his words were cruel, the pain in them reached her.

'Rafe . . . I . . .'

He looked at her then, their eyes locking. 'I want no sacrificial lamb, Laurel. Jordan may stay as long as he will . . . and I hope to God he never knows what price you were prepared to pay to have me say that! Now go to him. Go!'

Blinded by tears, she turned and ran, flinging herself through the guest-room door and on to the overstuffed armchair, pushing her fist into her mouth to stop the sobs from disturbing the sleeping man. She had offered herself and been rejected, and she did not know why she was crying so bitterly when she should have been rejoicing. She could not know that a thirty-two-year-old Austrian by the name of Sigmund Freud already had all the answers.

For Rafe, acceptable solutions came naturally in that era. To quench the fire that raged within him he strode out to where Saladin dozed, leaped on the stallion's bare back and rode down the road to where a velvet-eyed octoroon opened her door at his knock, then opened her arms, smiling, 'Minna bid you welcome, master.'

When the Frenchman awoke at last, cool browed and clear eyed, he received an altogether different welcome as dew-washed, long-lashed eyes bent over him and a voice scolded, 'How *dare* you nearly die on me!'

Being the man that he was, he reached up weakly and patted the soft cheek, giving the ghost of a smile as he correctly read the gaunt features and haunted expression earned through a week of sleepless nights beside him and restless days on the couch at the foot of his bed. 'There are no lengths to which a Frenchman will not go,' he murmured, 'to keep a woman he loves by his side.'

'You can't love me,' Laurel stormed, 'or you would never have considered doing such an irresponsible thing . . . and if you thought to . . . to divert me with a pet alligator, I must tell you, sir . . . they are quite out of fashion!' So saying, she bent her head and wept with relief.

'Laurel, *ma chère, ma petite*, compose yourself.' His own eyes damp, Étienne Jourdan, breaker of hearts, seducer, lover, libertine, realised for the first time in his life what it was to love and be loved in the purest sense of the word, *sans passion et sans réserve*. He, in his turn, hid his true feelings beneath a scolding tone. 'If you continue to soak my nightshirt I shall catch a chill, and then you will have to begin again.'

They exchanged shaky smiles. 'Are you hungry, Étienne?'

'Ravenous.'

'Will you dress for dinner or have it brought to you?'

Half-remembered moments of his nightmare returned: moments when a distracted voice called his name—sometimes Étienne, once, in terror, 'Papa'. He looked into those lovely misty eyes and said quite deliberately, 'If you were the loving daughter

I always wanted but never had, you would not ask such a foolish question.'

Her eyes widened, eclipsing her face, then a smile flashed out, so brilliant that it dazzled him. 'I'll be right back,' she said; then, impishly, 'Don't go away, now!'

The Frenchman relaxed into the pillows and closed his eyes. 'I wonder what Rafe will say?' he mused aloud.

'He wants *what*?' Rafe expostulated. 'Steak marinated in red wine and topped by three fresh eggs? A plate of cheeses and fresh-baked biscuits with a half-pint of my best claret? Is that what a sick man is asking for?'

'No,' explained Laurel gently, her cheeks a delicate rose. 'That is what I am asking for.' Her eyes lifted hesitantly to his, gauging the exact limit of her credit. 'I have heard also that a good brandy stimulates the heart, and he is still very weak.'

Rafe tried to conceal his amusement by saying dryly, 'The heart of a Frenchman, whatever his age, is always stimulated by the presence of a woman. I would therefore suggest that Mr Jordan has received a surfeit of stimulation over the past week. However, if you wish to take the responsibility, I am sure Leona will relinquish her keys to the wine-cellar for a while. The remainder of the meal is in your hands and those of the cook . . . Charm her if you can.'

'Thank you . . . Oh, Rafe, thank you!' and without thinking she reached up and brushed her lips against his cheek, ran to the door . . . then stopped, as her action registered. He was standing there, a statue, as she had left him, the glint of humour gone from his eyes, the mask in place. There was nothing to be said . . . and nothing that years of Victorian upbringing could overcome. 'Thank you,' she reiterated softly.

'You are both welcome,' he replied formally.

On winged feet Laurel ran to organise the meal, the solitary figure forgotten . . . almost . . . for there in the reaches of her mind dwelt the memory of his smooth skin beneath her lips. To think further would surely have been a sin . . . fodder for wantons and harlots. Half-way through pouring the wine her hand shook as, unbidden, came a memory of a few days earlier when she had seen him by the stable. The heat had been oppressive and the house still. She had wandered outside for some small breath of wind and heard the stallion snorting and cavorting on the stones. She had seen them then, the man with several buckets of water before him, and a large ladle. He had stripped to the waist, and his fawn trousers clung wetly to him like a second skin as he threw water over the horse that plunged and shook at the end of a long rein, evincing every sign of pleasure and soaking the man as well as himself. The watcher found her throat dry as the sight of the magnificent duo, both virile animals, muscles rippling under satin skin. An ember ignited within her, knotting her stomach and causing a burning in her breast. Blindly she had sped away before they could turn and discover her, fleeing to the sanctuary of her room. 'You are dreaming, child.' Steven reprimanded gently, his eyes speculative.

*   *   *

To keep the wounded man quiet during the next two weeks while he could not move, Laurel and Marie-Louise would sit reading or exchanging gossip. Marie-Louise became a different child as the light banter of the Frenchman and the eagerly offered love of her stepmother crept into her heart. Only Rafe seemed impervious to the slow transformation, still treating her every misdemeanour with unrelenting discipline and every small victory with apparent indifference. The child, therefore, retained her wariness when in his presence, and a formality that should never have existed even in those rigid times. Once Laurel ventured to reprove him, as gently as possible, on a cutting remark that had sent the child to her room in tears. 'Can you not loosen the rein a little? She *is* your *daughter* and I'm sure would be quite changed by a little more evidence of your love, for love her you must . . .' The angry look he had given her had brought the embarrassed colour to her cheeks. 'I meant only . . .'

'You are not yet in a position to judge my actions or the motives for them, Laurel. The child has my name and my care; she is well fed, well clothed and is given almost all she asks for.' Seeing her expression, his own hardened. 'Do not question what you do not understand. Marie has a good home; there is no reason for her to complain or you to condemn.' And with that he had retired, once again, to the library, leaving Laurel puzzled and more than a little worried. There were still undercurrents that she had noticed, not for the first time: half-frowning glances and long speculative looks directed towards the child and an unnecessary coolness. Not once had Laurel seen him touch Marie-Louise, either in affection or chastisement, and by his very attitude he discouraged any reciprocal contact. Her own feelings towards the child had deepened into a fiercely protective maternalism that made her resent her husband's actions. However, it was, she felt, too deep a problem, too dark a secret, even to mention to Rafe or the rapidly recovering Steven.

Marie-Louise's lessons were resumed at the bedside, and the novelty of it encouraged the child to try harder. Sometimes Laurel would join them and they would read playlets, each taking a role and often ending in helpless laughter, especially when Steven had to take more than one part, and one of those might be that of a woman. His exaggeratedly falsetto voice and grandiose gestures would convulse the following player with merriment and quite lose the sense of her lines.

On one such occasion there was a knock, and Rafe entered. 'I can hear that you are much improved, Jordan,' he remarked, taking in the chaos of pillows and the flushed faces.

The laughter had died at his entrance, and both Laurel and Marie-Louise smoothed their hair with an almost identical gesture. Only the patient seemed unperturbed. 'As you see, I am restrained by force. But for overwhelming odds against me, I should be on my feet and away.' His voice softened. 'Thank you for allowing me to stay this long; I am indebted to you.'

Laurel busied herself with the book of plays, yet

knew that Rafe's eyes were upon her.

'I had been considering,' he said reflectively, 'whether to make that debt a permanent one, until I appreciated that we would probably gain the benefit if you agreed to my proposition.'

She held her breath, sensing the Frenchman's puzzlement.

'Proposition?'

'Of a kind. It has not escaped my notice that your particular . . . talents are far more diverse than those of the average tutor. I have also become aware that a certain . . . affection, shall we say, has grown between you and my wife.'

For all his recumbent position, the man in the bed tried to struggle up. 'I will not hear . . .' he began, but fell back instantly, the perspiration breaking out on his forehead as the pain shot through the leg which he had twisted sideways in his surge upward.

Instantly Laurel was beside him, pressing him back and glaring at her husband over her shoulder. 'Say what you mean,' she shot out. 'You already know my feelings towards Étienne and the innocence of our friendship.'

'Loyalty personified—the she-wolf at bay,' Rafe mused. 'Very well, I apologise, Jordan, for my ambiguity: no insult was intended. I would hardly have condoned my wife's actions over these past weeks had I entertained any doubts at all as to her exact feelings for you. It is precisely those feelings, and also the esteem in which my daughter holds you, that prompted my visit. As Laurel so succinctly requested, I shall say what I mean to say. I wish you to consider this as your future home, if you will. There is no need for you to answer directly . . .'

'But I must,' the other insisted, his eyes curiously peaceful, 'for I have thought of little else of late.' His gaze went to a starry-eyed Marie-Louise, but it was the tightly clenched hand on the bed beside him that he covered with his own as he answered, 'I should be glad to stay, Mr King, and thank you from the bottom of my heart. You have made an old man very happy.'

Rafe concealed his embarrassment with a derisory snort. 'Old? An old man does not go chasing alligators through the swamps with only a bayou barbarian for company. Which reminds me . . . He, too, is still on my property, together with an evil-smelling hound of quite indeterminate parentage. You have a magnetic personality, Jordan. If I allow you to stay, I dread to think what flotsam may find its way here . . . However . . . you are welcome.' At the door, he turned. 'Perhaps, as a member of the family now, you will call me Rafe, though please do not expect me to wrap my tongue around Étienne,' pronouncing it with an impeccable accent. 'I shall call you Steven.' And with a short bow he left them to exclaim over their fortune.

Once outside the door, Rafe leaned back against the wall for a moment, listening to their excited chatter, and knowing that he could never be a part of it. He was not a man who could either give or take without thought of the consequences. The Frenchman, on the other hand, gave all that he had and took all that was offered with no thought at all other than that of the pleasure in the action. Sometimes, he reflected, there had to be a compromise.

Returning to his book-lined refuge, he soon became lost in his ledgers, weighing the possibilities of an early frost against the increased profits of a late harvest. Wondering whether there would be any cholera or 'yellow Jack' to lay the workers low this year. Wondering how the amount of cane-juice that was re-absorbed by the bagasse, the crushed cane from the rollers, could be reduced; last year, they had lost almost a third. There was the hope of a higher price than last year's three and a half cents for the 'plantation raws', and a wider market for the molasses, which was a by-product of the process that made the rich brown sugar. A frown marring his craggy features, Rafe soon forgot the moment of loneliness he had felt outside the guest-room door.

After Rafe and Marie-Louise had left, the latter to spread the good news about the house, Laurel said, 'You know how I feel about having you here, but I have wondered why it was you left Paris in the first place. You are so . . . Parisian.'

A cloud passed over the patrician countenance for a moment, deepening the lines there, but he made no attempt to hide it. 'It *was* my city . . . in my blood and in my heart. I had a little *belle amie* . . . very beautiful and very much a friend. She was as high born as I,' he went on, for the first time alluding to his birth, 'and each year she would attend the charity bazaar together with many of the French aristocracy.'

'At a bazaar?' Laurel queried, but he did not hear her, his mind already drifting through the mists of time.

'It was on the fourth of May last year. They had erected the hall on an empty piece of ground in the rue Jean-Goujon—so gay—with flags and bunting everywhere. They even hired eminent artists to paint the scenery round the booths . . . all to raise money for the poor, a dozen of whom could have eaten well for a year on the cost . . . but it has always been so. There were hundreds there . . . the papers said twelve hundred . . . all laughing and lavishly spreading gossip as well as money. I was unable to attend—a minor injury from a rapier—I had disagreed with a gentleman over the Dreyfus affair. The papers said afterwards that the cinematograph machine that had been installed for the children broke down. When the operator tried to light it, the other lamp exploded. The fire spread so quickly . . . so quickly.' His face was haggard, accentuating his years, and, tears in her eyes, Laurel took his hands between hers.

'Enough, Étienne!'

But he shook his head. 'There was only one exit. Panic spread as quickly as the fire. Men beat women to the ground in a bid to escape . . . Animals! Of the hundred and twenty-five killed, only five were men!' He gave a shudder, returning to her with an apologetic smile, then finishing, 'Our first lady, the Duchesse d'Alençon, died there . . . and a willow-slender brunette with eyes *comme un faon*, large and brown and velvet soft. Had I not fought that duel I might possibly have saved her—

who knows? I left France a month later and have never taken part in another duel to this day . . . nor ever shall.'

'Will you ever return?'

'No, *chérie*. There are too many places I could not visit, too many songs I dare not hear. I thought America a safe place for me . . . shallow and brash and with no heart. There was nothing here that I would have missed.' He smiled. 'How wrong can an old fool be?'

'And a woman too,' she responded. 'I never thought I should find another I could love as I loved my father. I'm so glad you came.'

CHAPTER
EIGHT

AUGUST WAS hot, with the steamy, sultry heat that
caused the mist to hang low over the bayous and
time to hang heavy on animal and human alike.
Saladin refused his bridle and savaged the short-
tempered negro who had kicked him. Fights broke
out in saloons, and knifings were a daily occurrence
in the city-of-sirens-and-sin known as Storyville.
Only the Cajuns in their cut-out pirogues rejoiced,
for the alligators lay comatose on the fetid, slimy
banks and the hunters reaped a rich harvest.

Laurel wore her lightest dresses, yet still they
clung to her, and she rarely left the house. Only
Rafe seemed immune, riding out each day to keep
the overseer alert and to sit in judgment on quarrels
and fights, returning soaked with perspiration, yet
appearing each evening at dinner coolly immaculate. Not for the first time did Laurel wonder about
his mortality, and she said as much to Steven.

For once he did not smile. 'Something is driving
him, *ma petite*,' and she remembered her father's
remark about the intensity of Rafe's card-play.

'But what can it be, Étienne? I am frightened for
him . . . and, I confess, *of* him at times, though I
would never dare to say so to anyone but you.'

They were in the drawing-room, and the Frenchman turned to glance up at the portrait of Hélène. 'Do you ever wonder about her? Not about the beauty of her, that is plain, or about her character—after Aurora, that is obvious too—but what she did to those about her and the effect she had on their lives?'

Laurel nodded. 'Philippe doubted whether there was real love in this house, not love as we understand it, yet somehow it is her home still, so she must have exerted an unbelievable influence over the lives here . . . so much so that they are still not free of her. I do not think Rafe ever will be; he, at least, must have loved her.'

'It doesn't always need love to leave such an inheritance, *ma belle*. No, it is the enmity she caused between Rafe and Philippe that intrigues me.'

'Surely, if gossip is to be believed, that is obvious?'

'Her running away to Castille, you mean? Yes, that would cause a jealous rage, but I feel that there is something more. Philippe seems to have no real dislike of Rafe, and Rafe's antagonism towards him is somehow not the rage of a jealous husband . . . and believe me, I speak from experience! Why, there are times when I feel that they might have been friends but for some past incident.' He gave a sigh. 'Perhaps we shall never know the truth, and it is far too weighty a problem for this oppressive heat. I wish the rain would come.'

'I thought I heard thunder last night. Even a shower would clear the air.' But Laurel was thinking of the gently refreshing rain of England, know-

ing nothing of the fierce storms that flooded the
Delta and tore over levées, sometimes pouring an
inch of rain every five minutes on the flat land.

Her dresses arrived the following day, but the
terrible memories they evoked were still too fresh,
and Laurel put them away untouched. Marie-
Louise fretted at her lessons and spent more time
peering at herself in the mirror . . . Laurel reflected
that Hélène and her kin had much to answer for.
One day she was passing the child's room and found
the door ajar. Tapping lightly, she went in, and
only by supreme self-control did she contain the
laughter that rose at the sight before her. Seated at
the satinwood dressing-table, Marie-Louise wore a
mask of congealing white paste from which her eyes
stared in woeful despair.

'It doesn't work,' she stated mournfully. 'Mama
used to put buttermilk on her face to make it white
and get rid of the freckles, but then she didn't have
as many as I. I've worn this stuff for nigh on an
hour, but I don't see any change at all.'

With difficulty Laurel kept her face straight and
her tone sympathetic. 'Some say that sliced cucum-
ber is as good, but I never found that either worked
as well as a large parasol.'

'It is all right for you, you don't have freckles, not
even one.'

'Oh, I used to—large brown ones in summer. I
get one or two still if I leave my parasol behind
when I walk out.'

'What happened to the huge brown ones?' asked
Marie-Louise, totally diverted.

'I honestly don't know, but when I was about sixteen I looked in the mirror—something I had avoided for quite a while—and they had gone. I suppose I had simply outgrown them without noticing.'

'Does that mean I have to wait another four years?' The cry was from the heart.

Laurel smiled gently, taking a clean cloth to begin removing the sticky mask. 'Maybe more, maybe less, but I think we can use the time. To be the toast of New Orleans takes a lot of practice and a little wisdom. You have to learn how to curtsy just so . . . one way to a visiting duke, another to a gentleman who has just begged to be introduced . . . and there will be hundreds of those! You have to know how to use a fan or a posy of flowers to hide your smile, and to reveal it in your eyes. It takes practice and then more practice: I don't know whether four years will be enough to teach you all you must know before you become a raving beauty.'

The tawny eyes were fixed, spellbound, on Laurel's. 'A raving beauty?' she breathed.

'But of course,' Laurel assured, as she finished her cleansing, revealing the already pretty features which would one day hold a feline fascination that her mother's voluptuous charms had never shown. 'How could the daughter of the most handsome man in Louisiana and the most beautiful woman be anything else?'

'Shall I have to learn the piano?' Marie-Louise queried, a slight note of rebellion in the question.

Laurel felt that she could make a point, since all

her previous suggestions on that topic had been studiously ignored. 'Yes, you will, without a doubt. Husbands like to be diverted after a strenuous day at work. You will play the piano and sing, read the classics fluently and discuss politics knowledgeably. You will know how to run a houseful of servants, control the ledgers—since not all men wish to give them the time your father does—embroider, and, of course, ride superbly.'

'When do I have fun?' said the child, mutinously, and Laurel's smile widened.

'You will also need to dance like a goddess, dress like a queen and recognise the finest gems; you must never accept quartz when only diamonds will do!'

'And we have only four years! Where do we begin?'

'Well, we could start by throwing out all this buttermilk!' Laurel suggested, and rejoiced in the child's laughter.

True to her word, Marie-Louise regained her willingness to learn, and the days passed more quickly. Laurel, too, felt uplifted in spite of the oppressive heat, for she held a secret. It had been during the second week in August when a letter had been delivered to her from London. She had taken it to her room, scanned it, then read and re-read it in growing disbelief. Finally, raising her head, she revealed eyes bright with unshed tears.

Abercrombie and Abercrombie, the Faver-shams' solicitors, had written sympathetically and warmly, offering condolences. They expressed sincere regrets that they must also bear the sad news of the untimely death of her uncle, Hayward Faversham, who, a month earlier, had been brutally murdered and robbed by footpads while walking home from the opera. Since Hayward had never married she, Laurel, was the last surviving Faversham and, as such, the sole beneficiary of his Will. Thanking her for her family's past custom and hoping that she would take advantage of their services in the future, they advised her that the hundred thousand pounds from her uncle's estate and investments awaited her direction. 'I am rich!' she breathed, as understanding overcame her initial sadness at the death of her last link with England. 'Oh, Papa, I'm rich!'

She had tucked the letter carefully down the side of a drawer, jealously prolonging the time until she told Rafe, and could watch his eyes. While dressing, she planned how it would be spent; so much for this room, so much for that, a complete redecoration of her own room, which she still regarded as Hélène's, and that horrendous guestroom that had thwarted all of its present occupant's attempts to brighten it. Marie-Louise would have all the beautiful clothes that she had ever dreamed of, and Rafe some new books. Then there were the uncleared acres on Moonrise, which could now be made productive . . . and . . . 'Oh, there is so much I can do!' Laurel enthused, the heat almost forgotten.

Yet the heat went on and on and the fieldworkers felt it more than any. The *bamboula* was danced and the drums sounded endlessly in timpanic rolls. 'Is that dance not forbidden?'

Laurel asked naively, having read all she could of the people under her husband's care, but still a long way from understanding them.

Rafe smiled, his eyes congratulating her on the small piece of erudition. 'We didn't *have* an August like this in sixty-five,' he remarked laconically, 'otherwise they'd never have issued such a fool law. You can starve and flog negro to the bone, but there's no way you're going to starve or beat his origins out of him. You Britishers abolished slavery in the colonies in thirty-three, but I'm told there are still piccanins clog-dancing in silk pantaloons for the rich in certain houses in London. Feed and clothe them, and they'll dance for you and serve you, but I'll warrant those piccanins will dance to the same drummer as my men when the white man turns his back.' His countenance hardened suddenly, and Laurel saw yet another side to him as his eyes belied the lightness of his tone. 'You know something, wife of mine? If you flogged a black man and a murderous overseer alongside each other they'd both drip red blood!'

'I don't want to talk of such things,' she protested, and gained an instant reprieve.

'Of course not, and I truly apologise. Let us discuss your Frenchman's progress in teaching Marie-Louise passable French . . . or perhaps, more important, the late arrival of your dresses.' His flippancy was not lost on her, but it was far too hot for annoyance.

A drum began in the field-hands' quarters and another took up the beat.

'The natives are restless,' quipped the Frenchman, but Laurel did not smile.

The drums had unsettled her with their pagan beat night after night and she had lain awake wondering at the identity and purpose of the unseen musicians. She was fearful, yet she knew not why, for she had often ridden the trails and passed a word here and there with the workers. The liking was mutual, and she felt no repugnance at the sight of sweating black torsos rising and falling with the hoe and machete. She returned their smiles and greetings, not knowing that they called her 'Missis Cotton-Top' for the colour of her hair, although this would not have offended her.

Yet still the drums disturbed her, especially on one particular night. Vainly she tried to shut out the sound, but as she lay rigid beneath the sheets their insidious beat called to her as surely as any Svengali. Finally she got out of bed. She had to see for herself, had to face this new threat to her peace of mind. Throwing a long black cloak over her ivory silk nightdress, she tied her hair into a careless knot and slipped through the silent house and out into the garden. She knew that, if she saddled the mare, Serena would whicker and cavort with pleasure and perhaps waken Rafe, so she made her way on foot through the trees, seeking the shadows, barely aware of clutching vines or trailing Spanish moss. There was a clearing at the edge of the trees where Rafe had begun re-claiming the land and it was from here that the sound came. Hidden by the enveloping cloak, she halted in the shadows, mesmerised by the firelit scene before her.

A long drum lay on the ground, one end covered by a stretched skin, the other open. A massive-shouldered negro bestrode it, beating out the rhythm slowly, yet with a concentrated vehemence that caused the veins to stand out on his neck. Another man held a smaller drum between splayed knees, his fingers and the heels of his hands doubling and trebling the beat of the other, his head rolling, his eyes tightly closed.

A line of young men faced their women, oiled skin gleaming in the firelight as they shuffled back and forth, barely touching, yet as sensual as though they had acted out their thoughts in another rhythm from time immemorial. A reed pipe joined the primitive rhythm, changing it subtly. A log was thrown on the fire and the flames leaped, causing Laurel to shrink further back into the shadows. Her scream was choked by a hand over her mouth that cut off the indrawn breath as another hand encircled her waist, drawing her back against an iron-hand frame.

'Easy!' Rafe murmured, relaxing his hold on the trembling body in his arms. 'You're a fool to be out here at all, but since you are you may as well see for yourself the creatures we are supposed to have tamed, and subjugated to our will. Look at them. *Really* look at them! Those two are from the Mountains of the Moon, that girl is a Fulani from the Cameroons, he's an Ibo from Nigeria. There are Ashanti, Dogon, Mbundu, Luba—yet to the average white man they're just "nigras" . . . once slaves, now by law free men. Free? They've always been free. Prison is a state of mind. Look at them, Laurel.'

In a vain attempt at normality she asked, 'But how do *you* know? Why do *you* care, Rafe?'

His expression was unreadable in the firelight, as though he had already revealed too much about himself. 'If I buy a hunting-dog, I want to know whether it is a cross-breed,' he stated evenly. 'If it is, it might prove a coward and either get killed in a hunt or have me killed. If I have a riding-horse I don't want any ancestral nervousness balking at a fence or rearing at the sound of gunfire. I know my animals and I know my people. Neither will be given the chance of betraying me.'

She wanted to ask what he looked for when he bought a wife, but a quickened drum-beat drew her attention back to the clearing. The night was cool, but beneath the heavy folds of her cloak she felt burning hot and a feverish perspiration broke out on her skin as she tried in vain to tear her eyes from the gyrating dancers before her. Rafe watched her, and when her nails dug into his arm he did not flinch; only those grey-green eyes darkened with his knowledge. Her lips parted with her tumultuous breathing as she fought the battle within her and her body ached with a hunger that nothing in her rigid upbringing could have prepared her for.

Suddenly one of the young men reached out, white teeth gleaming. His partner eluded his clutching hands with a burst of laughter and, whirling, made a dash for the trees. With a shout he raced after her, catching her just before the shadows, bending her instantly compliant body over his arm, his lips at her bared breast. A whimper was torn from Laurel's throat as the fire within her threatened to engulf every moral lesson she had ever learned. Turning, she buried her face in Rafe's shoulder. 'Take me away from here,' she begged. 'Oh, please take me back!'

His arm came round her strongly and she felt a tremor go through him, though his voice was quite even as he agreed. 'Yes, it's time, or we'll catch the storm.'

She had not been aware of the dull reverberations coming in from the Gulf, but now the spell was broken and the thunder almost overhead.

As they hurried through the trees, his supporting arm still about her waist, the first drops of rain began to fall. They came out into the road and lightning slashed a swathe through the darkness, heralding the first deluge. 'Will you run?' he challenged, his white teeth gleaming, his hair already clinging to his head.

'It must be almost a mile!'

He made no reply, yet she caught a recklessness, a contained madness, within him. They were standing, gazes locked, as the torrent crashed about them. They would not get wetter whether they walked or ran, and yet . . . 'My cloak,' she gasped, blinking the rain from her eyes. He held out his hand. For an instant she hesitated, then swung it off and handed it to him, asking, 'Shall we be runaway slaves with the dogs after us?'

He smiled then, really smiled for the first time since she had known him, without wariness or reserve, and her heart beat faster. 'No, we'll be lovers eloping from a vengeful father. Come, my love. Your hand.'

Hands clasped, fingers locking, they ran through that torrential storm, stumbling, shouting incoherent encouragement, laughing, defying the elements and the fictional father until they fell in through the front door. Without hesitation he swung her into his arms and strode up the wide staircase, releasing her only at the door to her room, letting her down against his muscular body, one arm still about her waist. There was still laughter in his eyes and a certain wildness that sought and found the gipsy in her.

He bent, and she flung her head back to present him with the white column of her throat. His lips moved in tantalising, mock-vampire bites and the gasp from her lips brought his mouth upwards to tease her further with tiny kisses and tongue-tip caresses until her arms surged upward and her fingers wound about his neck, holding his laughing mouth against hers. All of her being cried out for him and, unknowingly, her body moved against his in age-old sensuality. His hand came down her spine and lower, moulding her hard against him and she felt the desire rise within him . . . and suddenly . . . breathlessly, the fantasy was over. They were not runaway slaves—or lovers—and yet . . . Her eyes were wide and vulnerable, her breathing erratic as she searched his face for . . . she knew not what. He spoke her name, huskily, moving in even closer to her, his eyes the eyes of the loose-limbed pagan by the fire . . . and broke the spell. Panic-stricken by her own feelings, she spun

away. 'No!' running into her room and slamming
the door on her own dark desires.

She threw off the soaking nightdress and seized a
towel, rubbing her body until it glowed, punishing
her hair in the same way as though the violence of
her actions could assuage the violence of her mind
. . . and failed. Even crawling weakly beneath cool
sheets and burying her burning face in the
pillow could not still the uncontrollable shaking of
her limbs. 'What is wrong with me? I'm *not* like that
girl by the fire! I'm *not!*' Crying with fear and anger
and a bafflement that tossed her back and forth
with a fury as great as the storm outside, eventually
she dropped into an uneasy slumber.

But even in sleep the sound of drums reverber-
ated in her head. Her mind re-lived the leaping
flames and the sensual, writhing bodies. A sweat-
streaked black face appeared, looming over her,
teeth gleaming, eyes lust-reddened. Then she was
among the trees, running, running, gaining no
ground. There were bare feet pounding after her
and a man's laugh, sure and knowing. He was
reaching out for her. Terror-crazed, she screamed
out a name . . .

And then he was there . . . And she clung to him
in quivering remembered horror before she even
knew she was awake and the reality of the strong
arms about her.

'It's all over, Laurel. You were having a nightmare. You're safe now.' His eyes were deep and
dark as the night. She gazed mutely up at him, her
fingers still clinging to his shoulders, feeling the
warm strength of him beneath the black silk

dressing-gown. The eyes above her changed as they travelled down over the full breasts exposed by the tumbled sheet, and the hands on her bare back tightened. A shudder ran through his frame, yet this time she felt no fear, only an inexplicable breathlessness. Strange fires began at her stomach and surged through her to colour her cheeks, yet still she did not look away.

'I'm glad I'm not a poet or a great writer,' he said, his voice harsh with emotion. 'For if I were, I would live the rest of my life in torment.' Her eyes questioned and he raised one forefinger to her mouth, sliding it over her trembling lips, parting them. 'Because I could never put your beauty into words.' Laying her back against the pillows he lifted her hands to his mouth, kissing each palm, then each finger, the sea-green eyes never leaving hers. He said her name, his voice rough velvet, as slowly, almost mesmerically, he bent forward and under his mouth her lips parted in sweet surrender.

Different this kiss from any other . . . yet not so different . . . Passion, yes . . . yes gentleness in that passion as his hands caressed her ivory skin, bringing it to tingling warmth; moved down to raise that warmth to white heat. The mobile mouth moved over her temples and cheeks and chin, and her lips ached with neglect until he possessed them, savouring their inner sweetness. Slowly he aroused her, his lips and tongue following the line of those tantalising hands, playing scherzos on her flesh, and then returned again, slowly, to her gasping mouth.

That magnificent body rose, covering hers, and

lowered, but gently, moving slowly, then faster, bringing momentary pain, but immediately a tidal wave of feeling such as she had never imagined in her wildest dreams. She clung to him, crying out his name, rejoiced in his ragged breathing as again he raised her to that peak of pleasure such as she had never known . . . and again . . . and again, until she sank, satiated and breathing words of surrender, into enfolding, bronzed arms that held her close and rocked her to sleep.

The storm passed with the night, as did the wondrous storm within her. She turned to find him gone, yet there was no sense of loss. He was hers now; no separation could change that. She had to tell him, somehow finding new words for the emotions within her. Dressing, in too much haste to summon Vashti, she ran downstairs, knowing where he would be.

As expected, he was standing in his habitual place by the library window staring out at the fountain and the drive. For a moment she could feast her eyes on him, the broad, muscular back and slim hips, the very thought of which brought a weakness to her limbs. 'Rafe . . . I . . .'

He turned sharply, his features carved from granite, and the words died on her lips as he gave a short, formal bow. 'Your servant, madam. I believe I owe you an apology for my conduct last night and I freely give it. It is unprecedented for mc to break a promise. It will not happen again.'

Bound by tradition, by an era in which no lady was expected to find the soaring ecstasy that she had found in his arms, she could only lower her head in confusion. She wanted to throw herself against that massive chest and tell him that she was more than willing to be his wife if the fiery passion that had torn his name again and again from her lips was what marriage meant.

The tender warmth as, satiated, he had rocked her to sleep had gone from his eyes, and in this room they were again the cold green of the sea, yet not quite; there was a movement there, an echo of her own questioning, and his tone changed a little as he asked, 'Is there anything else you wish of me?'

Laurel felt, afterwards, that had she spoken then, even taken a step towards him, things might have been different, but pride lifted her chin as she met his eyes levelly. 'No, Rafe, nothing.' The chill emptiness enveloped her, freezing out the warmth within and sealing in a loneliness the like of which she had never known before. To have no love when love is unknown is a sadness, but to have lost love just when it had been discovered is a tragedy. In such agony of spirit Laurel returned to her room, walking rigidly and blindly up the suddenly endless stairs.

She did not see him come to the library door and watch her retreat with eyes that betrayed a pain as deep as her own. She could not have known that he had expected recriminations and coldness, rehearsed for them, armouring himself against them, and then had pressed his attack before defence was necessary . . . then had been unmanned by the luminescence in her eyes. Only the rehearsed words remained, those unfeeling, ill-timed words.

He had been wrong—terribly, irrevocably wrong. He had tried to right it, but only with a gauche question, and she had rejected it as he would have in her place. As he watched that slender frame ascend the stairs, his heart grew heavy. Would she ever forgive him? His knuckles whitened on the door-handle and ferociously he wrenched at it before slamming the door behind him and making for the stables. There was work to be done, and, cutting out self-recrimination as with a knife, he called to the groom to tack up Saladin.

CHAPTER
NINE

THE STORMS continued all that month and on into September. The planters worried lest the rising river burst its banks, bringing with it the same devastation of the 1891 to 1893 floods when many of them went bankrupt. 'Even last year was bad,' Rafe informed Laurel, sparing her nothing. Their marriage survived on a tightrope of studied courtesies and a formality broken only by rare moments of a strange, almost reluctant tenderness; the coolness instigated by Rafe alone, but accepted by Laurel as the only way to retain his presence. There was no further reference to divorce, but neither was there the pretence of a loving relationship, and never, by word or gesture, had he referred to that night of passion and pain.

Facing him now across the desk, where he wrote out pages of figures and she, with new-found skill, added and subtracted profit and loss, Laurel continued his line of thought. 'Shall we be able to make any profit at all? The crop looks good in spite of the rain.'

He flashed her a half-smile, warming her for a brief moment before returning to the pages before him. 'According to this, if we lose half our crops we may still break even, but there will be more than lean times next year.'

'Then we shall plant vegetables and buy some pigs and maybe a milk cow. Any money we make can then be used to buy more sugar: if the loss is great in the Delta, then next year's crop will surely sell at a premium.' She met his penetrating gaze with defiance. '*I* can manage a vegetable garden—I did it for fun as a child. I'll even learn to milk the cow if I have to. I can do it, Rafe, I know I can!'

Some indefinable expression crossed his handsome features, as very softly he said, 'I believe you could.' Rising, he came round the desk to take her hands and lift her to her feet, his voice deep and gentle as he stated, 'You shall not dig and plant and hoe, neither shall you tend farrowing pigs nor milk cows, though I have no doubt at all that you could.'

'What *shall* I do, Rafe?' It was a rhetorical question, since his mouth inches above hers overcame any desire for an answer, and when it descended, moving over hers with exquisite tenderness, she even forgot the question—but he answered it anyway—putting her from him with firm hands.

'You will cease distracting me from the making of those very profits of which we spoke, madam. Go now. I have work to do.'

Starry-eyed, Laurel turned at the door. 'Very well, Rafe,' she acquiesced, then daringly, 'But when the sugar grows and is harvested, when the profits are made . . . what then?'

'Go, witch!' he growled, his eyes giving the lie to

his tone, and with a heart that was lighter than it had been for many days she left him to join Marie-Louise in the school-room.

Incredibly the cane, higher than a man now, survived, and Rafe lost less than a quarter of his crop. With another quarter to be held back, placed in mattresses and covered with dirt for the new crop, it still meant survival. The cotton plantations, however, did not fare so well, especially those on the rich flat plain between the Mississippi to the west and the Yazoo River to the east.

Laurel should have been forewarned, yet still it was a shock when on the first Saturday in October the ominous black barouche drew up outside the house. Before Leona could cross the hall, Laurel had opened the front door, watching Madame Vautour climb the steps with a mixture of trepidation and anger. How *dare* she appear in this place again! Yet, as she noticed the new gauntness in the already too thin frame, the haggard look in the sunken, heavy-lidded eyes, she instinctively knew that this was a woman near the limits of her strength. There was still a touch of pride—or defiance—in the cold eyes that returned her look, but no longer the sure certainty of domination.

'I do not expect to be invited in,' she stated without preamble. 'I come to see Rafe on business, and what I have to say can equally well be said on the porch.'

Still Laurel did not speak, not from any cruelty, but from the simple fact that she did not know what to say. Could she say, 'Rafe will not see you'? or

'Leave this place and never set foot on our land again'?

A ripple of a sigh stirred the black bombazine, and the hand on the silver-topped cane shook, yet the flat voice was factual as she said, 'The rains have virtually ruined me, the field-hands are demanding their money, the bank has called in my notes . . . and Aurora had disappeared. I do not speak to my neighbours, and I have no friends.'

'It appears that you have reaped the whirlwind,' came Rafe's voice from the library door, and Laurel wondered how long he had been there, testing her.

She caught a haunted look in the tawny eyes, and a deep pity welled up within her for this indomitable, lonely old woman, drowning out all hatred as if it had never been. Impulsively she held out her hands. 'Please come in, *madame*, you must be thirsty after your journey.'

Doubt and a kind of respect mingled in the look the other gave her as slowly she entered the hall she had thought never to see again.

'Tell us of Aurora,' was Laurel's first question when they were seated, and Rafe spoke the words that were in Madame Vautour's eyes as he turned to his wife in surprise.

'I am surprised that you care what becomes of her after what has gone before.'

Laurel nodded, accepting an icy mint julep from the tray brought by Leona, before answering, 'So am I . . . but I simply can't go on hating; it just isn't in my nature. Hatred feeds off itself and destroys the hater, not the hated. Aurora tried to destroy me and, thanks to Philippe's timely arrival, failed. I know that she loves you, Rafe, in her own way; losing you to her sister must have been tragedy enough, but then perhaps she lived her whole life in the hope that you might one day be free again. No wonder she hated me. I confess I should hardly be inconsolable if something awful happened to her, but in pitying her, I would suffer a moment of remorse for what, quite unknowingly, I must have done to her.'

'No, Laurel, not you,' the older woman broke in. 'Nor any one person. If anyone is to blame, it is I, for not seeing her calculated softness as being just as deceptive as her sister's wildness . . . both were ambitious and quite ruthless in that ambition. *You* knew that, Rafe. She was always the quieter of the two, yet since our visit here when Philippe, the one she was sure would help, rejected her and saved you, Laurel, she raged quite as violently as Hélène did even in her worst moments. I thought at times that she had quite lost her mind.'

'But why would Philippe hate me enough to help her in such a vile action?' Laurel cried, the pain evident in her voice.

'Philippe doesn't hate you,' Rafe replied dryly. 'Quite the contrary, I imagine. No, it was typical of Aurora's thinking that, once she had given herself to a man, she owned him body and soul. In that too she resembled her sister.'

There was much unsaid beneath his words and Laurel knew that all she had heard of Hélène's affair with the handsome Creole was true. 'But how could she?' her mind repudiated. 'How could any woman prefer the shallow, gay beauty of Philippe to the deep complexity and rugged handsomeness of Rafe King?' But then she remembered that stolen kiss, the lips moving so surely over hers in that gaslit room, and she flushed. When she raised her eyes, Rafe was watching her.

'Don't you agree that there is a certain attraction in Philippe Castille that a woman . . . any woman . . . might find irresistible?' he probed.

Madame Vautour looked sharply from one to the other, missing nothing. She was a little surprised, therefore, to see the sudden flash of anger in Laurel's eyes as they challenged her husband's implication. 'Yes, I do,' she declared with a quiet dignity that yet held undertones. 'Philippe is an exceedingly attractive man . . . quite as attractive as at least a dozen others I became acquainted with on my travels round Europe. My one regret is that there must be enmity between the man who saved my life and the man to whom I have given that life . . . till death us do part . . . or had you forgotten, Rafe?'

A wry smile touched his lips. '*Touché*. However, for more reasons than you will ever know, there can never be anything else between Castille and me.'

'Then I shall have to accept that, but I fear we have digressed. Madame, you were saying that Aurora has disappeared. Could she have gone to Philippe, or might he know of her whereabouts?'

'It was the first enquiry I made . . . in person,' and Laurel knew what that must have cost her. 'He promised to put out the word. For myself, I must return to the plantation—what there is of it. The

banks offered me no more hope than Philippe. Last
year's flood took all of our crop and I had to borrow
heavily. This year they will lend me no more.' The
heavy-lidded eyes turned to Rafe. 'I am forced
therefore to turn to the one person who has the
least reason to help me. I would not ask for myself,
you know that, but there are others who will go
hungry or leave. I need at least ten thousand to buy
a new crop and pay wages, there is land to be
drained and buildings repaired. I ask nothing for
my own comfort; that is somewhat irrelevant at this
moment.'

His eyes were implacable as he rose and went to
pour brandy into a crystal goblet. 'Your daughter
used me to gain her own ends; your younger one
would have done the same. Would you follow their
lead?'

A spark lit the golden eyes, and Madame
Vautour rose shakily to her feet. 'Yes, Rafe, I
would. I would use anyone, promise anything, to
save my land. I fought the Yankees and lost. I shall
not lose this time. If you will not help me I have
heard that there are men in New York—Yankees—
who will lend any amount to anyone and do not ask
for collateral. I may be paying off the interest they
will undoubtedly charge for the rest of my life, but I
shall have my plantation!'

Rafe reached out a hand, then withdrew it, his
eyes softening a little, and Laurel guessed at the
closeness he once felt to this proud, beautiful
family. 'The rains have taken their toll here too,
though not to the same extent. If I am to survive
next year I must pay labourers for the harvest and

reclaim more land. I cannot help you, even in memory of more pleasant times.'

It was the instinctive peasant gesture, and his last words, said quietly and with sincere regret, that decided her. 'Yes, you can, Rafe.' They turned, eyes narrowing, as Laurel rose to her feet. She was unaware of the determination in her tone and the all too familiar lift of her chin as she told them the secret she had yearned to share, but had only now found the perfect moment. 'And so,' she finished, 'you may have your ten thousand; twice that, if you wish.'

The golden eyes looked into hers, not deigning to hide the tears there. 'My family has done its utmost to destroy you and your marriage. Why should you volunteer your own money now?'

'It isn't my money; it belongs to Rafe. As to your question . . . I never wanted you as an enemy, madame. Perhaps this will convince you.' A sudden and totally irresistibly impish smile tugged at her lips. 'Besides . . . I'm the daughter of a gambling man. If we lend you enough to start again and take a percentage of your profits over . . . say five years, I am betting on the river staying low, the rains coming in season and on your knowledge of cotton to bring us in a considerable profit.'*

Rafe let out a bark of laughter and even the frosty matriarch allowed a smile. '*That* I understand, and on those terms I will accept. Rafe?'

He bowed over the extended hand, touching the paper-thin fingers to his lips. 'What can I do but

---

The Mississippi Delta was not flooded again until 1903.

acquiesce gracefully in the light of my wife's forgiving nature . . . and undoubted business acumen?'

Laurel held out her hand, feeling it taken in a hold that was as fragile as a cobweb, yet with as much inner strength. 'Will you stay the night? It has been a long journey, in more ways than one, and you must be tired.'

'When I understand you, Laurel, if I ever do, I shall possibly regret my acceptance of your help . . . until then, I thank you. The debt, however, will sit heavily on my shoulders and I am not too sure that I shall be able to repay it, even after the money has been returned.'

Laurel nodded, her mind going back to a gambling-den in Marseilles—not the richly ornate halls that she and Wallace had been accustomed to, but a low dive where the worst denizens of Europe gathered. It had been one of the bad times and one of the lowest and poorest she had ever wished to see. A young man had been playing there, wildly, carelessly, his Byronic handsomeness puffed with drink and desperation. He had cheated . . . badly . . . Knives had been drawn . . . then Wallace Faversham had risen, laid his cards on the table and ordered, 'Leave him, gentlemen. Condemn him . . . to life . . . and let us continue our game.' The boy, for he was no more, had staggered from that room, and within seconds had come the sound of a shot. Laurel looked now into the baffled despair in those tawny eyes . . . and condemned them to life. 'Sleep well, *madame*,' she said softly.

*   *   *

Late the following day, when their visitor had left and the house was quiet, Rafe's light attitude was put aside. 'Why, Laurel?' he demanded, confronting her in the drawing-room. 'Why did you really offer her that loan? There was no need to reveal that you had any money at all: it could have stayed in a London bank or been invested with far more security. I don't believe in your apparent forgiveness either—no one is that saintly. You could even have bought your way out of this marriage, if you considered some dubious debt of honour still unpaid.'

'Is that what you'd rather I'd done? I'm sorry, Rafe, but for whatever reason I *did* make those marriage vows and, in spite of what I've said before, I don't believe that even in this enlightened society they are something one can dissolve with money. I *am* your wife for better or worse . . .' No longer able to meet his eyes, she studied the intricacies of the Aubusson, wanting to cry out, 'And I love you more than I ever believed possible.'

Eyes lowered, she could not see his expression, but caught an insistence in his tone as he repeated, 'Then why?' She turned away but was restrained by surprisingly gentle fingers on her arm. 'Why, Laurel?'

'I don't know. I thought . . . Oh, I know Hélène's family were here long before I arrived and you must have married her for love, whereas I'm all too aware that you married me simply as a convenience . . . as a governess for Marie-Louise. I thought perhaps if I could . . well . . . offer something more . . .' She raised those incredible smoky eyes to his and her voice trailed off at the expression there, a mingling of pity and understanding, frustration and wonder, and something else to which she dared not put a name.

'Laurel,' and his voice made rich music of her name. His hands came up to cup her face as his lips descended slowly, moving over her temples and cheeks, then down to her lips with an exquisite tenderness that brought tears to her eyes and an aching tightness to her throat.

'Rafe . . .' But already another expression had replaced the first, and she was released.

'On behalf of Hélène's family, I thank you,' he said quietly. 'We are unaccustomed to selflessness here.'

The 'we' alienated her, and she gathered her scattered emotions, putting down the ache in her heart. 'I thought I had explained my selfish motives . . . but I shall not bore you by reiterating them when I am sure you have work to do—even at this hour. Perhaps you will draw up the necessary papers for the transfer of funds, so that I may instruct my solicitors tomorrow.'

His eyes betrayed a bafflement at her coolness, having previously interpreted the bright tears with uncanny accuracy. 'As you wish. Will you retire, or shall I call for Leona to bring a tray?'

'It has been a rather eventful weekend. With your permission, I should like to retire early.'

All formality as he bent over her hand, that torturous rain of tiny bitter-sweet kisses behind them, each went their own way. And yet . . . At the bottom of the stairs she turned, but he had moved away and did not look round. As he opened the panelled oak door of the library, Rafe hesitated, swivelling to watch the stiff back already half-way up the staircase, but she did not turn. In such missed opportunities does the goddess Fortuna find her humour!

'At least they accepted your money,' comforted Steven the following day. 'It must have set a precedent for both of them . . . a little like the shock a spider might register if the captured fly begged to rebuild the web.'

Laurel smiled at his apt analogy. 'Dear Étienne! At least the rains have stopped, but I overheard Rafe talking to someone in the Delta who had lost everything. Their land had fronted the river and the levées had given way. Apparently we had a wet January and February which had already swollen The River as well as the Missouri and the Ohio. Then, when the late winter snows melted in May and June, they added to the problem . . . all that water flooding into an already full river. The drought of two years ago was terrible, so I heard, but surely these off-season rains are more devastating by far.'

'Don't trouble that lovely head, child; such problems are not for women. You should be thinking of starting that new embroidery frame for Marie-Louise, or whether we shall have a ball at Christmas. Women's minds are made for beautiful thoughts; no man worth his powder should trouble them with more.'

Laurel looked into the gently concerned eyes and

smiled. 'Well? Shall we have a ball at Christmas? Who would come? What shall we have on the menu and which wines? You must advise me, Étienne.'

'My pleasure, *ma fille*.' His old face lightened as he began enumerating the qualities of his various acquaintances, their likes and dislikes, the gossip surrounding them . . .

And Laurel watched him. 'It is so easy,' she reflected, 'to find a man's vanity and encourage him to indulge in it. Beautiful thoughts, he said . . . Even in these past few years . . . The death of my mother and father, the constant worry about where our next meal, or boat, or train ticket would come from; a marriage with a man who does not love me, overcoming the hatred of the family and household, a rescue from certain rape and possible death, the near death of my surrogate father whom I have come to love almost as much as the first . . . Oh, yes, dear Étienne . . . a surfeit of beautiful thoughts!'

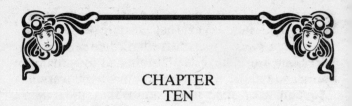

CHAPTER
TEN

To ASSUAGE her loneliness, Laurel began the herculean task of tidying the garden. She had discovered what must once have been a sunken Italian garden at the rear of the house and to one side. Now, it was a tangled confusion of weeds and flowers, brambles to tear and nettles to sting, poison ivy and deadly nightshade. Since October had almost ended there were no flowers to divert her from her task, so she took heavy gloves and scythe and began hacking vigorously at the miniature jungle. Fearful lest Rafe prevent her from doing such menial work, she went there only at times when she knew him to be away and the household fully occupied.

It was at the beginning of her second week of gardening. She had been uprooting one particularly recalcitrant weed when her eye was caught by a glinting near its roots, and brushing away the rich soil she unearthed an exquisite gold locket, heart-shaped and decorated with fine filigree work. Wonderingly, she brushed off the dirt with her sleeve, catching the material in the lock and causing it to spring open. Her breath caught sharply as Philippe Castille's handsome features stared up at her. It was an uncanny likeness, with the lips smiling and one devilish eyebrow raised mockingly, accusing the artist of over-flattery. But how had it come to this spot? Instinctively Laurel looked towards the house, and realised for the first time that it was out of sight behind a line of oaks and azelias: the Italian garden was within two minutes of the house, yet totally hidden from it.

Comprehension flooded her heart and mind. 'Oh, Rafe!' she murmured. 'Oh, my poor love!' So this was where they had met, not amid a two-year-old wilderness of weeds, but surrounded by sweetly-scented lavender and white oleander, observed by none but the stone cupid and the occasional wood-dove. Tempted to re-bury the incriminating piece, she nevertheless slipped it into her pocket in order to think out the problem. Perhaps she should send it back to Philippe; it was undoubtedly valuable and perhaps it had some sentimental value to him—though she doubted it. Unable to concentrate further, she returned to the house and slipped the locket into the finger of a pair of seldom-worn grey kid gloves. It would be safe there, and . . . 'Laurel, can you help me with this?' signified a minor emergency from outside the door. Hastily Laurel pushed the glove into a drawer and went to answer Marie-Louise's query. Instantly enmeshed as she was in the day-to-day minutiae of the household, the locket was forgotten. Once or twice over the following week Laurel thought, 'Yes, I must do something about that', but then November came and Rafe decided to harvest early.

*   *   *

'The old men forecast frost,' he said, weighing prophecy against profit. 'I don't think we can wait.'

It was then, as the lean, hard swamp-dwellers, fishermen and itinerants spread out over the land, that Laurel heard a language and a music, quite unlike any that she had already heard, which was enough to take her mind entirely off the gold locket in the glove. The drum-beat of the negro was there to remind her of that turbulent, wondrous, night two months earlier. There was the same atavistic barbarism in this new music, but also another sound, a deep, soul-searching, banshee sound which, a decade later, would be known as The Blues. The negroes already used the word in melodies such as 'I got de blues, but I's too mean to cry', and Buddy Bolden had been playing his down-beat trumpet in New Orleans for the past three years, but the plantation-workers had found a mid-way style. These hobo musicians had another instrument made of cane from the river-bottom, 'quills' they called them, and the breaks in their work would echo with the plaintive blowing of the quills.

'It's unsettling,' Laurel confided to Rafe one day. 'Are they always so sad? We treat them well, don't we, and pay them the rate for the job?'

'If you're paying a man, you are buying a piece of his soul,' he answered in that quiet way he had of reaching the basics. 'The only truly free man is the one who is not beholden to anyone, neither to receive nor to give.'

'But surely everyone has either to pay men to work for him or to be paid for work, doesn't he?'

The cool, grey-green eyes appraised her, assessing her desire to know, but then judged wrongly, thinking her avid thirst for knowledge to be mere curiosity, and he answered, 'It does seem to be the lot of mankind, doesn't it?' He was not going to tell her of his dream of a farm where every basic fruit and vegetable grew, where beef and dairy cattle, sheep and poultry produced meat, butter, milk and eggs. This land of his would have trees aplenty for building, and fresh water all year round. Herbs would grow, and flowers, too . . . food for the soul. The people on the land would share equally in its profits and its labour, and no man would be the inferior of another . . . But in 1898 such thoughts bordered upon blasphemy for a white Southerner—indeed, such thoughts would be castigated by the majority for the next century, though men like Rafe would dare to speak of them later. But not yet.

Much was changed on the plantation now, as the cane fell and the leaves were stripped by the deadly cane knives that just as often cut into long-suffering flesh. There had to be an outhouse raised near the fields where wounds were cleaned and bound, and anger between the diverse factions soothed. The grinding began then, a time when the men would work up to eighteen hours a day and on Sundays, too, racing to beat the frost, and Laurel's days were almost as long. She had found that her very presence could stop a fight before it began, and her nomadic upbringing gave her a feeling for the strange dialects that abounded.

Not all of the men who drifted down the Mississippi, however, were hard-working, law-abiding wanderers: some were human jetsam, discarded by society and washed up at the nearest large town where easy money could be made with no questions asked. One or two found their way to Moonrise but, for the most part, caused little trouble. Rafe's swift, harsh justice, backed by that muscular frame, solved any problem as it arose. There was one, however, who aimed to take more than money with him when he left. His eyes never left Laurel's slender form as she rode the fields, smiling encouragement and exchanging banter with the workers. They saw through the light cotton dress as though it did not exist, his mind's eye picturing white-gold hair tumbled from the neat chignon and lying over his arm.

As well as being a coward, he was also impatient. He knew that she had noticed him watching her, for a delicate flush would sometimes come to her cheeks and she would ride on a little more quickly than usual. He had no illusions about his looks either: the Runt they had called him, his three tall and handsome brothers. He feared that sooner or later she would tell her husband, and Rafe King looked too much like his elder brother, the one who had taken a bullwhip to him over that simpering school-marm.

It was not his fault, he reasoned, that he liked women far more than they liked him; it was natural for a man. The women liked him less now, since that bullwhip had slashed a ghastly scar into his cheek, bringing his mouth up into a perpetual sneer and half-closing one eye. He'd got even, though.

He always got even. He'd near crippled that school-marm who'd started it all. Caught him a rattler in a bag, like the Texas cowpokes did when they was funnin' a dude, and hid behind a bush on the trail she always took on her Saturday ride. Threw it out on the road just as she came into sight, giving it time to feel the vibrations of the horse's hooves and coil, rattling warningly. He grinned now at the memory of the mare's whinny of terror as she reared, and the woman's scream as she fell. His brother, too, had been well taken care of. A few dollars passed around a few dives had ensured a beating that he would never forget . . . but the alley-rats had gone too far and his brother had died. So here he was . . . on the run . . . because, like all rats, his 'friends' had squealed. But Miz Laurel . . . she wouldn't squeal, at least not after a while. There were fires under that ice, of that he was sure.

Laurel had noticed the scarred man and felt sorry for him, in spite of the uncomfortable feeling he gave her. She tried to put aside her instinctive revulsion and would give him an extra sweet smile when she saw him sitting alone with his lunch, knowing that the other workers seemed to dislike him as much as she did, although he worked well and spoke little. 'Perhaps he lost a woman he loved when he got that scar,' she guessed, 'and now feels alien.'

It was cool that day, and she noticed his lack of warm clothing. Determined to speak to Rafe about it, she bade the man a bright 'Good day'. He nodded, then suddenly threw her a look of shock and wide-eyed pain, doubling up and clutching at his stomach. He rose with a cry and, turning blindly, stumbled off into the trees.

'Wait! What's wrong?' Laurel cried, hearing his crashing path through the undergrowth. 'Please wait! Perhaps I can help.' There was no one in sight, though she could hear Rafe shouting orders to Ben, whose hearing deteriorated in proportion to the increase in work. Not wishing to bother them, Laurel dismounted and ran after the obviously sick man. The sounds had ceased and silence reigned. 'Hello?' she called. 'Are you hurt? Can I do anything for you?'

The low chuckle, when it came, was as much of a shock as his words. 'You sure can, Miz Laurel.' There was no trace of pain in his voice, or in his eyes, as she spun to face him. He was leaning indolently against a tree barely three feet from her. 'Oh, yes, Miz Laurel, ma'am,' he grinned. 'You sure can do a great deal for me—and I can do things for you that you'd never imagine!'

Laurel felt the icy fear raise the hairs at the nape of her neck, but forced herself to speak calmly and coldly. 'You are obviously not in pain, as I imagined. It is most ill-mannered of you to pretend to be so. Please step aside and let me return to my duties, and no more will be said.'

His grin widened, revealing blackened, uneven teeth. 'Now now, Miz Laurel, don't you get uppity with me, 'cos I understand women like you . . . all ice and touch-me-not on the outside and real chilli pepper under that starched cotton. You blondies are the best, so I hear tell. Come on now . . .' and his tone grew wheedling. 'You know I'm speaking the truth. Jes' you let that purty goldy hair down . . . I bet it reaches clear to your waist. Come on. It won't take but a minute.'

Laurel's fear turned to anger and the grey eyes were cold steel. 'Get out of my way,' she demanded in clipped, spaced-out words. 'My husband would have you flogged to within an inch of your life if he ever heard you speaking that way. So much as lay a finger on me, and he'll kill you, I swear.'

The leer faded and a snarl curved his already deformed mouth. 'He ain't gonna do nuthin', 'cos he ain't gonna catch me. Two, near three years, they been looking for me and they ain't caught me yet. They ain't gonna catch me now, neither, so you'd jest better give in graceful-like, Miz High-n-Mighty.' To add weight to his words he brought out the long-bladed harvesting knife that he had concealed beneath the sweat-stained shirt. In the instant that shock froze her, Laurel felt her arm seized and she was dragged close, the knife pricking her throat. 'That's better,' he crooned. 'That's much better.'

'It always was,' he grinned, remembering. 'Like that pale-skinned nigger wench I had the day before yesterday. Disappointing that one, though. Oh, she'd fought at first . . . A tough little thing, and I had to tickle her a bit with the long knife just to calm her down, 'ceptin' she went real quiet then, still as a stone, and just lay there staring at the ceiling till I finished.' He had hated that; cussed at her, then left her in the end feeling kinda funny inside, like he'd felt when his ma used to look at him in her pitying way.

Shaking his head, he cleared it of the years of accusing, pitying eyes, and looked into others just as accusing. He lost control then and with an incoherent cry threw aside the knife and slapped away the angry eyes, knocking Laurel backwards into the undergrowth, following her down, tearing at the cotton dress, choking off her scream with one hand while holding her body down with the weight of his own. With a harsh, rending sound the fabric gave and she felt the cool air on her skin. An incoherent, guttural sound issued from his throat at the sight of the full white breasts, and he rose up, his eyes lust-reddened. Laurel felt her senses reeling as she beat vainly against him, tearing at his face and chest. Suddenly his weight shifted. The mouth that had been about to ravage her tender skin opened in shock. An animal cry was torn from him as he rolled off her, staring in disbelief and horror at the brown-skinned girl standing over him. For an instant that seemed an eternity he hung there, half-raised on one arm—then fell sideways, the long knife buried to its hilt in his back.

Laurel's shattered mind would not understand; then the girl moved forward and, with a viciousness that told all, kicked the dead man in the head. '*Cochon!*' she spat. '*Bête!*' Turning to Laurel, she ordered, 'Get up. You are not hurt.'

With a shudder Laurel realised that she was correct, though had it not been for her timely arrival . . . 'Thank you. You're Minna, aren't you?'

The hate-filled glitter left the brown eyes, and

they softened a fraction as she saw the struggle the
other made to regain control. 'I'm Minna. I been
following this animal for two days now. Watching
and waiting.'

'Minna, I . . . I think I understand. I'm so sorry.
You saved my life, If there is anything . . . ?'

A half-smile touched the full lips. 'I didn't save
your life. We women seldom die of . . . that . . .
even if dying would sometimes seem better. I
should hate you, but I hated him more. I should
have waited a while, perhaps.'

Laurel met the brown eyes levelly. 'It might have
destroyed me for Rafe,' she agreed. 'But then it
might have brought us closer together and he would
never have left my side. Even had he done so, I
wonder if you could have faced him again.'

The other frowned, then put the problem aside
as being too hypothetical to concern herself with. 'I
have killed a white man and, whatever the reasons
for my action, they will blame me. I must go . . . get
far away from here.'

'I shall talk to them and tell them the truth. You
did it for me. Nothing will happen to you—I won't
allow it!'

Minna shook her head. 'Didn't do it for you. Did
it for me, and you will not tell anyone anything.
You don't know about the white man's law down
here if you think I'll just be allowed to go free. The
best they'll do is jail me and throw away the key. I
seen them jails, Miz Laurel. No, ma'am, I'm going.
That is, if'n you can keep hush 'till I'm gone. You
got reason to hate me too; you know what I mean,
even if you is a lady. When the law comes, you

could even tell them I was in it with this pig and lured you out here.'

'Minna!'

'Okay . . . I figured you for more of a lady than that. I'll go get a coupla bucks who owe me a favour and they'll make this animal vanish like he never was. 'Tain't nothing for these hoboes to come and go. I could get word to the house to have your cloak brought to you, but the less people that knows about this the better.'

'I'll manage, Minna, shall I see you again? Where will you go? I have some money at the house.'

An almost gentle smile flashed out and was gone. 'Better you don't know nothing. I can go places. I'll be okay. You mighty kind to offer money and, sure, you might sneak into the house like that without being noticed, but there's no way you going to sneak back out again and down here, and I don't have no time to wait for you to get yourself all changed. No, ma'am, best I go straight off. Told you I'll be okay.'

Laurel's hands went unhesitatingly to unclasp the heavy necklace that, miraculously, had not been torn off in the struggle. It was a chunky gold chain with tiny nuggets hanging from it—the result of a straight flush in Paris—and she handed it to the girl before her. 'It still takes money to . . . go places; if you break this up, no one will question the pieces, and it may take you part of the way.'

Tears appeared in the brown velvet eyes. 'I *did* hate you.'

'And I you, once or twice. Goodbye, Minna and good luck.'

She watched the girl disappear into the undergrowth, and then turned back—to see the twisted shape at her feet. A wave of nausea hit her, doubling her up, and for some minutes she retched dryly, hating herself for her weakness. 'I must get back unseen. I must give Minna time.' Pulling her torn bodice about her, she stumbled back to the road, to where a patient Serena stood waiting. For a moment she clung weakly to the glossy neck, revelling in the warm scent of normality before climbing shakily into the saddle.

'A snake startled the horse and she threw me,' she stammered out to an eagle-eyed Leona as she reached the house, ash-white and still trembling. 'I'm just a little shaken. No need to tell anyone.'

'You need a bath.'

'Oh, yes. I'll feel much better after a bath.' 'After washing the sickening touch of his hands from my flesh' her cringing mind finished, bringing another wave of nausea to wash over her. However, no amount of scrubbing could erase the memory of that brutal hand over her mouth or the weight of his body on hers . . . or the thought of what might have been. Laurel wept in shock and fear, hiding the ruined dress at the back of the wardrobe, but still unable to face Rafe or the Frenchman's searching gaze.

'Little fool!' scolded a concerned Steven when she refused dinner. 'You work like a field-hand and then wonder why you feel sick. What do you think you are, some two-hundred-pound negress? Enough! No more! You will go to New Orleans for a *vacance* and you will forget the plantation. I shall speak to Rafe at once.'

Laurel had not the strength to stop him and was secretly relieved to be escaping the stench of sweating bodies and the sickly-sweet smell of the boiling cane-juice, not to mention the terrible events of that afternoon. 'Do you mind?' she asked Rafe, later that evening.

'It may bring some colour back into your cheeks,' he answered obliquely. 'Will you take Steven with you?'

'I had not thought of that, but it would be wonderful for him to visit his friends.'

'And you yours, no doubt.'

'You know there is no one I would see in New Orleans unless Steven were with me. There is only Philippe Castille, and I would not distress you by seeing him.'

'I appreciate your concern for my sensibilities. However, should you meet him . . . accidentally, I trust that you will exchange no more than the time of day . . . this time.'

So he knew, or guessed, and even had he not, the colour that rose to her cheeks betrayed her. Aware that she was no match for him, she lowered her head. 'I cannot cross words with you, Rafe,' she said quietly, 'but I thank you for allowing me the visit.'

*   *   *

The few days planned, however, turned into ten: ten days that taught Laurel the meaning of laughter again: ten days in which the courtly Frenchman renewed his love of the cosmopolitan city and his acquaintanceship with some of its more cosmopolitan inhabitants. They stayed at the St Louis Hotel, taking adjoining rooms overlooking Royal Street, and spent much time watching the endless procession of street-vendors crying their wares and the black urchins clog-dancing to a banjo. 'Ragging' they called it, neither knowing nor caring that they had invented 'ragtime', and that in smart society the dance that went with it, the 'cakewalk', would sweep the continent and cross thousands of miles of ocean into Europe.

Laurel loved every moment of it, and Steven's presence added inestimably to her pleasure. He was the father she had lost, the brother had she never had, courtier and clown . . . and he gave her his undivided attention; something she had never received from anyone. She had not been eating well of late, yet, tempted by such delicacies as crab 'fingers' marinated in wine and sautéd in butter, lobsters in dry white wine and cognac with tomato and herb sauce, the colour returned to her cheeks and the flesh to the finely-boned frame.

'I'm putting on weight, and it's all your fault!' she scolded her smiling escort over her third crêpe in the French Market.

'It is good to see you healthy and happy, *ma belle*,' he replied warmly. 'But we cannot stay here for ever, much as I would wish to. As chatelaine, you have your duties, and as wife and mother you have even more.'

How could she tell him how few those duties were and how little they would be missed. 'You're right as always, Étienne. Shall we leave tomorrow, then?'

'I think we should,' and he laid a sympathetic hand over hers.

Laurel returned his understanding smile, drawing a deep breath. 'I must go back to the hotel and pack. Wouldn't you like the rest of the day alone? You have given me nearly all of your time without a thought for your own pursuits. It's early yet. I insist that you have at least one day in which to visit the people I'm sure you know but would never introduce me to . . . the kinds of people you must visit when you think I'm asleep at night and can't hear you humming to yourself and dressing in a certain way behind that closed door!'

His eyes twinkled. 'You know me too well, *ma fille*. However, you know also that I would gladly spend every minute with you if you wished it.'

'No, I insist, and please don't call a carriage; it's only a few blocks and I know my way now. No short cuts, I promise. I'll go along to the Square and spend a few minutes there before crossing to St Louis. I shall be at the hotel in less than an hour. If you're worried, you can telephone me there, Papa Hen.'

'I'll do that,' he confirmed, but the worry was still in his eyes as he watched her walk out into the bustling street.

Laurel breathed in the smells of farm produce

and fish, coffee and candles, feeling an excitement that only cities could bring her. Then she was in the Place d'Armes, raising her parasol against an unseasonably brilliant sun, but the awkward mechanism thwarted her, and she struggled with it for a moment, before a familiar voice requested, 'Allow me.'

Spinning around, her eyes betrayed her pleasure before her lips could say coolly. 'Philippe, how nice.'

'I seem destined to rescue you from yourself,' he smiled, adjusting the lace-edged parasol and handing it back to her, his eyes complimenting her on the saucy 'toque' that sat precariously on her upswept hair.

She had bought it the previous day, falling in love with the intricate jet ornamentation on the black chenille that contrasted stunningly with the silver brightness of her hair. A velvet bow of palest mauve was pinned to one side, perfectly matching the softly trained cloth coat. Now, more than then, she was glad of her small extravagance. However, remembering Rafe's oblique warning, she decided against lingering in the pleasant surroundings, and kept her tone formal. 'I was just returning to the hotel to pack. I have been here for over a week with Steven Jordan to chaperon me, but we must leave in the morning. What a pity we won't have time to talk. Perhaps, if you are not too busy, you would like to walk with me to the hotel.'

'Am I not to see you, then? Could you be so cruel? We could have the rest of the day together, you know, if you wished it.'

'No!' a little too quickly. 'I'm sorry; I must be back within the hour. Steven will be telephoning to confirm my arrival, in the light of past . . . events.'

The brown velvet eyes were serious, holding hers as he turned her to face him. 'You could tell him that you are safe . . . and you would be, Laurel, you have my word on that. From all that I have heard of M'sieu Jourdan he would not deny us a few hours together.'

'Oh, Philippe , I cannot . . . It isn't just Étienne . . .' She regretted the disloyalty as soon as it was uttered, blaming Rafe and not herself, as if she would welcome a day with the dangerously hand-some Creole.

'I see,' he murmured with more understanding than she knew, seeing the indecision in her eyes and assessing its strengths and weaknesses. 'Laurel . . .' and the caress in his voice was as though he had touched her. 'Laurel, just an hour. I cannot let you go so soon after having found you again. An hour . . . for lunch. Somewhere as public as you wish.'

She knew that she should not hesitate, for silence gives consent, but already the smile had flashed brilliantly in the tanned face. 'I shall call for you at two. Come, we shall return to the hotel and I shall leave you, however regretfully, to begin your packing.'

'Philippe . . . I really shouldn't.'

'Should not and shall not are worlds apart, *ma reine*! Now, while we walk, you can tell me all that you have done in my city.'

'First, I must know . . . have you heard of Aurora? Her mother told us that she had sought your help.'

For a moment his eyes darkened. 'No, I have heard nothing. I have eyes all over the State and beyond, but there has been no sight of her yet. It is possible that she may have gone to friends in Alabama or Georgia—I believe she has a cousin in Atlanta.'

Laurel shook her head. 'I'm certain they would have been contacted in the beginning. She is somewhere else, I'm sure. Sometimes in the night I hear a noise that isn't a hoot-owl or a crocodile coughing far off in the bayou . . . and I feel a chill.' She shuddered, and in an instant he was before her, holding her hands tightly.

'Stop those thoughts, Laurel!' he ordered, then smiled. 'It is a beautiful day and we shall not spoil it by talking of disasters and premonitions. Now, did you hear the latest about that new singer at the opera? Some say . . .' and he talked on, lightly, carelessly, until the slight frown had gone from her brow and a tiny smile dimpled her mouth.

Even later, words flowed easily between them, sparkling and heady, yet with deliciously dangerous depths, like champagne poured into the top glass of a fountain of glasses and allowed to spill over until all were filled. His eyes were eloquent, speaking volumes that his lips would not utter, and over lunch—as public as she could wish for—they brought a flush to her cheeks and a sparkle to her eyes that she could not restrain.

'You look at me as though I were some . . . some

piece of porcelain for your collection,' she remonstrated once.

'No, not porcelain, which is cold and fragile,' he corrected her softly. 'Rather a piece of jade which is ever warm to the touch and infinitely more rare and precious.'

'You must not speak so!'

'Then I shall not, though it will be difficult. What shall we discuss? Horses, perhaps? I am told all Englishwomen ride.'

She laughed. 'Not all, but I do. Shall I tell you of my silly childhood and my horses?'

'I want to know everything about you, especially your silly childhood,' he said, his eyes on her mouth.

And so the hour passed . . . and another, before she rose guiltily. 'I've stayed too long.'

'Never long enough. I must see you again, *mon coeur*.'

'I am *not* your heart; you mustn't say such things, and we must not meet again. Oh, Philippe, I am a wife and mother . . . I love Rafe . . .' She had never said it aloud, yet there was something missing in the words, something that recognised the pleasure of the past hours and the bitter-sweet impossibility of their continuance.

For the first time in his life Philippe knew what it was to want a woman for more than one brief moment of pleasure. He had taken enough women through that slow, horizontal gavotte to know every step, yet the great grey eyes that looked into his, pleading for honesty and understanding, conjured images of quiet firesides more than of quivering flesh. He put away the thought for his midnight fantasies, and said, 'I shall take you back . . . but I shan't let you go, Laurel. You must accept that, now. Étienne Jourdan may play chaperon, but I will not. You *will* return to New Orleans and, on whatever terms you stipulate, we *shall* meet again. I know your heart, even if you do not.'

'No, Philippe. No,' and there was a new note of firmness in her voice as she saw the wheel turning the full cycle. 'I am not Hélène . . . not for Rafe, not for you. I have failed both of you in that, but I will not fail myself.' She said it then, for the first time. 'Even if Rafe doesn't want me, and I doubt that he does, I am his. Even if you want me with all your heart, I can never be yours. I'm sorry, Philippe. Please forgive me and call a carriage now.' There were tears in those rare eyes, and his jaw tightened as he rose with her.

'Rafe never loved anyone, least of all himself, but he is one of life's possessors. Some possess, others are possessed. I too am a possessor, *chérie*. I am not yet ready to let you go, whatever you may think or say, and you may tell that to your boring, neglectful husband *and* that ancient roué you call a chaperon. *Now* I shall call your carriage.'

'Can we not part as friends?'

'We can never be friends, *ma belle*, when the very sight of you stirs my blood to white heat. I thought we could once . . . perhaps, in time . . .' 'when you are old and grey, and I am past the fantasies that haunt my midnight hours', his mind finished. 'But do not let it concern you; I have never yet conceded victory to Rafe King.'

Confused and guilt-ridden, Laurel returned to the hotel, saying little to Steven's gentle questioning and even less on the drive back to Moonrise the following morning. Phillipe's last words had been lightly spoken, yet seemed to contain a veiled threat that she could not put out of her mind. The bayou mist, dispelled by the rains, had returned again, creeping in from the swamps on grey cats' feet, silent and insidious, as elusive as her fears, yet quite as tangible.

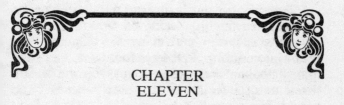

CHAPTER
ELEVEN

THE MOMENT she saw Rafe, the tight jawline, the steely eyes, she knew that her fears had been well founded.

'You are refreshed after your vacation?' No name, no softness, just the coldly formal enquiry.

She allowed him to help her from the carriage, wincing a little as his fingers cut into her wrist. 'Yes, thank you.'

'Steven? Are you also rejuvenated?'

The Frenchman searched his face for some hidden meaning that would explain the undeniably sneering tone. 'Thank you, yes. It was a most pleasurable visit.'

Rafe walked her to the long stairway up to the front door, and never had it seemed longer, his fingers still as steel bands on her arm. 'It is after luncheon, but I'm sure the kitchen will accommodate you both.'

'Not for me,' Steven put in quickly, sensing undercurrents. 'I should like to freshen myself, then I will see what progress, if any, Marie-Louise has made in my absence.'

'I'm not hungry either, Rafe. We left quite late and stopped for some fruit, cheese and croissants on the way.'

'There was obviously no reason to hasten back,' he agreed cuttingly, opening the front door with a sweeping gesture, 'and many for delaying your return, no doubt.' He led her forcibly towards the drawing-room. 'Perhaps, madam, you would care to tell me about your visit . . . those things that I do not already know of.'

The Frenchman was already half-way up the stairs, so was unaware of the frantic look thrown his way: Rafe, however, missed nothing. 'I would not call your chaperon if I were you; he has provided little protection so far, and even less chaperonage.' Thrusting her inside, he closed the door behind them and she was released.

Massaging her arm, which would undoubtedly bear the marks of his fingers, she retreated to a straight-backed chair where she sat rigidly, awaiting his next remark. He had gone to pour himself some brandy, even though it was only three o'clock. He turned, and she found herself imprisoned in that relentless gaze. He outwaited her. The silence dragged on interminably and it was she who had to break it.

'I saw Philippe Castille in town.' No reaction. His eyes said, 'Tell me something I don't know.' 'We went to lunch . . . Oh, I know I promised I would only pass the time of day, but it was my last day and the sun was shining and . . . well, he was so charming . . . It was quite harmless, Rafe, and quite public. No one could possibly have thought anything wrong . . .' She faltered to a halt, as she had done on other occasions before the contained fury in his eyes.

'Nothing wrong?' he queried icily. 'My wife is seen behaving like a wanton in the most famous restaurant in New Orleans with the most famous gambler and libertine in New Orleans, a man who, incidentally, is her husband's most hated enemy, and she says it was quite harmless. Madam, you would have done less harm had you put a snake in my bed: at least half the city would not now be apprised of your treachery.'

'Oh, no, Rafe! No!' and she ran to him, seizing him by the arm, shaking him. 'No, it was not like that. I know I should not have gone to lunch with him. I know I was weak and hen-witted to have thought you might not really mind . . .'

'Mind?' he grated, wrenching away from her. 'Mind? After all that has gone before, you dare to suggest that I would not mind wearing the horns?'

Again she took his arm, feeling the muscles iron hard beneath her clutching fingers. 'I'm sorry, Rafe, so very sorry. It will never happen again, I promise. I shall never see him again, not ever.'

The tears of fear and remorse filled those incredible eyes, brimmed over and spilled down, but in his anger he saw other eyes, mocking and triumphant. 'You are right,' he said, the coldness far worse than the white heat of his anger. 'You will never see him again, for, unless I personally accompany you, you will never leave this plantation again . . . and I rarely leave the plantation now for other than business reasons.'

She froze. 'You can't mean that. You cannot imprison me!'

His eyes locked on hers. 'Madam, if I chose to

horsewhip you to within an inch of your life, few would know, and no man would blame me. Think yourself lucky.' He tried to shake her off, the sickness deep within him, but in her desperation she had flung her arms about him.

'Rafe! Please! You must believe I meant no harm; not to you above all people, not when I . . .'

'Don't say it!' he almost shouted, eyes blazing. 'Don't resort to that final desecration. *She* would always swear undying devotion when all else failed and, God help me, I believed her. No more! Nothing you can do can match her in any way. Your tears, your lies, your duplicity . . . You are an amateur, madam, and I have been taught by a professional.'

Finally he freed himself and flung her from him. 'You are an amateur even in your hiding-places. She would have thought of somewhere far more original than an old glove . . . Oh, don't look so innocent. My ex-mother-in-law called to say that she had left a pair of grey gloves here after her last visit . . . Oh, yes, *now* you blush, and with good cause. Before we found them in the drawing-room, I sent Vashti to your room in case they had mistakenly been taken for yours. She returned with these.' He strode to the desk and pulled open a side drawer, lifting out the grey kid gloves and holding them as though they held poison. Laurel felt the shock freeze her tongue; only her eyes could stare in disbelief. 'A pretty bauble, my dear. A touch sentimental, but in keeping.' His sneer again turned to rage and she backed away from his forward stride. 'And how many other trinkets am I likely to discover? How many other "harmless" meetings?'

She could only shake her head. He would never believe her now. 'Rafe!' The cry came from the heart, but his mask did not change.

'Go to your room . . . Get away from me. I want no more histrionics and no more of your lies. Go!'

She was staring at him, the pain and shock deep in her eyes, drying her tears, freezing the words she would have spoken. He saw the colour leave her face and she swayed, then recovered and, with not another look, turned and went from the room. Numbly she climbed the stairs. 'So the suffocating tendrils of the orchid still enfold him,' Laurel thought despairingly. 'He hates her, loves her, is still totally possessed by her.' She could not cry; the hurt was too deep for tears. To love a man so longingly, so intensely, so completely, and have him belong to another was almost more than she could bear, especially when that other was a spectre she could not fight.

Making the excuse of a headache, she did not leave her room for the remainder of the day. She felt a little guilty when Marie-Louise paid a brief visit before dinner to leave a beautifully arranged bouquet of evergreens, but realised that the child had probably come at the suggestion of Étienne, so would not be too upset if a longer reunion were postponed. Sick with worry, she could not eat anything from the dinner-tray sent to her, and Steven came to chide her on her lack of appetite.

'Would you negate all my care and all that good food I have been forcing into you this past week? I fear that even the colour has gone from your cheeks. You have argued with Rafe again; he uttered no word over dinner and stared at Marie so intensely that even she was reduced to silence. Do not fret, *ma petite*, time cures all—even your jealous husband's temper. I assume you told him of your lunch with Castille?'

'Yes, but he is not jealous,' Laurel declared, still near to tears. 'He cares nothing for me . . . I know I should not say that, and it is only to you that I would, but you see . . . Oh, he is so blind!'

'Not seeing that you love him?'

'Yes.' And her voice came out barely above a whisper.

Comforting arms gathered her up from the corner of the chaise-longue and pulled her against him. 'Love is a frightening thing for the man who sees it as a weakness rather than a strength. Rafe is a man who cannot tolerate weakness, least of all his own, and as for love . . . the word means little when said so often that it cloys like molasses on the tongue . . . and he has had a surfeit of the word without the meaning over the years. He will believe only by example, not by anything you might say now.'

'New Orleans was a terrible mistake,' she acknowledged, but then, more fairly, 'No, Philippe Castille was a mistake.'

'Then why did you not tell me you were going to see him when I called?'

She looked guilty. 'You would have told me what in my heart I knew was true—that I should not have considered having lunch with him. Oh, but Étienne, it was so harmless and such fun at the time! We laughed and talked almost as if we'd known each other for all our lives. He made me feel . . . Oh, I don't know . . .'

'Like a beautiful, desirable, woman.'

'Yes, but more than that . . . or less. He teased me as a brother would at times, yet at others . . . ,' and the flush rose to her cheeks. 'But I still don't think Rafe would have been so angry had I not been so stupid earlier.' Then she told him about the locket, finishing, 'But now he will never believe the truth, and has forbidden me to leave the plantation.'

The blue eyes sharpened. 'Is that what he said?'

'Yes. I'm to be kept a virtual prisoner here, never going out unless with him, and you know he goes to New Orleans only once every month or so on business, and never, as before, to gamble.'

A thin smile touched the fine mouth. 'He did not need to gamble once he had won you, though I doubt whether even he realised how high the stakes would be. No, this matter of you staying on the plantation is the judgment of a frightened man.'

'Frightened? Rafe? He is afraid of nothing.'

'Save losing you, perhaps.'

'Losing a possession?' she said bitterly, and found her own anger reflected in his eyes.

'I think you're wrong. I shouldn't think he regards you in that way at all but, either way, it has cast doubts on my suitability as a chaperon, and that is a matter between Rafe and me.'

He raised her to a sitting position and brushed back the dishevelled hair from her face. 'I shall talk to your fierce, stubborn, and quite blind husband

and we shall, I hope, reach some compromise. I shall tell him of the locket later: he would not listen now. Come, call Vashti for some hot chocolate. You must look beautiful again, if only for me! Get some sleep now, and I pray for sweet dreams to take the worry from those lovely eyes.'

Was it a dream? A sound like rain . . . no, hail, against the window . . . there . . . again . . . Wide awake now, she rose and, pulling on an ice-blue peignoir, went to open the curtains, starting back in alarm as a tiny shower of pebbles hit the glass and, in the moonlight . . . 'Philippe!' She flung open the window, horrified. 'Go away! You'll be killed!'

'I think not,' he called softly, his face grave. 'I must speak to you.'

'No!'

'It's urgent, Laurel . . . I would never have compromised you otherwise. It's Aurora.'

'You must tell Rafe.'

'No,' his voice was adamant. 'I came to warn you, only you. Come down.'

'I can't,' she cried, wringing her hands in indecision and fear of discovery. 'I dare not.'

'Then I shall come up. I see a vine that looks tough enough to support my weight.'

'No! Oh, no!' Wretchedly Laurel ran her fingers through her hair. Aurora, he had said. A warning. Had he found her? Had something happened to her? Yet if Rafe saw him there, after all that had transpired . . .

'Hurry! I have little time.'

He was right; it was nearly dawn and the plantation would be stirring. 'Wait.' Taking a heavy cloak from the wardrobe, she thrust her bare feet into kid slippers and ran down to him.

His eyes lit up at the sight of her, and before she could anticipate him he had seized her in strong arms and crushed her mouth beneath his. 'That was my reward for a long, chill ride,' he said unrepentantly. Then, before she could speak, 'It's Aurora. She was seen two weeks ago in Natchez with the kind of man who would make me resemble the Angel Gabriel. Then, last week, that same man was found on the old dirt road going north. He had a knife in his back. An amateur job, because he lived long enough to tell the man who found him that it was a girl who called herself Dawn. He also said that she was clean off her head, sweet as sugar one minute and wild as a hellcat the next, but through it all planning revenge.'

'Revenge?' Laurel breathed. 'On me?'

'No, she had gone beyond that; she wants all of you to suffer. She is coming here, to Moonrise, and may be armed. I do not know when or how, but it will happen, believe me, and you must get away from here. Come with me now. Tonight. At once.'

Her eyes were shocked. 'I can't! I must warn Rafe and get the others to safety.'

His hands were fierce on her arms. 'You little fool, don't you understand? I don't care about the others. She is mad, and I trust my contact implicitly. She is coming *here*. She has killed once . . . at least once.'

'No, Philippe! Please let me go. It was courageous of you to come here, putting yourself in danger, but you mustn't stay. I shall be all right. I have Rafe.'

'Rafe!' he ground out. 'Damn Rafe! You have me . . . here and now.' Once again his lips descended on hers, fiercely, passionately, trying to wrest the love from her that she could never give, his arms bands of steel that held her helpless.

This time, however, there was nothing in her but the fear of what might happen to those she *did* love, and she brought up her knee sharply. Instantly she was released. He staggered, face greying as he bent double. 'Oh, Philippe, forgive me! I'm sorry, my dear, I really am. Please go. You must go!'

'Not just yet,' came a cold voice from the shadows.

'Rafe! Oh, no . . .' and she ran between them as her husband stepped into the moonlight.

His face was a mask, but his words cut them like a rapier. 'You are a traditionalist, Castille, so I believe I have the choice of weapons.'

'No!'

Both men ignored her horrified scream, and the Creole straightened with difficulty. 'You are not open to explanations or reason?'

'Please listen to him, Rafe. He came to warn us.'

'There is the front door . . . or in his case, a back door.'

Laurel was not fooled by the cool neutrality of his tone. 'I can explain everything.'

'Again? Your location, Castille.'

Something like a sigh, then, 'There is a place behind the St Louis Cathedral, St Anthony's Gardens. It is well known among Creole . . . rivals.'

'I beg of you, Rafe . . . Philippe . . . not on my account.'

A husky laugh came from that smooth brown throat. 'Not on yours alone, *ma chère*. This is an old wound re-opened. Rafe is quite determined not to lose another woman to me. Come, then, your weapons, m'sieu—though not the épée . . . I am too good for you and I have never particularly wanted *your* death on *my* conscience. Pistols, perhaps, since we are both creditable shots.'

The other's jaw tightened. 'I would gladly use a rapier on a gentleman, Castille, however accomplished. The lower orders deserve only horse-whipping.' A flame of pure joy lit the grey-green eyes at the flare of horror in the other's. 'However, since your family is quite as old as mine . . . even though you have managed to drag their name through every filthy, bottomless pit you could find, I shall make you a compromise. Bowie knives . . . the Cajun way.'

A fine sweat beaded the young Creole's forehead, but if Philippe Castille was anything, he was no coward. He nodded, 'Our left wrists tied by two foot of hide. Shall we say dawn tomorrow?'

'I shall be there.'

'I'm sure you will.' He turned to where his horse was tethered, then hesitated, 'By the way, King, do not make my journey here a totally pointless one. Listen to what your wife has to say.'

Laurel raised her hands in supplication. 'Oh, yes, Rafe! Please let me tell you; then you will see that there is no need to go through with this terrible thing.'

Ignoring her, Rafe met the Creole's eyes levelly, 'Whatever my wife has to say, I shall still be there.'

A resigned smile. 'I thought you might. *A demain*, m'sieu. Laurel, I *will* see you again.' She could not speak, but only nod. Springing into the saddle, he gave her one long look as if committing her face to memory, then with an unnecessarily brutal wrench at the reins he put the mare in a flat-out gallop back along the old River Road.

'Shall we go in, or will you wait here another twenty-four hours and more for one of us to return?'

His mocking tone inflamed her, and she seized his sleeve. 'You *must* listen to me, Rafe! You *shall* listen to me! I know your feelings towards Philippe, but there is more at stake now than old jealousies. It's Aurora: she has killed a man.'

That riveted his attention, and the craggy features grew alert. 'Go on.'

'That is why Philippe came . . . to warn me.'

'In the garden? Just before dawn? So urgent? So personal?'

'Yes . . . yes, to all your questions and insinuations.' Her eyes besought understanding as, unconsciously, her fingers dug into his arm. 'He heard that she seeks revenge on all of us, and fears that her mind is unbalanced. If she cannot have you, then no one shall.'

'Go on,' he reiterated, his tone neutral, yet still his eyes questioned, forcing the truth from her, and before that stern gaze her hand dropped to her side and she averted her face.

'Philippe feared, above all, for my safety. He . . .

he wanted me to leave with him.'

'Would you have, but for my untimely arrival?'

'How can you ask that?' 'I love you, only you!' she wanted to cry, but faced with his contempt she could say only, 'I have responsibilities here . . . duties. I had to warn you, arrange for Steven to take Marie-Louise somewhere safe until Aurora is found. Baton Rouge perhaps . . .'

'You think there is that much danger?'

'I don't know . . . yes, I do. I'm the one she hates, and I must be here when she comes. I must confront her. I cannot leave! Don't you understand?'

He nodded and there was a strange note in his voice, almost a regret, as he said, 'Yes, I understand . . . Your responsibilities. I appreciate your considering them: you have paid scant attention to them in the past. Is this where you usually meet him? A little public . . . quite within view of the house. But then I forgot . . . you prefer public places.'

'I have never met Philippe Castille here before tonight, or anywhere, any time that you don't know of.' Her head came up. 'I have said before that I am not like Hélène. You believed that I was, once before, and you were wrong. You apologised then because you were given proof. I can give you no proof this time, but only ask for a few moments of your time . . . it may well be in short supply. Will you follow me?'

Turning, without a backward glance, she picked her way along the dimly-lit, overgrown paths to the Italian garden. Feeling him close, she said, 'As you can see, even in this light, I have begun to reclaim it from the weeds. I didn't tell you because I was afraid you might prevent me or, worse, belittle my efforts, since you appear to treat me with contempt half the time and ignore me the other half. I was going to surprise you with it in the spring, when the flowers I would have planted came through. It is all too late now. However, it must have been a lovely place once . . . and quite secluded from the house as you can see.' She gestured towards the freshly dug earth. 'The locket was half-buried beneath the weeds. I didn't know what to do with it. I couldn't leave it here, lest it be found by anyone who . . .'

'Who might use it against me?' and his eyes were intent on her face, reading the truth there. But then he turned away. 'So this is where they met. I took away her carriage and put a man at the gates, but it was all too late. I kept her in, but could not keep him out . . . cannot keep him out . . . even now.'

'He came to warn us, Rafe, that is all. He has never been before . . . not to see me.'

He nodded. 'I have a penchant for accusing you wrongly. Once again I apologise.'

She brushed it aside with a gesture. 'I don't want your apologies, I want you to tell me that you won't fight this silly duel, knowing that Philippe only came to warn us.'

A sardonic smile touched the corners of his mouth. '*Silly* duel? As far as I'm concerned, Castille came to seduce and abduct you . . . in whatever order befitted the occasion. You are my wife, and his action must be considered as an insult to *me*, even if *you* saw none. Tomorrow's meeting, this silly duel, is long overdue.'

Laurel held out a hand. 'Is there nothing I can do or say to move you?' The misty eyes held an agony that was immediately misunderstood, and his jaw tightened.

'You have already tried that before to save another . . . friend. Don't worry, I shall not kill your Creole unless he gives me no choice.'

'Oh, you fool!' she flared up before she could prevent it. 'You stupid, blind fool!' and spinning, she ran back to the house, missing his narrowed eyes and the reflectiveness of the gaze that followed her retreat as dawn, possibly his last, broke over the gnarled oaks.

CHAPTER
TWELVE

'ÉTIENNE, PLEASE wake up! I'm sorry . . . so sorry, but you must help me!'

Sluggishly Steven Jourdan struggled from the arms, if not of Morpheus, then certainly of one of his better-endowed neophytes, and opened one eye. It was still dark. The weight on his bed lifted, curtains were pulled back and pale dawn crept apologetically into the room. He swore, regained full consciousness, and apologised as he focused on the white face above him. 'Laurel . . . what . . . ?'

'I'm sorry,' she reiterated, 'But Rafe and Philippe are going to kill each other. Aurora has already killed a man and is on her way here, and it's all my fault and . . . Oh, Étienne, I don't know what to do!'

'*Doucement, ma petite.* Easy now.' Sitting up, he took her by the shoulders and gave her a gentle shake. 'Now calm down and tell me what has happened. From the beginning, and slowly.'

The ice-blue eyes were sharp now as her first outburst registered, but his voice was still calm and a little chiding, as he said, 'It is not yet the end of the world . . . surely we have a few minutes more?'

Laurel gave a tremulous smile and, calming a

little, told him all that had passed since the rain of pebbles against her window had awakened her.

'Is Rafe in his room, or, more probably, in the library?'

'I don't know. He was so matter of fact, so cold, that for all I know he may well have gone back to sleep!'

The Frenchman smiled, yet with a certain sadness at the lack of understanding between these two. 'Go back to your room, little one. I shall seek out your vengeful husband and try to reason with him; though, knowing Rafe, I promise nothing. It is still a quite uncivilised hour and there is plenty of time for action, so you must take your time over your *toilette* and then we shall wake Marie-Louise and tell her to prepare for a short *vacance*.'

'Then you do think there is danger!'

'Laurel, Laurel, I only think that you and Rafe need some time together . . . alone, and that if Aurora does come here you will both be better able to cope with her that way. Allow me to talk with Rafe. Heaven knows, I have tried to talk more men out of more duels than I can count . . . usually with myself as the . . . almost . . . innocent party.'

Laurel felt better, having shared her burden, and could even raise a smile as she asked, 'And what kind of success did you enjoy?'

He gave a grimace. 'Pitifully little, *mon chou*, but there is always hope.'

She left him there, returning to her room to dress; praying for his success, but with little of the hope that he had prescribed. It was therefore no surprise when he called on her a bare half-hour later and exclaimed, 'Your husband is a fool!'

Laurel gave a sigh. 'No, Étienne . . . simply a man still possessed by his first wife. Will you take Marie-Louise to Baton Rouge?'

His patrician countenance registered defeat. 'Of course. You may wish to give the house-servants the day off, too, or at least the younger ones.'

Laurel nodded, taking a deep breath and, with that instinctive lift of the chin, became chatelaine with all the responsibilities that the post demanded. 'Yes, the young ones. Leona will stay, as will the plantation-workers who, God willing, may not have to know anything about it. Aurora cannot harm the cane now, thanks to the early harvest, but I don't think she would have done anyway. It is the family, myself in particular, that she will wish to confront.'

'Then you must accompany us to Baton Rouge and leave her to Rafe, who knows her so much better. I cannot leave you here, thinking that you may be alone with her.'

Laurel looked about the opulent room. 'I think, in coming to know Hélène, that I know Aurora as well as anyone can. Sometimes it needs a woman to cope with another woman, especially one as devious as Aurora. No, I must stay. If you take Marie-Louise away from here I shall know that two of the three people I love are safe. Whatever happens, I must be with Rafe tomorrow.'

A deep respect and love lit the gentle eyes. 'Had I known such a woman as you a decade ago, I might possibly have been a different man.'

She took his hand between hers, smiling into his eyes. 'But then you would not have been part of *my* life, and how could I have coped then?'

Gently his lips brushed her cheek. 'Very well, I suspect.'

But seeing him leave to make arrangements for the journey, Laurel doubted that his confidence in her was justified, and felt possibly more alone than she had ever done before. It brought no assuagement of her mood when she heard Saladin's angry scream and she knew that a fresh groom was attempting to saddle the hate-filled animal. Another bloodied hand or arm for the redoubtable Leona, another ember for the fires of resentment that drove the black stallion. 'Oh, why can't they all stop hating?' her heart cried. 'Why can't they all just stop?'

It was cool in the dawn air, and in the tiny gardens the rising cacophany of street-vendors and farmers outside was muted. Rafe faced his opponent with an easy stance, the great shoulder muscles rippling beneath the cream silk shirt. Philippe, too, looked relaxed, though a slight pensiveness showed in the deep brown eyes, a regret for this inevitable confrontation. Of slighter build than the man before him, he was yet solid muscle and had the advantage of speed from long practice with the épée. The two men were well matched and met each other's gaze levelly as the young Creole chosen to act as Philippe's second tied the length of hide about their wrists.

'Is Laurel safe at the house?'

Rafe nodded, accepting the other's concern.

'And Marie-Louise?'

At that, however, something stirred in the deep-set eyes and there was a strange note in the voice that asked, 'Why so anxious about the girl?'

'Should I not be? She is probably the only innocent in the whole affair.'

Rafe's eyes bored into his. 'No more than a courteous enquiry? Nothing stronger?' This time there was no mistaking the strain and subdued violence in the voice, and Philippe frowned.

'You talk in riddles. Here we are about to kill each other, and you talk of a child's welfare. I shall never understand you Americans.'

'You understand full well, Castille. Isn't Marie-Louise part of *this*?' And Rafe jerked his arm upwards, dragging the other's with it. 'You knew Hélène long before the girl was born. She . . . Hélène . . . told me so. She even laughed about it . . . laughed on her death-bed! "You'll never know," she said, and laughed.'

The Creole paled as comprehension struck him like a thunderbolt. '*Mon Dieu*! You think . . . King . . . I swear to God that Hélène and I knew each other then, yes, but not . . . not in that way. That came after, long after, Marie-Louise . . . You must believe me!'

'Why?' Yet there was a yearning underlying the anger, a longing for years of pain and uncertainty and hatred to be dissolved. 'Why should I believe such as you? Do you see anything of me in the child? Does she have a Southern name? Damn you

to Hell, Castille, I knew the type of woman I
married!'

Philippe flung away, only to be pulled up short by
the hide that bound them, and he turned back, his
anger as great as his shock had been. 'Knew her?
You knew nothing! You wedded her, bedded her,
then went back to your damned library . . . just as
you have done again. You're a shell of a man, King.
Hélène demanded more. And Laurel deserves
more. You empty your mind in case that festering
sore of doubt eats into your heart. You look at your
daughter . . . *your* daughter . . . and you see
Hélène's infidelity. You accept her lying insinuations, although you knew what a liar she was.
Your stubbornness will not allow you to reject the
child physically, so you reject her mentally, and in
time convince yourself that she is not yours at all.
Mon Dieu! If I had thought . . .'

His tirade was cut short by a sudden disturbance,
as Laurel ran into the gardens, hair flying, dress
dishevelled, eyes wide in fear. She slid to a halt,
momentary relief washing the anguish from her
features as she saw them standing side by side and
unharmed. Rafe had left just after midnight, not
telling her of his departure, not even waking her to
say goodbye. She had cried at that final rejection
. . . that he should go to fight and possibly die for
another woman, and not care even enough to say
goodbye.

Sleeping deeply after an exhausting day and the
effort of trying to stay awake, she had not seen him
enter her room and stand looking down at the
tear-washed face on the rumpled pillows, the bril-

liant moonlight showing him every feature clearly.
She had not felt him bend and brush his lips against
the tumbled silver-gold hair with aching tenderness
before he left, his eyes betrayingly bright. She
knew only that he had left without a word . . . knew
that she loved him still . . . helplessly, hopelessly
and quite completely.

Agonising lest she be too late, she had Hélène's
carriage brought to the front. A slender-sprung
spider phaeton, it was designed for the city streets
and intended to be drawn by one horse. Laurel,
however, remembering a disastrous accident on
the Brighton Road the previous year, knew the
potential of two horses being harnessed to the
vehicle. Ignoring the mutterings of the groom, she
had Hélène's greys brought round and within
minutes was driving at breakneck speed along the
River Road. The greys, unused to such exercise,
had enjoyed the run at first, but then, as whip and
voice were used unmercifully, had grown fearful of
the maniac at the reins and run ragged, their flanks
sweat-flecked and heaving. Their eyes rolled, as
ruts and rocks were ignored and curves were taken
with no regard for their necks or that of their driver.
Rearing and plunging, they were hauled to a halt
before St Anthony's Gardens and finally allowed to
stand, trembling and lathered, in the hands of a
wide-eyed negro who had been passing and was
ordered to hold them there. It was a measure of the
woman's appearance that the elderly negro did as
bid without question.

Flinging herself across the entrance, Laurel came
to a breathless halt. 'Thank God! I'm not too late!'

Then she saw the length of hide, and the glinting steel they held, and the colour left her face.

'You should not have come,' Rafe stated brusquely.

'I had to. I had to make one last attempt to stop you. Oh, I beg you both to reconsider!'

Philippe gave a thin smile. 'I think you are too late, *ma chère*. There is far more to this than even I was aware.'

'Go home, Laurel,' Rafe ordered. 'I don't want you here.'

Fists clenched, she fought down the tears of anger and despair. 'You don't want me at all,' she stormed. 'And yes, I *am* going home . . . back to England, so it won't be me that you are fighting for, though I know it never was nor ever will be. I'm not your servant, Rafe, and you want me as nothing more, and I never shall be your mistress, Philippe, and you want me only in that way . . . as a pretty toy. Since I can be neither the wife of the one nor the friend of the other, there is nothing to keep me here. My actions are my own. You may find another governess for Marie-Louise, and I hope you find one who loves her as much as I . . . or, if you hate her as much as you appear to, for God knows what reason, then I will take her with me and you can be alone with your books . . . the only things you ever wanted, anyway. We shall do very well together, for I do not think your pride will allow her to go hungry, even if you have starved her of affection. I sometimes think I hate you for your blindness . . . but not at this moment. Right now I am going to stand right here and watch you both try to kill each other. I shan't faint and I shan't look away. I want to see what kind of men fight over a ghost—and one who in her lifetime never loved either of them. Go ahead . . . fight . . . if she's worth dying for.' She stood, head erect, magnificent in her anger, disdaining the tears that now flowed freely down her cheeks, and did not flinch as Rafe turned to his opponent, raising his blade.

'Do you swear that the child is mine?' he queried softly.

Something moved in the brown eyes, a letting go of the tension wire-taut within, yet retaining enough of it to ask, 'Would you believe . . . such as I?'

There was a frozen moment when time stood still, as the goddess Fortuna rolled the dice.

Laurel watched them, her nerves stretched almost to breaking-point. 'Dear Lord, please don't let him die!' she prayed silently. 'I'll promise anything . . . do anything . . . go anywhere . . . die instead if you will, for there is no life without him.'

She saw Rafe's lips move and Philippe reply. A knife flashed . . . A scream was torn from her . . . And the leather thong binding them parted. Philippe turned as if in slow motion and gave her a low bow, never taking his eyes from her face, and there was an air of regret and finality about him as he walked away. She barely saw him go, her whole being absorbed by the tall frame crossing the turf with that tigerish stride. He reached her as the sky began to spin above her head. 'Rafe . . . Oh, thank God!' she murmured brokenly, her words betraying her unspoken love as she crumpled slowly to the ground.

Swiftly he knelt by her side, gathering her into his arms. Gently he smoothed the tumbled hair from her face, his eyes troubled, yet more tender than even he realised. Her outburst, her vow to return to England, had resounded in his ears like a death-knell, yet as a scrupulously honest man he knew the truth of the accusations against him. Even Hélène, fiery and passionate as she had been, had eventually withdrawn from his introverted nature. How much more alienated must this quiet and gentle Englishwoman feel? Hesitantly, almost against his will, he bent and kissed the parted quiescent lips, an inexplicable ache in his throat as he savoured their inner sweetness.

Laurel stirred with a soft moan, coming reluctantly back to reality, attempting to hold for a moment longer the wonderfully impossible dream she had just experienced. For a moment, dream blended with reality as she opened her eyes to the granite features inches above her, and her eyes went for an instant to his lips, but they were tight and stern and she knew that it had been but a fantasy. 'I'm sorry,' she murmured, 'Foolish of me. I promised I wouldn't.' Allowing him to lift her to her feet, she revelled for a few seconds in the strength of the arms about her, but then they were removed and his normal neutral voice enquired,

'Are you strong enough to walk? My carriage is not far.'

'Yes . . . yes, thank you. And Philippe?'

He frowned, his jaw tightening. 'Will not appear

on my property again. Since you are returning to England, I can scarcely forbid you to see him again in the meanwhile: I only ask that you be more discreet than your predecessor. I would appreciate as little scandal as possible, for Marie's sake, if not for mine. She shall stay with me . . . I feel that we shall fare better this time.'

They were at the carriages now, and she turned to him, raising her hand to touch him, then dropping it again at the strange look in his eyes. 'There will be no scandal, Rafe, for I shall not be seeing Philippe again.' And she knew that in Philippe's last look there had been the same knowledge, even though she had not been aware of it at the time.

Rafe's eyes went to the spider phaeton and the still steaming greys being walked by the negro she had terrified into taking them. 'You came in that?'

'You took the other. Marie-Louise took Serena to Baton Rouge, and I could hardly ride Saladin.'

'Was it necessary to put two in?'

Their gazes locked. 'I thought so at the time. I was under the naïve assumption that I might stop you . . . either of you. I should, of course, have known better, should have realised how little influence I have had from the beginning. Shall we return? You can send a man for the other carriage if we arrange for its care until then.' Her voice was level, almost emotionless, and gave no indication at all of the agony within.

No word passed between them for the whole of the long drive back; both too lost in their own thoughts to notice the beauty of the bayou morning, the mist floating upwards to envelop the trees in a gentle haze, the rising sun reddening the sky . . . But *so* red? . . . 'No!' Laurel cried, as the full import struck her seconds before Rafe lashed the bays into a gallop. 'It's Moonrise!'

Careering madly through the gates and up the long drive, the animals almost overturned the carriage as they slithered to a halt, rearing and fighting the reins at the fearsome sight before them. From ground floor to eaves the house was ablaze, and before the conflagration men moved about like silhouetted puppets in a shadow-play. All was in turmoil. Men were shouting incomprehensible orders, passing pathetically small buckets of water and cursing automatically and without feeling as pieces of wood crashed about them. Hungry tongues of flame had licked up from the ground-floor inferno and, within minutes, caught at the dry eaves. Black clouds of smoke belched out from shattered windows and swirled up into the still dawn air. A bedroom window exploded as Rafe controlled the terrified animals, and a groom ran up to take their heads, ducking through the deadly rain of glass that fell on the men below. The field-hands did not withdraw, but only cursed the louder and redoubled their efforts.

'Leona!' Laurel screamed, leaping from the carriage unaided and stumbling towards the flames. 'Leona?' she shouted at a passing man, but he shook his head and ran on. 'Have you seen Leona?' she asked a bruised and bleeding negro being tended by another. He shook his head, coughing smoke from his lungs, but the second man pointed to where a group of wounded and burned fire-fighters had been brought to the fountain and were being tended by some of the younger women. Among them, lying on a blanket, 'Leona!'

The housekeeper turned her head as Laurel ran forward . . . and brought the girl to a shocked halt by her appearance. 'Oh, Leona!' Slowly Laurel moved to her side, sinking to her knees, lifting trembling fingers to the terribly burned face, not daring to touch her. Someone had covered the burns in axle-grease for want of anything better, accentuating the awful appearance of those once noble, classically beautiful, features.

'I'm sorry, Mrs King,' the woman whispered through broken lips. 'I didn't even see her.'

'Aurora did this? Oh, of course she did. What happened?'

'Don't know exactly. I was in the kitchen. You know how that outer door is always sticking . . . Well, when I smelled the smoke I tried to get help, and wasted lotta time pushing at that door before I realised it had been jammed up by someone from the outside. She didn't mean for anyone to get out that way.'

Laurel momentarily closed her eyes, imagining the terror Leona must have suffered in that moment of realisation. knowing she was trapped in that inferno and that the only way out was through it, across the already blazing hall to the front door. 'Miss Aurora, she was upstairs. I heard her shouting and laughing wild-like, crying and laughing at the same time, and calling to you and Mr King to come find her.' Exhausted, Leona fought the pain and shock, finishing, 'I couldn't reach her, Mrs King, and I couldn't save the house. I'm sorry.'

Laurel looked over her shoulder, and tears pricked her eyes. 'No one could have done more, Leona.'

'You better go back to Mr King now. I'll be all right, and he will be needing you more'n me right now.'

Reluctantly Laurel left her there, and pushed her way through the chaos to where Rafe's tall frame could be seen working with the energy of ten men. His features were set in an emotionless mask, and it was only when the upper floor gave under the onslaught and fell with a thunderous crash of timbers that he swore, coldly and harshly, tearing off his shirt to smother the flames on a badly-burned negro caught in the exploding debris, before telling the man to withdraw. There was no longer any hope of saving the house, and in the still air even the sparks fell back safely to the damp earth.

Laurel turned her tear-washed face to the stony countenance of the man beside her. His name emerged as a bare whisper above the cacophonous nightmare about them, but he heard and turned. 'It's all my fault,' she whispered. 'I should have stayed.'

A flicker of some indefinable expression crossed the grey-green eyes, then wordlessly, and with a gentleness she had never thought to feel again, he gathered her into muscular arms. 'No,' he denied. 'No.' Nothing further was said as one hand smoothed her hair rhythmically, holding her head against his chest, where she could feel the strong beating of his heart. Gradually, in spite of itself, her body relaxed against him, moulding itself to the length of him . . . And the beating of his heart changed, quickened into a roll of thunder as, with his free hand, he lifted her chin. The long-lashed, deeply-set eyes were almost all green, and Laurel could not tear away from that look until it was blotted out as his lips came down on hers.

'Marse King! Marse King! You come quick!'

Almost angrily, Rafe tore his mouth away and faced the burly black. 'What is it? What more, in God's name?'

'Lady, Marse King . . . lady dead . . . You come quick!'

For a space out of time their eyes met in comprehension, then, as one, they turned and raced after the negro. It was Saladin they saw first, the makeshift bridle caught in a low-hanging branch, his angry snortings and drumming hooves drawing their attention to what lay at his feet. Laurel choked and turned away, gagging, as Rafe dropped to his knees, fighting down his own nausea, beside what was left of Aurora.

Having fired the house, she had been caught by the flames of her own making. Burned and half-blinded, her mind almost gone, she had staggered to the stables, unaware that the mare had been taken by Marie-Louise, unaware that only Saladin was left. The noise, the screams of the servants, the shouts of the field-workers as they discovered the blaze, had all served to unbalance her further. Throwing a noose over the stallion's nose, she had mounted with the instinct of a born horsewoman, her one desire to escape her burning flesh and the reprisals she knew would come. She had lashed the horse towards the trees, heading north, but only Rafe rode the half-broken stallion, and the horse had rebelled. As the demented woman had lashed him harder, he had bucked and reared, no doubt screaming his fury to the sky. Aurora had been thrown and, with an atavistic survival instinct, coupled with his own hatred of mankind in general, the animal had turned on his enemy, crushing almost every bone in her body beneath trampling hooves.

Rafe rose quickly, turning to shield the terrible sight from Laurel, but too late. She was sobbing in pity and horror, retching dryly, arms folded tightly across her stomach, her eyes wide in secret fear. Wordlessly he lifted her, carrying her away from the place, away from the field-hands and their pathetic bucket chain, away from the noisy, belated arrival of the fire-fighters, away from the snorting, still angry, horse which had, in its way, rendered them all a service.

By a moss-draped oak he lowered her to the ground, drawing her close against his bare chest, protecting her from the cool breeze and stilling her trembling. Laurel clung to him, her arms wound about his neck, eyes tightly closed to shut out the memory of the sight she had just witnessed. She felt the hold loosen, and clung to him even more tightly. 'No . . . Not yet . . . Just a moment more . . .' Immediately the strong arms tightened.

'For ever if need be,' Rafe murmured, his lips against her hair. 'For the last time . . . not for ever,' he thought. 'What a fool I have been; what a cold, arrogant fool!' Hating himself, he confessed, 'I've given you nothing but pain and misery. I've offered you nothing but Moonrise, and now even that has gone. I've nothing left. There is nothing to keep you here, even had that incident with Castille never occurred. I shall make any arrangements you want of me for your journey home, and make the divorce you seek as easy as possible.' His voice was harsh with the remorse that twisted like a knife within him.

'But I don't want you to make it easy!' her heart cried. 'I don't want to go at all.' Memory seared her and unconsciously she turned her head to taste the salty sheen of perspiration on his skin, the masculine scent of him mingling with the smoky odour of the fire in her nostrils. Held against the muscular hardness of his chest, the tanned skin beneath her lips, Laurel felt the sudden sure warmth within her. 'It seems we are both forgetting something about "for better or worse, for richer or poorer".'

'That was the past,' he grated, turning away from the gently chiding gaze that was raised to his. 'This is cold reality, and I have nothing! Nothing but . . .'

'Say it, Rafe?'

And he did so, quietly, slowly, the agony of it in his eyes and in the rough velvet of his voice. 'Nothing but my love for you; a love that even I was unaware of until I was confronted with losing you.

You filled an emptiness in my life; took my doubt and turned it to faith, converted my prejudice to discovery and my arrogance to the deepest humility. Laurel, I can never ask you to stay. It will take me a year to re-build and years more to repay the loans I must take.'

'But if you could,' Laurel interrupted, 'How would it be . . . The house you would build?'

A tiny flame of hope touched the deep eyes that searched hers, and a new concern was in his voice as he said hesitantly, 'Smaller than this one, but with a great chandeliered hall where we would entertain the friends we would make together. It would have white walls to reflect the sun on to your flower-garden and Doric columns to support the second floor, which would extend over a wide, cool porch where we would sit in cane rocking-chairs and sip mint juleps. There would be high ceilings for coolness, and large shuttered windows. Inside, shades of blue and grey, and palms in white tubs would rustle in the breeze from the windows. There would be a small music room where Marie-Louise could practise her piano and,' he smiled, 'if the noise became too unbearable, we could banish her to her room—a young woman's room, not a child's. It would have carpet and curtains of pale rose and the bed would be covered with a scattering of silk cushions which she could throw at Stephen or her maid—whichever annoyed her the most. It would face the fields where she could watch the men working—a lesson in art and a reminder of how mutual respect reaps its own rewards.' His fingers came up to brush her cheek and she remembered those same fingers trembling a little as they had parted her lips on that one unforgettable night. 'You could even have an *Art Dèco* bedroom.'

'There would be only one bedroom for us,' she dared, and his eyes flared with a desire too long contained; yet still he questioned the love he saw in her eyes.

'How can you want a man who has treated you so harshly?'

'How can a flower grow in the desert, needing only the slightest touch of rain to make it bloom?' she countered with a smile. 'One look, one touch from you and my heart grows strong again. Feel how it beats just by being this close to you,' and deliberately she moved his hand to beneath her breast where he could feel the erratic fluttering as of a bird trying to escape.

Almost of its own volition his hand curved upwards and her breath quickened as she felt the heat of his fingers through the thin fabric that covered her breast. For a moment out of time their eyes met and held, then slowly he bent to capture her parted lips, moving his mouth caressingly over hers, feeling a kind of wonder at the instant response he found there. The kiss deepened, and it seemed that her every sense was accentuated a thousand times. She felt every nerve vibrating at each point of contact: her nostrils flared at the myriad scents about her, the flowers and leaves, the damp earth and the smoke in the air and, above all, the tangy scent of the bronzed body beside her. Stars flashed behind her closed lids in a kaleidoscope of colour and she felt tears of happiness pricking her eyes. He loved her, and her world was therefore complete.

Breathing raggedly, Rafe finally raised his head, awaiting the slow opening of those incredible eyes, torn apart inside with the love he saw there, knowing that still he could not accept it.

'No!' he groaned, shaking the leonine head in repudiation. 'I'm merely fantasising—I have no future to offer you, Laurel, none at all.'

Now was the time, Laurel knew, and a small, secret smile curved her lips. 'We shall rebuild with the rest of the money from my inheritance. We'll find a small place in town—though I'd live with you in a field-worker's hut if I had to. As for the future . . . Oh, yes, my darling . . . we have a future, one we made together on that wonderful stormy night in August.'

As understanding dawned, the disbelief, incredulity, love and wonder that chased across the rugged features were all the reassurance that she would ever need, and her fingers lifted to curl in his hair. 'He'll be as handsome as a Greek god, with hair the colour of ripe corn and eyes the grey-green of the sea.'

He chuckled softly, jubilantly, no longer afraid, no longer alone. 'Perhaps she'll be a flaxen-haired beauty whose mysterious bayou-mist eyes will take New Orleans by storm?'

'Shall you mind if it's a girl?'

He gave a deeply contented smile. 'Laurel, my Laurel, our baby, boy or girl, could not be more loved than its mother is now.' The proof of his statement was in the mouth that moved over hers and the strong, loving arms that held her close to his heart.

Mills & Boon

Your chance to step into the past Take 2 Books FREE

Discover a world long vanished. An age of chivalry and intrigue, powerful desires and exotic locations. Read about true love found by soldiers and states-men, princesses and serving girls. All written as only Mills & Boon's top-selling authors know how. Become a regular reader of Mills & Boon Masquerade Historical Romances and enjoy 4 superb, new titles every two months, plus a whole range of special benefits: your very own personal membership card entitles you to a regular free newsletter packed with recipes, competitions, exclusive book offers plus other bargain offers and big cash savings.

AND an Introductory FREE GIFT for YOU.
Turn over the page for details.

**Fill in and send this coupon back today
and we will send you**

2 Introductory Historical Romances FREE

At the same time we will reserve a subscription to
Mills & Boon Masquerade Historical Romances for
you. Every two months you will receive Four new,
superb titles delivered direct to your door. You
don't pay extra for delivery. Postage and packing is
always completely free. There is no obligation or
commitment – you only receive books for as long as
you want to.

**Just fill in and post the coupon today to MILLS & BOON
READER SERVICE, FREEPOST, P.O. BOX 236, CROYDON,
SURREY CR9 9EL.**

**Please Note:- READERS iN SOUTH AFRICA write to
Mills & Boon, Postbag X3010,
Randburg 2125, S. Africa.**

- -

EPS

'Now ladies and   young lady here   pretty dress, an   you're all going   she's also very new and very nervous.

A few titters, a round of applause, and then everyone turned back to their conversations. Several couples, restless after the ballet, took to the floor. Most people were too drunk to notice more than an increase in well-being: Ida's voice blended sweetly with the swell of pleasure around them. But Tommy Trevino glowed with encouragement . . .

He caught her mood, and played it back to her on the keyboard . . .   In return, Ida heard her own voice fill out with warmth. The louder she sang, the sweeter, more exciting she became. Now her voice did not sound accomplished, but was a cry of youth, eagerness and a hunger for good times. Ida lifted her arms from her sides and held them out to the audience, like a welcoming embrace to someone familiar. Tommy did not take his eyes from her. That was her moment of realisation. She was in the right place, not by choice, or chance, but by decree: her own very special inheritance.

*Also by Frances Kennett
and available in Sphere Books:*

A WOMAN BY DESIGN

FRANCES KENNETT

Lady Jazz

Sphere Books Ltd

A Sphere Book

First published in Great Britain by
Victor Gollancz Ltd 1989
This edition published by Sphere Books Ltd 1990

Printed and bound in Great Britain by
Cox & Wyman Ltd, Reading

ISBN 7474 0575 1

Sphere Books Ltd
A Division of
Macdonald & Co (Publishers) Ltd
Orbit House
1 New Fetter Lane
London EC4A 1AR
A member of Maxwell Macmillan Pergamon Publishing Corporation

For Jane and Maxine

Do as you did in the past
And play.
Cheer up the state of the angels,
And so the sinners won't get too
    unhappy in Hell
Make their lives a bit more hopeful
And give to Armstrong a trumpet
Angel Gabriel

Yevgeny Yevtushenko,
on learning of the death
of Louis Armstrong

1

'He's the worst yet,' Jack said, and Ida had to agree with him. The two children stared at Mr Ottley from their hiding place under the parlour table.

Friday night was the regular date for the Garland family's *musicale*. It took place at One, Salamanca Street, Gran Garland's theatrical boarding-house, which stood on a corner of the Bayswater Road overlooking Hyde Park. Artistes liked it because it was nicely placed between West End theatres and the entertainment palaces to the west of London, round Shepherd's Bush and Hammersmith. Besides, Gran Garland was an ex-music-hall girl herself, and a sympathetic landlady when it came to late hours and the non-payment of bills.

On the sofa by the fire, unaware of the staring eyes of the two hidden children, Jack's mother Josephine sat clinking glasses with her latest, the lubricious lodger, Mr Ottley of the First Floor Back. They both raised a toast to Gran Garland, seated a little distant from them in the bay window. Then Josephine crossed her legs, negligently revealing a roll of oyster silk stocking top above the knee. Josephine was the only girl in a family of six boys. Perhaps that was how she knew how to manage men so well. Ida and Jack watched the couple with interest. There was as much entertainment in the grown-ups' so-called normal behaviour as there was in their musical turns.

Then George, the youngest (and their least favourite) uncle came into the room. He saw the scene on the sofa, rolled his eyes to heaven, and moved the coleus, the Spanish shawl and the fern off the grand piano, in preparation for the evening's performance. He banged down the plant pots on a table right next to Mr Ottley so that fronds of green interfered with his glazed viewing of Josephine's knees.

Gran Garland did not respond to George's crude facial grimacings. With a large family to rear single-handed, she had

9

learned early not to be seen to take sides. Josephine's flirtations were, however, boringly predictable. Instead she leaned back in her seat at the bay window, pulling the curtain to one side, hoping to see something more interesting down below. Ida knew she was waiting for the arrival of her most mothered sons, the middle ones of the family, who still lodged with her, as did George. Gran let the curtain drop, impatient with the latecomers.

Josephine giggled again. 'Ooh Sidney — you are a scream!' she said, turning to Gran Garland. 'He wants to know if he can smoke — seeing there's no ladies present. He means me of course — shocking, isn't he?'

'Joke, of course, Mrs Garland . . .' Sidney stuttered, spilling champagne as he struggled with his lighter. 'I mean, I don't suppose you theatre folk mind a little smoke . . .'

Gran maintained a dignified silence. Next to Ida under the table, Jack muttered an adult, newly acquired expletive, 'Strewth!' as disgust welled up inside him. Ida dug him in the ribs with a sudden and familiar warning.

'Shut up! Or they'll remember we're here and then I'm done for! It's always your fault — be quiet!' She gave Jack a stony look then went back to her task, twisting the loose spirals of fringing on the red chenille table-cloth that hid them.

Every Friday night, the same ritual, Ida thought: more tassels unravelled, more flirting to watch from Jack's Ma Josephine, and always the anxiety that someone would be in a bad mood and send her and Jack off to bed. She had missed three Fridays in a row, sent home for various small wrongdoings — and it was always Jack's fault, never hers.

Conjured up by her worries, Ida's parents appeared in the parlour. They lived very close by — in a mews cottage at the back of the property.

'You're late,' stated Gran, with a baleful eye at her eldest son. 'Mr Ottley's had to drink on his own. Now, Mr Ottley, don't bother to get up.' (Too late, Ottley tottered to his feet, dropping ash on the carpet, and spilling more champagne.)

'You're Josephine's big brother, aren't you? And her agent too, she tells me. How de do.'

What a contrast they presented. Ida's daughterly heart filled out in her chest. Her Pa was so elegant. Tall, thin, immaculately dressed. Dark suit, spats, shiny shoes, watch-chain. Thin fingers gently touching his wife's bony elbow as he led her to the other sofa by the fern-filled fireplace.

'Earl Garland; delighted. May I present my wife, Mrs Denise Garland?'

'Oh Earl, relax,' said Josephine. 'It's Earl and Denise. Let's be cosy . . .' Josephine sloshed out more champagne and shoved a glass at him.

Ida's Ma and Pa sat stonily side by side on another sofa, facing Mr Ottley and Josephine. Earl and Denise: the only married Garlands. Ida's Pa was the eldest son, known always as Earl, for reasons that had never been explained to her. Her Ma, Denise, was the kind of light, bird-boned blonde that turned heads in the street when she was dressed to kill — and she liked to go out man-hunting on her afternoon walks. Just to enjoy admiration, that was all, but it caused great friction in Ida's household, for her Pa adored his wife and never knew where he stood emotionally at all.

Aunt Josephine's performance was uniting Ida's parents (a rare event), if only in disapproval. This gave Ida more chance of being forgotten, to stay unnoticed and enjoy the Garland family *musicale*.

Josephine refilled Mr Ottley's glass, bending well forward so that the sight of the dark line between her breasts caused him some difficulty in saying 'when'.

'Here we go again!' he cried, so vain that in the middle of raising his overflowing glass to toast Aunt Josephine, he ran a thin white hand over his greased hair parting.

'Here's to success in your new show, dear Miss Garland!'

'Yes Josephine. Well done.' Earl fingered the tiny diamond in his silk tie. 'I'd have had to hock the rocks if you hadn't landed this one.'

'Ooh, never! You'd die!' She grinned at her brother.

Ida knew Aunt Josephine had been 'drawing against' with her Pa for weeks . . . this was a grown-up way of borrowing money. Jack shivered a little and Ida took his hand in sympathy. He snatched it from her, suddenly angry that he looked as if he needed comfort. Ida ignored this gesture and whispered,

'That's why they've got the champagne tonight. I heard Pa say, your Ma's got a six-month run now, for certain.'

'Good. That means I can stay here with Gran,' Jack muttered. He had learnt the hard way how to cope with his mother's theatrical wanderings, and turn the situation to his own advantage. Whenever his mother went on tour, or got into a long-running London show, he moved from home into the Bayswater boarding-house so that Gran could look after him. He loved his grandmother, but he enjoyed the freedom that living with her allowed him even more. 'I can't stand another adopted Dad in our house. I'm sick of it.'

'Ssh! Quiet! Look! Uncle Ted's come in! Oh good, they'll all start singing now!'

A cheer went up from the ladies: Josephine, Denise, even Gran, when Ted came in. He carried an enormous bunch of daffodils.

'Here you are old girl. Spring flowers.'

'George, get a pot,' Gran ordered, and George, who hated being treated like a skivvy because he was the youngest and least talented, scowlingly grabbed the bunch of flowers, and slunk off to the scullery.

'Come on Ted, give us a tune while we wait for the boys,' Josephine said.

'I'll play girlie, but you'll have to sing with me, how's about that?' Ted agreed with a wink, as if to say: The boyfriend wants *you* to perform, not me darling! Then he took his place at the piano, touching it into suggestions of notes, half-sentences of tunes, while he decided what would suit the mood.

The evening showed every sign of mellowing quicker than usual. The day before had been momentous, and was worth celebrating in style. That day, Thursday May 13th, had seen the end of the General Strike, which had suddenly brought schoolchildren like Ida and Jack two weeks of extraordinary holiday atmosphere in the midst of a boring term. But for Aunt Josephine, things had been bad: no management would commit to new shows with audiences dwindling in the chaos. Few buses, no trams, sometimes no tubes; huge traffic jams, because of a curious and unseasonal fog, and people off work lounging in the streets, not allowed into Hyde Park over the road because it was being used as a milk depot. Now it was all over, and Josephine's show could go ahead.

Ida and Jack watched as their uncle Ted, their favourite, broke into a boisterous rendering of one of their grandmother's best-loved tunes:

> 'Runnin' wild, lost control,
> Runnin' wild, mighty bold,
> Feelin' gay, and reckless too,
> Carefree all the time, never blue . . .'

Ted's hands ran vigorously over the keyboard, his left setting up a rumbling striding rhythm that made Jack's blood beat a little quicker and Ida feel forgetful and happy for a moment. Ted always sat so straight, never moved his head, and played with just a thin smile on his lips, and that pounding, joyous sound flying up from his fingers.

'That'll do Ted! What'll Mr Ottley think?' Gran flapped her hankie at him, then spread her hands on her ample thighs. 'I'm too tired for that kind of nonsense, all the walking and queueing I've had to do with this strike on . . . Besides, you shouldn't upstage your sister. This is *her* night — what will Mr Ottley think of us?'

Her mirthless smile revealed she could not care less; all her sons saw it and chortled, stage laughter, which Mr Ottley could not join in and which left him feeling confused.

'I don't play anything, I'm afraid,' he said, standing up in spite of himself. He posed like a paterfamilias, legs straddling the fireplace. Ida had a good view of those legs, thin bony shanks, with a stain near the zipper. She was repelled.

'Oh, that's all right, old man,' Ted broke off at the piano and replied casually, as if he were a close friend of Mr Ottley, instead of the disinterested relative of the object of his fancy. 'There'll be enough of us at it to keep you happy till morning. Wait till Jim and Billy turn up! We like to do it to give Ma a stir — it makes her feel better, telling us what hams we all are . . .'

'There they are! About time too! Go and open the door, Josephine, Dot's got her night off.' Gran Garland gave orders ignoring Ted's teasing.

13

'Oh, do allow me, Mrs Garland.'

Mr Ottley, by now well-oiled in every sense, gave Gran and Josephine a fatuous smile and walked a little too carefully into the hall, legs jerking like a string-puppet's.

At present Mrs Garland was using the First Floor Front of her boarding-house as parlour: the front room downstairs was going to be redecorated for her own private use after the death of an old singer friend who had long ago stopped paying rent. Two more boarders had the big bay room on the other side of the hall. These were a couple of African law students who kept themselves very much to themselves. In the middle of the hall was the lodgers' dining-room and Gran's own bedroom or snuggy, as they called it, was at the back, near the kitchen and the old outside privy in the yard.

Mr Ottley occupied the First Floor Back, Ted had First Floor Middle, and Uncle George was on the floor above. The other uncles, Billy and Jim, were uncomplainingly crowded into Second Floor Back so that two acrobats currently appearing at the Shepherd's Bush Empire could take over Uncle Jim's top floor quarters. Three chorus girls, from the West End show in which Josephine had landed a small featured role, occupied the tiny Top Landing Room next to the live-in maid, Dot. Normally Mrs Garland segregated the sexes on each floor, but the spring theatrical season was in full swing and she wanted to make the most rent she could from full boarding. The chorus girls only had enough money to share one small room, and worked too hard to make trouble. Besides, Mrs Garland knew her sons Billy and Jim were timid, however enthusiastic, and would never try anything on in their own home. And the acrobats were unlikely to cause the girls any bother at all.

Ida knew why and had explained it all to Jack.

'They're in love with each other and they don't like girls because girls give them babies and then they can't be acrobats. And they're not the Esmeralda Brothers at all: one's called Joe Diamond — got it?'

Jack ignored this slur on his intellectual capacity. He was puzzling over Ida's explanation of the acrobats' love-life.

'It's nothing to do with babies. They're just nancy boys. We've got one at school, teaches English he does. He goes to concerts and reads the score while the orchestra play. I've seen him do it in the park.'

To children brought up with the latest in sheet music as a professional tool of trade, this seemed particularly eccentric. But then all adults did stupid things with no meaning: the Garland family above all others.

Take Ma, Ida reflected. There she was, on the sofa facing Josephine, sitting all neat and elegant beside Pa, tapping her foot to Uncle Ted's medley of London show songs, and watching with deepest pleasure how her profile was reflected in the mirror over the fireplace. As if she had not already spent an hour at home in front of the dresser doing just the same thing, and knew her face backwards. Even worse, Pa was watching Ma watching herself, and seemed to be enjoying the whole boring performance. Ida did not understand this silent game between her parents. She had always been excluded, as long as she could remember, from some private communication between them that made her feel like an intruder in her own home. Silent yet powerful, Ida thought of it as an unknown law of attraction like the magnetism that made waves go in and out on the shore. The sea moved so accurately, men could put the times of the tides in the newspapers. Her Pa ebbed and flowed with her Ma, just like that.

Lunacy — of a sort, but not just sex, either. Ida knew all about that business from her uncles' jokes. She was unemotionally well-informed about the facts of life. The secret between her parents lay in something far more important than those contortionists' tricks, when two bodies somehow fitted together and did things. Ma had a hold on her Pa that made Earl worship her, and made Denise cruel then playful by turns. How could a man as clever and proud as her father love a woman who was silly and selfish? Even if the bed thing *was* good. Ida was old enough to guess the times when it was. Her mother would drift around the house in rayon négligés, humming for a few days. Then there would be an argument, and Ma would stay in her room for breakfast, while Pa came down dressed early and ate his toast in silence across the table from Ida without so much as a glance . . . Ida had got quite used to growing up invisible. It was like that most of the time.

'Where are the kids?' Denise's sharp question interrupted Ida's musings, as if she had sensed illicit thinking going on in the air around her.

Gran was sitting upright in her high-backed chair by the window, still waiting for Billy and Jim to come up from the street. Now she looked slowly around the room, guessing where the children's hidey-hole was. Her gaze fell on the table, and she peered at the hunched figures beneath it. She almost made contact with Ida's wild, pale eyes, staring out under the red fringe as if she were a tiger spied in a jungle thicket. Gran caught a glimpse of Jack also hunched beside Ida, and he had a child's stillness, that intent, frozen-rabbit tension of someone waiting for a sentence. 'Not bed Gran! Not bed!' he pleaded silently. Gran Garland granted the reprieve.

'Hiding somewhere.' She answered Denise with a shrug. 'Leave them this once. It's nice to have the whole family together.' Gran turned back to her window view without smiling. If Denise caught her looking conspiratorial, the mean bitch would be tempted to spoil the fun.

The two missing brothers, Billy and Jim, burst in, making the Garland family gathering complete. They pushed Denise unceremoniously to the end of the sofa, squeezing in cheerfully beside her and Earl, timing their 'excuse me's', bum-bounces and trouser-jerkings so comically with each other that Ida and Jack, feeling more sure of their treat, began to burst with silent giggles again.

'This won't do,' Gran said, irritably. 'For goodness' sake, Jim, Billy, pull that other sofa up so you can sit properly and stop fidgeting. You should be ashamed of yourselves, still horseplaying at your age.'

Punching each other as if they were still in their teens, not twenties, Billy and Jim fetched a dilapidated *chaise-longue* from a far corner and made a third side to the square in front of the fire. The fact that Billy carried the frame and that Jim brought two piles of books instead of legs for it to stand on did not cause comment. Every object in the parlour was a cast-off from one of the lodgers' rooms, and had some interesting defect. Ida experienced great satisfaction in noting a lump of horsehair poking out of the upholstery behind her mother's lace sleeve, as if the hairs in her armpit had sprouted into an unseemly pubic bush.

'Right ladies! Give us another, Ted!' Uncle Jim called out. 'I'll join in!'

Now Jim, the Wind Man, pushed up his cuffs and pulled two sets of ivory bones from his blazer pocket. He clasped them firmly between the thumb and forefinger of both hands. A short, rotund man, yet very nimble, he danced around the sofas, weaving in and out, shaking his clappers clickety-clack and accentuating the rhythm of Uncle Ted's piano tunes.

'He's lovely, isn't he?' Jack whispered, and would have crawled out from under the table to join in if Ida had not held him back.

'Not now! You promised! You know I'm going to do a surprise tonight!'

'Ooh! Forgot! Sorry.' Jack put his head in her lap, sighing, curled up in front of her so that he had a clear view of the rest of the room and Jim's performance. Ida began to run her fingers through his hair, but finding too many tangles in it, had to give up.

She tugged at the curly black mass on his head. 'You've got hair like a tinker's,' she said with affection. Jack shrugged but he did not move. Ida looked up: on the dresser near the table was a row of family photographs. When Jack was born, his hair was fair, to match his blue eyes. As he grew older and bolder, it turned black and wiry, impossible to comb flat without a dollop from one of his uncles' pomades. They all had a particular concern for appearances, the uncles. This trait had clearly not been passed on to Jack. But there were many other talents to inherit, one way and another . . .

Family legend held that grandfather Joseph Garland was a negro vaudeville performer from New York, who had come over in the 1890s to play a London theatre. He had met Gran, then Sarah Ann Alder, backstage, during her appearance in a family song and dance act. They fell in love, married, with little opposition from her parents who found Joseph Garland handsome, gentle, talented and generous. How lucky Gran was, Ida thought, to have been allowed such an extraordinary love-match in those days. But there were no pictures of her grandfather on the dresser, among the other family portraits.

Ida studied the line of photographs. The six Garland brothers were there, jostling at angles the china souvenirs from summer seasons on the coast. Ida's father was the eldest and looked responsibly miserable even as a child, sitting bolt upright, in a high collar and dark tie. In another studio portrait shot, Edward (Uncle Ted now), and his little twin brother Charles laughed gleefully, two round bundles in a wicker cot, happy to be squashed in. Ida did not remember Uncle Charles because he was killed in the Great War, when she was just a baby. Then there was Josephine, the only daughter, who was all eyes for her photograph, and posed clutching her younger brother James very firmly round his soft stomach, to keep him on her lap. Uncle Jim was plump and happy even then.

Ida's two youngest uncles, William and George, were in separate frames, relegated to a position at the back of the dresser, propped up against a broken metronome. Billy was myopic, and George had a very slight cast in his left eye, that only showed up through a camera lens or when Ida looked at him in a mirror. Uncle Billy had grown up shy and silly; Uncle George's little cast in his eye seemed to suit him, always at cross-purposes with everyone. Mean. These two brothers were always casual, unambitious, and less inclined or not sufficiently talented to follow the theatrical tradition. Which way would Jack go? Ida for herself was quite, quite certain. She was going to be the Garland family's most famous name.

'Ooh!' squealed Aunt Josephine when it was her turn to sing again. 'Let me see now, what'll it be, Sidney?' It was a wonder to Ida how her Aunt Josephine could imbue an innocent remark with such potential for sin. Unconsciously Ida leant forward over Jack, licking her lips the way her aunt did.

The young boy watched her drily: Ida had no idea that she was imitating Josephine's every movement. Her head mirror moved from side to side; Jack did not need to look at his mother to know exactly what she was doing. Ida in her dreamy state just fascinated him. He had noted before that Josephine and Ida had one special thing in common (it saddened him too, because he liked Ida so much better than his mother). They had arresting eyes capable of turning slow and mesmeric when they concentrated on performing, eyes that for all their warmth and shine told of something withdrawn and secret behind them. Ida's eyes were not dark black pools, like his mother's: they were almost yellow, tawny, flecked like tortoiseshell, fascinating.

> 'Oh, Baby won't you please come home?
> Oh honey, I'll do the cooking, I'll pay the rent,
> I know I done you wrong . . .'

Josephine was burlesquing her way through Mr Ottley's favourite number, pursuing him vocally round the grand piano. Her need always to have a man like a dog on a leash was a source of mild boredom to all present, including the children, but because she had landed a job for the next few months, they humoured her.

Suddenly, Ida got a signal from Gran, pushed Jack off her knee and scrambled out from under the table.

'It's my turn Jack! Ooh, wish me luck!'

'There you are child!' said Gran, acting surprise perfectly. 'I thought you'd gone to bed long ago! Come to me, there's a good girl!'

She waved Ida forward. Ida glanced at her mother, hoping not to be reprimanded, and moved quickly to her grandmother's side. As she expected, Denise began to whine.

'Really, she shouldn't be encouraged to show off, a girl her age . . . you know I don't approve, she's too full of herself as it is . . .'

'Now, Denise, don't get so worked up. She don't have school tomorrow, and I asked her to give you all a treat. Get up from that piano Ted, let your mother show you how to play properly, for once.'

It was a rare occasion for Gran Garland to soften and perform herself. Her rough words were a sign the whole family recognised; Gran was in a good mood tonight. Normally she was strict, a tongue-lasher who never needed to raise her hand (except to Jack who was beaten by everyone). Ida felt sudden apprehension, hoping she would do well enough to satisfy her.

Seated expansively on the piano-stool, Gran gave her a proper introduction. She had a clear, old-fashioned London voice, a real crowd-catcher. 'Miss Sarah Ann Alder, late of Daly's, the Gaiety, and latterly the Winter Garden, now introduces her very own protégée, who will sing the hit of *Chu Chin Chow*, in which the gel's dear Aunt Josephine scored such a notable success. That famous, record-running musical, known to all of us as a more navel than millinery production, will never be surpassed. Let me present, my best grandchild, the lovely young Miss Ida Garland.'

Jack was impressed: his Gran was surprisingly good at music-hall patter — all the more so because she was usually so grim. Could she really once have been a pretty young girl singer, Miss Sarah Ann Alder? It was a girl's name. His Gran was never a girl, never. At least, not one he could imagine.

Jack looked at Mr Ottley again. He was tall and bony, leaning forward eagerly on the edge of the bald sofa, his mouth slightly open and his mild eyes pink with alcohol. His fingers were stained orange with nicotine and his cuffs were very long. The man seemed to have a lot of money; his clothes were expensive, even if dirty, but he struck Jack as tight-looking and ugly. Strewth, his mother had no need to scrape the barrel. Although she caused him grief, he wanted to be proud of her.

Only Mr Ottley did not know that Josephine Garland had appeared in the slave market scene of *Chu Chin Chow* for four whole years! She understudied a succession of female parts for nearly as long. She even sang the lead, Marjanah, at a few matinées; she did well, got noticed. Everyone in the family said his Ma had deserved her success after such untypical patience.

Ida stood by the piano, enjoying her Gran's flowing bars of introduction so much that she missed her cue. Everyone laughed. Ida flushed, but Jack knew that was all right — she would do even better if she was cross.

'Would you give me that again, Miss Alder please?' Ida mimicked her Gran's professional manner, and Jack shouted 'Boy, oh boy, oh boy!' rolling out from under the table on to the carpet where his Uncle Ted grabbed him by an elbow and sat him on the floor pinioned between his legs.

'Shut up yer young hooligan,' Ted said in an uncritical

fashion. He had a very thin, neat black moustache, in the style of Douglas Fairbanks, a deep brown skin like a sportsman and a million girlfriends. Ted could also move his eyes in different directions, besides play the piano like a dream. He composed dirty ditties for Jack and Ida on all the black notes. Of all the uncles, Jack loved him best.

Ida did not look at Jack again. She stood as tall as she could manage, which made her look fragile and bold, like a springtime tulip in a park flowerbed, straight-stemmed. Her black hair was pulled back in a floppy bow and her dress was not very clean. But she licked her lips, pink, full lips, closed her shiny eyes for a moment, and began to sing. Jack grew horribly confused. She was no longer his lovely cousin Ida, a thin twelve-year-old girl with a hint of a figure: she was a lady, remote from him, and sounded unlike anyone he had ever heard before. Her voice made him think of beautiful things, of some sort of heaven, or at least a place where people would be good to each other. In a brief moment of peace, his usual bullishness left him and he hoped he would remember the sound for ever.

Ida's singing was like someone half-sad, trying to break into joy all the time, and you wanted to tell her that joy was just around the corner. It made him desperate for her to be happy. Jack screwed his head round to look at his Uncle Ted: he must have been feeling something like that too because of the stillness of his face. In fact, now Jack had a good look, everyone in the room seemed different, quite changed from their usual teasing, petty selves.

> 'Although I've often asked before,
> And thou hast answered yea,
> Oh do not say me nay,
> Wilt thou devote thy life to me
> And always for me care,
> And take thou as wife to thee?
> Let me hear thee swear,
> I love thee so, I love thee so . . .'

Ida held her hands down by her sides, with a presence of great simplicity that Jack, for all his youth, knew was the mark of a naturally compelling performer. That much was plain to him because he had heard Gran pass terse comment on every single female singer at the Shepherd's Bush Empire since he was five years old, and first went there for a matinée to see his mother. Supposing Ida became rich and famous, better than all of the Garlands put together?

Then of course, he would lose her. She would not want to mix with the likes of *him*, or the rest of the Garland family. Suddenly Jack was fed up with the lot of them, the teasing and the sighing, men making eyes at women and girls trying to express their feelings all the time. Ida had just finished her song, and there was an irritating lull in the room. Jack wriggled and kicked until Ted had to let go of him, causing him unintentionally to knock over a rickety bamboo table laden with the champagne. Jack had to get out: he crawled swiftly from the room, howling like a mournful dog, just for the hell of it.

It was a mistake: Jack knew that as soon as he had started on his run. It would be George who came after him — the least kind of all his uncles, because he was the youngest and needed someone to pick on. George was small, with neat hands, small white teeth, and a pinched look about him. What he lacked in physical strength was compensated for by dirty punching. He caught up with Jack just as he tried to bolt himself into the outside privy.

'D'you know what they should do with you,' George said evenly, putting his foot in the door and standing over the boy. 'Rub your pasty white face in some nice heap of dog shit, just to teach you a lesson. Barking like that. Shall I do it for you, shall I? Or better still, I could take you round to the knacker's yard and bury you headfirst in a big pile of horse shit. Do you a power of good, that would. What do you say, sonny Jim, eh? What do you say?'

'Get off me, you great bully. Gran'll kill you. Can't pick anyone your own size, can you?' Jack bawled. He threw a bar of soap at George, then a scrubbing brush from the yard bucket, temporarily preventing his uncle from laying a hand on him.

Another voice, a woman's: 'Get in there and give him a hiding George.' Josephine stood behind her brother, pushing him in. She was a plump, petite woman, with thin limbs and tiny feet, but framed in the doorway with the low sun behind her, she looked massive to Jack.

'It's not fair! Not fair!' he shouted, feeling that his bad behaviour was wiped off the slate by this show of force.

'Right! That's enough!' Gran shouted down at them. 'Back upstairs at once and leave him be. Josephine, open up some more champagne — but do have your Mr Ottley go a bit steady.'

Gran was leaning out of the landing window overhead. It was some achievement that she had manoeuvred the big bun on the top of her head through the narrow gap without disturbing one hair of it. But bending down made her old face fall forward, and she looked peculiarly threatening. Jack cowered further behind the toilet until his mother and uncle left the yard. A silence ensued.

'Come out of there,' Gran ordered.

He stood sniffling, refusing to rub his eyes clear of anger and look like a sissy. He never cried of course.

'I'm not talking to you from ten feet up. With *my* back.' Gran banged shut the sash-window, and Jack knew he would have to go up. She had saved him from a thrashing, and it was only fair to do as she said.

He climbed the stairs slowly, hearing the laughter behind the parlour door, the now insistent jollity of Ted's tinkling piano, and Jim's light tenor joined with Josephine's high notes in the *Kissing Time* duet.

'Come here,' Gran said, seated on a bench on the turn of the stairs, waiting, rubbing the small of her back.

'I know why you did it,' she said. She cleaned his face clean with two firm swipes of her handkerchief. 'Ida makes you feel cross at times. It's perfectly natural for a boy to feel cross with a girl. When he likes her, and she's a friendly cousin. Most people hate theirs.'

No answer meant he agreed with her.

'Well, it's not so easy for her either. Her mother's a right bitch and Earl's too hard on her. You mean a lot to Ida, you know.'

Jack stared at his grandmother. He had never heard her criticise an adult before. It made him believe she meant every word she said, and he felt happy again.

'Now, go in there, and do your party piece. Go on.'

'Not for Mr Ottley I won't. Why should I? I hate him.'

'Do it for your mother. And for Ida. Don't let us down. You don't like Mr Ottley? Well let's get rid of the blighter then.' She pressed a champagne cork into his hand, and winked at him.

Jack did not understand why his party piece might do away with Mr Ottley, but he did as he was asked. Gran had some scheme which promised embarrassment at least.

He rushed into the back kitchen, opened the range oven door and heated the champagne cork in the blue flames. None too thoroughly he smudged his face all black with the sooty stub. After a moment's thought he took two tea-towels from the kitchen-table drawer, tucked one into his leather belt like an apron, and pushed the other one behind his braces like the folds of a toga.

He burst into the parlour, and scrambled on top of the table. Ted, suddenly seeing what he was up to, moved some trays of buffet snacks to one side before Jack sent another object flying. Jack began his party piece, his speech, rolling his eyes in the burnt-cork tradition of the minstrel show, a recitation from an Ethiopian drama. A heavy darkie accent was essential.

'Friends, Romans, Countrymen! Lend me your ears. I will return them next Saturday. I come to bury Caesar, because the times are hard and his folks can' afford to hire an undertaker. Brutus has tol' you Caesar was ambitious. What does Brutus know 'bout it? It sure ain't none of his funeral . . .'

'Ooh,' shrieked Josephine, rolling about and clutching Mr Ottley excitedly on his knee. 'Isn't he a scream? My boy!'

Earl and Denise drew heavily on their cigarettes in an effort to maintain sophistication. 'An old family joke, Ottley. Sorry, I'm sure you don't find it at all amusing,' Earl murmured across the sofas.

Jack had lost his place when his mother laughed at him, and was desperately trying to carry on.

'Brutus is an honourable man, 'pon my honour he pays me back every time. Thou art fled to brutish beasts, don' the horsetrack make a dog of every man . . . ?' He could not remember any more, yet frowning and searching for his lines seemed to cause as much uproar as speaking the ancient words now fading fast.

'Well done, boy! I didn't think you'd get so far!' Gran smiled a little sadly and signalled for him to climb down. Jack, grinning so that he looked even more comic, his white teeth gleaming, strutted about the room.

Mr Ottley was completely confused. 'Gosh, I say, I've never seen anything quite like that before . . .'

'Old American vaudeville act,' explained Earl. 'My father used to do it, and Gran taught Jack. I just remember my old Pa doing it for us, a few times. Poor old man. Think of it, having to black your face when you were already — still, it was one way to become a professional.' Earl grew a little stiff, and reached for his glass again. Denise yawned obviously, and this time, Ida knew that her time had come. Her mother's good mood was dwindling.

'Off to bed, young lady! That's quite enough from the pair of you!' Her maternal duty had been exercised in one remark, and was at once forgotten. Denise wetted her fingers absently with her champagne, and placed them between the crimps of her bottle-blonde Marcelled waves to refresh them. Ida watched her Ma's varnished fingers squeezing the corrugations precisely. Denise's nails were small and pretty. But if Ida were not to obey — why then, Denise would get up from her seat, grip Ida's wrist so tight that those red fingernails left marks as she dragged her out of the room.

'Come on, Jack,' Ida called. 'He can come over, can't he, Pa?'

'Very well then. Sleep in my study Jack.'

Ida's family had the mews cottage at the back of the Bayswater boarding-house, which was where the original grand owners kept their horses and livery servants. To Ida, the whole establishment was one. Being so close to Gran made up for her Ma's severity. Two houses, lots of lodgers, and *musicales* with the uncles. They made up for a lot . . . She started down the stairs to the yard, where she and Jack could go across to the other house, through the garden. The fence between the two buildings had collapsed long ago.

Jack lingered for a moment, because Gran was watching Mr Ottley in a hard, calculating way, and he knew she was not finished with him yet.

'Minstrel shows, coon acts, Mr Ottley — before your time I expect. He was a fine musician, my Joseph.'

25

'Come *on*, Jack,' Ida called from down below. 'I'll mix my cocoa powder and sugar in a cup and we can suck it on our fingers in bed.' Ida was being nice to him again, all puffed up because she had been the centre of attention.

'Hang on a minute,' he replied, but Ida tossed her head and ran on into the yard. It was cool outside, with a comfortable smoky smell left over from several nights of fog.

Jack waited by the parlour door, forgotten by all the grown-ups. His uncles were looking a little sheepish. Ted was smoking a cigar, with his long-fingered hands dropping between his knees, his well-groomed head bent forward. Young George had gone to fiddle with the gramophone on the sideboard and was sorting through a pile of new jazz records. But it was Gran's persistence that held Jack to his place. What was she on about?

'. . . Lynchings and riots, poor man. Broke his spirit. Came here from New York with the Bohee Brothers, another coloured song and dance act. They all decided to stay here for a while, avoid all that trouble back home. Played in a lot of clubs, and for a few shows . . . what a man, a real gentleman my Joseph was. The Bohee boys ran a night-club in Leicester Square. All the best people went to it for dancing in the small hours.'

'So that's why Jack's the only one who . . .' Jack saw Mr Ottley thinking hard, staring at Josephine. 'His Dad must have been an Englishman, through and through . . .'

Jack's heart jumped a bit, for he knew nothing about his father, except that he was a white man. He must have been . . . Josephine tossed her head, gave no answer. She did not like to be reminded of her age, her maternal role.

Gran continued. 'Edward the Seventh learned banjo with the Bohee Brothers. You didn't know that, did you Mr Ottley? They were so popular, they taught the banjo to Royalty . . .' Her memories were getting the better of her desire to make Mr Ottley feel out of place.

'But you don't remember your father well,' Mr Ottley said, worrying, turning to Earl for confirmation.

'Oh yes, I do. He was out a lot when I was a kid, playing for shows. He tended to be asleep when I went to school. But I remember the way he used to sit at that very piano, one foot

tucked up behind the stool, and play ragtime tunes for us at tea.'
Denise was frowning at Earl, and his voice petered out.

'So, do you really mean . . . ?' Mr Ottley's shiny face had
turned waxen with the effort of absorbing difficult information
on top of a bottle of champagne. 'You're all *negroes*, really?'

'What of it, dear?' Josephine said, standing over him and
smoothing her dance dress down over her hips. 'Red, white,
blue, what's the difference? We all like the same things, under
the skin, don't we . . . Come and have this dish of mussels with
me. All that lovely food will dry out if we don't eat it up.'

'I'm allergic to shellfish,' he said, suddenly uncooperative
because he had heard something he did not like. Jack, still watching from the door, recognised the expression on his mother's face.
He saw it often just before she gave him a clout. It seemed an ugly
moment, till she turned her back on Ottley in a sulk.

Billy and Jim stood up and took turns with the plates for
Josephine's guest.

'Pork pie, Mr Ottley?'

'What about a little herring instead?'

'Oh shut up, you two, get off and leave him be!' Josephine
exclaimed, unwilling to be humoured.

'That's enough Billy. Jim, get me a cup of tea.' Gran
intervened. 'Would you like to quench your thirst, Mr Ottley?'

'I do think you should all call me Sidney, as I'm going to be
here for the rest of the summer,' he replied, dragging his
mesmerised gaze from Josephine's wonderful satin bottom, now
bent for his benefit over a tray of food. Josephine beamed, but
Gran fell silent. Mr Ottley had an unusual streak of tolerance, or
perhaps he was too infatuated to pull back.

'Stick a record on, Georgie-Porgie,' Jim said, going over to his
mother, and putting a comforting arm round her shoulder.

'Huh! Look who's talking!' George retaliated.

Gran was looking old and harassed again, locked in her
memories. Jim, chubby and kind, was the only son not shy to
show her physical affection, and he kissed her cheek with a big
smacking sound.

'Lovely buffet, Ma, and wouldn't our Dad have been proud of
those two young ones? Chips off the old block, they are.'

Jack knew Gran was thinking of his grandpa, the man he had

never met, but whose shadow hovered over all the family. Now Mr Ottley was holding his Ma close, and trying to quickstep with her in a corner. He was neat on his feet, and she tucked her face into the crook of his shoulder. With her eyes closed, and her face turned up to enjoy the music, she could have been a baby on someone's arm. Jack was disappointed. Whatever Gran had planned to achieve, it did not seem to have worked. Ottley was still keen on his mother and did not mind showing it.

Ida called him. 'Jack! Hurry up! I don't like going over on my own in the dark! There's slugs on the path!' Her voice was a hiss from the bottom of the stairs.

Such an appeal to his manhood, from a girl of twelve, had a stirring effect on Jack. (He was going to be eleven in August himself.) He could not understand the awkwardness in the parlour anyway — grown-ups were always lying to each other, not meaning what they said. It was clear to him no one liked Mr Ottley, and yet they were all making such an effort over him.

'Jack! I'm freezing!'

He led Ida past the privy and the pile of chairs waiting for Uncle George to mend their broken struts. On what was once a lawn, a bedstead lay rusting, and foxgloves were spreading thick fluffy leaves among the paving stones beside it. The music of the gramophone was loud enough to be heard all down the stairs and out over this wreck of a garden, but the children were too tired to pay attention to it, and they had to brave the darkness to the far corner of the fence. Up two steps, where shafts of ancient gladioli and leg-whipping grasses practically met across the path. It was on these broad blades of green that bugs and slugs regularly lurked, and for both of them it was a night-time terror, getting slimy wet patches on their shins. Distaste turned to disgust, because there was no light to see what sickening muscly thing had left the ice-cold smear; nothing but darkness till they reached Ida's back door, and fumbled with the lock.

'Ooh, it got me! It got me!' Ida squealed, and Jack bent down to rub at her shins.

'There's nothing on yer,' he said, shoving her into the kitchen, and turning on the light. It was a terrible mess: Denise was a slut who could emerge immaculate from domestic filth.

Ida clambered on to a chair and pulled down a cocoa tin. She stirred two spoonfuls of powder, two of granulated sugar, into a cracked cup. Then she took off her shoes and socks, and climbed into the sink among the dirty plates.

'Turn on the tap,' she ordered him, 'wash it off, there's yick-slick on my legs! Ugh!' She stood high above him, dipping and sucking her fingers in her favourite chocolate mix.

Jack ran the cold, and she squealed again. But Ida had the prettiest ankles and pure feet without lumps on them like Gran's. He splashed her and tickled her, until her legs were frozen and it was time to go upstairs to bed.

'Give me the cup, Gut's ache, it's my turn,' he said, and climbed into Ida's unmade sheets while she took off her dress. Ida put on her night-dress over her liberty bodice and knickers; the thought of stripping to a bare skin for bed never appealed to her.

Jack was not in the least worried that he would be found. Earl and Denise never came up to say good-night to Ida — they were always too drunk or too keen to be alone. Besides, he would be awake before anyone else in the house had stirred. Gran would be up early to serve the lodgers' breakfast. He would eat with her. Then, tomorrow being Saturday, and his mother in a matinée at her theatre, he could disappear all day into the streets with his friends. The gang might like to go fishing on Paddington canal, opposite the barges in the basin, or tie door-knockers together across a street for a quicker diversion.

'Shove up,' Ida said, sitting on the edge of the bed to brush her hair.

'Them's me feet,' he argued back.

'You really gave Mr Ottley a turn with your routine, Jack.'

'What's she see in him?'

'It's just a game. Your Ma's like that. Don't worry — there's nothing in it. You mark my words.'

Jack finished the cocoa cup and turned towards the wall, without an answer for her.

'Good-night,' she said.

Ida slipped in next to him, and wound her cold legs round Jack's bony shins, which gave off very little heat for her. But as he was still fully dressed, having removed only his shoes, his back soon heated up inside his flannel shirt and they both fell asleep, sweating.

2

Ida waited for Jack outside Luke Road Baptist Chapel, in Hammersmith, a nondescript, sooty street, lined with identical villas. An old laburnum shook its dusty yellow petals on to the pavement, and window-boxes of half-dead marigolds suggested the tired housekeeping struggle of low pay and too many mouths to feed.

It was a long way west of Bayswater, but close to Aunt Josephine's house, a tiny terraced place a few streets from Shepherd's Bush Green. Jack was at practice with the Sunday School boys' choir, after the morning service.

Earl was standing at a distance in conversation with a stranger. It was hot: Ida jumped off the brick wall where she had been sitting because her thin dress was sticking to the back of her legs, and she could feel the imprint of the stonework on her skin, even through a layer of cotton.

At least she was spared this one duty. Ma and Pa did not force her to go to church, the way Gran and Aunt Josephine made Jack. In fact, only her Pa liked to take her out. The rest of the time she stayed at her schoolwork or sometimes Jack came round.

One day she had gone to listen to him sing a solo anthem, just for encouragement. The church was dark and dreary, heavily scented with a sour, old-fashioned beeswax and evaporated turpentine. Ida had gone into a trance, listening to the preacher, staring ahead at the pews where Jack and the boys were making an effort not to fidget. Dressed in Sunday suits with white collars, restless, they distracted her, for a white cuff flashed if an arm moved, and a crooked collar stood out in the gloom.

Their pews had curved ends, with curling leaves of ivy or some other formal foliage carved on it . . . but then Ida realised, with a shiver, that a dark shape with deep-etched wrinkles was a boy's forehead, his head craned back to ogle at her, his eye raised to such a monstrous angle that he looked like a gargoyle, a grinning grotesque on the woodwork. That eye feasted on her until she had felt dizzy with embarrassment. It had taken her a long time to understand that she had the kind of face that attracted male stares. Some were nice, admiring ones; others were baleful, even hostile. Sometimes she heard evil words, but she made herself forget them.

Jack did not question why she had stopped coming to listen to him. Since that day she would only wait outside. He put up with the endless teasing of the other lads about his beautiful, unusual 'cousin'. No one believed they were related because she was dark and he had bright blue eyes. He ignored the jibes. In the end, being a Garland held him and Ida together, against everyone else.

'Can we go by the river on the way back, Pa?' she called out. Perhaps down there it would be cooler, and maybe someone would be selling ices . . .

'Maybe.' The stranger slipped notes into her father's hand and winked at her. Pa must have lent someone money. How good he was to old friends. In spite of a smart office in town, where he ran his theatrical agency for the Garland family and other artistes, Pa did not give up certain of his old corner-boy habits.

'Jack's late. I'm getting so hot, Pa.'

'Stand with me here then, it's in the shade.'

Ida joined her father under someone's front-garden lilac. Earl looked slick and pale this morning, in his grey flannels and blazer. Hammersmith locals sneered at him for his fancy clothes (dark serge suits were the only permissible Sunday wear for a man of their low class, and besides, Earl was dark-skinned, giving him even less right to put on airs), but Ida was glad, just at this moment, that he looked so elegant, like a West End gentleman. It separated them from the crowd gathering further down the street, near the Sun pub, for it was almost closing time.

The street and its inhabitants had a lazy, desultory air, bred of enforced idleness and an unusually strong sun. Sunday was an aggravation to people without work, nothing to do all week except wait for the next one. Ida observed the ordinary things, for lack of anything more compelling. Two boys in flat caps

31

waited for their fathers to come out of the public bar. One pushed an enormous black pram, on curved metal springs, filled with washing bags instead of an infant. The other picked his nose while he meditated, then ate the findings. A couple of young girls, perhaps Ida's age, were biffing and cuffing their smaller brothers and sisters, squabbling at the gutter's edge over a set of stones. One by one, slowly, the last drinkers spilled out of the pub, blinking in the sunlight.

'There's the lad now,' Earl said, for at the same moment the choirboys came out of the iron gate beside the church. 'Look at the state he's in,' he added, disapproving.

Ida stared at Jack, who appeared to have been scalped.

'What've you done to your hair?' she asked in a loud voice as he came near. The other choirboys overheard her and began to titter.

'Shut up, Ida,' Jack said, swinging at her with a string shopping bag stuffed with his starched collar, tie and jacket.

'That'll do, my lad,' Earl said, disinterested, for a commotion outside the Sun had caught his attention instead. Two dingy old bar hags had jostled each other coming out of the public bar, and were beginning to argue heatedly in front of a crowd gathering on the pavement.

'Oh Pa, let's go for our walk,' Ida said, pulling on his hand.

Earl stood back, observing the scene with disdain. All the other men and boys were drawn to watch: Jack ran off from Ida, obviously annoyed with her about the haircut remark, and huddled forward with some of the other choirboys. Wedged shoulder to shoulder, the boys felt braver, and shouted orders. The two old women began to sway, making circles.

'Have a go, Grandma. Have a go!'
'Give her a left, give her a left!'
'Pull the other one, Gran, over 'ere Gran!'
'Gwan, gwan, let's be havin' yer!'

A cheer went up as one old woman, brought to the boil by drink and encouragement, let fly a fist at the other's head, knocking her hat off. The small kids snatched it, and unintentionally tore the ancient brim in half. Instant hand to hand combat started.

Women fighting stirred everyone's blood: even Earl began to laugh, and other men said bawdy things that Ida understood more by intonation than by the words. It was a fearsome thing, to see a woman's stockings down round her ankles, the purple-mottled markings on her legs; a flopping bosom jerking this way and that when tired straps and buttons began to burst. Bleary eyes, saliva at the mouth, thin scraggy hair unpinned in greasy coils . . .

'Oh my Gawd, it's the police!' someone shouted.

Earl turned round, and swung Ida to safety by standing her on a garden wall. This was such a good place for a view that the choirboys scrambled up to join her, grabbing one another's arms and pushing each other off. A sudden wave of bodies pressed back on them; the police officers ran hand-barrows fast through the crowd, expecting the onlookers to stand off. The metal rims on the wooden-wheeled 'ambulances' clanged on the kerbstones. Ida was lucky not to be down below with bleeding elbows, scraped up against the wall like other smaller children.

It took strength to separate the women. Ida was now beyond disgust, fascinated by the strength that such old bodies showed. The older thin hag was turning quite blue; she was forcibly pinned to the barrow with leather straps and run juddering over the cobbles to the Hammersmith police station in the Broadway. A gurgling noise churned in her throat and the dirty hands by her sides demonically flapped, like a wicked old bird.

Ida did not feel sorry for them: she was captivated by their wildness, appalled by their physical decay. How could such decrepit, almost inhuman, bodies have feelings? The fat one was giving much more trouble, oaths and elbows rotating without end. Her boots had never had laces, now one fell off in the gutter, and her deformed foot was visible, all black and bleeding.

'Yer fuckers, yer fuckers! Wot've yer done wiv me sister!' she cried, a dry voice, like a parrot choking.

They were *family*! No wonder they fought! All families had people who hated each other — that was the way of Ida's world. The second hag was finally secured to a barrow too, and disappeared foaming at the mouth.

Men wiped tears of laughter from their eyes, trying to remember what they were doing before they were distracted.

Jack stayed beside Ida, while the other boys ran after the barrows shouting. In an old habit they had, Jack and Ida fell silent at the same time.

They walked a few paces. 'Sorry about the hair. Who did it?' she asked finally.

'That bastard Ottley. 'Cos I didn't comb it when he said. He came round last Sunday for tea and started straight in, givin' me orders.'

'Oh Jack.'

'I'm going to kill him. I swear. You'll see.'

'I haven't got all day,' Earl called, sauntering in front of them with his hands in his pockets and a cigarette in the corner of his mouth. Ida did not like it when he relaxed this much: it was too easy to imagine him as a villain — the kind of crook that drove a big polished Bentley car round Shepherd's Bush.

'Fancy a stroll by the Bridge?' Earl said over his shoulder to Jack. Earl seemed to understand the humiliation of the haircut. He did not say anything direct, but his voice let Jack know that he was sorry about it. Jack nodded.

But he was still angry, and walked beside Ida swinging his bag into all the garden bushes.

'Don't do that. You'll break something,' she said.

'Fucking break his head, you see if I don't.'

'Why can't you go back to Grandma's? Won't she have you instead?'

'Ma's got this idea about Ottley, her and me. Family life, she calls it.'

'I suppose your Ma's got a right to want you to live at home with her.'

'Why can't she just hole up with her fancy man and leave me in peace? She's never in, what with the show, and going out all night with Ottley. I wish I could be at Gran's like before.'

'Well, perhaps Aunt Josephine wants to do her duty. Try to be a mother to you. Perhaps she wants to make up for all the long times away.'

'Well, she's no mother to me, never has been, and never will be. I'll run away. I'll join the Navy. I'm not going to be beaten up by that bugger every time I spill me tea.'

'Does he really Jack?' she said, with sympathy.

'"Does he really Jack?"' he mimicked her, looking savage. 'Nah, he polishes me boots and reads me bedtime stories. What do you think he does, eh? What do you think this is?' He glared at her, pulling at the neck of his shirt so that Ida could see big bruises on his collar bone.

'But Ottley's such a weed,' she said, disbelievingly.

'He looks feeble because he can't help it; he's as sharp as rat shit underneath. D'you know how he makes all his money? He's a card-player in a club. That's why he and Ma get on so well. You know how much she likes throwing her money around. They spend all morning in bed. Doing it. I hear 'em.'

'That's disgusting.'

'I know it is.'

They skirted across the Broadway, which was strangely peaceful without traffic as it was Sunday lunch time. Following Earl (who would never walk alongside children, beyond his style), they walked down through the fusty, tree-shaded lanes of what older locals called Little Wapping, the dock and mill area beside a creek that fed into the River Thames below Hammersmith Bridge. Barges still came up the creek here to unload building materials at Sankey's wharf and the breweries nearby; in weekdays the shrill hooters of Dutch tile boats split the river breeze as if they wanted to cause a shock, stop all motion of time, and keep this shabby corner of London the same always.

After dark, Earl would never have brought them to the river by this short-cut. Prostitutes and tramps lay together in damp corners for the night, hurling abuse at anyone who passed. But by day the place was civilised and family folk could watch the rowing boats and have an ice at the Dove Coffee House. But Jack and Ida always hoped to see something sinful on the way.

They sat together on a bench looking across the muddy, low-tide river at poplar trees, green then silver as the wind turned their leaves. Earl bought them ice-creams.

He watched the children eating. Jack looked like a slum boy, more due to his hard blue eyes and cool expression than any defect of clothing. Ida was two years older, almost thirteen, but she was younger than the lad in other respects, more innocent, and he wanted to keep her that way.

'I think I could get your Ma a second job,' Earl said to Jack, apropos of nothing at all. 'I think she could do a club after the show.'

'Anything to keep her busy,' said Jack, scowling.

'I could look round for a slot as featured singer,' Earl suggested. 'It'd be more money.'

'I'd like to do that when I'm older,' Ida said, eager.

'No you won't,' Earl replied quickly. 'I'm not working this hard to see you waste yourself. You get an education.'

Ida did not dare contradict him. Her Pa had a grand plan for her, a scheme dazzlingly brought to his mind one day last summer when he met an old, once-famous opera singer, reduced to doing the rounds of the music-halls. Madame Albani. Earl brought her home for Sunday tea, and made Ida sing for her. Madame Albani praised her voice (what else could she do in the circumstances?), and gave Earl the incentive he needed.

'Madame Albani said you had promise,' he reminded her again. 'I don't like to think of talent being undeveloped. I want to see you make something of yourself, in a proper walk of life.'

Jack listened carefully, but he kept his eyes on his ice-cream. He could not understand words like 'promise' or 'undeveloped'. He thought only about coping. With no father to look after his interests, he relied on the goodwill of his uncles for his future. He was trying to learn how to deal with all of them, to find out what favours they were differently good for. He had discovered there were topics about which it was useless to argue with adults. He had to wait for attention, wait for the right moment with each one of them. The timing varied with every uncle.

'Well, why doesn't Jack go to Dawson Court like me next year then instead of the Elementary School?' Ida asked. 'Why doesn't Aunt Josephine think the way you do? It's not fair.'

'Because Jack refused to go. That's right, isn't it, my lad?' Earl answered.

'Me with a bunch of swots? Not likely,' he muttered. 'I don't want to go into book learning. Uncle Billy's going to give me a job when I'm big enough.'

'You can't work in a music shop if you can't add up,' Earl retorted.

'Test me then. Go on, test me.'

But Earl stood up, bored with the boy, and conscious of the church bells in the distance.

'Three o'clock. It'll be time for dinner soon. Don't let your ice-cream drip like that, Jack; I don't know why I bought you a cornet in the first place. It'll spoil your appetite. Clean him up.' He spoke sharply to Ida, then walked ahead.

Ida, as always, had a fresh handkerchief, but it was easier to suck Jack's shirt-front on the dirty spot.

'There, it'll dry by the time we get back. Hold my hand just to cross the road.'

Jack absent-mindedly forgot to let go once they were over the Bridge, heading north towards the Broadway and the bus.

Ida squeezed his sticky fingers, conscious that this was a big sign of affection from her cousin, to hold her hand in public. She did not pity Jack exactly, because he had certain compensations for his erratic life. It was exciting to have a mother who was on the stage, made lots of money sometimes, and gave him big treats when she was in a good mood. Better than having a slut of a mother who hated you. Day in, day out. Ida had no idea why Denise disliked her so.

Jack found benefits in any situation. He got lots of money, bribes from Josephine's men friends, to stay out of the way. He also knew how to steal. He had shown her how to pilfer pockets and purses; not too much to be found out, just a few coins each time, plenty left behind. He had over ten pounds buried in the yard at Gran's; double what some people earned in a week in the factories . She had accumulated only two pounds sixpence, but if her Ma found out, she would be flayed alive.

'Shall I try to have a word with Gran about it?' she asked.

'About what?' he said, sharp-eyed and defiant.

'Mr Ottley.'

'I can handle it.'

She sighed. 'All the same, it must be nice for Aunt Josephine, having someone treat her like a duchess, buy her flowers . . . I'll be like her when I grow up. She has such a good time, your Ma does. Apart from the bed thing. I wouldn't do that. Not even for a fur coat.'

'When you grow up you won't be like her, you'll get married.'

'Maybe. Maybe not. Pa wants me to go to singing lessons next.'

'Blimey, you'll be in the opera before he's finished with you.'

'Honestly Jack, I do wish you'd mind your language.' Her Pa's great ambition for her was alternately a worry and a source of pride.

He let go her hand, dashing forward to swing round the bus stop.

'Yer-yer, yellow eyes, cat's eyes, piss eyes!'

She rushed at him and clapped her hand over his mouth. Ida had the advantage of at least four inches in height, and she suddenly felt hateful towards Jack. He was so stupid, always looking for trouble, even when people meant well towards him.

'Say sorry. I'll smother you. Say surrender or else . . .'

Earl separated them at once, his hands unusually rough.

'In the street! People staring at us! Who d'you think we are! Your mother'll hear of this!' It was the worst threat he could use, and he knew it.

'No Pa, please!' Ida cried. 'It wasn't my fault! He was teasing me, honest!' She gave Jack an accusing look.

'That's enough. That's *enough*. Let me tell you something Ida. *Any* trouble, and the police will come down on us like a ton of bricks. It happened to Ted and me, when we were kids. Listen. People like us, we have to prove we're English. Folks like us who can't prove it, *they get put on a list*. If they get into trouble again, that's it. Deported. Kicked out. Got it?'

'Yes Pa.' Ida's lip quivered.

'It's all right for old hags and other white folk to be law-breakers. Jack can be a hooligan if he likes. There's no risk for *him*. But you'd better not forget, Ida: you're different. There's only two places for you. Right at the top, or right at the bottom. You have to be *good* to get to the top. Better than any of them.'

His voice rambled on, angrily repetitious. At first Ida thought he was exaggerating, just to impress her with his message. But the notion of being 'put on a list' seeped into her, like cold water in a hot bath, gradually more chilling. The bus came at last, and they continued on their journey home in a subdued silence.

Jack sat in the front seat upstairs on the trolley bus, pretending to be the driver and busily steering round corners. He had already forgotten about her Pa's words, but Ida was still wondering what the trouble with the police was, when Earl was young. She wanted to ask her Pa, or her Gran maybe, but she did not think she had the courage.

When Ida was very small, the power of her grandmother's authority on the whole family was one of the first absolutes of life she had learnt. Her father had told her about the poverty of his childhood, a life she recalled almost as a fairy-tale.

Once, he described it to her: 'After Dad died, Gran was left with all seven of us under the age of twelve, in a big empty house. All those naughty little lads . . .'

'What about Aunt Josephine?' she had prompted.

'Oh yes, well, a girl, I forgot. We stayed home while your Gran went out to find work.'

'And who looked after you?' she had asked, concerned as children always are when adults are careless about important details. Ida smiled to herself as she relived it.

'She got a neighbour in for the day I suppose. Anyway, then she went round all the theatres, all the agents, and put us down on their books,' he continued. 'Just us older ones at first, me and Ted and poor old Charlie, because Billy was, I dunno, about six and George would have been four or five.'

'What happened then?'

'Well, because they knew her, and felt sorry about Dad, they'd send someone round whenever they needed a walk-on lad — you know, someone in a crowd scene, with a dog, or a messenger boy for a whodunit. "Send for a Garland boy," they said.'

'Who done what?'

'Who done the old boy in — cops and robbers, detective plays. Like Charlie Chan.'

Ida had nodded, understanding.

'I tell you what, I've delivered more cables than spoken lines! Never could say much on stage . . . Mmm-mmm,' he shook his head, making Ida laugh at his nervous face and dried-up words.

'With all the money, we got music lessons: Ted was best, then Josephine, for the piano, then later on, Jim for clarinet and sax. Handy lad, he was. Still is, of course. I can always get a gig for Jim, any time.'

'And what about you, Pa?'

39

'Oh, I'm tone-deaf and flat-footed. They always thought the Garlands would be naturals, what with Pa, but I broke the rules . . .'

Ida looked back at her father now, staring down at the street below. He looked sad and drawn as grown-ups often did when they thought no one was looking at them. If someone were to speak to him now, he would suddenly beam like a floor manager in a big shop. Ida liked him better when he was not making a false effort. He was more handsome then. Grown-ups lost in thought looked capable of momentous decisions, as if they might turn the world upside down.

''Ere we are! Get off!' Jack pulled on an imaginary handbrake and shot down the stairs, sliding down the brass rail of the spiral steps with his arms stretched taut and his legs swinging free. 'Race yer to Gran's!'

Lunch with Gran Garland was the usual steamy, greasy shout-up: all the brothers could cook quite well; Gran had brought them up to fend for themselves. Consequently they argued over their different culinary methods, Billy, Jim and George being the most rivalrous.

Billy ran a music shop in Shepherd's Bush, and liked to liven the lunch hour with a collection of the latest 'hot' records imported from America, before selling them to his fanatical clients. Billy put Uncle Ted in charge of this musical accompaniment for the cooks, telling him in what order to put the 78s on the gramophone. Strains of Jelly Roll Morton followed by Bix Beiderbecke filtered down the stairs.

'Don't put bicarb in the greens — you're ruining the flavour and it makes them tough!' Billy ordered George as he hurried back to the cooking and they both clattered about in the green-swampy scullery.

'Balls. Preserves the vitamins. Ask Gran,' George said in an equable tone, tipping fat from the meat on to the batter for the Yorkshire pudding. His thin mouth worked in and out with the effort of dividing the juice equally between the little tin pans. 'Move out of the way — d'you want me to burn myself?'

'And you two can steer clear of here as well,' Uncle Jim said, waving a wooden spoon coated with gravy to threaten Jack and Ida.

Uncle Billy turned to them in a more friendly fashion. 'Here's a little job for you. Go and pay your respects to your Gran. Take her up the sherry, there's a good girl Ida.' His tortoiseshell spectacles steamed up and dispelled the moment's awkwardness Jim's short temper had created in the kitchen. Uncle Billy was a soft man.

No small doses: Ida poured 'Gran's mellower' to the top of a gold-rimmed tumbler and followed Jack upstairs. On the landing, without speaking, they stopped and each took a large swig from the glass, rubbing their chests as the liquid went down. It had an instant effect on them; Ida felt the sweet juice coursing through her and within minutes she was happy, slightly numb, as if her skin had begun to thicken. Sherry always made her a little deaf too.

Gran Garland sat in her customary place by the window. She stared at them as she sipped her drink, and Ida moved back very slightly in case Gran should smell the 'nip' on her breath.

'Get on all right at school this week, Ida? Doing your homework? No bother?'

'Oh yes, Gran. Got an A for English on Thursday.'

Gran stared meaningfully at Jack. No question was directed at him. Ida hated the way everyone treated him like a lost cause.

'Here, Jack me lad, wind this up for your uncle,' Ted called him to help with the gramophone. 'I've got to change the needle.' He took a small tin of steel needles from the dresser and twisted the head on the gramophone. Jack liked to watch Ted doing anything with his hands, because he was neat and deft in all his movements.

'Did Earl see anyone on the way here?' Ted whispered to him.

'Like who?' Jack asked loudly.

'Keep your voice down, for Gawd's sake! I mean, he didn't have a quick one with anyone, at the Sun, or down by the river, did he?'

'How much?'

'What?' Ted responded, puzzled.

'How much is it worth to yer?'

'Get off, you young bleeder.' Ted raised a hand as if to cuff him not too affectionately across the ear. Jack bounced out of the way with the reflexes of a trained boxer. Ted stopped smiling.

'Been getting at you, Ottley, has he?' he asked quietly, putting a hand on Jack's cropped hair.

'Leave go of me.' Jack twisted out of his grasp.

'You shouldn't ask for it. He's got a shocking temper,' Ted said. 'Uncontrollable, that's him.'

Ida was half-listening to this conversation; Gran was still making her ritual enquiries, but the sherry was working on her too, and she was taking longer to think of each question.

'Gran,' Ida whispered.

'Eh?' Gran rubbed her strong, tired face, working into her eye sockets in a way that always alarmed Ida. One day Gran might push her eyeballs right in.

'What does Aunt Josephine see in Mr Ottley? I don't like him and he's mean to Jack.'

Gran looked sober. 'She's got in a spot of bother, gambling. He's a croupier in the club. He could cause her a packet of trouble. It's best not to interfere. As for Jack — I can't have him back dear. He's too much of a handful. I can't control him. Maybe he needs a strong man.'

'Oh Gran . . .'

'Don't argue with me. Jack's going to make his way in the world all right. Never you fear. Now you go and tell those boys if dinner's not on the table in five minutes . . .' She wagged a warning finger and drank deep, gusty gulps.

'Gran.'

'What is it now?'

'Will you buy me a new dress at Whiteley's? Pa's taking me for singing lessons, he'll give me the money. I want to look smart, and Ma chooses me such awful things . . . you know, something so he'll think I'm smart . . .'

Gran laughed. 'Twist everyone round your finger, you do.'

Ida knew she agreed. 'After school, Monday, then, I'll come round . . .'

'Cash I want — tell your father it'll be ten pounds. We won't go to Whiteley's — I'll take you to Allaine's.'

On the following Monday Ida and her grandmother walked the short distance from the boarding-house to Lancaster Gate, at the smart end of the borough. It was a bright sunny day, the

London plane trees dappling the pavements, but the cars throwing up too much grit into their eyes. Once they had turned off Bayswater itself into the quieter streets, they could slow their pace and chat.

Here, the roadways were unusually wide and sedate, for they formed part of an estate of grand town houses, white stucco with imposing pillared porticoes. This area had been called Tyburnia when Gran Garland, as Sarah Ann Alder, had begun her life on the stage. Tyburn was where criminals were hung in the old days, Ida knew that from school. But her Gran told her more interesting details than that. This estate, near Marble Arch, was owned by the Bishops of London; they built the grandiose town residences, many overlooking Hyde Park, to sell to the wealthiest families in England. On its fringes (where the Garland family lived), prosperous merchants and businessmen had also built their homes; Greeks, Maltese, Jews, a mingling of nationalities. They were drawn to the area by its newness, which made it comfortably less exclusive than Belgravia, and by the commerce growing up round the Great Western Railway Station, Paddington.

Tyburnia gave up its grisly name, and the homes facing the park remained polite, but much of the rest of the Church's property west of there was soon sub-divided into some of the worst slums of London. Cockney, Irish, or unemployed northerners drifted from the trains into the back streets of Paddington. The Bishops of the Church of England lived off the rents paid by prostitutes, immoral earnings, at the turn of the century.

'We bought our house from a Greek family, Petrocochino, they were called,' Gran told Ida as they walked along. 'That was when the Alder family was earning a fortune, top of the bill we were in those days . . . and then, when my Pa died, it came to me and Joseph. He had no trouble living here. The whole place was a nice mix of folk, and no one bothered him. Still is a nice mix, don't you think Ida?'

Ida had never given the subject much thought: her school had its sprinkling of other nationalities, Italians, Greeks, and some well-off Africans, whose fathers were doctors or studying to be lawyers, and no one found significance in it. But her Pa's words about behaving herself, and those 'lists' for people not born

British, were ominous all the same. Perhaps a 'nice mix' was another way of saying that people with a certain problem stuck together. They were all different, one way or another.

'Tell me about Grandpa dying, and coping with the boys,' Ida urged, hoping for more details. Growing up was all about learning the past, not heading into the future in a funny kind of way: getting grown-ups to tell you who you were. After all, her Gran had known her before she knew herself.

'No. I'm out and about, I don't want to feel my age,' Gran replied, changing her mood.

So unpredictable. Grown-ups. They loved talking about the good old days, and then all of a sudden they got bad-tempered because they were so ancient! Ida sighed.

'One day I'll tell you, but not now,' Gran said. 'Here we are: they'll remember me, they will.'

Sandwiched between a Catholic Church and a gentleman's outfitters, was the small curtained window of Allaine et Cie.

Two sisters ran the establishment; two tiny east London ladies, one a wordless craftswoman with pins in her mouth, the other an opinionated Madame with a memory for names.

'Mrs Garland! What a nice surprise — isn't it, Emmie, and this must be your granddaughter. Do come in, just in time for a cup of tea.'

'I could do with a cuppa, thank you Celia, with this heat.' Gran sat down, pleased to be served, and indicated to Ida that she should offer help in organising the refreshments.

'Don't you move, young lady. Take a seat, I can't have that. You're customers!' Celia nodded at her sister, who stopped work instantly.

Emmie, plump and white-haired, moved slowly to the kitchen at the back. Ida looked round with curiosity. The shop was one big, bare room, a faded place, with the trimming working loose on the edge of the brocaded chairs, and a dingy grey carpet that was once light blue. In a corner by the window-platform, fungus grew in a patch of damp. Curtained brass rods dividing the shop window from the interior were speckled black with rust, and the pink chiffon upon them was nearly rotted through. But Allaine et Cie were busy; a clothes rail was full of the very latest lines, and Emmie's chair and table were covered in a pile of alterations.

44

'Just like your mother,' Celia nodded, brittle-featured, tight-lipped, in approval at Ida's face. 'What's it to be — an audition, have we?'

Gran tutted noisily. 'Not yet. She's to have lessons with Harvey Johns. The composer, you know.'

'Well, fancy! The one who lives near the Park? Saw his picture in the evening paper once, giving prizes at Dawson Court,' Celia said, impressed.

'Yes. That's what gave Mr Garland the idea,' Gran volunteered. 'He saw him at Ida's Speech Day.'

'I didn't know composers gave lessons,' Emmie said, presenting the tea.

'Well, only to hand-picked people they like,' Gran could not help boasting a little.

'Moving up in the world, aren't we?' Celia said.

Gran kept smiling, but Ida noticed that her hands clutched her handbag a little more tightly. Gran saw Ida looking, and in studied fashion opened her bag and considered its contents, as if there was nothing barbed in Celia's comment.

'I'd thought . . . something like this,' she said, pulling out a cutting from a magazine. Ida felt deep affection for her grandmother at this moment. She took all the trouble that a mother should — and of course Denise had no notion that this expedition was taking place.

'Can I see, Gran?' Ida asked, blushing, because as she stood up the dressmaker looked her up and down, from her ankles to her new breasts, and she was 'typed' on the spot.

'Now don't argue with me, Ida. I know what I'm doing.' Gran handed over the slip of paper. Ida stared: it was a picture cut from a magazine of an unknown film star wearing a creation of pleats and bows.

'It's very smart,' she said, uncertain.

'It's quality,' Celia agreed. 'No trouble Mrs Garland. But I might fill in the V at the neck.'

'Piqué,' Emmie managed through bristling lips of pins.

'Just for the neckline,' Celia added, nodding approval.

Ida tried to stand still while she was measured, but she felt flushed and ticklish when the dressmaker, no taller than she was herself, pushed the tape into her armpit to measure the length to her hips, and then wound it round her bosom, brushing it this way and that for a tactfully loose fit. Miss Celia smelt of lavender and tobacco smoke, and her precise soft voice was full of careful aitches and Essex vowels so that she said 'stand ap strite' and 'littul' instead of 'little'.

'Right-o. And now, pastel or predominant?' Ida did not dare to offer an opinion, while the three women tossed aside bolts of pigeon colours, pink, grey, blue, looking for a 'young shade'. In the end the ladies chose cerise, a word Ida did not know, any more than she had heard of taupe, magenta, or écru. Although Ida knew that there were far more exclusive places in which to buy clothes, in Bond Street or Piccadilly perhaps, she believed that no other women in the world could compare with the Allaines and Gran Garland for good taste and a perfect sense of style. She was learning the first principles of womanhood from experts, and she hoped she would remember everything they said.

Her grandmother paid the deposit without any reaction to the price asked. Two pounds seemed an extraordinary sum to Ida, and she hoped her father need never know exactly what had been spent. Gran Garland pursed her lips and shut her bag with a click, to let her know that this anxiety about the cost was meant to be put aside. At home, people complained about money all the time — but now Ida realised that in public one never showed the slightest hint of unpreparedness, if one was proper and smart. She wanted more than anything in the world to be a real lady, at that moment.

'And how's Josephine?' Celia enquired. 'We haven't seen her in a long time. When was it, Emmie, we altered her, before Christmas, the red lace?'

'She's still got to see us about that,' Emmie nodded, by which they all understood that Josephine had not paid.

'I was just coming to it,' Gran answered quickly, 'five, wasn't it? Isn't that what she said, Ida? This morning?'

Ida was eager not to fail her grandmother in the lie. 'Five guineas, Gran,' she agreed. She felt like a great actress; deception in league with a grown-up gave her a thrill quite unlike doing wrong with other children. Her Pa's ten pounds was being well used, paying two bills.

Celia took up the game. 'Ooh, no, she's having you on! It wasn't anything like that much, was it Emmie? More like four guineas, but I'll take the rest if you insist — I don't mind, if you really want me to rob you!' Both dressmakers laughed brilliantly at the notion, but Celia dabbed a tear from her eye to mask the close look she kept on Mrs Garland's hands, counting out the pounds and shillings.

Then everything was in order, and the Garlands left the shop. 'See you Thursday then Celia.' Gran Garland waved, squared her shoulders and led Ida firmly down the street.

'Pricey, but good,' she said. 'Always go for quality, spend more than you think you can afford, it's worth it,' she instructed. 'Don't do what your mother does, don't buy cheap frills. She's a small blonde and can get away with it. I'm relying on you, Ida, to set a tone as you grow up.'

Ida had no idea what 'setting a tone' meant, but instinct told her that Gran Garland was an ally where her mother was not, and that for all her pretension to glamour, Denise had an uncertain grasp of all right matters compared to this aged, plump, old-fashioned woman, still wearing a long black coat and a deep-crown hat. (It was a style of millinery she could not give up on account of the size of her bun.)

'Now you go round the back,' Gran ordered as they reached the corner of their street. 'Say I called you in for tea on your way home. And mind you get your homework done this week, I can always go back and tell Allaine's to sell it off if you don't.'

'Sell my dress? Gran, you wouldn't.'

'Don't try me then.' The big, emphatic features of her grandmother's face had gone hard again. It's the boarding-house, that does it, thought Ida, she's much more friendly when we are out on the town.

'Thank you Gran, I'll be ever so good.' Ida leant up to kiss her dry, fleshy cheek and skipped away.

Gran Garland worried that Ida looked too thin; her elbows jutted out white as she ran and her legs were too long. She did not see herself in Ida. At the same age she had been a big, handsome girl, with thick brown hair, a wide smile, and a strong singing voice capable of filling any theatre. Physically, Ida took after her own husband, Joseph, and reminded her of Josephine

47

before she had her baby and ran to fat. The dark side of the family, in more senses than one.

Gran Garland saw a special quality in Ida. She had the natural refinement of her grandfather Joseph. And when she sang, no one was immune to a soft feeling, a moment of stillness in the tumult. Joseph did that to audiences too, until he grew too sad and sick, and died. Ida had spirit. With her musical talent, she could succeed where none of them had dared to try — in society, be a proper person. Gran Garland hoped she would live to see the day. For Joseph's sake, so she could tell him when she joined him on the other side, among the great majority.

Ida ran home from school for lunch one day and found the new dress left in a box standing in the doorway. She rushed straight round to Gran's house, but, unusually, she was out. Only Uncle Ted loitered in the hall, waiting for the maid Dot to serve the lodgers' meals.

'Uncle Ted! I've got my new dress! Where's Gran?'

'She's round the corner, about her chest. She should have been under the doctor weeks ago,' he added. Ted seldom interfered with other people's lives, although he kept a close account of their mistakes. 'Why don't you put it on for me? I'm an expert on fashion. All my girlfriends like to take me on shopping sprees. Come on, let's have a look at you. I'll give you an expert opinion.'

'Oh. All right. But don't you dare say anything rude 'cos Gran designed this all by herself.'

Ida changed in Gran's snuggy, full of expectation. Gran's room was very plain: a chest of drawers, a velvet-covered nursing chair, linoleum on the floor and an old rag-rug Gran had made herself. More baby portraits covered the top of the chest, next to a couple of small china pots. A string of crystal beads hung from a hook and above the lead fireplace hung a *Way of the World: the Straight and Narrow Path* that some grateful lodger had given her.

There was no full-length mirror to see the total effect, so Ida had to be content with a head-and-shoulders view above the chest of drawers.

'Are you ready?' she called out. Then she sailed forth into the hallway trying to do a mannequin's glide.

Ted gave a long low whistle. Ida's leggy slimness was perfectly set off by the dress, which fell straight to the hips, and filled out with rows of horizontal pleats over her thighs. The cherry crêpe glowed against the honey-dark tones of her skin, and her frail long arms seemed to become elegant, not angular. But most of all, Ted could not help noticing Ida's wonderful breasts, small and firm, the nipples erect because of the coolness in Gran's bedroom. Ida blushed and instinctively covered herself, pretending to fiddle with her hair.

'Awful mess. I should get it cut, really . . .' She sensed that Ted was looking at her with a new appreciation, and it both pleased and embarrassed her.

'I tell you what,' he said, breaking off to clear his throat, unaccountably gruff all of a sudden, 'you're a stunner. You could pass for sixteen at least in that dress. Doesn't half show off your — er, *features*. Give us a hairbrush. You haven't got a clue, have you?' He pushed her back into Gran's room, and rummaged among his mother's china pots with the familiarity of a favourite son. Eventually he found a cache of long hairpins.

'Sit down.' He filled his mouth to bristling and started to plait Ida's thick bushy mop into two tight clusters of hair. With a deft hand, he twisted each one round and round, pinning them back to make two neat 'earphones' just behind her ears.

'All my girlies like me to do their hair. They think it's "swoony".' He winked at her so that Ida aimed back with an elbow at his stomach. Ted moved out of range, too experienced.

'There. Makes your eyes look big. Always keep it off your face. And walk with your chin up. That's what stars do. Makes people think you think you're beautiful. In your case, you're entitled to.'

'Ooh Ted. Really?' Ida could not help batting her eyes, practising on Ted — it was all such an exciting, different mood between them, not like other days. Before the Dress.

'Sure! Look, I tell you what. Forget school. Let's do something daring to celebrate. Let's pop into town, have a spot of dinner, give Earl a surprise. He paid for it — he should see the finished article!'

Ted was the only grown-up in the family who would have the nerve to suggest she play truant.

'Really? It would be so wicked!' She clapped her hands to her mouth, bursting with excitement.

'Sure. I could pop along to see about a gig while I'm there. No trouble! Hurry up.'

What a comedown, to have to stick her miserable school blazer over the glories of the cerise crêpe! On the other hand, she certainly did not want to swan into town with other men looking at her nipples the way Uncle Ted had. She covered herself up. He seemed to have got used to her 'features' now, however, and she felt more comfortable with him, as they strolled arm in arm to the bus stop on Bayswater.

It was clear he did not know the rules: Earl *never* took her into town, to see his work at the agency. She now had a perfect opportunity to discover why for herself.

The bus ride took them along Bayswater to Oxford Street, a tempting mile of goods in shiny shop windows.

'Ooh look, Lyons Corner House! Selfridges! Look, John Lewis's!'

'Shut up, Ida. Anyone would think you'd never been up West before,' Ted said, bored by her loud voice.

'I haven't, since last Christmas. Gran took me and Jack to see Father Christmas at Selfridges. I bought a glass ball with snow inside it, you know, you shake them, in the basement.'

'Surely Denise takes you shopping, doesn't she?'

Ida shook her head and imitated her mother's flapping little hands, fussing with her haircurls.

'First, she didn't like "pushing a pram all this way". Then I "walked too slow" for her, and now I'm "far too big to be trailed about". She doesn't like to be seen with me. Maybe it's because no one fancies her then . . .'

'Jesus, I didn't know she was that bad.'

'Well, anyway,' said Ida, feeling she had portrayed her family difficulties a little strongly, 'Pa takes me out on weekends, and so does Aunt Josephine, and last term we went to the National Gallery with the art master from school. And now there's you. Thanks, Uncle Ted.'

Ted sniffed, suddenly conscious that neither Ida nor Jack

50

were having ideal childhoods. Not that there was much he could do about it, being on the road or out of town so much . . . They would have to survive, like everyone else. There were thousands of people without even the food to put in their mouths . . .

'Hungry?' he said, and Ida nodded eagerly.

A brief walk led them into Soho, into the heart of the night city.

Bayswater Sunday lunches were strictly British traditional. Now Ida's nostrils were assailed with a *mélange* of rich, foreign smells. Brandy gravies floated out of the French restaurants, where Ted said West End stars and their agents or producers plotted glamorous new films over lunch. The corner pubs smelt of spilt beer, the sticky aromas of pie and mash, pickles and pasties. Ted said a pub had been closed down for putting cooked London seagull in the sandwiches. Garlicky tomatoes and bubbling cheeses emanated from Italian and Spanish snack bars. Ted said the Maltese ran the white slave trade in Soho, and slit people up with long thin blades. Ida gawked at the over-painted girls sitting in the windows, vulgarly munching a quick bite between auditions, or what Ted called 'assignations'. Their red lips worked in and out, now looking like a kiss, now looking like a clown's grimaces . . . 'Assignations.' Ida did not ask Ted to tell her more about those . . .

She loved all these sights, and tried not to look shocked about the 'ladies of the night'. But she was completely taken aback when she and Ted turned a corner, and saw a man in a mackintosh open the door to his flat with a latchkey. Beneath his gaping coat, he had on nothing but pyjamas, with an interesting dark, hairy gap in the middle.

'Look, Ted!' she gasped.

''Spect he's a writer. Been out for his milk and paper. They always do that. Work at night.'

Brewer Street had butcher's shops, where tiny pale birds lay trussed in rows, waiting for someone's cook or butler to take a fancy. Ida saw a gentleman's gentleman in striped trousers and a bowler buying one perfect lamb cutlet.

'Have it delivered,' he said. What a luxury!

Then there was Berwick Street, a long narrow tunnel of barrows, filled to bursting with fruits and vegetables many of which Ida had never tasted. A frowsy woman, who was without

51

any shadow of doubt an older, more desperate kind of prostitute, unpeeled a banana at one of the market stalls, shouting, 'Is it ripe?' This provoked some rich Cockney responses that Ida memorised, just for Jack's ears. Ted was forced to pretend the street was deserted.

'What's that, Uncle Ted?' she asked, pointing and poking him eagerly.

'An artichoke.'

'Can I have one?'

'Don't be daft, it needs boiling. Have a toffee-apple instead.'

She agreed, and followed up with a bowl of cockles, a hot sausage-roll from a market-workers' stall, and an ice-cream cornet from a lovely Italian shop, where a fat man pinched her cheeks rather hard.

'Full? Good,' said Ted. 'Earl's office is down this way.'

Suddenly Ida lost her nerve. 'Um. Must we? I've had such a nice time. Couldn't this just be our secret day?'

'You haven't been before, have you?' Uncle Ted guessed. 'You should have said.'

Ida blushed. 'He doesn't like me being in Soho.'

'For God's sake, there's nothing wrong in seeing a bit of life. He won't mind — not when he sees you looking so smart and ladylike.'

In an alleyway in Soho, Earl had one nameplate among ten others beside a battered doorway. Curious yet terrified, Ida followed Uncle Ted up the smelly stairs to an attic room. It held no more than a desk, a telephone, and a view from the window over pitched glass roofs, the workshops of the Jewish tailors. In the distance the domes of theatres in Shaftesbury Avenue rose high. Ida was disappointed. The 'office' was silent, shabby and unimportant.

'Not in,' said the messenger boy coming up the stairs behind them. He hissed on a cigarette, so sunken-chested that it was a tough job for him to breathe the smoke out again. 'Round at the Pumpkin Club. I just seed him.'

'Come on, Ida,' Ted said, winking. 'We'll just go by Archer Street first, it's on the way.'

He led her to the 'Street of Hope' as the musicians called it, the alleyway in Soho near Rupert Street where players congregated to hear about new bands forming, swop gossip about good gigs and bad, and where new aspirants stood around trying to look like old-timers. Ida stood shyly while Ted got into some incomprehensible conversation with another snappy pin-striped dresser carrying a huge instrument case. The pavements on both sides of the street were impassable, jammed with men in clusters, trying to find jobs and swopping details of band changes. Carts and taxis had a hard job getting through, and the air grew filthy with exhaust fumes and the clouds from anxious chain-smokers. The men stamped savagely on the butts every time they aired an opinion.

Ida dawdled by a tobacconist's window, looking at a display of cigarette cards, the sort that Jack collected. She got a few curious glances, for the cerise crêpe was certainly a vivid, summery colour to be seen in, but incongruous with a blazer trimmed in yellow braid. Ted was just doing a deal with a man who needed a relief pianist for a fancy club for a few weeks, when, as if to a magic password, the gangs of musicians suddenly evaporated. Ted grabbed her hand and pulled her to one end of the tiny street. 'Quick-march,' he said quietly, 'time to blow.'

'What is it?' she asked.

'Police. They don't like us all loitering.' He feigned interest in a sweet-shop window until the two coppers had walked away. Just like urban termites, the gig-players swarmed out of the brickwork back to the pavements, and Archer Street once more was thronged.

Ted finished his chat and set off as promised to the square nearby where Earl was said to be. It was a 'hot spot' — not really a night-club, but one of the dozens of Soho 'bottle parties'. Ted said these evaded the licensing laws by being open only to members. They ordered their drinks in advance of the evening from the 'host' or owner. Tea and sandwiches, a floor show, a good dance band, and limitless alcohol were thus available till dawn.

'Mrs Cavendish never gets raided,' he added, as they went down another set of narrow stairs to a basement room. Life in Soho seemed to go on above, upon *and* underneath the buildings. 'Half the bleedin' force of Scotland Yard comes here of an evening, besides half the Life Guards or half of Westminster.'

'Hallo Mr Garland,' a stranger said, as Ted passed him on the stairs. Ida was thrilled. It was true — a Garland could cut a figure in the West End!

Her Pa was there, standing by the bar, nervously running his hands round the brim of his hat. Mrs Cavendish, a tired, thin-lipped woman with a kimono over her wool suit, waved a cigarette holder at him, disagreeing about something. At the far end of the long, dark room, a tall, blond young man in flannels and a check shirt was shouting at a small troupe of girls, tap-dancing on a stage the size of the scullery in Bayswater.

'Can I watch them, Ted?' Ida whispered, forgetting all about her terror of her Pa, edging forward through the stacked up tables and chairs.

'Just for a mo,' Ted nodded, 'Earl'll be finished soon. She's very tough, that old bitch Cavendish, never pays a penny more than she needs to.'

Ida sidled forward without her Pa catching sight of her. 'As long as it's clearly understood, no gambling!' Ida overheard Mrs Cavendish's reedy upper-class tones; it occurred to her that her Pa was keeping his promise, trying to find a late-night job for Aunt Josephine.

She tried not to look at Earl as he bent forward to light Mrs Cavendish's cigarette. It was embarrassing to watch his ingratiating looks, his persuasive smiles being employed so skilfully for a purpose. Mrs Cavendish had ordered some drinks, and was allowing a thin smile to lighten her face — watery and pale, like a winter sun in a grey sky. Her Pa and the lady disappeared into a small office behind the bar.

Feeling that the day had already been too tremendous for shyness, Ida got near the stage and composed herself by a table piled with chairs, trying to be still so that no one would pay attention to her. She watched the girls rehearsing and her foot began to itch in rhythm to the tap-dancing. The young man banged a stick on the floor to the beat and the girls kept time, rehearsing the same sequence over and over. They looked like clockwork toys, mechanically sprung, their faces blank in concentration.

'Nearly there girls, only Mona's not with us yet — buck up Mona, now, one two three and one two three and a one two three . . .'

'Ooh!' squealed Mona, stopping in the middle of the number, and flicking her sweaty black fringe from her big brown eyes, 'if it isn't Ted Garland!'

A chorus of 'Hallo Ted!' forced the young man to turn, irritated, but when he recognised Ida's uncle he ran forward and shook his hand in a friendly, accepting fashion.

'Do me a favour Ted — run through this number, the pianist failed to show up today and I'm tired of shouting.'

'For you girls, anything!' Ted said, blowing Mona a kiss and sitting at the piano. 'Let's have you . . .'

With an audience of one, whose admiring glances caressed their legs, the dancers came alive. Ida was fascinated. The four girls radiated good humour and fun, throwing sidelong glances at the piano, nudging each other with their elbows as they held their tight spaces on the platform. Feet flew in precision, without thought from any of them.

'I see . . . Ooh-ooh-ooh, what a little piano can do-oo-ooh,' the young man mocked, when they had finished. 'Topping. Great stuff. Break for lunch.'

He caught sight of Ida. 'Hallo there young lady! Who might you be?' He spoke as if she were a person, not a child at all.

'I'm Ida Garland, sir,' she said.

'Another one! Not this rascal's daughter!'

'No sir, Earl Garland is my Pa.'

'Well, well. What a family. And do you sing or dance, young lady? I'm sure you do.'

'I sing, sir.'

Behind her, Uncle Ted trilled on the piano, inviting her to be brave, and Mona said cheerfully, 'Here sweetie, give us a song. Have some of my lemonade too.' Mona threw Ted a glance, hoping for his approval.

Hot with excitement, Ida had a sip of the drink, and the young director man lifted her on to a bar stool by the piano. Ida slipped out of her blazer, her heart beginning to thump with self-consciousness as she did so.

'I got a new dress today,' she blurted.

Mona giggled, but the young man folded his arms, surveying her with a genuine, conscientious interest. Luckily he was a bit less girl-mad than Uncle Ted, and did not stare at her bosom, at least, not that she noticed.

'It suits you,' he said, gallantly. 'Quite the thing for a day in Soho. Smart, isn't it girls?'

'The latest!' They all crowed and giggled, enjoying a moment's sentimentality over an innocent child.

'What'll it be, Ida?' Ted nodded encouragingly, before any of the chorus girls said something suggestive Ida ought not to hear.

''Alexander's Ragtime Band'?' she asked.

'Topping!' the director repeated, laughing.

'Corny!' said Uncle Ted. 'Four bars intro, are you ready?' and he led her into 'My Melancholy Baby', waving a warning so that Ida sang very softly. Perhaps Uncle Ted did not want Earl to know what was going on. The girls leaned on the piano cupping their chins in their hands and turning moist-eyed. Ida began to sing more confidently, loving this intimate, indulgent audience. Mona casually draped an arm round Ted's shoulders as he played. Uncle Ted certainly had various ways of winning hearts . . .

In an instant Earl was behind her. 'Ida! What are you doing here!'

She turned a shining, animated face to him, 'Uncle Ted's been showing me all over the place, and I had a toffee-apple, and cockles, and I wanted you to see my new dress, and look Pa, it's so pretty!'

'Don't she sing beautiful, Mr Garland!' one of the chorus girls offered. 'What a lovely voice, made me go all funny, just listening to her!'

(Ted meanwhile led Mona away into a quiet corner to avoid Earl's indignation.)

'This is no place for you. Come on, I'll take you home.' Tight-lipped, Earl took her firmly by the hand.

Ida gave the young director a reluctant, big-eyed farewell.

'*I* liked the dress,' he called after her, 'and I loved the song.' Then, out of devilment, he added: 'Come and see me in two years' time!'

'Ted, are you with us?' Earl said in clipped tones as he prodded Ida towards the stairs. 'I'd like to talk to you . . .' His voice had that mean, big-brother's superiority for a minute, even though they were grown men and fairly good friends.

'Er, no — I'll get you later, old man.' Ted, hovering protectively over the diminutive Mona (or was she a protection from Earl?).

Earl strode along the street, and Ida had to skip to keep up with him. Of course, now that she was with her Pa, she began to see all kinds of evil, ugly things. A drunk, fallen asleep in a doorway. Another prostitute, adjusting suspenders on bloated, bruised legs, in full view of a gawping Chinese child at a window above an emporium. Three ex-army men, all mutilated, hustled off a doorstep by a short-tempered shopkeeper.

'Did you get Aunt Josephine a spot, Pa?' Ida said, hoping to deflect Earl's anger by showing interest in his affairs.

'Oh yes. Mrs Cavendish likes her well enough. She's a great late-night entertainer, your Aunt Josephine. Grand company. Ten quid a week extra,' he replied with satisfaction, forgetting to sound annoyed.

'It must be fun, Pa . . .' Ida could visualise the room, smoke-laden, filled with smart people in sparkling gowns, starched collars, shiny shoes, like the people she had glimpsed, stepping out of limousines and taxis . . . A scene of animation — and above all, a setting for that funny, sexy playfulness which Uncle Ted and the girls at the Pumpkin Club suggested. Naughty but light-hearted attraction, not the unpleasant, unkind tension that existed between her Ma and Pa.

'I don't want it for you, Ida. For every girl who makes money, there's two or three end up in trouble. Big trouble. Falling for some shady character, or worse. I know. I have them on my books — for a while.'

'Are all your clients chorus girls, Pa?'

Earl was affronted. 'Of course not! I've got Josephine, and Uncle Jim, and a couple of comics, a small band — Jamaican boys from Cardiff who are beginning to do all right — and then there's a few music-hall acts from the old days.'

On the pavement in front of them some unemployed men were busking, a raucous excuse for begging. 'Ted's going to hear from me, bringing you to a place like this.' Earl gave vent to his displeasure once more.

Ida followed him dutifully up the busy Soho street. It was best not to argue. It had been a great moment in the club, when she sang, but now she wondered if some of the grown-ups had been laughing at her, especially the young director. Perhaps her Pa was right, and she should keep well out of London's heart. It was not like her end of town, where poverty was mundane, violence a Sunday morning anecdote, and unemployment a way of life. In Soho the very rich and the very poor were on kissing terms, and everyone was greedy. Ida did not want to end up adjusting tattered suspenders on legs mottled with bruises.

3

There were occasions when Jack's admiration for his mother overcame all his bad feelings about her — sitting on a hamper backstage for a matinée at the Shepherd's Bush Empire in a smart sailor suit, was one of them. Ida was impressed too, as she hoped to be a singer herself. She stood beside Jack in her new dress, which was beginning to look a little shabby from all its adventures.

When she was announced, Aunt Josephine took deep breaths and worked her shoulders, like a Paddington locomotive building up a head of steam. She did not walk on to the stage; she arrived in a burst of energy and warmth that demanded a rapturous reception.

Josephine would never be a great performer, but she was what Ida's father Earl referred to as 'useful'. A place could always be found for her second or third on the billing in a music-hall, or for a small character part in a West End musical, and she performed equally well in front of raucous or refined audiences. She was perhaps destined to save situations, rather than be a big star herself.

Being born and bred in Bayswater, not very far from the Shepherd's Bush Empire, made Josephine a great favourite with the local audience. As this was a matinée on a balmy Saturday the place was full of faithfuls.

> 'Am I wasting my time
> By thinking you're mine,
> And dreaming the way that I do?
> Am I wasting the tears,
> I've cried all these years,
> Just wond'ring if your love is true . . .'

Josephine exploited her warm welcome to the full. The house

was still, and if it had been possible to peer into it, the children would have seen shiny eyes and rapt, parted mouths. But they never peeped round the curtain — it would have been unprofessional. Jack watched in a curious mixture of embarrassment and happiness as his mother became someone else: her face was so vitalised that it was as if she had put on a magic mask that made every change of expression more intense and discernible.

Ida, too, liked Josephine's altered state: she resembled Gran Garland in a strange way. Gran had an English country face, broad cheeks, honest grey eyes, and once her hair had been a soft brown colour. Josephine was small and wide, with stubby crinkly black hair. Today she had it rolled up over thick pads, with feathers and brilliants pinned in it. Her mouth was big and fleshy, far redder than Gran's. But what made both women seem alike to Ida was that air of knowing what they were doing — being confident and open-hearted in their performance.

Josephine's song finished to an audible sigh and a rush of applause, hoots and whistles. She bowed gratefully, exited grandly to the side of the stage — and the mask fell off at once. Jack had a sudden fear that she had remembered some dreadful sin he had committed, which she had put out of his mind till the end of her performance.

'I'm dying for a plate of jellied eels,' she said, much to his relief. 'Just a tick, kiddies, and then we'll be off. Oh Jack, you do look a dear in your sailor suit. Come here! Happy Birthday love!'

She rumpled Jack's head, and pressed him to her bosom (for the benefit of the audience of stage hands no doubt. There always had to be someone watching). Jack scowled and rubbed his cheek where her necklaces had scratched him. He was actually quite proud of his neat navy outfit, but now his mother had made him feel like a complete idiot in it.

Ida jabbed him with a sharp elbow to make him appear more gracious; Jack never seemed to understand that adults needed humouring to make them indulgent.

'It's so hot,' complained Josephine, 'what I need is a breath of fresh air. We'll pop round the corner, what d'you say? Half a tick while I change.'

Ida and Jack sat obediently on the hamper until she returned. 'Round the corner' was the Goldhawk Road, a smoky, smelly mêlée of bikes, trams and market barrows — hardly the place to find fresh air, but it did have Josephine's favourite pie shop. Ida and Jack squeezed fingers with excitement, because Aunt Josephine was always extravagant with food.

All round them the stage was being dismantled in a spell-binding show equal to the matinée just ended. Thick ropes uncoiled and flew skywards as backdrops were returned to running order. Perspectives painted on scrim suddenly fore-shortened as the overlapping flats were stacked into corners. Stage-hands ran up vertical iron wall-ladders into the lighting gantry, like nimble sailors before the mast. All transformations were accompanied by piercing whistles or bursts of song from the props men and a bravura display of thuds and swear words that entranced Ida and Jack.

This private performance only took moments. The children were left in semi-gloom, an eerie silence in which great songs, comic laughter and the clatter of dancing feet waited to be summoned on all sides. A terrible expectancy hung about the place.

'Look lively you two! I'm dying for a cuppa tea.'

Josephine was wearing a smart blue wool coat and flowered cloche. Unfortunately, her attempt at style was spoilt by the gigantic fur collar that made her look bizarre rather than elegant. There was always a note of rapacity about Josephine that attracted many men but made women and young children cautious.

It was splendid to walk (or rather, allow oneself to be frogmarched arm in arm) beside this magnificent person, while everyone in the street smiled or stared, or even had the nerve to shout a greeting.

'Hallo Ducks! Who's looking gorgeous then!'

'Hang on tight, kiddies, yer mother does!'

'Don't be so filthy, don't take any notice of *him* will you darlin'!'

'Ooh — can I come?'

All these remarks from shopkeepers in doorways, sign-painters, street-sweepers, car-minders, dog-walkers, gold-watch-sellers and window-cleaners had a predictable mollifying effect on Josephine. By the time they reached the eel and pie shop, she was ready to buy them anything.

'Now, what's it to be? Lemonade and jellied eels, three rounds of bread then ice-cream . . . that's just the job, but waitress, I'll have a pot of tea,' Josephine ordered, joining the children once more.

They settled in a booth facing the street; on the top window above them shadowed lettering arched in reverse: 'ƨlɘƎ' looked more like eels really were, in reverse, especially next to an ampersand backwards. For privacy the glass was opaque and rippled; the sun fell in golden strands like curls of hair on their table-cloth. Jack immediately started tracing the patterns of it on the linen with his fork.

'I can't take you anywhere,' Josephine said, only half-mocking, smacking his fist. 'You're a disgrace. Anyone would think you'd been dragged up.'

'Well, I have, haven't I?' Jack said defiantly, unwilling to let her have fun at his expense.

'Look here, my lad . . .' Josephine began to look threatening.

'Oh, don't be cross, Auntie, he didn't mean it, and Jack don't be horrid, because your Ma's really kind to give us a treat and you shouldn't spoil the fun. Please, Jack, for me? I put my best dress on, specially.'

'Yes, and it's very nice too, Ida. How old are you these days?' Josephine asked Ida, as if they had not met for months.

'I'm thirteen next month, September 24th,' she added hopefully.

'Quite a big girl. Mmm.' Josephine sighed, as if Ida's age made the passage of time (and that stage of 'promise' in her own career) too clear.

Josephine finished her dish, then sat back and watched the children messing the food inefficiently with their forks, spending far too much time on the lemonade and less on the jellied eels. Ida caught Jack's eye and warned him to finish quickly. It had not occurred to Josephine that jellied eels was not their favourite dish — it certainly was hers, and therefore had to be the family treat. Ida and Jack endured it for the sake of the ice-creams she had promised afterwards.

'Jack,' Josephine began, placing her teacup carefully in its saucer. The two children were alerted like wild animals to danger. Aunt Josephine was going to say something important.

'Yes Ma?' Jack said, his blue eyes direct yet wary at the same time. Ida felt sorry for him.

'I thought I should tell you first, and Ida's our special girl, isn't she, so she should know too. I'm getting married. What do you say to that, eh? A real father, for a change!'

'Not Mr Ottley!' Ida blurted.

A darkening expression, like a cloud passing over the sun, changed Josephine. 'Yes, Mr Ottley, Sidney. Don't all rush to congratulate me.'

'But Pa said, I mean, you don't owe Mr Ottley money any more, do you Aunt Josephine? I mean, now you're at the bottle party, you're not allowed to gamble there . . .' Ida blathered.

'What's Earl been saying? My Gawd, that man don't half poke his nose in sometimes. I know he's my agent, but he takes real liberties . . .' She fumbled in her bag for a handkerchief, letting out a whiff of violet perfume.

'Look here, I don't have to explain anything to you two!' Josephine was growing indignant, genuinely hurt by their lack of enthusiasm. Her big black eyes began to shine with tears. 'I just told you two first, out of the kindness of my heart, you Ida, and you Jack, my own son, so you'd be pleased for your mother, and that's all I get. Accusations. I don't know what to say. I really don't.' She blew her nose vigorously, and made a great show of drying her eyes.

'You'll see, my girl,' she continued, turning her attentions to Ida's solemn face. 'You think it's so easy to be successful and beautiful, fame and all that . . . well let me tell you, it's hard. It's a hard life, and it's even harder to find a good man who'll stick by you. Mark my words.'

Ida and Jack bowed their heads. Every adult in the Garland family had this maddening habit of asking them to 'mark their words' when seeking to justify actions which as far as they could see, were sheer lunacy. If Earl bet on a horse, he'd say, 'He's a clear winner, a dead cert, you mark my words . . .' and then he would lose every penny. If Ted was making a play for some girl he fancied, he would say, 'This is the one for me, no fooling around any more, I'm going to marry this one, you mark my words . . .' and within three weeks Susie, Ruth or Betty would be on the way out to make way for some new Doreen or Daisy.

Jack spoke first. 'I hate Mr Ottley, I always will, and he's not my Dad and I wish I'd never been born.' He uttered these words with great deliberation, knowing that he brought the roof down on his head with them.

His mother leaned forward. '*What* did you say?'

Josephine was wavering between anger and depression. She looked darkly at Jack, and Ida was sure she would hit him. Ida flung her arms around her cousin. She had a great dislike of being vulnerable herself, and could not bear to see him being hurt. Jack was so dejected he did not move an inch. His body felt heavy as if he did not care what happened to him.

'You needn't do that,' Josephine said, offended. Her broad shoulders slumped. For a moment she looked pretty in a new way, as if she were someone unknown, more sensitive and soft-featured than when she was 'acting up'.

'Look here, Jack,' Josephine said, almost pleading with him. 'I need a man. I mean, I need someone to look out for me. You understand that don't you? He's not a bad fellow Sidney, it's just that he's not used to children. If only you'd try a bit, just for me. Eh? What do you say? Eh?'

Ida squirmed with embarrassment at this conversation. Her parents never spoke to her in such an adult fashion and certainly never talked about their own emotional life. Josephine seemed smaller, more pathetic, confessing.

Josephine reached across the table and took Jack's arm, her big brown hand covering his slim wrist. The boy looked down, suddenly aware, in spite of his clean clothes, of his own puny size and the dirt under his fingernails. He drew his hand away, clenching his fist to hide his grubbiness. With a sidelong glance he muttered at Ida, 'Go on, you ask her.'

'What? Ask me what?' Josephine encouraged them, hoping for a positive suggestion.

'Er um . . . well . . .' Ida knew this was a mistake, not the right time to say what Jack wanted. Aunt Josephine would take it the wrong way, and he would certainly suffer for it.

'Come on, out with it. I haven't got all day.' Josephine pushed her plate away.

'Oh Jack, not now,' Ida resisted.

'Right, I'll do it myself then,' he said, drawing a big breath. 'I want to go back to Gran's. I don't want to live with you and your fancy man. I don't like him, he's not my Dad. I don't think I had a Pa anyway. Uncle George is always calling me a little bastard. That's what I am, aren't I? Gran's got to have me. Gran's got to have me.' He became agitated, kicking the chair legs of the seat opposite and pushing Ida away. 'I never had a Dad, did I?' he asked his mother, at last, directly.

'Oh Jack doesn't mean it, honestly Aunt Josephine,' Ida hurried in. 'It's just the surprise. I mean to say, with you being so famous and everything, and touring and not being at home very much, and Mr Ottley being well, not exactly handsome, though I'm sure he's very nice, when you get to know him, and if he didn't hit him so many times . . . Please don't be cross with him!' Ida babbled on, trying to help Jack, trying to make her aunt understand.

Josephine stood up slowly, and leant across the table till she had her son by one ear.

'Get out of the way Ida. I'm not standing for this. Talk to your mother like that — who do you think you are! Who *do* you think I am?'

Ida was struck dumb by Jack's bravery. His ear was burning red, but he did not howl at all: he moved as nimbly as he could to avoid being injured, to be led cruelly from the pie shop. Only at the edge of the kerb did Josephine let go her fix on him. Then in that ugly, unavoidable way grown-ups impart serious information, she bent down, and pressed her big face two inches away from the tip of Jack's nose.

'For your information, you horrible little person, I *was* married, and your Dad died in the trenches, doing his bit for England, poor sod. And that's all you can think of him and me. You've got a dirty, nasty little mind, and I'm ashamed of you. So help me I am.'

She drew herself up, and turned to Ida. Inflated with injured pride, she addressed the girl as if Jack had ceased to exist.

'I'm sorry about this Ida. I was enjoying your company. I think you'd better take a trolley bus back to Bayswater and I'll go home for a lie-down. I've developed a shocking headache. I can't think why.'

'Sorry Auntie. Jack didn't mean it. Really.'

'Don't let's talk any more about it. *Sanny fairyann* as the French say. What's done is done, and what will happen will happen.' Josephine was moved by her own calmness, and hailed a cab without a backward glance. The taxi brakes squealed, the cabbie eager to pick up someone he recognised. Horns hooted, oaths were flung about by various drivers, and Josephine disappeared.

Passers-by jostled the children as they stood forlorn on the pavement. Ida felt herself grow insignificant, parted from her famous relative; within seconds, no one knew that she and Jack were attached to 'Josephine Garland of the Shepherd's Bush Empire'. They were just London street children, in the way, probably up to no good. Ida felt her unimportance so keenly that she hated Josephine for depriving them of status in this vulgar, commercial road.

'Come on, we'll have to walk all the way back to Uncle Billy's shop. I haven't even got a penny for the bus ride so we'll have to ask him to lend us a bit. You shouldn't have said those things to your Ma, Jack,' she said.

He looked positively comic now in his sailor suit. It was an old-fashioned outfit that required slick hair and an assertive, well-behaved manner. Jack slouched and rubbed his ears like a lout. Ida walked in front of him, angry and unwilling to admit to herself that she was ashamed to be in his company.

A policeman kept his eye on them as they negotiated the crossings at Shepherd's Bush, a maze of trolley lines, horse-drawn carts, and belching cars. Uncle Billy's record shop was on the north side of the green, and the dirt of the streets was forgotten as soon as they pushed through the heavy glass door.

'Well! The kiddies! Hallo you two!' Billy cried, bustling forward, removing a short pencil from behind his ear as if he meant to take mental note of them. The children were always shy when they were alone with this particular uncle. Billy found it difficult to be amusing. The comic double-act he resorted to with James was his only way of letting off steam. On his own, he had the air of someone who had just lost a telephone number and had no means of finding it again.

'Handy, you two turning up,' he said, beckoning them both into the gloom. 'Give us a hand — pass up the pins, will you Jack? And Ida, be a good girl and make us a cup of tea. Ask Mr Foster in Number Two if he'd like one. Now, where's that sheet of paper . . .'

Ida went to the back of the shop where her Uncle Billy had built in two heavy mahogany listening booths. She could see Mr Foster through the glass, a mild man of clerking appearance, sitting rapt in a well-lit corner. As Ida opened the door to speak to him, he looked startled, and the earthy complaints of some fierce woman shouting a blues song came out at her.

'Tea, Mr Foster?' she mouthed.

'Lovely, ta!' he called back, delighted.

Uncle Billy, meanwhile, climbed up a wooden step-ladder with a poster in his hand, not waiting to see if either of the children obeyed him, the way a parent or a teacher would, but merely assuming they would both do as they were told. Uncle Billy lived in a world of his own: the walls of the small dark shop were plastered with the illustrated fronts of song sheets — young ladies swooning in the arms of sheikhs; romantic songs that made heavy-lidded ladies bury their faces in flowers; and ragtime piano collections publicised with big-teethed prancing negroes on the covers.

Pinned in between were Billy's own cartoon sketches of film stars, drawn from photographs, and his hand-written opinions of favourite records: Buy the bluest jazz — Morton's records are here!; Red-hot syncopation — Savoy Orpheans; Great British Jazz — Hylton's Kit-Cat Club Band — only on HMV Records. Hear It Here Any Time!

'Pass us up another,' he said to Jack, a hand stretching out behind him, fingering the air.

Uncle Billy's life was devoted to his record-buying public. The shop was never full, because most of his profit came from sending out special records to his suburban clientele who hung over their gramophones in chintzy sitting-rooms to catch every beat of some 'hot' American orchestra. A few resourceful customers managed to find the shop on the day a small consignment of new 78s arrived and were quickly sold out. A privileged individual occasionally got invited upstairs where

Billy would happily drink away a day's profit in whisky, listening wordlessly and with strong emotion to some New Orleans soaring solo.

Having adjusted the last poster to his satisfaction, Uncle Billy climbed down and sat on the lowest rung of the ladder to talk to them. Ida brought his tea.

'What can I do for you?' he said, looking helpfully at the two children staring at him with an obvious need for something.

'Can you give us the bus fare home?' Ida asked without hesitation.

'What? I thought you were spending the day with Josephine.' The children glanced at each other.

'Change of plan. She's feeling poorly,' Ida said innocently.

'Mmm,' Billy murmured, doubtful, stirring his tea and considering the pair of them. He was a neat man, with little round spectacles; still only in his twenties he seemed very old to the children — much older than Josephine.

'Did you know she's getting married?' Ida announced, for it was impossible not to pass on the information.

'No! You don't say!'

'To The Uncontrollable Mr Ottley,' Jack reminded him, superfluously.

'Well I never.' Billy still circulated the spoon in his cup, and his eyes began to shine glassily. The children knew they had lost him.

'Uncle Billy,' Ida persisted.

'Mmm?' He smiled in such a kind, innocent way that she could not be cross with him.

'The money — can we have a penny?'

'Of course you can — I was just thinking, we'll have to get a good band for the wedding reception. You think she'll have a proper send-off, don't you? We ought to do her proud, not like the last time.'

'The last time?' Ida prompted, wondering if Jack's suspicions had some real basis after all.

'The war and everything.'

'Oh.' No one hardly ever talked about the war to Ida, least of all her Pa. There were the facts: only two of the eldest Garland boys had gone off to it — the twins, Ted and Charles. Earl was declared unfit and did not like to be reminded of it. The other brothers, Jim, Billy and George were all too young. Ted's twin, Charles, had died in the trenches. Beyond this information, no one ever described the war and no one asked anyone for more detail. At school the children were taught that war was shocking and ugly. Life showed them it was a necessary evil. Ida and Jack hated 'the Boche' and Jack spent a good deal of his street-time killing imaginary hordes of them.

'Look, I've got to get on, you kids run along. I can't think what she sees in him, but it's her funeral, not mine,' he said, smiling cheerfully. Ida noted that she had never seen Uncle Billy in love with a woman or a man. However, she decided this observation was a little too adult to confide to her cousin Jack just then.

Josephine's wedding was a joyful occasion for all the Garlands, except Jack. He was made to sing an anthem during the signing of the register at the Luke Road Baptist Chapel. Given his frame of mind about the event, it was hard for him to do so with enthusiasm. All the Garlands could recognise a lack-lustre performance, whatever the style of music.

Josephine shone in gold lamé, Sidney Ottley hovered in a frock coat and tails, which he wore with a lot less distinction than the Garland uncles. (Ida could not help thinking that her relatives looked like a tap-dancing line-up from a musical, an image very much reinforced by Billy and Jim playing leapfrog over tombstones as they left the church.)

The reception was held at the Perth Court Hotel in Bayswater, not far from the Garland boarding-house. Its interior was frozen in Victorian splendour with pink marble fireplaces, and golden bobbles round the curved curtain pelmets. Through glass doors was a palm court for dancing, where bronze flamingoes pecked round a water fountain. The décor's excess suited a Garland family event perfectly.

The guests included a few West End agents and out-of-town theatre owners (a mixture of Josephine's ex-lovers and former employers). Her chorus girlfriends, some from the Pumpkin Club, were blatantly displaying their charms to the older, powerful men with an eye to autumn bookings. They sat on their knees, ruffled their hair, fed titbits into their rubicund faces — anything to please. Ottley's cronies, gamblers, 'musos' and bit-part actors, tried to lure the prettiest girls away to the dance floor, offering their more muscular attractions with not much success. The band organised by Uncle Billy played 'hot' music noisily and the champagne bottles swivelled light and empty in the ice-buckets.

In a velvet-upholstered corner, Gran Garland watched the scene with her customary phlegmatic expression. Ida, bored by grown-ups slurring their words, went over and offered to fetch her some pudding or water-ice.

'I don't mind if I do,' Gran said, 'I'll have a spoonful of that trifle with the cherries. What a good girl you are . . . Are you having a good time?' she asked.

'Oh yes, it's grand!' Ida said gamely, though in truth she was bored by the shrieking and sexual grappling that was going on. As midnight approached she felt sleepier. She edged round the dance floor to fetch her grandmother's dessert dish from the buffet next door.

A dressing-up version of the hokey-cokey was taking place. Uncles Jim and Billy had prepared a large tub specially for the occasion, and placed it in the middle of the dance floor. Every time the music stopped some poor fool of a man had to remove his jacket and give it to a young lady. Then he had to reach blindfolded into the basket for a piece of substitute clothing. By the time Ida got back to her Gran's seat, the entire male contingent was cavorting about in oyster-pink ladies' corsets, outsize bras that contrasted obscenely with hairy chests bursting out of cracking shirt-fronts. For a laugh some rolled up their trouser legs, revealing hairy black legs and suspendered socks. The hotel waiters looked scandalised, and the manager put in an appearance.

'I ask you,' Gran Garland said, rising in defence of family honour and expenditure, 'what's the point of spending all this money if you're going to be treated like *hoi polloi* in a pub?' She nodded curtly to Earl, and they both accompanied the manager outside.

Just in time, it seemed, Josephine and Ottley appeared in their going-away clothes. The band struck up 'If You Were the

Only Girl in the World'. Josephine hugged Jack in a guilty rush of affection, and the couple fled in a shower of confetti and shoes.

'Didn't they look lovely?' someone near Ida sighed: it was Mona, from the Pumpkin Club. 'Hallo dear! Enjoying the party? Aren't you going to sing for us today?'

Ida shook her head. 'No fear,' she said, 'I've got to find my cousin.' She had spotted Jack darting off through the crowd in the hallway, and knew he needed her.

Earl had obviously pacified the management: after shouting their farewells to the bridal couple, guests were piling back into the party rooms, intent on seeing the night into the morning. Ida struggled through the crush, worrying about Jack.

Eventually she found him under the drinks table. He was crying, his head buried in a pile of wine-stained table-cloths. It was a long time since Ida had seen any evidence of heartfelt emotion in her cousin, and it made her feel very depressed.

'Don't cry,' she said, gathering his body on to her knees. The poor boy was so pathetic, weeping over his mother's marriage to someone he hated.

Suddenly Jack punched her hard. 'Gerroff!' he hissed. 'Leave me alone! You're all the same!'

Ida was scared. Jack had never turned on her before. They wrestled silently, until she got his arms pinioned.

'Shut up. I'll bite you.' She meant it too.

Jack kicked at her savagely, but she wound her legs round his. He tried butting her like a wounded animal. Gradually he subsided, he settled in her arms, his body became heavy. The raucous din of the Garlands having a whale of a time crashed about them. Jack slumped against her, defeated. Ida watched the feet of the barmen, running backwards and forwards, their shoes stained with splashes of beer.

'Don't you worry, Jack,' she muttered. 'I'll look after you. Bugger Ottley. Bugger your Ma. Bugger my Ma too!' He did not answer, and Ida cuddled him till he fell fast asleep.

With a crash, more trays of dirty glasses were dumped beside the table. She did not want Jack woken up. Savagely Ida stuck out a hand to push the smelly pile away. Then in a mood of bored defiance she had a taste. A sip. First one glass, then another. Whatever it was had a sharper kick to it than 'Gran's mellower'.

71

Perhaps she too fell asleep: there was certainly a lapse before she felt someone poking her sharply.

'What the hell do you think you're playing at!' Denise peered at her, under the table-cloth, and prised Ida's arms off Jack.

Ida tried to speak but something had happened to her tongue. 'Bugger Ott . . .' she mumbled.

'You're disgusting! Thirteen, with your legs wrapped round your cousin! Evil little slut! Seeds of filth. You've got your father's seeds of filth all sprouting up inside you!'

Jack stirred, and on hearing Denise awoke in an instant and shot out from under the table.

'Come here, you little guttersnipe!'

Denise let the cloth fall and ran after him.

Ida stayed where she was, unable to move, her head spinning. What did her Ma mean, 'seeds of filth'? She felt scared and sick.

The next person to stick their head under the table was Uncle Ted, and beside him, Jack.

'O my Gawd, she's blotto,' Uncle Ted said. 'Come on, we'd better get her out of here before Denise finds Earl.'

They hauled her out. Jack was revived by his sleep — finding Ida so close to him had been a particular restorer.

'Your best dress and all,' he said, smelling a streak of whisky on her flopping bow.

Jack held one hand while Ted steered Ida through the waiters' door out into the courtyard at the back of the hotel. The ground was wet and the wind blew, but Ted ignored Ida's shivers and trotted her up and down.

He staggered a few times himself. 'Works a treat,' he said thickly. 'Fresh air. Sobers you.'

It had the reverse effect on Ida. She became a fantasist, light-headed, imagining herself in a white mink coat, accompanied by a man in tail coat, striped trousers and spats. She was being escorted to a chauffeur-driven car for a night out in Soho. She stumbled; Ted held her up, they swerved and woodenly walked back the other way.

No, that would not do, thought Ida. That was what the Monas did. She'd be different. She'd show her Ma and Pa, make all the Garlands take notice of her. She'd buy a nice big house for her and Jack, and they would let only Gran and Uncle Ted call on Sundays, and have cockles and ice-cream for tea. She'd be a famous opera singer like Madame Albani had said, and people would give her diamonds, and she'd throw them at Denise's feet as cast-offs. That would show her and her seeds of filth.

She had only a muddled recollection of how long it took to move from the hotel yard to the vehicle, to the house, then to her bed. Ida thought she had grown up, expanded her mind into an adult mode all in one night. In some ways this was true. Next morning when she shivered and her eyeballs creaked when she looked at the light, she knew she had indeed changed: she was suffering from her first hangover. Ida did not regret the act of getting drunk, only the misery of sobering up. It meant she had lost that moment of wildness, when everything in the world seemed possible, and she was not just an insignificant girl.

Her head was not hurting, but she felt very sick. She was also scared of what Earl and Denise would have to say about her behaviour. It was pretty alarming not to remember going to bed, or saying good-night to anyone. Ida got up and stumbled down to the kitchen for some water. While on the stairs she saw the outline of a man shadowing the red lily-shaped glass on the front door. Uncle Ted: she ran to let him in before he banged on the knocker.

'Oh! Uncle Ted! Morning!' she said. She felt faint with the effort of speaking cheerfully.

'Well! And how are we today?'

'I'm perfectly fine — why shouldn't I be?' she said.

'Ah yes, well . . . like that is it? I suppose you don't remember being poured into my car?' he grinned at her.

Ida tossed her head (this was a mistake), and led him into the kitchen. The sink was piled high as usual, and she rummaged ineffectually for the least dirty cup she could wash out for him.

'Ma and Pa aren't up yet. Shall I make you a cuppa?'

He shrugged. 'Don't bother. I'm on my way to meet a man about a dog,' he said, miming the large glass of beer he would soon be swallowing. Ida shuddered.

'Look here, duckie, I won't let on, but I just want to put you straight. Keep off the drink. Just for me, will you? I won't let on to Earl if you promise me it won't happen again. You're far too young to be on the hard stuff.'

73

'You wouldn't tell!'

'I might . . .'

'Of course I promise! It was all an accident! I had no idea . . .' she lied.

'So. No harm done then.' He looked at her with sympathy.

'Oh no, Uncle Ted.' But Ida remembered her Ma's words under the table and felt that something important had happened to her. Her Ma was all wrong. She and Jack were good to each other. She'd look after him, and they'd both get away somehow.

'So. I won't tell, and you'll keep your word to me. It's not right, a girl your age . . .' he looked genuinely concerned for her, and rubbed her cheek in a friendly fashion.

Ida was beginning to feel ill, and his kind touch only increased her feebleness. She nodded agreement, unable to find the right tone of voice either to thank him or to apologise. Uncle Ted winked, and kissed her goodbye.

Earl appeared soon after, neatly dressed, if a little paler than usual, and Ida went back to the kitchen to help him make breakfast. Her father had a knack of stepping through the debris of his wife's poor housekeeping without it impinging on him. His clothes were always well pressed, his ties unstained, his shoes polished. He found just enough clean cutlery and china to set a table for himself and Ida, brew a pot of tea, and serve up toast.

'I suppose there's no chance of Mrs Black coming in today,' he asked Ida coldly.

'Pa, she left last week, didn't Ma tell you?' Ida was pleased to have some bad news against her mother to pass on. One of her lifelong campaigns was to convince her father of her mother's worthlessness.

'Why Denise can't hang on to domestics is beyond me,' he said, with a look of dismay. 'Lord knows we pay them enough.'

'Mrs Black said she wasn't going to clean up after a woman who stayed in bed till lunch time every day,' Ida said, in a self-satisfied tone.

'That's enough Ida. I'll thank you to speak respectfully of your Ma. Specially after what I hear. I'll deal with you later,' Earl replied in an even tone.

Oh Lord, he was going to make her wait, make her suffer. Ida ate her breakfast in silence, though each lump of toast made her want to retch.

As a penance, she tackled the filth of the kitchen while he attended to his letters in the parlour. She was half-way through the china, with a mountain of pots and pans still waiting untouched, when Denise descended from her long lie-in.

'Earl?' she summoned him as she minced in high heels, click-clack over the hall tiles towards the kitchen. Ida's heart sank: she knew that tone of voice meant she was in for it. She did not turn round when her mother came into the room.

'You needn't think *this* wins any favour with me!' Denise snapped at her. 'You only lend a hand when you're in trouble — never out of the goodness of your heart. You needn't think you can fool me!' Her words burned with anger. 'Earl! Oh. There you are. Well, what are you going to say to her?'

'I said I'd deal with her. Don't shout.'

'Don't take that tone with me! You're far too soft with her. She was blind, stinking *drunk*. I saw her. What are you going to do about it?'

Her Ma was up to something — Ida knew of old that she could be very ingenious when thinking up punishments. Denise was angered by Earl's refusal to do any beating, and spent a lot of time creating other longer-lasting miseries. Like forbidding Ida to speak to her for a week, or not letting her eat proper meals for several days. Ida scrubbed steadily at a mouldy pot, wondering what her mother's latest 'game' might be.

'You spend money on her, trying to smarten her up, and look what happens! She behaves like a trollop!' Denise was well into her speech: insults came readily to her lips.

'Drunk? Just because she and Jack . . . we haven't heard her side of it . . .'

'There you go again, always ready to accept excuses! It'll all be lies and you know it! Well, I tell you what I think. I think this girl's getting too big for her boots and needs taking down a peg or two. And if you won't do it, then I will!'

Ida's head hurt abominably, not so much from the effects of alcohol as from the effort not to let her bad feelings for her mother show in her face.

'I'm not letting you out of this house for weeks!' Denise screamed. 'I don't care if it is your summer holidays, you'll stay in, make yourself useful for once, no nicking round to your Gran's, no Jack — and no singing, neither!'

That was it! It was all an elaborate (or rather, an obvious) scheme to stop the plan for singing lessons with Harvey Johns! Ida could not tolerate such envy and meanness.

'I didn't do anything! Jack was all alone, and I was thirsty and tired, and I didn't know what was in the glasses!' she cried, angry and distressed, yet knowing that she lied.

'Oh ho, ho!' her mother roared in mock disbelief. 'Don't kid me, Lady Muck! It isn't from my side of the family you get these tastes and habits! We all know about that!'

'Shut up, shut up!' Ida screamed, pressing wet hands to her face to avoid her mother's look and voice. Her fingers were soggy and wrinkled from the washing-up, and the dirty sink water on them made her want to vomit.

Earl intervened. 'Go to your room Ida. I never want to see you in that condition again. That's all I have to say about it.'

'What about Mr Johns? Oh Pa, please don't make me stop!'

He looked surprised. 'I thought you weren't so keen.'

'Ha! Now he's got you, hasn't he?' Denise exulted. 'You're a fool, Earl. She only wants to go 'cos I've said she can't, it's all done just to spite me! She's no good, I keep telling you! You're far too soft on her. I know her type, and you don't believe me. Give her an inch, she'll take a mile. Look at her, looking at me! I know what you're thinking, my girl. Earl, Earl! Listen to me — are you going to stand by and let her look at me that way? Are you? Oh my God, I don't know why I had her . . .'

Ida had heard this litany before, and ran up to her room to avoid it, sobbing.

She heard the doorbell and her mother's heels staccato with anger going across the hall to see who was there.

It was Jack. 'Um, can I play with Ida?'

'No, you bloody well can't!' Denise shouted. 'She's been sent to her room, and you're not to come round here for a week — d'you hear me? You should be ashamed of yourself, your age, egging her on like that. I saw you! Fiddling under the table with her! Now bugger off! I'll tell your Ma when she gets back from her honeymoon!'

'So what! It don't bother me! I done nothing! My Ma won't like it, you telling tales on me, and no one likes you, not no one in the whole bleedin' family!' Jack roared, walking backwards step by step away from the door, stopping now and then to get breath enough to shout some more. Ida watched him through the landing window. She wanted to cry even more then, for Jack was so loyal to her. He would bring wrath down on his own head, share her bad days in some way, if he was not allowed to be with her.

4

A week later, an extremely sober young lady followed her mother down a small square in Notting Hill Gate to a tall Georgian house at the far end. Harvey Johns' name was etched in brass beside the door, and under it, Top Studio.

'Stand up straight. Wipe that sullen look off your face,' Denise ordered. 'I didn't want to bring you here, but since your father insisted, the least you can do is act decent.'

Denise rang the doorbell and waited, her fingernails rat-tatting with impatience on her patent handbag. Ida sighed, and turned her face towards the sun and a light breeze. The house stood in a corner where the backs of two streets met the end of the square. The triangle of space between was filled with odd-shaped gardens, all neglected because the surrounding prop-erties were divided into flats and one-room tenancies, and no one cared for flowers.

'Come up!' A woman's voice called down to them. 'The door's on the latch.'

Upstairs they were shown in by a cleaning woman in a flowered cross-over pinafore. Ida was not being truculent: she was terrified. She stood by the window looking down over the gardens she had glimpsed in the street. In the midst of weeds and overgrown hedges, giant sycamores creaked. She watched them sway back and forward, and worried that if ever they fell, they would land right on Mr Johns' studio.

She was too shy to look around the room in detail. She noted that the composer had only an upright piano, but it was white, very modern. The room gave her an impression of shabbiness but formality too. There were bookcases, several vases of flowers, a real oil-painting over the fireplace, and no family photographs. Ida spent most of her time snatching looks, hovering by the window, trying not to appear nosy. Denise sighed impatiently, but made no effort to chat to her, to pass the time. Then Ida heard a murmur of conversation outside the room, and a high, thin, girl's voice belled out. It was such a clean, pure sound, repeating one small phrase perfectly. A man laughed and clapped, then called out 'Goodbye'. A tall, thin man sauntered into the room.

'Mr Johns?' Denise said, charming him with her smart clothes and her soft voice. She was a monstrous chameleon, her mother, Ida thought, for she could not help admiring how neat and correct Denise could be when she wanted to be liked.

'How do you do, it's Mrs Garland, isn't it? Sorry, I just had to finish something . . . another pupil.' Johns was wearing baggy corduroy trousers, a cravat and a shamefully ancient knitted pullover. Ida was awed by his appearance. It took utter self-confidence to be seen in that condition. Her mother looked radiant in contrast.

'I'm sorry my husband could not meet you himself. He had an urgent business meeting. Still, here's Ida. I do hope we're not wasting your time . . .' Denise fluttered prettily, but Ida was pleased to see that Mr Johns was responding less eagerly to her mother's charms. Then in a curious reversal of loyalty, Ida felt cross with him, and defensive about her Ma.

'I'm sure that's unlikely. Mr Garland spoke very highly of his daughter on the phone, and he's a man of some experience in these matters, I understand . . .' He encouraged Ida with a kind smile, but she looked steadfastly at the pleats of her best dress.

'Oh, yes!' Denise agreed, without any hint of boasting about Earl's business life. 'But there's a great difference between the popular stage and the concert hall, isn't there Mr Johns?' she said.

'Let's give Ida a chance, shall we?' he said. Harvey Johns sat down at the piano and trilled up and down extravagantly. 'We all have to start somewhere. In your case, Ida, I understand you know how to sing popular songs.'

'Yes, sir. Only at home though,' she replied in a thin voice.

'At least you enjoy singing. But to do it professionally you have to be prepared to work very very hard. To practise every day, for the rest of your life.'

Ida could not imagine this, but nodded dumbly. It seemed the only thing to do.

'You must be very determined, and also very strong. I studied for years to be a tenor — the Vaccai method, which I still follow with my pupils. Unfortunately, I had a very low resistance to infections, and illness ruined my vocal chords. So I content myself with teaching, and my compositions, of course. You look very fit, Ida — no history of health problems in your family?'

'My Pa . . .' Ida began, but Denise interrupted.

'She thinks because he didn't fight . . . but it was only his feet, Mr Johns, honestly.'

Harvey Johns was obviously amused by this admission, and turned to Ida again.

'Would you mind just opening your mouth for me? Mmm. A high palate. Good. Now, let me hear you sing. Start with your favourite. Nothing fancy. I want to hear you when you're happy,' he said, smiling.

This was difficult. Ma was watching her with a deceptively interested expression. Behind that polite, falsely hopeful face, Ida could make out the intensity of her mother's desire for her to fail. Ida was sure she *would* do badly, because Mr Johns frightened her with his easy upper-class manners and the civilised modernity of his house. But she did not want to give her Ma the victory.

'Well then, I'll sing a song from *Chu Chin Chow*. My Aunt Josephine was in it,' she added with defiance.

'I don't have the music, just give me a refrain,' he said, in a friendly way. 'I'll follow you.'

'How can I sing from a heart that's cold,
From a heart that's bought by a bidder's gold,
A song of passion, of love, of life,
With a will at war and a soul in strife,
I long for the sun, and for freedom's breath . . .'

Harvey Johns stared. He could not believe the purity of sound coming from this shabby-looking, sulky girl. Her mouth had a perfect shape.

'Oh Lord!' Denise interrupted, 'I don't think Mr Johns wants to hear that kind of thing at all, my girl. I don't know what's come over you, choosing something so unsuitable.' She tittered cheerfully at Harvey Johns. 'So sorry! Do excuse us! She's got all the records at home — her Pa's bought her Patti, Melba, all those . . . Calvé . . .'

Mr Johns lit his pipe while her Ma ran on, and Ida began to feel extremely foolish, comparing his soft gestures with her mother's brittle manners and insincere voice. Denise was spoiling the first impression she had made; the composer was looking doubtfully at her.

'Mrs Garland, perhaps it would be better if I had a little talk with Ida by herself, I need her to sing a few scales, that kind of thing . . . would you mind very much leaving her here with me for a few minutes — say half an hour? I'm sure you'll find it terribly boring . . .'

Denise opened her mouth as if to protest, but he bounded up at once, deftly placing a hand under her arm to guide her to the door.

'So kind of you, one has to take such a long time with younger girls, and I'm sure you'd like me to be quite, quite sure, not to build up false hopes . . .' He manoeuvred her down the staircase in such an engaging manner. Denise left, nodding agreement with him because he hinted at refusing Ida. She only realised on the doormat that he had got his own way and was rid of *her*.

Harvey Johns shut the door. 'She's right of course, your dear mother, it's rather a gloomy choice of song, I think? Do you know your name-song?' He began to play 'Ida, Sweet as Apple Cider', and to sing in a light tenor. Ida found herself laughing and joining in, pulling a little face because the song was old-fashioned and datedly romantic. But Harvey Johns was kind: he ran on into 'Shine on Harvest Moon'; 'You Made Me Love You', and 'Oh, You Beautiful Doll'. Before Ida could think about it, she was singing her heart out in a medley of popular old numbers.

Harvey Johns was in a state of barely suppressible excitement. When the girl sang, she lost all her inhibitions and was positively illuminated with music. Her pitch was fantastic, somehow accurate and yet she had this knack of sliding all over the note, as if she were inventing it. Her strange leonine eyes sparkled and her pink tongue glistened against her white teeth. She was exotic, with a dusky hue, and yet such vocal potential.

'Fine!' he said, suddenly stopping, running a thumb down the keyboard like a zipper opening. 'Now, listen carefully . . .'

He gave her the note for a series of rising scales, and asked her to repeat them. Then he played many phrases, which she had to repeat from memory, unaccompanied.

'That's a little tune by a man called Tosti. Do you think you could try to sing all of it for me now?'

She did her best, and only muffed two parts of it.

For a while, to give her a rest, he played some lilting classical music, humming the tune to her. Ida forgot the purpose of the meeting, and sat by the window, listening to unfamiliar music, feeling calm and happy.

'Back to work,' he smiled. 'Will you sing for me again?'

Ida attempted several scales, and having tried her best to sing out, was disconcerted when he told her she was shouting, which was not the same thing at all.

'Can you try to come down on these notes, not reach up to them?' he said, growing serious and allowing dissatisfaction to be heard in his voice. 'Think of the notes like a wheel turning, you're at the top, descending on them . . .' She started again, but before she felt she had satisfied him, a bell rang, and her mother reappeared at the door.

'Mrs Garland! How good of you to be so prompt. We've just finished.' He turned to Ida, and took her hand to say goodbye.

'Thank you for coming to see me. I'll write to your father before the end of the week. It was fun, wasn't it?' Ida thought he winked, but she decided just to nod in reply, so that her mother would not press her with questions about what had happened between them.

When she had gone, Harvey Johns sat thoughtfully planning how he could best use this diminutive original. With a mother like Mrs Garland, her education would be an uphill task. He did not like complications, but Ida's voice might make the effort worthwhile. He lit his pipe, slowly savouring all possibilities. Then he frowned. Too unconventional. Her looks would be definitely against her, unless he could turn them to some sort of advantage . . .

Her Ma had to take a taxi back home. Denise was furious at having to pound pavements while Ida auditioned, and her toes were hurting her. (Ma liked to wear shoes one size too small to make her feet look elegant.)

'Complete waste of time,' she grumbled. 'Earl's mad to send you to him, ideas above your station, that's all will come of it.'

'Well, you always want Pa to be posh and everything, I don't see why you should complain . . .'

'Enough of your lip, my girl. I brought you to this man Johns as a favour to your Pa, not because I approve or anything.' Her Ma pressed her waves against the brim of her hat, and her lips tightened. Ida watched her staring idly at the shop windows as they headed back home. Then she knew that her mother had only come to flirt with Harvey Johns, and she felt pain for her father. She began to form a general dislike for pretty, small blonde women, and at the same time, a clearer desire for Harvey Johns to accept her.

Earl came back from his office early that evening, anxious for a full report on the audition. Denise sat smoking and described in a cool way how silly Ida had been to choose a melodramatic show song, and how Harvey Johns had been so kind to overlook her stupidity.

Earl perched on the edge of Denise's sofa and looked at Ida anxiously. 'But you did better after that, didn't you?' he asked. He ran his slim fingers over his chin and lips, as if he needed a shave, a habit he had when he worried about something.

'He was really kind to me, Pa! We sang lots of songs together, and I sat beside him at the piano, and he showed me some of his own compositions . . .' she glanced at Denise to see how she was taking this good news. As she anticipated, her Ma was looking at herself in a mirror, smitten with deafness.

'I tell you what though Pa,' Ida announced, growing more confident. 'I think we should have a few more busts about this place.'

'What?' said her parents in unison.

'Busts!' Ida repeated, impatient. 'You know, women with breasts and drapery, that kind of thing . . .' Ida could not understand the blank, fascinated looks on her parents' faces. 'Mr Johns' studio is ever so smart,' she went on, 'he has real paintings on the walls, and these two bare white ladies, statues on pillars, I think they're real marble or something . . . Why can't we be smart like that, eh Pa? We could put one in the window, it would be really elegant!'

To Ida's dismay, both her parents started to laugh at her, with that throaty, pleasure-loving sound that she particularly hated. Denise put out a hand and stroked Earl's hair into the nape of his neck. He responded to her at once, turning from Ida and laying one hand possessively on Denise's thin hip.

'Up and do your schoolwork, Ida.' Earl kissed Denise's fingertips; Ida left the room. It was obvious that her father had not taken her to Harvey Johns himself for some hidden, personal reason. Her Ma had done him a favour for which she would now exact payment, of that very particular kind.

She was still forbidden to talk to Jack, so she had to spend the whole evening by herself, reading her cinema magazines, waiting to feel sleepy. Ida was not as lonely as she might have been. She had caught a glimpse of another kind of life, and the purity of that girl's voice, echoing in the corridor, had impressed her. She felt despondently unfit to move into this new world, away from the confusing, highly-charged atmosphere of home. Up till now living in the Garland family had excited her, but she began to feel she had been wrong. A more proper response might be one of shame.

Next day, while her Ma took an afternoon nap, she sneaked over to Gran's house hoping to find Jack. She judged she had half an hour. Ted, Jim and a friend were in Gran's parlour upstairs, practising new tunes. The gramophone had been moved to the middle of the room, and a brassy big-band number blared forth. Stop and start, up and down, went the needle head: Ted hopped between the record and the piano, trying to copy phrases. Uncle Jim blew twiddly bits on a clarinet, and the earnest young man in a cricket sweater, holding a newer model of the same instrument, followed him with great interest.

'How does Jim play that gobstick?' the young man demanded of Uncle Ted. 'Half the keys are held on with rubber bands . . . I couldn't get a note out of it!'

'He copes,' said Ted laconically. 'He's picking it up quicker than you are at any rate. Hallo Ida, what's new! We're just working up a couple of good ones!' Uncle Ted turned and beckoned her into the room.

Ida moved forward shyly. 'Pardon me, I was looking for Jack.'

Ted shrugged. 'Not here, duckie. He's down at the boating lake in Kensington Gardens.'

'Thanks. Who is it, Uncle Ted, on the record? I like it.' Ida wanted to hurry, but she was held by the music.

'Fletcher Henderson. One of Uncle Billy's latest imports. Bloody marvellous. Hang on fellers . . . did you get it, Jim? Jesus. Those riffs prod along, don't they? Great bridging to a hot solo, this is.' Uncle Ted tapped the end of a fresh cigarette on his silver case, to pack the tobacco tight before he put it to his lips. It was one of his little gestures, a way of disguising enthusiasm, but his whole body could not conceal his strong liking for the music. He was a very handsome, flashy man, a great piano player. Ida knew all his little ways and she was proud of him.

'Yep, I think I got it,' Jim replied.

'Yes, but Ted, you've got to make it swing . . .' the young man in the cricket sweater was pacing up and down, looking intense.

'Like this, d'you mean, my lad?' Uncle Ted winked at Ida and stuck the cigarette behind his ear like a road-mender. He sat down at the keyboard to thunder his way through an improvisation on the two bar phrase in question.

The young man gulped slightly. 'Yes. That's it,' he muttered, and bent low over the gramophone to cover his mistake.

'I'll leave you to it, then,' Ida said laughing, backing away, but no one took any notice.

'Ida! Hurry up down here!' Her father called her to breakfast earlier than usual. A week had elapsed since her visit to Harvey Johns; perhaps there was news at last.

Ida hurried down from her room, hoping her Pa was alone.

'Morning. What's up?' she asked too brightly.

He waved the letter at her. 'He said yes. Starting in September. I hope you realise what this will cost . . .'

'Ooh Pa! I'm so glad!'

'Well you're a funny one, I'll say that. First you can't stand the idea, and now you're all for it. He says here you've nearly ruined your voice with all this family singing. No more Friday nights, and I'll put a stop to Ted encouraging you. You've no breath control and no top register. But there's a possibility. If you work hard, he says.'

Ida was thrilled by these criticisms, not a bit downcast. Someone was offering to give her a special voice. More important, her Pa was pleased with her! Denise would be furious . . .

'He also says, which I knew of course, that you're too young to have your voice trained. But I want you to make a start. So he suggests he gives you musical theory lessons, a bit of singing, some repertoire work, and later on, when you're over fifteen and your voice has settled down, then he can begin training. That's what I want for you Ida. A good start, on the right path. I want you to end up with a better class of people.'

'I'll try really hard Pa. I want you to be proud of me, I do . . .'

On impulse she ran forward and flung her arms around him. Earl resisted, and would have pulled her away, except that he was too pleased with the news to keep up his usual coldness. It was all an act anyway. He adored Ida; he was strict because he had big plans for her, and she was under his thumb — unlike some other people in his world.

But all this emotion could not be allowed to go on too long. Earl held her gently for a moment, then broke away.

'That's enough of that. I'll be more impressed by results than fine words.'

Ida sat huddled in her own small space, at her bedroom mirror day-dreaming. She stared at her reflection, for a few seconds longer, smoothing over her nose with a pink powder-puff Jack had stolen for her from Aunt Josephine's dressing table. She replayed a scene from a recent new picture, Gloria Swanson, dusting her cheekbones, this way and that, adding softness to perfection.

'Ida!' Her Ma's call was sharper the second time. It was Sunday, and they were to go to visit Gran, laid up in bed.

'I'm not waiting here all day while you make faces in the mirror! Who do you think you are!'

She did not bother to reply. Nowadays there were no new savageries from her Ma. Just the same old blurred sounds of spite and hopelessness. The fact that she was working hard at school, working hard with Mr Johns, and had nearly finished a whole year of lessons, only increased her Ma's irritation. Ida could see why: it was because she was making *plans* for herself.

According to Ma, this was a sin. According to Ma, a force called 'Life' could pop out at any moment and perform its ritual task, which was described in vague, stale phrases that had little meaning. Life 'pulled the rug from under your feet' or 'knocked you for six' or 'put a new complexion on things'. Worst of all: 'you never knew'.

But Mr Johns never said things like that. In his world, a person studied, passed exams, built a career, block by block, and generally speaking felt pretty pleased with the result.

'I'll go on then! I'm not waiting for you any longer!'

Ida was pleased to deny her Ma her company. Besides, she wanted to talk to Gran alone, about Jack. It just was not right that all this money was being spent on her music lessons, and he was growing up like a vagabond boy.

Jack had spent barely any of the last year under his mother's roof with Sidney Ottley. Arguments had become routine and increasingly violent. Then Gran took sick, and Jack grew desperate. He pleaded to be let back to her house, so that he could fetch fresh milk every morning from the local cowkeeper in Star Street, as the doctor recommended, and be sent on other errands when needed. Oddly, he was good at these jobs for Gran, but his schoolwork was hopeless.

He kept Gran company when the uncles of the house were all working — Ted had gone to a hotel band out East, Jim was in a show in town, Billy had his music shop. George was involved in something time-consuming and nefarious which made him unavailable. The least Gran knew about that the better.

As Ida went out to the street, she saw Jack sauntering back from the Edgware Road where he had been sent to buy pease-pudding for Uncle Jim. Ida caught him licking a large dollop out of the folded cone of paper, prodding the surface flat so that it looked untouched.

'You should be ashamed of yourself,' she said.

He ignored her and took the package into the house, leaving it on top of the coal range to keep warm.

'Wait with me outside,' he ordered. 'They'll be back in a minute, to do the dinner.'

They sat together on the wall and for a while they had an enjoyable tussle trying to push privet leaves down each other's neck. Front-garden hedges along Bayswater were full of grit and dusty small spiders' webs; this was a city game with a touch of malevolence. But it had to stop when the loop on the collar of Ida's dress snapped.

'Look what you've done now! You're an idiot Jack Garland! I'll cop it for this!'

'Could have happened in the wash. She won't notice.'

Ida had to admit this was true: Jack was always quick to see ways out. That was one of his strengths.

'I gotta get me wages,' he said.

'Wages?'

Jack put a finger to the side of his nose giving Ida a distinct impression of what a good villain he might make in ten years' time. He squinted into the sunlight, in a vain attempt to look manly.

'Wait and see. Look, here's Uncle Jim.'

'Did you get my penn'orth, Jack? I've been for a walk in the park to work up an appetite.' Jim patted his beer belly in a friendly fashion.

Jack ignored this obvious lie. The smell of brown ale from his uncle was warm and pleasant. 'I did. It's on the range.'

'Good lad.' Jim flicked a small coin into the air and Jack caught it without losing balance.

Jim went into the house, but a moment later a great roar went up.

'Bugger's given me short measure again! I said a penn'orth, not a bleedin' spoonful!' Ida and Jack smothered their giggles and eyed each other over their dirty green knuckles.

One by one the uncles staggered back to the house, in various stages of inebriation. (Only Gran's absence from the dining-table made this possible.)

After a while Uncle Jim, wearing a large frilly apron that strained across his stomach, yelled from the doorway, 'Dinner!'

As they trotted up the path, Jack's face broke into an engaging smile, and he drew his fist out of his pocket.

'For you,' he said, giving Ida something that felt warm from the heat of his palm. It was a poodle-dog brooch with diamantés in its eye sockets. She did not ask where it came from: it was obviously shoplifted. The cheap metal smelt tinny from the sweat of his skin.

'Thanks,' she said, genuinely pleased at his gift. She pinned it to her dress and went in to eat with her arm round Jack's neck.

'Hallo Gran,' Ida said, slipping into the snuggy after lunch to pay her respects. She sat on the thin white bed cover.

'Hallo dearie,' Gran said, in a chesty, wheezing voice that made Ida uncomfortable. So did the sight of her ample chest, unbound and sagging in her night-dress. Her let-down hair was surprisingly thin and unimpressive in a grey plait.

'Are you feeling better, Gran?'

''Course I am. Soon be up and about. Pass me my handbag, there's a good girl.'

Ida fetched it from the chair, hoping she might be given a penny or two. Sunday was always a day for treats.

'Look, I found this when I was going through my old albums last week. I thought you might like to keep it, dear.'

It was a little photograph from a seaside summer theatre, all the leading players lined up in costume against the knobbed white rails of the pier. There was Gran in a picture bonnet, with her wide country face and bright eyes, and next to her a tall man with his face blacked up and his smiling lips enlarged and whited.

'That's my Joseph. Handsome, wasn't he? and look, there's me, on the end.'

Ida did not see anything handsome about Joseph's sooty, comic face, but Gran was wearing a pretty bonnet.

'You look just the same Gran,' Ida commented, trying to be complimentary, though there was little similarity between the generous smiling face and the tired grim person sitting up in bed.

'Rubbish. All that flimsy clothing. No wonder I've ended up with a bad chest,' Gran sighed.

Ida stared at her grandfather, the thin, cheerful minstrel waving his boater in the air. None of Grandpa's pictures made him look like a real person.

'I'd forgotten that show, it was the first we did together out of London,' Gran went on. 'The Isle of Wight. He didn't like the cold — it was a dreadful summer. He was never strong, even as a young man.'

'Was he homesick? Didn't he want to go back to America sometimes?'

Gran shook her head. 'No. It wasn't a good place for him to be. He was happy with me. Then when the babies came along, he just fell for 'em. He only got downhearted when his health failed him.' She thumbed the picture, smoothing dust off its surface, as if warming the image back to life. Just then Ida saw such an expression of love in Gran's face, that she became the girl in the picture, with a soft smile, and a shining hope in her eyes.

Ida had a sudden urge to cry. She was old enough now to see how happily married Gran had been. She could not understand why it had been so easy for her grandparents to be loving, even when they were precariously employed in the music-hall business, and had a big family. Ma and Pa had no money worries, and just one child, but their home was an unhappy place, full of tensions. Gran missed her husband, every day, was a stoical presence of sadness, but that did not make her sharp the way her Ma always was.

'I didn't give a damn what people said. He was enough for me. People stared, pointed at him, but he'd been brought up with a lot worse than that. Segregation. Then sometimes a woman or a child would come up and touch him, because a 'darkie' was supposed to bring good luck. And all he ever did was give my hand a squeeze and tell me not to mind.' Gran murmured on, but Ida was not paying attention. She had fallen into one of those self-centred reveries that the grown-ups irritatingly dismissed as 'just her age', when she was actually trying very hard to find answers . . .

'Keep the picture. I'd like you to have it,' Gran said, nudging Ida's arm.

'What? Oh. Thank you very much.' Ida did not particularly want the sad little picture, but if Gran thought it was important, she would look after it.

'Gran,' she said, trying to raise her main concern, 'what's to be done with Jack?'

'I told you I'd look after him, didn't I? Though I didn't think the flu would do the trick.'

'Oh Gran, he was so pleased to come back to you. Ten months with Ottley! I hate that man.'

'You don't understand, duckie, he only does what he thinks best for the boy. A firm hand.'

Ida shook her head, but did not argue with Gran, for she could hear the old woman's chest wheezing, and her head fell back on the pillow in a tired way. 'You know I think the world of Jack,' Gran went on, 'but he's a handful. He's different from the rest of us . . . and I tell you something else.' Ida moved closer, as her Gran's voice was getting tight and breathless. 'It won't do any good, lecturing and hectoring that one. Don't you see? It'll only make him do exactly the reverse . . .' She chuckled, but the laughter ended in a spasm of coughing, and she waved Ida out of the room, suddenly angry.

'What do your schoolfriends think of your singing, Ida?' Harvey Johns asked next day, noticing her bulging satchel. Ida blushed: he had guessed that she changed out of her school uniform just for him, and she felt awkward. She put her fingers to her poodle brooch, to make sure she had not lost it.

'Oh, I don't really talk to them all that much.'

'Why's that?' he asked idly. He began to tap out one of his curly briar pipes. Try as she might, Ida did not find this masculine taste in the least attractive. Bits of black tobacco spilled down his flannel trousers.

'They're silly. I mean, they're nice, but they're babies compared to me. Not that I want to pretend to be grown-up, Mr Johns, honestly . . .'

'I think you mean pampered,' he suggested. Ida, whose vocabulary was sadly limited, felt a thrill of admiration for him that the pipe-smoking had stifled.

'Yes!' She giggled. 'They're real Mummy's babies!' Then she felt stupid again, and made her face serious, feeling the dryness of her gums as her lips closed nervously. 'Mr Johns, can I ask you something?' she ventured.

He looked up, she was not sure if he was excited or merely surprised. This was the longest 'outside' conversation they had shared since she began lessons a year ago.

'Am I improving?' she asked. 'You said my chest register was overdeveloped. Do I sound any better? Am I old enough now to start proper voice training? I've been coming for nearly a year . . .'

His expression of curiosity did not change. He sucked on his empty pipe, waiting.

'I mean, Pa wants me to be a concert singer. D'you think I'm not going to be good enough, or something?' she blurted.

He almost laughed at her, then changed his mind.

'What gave you that idea? Haven't I always been pleased with you?'

'Yes, but . . .'

'Well, believe me, I think you'll go far. I'm not sure yet in which direction, and I don't believe a voice as pure and strong as yours should be developed too soon. You have a clarinet-like quality, and a certain agility too. You may have coloratura possibilities but it's far too early to say anything definite . . . all we can do is work on the breathing, the diction, study a broad repertoire . . .'

'Is that why you still like me to sing these jazz things for you?' She finally got it out. 'It isn't because you think I'm not good enough to be — classical?'

Harvey laughed a little too richly, Ida thought, and felt foolish.

'My dear! You've completely missed the point! You know, a lot of serious composers are interested in modern American music. Poulenc, Milhaud, Stravinsky. I was actually considering writing a special composition for you in that vein . . .' He turned away to light his pipe, and puffed a couple of times while the match flame spurted. He stood in thought for a moment, offering her his profile. Ida studied his fine-boned head. This was the sort of scene that happened in films: The music master and the budding pupil. Yet somehow she was not sure of Harvey Johns, and could not give herself up to the undoubted elegance of the moment.

One telling objection held her from that. Sometimes Harvey Johns played a 'hot' tune for her on the piano, to be friendly and to give her voice a rest. Sometimes he asked her to 'bend' notes when she sang, imitating American blues singers, which Ida could do quite well. But he had a bouncy, over-correct style that sounded far less 'right' than Uncle Ted's playing did. She had always suspected he was being condescending when he admired her uncles' music, or just gave her lessons because he liked the money.

'Gosh. I never thought it was because I could do something special . . .' she murmured, but he did not hear.

'Look at the time!' he interrupted. 'Let's continue our chat about colouring — do you remember what I said last week?' He led her to the piano-stool, and they sat side by side. Was Harvey Johns thirty or forty? Ida wondered, and found her brain empty of other thoughts.

'Er . . .' she said, blushing. He did not notice, fortunately, and she made an effort to concentrate.

'There are three kinds of colouring,' she began.

'Yes. And what are they?'

'There's a warm tone for serious songs, a lighter shade for happier ones, and a clear, transparent colour for telling stories . . .'

'Without any emotion at the back of it,' he added. 'And why is that?'

'Because often I must learn to let the words do the colouring themselves . . . and not overwork a song.'

'Yes, just the way a painter has to know when to stop touching up his canvas.'

'Oh I remember! You said you can't sing a sombre song in a bright voice, nor a happy song in a dark voice without looking stupid.'

'Yes, well, I don't think I quite said that but you've got the general idea all right . . . Now, I'll tell you something else today Ida, and I want you to pay close attention . . .'

Ida was absorbed, and happy to be someone's entire focus.

'In most people, thought and speech are the two functions most swiftly co-ordinated. That's why the tone of a person's voice betrays what he is thinking, whatever the words he speaks. You have this same quality in your singing. In speech or in song, the last control we have over the sound is in the muscles of the mouth . . . Let me ask you something. How can you tell if a person's lying?'

Ida thought of Jack for a moment, then suggested, 'By the light in his eyes!'

Harvey Johns shook his head. 'Next time, look at the mouth. I don't believe it's in the eyes. I think it's the small alteration in the skin round the mouth, a little tautness — maybe this muscle tightening pulls the eyes open too. My advice is, if you want to know what a person is really like, watch the mouth as he speaks to you.'

Perhaps it was just as a result of these words that Ida and Mr Johns, from that day on, always watched each other's lips as they conversed.

The next time Ida went to Harvey Johns she had an unpleasant shock. He was just saying goodbye to a tall, fair-haired girl, giving her a peck of a kiss on her forehead. They held both hands, in a formal pose like old English country dancers, exchanging words. The girl was just a year or two older than Ida.

'What was it again, Harvey?' she said in refined tones.

'La la la?' he sang for her, up the notes.

The stranger waved merrily and trilled the phrase as she ran down the stairs. Ida recognised the sound at once: she had heard that voice a year before, on the first day she visited. She only had a glance at a hand-knit Fair Isle sweater and a neat kilted skirt to know the type: mothered. What offended her most was that the girl passed her on the stairs without a glance, as if she were insignificant.

In all the months she had attended classes she had never met any of Mr Johns' other pupils. Her feeling of being special rather abruptly died.

Harvey Johns led her in and went immediately to the piano.

'Listen to this,' he said, playing a lyrical tune. 'It's French, by a man called Debussy. Do you like it?' he asked. The notes tapped lightly on Ida's ruffled nerves.

'Mmm.' She began to feel apprehensive.

'Look, I've had the most wonderful idea. You're not used to public performance, and I'd hate to make you nervous. Why don't I ask you to sing a duet with Janet — that girl who's just left? One of my own compositions. I've written a suite, 'On Syncopation'. I want Janet to sing the conventional themes and you to sing the improvisations. Janet's two years older than you — she's sixteen — and as it's your first concert, I thought you'd be happier to sing with someone more experienced.'

Ida was confused. Johns began an obvious effort to soothe her feelings. He played seductively light phrases, like a woman's laughter heard in a sunlit park.

'It's interesting how many ways there are for young ladies to be beautiful,' he said.

(He's not talking about her and me of course! Ida thought, but her spirits lifted.)

'Take Janet, now. Some people might like her classic, almost ethereal looks. But then, you have such strong dark eyebrows, such expressive eyes, and *perfect* singer's mouth. A high palate, perfect teeth and a small tongue . . .'

He merely suggested (or was Ida hearing only what she wanted desperately to hear?) that he thought Ida superior by far.

'The contrast of your voices will make the piece most interesting . . . You know, don't you, this modern business of improvising is not entirely new. Handel, Vivaldi, in their original forms were intended for improvisatory embellishment . . . and your voice is very suggestive, flexible. It has immediacy.'

She felt a lump rise in her throat, and became angry at once. Harvey Johns was old, thirty at least; he had dandruff on his collar, and his trousers had tiny burn holes from his pipe-sparks. He just happened to be an educated man, however, and she needed his praise. She needed it so much that the thought of failing him was beyond her.

'I couldn't do it, Mr Johns,' she said it as a matter of fact, not an expression of doubt.

'Why on earth not?' Harvey Johns suddenly looked angry.

'I can't explain. I just can't do it, that's all.' This was true. Ida did not know how she had the nerve to refuse her teacher, when he had written something specially for her. She was responding entirely on an instinct. It wasn't just stage fright. She did not know why, but the prospect of singing with this other girl horrified her.

Harvey Johns struggled to be patient. 'I leave it to you, Ida. You know I want your first appearance at my Christmas concert to show you at your best. But there'll be plenty of other occasions.'

'I'd do a little piece, Mr Johns, I'd not be nervous — couldn't I do that song of yours that I tried last week?'

He was surprised. 'My setting of the Milton poem? It's not very long, and it hardly demonstrates how your range has improved.'

'Yes, but this is the first time — please!'

'If you insist.' She could hear the disapproval in his voice, and still did not know what compelled her to defy him. 'But Ida, if you are to become a concert performer as your father wishes, then you must grow accustomed to the idea of displaying your talents without being over-modest.'

Ida nodded, unable to express her thoughts. The rest of her lesson passed in a subdued atmosphere.

That night, Ida thrashed, sleepless, in her bed. Discontent brought suspicions to the surface of her thoughts.

Seductive snatches of Harvey's 'Syncopation' duet floated through her head (for of course he kept playing bits of it, to get her to change her mind). How mean of Harvey to keep playing her the music, full of blue harmonies, swervy, flattened thirds and sevenths, as if flirting with her natural, untutored love of the real jazz music. But Ida knew she did not sing like those big sorrowing shouters she heard on records in Uncle Billy's music shop and if she could not do the real thing, she would not be a poor copy.

Now she wondered why Harvey Johns had suggested she should sing alongside Janet. Was it contrast? She would have the worst of the comparison; she was only medium height, getting a little plump and horribly dark-skinned. Her hair was a disaster too, thick black handfuls, an unmanageable thatch compared to Janet's smooth blondeness. Its colour was not a brassy bottle yellow like her Ma's but a classy, fawn-grey tinge. She hoped Denise would wear a hat for the concert. (Pa was not coming — a great disappointment.) But then, if Denise wore a hat, there was the risk of *feathers*!

Disconcerted, Ida got out of bed and crept downstairs. There was no one in the house. Typical of Ma and Pa not to tell her they were going out. It was a blustering winter night so it would take especial courage to crawl through the fence to Gran's house. Ida pulled her night-dress tight round her legs and waddled through the yard to the boarding-house back door as quickly as she could. The scullery was unlocked. It did not even creak as she let herself in. Jack was sleeping up in Uncle Ted's vacant room and she would creep into his bed . . .

But on the stairs, Ida froze still. Denise and Earl were talking about her in the front room.

'Mr Johns told me on the phone, she flatly refused. What d'you make of it?' Earl asked, worried. Ida shivered at the note of concerned interest in his voice. She listened, all eagerness. They were actually talking about her!

'Maybe it's stage fright. She'll grow out of it. She's only fourteen — after all, it's a big step singing in a formal concert,' Gran said.

Earl obviously disagreed. 'I hope she's not going to let me down. I know I'm right about all this. She could do well. I know she could go straight.'

'Ha!' Denise wanted to end this discussion quickly. 'You're both wrong. She did it because she didn't want to share the limelight with anyone. That's not good enough for Miss Ida Garland!' She gave an amused, dismissive laugh. 'Didn't you guess? I know her better than both of you! Centre stage or nothing for that one!'

Not one word was spoken in her defence. Ida was so hurt she could hardly breathe. There was an accusing silence from the room, the moment was endless. She could picture Pa stroking her Ma's hand, to calm her down, and Gran, tight-lipped, knowing it was futile to waste words.

Now it was even more important that she get upstairs without a single board-squeak. Willing herself almost to float, Ida crept up, rejection and anger rising in her on the dark staircase.

Ted's room had a big bed and a small divan against one wall where he often put up a friend after a late night. Ida did not get in with Jack in case she woke up. She needed silence. She lay on the divan facing the wall and painful tears welled up. But then, heavy doubts made her stop crying. She hated to think there was any truth in her mother's words: in her heart her motives did not seem quite as ugly as Denise had made out. But her Ma was probably right, in the end. It was pride that had made her refuse. Suddenly aware of her conceit (for apparently that was the true name for her feeling, not self-consciousness or shyness), Ida lay still, not seeing anything in the dark, and losing her pleasure in her voice.

5

Ida watched her father reading Harvey Johns' report. He was standing by his desk wearing a dress suit, tails and white tie, waiting for Denise to finish dressing.

'Can't I look?' Ida moved forward as if she would read the letter over his shoulder.

'Sit down.' Earl spoke quietly. 'Let me finish it in peace.'

Ida could not imagine why he was taking so long. Harvey Johns never wrote anything sensational; he had realised long ago that he should never overpraise her or criticise her too specifically in these letters home. The first encouraged Denise's verbal cruelty, the second caused more pressure from Earl. Her teacher knew that Ida lived in two worlds: that of her family and of her future. He was mindful to avoid any conflict that would discourage her from leaving the old one and making a success of the new.

'You must have finished with the first page. Couldn't you pass it over?' she asked again.

'Be quiet or I'll have you leave the room.' Her father had no need to raise his voice.

Ida sat on her hands. Harvey Johns did not see that in the past three years he had taught her quite the opposite of what he intended. He had this vision of her as his 'avant-garde, syncopated interpreter'. Ida resisted him, and worked at a more classical repertoire almost in spite of him. Her mother's hostility drove her to want to succeed in a proper way, to cut herself off from everything to do with the Garlands. To win respect more than fame.

Ida knew that people like the student Janet, and presumably several other of Johns' protégées, would never have to work as hard. Because she had more talent than any of them. Only people like her had to make this leap of the imagination, to believe they belonged somewhere else and to give up everything familiar. Most of the time she wanted to, at other times, she felt the strain of her compulsion.

'He thinks you should start singing in public,' Earl said, breaking in on her thoughts.

Ida was stunned. 'What? He couldn't have suggested that!' Johns had not spoken to her about this at all.

'Well, you are sixteen. It's time you moved on, broadened your perspective musically. He wants to take you to some summer school for a week, in a country house, private affair. I expect you'll meet some useful people.'

'Are his other pupils going?' Instant rivalry.

'Apparently not. But there will be several teachers bringing their best students, and you'll share a room with a group of girls.'

Ida thought of the state of her night things and rejected the idea at once. She did not own a dressing gown and layered herself instead with her Pa's old cardigans.

'I don't want to go,' she said.

'Oh Ida, don't start all that again. You know you want your chance to be in a better class. Won't you be glad to leave all this behind?' He smiled thinly, and Ida felt a pang of guilt. She did want to get out, for a reason she could not tell him. To please him, yes, but also to get back at Ma — his wife, but her mother — who did not care for her in the least.

'Earl?' Denise tottered downstairs and appeared at the door. 'Oh. There you are!'

Her Ma had a way of saying those three words that conveyed to Ida quite plainly she would have preferred her not to be present.

'You look terrific!' Earl said.

Denise paused in the doorway, wondering what they had been discussing. Ida did not add a word of praise, for she was trying to sneak a glance at Johns' letter while her Pa was not looking. He pulled down the bureau lid, clicking his teeth with irritation.

'New dress? I like it.' Earl hurried forward to kiss Denise.

She smiled. 'Don't ruin my hair-do.' But she put up her cheek for his lips all the same. Still Ida said nothing, to annoy Denise — that dress of silver satin demanded attention, and made her Ma look appealing in a fragile sort of way.

99

Ida had reached a state of mind where she was happy only if her parents were arguing. Harmony disgusted her, a reminder of all that was seedy and distorted between them.

In a second she recalled her Ma's tiresome whine: Ida had overheard them arguing in the middle of the night.

'I've had it! Up to here!' Earl had shouted, running downstairs.

'Oh sweetie, come back to bed. I'm sorry. I'm sorry I was mean. We were lovers last night . . . don't you want me any more? Oh Earl . . .' Denise's teasing voice twisted and twined, as her body did.

When Ida heard her Pa go back upstairs with Denise, she could not forgive him . . .

'We'll be late,' Denise said now, gathering up her fur wrap. 'Be sure to turn off all the lights, Ida.'

'And get on with your practising,' Earl chipped in.

They were going to see a play in which one of Earl's pretty girl clients had taken over a modest role. *The Love Race* at the Gaiety starred Stanley Lupino and was full of quick jokes, but Earl would probably fall asleep before the interval, and Denise would be irritated with him all evening. There might be a small dinner afterwards. Ma would be grand with the actresses and flirt with the young men. Ida imagined the whole scenario, including Earl's suppressed fury in the taxi on the way home. At least tomorrow she and Pa would have breakfast alone, and could talk about Harvey Johns again.

Ida got out one of her musical scores, Mozart, and started to memorise the words. But no sooner had the front door closed than the back one opened. Jack had seen her parents leave and timed his arrival by that.

'What do you think?' he said, strutting around in a new mess jacket, decorated with a gold-braided, fairly vulgar badge on the breast pocket.

'Isn't it just a little loud?' Ida said. Harvey Johns always said 'a little' instead of 'a bit'.

'Get off Ida, it's for the band. Have to put on a show. Whaddya think?' He turned again, and stuck his hand in his trouser pocket for a more nonchalant effect.

'I think it's fine,' she agreed. The band was Jack's new

venture: he had left school that summer at fourteen, hopelessly uneducated, and gone to Uncle Billy's shop, where the music bug had got him, but strictly as a money-earner. The idea of him managing to get his arms round a double bass, let alone make a sound on it, amused her. (Not that he produced music, more an efficient two-in-a-bar rhythm, tonic and dominant, dum-dum, dum-dum.)

'Got a booking!' He pulled out a letter of agreement with a sprawling signature across a two-penny stamp. 'Official!' he beamed, holding it up. 'Saturday, two weeks from this one. Ida, do me a favour. Will you come?'

'To listen, you mean,' she smiled at him, knowing full well he had something up his sleeve.

'Well, not exactly . . .'

'Jack, you've never said I'd . . .'

'Look, this is dead important. You remember that feller used to play with Ted — the student who was keen on hot music . . .'

Ida remembered the young man's cricket sweater, and his awkward blushing over Uncle Ted's piano playing.

'Henry Palmer. He came into the shop the other day. He's getting married, parents have a big place down on the river near Maidenhead. Uncle Ted being back from the East, naturally I said we'd do it: Ted, me, Uncle Jim and Terence Bageshaw. You know Terence,' Jack concluded. He refolded his much-thumbed contract and tucked it into his pocket.

'Yes. I know Terence. That awful little crony of yours who had the cheek to make eyes at me on the bus. Don't know how he had the nerve, the size of him. He's a shocking influence on you, Terence is.'

'He's all right. You have to know how to handle him. Heart of gold, he has, and he's not half bad on the drums. And Uncle George is getting me some extra sound equipment, he knows a man with a — well. Anyway.' Jack's mode of speech was in general improving as he began to go about in the world. Occasionally London emphases still slipped into his speech, and Ida lapsed with him.

'Will you say yes? Just this once? It could mean me moving into the big time! Lots of smart parties, they pay really well!' he begged, his blue eyes pale and bright with the possibilities.

'I couldn't, really . . . you know Pa's rules . . .' But she wanted to help. She was also curious to see what a smart wedding reception was like. On the other hand, she was less keen on singing her way into it.

'Oh, come on Ida. Don't be a spoil-sport. I hardly see you these days, what with work and all, and I really need you to help. You know you've got the best voice ever, and Ted's playing, so it'll be fun for all of us. Just this once . . .'

'Well.' Ida hesitated, but old loyalty to Jack made her yield. 'I suppose I could wear that black thing I made for my last school concert . . .'

'Great! You'll get paid a bit, of course, and lashings of free food from the buffet, good nosh, and free drink — wedding champagne, eh?'

'"Paid a bit"! I'm not doing it for shillings! You pay me a guinea at least.' (Guineas made her sound more of a professional.) 'How will you fix it, about Pa I mean? You know he doesn't like me singing popular stuff. Especially with a band. It's bad for my voice . . .'

'He need never know. I'll get Uncle Billy to have you instead of me at the shop for my Saturday job. Then at the last minute you ring in sick. Billy'll cope just once. If Uncle Earl comes looking for you, you just say you took the bus, got ill and had to get off for a lie-down in the park instead. Dizzy, you know, a female turn . . . time of the month or something . . .' He winked at her. Ida blushed. There were moments when his long-standing familiarity with her enabled him to be too crude.

'You would think of that.'

'I would.' He grinned, knowing she was going to agree to do it. 'Give us a kiss, Ida. You're a great girl. You know that.' He gave her a smacker on the cheek, blowing a raspberry with his lips. Ida pushed him aside. 'Means a lot to me, this. Now I've got to go — got to keep in with Ma for a bit, in case she turns nasty before the weekend.'

'How's The Uncontrollable?' Ted's nickname had stuck.

Jack shrugged. 'Don't see much of him.' Ida let it go — he did not want to talk about Ottley when he was looking forward to a good time. She knew the arguments worsened as Jack grew older. The only difference was that now Jack could occasionally hurt his stepfather in a fight, especially if the older man had been drinking. Unlike the Garland boys, Ottley grew less effective with his fists after a couple of glasses.

'I've got a date to see on my way home. Have to go, sorry and all that.' Jack adjusted his jacket, self-important.

'Who asked you in?' Ida retorted; she did not believe in the 'date' and she was angry that he left her alone for the evening. Just when she was doing him a favour and feeling concerned for him, he always hit another note and had to swagger. Jack was turning into a right show-off: he could not possibly have a girlfriend at his age. Just someone cheap to neck with in a shop doorway in Shepherd's Bush.

'Don't let me keep you,' she said, flapping him out of the room with a piece of Harvey Johns' sheet music as if he were an annoying wasp. Only after he had left did it occur to her that he had deliberately annoyed her: because he needed her help, and it rankled in his growing manly pride that she had felt sorry for him.

The wedding reception was not remotely as Ida had imagined. Firstly, Henry Palmer and his bride were very progressive and would only agree to a ceremony in a registry office. The family were scandalised, and forced the newly-weds to hold a small, formal reception at the bride's home in Chelsea, for the more conservative relatives. In return they got their own 'thrash' at the Palmer mansion. Henry's parents absented themselves: stayed up in town to console the other in-laws with a visit to the exclusive Milray Club in Regent Street . . . much more the thing.

Ida wandered in the garden while her two musician uncles argued with young George about the amplifying equipment in the large marquee erected for the dance. When everything was satisfactorily arranged, all the men went off to dispatch a few beers swiftly before the party called for their services.

It was a sultry, late summer afternoon, and someone had arranged fairy-lights in swags between the trees. A weedless, springy lawn stretched down to the edge of the Thames, for the river ran literally at the end of it. There was a narrow boardwalk and a few boats tied up in readiness for midnight paddlings.

Shrubs unknown to Ida made cosy blobs of colour along the side walls, all neatly tied up with pea sticks and cosseted with dung. Here was beautiful order: yet Ida could see that the hosts, young Palmer and his bride, hardly took notice of their surroundings. In fact, their set positively despised it.

The guests had started to arrive in large gangs, spilling out of sports cars. Ida lost all her manners and gawped.

'What ho! Henry!' someone yelled.

'Bourgeois little pad, eh?' called another.

'Too dull!' someone else agreed.

How rude! How odd! was Ida's response. To her, the house was anything but dull. It was proper — a really proper home! She began to pry, thinking that lying to her father was not such a bad thing to have done if it enabled her to see how other people lived. She strolled about, imagining the house was hers and that she was a real lady — not like these wild young rebels.

All the couples were dressed as sheikhs and slave girls. She had only ever seen such undress on stage where artificiality made it much less shocking, almost anonymous. The carry-on at Josephine's wedding was positively coy by comparison. These people went about half-nude, recognising each other's bodies! Ida spent a long time staring at belly buttons, men's nipples and girls' half-bare breasts. The men looked ineffably silly, but the girls were in the main stupendous.

Ida heard the band begin to warm up, and hurried back to the marquee. Jack was craning his neck, looking for her, and the flushed young bridegroom, Henry Palmer, was waiting to be introduced to her again. 'Well hallo!' he said, nodding approval. Ida had put up her hair under a paste-diamond headband, and her simple tunic emphasised the glow of her skin.

'We met,' she said shyly, 'but that was a few years ago, in my Gran's parlour.'

Henry Palmer did not remember, but he smiled very brightly as if the moment had just come back to him. He had the same easy charm of Harvey Johns, but spoke with a more vigorous, sporty voice. 'Of course! How do you do! So glad you could come!' He pumped her hand. 'Drink anything you like — have a good time! Terrific you could all come. Hope you won't mind the crowd, I do hope they pay you jolly close attention . . .' he winked, adjusted his head-dress coiled with a gold rope, and gave Uncle Ted the thumbs-up sign.

Uncle Jimmy stuck his clarinet into a paralysingly fast version of 'Royal Garden Blues', to attract the guests being served drinks in the house and the rest sauntering on the lawns. Uncle Ted played piano with a cigarette dangling from his lips. Ida noticed that the cocksure Terence Bageshaw had his head bent low over his equipment, hanging on to Uncle Jim's coat-tails, musically speaking, and making a noise on a trap drum like a steamroller over cobblestones. Jack thudded about on his double bass, and to give him his due, he produced a surprisingly firm slapping rhythm. He must have been practising.

It was rough music but very contagious. However, Ida noticed that the sudden changes of rhythm were irritating the keen dancers in the crowd. The Arab sheikhs and their skimpily-clad harem girls jiggled about, getting too flushed.

'Uncle Jim!' she hissed. 'Dance numbers, that's what they want!'

'Orders from the host,' he winked, picking up his saxophone for the next classic piece.

A succession of popular 'hot' jazz numbers followed, many indelibly scored on Uncle Jim's memory from the day he had heard the Original Dixieland Jazz band at the Hammersmith Palais in 1919 — when he was seventeen. Uncle Ted took him to that first occasion, but Jim was so wild about the band that he followed them around London, to their Palladium show and to a few bookings at a club in Tottenham Court Road.

Of course, when Jim started to get jobs himself, as a multi-instrumentalist, he played written, commercial music, on variety stages, or in theatre pits for shows. But after hours that was another matter. He and Ted joined that small coterie of professional musicians who liked to play jazz in their own way whenever they could, and found a certain audience among middle-class intellectuals and amateur musicians like Henry Palmer.

'Come on Ida, you're on,' Jack called to her. He helped her clamber on stage, and patted her shoulder. 'You look really pretty Ida. Come on, now let 'em have it — the Garlands!'

'Back to jig tempo, fellers,' Ted called out, as Ida moved to the front of the tiny platform. She was not before time, for the crowd were looking a little ragged, even stunned, breathless after their authentic jazz session.

'There's nothing to be scared of, Ida, just pretend you're in the parlour!' Ted encouraged her.

Here goes! I must be mad! Ida said to herself. She closed her eyes, took a deep breath and *belted*. She had rehearsed a whole programme of songs suitable for the occasion: 'Everybody Loves My Baby'; 'I Found a New Baby'; 'I Can't Give You Anything but Love'; 'I Can't Believe that You're in Love with Me', and so on. Ted had pitched them all several keys down from where she first wanted to sing, to make her voice sound more natural. Every time she opened her eyes, and peeped out, it all seemed to be going down well. Henry Palmer's bride, a pretty, plump girl with a flashing smile and a row of gold coins on her straight fringe, kept circling with different men in front of the bandstand, mouthing all the words vacuously.

Ida began to relax. Jack was jogging about, looking utterly delighted. His pleasure was so physical that he looked like a little boy, all fresh and full of joy. It meant so much to him, because he had arranged everything himself, and was being a somebody. Happy for him, she began not to mind the rising hum of conversation. Guests were getting exceedingly drunk and loud-mouthed. The band was occasionally nerve-wracked by people who came up to the bandstand and asked for songs by the wrong names. 'Grab Your Coat' was easily identified as 'On the Sunny Side of the Street', a new Depression favourite. Uncle Ted spotted 'You for Me' as 'Tea for Two', and 'You are the One' as 'Night and Day'. As the evening grew longer, memories weakened and song lyrics blurred into one long, sentimental cliché.

At about midnight, when Ida was beginning to feel the sweat pouring between her shoulder-blades, Palmer signalled for the band to stop, and a small *divertissement* took place on the dance floor. Two escapologists had been hired for the Arab guests: the whole scene struck Ida as absurdly fashionable and grotesque. At first she was shocked, then disappointed that smart, wealthy people liked to watch this common kind of side-show. It held no charm for someone who had seen drunks fighting in the street at an early age.

The 'expert' and his 'victim' were a pair of unsavoury East End villains who liked entertaining the wealthy classes; they enjoyed the *frisson* their violence gave the ladies. Ida could see that from the way they had dirtied and greased their muscles, rippling their arms suggestively to test their locks and chains.

'They're a pair of hams, if ever I saw them,' she whispered to Uncle Jim. Ted had already disappeared to the bar.

'I'm not at all sure I should let you watch this, Ida,' Uncle Jim said with a mocking note of prudery.

'I can't see why anyone wants to anyway,' she replied, coldly. 'Horribly vulgar. Pa would die if he knew I was here.'

'This is only half the show, dearie,' he winked at her. 'I expect they specialise in a few other tying up sessions for private customers — you mark my words.'

'Uncle Jim! What a thing to say!'

He stood back beaming, drinking his beer like a child at bedtime with a mug of milk. He licked the white foam from his upper lip. 'They're all the same, these nobs,' he added. 'It's always got to be unusual to get 'em going.' Nods and winks made plain he was referring to the 'physical department', as he tended to call it.

He never would have told her at home in Bayswater! All at once Ida felt a thrill: she was being treated as an equal, a paid performer to whom the world's secrets could be passed on, not as a studious little innocent.

'Well I never,' she said, an inadequate response.

''Sides, I bet they do a few jobs. Burglaries. This gets them into the right houses, see? Poor old Palmer thinks he's being so advanced. His Dad won't thank 'im when this pile's done over six months from now.'

Ida watched the two blue-oiled men flailing about in torn clothing. The older, savage one was busily tying straps round the pretty, young one's body, pinning his arms to his sides. He put a boot on his chest and snarled realistically. Some tipsy girl screamed, and a wave of banter ran through the audience. At a given signal from the torturer, Terence Bageshaw began a threatening roll on the drums, while the young boy writhed and kicked on the boards. A magnificent cymbal-crash signified his escape, the end of the floorshow, and caused a general stampede for more drinks.

Henry Palmer swayed up to Ida with a pink grin on his face and a large glass. 'This is for you, me dear. What a knock-out you are! You sang the last one a little bit like Ethel Waters.'

'The one who sings with the Fletcher Henderson orchestra. I know.' In spite of her pretensions to be a great concert singer, Ida was complimented. He had good taste in the real bands, Henry Palmer . . .

'Just a little punch! Keep up the good work!'

Ida knew all about mixing her drinks. 'Thank you very much,' she replied. As soon as his back was turned she stepped out on to the lawn and poured the frothy mixture into a tub of flowers. Uncle Ted would be pleased with her.

But Jack was not so easy to avoid. He found her by the river's edge, and sat beside her with two glasses and a bottle of champagne.

'Have some,' he said. 'You'll never keep up otherwise, we've got to go on again till five.'

'Jack Garland! You never said it would be all night long! What'll Pa say when I get home!'

'I sent a telegram. I told them Uncle Ted accepted full responsibility for you. They won't kick up a fuss if they know you're with him.' Coolly, he poured a glassful.

'You planned this all along!'

'Oh Ida, lay off, will you? What's done is done. You might as well have a good time. What d'say, eh? Smart do?'

'Are they always like this?' Ida blinked in the direction of several tangled bodies with what she hoped was bored hauteur. Unfortunately, Jack saw fascination in her eyes.

'Naughty, you mean? What's Uncle Jim been saying to you.'

Ida found herself blushing.

'You don't want to listen to him. Vivid imagination, too shy. That's his problem.' Jack poured her another glass with confidence. 'Go on, before they call us back again.'

'Oh blast it. Why not?' Ida could not believe she was two years, three months older than Jack. She was a stiff little simpleton who was missing out on life. It was all the fault of her

Ma, making her feel she had to fight against her sinfulness — all the fault of her Pa, driving her to be respectable. All the fault of Harvey Johns with his grand and perfect plans. All the fault of — someone!

Jack was right about the champagne, too. Ida did not know how she would have continued for another four hours without the numbing, fuelling effect of alcohol. The crowd grew raucous; sheikhs disrobed and danced in their baggy trouser bottoms or even in their underthings. The girls did not actually undress, but grew prone to mishaps: quite a few breasts burst out from jewelled casings, and chiffon harem leggings were torn to shreds. The noise was deafening. Ida closed her eyes, and at ten to five, by popular request, sang 'Honeysuckle Rose' for the sixth time.

Only now she felt quite different. Uncle Jim was accompanying her on the saxophone, Uncle Ted on the piano, and Terence Bageshaw even had the tempo (after all, they had never performed together in public before). Ida threw back her head and thought of nothing beyond the effect of her voice and her dear uncles' truly beautiful instrumentation. The music *happened*: she knew because Jack's bass-playing was soft and swinging, and the whole band stopped peering anxiously at each other for cues.

Most of the dancers left were exhausted or very drunk, and all gathered in front of Ida for the pleasure of her song. She was hardly aware of a crowd, just conscious of a oneness with the people out there beyond her. And yet, at the same time, she was utterly at peace, alone with her voice. Joy in song returned to her, wrapped itself round her like someone's sun-warmed arms.

When she finished, a spontaneous round of applause thrilled Ida. As she bowed a rush of tiredness made her swerve. Her shyness, her bodily presence came back to her.

She longed for a warm drink — tea was being served with bacon and eggs on the lawn. Inconspicuously, Ida helped herself, and walked to a dark patch of grass to sit down. Behind her in the shrubbery, a couple sounded as if they were copulating inefficiently, complaining to each other about their lack of success.

'I'll have to stop! My back — my back!'

'Darling! Move over! Aah — not so quick!'

On the river, a more romantic vision of love floated past; a man lay stretched on top of a woman in a punt, both sound asleep like corpses in a medieval funeral barge.

Ida moved away tactfully from the struggling couple and sat against a side of the tea-tent with a pole at her back. That final solo still soared in her head, and she sipped her tea, trying to calm down. Phrases from Uncle Jim's saxophone came back to her, causing tremors of excitement inside her again. A rumble of drums thudded faintly in her mind. Cold air made her shiver, but the warm drink was soothing. Bit by bit, pleasure faded and she began to notice people in the darkness all around her. Giggles, mumbles, spilt drinks, and the slapping of naughty hands.

'What would you say? Arab? Greek? Latin American?' she overheard a peremptory voice inside the tent, behind her. All the guests talked loudly, even about mundane things; they had the unselfconsciousness of the privileged.

'Oh, most likely negroid, old chap. I agree, some sort of native element. The old boys look positively swarthy,' a second man commented. 'But they play a ripping tune, don't they?'

'Luscious little thing, isn't she? Exotic — definitely a touch of the tarbrush there unless I'm very much mistaken.'

'Probably right. But what a terrible handicap. Poor girl — with a voice like that.'

'Oh, I don't know. They're feckless you know. Simple people, these darkies. I don't suppose she's particularly ambitious. They just love a good time.'

Ida turned to a block of stone. How dare they talk about her that way, when she was Mr Johns' star pupil! She should never have come, never ever got herself involved with such a hideous set of people.

Up until this moment, Ida had never really seriously considered what being 'different' might mean. Exotic, colourful, talented, maybe. Now she knew — not 'colourful', but 'coloured'. She was a 'native', touched with the tarbrush, a handicapped thing, simple, mentally deficient, without normal feelings.

It was utterly stupid of her — of course she had an awareness of a family tale, even a romantic pride in her Gran's stories of the music-hall and Grandpa Joseph. A touch of the tarbrush. In Baywater, in her claustrophobic, chaotic life, all that mattered very little. It was just a yarn like a million others. Gran's boarding-house was full of performers who accepted anyone unusual. African students came and went as lodgers, perfectly dressed and quiet, with their rolled umbrellas and their copies of *The Times*. School was a crowd of girls with socially dubious origins, Greek, Maltese, other southern Europeans. She fitted in. No wonder her Pa got her an expensive education. If she were poor and tarbrushed, she would have no chance . . . people called them 'darkies'. Natives.

Growing up meant learning hard truths, like the awful things her Ma said to her. Harvey Johns had given her some hope that she could change for the better. But what this party man said was altogether harsh, something she had avoided all her life. The world was against her.

Ida began to focus very sharply on her discovery. Aunt Josephine traded on looking exotic — and according to the stranger, she might too. Imagine if that was *all* she could do!

No wonder the Garlands stuck together. They were all tarred with the same brush — except for Jack. Ida stood up quickly, feeling chill from the dew under her, but colder inside, for certain family attitudes were clear to her now, like a prism turned in a shaft of light. She knew now why everyone was down on Jack. He was the first one among them who could unquestionably pass for white.

'Jack!' she called out, in a panic. He had gone off drinking somewhere — she had to talk to him — they had to talk about this properly, right this very minute. Ida took a deep breath, feeling dizzy but strangely clear-headed. The champagne had caused a sudden expansion of her understanding — secrets long hidden from her now seemed so obvious that they exploded in her head like fireworks.

They were shooting all over the sky: all colours of the rainbow. Rockets, catherine wheels, bangers darting across the Thames. It was an explosive display, childish luxury for the parting guests, who roared, bellowed and belched their way to their cars. Noise was one of the party's most memorable achievements: Ida had never heard pandemonium before.

Suddenly desperate, she ran about looking for Jack. Her uncles would all be in the bar, no doubt, making up for lost time. She peered through the french windows into the smoke.

Jack was sitting on a bar stool and a tottering sheikh with a cigarette holder was flirtatiously pouring whisky straight from a bottle down his throat. Jack spluttered and jack-knifed forward, laughing.

'That makes nine! You're winning my boy!' the Arab said in collegiate tones, and raising the bottle to his own lips, challenged him again.

Jack winked at Terence Bageshaw and Uncle George, both of whom were slumped against the wall, unable to do more than offer mute support with a titter or a weakly raised hand. Then he saw Ida coming in.

'Ida! Where've you been? This is Freddy. Say hallo to Freddy . . .' His words were slurred, and he held on to the older man's sleeve for support.

'So this is your big cousin,' Freddy murmured. 'Fine-looking girl!' he said, carelessly blowing smoke in Ida's face.

'Leave him alone!' she stormed, grabbing Jack by his sodden lapels.

'I say, what's the problem? Just a joke, just a joke . . .' Freddy the Sheikh shrugged and felt his way across the room, arms outstretched like a bedouin in a sandstorm.

Ida pulled Jack outside, into the garden again.

'Look at me! Look at me!' she demanded.

'What's up? Leave go! You're wrecking my tie!'

'Those things the boys at your church used to say — about me — on Sundays . . .'

Jack stopped struggling. 'Jesus. What's got into you?'

'Nigger. Darkie. Nig-nog. Was it that?' She punched him hard to make him listen.

'How the hell would I remember! What's the matter with you! No! It wasn't. I'd kill anyone who said that!'

'Someone just did — "Definitely native!"' she mimicked.

'What? Who! — I'll . . .' Jack was a Bayswater lout in an instant, spoiling for a fight.

'No!' Ida grabbed him again. 'Look at me! Look at me!' she repeated, hysterically. She seized his hand, almost crying at the sight of it, dirty yet white against her own. 'It's true, isn't it? It shows — on me, but not on *you*, it doesn't!'

'But you knew . . .' he said, his brain clearing slowly. 'You knew.'

'Grandpa.'

'What's all the fuss? It's history! Think of Ma! She's done all right. Stick with the family. They'll look out for you . . . more than they do for me . . .'

'I can't! Pa won't — why does Pa want me to do all these fancy things?' Tears were streaming down her cheeks, and she hit him again, futile little blows.

'Ssh,' said Jack, pushing her against a wall, sacrificing the white triangle of a linen handkerchief in his top pocket. 'Come on, old girl, blow.' He stroked her head, until her sobs subsided. 'I think,' he said slowly, frowning in an effort to talk properly, 'maybe Uncle Ted can tell you a thing or two . . .'

'Uncle Ted! Uncle Ted!' Ida called out, reacting at once, dragging Jack behind her unresisting.

They found the uncles playing cards in the billiard room. Uncle Ted responded to her distress, threw in his hand.

'What's up sunshine? Blotto again?' But he was only teasing.

'Ida's tired,' Jack said, offhand. 'Come on, we ought to go.'

'Quite right.' Ted agreed. 'Been a good show, though.' He steered them through the crowds to the drive outside the house. He found his car, a vintage AC large enough to carry men and several instruments. He unlocked it, sat Ida inside and gave her a blanket.

'Wait there Ida, I'll get Jim and the cases. Jack'll give me a hand — won't you lad?' He grabbed Jack by the collar and marched him back to the marquee.

Ida sat shivering under the rug, listening to the revellers going home. Nearby a car backed into another, metal buckled and glass fell in splinters. A girl's voice shrieked into giggles. Ida did not look out of the window. She breathed heavily on the pane so that it misted over and she could write her name. But the air inside the car was not very cold, and the mist faded as soon as she formed her letters. Headlamps swooped past the car, illuminating her brightly for a moment. A vehicle stopped alongside, and a friendly man's voice said:

'I say, you were smashing! Jolly good luck young lady!'

She did not reply. Gradually the car-park fell silent. The

uncles did not come — perhaps they were finishing their game, had actually forgotten about her, in spite of everything.

Ida was so tired she nearly passed out. Control snapped in her. She beat her hands on the steering wheel. 'I want it to stop! I want to go home! I want it to stop! Stop! Stop . . .' Her voice moved out of her body; it was another girl's voice screaming, and Ida knew that it would go on screaming in the darkness for ever and ever. This other voice had the monotonous energy of someone desperate, begging not just for the end of the party, but for the whole hard world to stop turning too. It was the cry of a frightened soul, lacking spirit, very small, a person she did not listen to very often . . . Her fists beat in rhythm — then Uncle Ted got in the car and held her tight.

'Ida! Cut it out! Gawd's sake!' Ted spoke with hostility and shoved her hard back against the passenger seat. He unhooked the roof and lowered it back. Cool air overcame her, Ida gasped, and shut up.

'We can't have this,' he said evenly, pulling her to his chest, relenting. 'Jack says you've been upsetting yourself. Some fool said something stupid. Well, you'll have to learn not to notice. You're a big girl now.'

'I'm so ashamed,' wailed Ida. 'I wish I was dead.'

'Don't say that! You're a great little singer! Your Pa's got it all planned. You're worth a lot Ida.' He hugged her, trying to force pride back into her. 'It's tough. I can't say it isn't. And Denise doesn't help, I admit.'

'Is this why she doesn't like me? Because — we're dark?' Ida asked, simply.

'Because we're *darkies*. You want the truth? Why not. She never meant to have you Ida. I was around when they met . . . She made a mistake. Now you've got to show her she was wrong. That's what your Pa wants. Get it?'

Ida, paralysed by this information, heard only one phrase, drumming in her head. Seeds of filth, seeds of filth . . .

A blast from a rocket above her head: as it cracked, so did her innocence. Exploded, then vanished, little burnt-out fragments of her heart.

'I'll show her,' she said.

'That's the ticket.'

Uncle Jim came running up. 'What's all the hurry?' he said, panting. Ted let go of her abruptly and started the engine.

'Girl's tired. Get in. It's been a long night.' Ted's voice was curt. Her uncles were not people for too much talk; they were legends from a childhood. Now she, too, was entering the myth.

Terence Bageshaw, sniffing, was tying his drum kit on to the spare-tyre shelf at the back of the car. He himself had to ride on Uncle George's second-hand motor bike, pillion seat. Uncle Jim and Jack sat with the double bass lodged between them in the back of the AC. Everyone fell silent, morose for lack of another drink. Ida sank low into her wool blanket and the car jerked forward into the night.

Naturally there was a family row as a result of the Palmer party. The Garlands involved gathered in Gran's parlour for a post-mortem, as Ted put it.

Earl was enraged that his next-eldest brother had acted so irresponsibly. 'I might have guessed you'd be stupid. You've done it before.'

'I always said so,' Denise added, sarcastic as ever. 'I've told you before, Ted's the one to watch. He's been a major source of bad influence on Jack and Ida, right from the start.'

'Aw, leave off, Denise. Kids have to grow up sometime. At Jack's age I was in Picardy, up to my neck in mud. What's so wrong with a bit of fun?'

Earl looked sensitive. Ted had come up with a perfect line of defence, mentioning his military service. 'Don't exaggerate. The boy's not yet fifteen,' he protested.

'Fifteen, sixteen, what's the difference? The principle's the same.' Ted frowned, untypically serious. 'Don't you lot take a high tone with me. We haven't done right by Jack. Just because he's got every advantage, regular whitey, blue eyes, and so forth. Doesn't mean he doesn't need a helping hand. It's no wonder he's a terror when you think how he's been . . .'

Now Josephine flared at him. 'It's none of your business! I did my best! What do you expect? It's easy for you to talk! Sidney — are you going to listen to this?' Ottley seated beside her reacted at once as if he might rise to his feet and throw a punch, as her protector. He had a very narrow view of manly behaviour.

'Don't try me, Ottley. Just don't try me.' Ted lit a cigarette with great deliberation.

Ottley's Adam's apple wobbled. Force was out of place; frustrated, he spat into the fireplace, slumped in his seat and murmured: 'It don't matter how many hidings I give him . . .'

In sympathy, Josephine brushed the specks of dust and dandruff from the back of Sidney's neck. Uncle Ted breathed disgust into the air in a cloud of smoke. 'I don't suppose you can think of any other tactic besides larruping him?'

Sidney looked at him with genuine surprise as if the thought had never crossed his mind.

Outside in the hall, Jack gave Ida a dig in the ribs. Mentally they were under the chenille table-cloth again, eavesdropping. Dot the maid was breathing hard over both of them.

'You come away from there,' Dot said, but she spoke the words too slow, so they knew she would not force them to go. Ida put a finger to her lips, and turned back to the conversation.

'Well,' said Gran. Her voice trembled more than usual — Ida and Jack looked at each other warily. They could not tell if her unsteady tone came from great anger, or an attack of old age. 'Jack's earning a living, which is more than can be said for a lot of boys these days. His way is clear. And Ida's always been a good girl. One night won't have done her that much harm. But what you did was wrong, Ted. Going against Earl's wishes.'

Earl looked satisfied with this judgement; Ida thought he had probably behaved the same when he won a point over Ted at the age of six. Gran soon took away his complacency.

'Personally, I'm not sure what Ida thinks about all this concert singing business. Have you ever asked her Earl? Really talked to her? I don't suppose you have . . .' she sighed.

Ida gave a shudder. Jack noticed. 'What's up? You cold?' he whispered gently, putting an arm round her.

'No. I'm not listening to any more.' She was not going to stand there, being discussed, one minute longer. There had been far too much of that recently. Too many truths, too many hurtful remarks.

She walked directly into the parlour. 'If you're going to discuss my future, then at least you might ask me in,' she said, plonking herself down on Uncle Jim's knee. He seemed to have escaped criticism for the party episode, but Ida's claim on him made him nervous that he too would be found guilty.

'Ooh, you are a big girl,' he said, with a nervous giggle.

'Ida! Get up at once!' Denise snapped.

Ida did as she was told, but in such a manner that it seemed her own choice. 'I do want to be a concert singer, Pa, and Harvey Johns has been very good for me. Do you know Gran, he wants to take me away to a fancy house in the country, so I can sing for some important people. His friends. So I must be good, mustn't I?'

'Well I never!' Gran exclaimed.

'What's this Earl? You never told me!' Denise had been caught unawares; surprise made an eyelash fall into her eye. In tears, she had to dig about with her long fingernails. Ida felt her spirits lifting; this was how to make her Ma regret her existence!

'I hadn't thought it over,' Earl said, but when he looked at Ida, she could see how relieved he was. This was the first time that Ida had side-stepped her mother, getting the rest of the Garlands to bear witness.

'I say!' Uncle Jim got up, cheerful now that good news had changed the family mood. 'This calls for a celebration!'

'Where's Jack? Send him down the road for a few beers,' Uncle Ted suggested.

Jack turned into the room slowly, and leant against the door frame. He looked at Ida and nodded in praise. 'Atta girl!' But his words were a little flat, and he went off to the pub looking muted. Perhaps he had hoped for a few more jazz dates . . .

'Of course,' Ida said, ignoring her Pa's warning cough and pushing her luck, 'I'm going to need a lot of things. It's lucky I got some wages from Mr Palmer, because I can buy my own bathroom things. I'll need a sponge bag, and a pair of slippers . . .'

'A toothbrush, more like it,' Uncle Ted said with a wink.

'Uncle Ted! I always clean my teeth!' Ida's dignity vanished: hands on hips, she glared at him. 'Better'n you, at least I use toothpaste, not gin! That's all you've got by the glass in your room!'

They all cackled and shrieked at that one, and the Palmer affair was forgotten.

6

Ida waited in the car as the taxi-driver carried her luggage to the stone steps: one embarrassing battered suitcase, plastered with hotel labels, lent by Uncle Ted. She tried to move graciously, hoping to look suitably adult and correct as Harvey Johns helped her out. Some wealthy opera patrons had financed the summer school for young singers in what seemed to Ida an ancient stately home. She had no idea where she was — somewhere south of London, but not near the coast. A picturesque herd of deer nibbled the trees and fat pheasants lumbered about fearlessly, not having heard a rifle shot in years.

'This way, Ida, I'll give you a quick tour. It's wonderful to be here again. Quite an old home to me . . .'

Harvey Johns took her suitcase and walked ahead, thoroughly at ease. Ida trotted a few steps to be close to him. She was surprised to find everything very basic. There was a baronial kitchen, but no servants: some of the students were buttering bread and making tea. Nearby was a very grand hall, covered in gilt and plaster, but the carpet was threadbare and metal seats were stacked up by the walls. On the middle floor the music tutors occupied the only reasonably appointed rooms. 'This is mine. Yours is up here.' Johns led her up another bare staircase to a set of boarded rooms that were the students' dormitories. Iron beds, like hospitals, and only a set of hangers on hooks, no shelves or cupboards.

'This is your room, I'll leave you to get sorted out, shall I? You come down for tea at four. In the kitchen. No standing on ceremony!'

Johns left her alone. Ida felt very shy. She put her suitcase down uncertainly on the bare boards, not assertive enough to claim a bed when none of the other girls had arrived. She looked out of the window, a lovely round one with a deep sill. The gardens were sadly unkempt, and the ornamental pond was covered in a vivid green substance. Fields round about looked more tended, full of ripening wheat.

She did not know what to do. Did Harvey Johns expect her to change clothes for tea? She tried to recall what he had said for a clue. She thought she might wash: people did that very often in proper circles she supposed.

'Hallo! I'm Veronica. What's your name?' A girl came in, leaving the door wide open.

'Ida.' She blushed, for she was in the act of unbuttoning her cardigan, and felt exposed.

'Been before?'

'No. Have you?'

'A couple of times. I'm practically tone-deaf, but we know the people who arrange these concerts. It's their house, actually — we used to come here for weekends when I was a girl. Before they lost their money.'

'Oh.' What else could she say to someone so comfortable? Veronica was evidently well-off, but her clothes had a nice wrinkled look, her heavy hair was attractively lopsided, and her voice warm and soft.

'What a pretty dress. Is that your afternoon frock from school?' Veronica asked with unaffected interest. She was rich enough to go to boarding-school, but not offensively stuck-up like others of her type. Ida was surprised.

'No.' Ida was about to say that it was her one best dress of the moment, courtesy of Gran and Allaine's once again, but that sounded too mundane.

'Gosh you should see what we have to wear on Sundays. It's got this huge white collar — makes you feel like a nun! I'd hate to be a nun, wouldn't you? Thick bloomers, for the rest of your life . . .'

Ida had never given the subject of underwear very much thought — négligés, as in films, perhaps had been the subject of fantasy, but as to her own personal choice . . .

'Cami-knickers! In pink silk. With cream-coloured lace all round the legs,' she suggested, inspired. 'That's what I want when I grow up. Not rayon or anything like that.'

'Pink . . .' Veronica thought for a moment. 'I've got a yen for a silvery grey petticoat. Imagine, with white lace over it.'

'No — White chiffon!' Ida dared to disagree. 'Like Ruth Chatterton in *Sins of the Fathers*. I saw that film four times.'

'Did you? Lucky thing! I wasn't allowed . . .' Mutual admiration was developing.

'My Aunt Josephine gets me in. The ticket lady at the Silver Cinema is a personal friend of hers. My aunt's a singer too — but not this kind of thing . . . on the stage, you know. Musicals, dancing.' Ida was diffident about revealing these facts but she liked Veronica and decided to take the risk.

'Gosh. So you're a bit of a professional then. How old are you?'

'Sixteen. I'm only just beginning.' Ida was embarrassed, for she had not meant to show off; she could not tell whether Veronica was truly impressed or just sounding politely enthusiastic. Harvey Johns was her only previous contact with a world where people did not say exactly what they meant.

'Which bed do you want?' Ida asked. She stood by her suitcase in the middle of the room so that her question had no prejudice in it.

'Oh Lord, I don't mind. At home I sleep on the floor most nights with my dog, my chum, and at school I sleep with twenty other girls. You choose!'

'Could I have the window, then?'

'Certainly! Go on, get it before the third girl comes, whoever she is.'

'All right. Then shall we go down for tea? I'm very thirsty.' If Veronica changed, then so would she.

The other girl pulled off her clothes and rummaged in her suitcase, quite nude. It was so strange to see limbs perform domestic actions, without the cover of the right clothes to lend efficiency. Veronica's breasts bounced rather pathetically as she tossed out her belongings. Ida was embarrassed and felt her heart begin to thump. Veronica looked so very beautiful, all creamy white with a puff of black curls between her thighs. Ida could have stared for ever; she had never seen another girl utterly naked. Her school did not encourage that sort of thing.

'There's a stream round the back of the house, and a bit of a pool by the bank. Come and have a swim first!' Veronica suggested.

'I haven't got a costume,' Ida confessed.

'That means you don't know how to, I expect,' Veronica said uncritically. 'Never mind, this is a really good place to try. I'll show you. Never let a boy teach you how. They always play tricks. I should know. My brothers were horrible and I nearly drowned twice. Look, you wear this one, and I'll put on my leotard, I brought it just in case.'

'I couldn't do that . . .' Borrowing was a forbidden thing — Ida did not know how to do it without being 'beholden', according to Gran's code.

'I'd have a much better time if you came too. It's so boring being on one's own.'

'All right then.' Ida pulled out her new dressing gown from her old suitcase, a silk wrap with brilliant oriental embroidery. Uncle Ted had brought it back from the East for some girlfriend but gave it to Ida in honour of her advancement and to make up for the Palmer fiasco. She undressed swiftly underneath it.

'Ooh! How pretty! Gosh, you look like . . .' words seem to freeze on Veronica's lips.

'What?' Ida asked, cheerfully. 'Like what?' She stood up, holding the robe self-consciously round her shoulders. 'Not like Madame Butterfly . . .' she smiled, baring her teeth in mischief, a row of slightly gappy teeth that made her look like a happy mouse.

'It's the colours . . .'

'I'm very dark.' Ida said it first, said it at once. 'It runs in the family.' (What a handicap! With a voice like that! The words whispered in her brain.)

'Come on, or we'll miss the sun,' Veronica said, giving up whatever passing thought she had and running out of the room. 'Do hurry!'

Ida followed, bouncing on the steps as Veronica did, as if she owned the house. On the ground floor she could hear someone playing unfamiliar music on a piano, and a small group of male voices singing, recognisably Verdi, in another room. She was excited by this new world, and followed Veronica straight down a back corridor and out the kitchen door with increasing confidence. She tried to catch up with her new friend, who ran pretty fast, shaking her black hair loose from its ribbon.

On the lawn at the side of the house Ida stopped for breath just for a second and heard another taxi. Pulling her silk wrap tight about her, she looked back and saw the angel-haired girl, Janet, step out and Harvey Johns run forward to welcome her.

'Oh bugger,' Ida was furious. Pa had said she was the only one of Johns' students being taken to the summer school and Mr Johns himself had not mentioned the girl as they travelled down. Supposing that creature was the third person in their room. Ida ran to the back lawn, to the pool. Veronica was such a wonderful discovery that she was determined not to let this unpleasant incident spoil her first day.

Veronica had plunged in, swirling forward through the water without effort. Ida thought that falling in love must be just like she felt now: this seeing of grace and sensation of pleasure in everything a stranger did. She lowered herself into the water and bobbed up and down a few times, kicking her legs out, but her body remained resolutely vertical.

'Mmm.' Veronica looked doubtful. 'Well, try floating on your back, just to get the feel of it. You do stay up, eventually. It's all a question of believing you will. I'll hold you. And I swear I won't let you go.'

Ida kicked her legs up, Veronica held her underneath, and the two girls floated round in circles.

'I'm floating! I'm floating!' Ida cried out, and Veronica began to bounce her body a little in the water, so that for a few seconds at a time Ida did not feel contact with her firm hands.

'You'll do it before the end of the week!' Veronica said. If it would earn this girl's pleasure, Ida swore she would.

'Hallo! Tea time!' A man's voice resounded in the warm, absorbent air, and a male silhouette against the sun walked towards them.

Ida shivered. She recognised Harvey Johns and was reminded of his new arrival. She had avoided the other girl, Janet, for three years, ever since her first concert. Without words on the subject, the two girls had set themselves up as rivals.

Johns came nearer as Veronica swam a little showily back to the edge of the pool. He looked more attractive in the countryside; his usual baggy trousers, sleeveless sweater and a worn shirt made him appear relaxed rather than untidy, and the ubiquitous pipe added a jaunty note. 'Would you mind awfully walking ahead of us, Mr Johns? I'm wearing a rag of a thing and I'm hardly decent.'

Harvey Johns was much amused by Veronica's suggestion that the sight of her youthful body would inflame him. He was kind enough to take her seriously and walked ahead without sneaking a backward glance. Ida thought that was nice of him.

Veronica followed with Ida: 'I shouldn't let on that you've never swum before,' she whispered, 'or he might not let us go near the water by ourselves again.'

'You remind me of my cousin Jack,' Ida whispered back. 'Brilliant in tight corners.'

'I've got two brothers! And I get into loads of trouble at school.' Veronica confessed, shrugging her shoulders to indicate a dismal educational record, but some training in resourcefulness. Ida doubted that she was as hopeless as she made out, and became suddenly curious about her singing voice. She would have to ask Mr Johns when they had a moment. This overlaid thoughts of Janet as they hurried back to their room. Consequently she reacted with surprise when she saw the very girl unpacking in their room.

'Ah! It's — Ida Garland, isn't it?' Janet said, for confirmation, not really as a welcome.

'Yes. And you're Janet Sheldon.'

For a moment Veronica watched them. Ida supposed she was wondering if they were old friends and whether she would be left out. Ida busied herself with her clothes, hoping that Veronica would sense they were not at all close.

'Gosh, that's a good name,' Veronica said. 'It will look good on posters, a name like that. Janet Sheldon.' She waved her hand, mapping the word across the room.

'I do hope not.' Janet's tone was even, as if to tell them both that she was considerably older then they were and unlikely to share their fantasies.

'Aren't you ambitious at all?' Veronica was not easily squashed.

Janet sighed at her persistence. 'I'd like to be considered good, but fame is rather vulgar and a dreadful imposition on one's life,' she said.

('You'd never have the choice,' Ida thought darkly.)

'What about you, Ida? Your name's pretty starry too . . .' Veronica drew her into the conversation.

'Yes, but better for neon, not printed programmes.' Ida laughed at herself.

'You could always change it,' Veronica persisted, 'but I think it's very pretty. What's Garland in Italian?'

'*Ghirlanda*,' Janet supplied tonelessly.

'Mmm.' Veronica considered it.

'Sounds like an acrobat!' Ida began to giggle, annoyed with herself, for she was giving Janet the advantage. But then she stopped, for an Italian name might indeed be good for her — considering her looks. After all, Melba had created a foreign name for herself out of her unlikely birthplace, Melbourne. It was the fashion among great divas to have romantic names.

'Ready?' Veronica asked the room at large.

'Yes,' Ida joined her, and for a second they both looked back, in case Janet would come too.

'I'll be down in a moment,' she said.

Harvey Johns was waiting for them at the foot of the stairs. 'You've met Janet — she hadn't expected to come, her mother has been ill. Jolly glad she could though. My star pupils!' He took Ida's arm in a kindly way. 'Veronica's a wonderful character. You'll get on with her very well,' he murmured.

Veronica had already inserted herself in a long queue for buns, tea and bread, and was waving for Ida to join her.

'She knows the ropes,' Johns grinned, and pushed Ida forward. 'Go on. Enjoy yourself.'

'Aren't you going to sit with us . . . ?' Ida's words were lost and he walked off. In front and behind them in the line musical conversations made a hubbub, like an orchestra tuning. One listed the virtues of a particular mender of violins; another spoke of a recent operatic performance and discussed 'rallentandi' and 'rubato'. Someone else demonstrated a point with a snatch of song, unafraid to be overheard, and then a pile of music-stands crashed off a bookcase. The faded country house and its enthusiastic guests were perfectly matched in a scruffy English cheerfulness; echoes filled the bare-floored room, voices and scraping chairs sounding loud and unharmonious.

The girls found a window-seat overlooking the stream and pool where they had swum. Ida munched her bun. Veronica was silent too: boarding-school habits persisted and she ate possessively like a prisoner afraid of losing his food ration.

They both looked up when they saw Janet conversing in the doorway with Harvey Johns. Ida was smitten with jealousy, and then suddenly began to dread her first semi-public performance.

'She'll change rooms,' Veronica said.

'Why?'

Veronica laughed, a forced, knowing sound.

'Let's just call it a matter of taste,' she said.

'Why? Because we're younger than her?' Ida was still puzzled.

'That's it,' Veronica agreed flatly, but Ida suspected there was something else.

She struggled with her first impressions. After tea the crowd gathered for a welcoming talk by the organiser, Mrs Rose. Ida learnt she was to have a class with Mr Johns every morning, a group master class with a distinguished soprano whose name she did not quite catch, a musical appreciation session at noon, and a general dance and expression class in the afternoons. The concerts would take place on the following Thursday, Friday and Saturday nights. Sunday would be devoted to an excursion to a place nearby of historic interest and then she would be free to go home.

'Honestly, it sounds worse than it is,' Veronica whispered, seeing the appalled expression on Ida's face.

Ida felt a wave of homesickness at the thought of so much culture in one week. She was tired, ate little at supper, the repetitive impersonality of meals in a crowd making her withdraw. She had not realised that Mr Johns would be so distant — occasionally he smiled across at her, nodding encouragement when he saw her talking to Veronica. She began to see him in a new light, surrounded by others of his kind. He was very popular; he told good jokes; people listened to him eagerly and loud laughter came from the animated group at his end of a long table. Ida felt quite proud of him.

Then she began to hanker for his attention. She had not realised that she would be dropped in the deep end, left to fend for herself socially. Veronica was a great bonus, but Ida had hoped

Mr Johns would whisper things to her, explain who was who and what was what. For example, she had no idea how 'important' everyone was. The music school appeared so rough and ready, not grand at all. Ida felt uneasy, because distinction obviously lurked beneath the bluff appearance of things, and she could not measure it at all.

Veronica obviously knew a thing or two. When they went to bed, they discovered Janet had disappeared.

'I told you!' she said, with a bitter exasperation. 'Well. I can't say I'm sorry. I'm more at ease with just you.'

Ida blushed, because it was wonderful to be liked by someone for whom she felt such an instant sympathy. She wanted to ask more about Janet's departure, but the hardness of Veronica's reaction made her decide to leave questions till later.

'I like to read in bed,' Veronica said. 'Will the light bother you? Or we could sit up and talk if you like.'

'I don't mind the light, but I'm cold, and that makes me tired. I'll pull the covers over my head. It's freezing in here,' Ida said. Cold and heat were reflections of a state of mind in her. If she felt depressed or unsure of herself, it was as if her body temperature fell. She curled up, shivering under unfamiliar, thin blankets. 'Goodnight.' She'd faced up to enough new things for one day.

Madame Amate brought further surprises, next morning. An aging Italian singer, trained at the same Parisian school as Harvey Johns, she had come to England to show off her star pupil, Emilio Brin, a young operatic tenor whose repertoire she was building up.

'Emilio thinks this little country house is so strange and cold!' Madame Amate laughed at her class of girls, huddled on a disappointingly dull Monday morning in one of the barer rooms. 'I don't think he's impressed. I told him, wait till Thursday night, wait till your audience listens in silence, ready to frown, at every single note!'

'Won't they like us, Madame?' Ida could not help asking. Madame Amate's soft, chattered English encouraged forwardness. She noticed Janet's hands tighten in her lap, disapproving.

Madame Amate laughed, shaking her head. 'You misunderstand! My English is not very good . . . Perhaps your teacher doesn't like to frighten you too much. You are Harvey's, aren't you?'

Ida nodded, blushing because she had not meant to draw attention to herself.

'They'll be critical, difficult, but very good for you. And somebody may remember you. There will be agents, an opera company representative, a few patrons . . . who knows. Now, to business.'

'I'm going to help you with the "habanera" from *Carmen*. The opera is popular, and those of you who will sing it in concert must concentrate most particularly on character and expression. If you intend to make a big voice for the stage then you must also be good actresses too. I am an opera singer, so I can only teach you what I know!'

Ida's thoughts were focused at once. If only she could go home with some impressive report for her Ma and Pa. So much promise, and as yet so little result. She began to feel impatient, her timidity dissolving into excitement.

She glanced at Veronica, who was as relieved by Madame Amate's friendliness as she was herself, and they both settled down to work.

On the night of the first concert Ida was dressing when Veronica came into their bedroom carrying a large bag.

'I asked Mother to bring these. I thought perhaps . . .'

'What is it?'

'Two dresses. She hired costumes for us, for our duet. We don't have to wear them if you don't want — but Madame Amate agrees, so don't worry about her.'

'They must have been very expensive . . .'

'Well, actually mine was, but yours was nothing — it's just a simple maid's dress.'

'But it's beautiful!' Ida held up the silk stripes.

'So you'll wear it . . .'

'If you really want me to.'

'And look, she just happened to stick these in. I thought you might like to wear one when you do Mr Johns' new songs. Don't if you can't bear the idea of borrowing, but really, I just want to crush the competition! Don't you?'.

Veronica had such charm, it was difficult not to do just as she said. 'The competition', Janet Sheldon, was already furious that Ida had been given Harvey's new solo compositions to sing, because she had not been expected to attend. To have something confidence-inspiring to wear would help Ida to ignore her baleful face.

Veronica threw three silk crêpe dresses on the bed, blue, black, a rich dark maroon. Ida began unbuttoning her latest Allaine creation. As she laid it aside she felt disloyal.

'My Gran got me this one specially.' Suddenly it looked all wrong, too many frills in an effort to be smart.

'Just as you prefer. It doesn't matter, really.'

Veronica's not insisting made the offer more tempting.

'I suppose I could just try one on.'

'Which colour do you like best?' Her friend spread the skirts of the dresses, like big fans.

'The deep blue.'

Veronica's parents sat in the front row of the golden salon, on the seats reserved for important guests. Ida studied them through the open door of the rehearsal room. She saw at once that Mrs Summers was exactly the type her Ma tried to imitate: cool and expensive. She wore a long black dress and a tiny hat with an assertive coquetry in its veiling. When people were introduced to her, she paid attention, replying in conversation with great care, allowing their presence to take effect. Languid and confident.

Mr Summers was much older than his wife, and hovered about her in a way that fascinated Ida as much as Mrs Summers did herself. In Ida's world men did not show affection without being diminished by it — like her Pa. She stared at Mr Summers, bending very close to his wife, touching her arm, whispering seriously in her ear.

The room was filling up. To Ida's pleasure real candles had been arranged all around the room, replacing most of the electric lights. All the curtains had been taken down, leaving great arcs of black glass, to make it easier for the singers (Ida knew how much draperies absorbed sound and forced a singer to strain for effect). The event was taken seriously enough for no one to be allowed to smoke.

Harvey Johns came to find Ida. She had never seen him in evening dress, and it brought home the importance of the event. *He* looked really rather handsome in an effete, English way; *she* could not help blushing at his unguarded stare at her dress.

'My goodness! Where did you get that?' he said, his surprise implying it was far too expensive and elegant for the likes of her.

'Veronica's mother brought it down with her, and some lovely costumes for our duet . . . is it all right?'

Harvey Johns had difficulty in finding a reply. He was totally thrown by a discovery. His humble Ida had the most nubile, succulent body: sweet, high breasts, just the size to cup in one's hand; a skin that made you want to take off all her clothes; and those strange, wild eyes, that never gave away all their secrets . . . He had never seen her as anything other than a promising protégée, a great voice in a slightly distasteful exterior. Blue crêpe, a night-time colour, sophisticated and subdued, had transformed her. Clothes maketh man, he thought, aware that he had taken her for granted, and not noticed her growing up. He would have to rethink his plans, he realised, irritated, before a certain person got big ideas . . .

'You look very lovely. Very lovely.' His dismissive tone was half intentional. 'Now remember, keep the tempo steady in the first song, won't you? Now, I must have a quick word with Janet.'

Ida was disappointed in his lack of enthusiasm, and stood alone, listless, vacant.

Madame Amate hovered in the room; she was straightening Emilio Brin's cravat like a devoted mother, but at the same time taking note of other exchanges about her. Ida was aware of her eyes, and grew even more self-conscious when the great lady summoned her to a corner.

'Don't sit down, you'll crease that beautiful gown. I may not have a chance to talk to you later this evening — there will be others who will claim you!'

Ida was grateful for her kind words. 'That's very kind of you, Madame Amate. But my family haven't come.'

Madame Amate brushed aside this information. 'You know why he spoke that way about your gown? Harvey? Mr Johns?' Madame Amate was abrupt.

'No.'

'Because he's jealous. Not of the dress, my dear. Of the Summerses. The father is wealthy, and Jewish. The English are funny about the Hebrew race. I thought perhaps you should know this. It isn't because you don't look pretty. You do. You look stunning — that deep blue, your big dark eyes, your lovely hair!'

'Veronica fixed it up for me,' Ida said, embarrassed by Madame Amate's frankness. Then it occurred to her that perhaps Janet Sheldon had moved out of their room because she too did not like 'the Hebrew race'. Another reason to hate her . . .

'But Mr Johns was glad that I made friends with Veronica! I thought he'd . . .' her voice trailed away. Of course: they were both outsiders.

'He wanted you to have a good time! Perhaps I should not have spoken . . . Harvey will positively adore you after this evening!'

Could there be a small threat in Madame Amate's voice? She patted Ida's cheek, and her dark eyes gleamed suggestively.

'You're so young. Don't be scared, I think you will have a good life . . . You are very talented, Eeda.'

Harvey Johns had told Ida that many singers did not speak for hours — even a day — before performing. She now wished she had been able to do the same, to stay in her room and avoid all these criss-crossing verbal currents.

Banging chair legs and a spate of clapping warned them all that the chamber orchestra was taking its place. Veronica appeared quickly beside her but Ida put her finger to her lips. She only needed her friend to be near her to feel reassured and happy about herself.

After a little Haydn from the strings, Janet Sheldon sang a song by Giordano. Ida listened carefully, understanding why her rival might mind desperately that Harvey had transferred his attentions (professionally speaking) to her instead. Janet's perfect, clear voice suited his cool, complex songs. She had meticulous diction, a smooth range from middle to top register, and a correctness in her phrasing. All Harvey's pupils were noted for their diction — English singers did not often learn to pronounce French and Italian so accurately. Madame Amate had been pleased with both Ida and Janet on that score, but she obviously preferred Ida because she was the better actress; Ida disliked Janet because she was such a snobby little puritan — and not only in her voice.

A tenor and a baritone sang a duet from the last act of *La Bohème*. Ida did not listen to it or the piano solo that followed, because after that, she would have to give the first performance of Harvey Johns' latest compositions.

Warm applause for the pianist. It was her turn. Panic and nausea rose up in Ida's body, making her hot and trembly. She stepped forward, afraid of tripping in her unfamiliar long dress. Somewhere in her terrified thoughts a warm rough voice spoke up at her: I give you Miss Ida Garland — Gran on a Friday night. She looked at the audience, reduced to dots of glossy, civilised eyes, their eyebrows raised in interest like a row of question marks: Well, who do you think *you* are? Harvey Johns finished his introduction on the piano, but Ida failed to open her mouth.

The heavy silence of the room rolled forward like a giant wave: only Ida could hear that roar of tension.

'Please can you start again, Mr Johns?' she asked him as loudly as she could. The wave receded, and in the emptiness it left behind, Ida's voice poured forth.

There were three songs, not a suite, but no one responded in between them. Ida was not disconcerted by the silence, because Harvey Johns had warned her this could happen. The music was unfamiliar to the audience, with hints of sensual, jazzy harmonies, and sudden 'hot' intonations. Normally, Ida found it odd and uncomfortable to sing this classily controlled composition on a blues, with Harvey's dissonant accompaniment. But tonight she poured her feelings into it, and for once, it sounded exciting, as original in effect as he intended.

Her final notes died away. Again a silence, in which Ida panicked, thinking they all hated her. She looked quickly at Harvey Johns, and understood that it was the lull that comes when someone has made a deep impression. He stared at her; if she had not known better, she would have thought he was in love with her then. His expression was one of intense possessiveness, as if she were a beautiful prize that he wanted to seize. Ida was overcome with excitement — could it be that he *did* value her? That she was important to him?

The room erupted in loud clapping, and she hurried from the side of the piano, her eyes filling with tears of relief.

But Harvey Johns was terribly cool when he came up to her in the interval. 'Well done Ida. Pity about the fluff at the beginning . . . we'll have to work on that. Have you seen Janet?' He hurried away, and took with him all her satisfaction.

The rest of the evening passed in a nervous blur. She and Veronica sang their duet, the letter scene from *Figaro*, with herself as Suzanna and Veronica as the Countess. They sang in their hired costumes towards the end of the second half, by which time the audience was entirely relaxed, and did not mind that Veronica cracked on a note, and Ida wobbled because she was over-acting. Emilio Brin brought the evening to a fine conclusion singing a heart-rending solo from Donizetti's *L'Elisir d'Amore*. Madame Amate had trained him well; the tenor could adjust his big operatic voice not to sound too hard in a smaller concert room. Ida was proud to have performed in such company.

When the final applause died away, Veronica hugged Ida, then led her straight to her father.

'Here she is!' she said with pride. Mr Summers bowed a little and put out a hand to grasp Ida's firmly.

'We all thought you were marvellous. I have to say that you managed to get this young delinquent here, my daughter, to sing better than I have ever heard her sing in my life. I'm grateful to you for that too. You must wait here with me, and meet my wife.'

Ida nodded dumbly, wishing that her hand did not feel clammy with nerves in his confident grasp.

'I wasn't so good,' she said. 'I've never sung formally before . . .'

'Harvey Johns no doubt has great plans for you,' Mr Summers went on. 'His songs were — interesting. He seems to have tutored you to be the perfect exponent of them. Reminds me of Poulenc, just a little, but of course they're very English, less decadent. I'm not wildly keen on modern music . . .'

Ida had heard Harvey Johns expound in this way before, and could at least nod with familiarity.

'I don't really find it too difficult,' she said, attempting to chat. 'I just listen until I hear something in the sounds . . . shapes, meanings. Then the words sort of work by themselves . . .'

'Mmm.' Mr Summers looked pleased. 'A natural talent. A true singer's explanation.'

Veronica interrupted. 'Mother's busy with Mrs Rose. Can't we get a drink and come back later?' Ida began to sense the battle. Veronica wanted her exclusive friendship (she could not think why!), but she was too tied to her parents not to want them to admire her 'discovery'.

'No, that won't do at all.' Mr Summers still had a discreet hold on Ida's hand. A nod summoned a waiter. 'I think champagne is appropriate. You too Veronica. Here's to your success, young ladies.' He let go so that Ida could enjoy his toast.

Harvey Johns pushed through the crowd to join them.

'Ida! There you are!' Curtness revealed his aggression. Seizing a glass from the passing tray he drank from it in one gulp. 'Apologies for the weed,' he added, lighting a cigarette.

'I'll join you,' said Mr Summers, pulling out a very fat cigar. He now looked irredeemably like a very wealthy Hebrew, and Harvey Johns recoiled at the sight. Ida read her teacher's thoughts, and was upset that Madame Amate had made her aware of her idol's faults.

'So. What next, young lady?' Mr Summers asked her.

'I don't know sir, it's for Mr Johns to decide . . .'

Mrs Summers overheard this last remark as she came up to the group. 'How very sweet you are,' she said. 'Mr Johns must be pleased to have such an obedient pupil. Most sensible.' More praise followed, like the edgy purring of a cat.

Ida did not fully absorb the rest of the conversation, it was all too overwhelming. Mr Summers talked about a private concert at his house. Financing further studies. Mrs Summers murmured about how lovely she looked, how they ought to go to Paris, her Veronica and Ida, buy clothes, see the sights . . .

'Ida has only just started to sing in public,' Harvey insisted. 'We mustn't move too fast.'

'But you like it, don't you? You enjoy an audience?' Mr Summers demanded. 'You certainly look as if you do.'

'I don't know . . .' Ida felt inarticulate, over-examined in this verbal tug of war. 'Well, no. I can't say enjoy it, exactly, because waiting to go on is so awful . . . but when I'm doing it, I forget everything else. That's a nice feeling . . .'

'If you don't mind, I think these girls should go to bed,' Harvey Johns interrupted. 'They have another concert tomorrow. And I have to rehearse Ida again. She wasn't too sure of some sections . . .' He was looking critical again.

'Good-night, dear girl. We'll see you in London very soon. We'll most certainly arrange something before you leave here. I'll speak to you in the morning, Veronica.' Mr Summers gave his daughter a hug, and she nodded obediently.

'Good-night Daddy.'

Two quiet young women went up to the top floor. It was a relief to be alone together, and not to talk too much.

'Daddy was awfully impressed,' Veronica said, a little reluctantly.

Ida was so overwrought that she dropped her dress in a heap on the floor and took to her bed without bothering to wash. She watched as Veronica, not fastidious as a rule, picked up the blue crêpe and hung it up for her.

'Sorry,' Ida said quickly. 'How could I forget!' It came to her that in less than a week she had grown so well used to this girl that she could be wholly herself in ways that were unthinkable at home. Denise forced a deliberate, mean tidiness from her out of revenge, not virtue. Ida lay still, thinking of her family, a world apart from her now.

'Does Jack mind about you becoming a singer?' Veronica asked. She sat on the edge of Ida's bed. Her face was strained, the question too casually presented.

'How funny you should mention him!' Ida was unnerved by this coincidence. Up until this moment she had only related a few silly pranks about her cousin but no doubt Veronica had guessed how fond of him she was. Just now Ida thought of Jack with conflicting emotions. Nostalgia for their closeness, envy because he was so much bolder then she was, and a certain hostility, because of the tarbrush . . . 'He might be jealous. He wouldn't like all this. Including you! He'd behave like an oaf. Maybe not. He is proud of me, is Jack.'

Veronica rolled a bit of her night-dress into a pleat between her fingers, nervous, trying to sound casual. 'Is he the only one in your family you care about? No one else? No one who'll mind if you . . .'

There was something important behind this questioning. All at once Ida saw clearly what was going on.

'You mean, you want to know if I'm prepared to leave it all behind? My awful Ma, my bad uncles, the music, the lodgers . . . not to mention the drink. I've told you everything! Did your Pa tell you to ask me?'

Veronica looked up suddenly and her eyes were full of tears. 'I wish he wouldn't do it. I lose everyone to him in the end. Perhaps I should be the one, but honestly, I couldn't bear it, trying to please Daddy all the time, trying to pretend I'm the best when I'm jolly well not.'

All this was too much for Ida. She was old enough to catch the implications of Veronica's words, but not old enough to see her own way forward. She understood something of Veronica's anxiety, for she too had been pushed into a career by her Pa. But Mr Summers had real influence. He could pull strings and turn a person into anything he wanted. Perhaps Veronica's best defence was to be sure she was unworthy of his interest.

'It's not the same for me,' Ida said. 'I mean, Pa wants me to do well, but he can't force me. He hasn't got the power. He's strict, but I think he means well . . .' Earl Garland was not Mr Max Summers . . . Ida began to wonder if her Pa was perhaps a weak man, but the thought upset her and she pushed it aside.

Imagine Mr Summers turning his attention to her, the latest in a long line of protégées! Ida was impressed by their proprietary manners. Both he and his wife made it clear they had little time for Mr Johns. He'd been very cross, jealous even. But then, he had also been pretty mean about her performance . . . perhaps she was not as good as they thought she was.

'Veronica, whatever happens, I mean, even if your father

135

isn't pleased with me in the end . . . could you still be my friend?'

Veronica took herself to bed. 'I'd try. But it won't be like that. You'll see . . .'

They both fell silent again. Ida was more perturbed by Veronica's deflated manner than by thoughts of fame ahead. She lay still, imagining the moment when she would relate all this splendour to her Ma and Pa. Gran would sit back in her rocking chair impassive as usual. Jack would prop up the door, murmuring: I knew you'd do it, atta girl . . . ! but give her a sad smile too, because each of her triumphs meant they grew further apart.

Ida listened. Unlike other evenings Veronica had fallen asleep first. It seemed like an act of betrayal to be glad that she, Ida, was still awake, alone with her thoughts. Veronica was the first person outside her family circle to whom she had made a strong attachment, and now all this drama with Mr Summers made her doubt the friendship. Then there was Harvey Johns: he had been behaving oddly all evening. Pleased one minute, cold the next. Was there anyone she could trust?

In spite of exhaustion, Ida could not sleep. She was annoyed with herself about the mistake at the beginning of the song cycle. But when she stopped singing, Mr Johns had looked so — so proud of her. More than proud, just for a moment . . . *smitten*. Then why was he so cool with her after the performance? Ida began to feel quite scared that she was losing her bearings, being swept along into situations beyond her grasp.

Then it came to her that she really needed Harvey Johns. All week she had been pining for his company, his acceptance. How could she possibly go forward with all these concerts and interesting developments if he was not in her corner, supporting her? This was the first time she had been away from home, with no one to fall back on. No Uncle Jim explaining people's wicked ways, no Uncle Ted to whisk her off when the going got too hot. No Jack to say something basic, pretending so hard that he was worldly wise.

Here she was, all alone, surrounded by cultured voices and unreadable signals of privilege, and the strain was beginning to make her crack. She just had to talk to Harvey Johns.

Ida pulled on her silk wrap and crept out of the room, padding noiselessly down the corridor. She felt the dust clinging to her hot, bare feet, and saw that her footsteps left clean patches on the wooden floor. Perhaps she should not go to his room at this hour . . . but as Ida crept on, she realised she knew exactly what she wanted from her tutor. She wanted him to be just a little bit attracted to her. Surely she had not been wrong about the way he looked at her tonight. Did he mean that she was — a *woman*? The kind of woman he might actually be able to love?

She could hear a few people still moving about downstairs, clearing up. Holding her breath, seated on the middle landing, Ida listened hard, identifying the voices. Harvey Johns was not among them.

She moved quickly along the first floor corridor to his room, and with a soft tap on the door, opened it and let herself in. Johns was lying on the bed, fully clothed, smoking and reading a magazine.

'Ida! What's the matter! What are you . . .' His tutor's voice failed as he took full stock of the robe she was wearing.

'Mr Johns. Oh, what am I to do!' she rushed forward and flung herself upon him.

At first he behaved impeccably. He sat up and pulled her gaping wrap more tightly to her neck, before jumping up and fetching her a cooling glass of water.

'Drink a little of this. What about an Aspro? I'm not surprised you're, er, over-excited. But really Ida, should you have come to me like this? It's awfully late. Couldn't we talk in the morning?'

Obediently, Ida folded the silk around herself more modestly and stared at him, mute, innocently pleading.

There was an element of calculation in her. She decided that complete honesty might disarm him. Her intuition was so strong that she decided to trust it. Act boldly. If Jack were a girl, this was what he would be doing . . . After all, everyone was up to it at the Palmer party. Smart people did it. Not just furtive people, like her Ma. An ache for acceptance drove her on.

'Mr Johns. I have to tell you everything! You know Mr Summers wants to take me on, oh, how do you say, it's not managing me exactly . . .'

'He wants to be your benefactor.'

'There you are! You've always told me the right words, haven't you, Mr Johns?' She smiled, in tears of admiration.

'If we must continue this conversation, which I'm not at all sure is the right thing to do in the middle of the night, then I insist you call me Harvey. Can you do that, do you think?'

His eyelids fluttered a little; for an instant Ida saw the vanity in him, the enjoyable exercise of the power he held over her. But then his eyes lowered to the softness of her breasts filling out folds of silk. This gave her the courage to take the next step. Was she seducing him, or was he leading her on? This was another of the night's questions which she could not begin to answer.

'Mr Johns. Harvey. You know I'm sure that my family are a little bit, how shall I say it? *Coloured*? Not on my mother's side. My father, and his father . . . I've never spoken about it to you. Some people say such stupid things . . . will it matter, Mr Johns, I mean, Harvey — does it spoil anything? I have to know. I had to tell you. Of all people . . . ?'

He straightened up, fascinated, and stood over her with his hands bolted deep in his pockets.

Three lessons a week, for three years . . . there were few nuances in his facial expression that Ida could not interpret before he hid them, and she studied him closely. She saw his reactions, one by one: embarrassment; curiosity; prurient attention; mild sadness; a revival of interest and finally, nonchalance.

'It has often crossed my mind, obviously. You're . . . of a suggestive complexion. And there's a slight timbre, a shading in your voice that sometimes bothers me, but on the whole I like it.'

'I don't just mean in my voice! Harvey — what will people think of me, as a — as a person? I mean, *personally*?' Her rather desperate desires made her tremble. What if she had miscalculated? Suppose she disgusted him. Suppose he sent her back to bed, like a stupid child.

He smiled. A slightly unpleasant atmosphere came over him. 'You did notice the way I looked at you tonight! I wondered. You want to know if this makes any difference to my feelings for you . . . is that it? Well well, Ida. If I've made a mistake about you, it was not to see that you were ready for love long before I thought of it.' He lifted her chin, and in a cool, savouring way, kissed her.

Ida responded, but she was disappointed. His lips were wet (she expected that), but not as fierce as she might have wished her first man's lips to be. They smelled of smoke. On the other hand, he was an important person not just to her, but to many other people. A composer. She put her arms round his neck and drew him down to sit beside her. Harvey pulled himself free and sat back on the pillows, considering her. How cool and elegant he looked.

'Has anyone been talking to you about love?' he asked.

'What do you mean!' she exclaimed. 'You think this is a prank, do you, something I cooked up with Veronica? For a bet? Come off it!' Bayswater speed of thought produced Bayswater language. She was not ashamed of either.

Strangely this had the desired effect. Harvey Johns lunged at her, laying her full back across the bed.

'What am I going to do with you!' he muttered urgently. 'You've got a freak of a voice, and yet you're still so dreadfully uncouth!'

'Mmm!' Ida was insulted, and tried to get out from underneath him, but now Harvey Johns had made his mind up too. His lips spread greedily across her mouth. His tongue sank deep into her throat and she felt foreign-tasting saliva slide into her gums. It was bizarre, but most horribly exciting.

She did love Mr Johns, because he had tremendous influence over her, and she admired him. But that did not make her want him, sexually. Kissing was her victory — all the rest happened with Ida in a state of awed submission. What happened made her shy, unresponsive. She let him do all the things he wanted with her, out of elation, curiosity, and not a little fear. He stripped, and fell on top of her again, grabbing at her breasts as if he had been wanting to touch them for an eternity. He entered her briefly; it did not hurt because he was a very small man and did not seem keen to do it that way. Suddenly he withdrew and ordered her to lie face down across the bed. He grabbed a pot from his dressing table, and stood behind her, urgently applying cream to himself.

'The cheeks of your bottom are ripe, ripe apples for the teacher,' he whispered hoarsely, deep in some erotic dream all of his own, rubbing himself into a state of remote agitation. Then he poked his stiff little member at her bottom.

The shock of it deadened her physical reactions. She felt only a cold detachment, impressed to learn that a London street word had genuine violence behind it, unparalleled among the curses she knew. Harvey Johns stood behind her, moaning, and barely managed to enter her before coming — a convulsive, saddening experience that reduced him to a heap.

'Oh my God. What have I done,' he said, falling to his knees. He fumbled for his cigarettes — for a moment he regarded his pipe, and Ida saw, despairing, that he almost reached out to light it, such was his desire to return to his civilised self.

Ida curled herself up, hurting. It had to be all right — he had to know what he was doing. She could not bear it, that he was embarrassed. The whole point of doing it was for them to belong to each other. Surely he was not going to regret anything — throw back her offering? It wasn't a gift that could ever be returned.

Ida sat up, worried. 'Wasn't I any good?' she asked simply. 'I'm sorry. I'll get the hang of it. Anything you like can't be bad, Mr Johns. I'll do anything for you.' She was so grateful to him for this new world, her opportunities, her future . . . passionately grateful that he found her attractive. She was lovable! 'I won't tell anyone. I promise.'

He looked thoroughly alarmed at the suggestion. 'Christ!' he groaned, sitting on the floor and rolling his head back on the bed.

There was a footstep in the hall. Mrs Rose on night patrol.

'Mr Johns? Is everything all right?' she called out.

'What? Oh, yes thank you Mrs Rose. I stubbed my toe. Sorry! Good-night!'

Ida pressed her face to the pillows and giggled. Then it was all right: Harvey climbed into bed and took her in his arms. She looked up shyly: from certain angles, he was quite handsome, even though his body was thin and felt much older than hers.

'Ida. You're a very beautiful girl. I had no idea . . .' This time he wooed her into making love as she had imagined a gentleman would, with soft kisses and persuading hands. 'You mustn't worry about getting pregnant,' he murmured. 'I'll take care of you. I have something in the bathroom.'

Ida covered her face with the sheet and waited for him to return. She hoped he would not appear with some incredible apparatus. With much relief she glimpsed what she knew was a condom, though she had only ever seen it as tawdry litter in the mud of the River Thames at Hammersmith, or as a plaything. Jack's friends inflated these skins on Paddington Canal, and sent them floating down the stream attached to twigs. They told her stories about the slaughter of pigs . . . packets of the things were hidden on Uncle Ted's bedroom mantelpiece in a Havana cigar box . . . Jack stole them so that he could act big and sell them to the older boys.

She knew she had not experienced the whole of it — but enough was hinted at in her body to tell her that soon she would discover the secret of sex, and then she would explode like a thousand stars — all for nothing, all for free, and it would be the tastiest, happiest moment of her life. It would be her own ecstasy — and Harvey Johns would teach her, as he had taught her so many other things.

Sometime later, he did light his pipe, having the safe cover of his tartan dressing gown and a pair of old slippers. He sat by the lurid castellations of the gas fire and told Ida of the future he planned for her.

'Look, to be perfectly frank, I think you should come to Paris with me. I'll find a decent family for you to board with, *en pension*, and I'll get you into classes with a good old tutor, Boinvilly. Madame Amate trained with him, Mary Garden spent a little time there — he's an old man now, but it would do him good to see someone young and exciting again.'

'Paris!' Ida was entranced, sitting up in bed, wrapped in sheets like a fragile parcel in need of protection for the post. It was all going to be perfect, just as she planned.

'But really, the reason is, you need an education. You need — culture. Painting, literature — not just music! Taste! Experience! Though not, I assure you, of this nature . . . I'll look after that. This is just us. Just our little secret love, isn't it, Ida?' He pulled at the sheet slowly, and stood over her, admiring the perfection of her youth on the stained and tangled linen.

Ida looked up at his face, at a scrutinising expression of purely physical interest. She tried not to see that Harvey lied. It was in the lines of his mouth. She could not deceive herself. They did share a secret, but it wasn't true love. Bleak in her suspicions, Ida wondered how much of what he planned was out of real affection, or how much he wanted her to grow up, experience things, belong to him in a number of ways. In lust. No! It had to be beautiful and good! He was civilised, famous, and he could pick *anyone*.

He handed her the silk robe, and began to pace the room. 'I know I'd have to convince your father of my plan. I've never met him face to face. I do quite see, from what you've told me, how deeply he must feel about your — your succeeding in this new world. Of course, in Paris, people are less sensitive about these things, and quite honestly, if you had the proper bearing, no one would think you . . . I tell you, sometimes it's better to make a name out of England. People resist home-grown talents . . .'

'Except people like Mr Summers,' Ida suggested, half-aware that her remark was telling.

'Ah, yes, well. I think that could be a — a complicated situation.'

'I haven't mentioned my family to anyone else.' Ida had held this back even from Veronica. 'Jack's the only one it doesn't show in,' she added. The thought of him suddenly made her cry, remembering his concern for her, his muddled, intense efforts to look after her at the Palmer party. What on earth would he say to what she had done? 'Oh! I don't know what's the matter with me!' she exclaimed.

'You must go back to bed. You'll get hysterical if we go on much longer. God, I've been a brute. I shouldn't have talked to you about all this, straight after . . . Well. We'll talk more sensibly tomorrow.' He tied her silk sash, then ran his hands over her head, down her shoulders, down her hips, and pecked at her tear-wet cheeks.

'Are you all right? You're a very, very lovely girl . . .'

There! He *was* genuinely concerned for her! Ida curled her hands around his neck and made him kiss her on the mouth again. It seemed like the right thing to do.

'I'm just fine, Mr Johns . . .' she smiled, coy at being womanly, tender, after the bold event. She found it very strange to see him as a lover and half wanted to go back to how things were before it happened, when she had only romantic thoughts about Mr Johns. Sex was more complicated than romance.

In the morning she was woken by Veronica sitting on her bed again, patting her hand and waiting, impatient for their day to begin.

'Just two more concerts, and then a day off! And look, the sun's shining! Fancy a swim?'

'Before breakfast? Won't it be cold?'

'No, honestly. It's brilliant today.'

Ida was aware of discomfort, some pains in hitherto insensate regions. The day was too vivid: it made her amazed at what she had done. It all seemed like a dream, one in which she could not possibly have taken an active part. Excitement thrilled her like a cold sword. Paris with her lover! How fantastic!

Then another mood. Deep, deep shame. Seeds of filth, seeds of filth: her Ma's words taunted her. Then her Pa's face, grave, worriedly hoping for the best in her. Self-deception hurried on behind shame. If anyone asked (that is, if she asked herself), Harvey Johns had seduced her, and she was a victim.

'Oh God!' Ida muttered, running across the lawn. 'Which is right? Should I be madly happy or am I just steeped in sin?'

She followed Veronica to the garden wondering how she could face the man again. She did not know if he expected the physical thing to be repeated, or if it had been a moment's abandon. She had a rough idea about sex, positions and all that . . . but how did a girl behave? Sexual manners were a complete mystery. She had no idea what to do or say — whether to act as if nothing had happened, or to assume that she and Harvey were 'one'.

Ida wanted desperately for Harvey Johns to be a faithful, passionate lover. Some instinct — or was it imagination only? — told her he had strange feelings about sex, was perhaps promiscuous, and likely to cause her unhappiness, the way villains did in films. But she did not want to listen to her heart. She wanted all the bright wishes in her clever head to come out right.

The girls' morning was like any other; its very sameness made Ida value it the more. Veronica swam beautifully to the far bank, and Ida followed, more weighted down by her body than she liked. She exerted herself, pushing at the water so that it refreshed and purified her. As she reached the far bank, she felt a desperate impulse to tell Veronica everything. But there were too many reasons not to, the most important being that Veronica might be shocked.

'I spouted a lot of rubbish last night,' Veronica announced, lying back in the sun. 'I was tired. Don't make a thing of it, will you? It's all going to work out jolly well.'

Ida lay back next to her and closed her eyes. She wanted to believe her. If Harvey would look after her, as he promised, everything would be fine.

Someone blocked the sunlight: for a thrilling instant Ida thought it might be him. But she opened her eyes to see Janet Sheldon beside them.

'Breakfast. You're late for breakfast,' she said, in unfriendly, precise tones.

She knew. It was obvious: Ida felt revulsion because she had forgotten that Janet had moved down to the floor below, perhaps even next door to Johns' room. She could have heard everything. Then she wondered if Janet had been his mistress too. The very word made her ten years older. Impossible: surely the angel girl was too perfect, too ladylike to be tempted. Ida could not tell.

Hurrying back across the lawn Ida realised that losing her virginity had changed not just her own body, but the world around her. Now she had to contend with undignified, alarming visions of people's sexual preferences. She would never again be thrilled by the kissing profiles of celluloid lovers. It made her sad, but then, having the talented and famous Mr Johns as her lover, was surely a reward for her loss of innocence.

7

Their last morning. Ida was packing her few belongings when Madame Amate came into the bedroom.

'I just came to kiss you goodbye, my dear Eeda,' she said. 'Dio! You slept up here? How cold it is!'

Ida blushed. She had spent too little time in it . . .

'Now. We have a little chat. Harvey tells me he is going to take you to Paris, to my old tutor, Boinvilly.'

'Yes, Madame.'

'This is very good.'

Ida smiled happily.

'But tell me. What will your mother say? She will go with you, your Mama?'

'Gosh no!' Then Ida blushed again, for Madame Amate's tone suggested there was something not quite right about this arrangement. Was she going to give her a warning when it was already too late? 'I think the idea is for me to stay with a family, have all sorts of lessons . . .' Ida spoke too quickly trying to cover her embarrassment.

Madame Amate's whole body expressed disbelief, as to a lie in an opera. 'Lessons! In Paris! And you're nearly seventeen! Ha! He will take you to the Louvre and to Versailles, *à deux*?'

Ida was not at all sure if Madame Amate was being ironic: the Italian lady's uncertain grasp of English did not help her when she wanted to be suggestive.

'Listen,' said Madame Amate, leaning close and wagging a finger, 'I say this to you, forgive me, maybe nobody else do. Sex will not give you a bigger voice or make you a better artiste. Many women are told this by their masters. But it is not true. I am very fond of Harvey, he is my friend and I love his music. But in this matter he is a man, like other men. They lie to you. I like you, so I warn you.'

Ida was hot with shame. Her guilt was made worse by the fact that Madame Amate obviously believed her to be a good girl, about to be led astray — not a hussy who had already done the deed.

'You won't reach the heights of your art in someone's bed!' Madame Amate declared. 'Let us be frank! Don't think of it!'

'Madame Amate! How could you suggest such a thing, of me, of Harvey . . .' Ida had to avert her face in a youthful fling of annoyance, pretending that her blushes came because she was offended.

Madame Amate gave her a sharp look and brushed the subject away with a flick of her hands.

'Bene. Bene. Dear Eeda. I wish you luck.' She gave her a final hug and left the room.

Ida was sorry to see her go abruptly, sorry for the awkwardness of their final words. Sadly, she finished packing. Veronica reappeared. 'Hurry up. Cars are waiting.'

'Goodbye room,' Ida said. 'Oh! How awful!' A sudden thought stopped her dead in her tracks.

'What is it? Left something?' Veronica asked.

'No.' Ida blushed furiously and rummaged with her bags so that Veronica would not see her shame. She had said Harvey instead of Mr Johns to Madame Amate. The kind old lady must have guessed the truth.

All the way to London Ida grew more and more anxious. Back home, everything might revert to the same old dreary pattern. Would her parents be able to tell? Would Harvey Johns fulfil all the promises he had made her? Would Veronica forget all about her, and the Summers family disappear with all their offers and attractions? Ida looked at her companions in the railway carriage. They all looked so boringly normal and decent that her frantic thoughts seemed laughable. Veronica was munching chocolate and reading a detective paperback, leaning comfortably against her shoulder. Janet Sheldon was working through a musical score, pointedly ignoring her. Harvey was dozing in a corner, looking his age. Ida quickly looked out at the view rather than take note of his sagging jaw and middle-aged, blue-veined eyelids. Her care not to hold this unpleasantness against him, restored her equanimity, and made her feel grown-up again.

Unfortunately, calm deserted her when they arrived at Waterloo Station. As soon as she had been helped down in a mock frail ladylike condition by Harvey Johns, she caught sight of two familiar but unexpected figures. Gran and Jack stood waiting.

Gran had a forbidding air, due to a large black hat and the fox poking its nose round her neck (Ida knew this belonged to Josephine). Two sets of eyes, Gran's grey-blue ones, and the fox's glassy amber, saw straight through Ida's falsely female manners. Jack waved at her frantically, then let rip a piercing whistle, two fingers in his mouth.

'God!' she said in disgust, but a lovely warmth spread where cold anxiety was before. He really was a shocker.

'Veronica! I have to go!' She clung to her friend, yet wanted more than anything to get away from everyone: she was home!

'Goodbye old girl! See you soon! Don't forget, Daddy's planning the concert for next week!'

'Oh Harvey! I'm being met!' Ida called out. 'Bye!'

He turned round slowly, still sleepy from the train. 'What?' But Ida was on her way. She picked up her case and scrambled for the ticket gate. Jack ran forward, and grabbed her luggage, pretending it was not too heavy for him, though Ida could see how his neck strained in its fresh paper collar. She flung her arms around him in a big hug.

'Sunday best — gosh, you are smart,' Ida teased him.

'Get off. I got a gig later. Hurry up, I haven't got all day.' Jack glowered as Ida blew a last kiss at some dark-haired girl striding up the platform to a waiting car. (Ida did so out of nervousness: she could see Veronica looking at Jack, smiling in recollection of the wicked things she knew about him.)

'Over 'ere lad,' Gran boomed, holding on to the door of a taxicab as if it were a worrisome horse that might bolt from her grasp. 'And you get in, Miss. I can see we've got a long story to catch up with.'

Once installed, Ida looked back to Harvey Johns and Janet Sheldon gazing into the middle distance from somewhere in the queue for cabs. It was rude and irreverent to laugh at them, but that is what she wanted to do, out loud. It was so nice to be back with Jack and Gran.

'What's the joke?' Jack asked.

'Nothing really,' she said.

'Bring me a present?'

'Jack Garland! Wait till you're given!' Gran said, smacking his hand loudly but smiling at the same time.

'I didn't go near any shops,' Ida said. 'So all I could bring was this — from the house we stayed in. It's all right Gran, they were put in all the rooms as gifts for the guests.'

She pulled the trophies out of her vanity box, which she had kept close by her on the train. A bar of Harvey Johns' spicy soap, a packet of his cigarettes, and a bottle of eau-de-Cologne. The first she had wheedled out of him as a gift, the other things she had stolen from his room. For Gran she had a lace-edged handkerchief and a jar of honey that Mrs Rose had given her as souvenirs from the country. 'I don't think I'm a lace hand-kerchief sort of person, but I know you are, Gran,' she said, smiling.

It gave her an illicit, sensual thrill to be handling Harvey's possessions in front of Jack and Gran, who did not have a clue what she had seen and done. A vision of Harvey Johns' naked body flashed into her mind, making her desperate to be close to him again. Ida began to feel a creepy, crawling excitement between her inward visions and her outward calm. Then she wished she had been better behaved, and said goodbye to her music master properly.

'I've got the programme of the concert for Pa, and something really fine for Ma.' Ida was going to offer her the blue crêpe dress from Mrs Summers. She would really be impressed with that.

The ride in the taxi sobered her. Trying to explain her week to Gran and Jack was difficult, for it was her first attempt at not telling the whole truth to people who knew her well. Like Madame Amate, Gran was hard to deceive, and Jack would keep asking exactly the wrong questions, making Ida's fishnet of happenings fall to pieces.

'Doesn't sound as if Mr Johns likes the idea of the Summers family. Isn't he pleased someone rich is on to you?' Jack asked her, staring in a way that was unsettling.

'Well, I suppose he doesn't want things to move too fast.' Ida defended her tutor.

148

'It sounds very promising. All this. You're a smart girl,' Gran said. But her benign smile faded. For a moment Ida thought Gran suspected, but the old lady tapped the glass between her and the driver. 'Now what's the matter, cabbie?'

'Been a demo, I should think. All this talk of a National Government.'

'National Busybodies,' Gran passed judgement.

'There's not one of 'em in Westminster can sort it out you know. Haven't a clue. It's chaos, that's what it is. Chaos.' The taxi-driver looked satisfied.

'To think we fought a war. That my sons should . . .'

'To think, madam, we have an Empire!'

Gran and the taxi-driver continued to exchange comfortable comments on the ineptitude of politicians. The taxi stood still in Park Lane. From her position on the folding seat, Ida craned round to see what was going on. A crowd of unemployed men with placards surged across the road on their way to Hyde Park for a final rally. They were singing in unison as only desperate, out of work Welshmen can: with pride, anger, and a wild beauty.

'Ooh look, there's hundreds of police!' Ida was sorry for the men, but happy to be at the centre of life again, pleased to live in London.

'Men out of work. It's a disgrace. Ramsay MacDonald hasn't got a clue. The Welsh Wizard — what he's done for 'em!' Gran went on.

'It's not his fault,' Jack interrupted. 'I read it in the papers: it's all over the world, an economic depression. Look at what happened on Wall Street last year. It's only now hitting us hard.' He folded his arms, suddenly looking intent, quite sensible for once.

Ida looked at him with surprise. 'Wall Street? *You*, reading? *Very* mature.'

'Drop dead.' He dug her in the ribs, scowling, and the two of them sulked all the way to Bayswater. How odd. Only a week ago, and yet everything was different. *She* had changed, but she expected everything at home to remain exactly as it was.

'Here we are at last. Now, you get out Ida,' Gran said as they stopped near the boarding-house. 'I've got to get back — it's feeding time for the lodgers. We'll see you later.'

'Can you handle your bag?' Jack turfed it out on to the pavement, paying her back for teasing him, his eyes hard and bright.

''Course I can. Thank you Gran. Bye.' Ida turned to the red lily glass on her front door while Jack and Gran headed for the boarding-house, arm in arm. Her spirits sank. She found the front-door key under the milk churn on the step and let herself in.

'Is that you Ida?' An idle enquiry floated downstairs.

'Yes Ma.'

'I'm putting on my face. I'll be down in a minute.'

That was a relief. Ida went to her room to prepare herself for the challenge of her mother's questions. It looked exactly the same, the bed had not been made all the week she was gone, let alone the sheets changed.

Ida sat at her dressing table, seeing herself repeated sideways, endless vistas of sexual deception in the wing mirrors. Under the table-top glass, photo-postcards of familiar faces encouraged her secret self, now quite changed: Mary Pickford, Gloria Swanson, Ruth Chatterton. Their knowing eyes all seemed to say: We share your double life. You're a woman now, like us. But next to the meaningful glances, there were other faces that made her dubious. Little snaps with serrated white edges: Jack and Gran on a day trip to Brighton. Jack poked his tongue out at her. Pa, in a slouch hat leaning against Ted's vintage AC, trying to look disreputable and only looking awkward. His face made her feel particularly bad. On top of the glass was the embroidered mat her Gran had given her for a birthday (it seemed so long ago now). Three children, hands joined in a ring of roses dance, in a shaky chain stitch. The colours had faded in the wash. It looked so pathetic and childish.

The whole display was coated with a fine dust of talcum and face powder, exactly as she had left it a week before. Ida chucked her suitcase angrily on the bed, unpacked in a minute, and set about making all her possessions shine, temporarily at least, with a wet face flannel.

She heard the front door shut again, Pa returning from a shady Sunday encounter. Betting or drink.

'Denise?' he called first, as he always did.

Ida stopped making rummaging noises, for he did not know she had come back yet. She crept to the door to eavesdrop, hearing her mother descend the stairs, sighing in response to him.

'Baby.' The tone of her Pa's voice curled into her being.

'Don't touch me.'

'Oh Denise, not again. What is it this time?'

'You know very well. Don't pretend.'

'You mean, because I didn't sit next to you last night? But honey, I had to talk to Bernie, we had trouble, the booking for the Oldham theatre. You know, 'cos I told you.'

'You don't understand. Those people. They're clods. They're dirt compared to me. I won't go out with them unless you protect me. You're no gentleman! I only went for you. And then you neglect me . . .'

'I'm sorry, don't be hard on me . . . how about . . .'

A muffled, physical silence followed.

Unheard and unseen, Ida spat on her flannel, and rubbed at a dirty ornament.

'Earl! For goodness' sake! She's upstairs — Ida's back.'

'My girl? That's nice.'

Ida was undone by this remark, and flung herself on her bed groaning into her pillow, overtired, and full of regret. When Earl put his head round the door, she pretended to be asleep, and he left her alone. Moments later Ida could hear the two of them creep up the stairs and lock their bedroom door. Imagine going to Paris with *her*!

'Mr Johns? Harvey?' Ida whispered into the telephone. It was dark, she was alone in Bayswater, at midnight.

His voice broke sleepily. 'Ida! Why did you run off like that?'

'My family . . . I had to be with my family . . .'

'We need to talk. Are you coming tomorrow, as usual?'

'Can I leave it till Thursday?' Ida did not know why she said this. When she lifted the telephone she had every intention of running away to Harvey Johns that very night.

'Thursday?' He was puzzled.

'Look, my money's run out. I can't speak any longer. Thursday!'

'Ida . . .' The line went dead.

The three of them were having breakfast: Earl and Denise together for once.

'Gran said you did well, Ida, had a good time. I'm glad,' Earl said. Denise was playfully dropping sugar cubes into his cup of tea.

'Here's the concert programme Pa. And — this is the card from Mr Summers. He's my friend Veronica's Pa, and I'm going to sing for him. At a do. A private concert!' Ida flushed with pride. Earl took the programme, read its contents carefully, like a racing page.

'Look Ma.' Ida grew bolder. 'I got given this dress. It's very expensive and will fit you much better than me. Try it on, if you like it, you can have it!'

'Second-hand? How could you! It's filthy!' Denise was peering with distaste inside the neck, looking for a label. When she found it, her face froze.

'Who gave you this?' she asked.

'Mrs Summers, for the concert. I . . .'

'Charity! Have you no pride? And modesty! Dolling yourself in *Chanel*! Earl!' Denise nudged him hard.

'Eh?'

'French models!' She thrust the crêpe at him, but Earl was being very slow. Denise dropped the dress on an empty chair, like a pair of dirty knickers. Then she looked across the table at Ida, upright and prim. Ida could see she was taxed by this development. New lines of attack were being summoned, it was in her eyes.

'Ida,' she said finally, sorrowing.

'Yes Ma?'

'You know what my job was, when I met your Pa?'

'Yes Ma. You were the cloakroom attendant in a restaurant in the Strand.'

Denise went white, but held herself back.

'I was receptionist in a private dining establishment. I met all kinds of people. Society. The very best. Lovely to me, they were.' She raised a cigarette with studied self-approval. Earl had chosen to hide in the concert programme, and did not provide a match. Ida quickly fetched a box from by the oven. She knew this conversation would end in some cruelty, but her mother's elaborate methods somehow always caught her up. In the centre of her will (now more than ever with a sin to conceal), was the desire to cause a reaction in Denise. Admiration or interest. Even anger would do.

'There's nothing more common than a girl who does not know her place. A real lady only wears discreet dresses. Anyone who shrieks money,' a tilt of the head referred to Mrs Summers' wardrobe, 'is either on the make or on the game. Which will it be for you Ida?'

'Ma!' But Ida's guilt made her redden so deeply, she felt her hot blood and her shame were one, all over her skin.

Denise's voice dropped to a tired, saintly whisper, knowing that she held her audience.

'I've tried to bring you up decent. God knows, I've tried. But it's an awful battle with you Ida. You see, I was never one for evil myself. Too shy, too sensitive. So I may not be able to guide you now, dear. You're moving into another world — far too smart and complicated for the likes of *me*.'

She stood up slowly and left the kitchen. Earl raised his eyes to Ida, who was visibly trembling.

'She was beautiful, your mother. She could have married anyone,' he said. 'She still is a very fine woman. Highly strung, that's all. Highly strung.'

'She hates me. I wish I'd never been born.'

'Don't you ever say that again! I'm your Pa! Pa needs you honey. You're going to make me a proud, proud man.'

'Am I Pa?'

'Of course you are! Now, sit down and tell me all about this Summers deal, and we'll see where we're going . . .'

Fighting back tears, Ida moved closer to him. Above their heads, they could hear the sound of Denise's petulant crying.

'Darling!' Harvey Johns fell on her as she entered his music room. Ida was inhibited — this was the room of her girlish aspirations, the room of singing rules and difficult music.

'Oh Harvey, you're hurting!' Accidentally he had caught his signet ring in a knot of her hair.

'Sorry. Look, sit down. You look fine, Ida — no repercussions from our trip?'

Ida was puzzled by this turn of phrase. 'Pa was very pleased, if that's what you mean.'

Harvey laughed softly. 'Jolly good.'

'Mr Johns, I mean Harvey, what are we going to do? Are you going to talk to Pa about Paris and all that?'

He jumped up, searching for his pipe. 'Have you told him about our plans already? I don't think you were altogether sensible, darling . . .'

'No, I haven't. 'Sides, I'm not sure I want to go just yet. I'd like to do the concert at Mr Summers' next week first.'

'Is that wise?' he bridled this time.

'I don't know if it's wise, but I want to see Veronica again, and it was a proper invitation. It would look rude not to go, wouldn't it?' Ida could feel that hint of manipulative power she had found in herself returning, now she was alone with her lover again.

'How sweet you are. So eager to please . . . haven't you got a kiss for me, Ida? I've been thinking so much about you . . .'

'Do you want to go to bed with me again?' Ida suddenly discovered that she did: she wanted to know what his bedroom looked like, and she needed to make her attachment to him real in their London setting.

'Sing for me first. I've written you a new song. It's an interesting new development.'

That made Ida proud, and she wanted to thank him in the way he liked best. She would try to be daring and passionate today, and perhaps, because of a few days' rest, it would not hurt, and she might like it better herself.

'Afterwards. I've got all afternoon,' she said, invitingly.

But love-making was no better. He kissed her, and the familiar taste of tobacco filled her mouth; his saliva coated her tongue. His small, urgent erection pressed against her and Ida allowed him to apply her hand to it, kneading even greater life into those strange, foreign parts.

All that week, leading up to the Summerses' party, she felt she was being treated differently by the Garlands. Reactions to the news of the invitation varied. The address of the house alone was enough to make Josephine's eyes globular. This was patronage of a kind she had never been lucky enough to attract. At least, not on the right terms.

'The first time I was asked to sing at a party, they wanted me to do it in a corset!' she laughed, smacking Ida's arm when told the news. 'You're made, you are!'

Then Ida was puzzled, because she knew the Summerses were not so very grand, and she had learnt from Madame Amate that they were considered undesirable in certain circles. How confusing it all was.

Gran continued to be phlegmatic in her acceptance, as if it was all turning out as she anticipated. Occasionally Ida wondered why Gran never questioned her closely. Perhaps she was biding her time.

Uncle George sneered at her for fancy ideas, talked about foreigners and toffs turning people's heads . . . Uncle Jim's eyes popped; like Josephine, no doubt he was worrying about the likelihood of after-brandy orgies.

Uncle Ted, sadly, was not there to share her news; he had gone back out East at short notice, this time to lead a dance band on a luxury liner full of tea-planters and colonial wives heading for Malaya.

Uncle Billy seemed the least concerned, but then he was not impressed by the upper class. Jazz was the almighty leveller to him. Quite a few Guards officers from the best society regiments brought their girlfriends to his record shop and chatted amiably about their musical preferences. He thought 'nobs' were almost mortal, when you got to know them.

'Fancy a walk, or shall I call a cab?' Earl asked when it was time to leave.

'Let's walk, Pa — I'll wear my laced shoes, and change when I get there.'

'OK. Sorry Jack can't take you. I did ask him, but he's got a gig.' His refusal to come face to face with this world he was pushing her into got on Ida's nerves. Why couldn't he be himself, instead of using others to create a better impression?

'Honestly, once I used to wipe that boy's nose, now suddenly Jack's old enough to take me places!' she exclaimed.

'He's six inches above you — or hadn't you noticed?' Earl teased her, stature being another sensitive issue to Ida.

'His neck's very long,' she sniffed.

Earl laughed, a warm, relaxed sound. Ida thought he looked very handsome at that moment. She put her hand through his arm, wondering if passers-by might think she was his girlfriend, especially when he kissed her cheek in response. His coat was thin, something expensive, soft and silky to her fingers.

'It's all right Pa, I'm glad Jack's working. Keeps him out of trouble. And the band's not half bad, don't you think? Is he getting a lot of gigs?'

'No. Not yet. He larks about too much, I can't have that. I've told him, I want to see him behave like a pro before I'll take him up to Archer Street and introduce him to the real circuit. They know there's nothing a dance hall hates worse than a band breaking an engagement.'

'But Jack must have some talent, to get any dates at all, and he's still really young.' Ida loved having business conversations with her Pa. It made her feel close, useful to him.

Earl looked very knowing, yet casual. 'At fourteen he should be sensible, not wild. The lad's got a name to keep up. He only has to mention he's a Garland boy. It doesn't do him any harm, I can tell you.'

Ida shivered as they turned a corner and the wind from the river hit full at their bodies.

'Cold?' Earl asked her, and pulled her coat collar up to her ears. 'Must be careful, with your voice. You know how pleased I am for you, don't you Ida? Very pleased.'

'Oh Pa . . .' Ida felt so ashamed of herself. All week she had been despising her family, most particularly despising Earl for his self-effacing gloom, his utter weakness in loving such a dreadful woman . . . now that she knew about sex for herself, his infatuation seemed all the more ignoble.

'I told Harvey Johns, you know, about the family background . . .' the words popped out of her thoughts.

'There was no need for that.' Earl dropped her arm abruptly, lit a cigarette.

'I wanted to be sure . . .'

'You've no cause to worry. No one would think of it if you didn't tell them. Besides, in smart circles, people find that kind of thing — interesting.' He looked at her in a hard, almost hostile way. 'Don't go making a rod for your own back. You're always inclined to fuss, Ida.'

For a moment she was angry with him. 'You're the one who won't come to Mr Johns' concerts, always sending Ma instead! You're the one who won't go beyond the door tonight! So people don't see you're darker than me!'

His smile was bitter. 'I know what I am, and it's nothing to do with my skin,' he said, poking at his cheekbone. 'I'm OK in my world. I'm a good businessman, don't you forget it. I'll talk to Mr Summers in my own time, in private. I just don't go sticking my nose in where I'm not going to be wanted . . . The women of the family do that well enough.'

He had never said a worse word about Denise. Did he mean he saw her Ma as she did — cheap, full of pretension? Ida did not dare to ask. She actually did not want to hear her Pa admit to his weakness. If it was spoken about, he would shrink, right there before her, into the size of a dwarf. They stood together, silent for a moment, trying to avoid the knowledge that Denise enslaved and belittled him.

The Summerses' house lay facing the river, at the bottom of a dimly-lit street. White garden walls decked in thick ivy gleamed as they walked down it. They crossed to the pavement opposite the house, to look up at its brightly illuminated windows, the curtains all open in ostentatious welcome. But then, there were no ugly terraced houses built across a mean space of street, nets twitching on their windows. Only water. Beyond a small public garden, Ida could make out the black unreflecting mass of the River Thames. It was quite full and silent in this stretch; not worked like the part by Hammersmith. No rowing boys, no slow barges, no ice-creams on the embankment; no pubs, with beer glasses lined up on the window-sills, a lacy pattern of froth in their empty insides. She felt apprehensive.

'Off you go.' Earl kissed her again. He did not give her a hug, but stood back with his hands in his pockets, gesturing, like a gangster in a film. 'You go ahead.'

She wanted him to say something more, give her more to hold on to. Then Ida heard a taxi draw up at the garden gate, and four people in evening dress stepped out. A glimpse of a glittering hem, a high-pitched laugh, the click as the taxi-driver flipped his For Hire sign up again . . . 'A trip to the moon please,' Ida could have said. Earl gave a piercing whistle, climbed in the empty taxi as it swung past them, and disappeared without one look back at her.

Ida followed the four guests up the garden path and the door opened as they arrived at it. A butler stood back as the couples passed, but took a perceptible step forward when he saw Ida just behind them.

'Ida! Spiffing!' Veronica bounded on to the threshold. 'Oh? Where's your Pa? Daddy was asking for him.'

'He couldn't come,' Ida said firmly.

'Well. Another time. Golly it's good to see you. Up this way . . .' She led Ida straight past the guests towards the staircase. Ida glimpsed a large gathering in the front room. Bare arms, cigarette holders, red lips, furs . . . one man with a monocle, shouting a joke in Yiddish. Everyone laughed at him. Ida craned forward, staring, while the butler drew off her coat.

Veronica tugged at her arm. 'Awful aren't they? Daddy thought it might be nice if we had supper together in my room, and then you could join the others for coffee, and sing your pieces for them.'

'All right.'

Ida was disappointed: she had understood she was to be a guest at the party, but one glance at the room, and she realised that she could not possibly have been included. She had no conversation. What did people talk about all evening, standing up, so animated? She followed Veronica, feeling cross at her inadequacies.

'I say, I cleaned my Gran's brasses yesterday,' she minced, under her breath, making Veronica laugh nervously and put a finger to her lips.

'Honestly, Ida!' she said, non-committal.

'Guess what Freddy,' Ida grew bolder, 'I read this simply thrilling cartoon in the *Daily Mirror* while my toenails dried this morning.' No one could see her feet, they were hidden and radiating confidence, tipped with bright red nail varnish, purloined from Denise's dressing table. She glanced at her feet and was horrified.

'Oh Gawd, Veronica, I haven't changed my shoes!' No

wonder the butler had eyed her. She was still wearing lace-ups, as battered as a tramp's brown paper parcel, and her satin pumps were stuffed into her coat pocket. She could have been looking for shelter from a rough night on Shepherd's Bush Green.

'Why didn't you say something?' she said, deflated, but her dismay only made Veronica laugh more freely.

'I'm sure no one noticed — and anyway, who cares? Don't be so nervous!' Veronica was happy to be slightly more in control.

Ida decided she would definitely go to Paris just as soon as she could run off with Harvey Johns. He was right — she was hopelessly uncouth. She kicked her shoes off on the top landing. One of her scarlet nails poked through a hole in her stocking.

'Can we practise?' she suddenly changed tack, deciding to be professional. Veronica had agreed to be her accompanist for the evening.

'I suppose we should. I do wish you'd have come earlier in the week, why didn't you? We'll have to go back downstairs to the playroom. They won't hear us there. And I'll get your shoes from the cloakroom.'

Veronica led the way past the party down a long corridor to the garden side of the house, a back room, full of books, leather chairs, a big globe in the window, and an old upright piano. A large gramophone occupied another corner, and piles of records were strewn on the billiard table.

'Used to be our nursery. The boys use it in the hols,' Veronica explained. 'Look, these are my horrible big brothers. That's Simon, and that's Felix. He thinks he's a dish.'

Ida looked at the silver-mounted portraits, so different from Gran's motley crew in their broken frames. Cricket elevens, boating crews, dining-club nights, and cap and gown occasions. 'Magdalen,' she murmured, reading a caption.

'*Maudlin*' is how they say it,' Veronica corrected. 'Felix is reading law at Balliol. Frightfully clever.'

'Frightfully handsome too,' Ida smiled. 'He'll introduce you to tons of smart young men. How lucky you are.'

'No he won't. I'm far too clever to suck up to him, and I'm not the English Rose type. Besides, he'd rather die than bring any of his friends here!'

How disappointing, that she might not know this regular-featured, smooth young gentleman. Perhaps he found his home bourgeois — that word the people at the Palmer wedding had used in judgement.

'He does smirk a bit,' she suggested, and Veronica sniggered happily.

'Come on. The piano's pretty good.'

'Here's my music.' Ida fished in her bag and pulled out her song books; on Mr Summers' advice she was singing light things, some sweet melancholy pieces by Landon Ronald, a lullaby by Peter Warlock, the beautiful 'Oft in the Stilly Night' and, if she were asked for an encore, 'Believe Me if All those Endearing Young Charms'.

'Your father said you'd be able to play all these,' Ida said, giving Veronica the music. 'They'll all be asleep by the time I've finished,' she laughed nervously.

'They may look asleep, but be warned. The brains still function.' Veronica gave her a long look. 'You didn't wear Mummy's crêpe?'

'I'm sorry. Did you want me to?' Ida did not wish to hurt her feelings. For some quirk of reasoning, she had decided to wear the dress her Gran had bought for her to wear at the summer school. It was a soft mauve, bias-cut with ruched sleeves and complicated panels over the hips. Ida felt more of a schoolgirl in it, in her party best, a little gauche, which, given her all-too-aware frame of mind, was a better impression to leave with these strangers. Protection of a kind.

'No, it doesn't matter. You look lovely in anything.' Veronica was too good natured to have planned an insulting *double entendre*. Ida smiled in satisfaction, and they went on rehearsing. It was fun; Veronica was an accurate pianist, and seemed to be able to anticipate Ida's phrasing pretty well.

After a while the girls shared a relaxed, enjoyable supper in what Veronica astonishingly referred to as the morning room (presumably the house contained afternoon rooms, evening rooms, who knows, a dawn room too), where Mr Summers came to find them.

'There you are! Very sweet you look too! I'm sorry not to meet your father. Are you ready? My guests are looking forward to you!'

Ida could see he was a little drunk; she wished he had been a bit grander with her. She'd imagined him sweeping her into the salon, announcing her like a new star. All these private chats in back rooms were tantalising, too small glimpses of a world to which she did not belong.

'We've just had a rehearsal, and a little supper, though I don't like to eat too much before I sing,' Ida attempted conversation. 'Mr Johns says it isn't wise.'

A small shadow of irritation winged across Mr Summers' face at the mention of her singing master's name.

'Quite so, good man. Good man. This way.' His big hand in the small of her back made her spine tingle. Ida began to enjoy herself.

Somehow, she knew that singing would be effortless. She stood by the piano, smiling as Veronica arranged her pages. Ida tried not to look at the guests, coughing, drinking, chatting to each other and laughing loudly without paying attention to her arrival. There was a fuss about someone's seat; a flirtatious, beautiful woman ended up perched decoratively on the arm of a man's chair, so that her legs looked particularly fetching. She had a curious way of tucking her elbow into her hip as she held up her cigarette-holder.

Ida watched the woman posing and it provoked a combative mood. She smiled sweetly and asked, 'Would you mind not smoking, just for my first song please?' Someone laughed at her effrontery, but the beautiful lady recognised a competing spirit, and stuck out her elegant chin.

'Why of course! I don't suppose you're used to it at all! How brave! Come on everybody! Lights out! Harry, be a good boy! It will do you good!'

There was yet more commotion while ashtrays were found and a glass of liqueur was spilled. Ida felt her boldness fading, mocked by the exaggerated courtesy of the guests. To steady herself, she tried looking around the room, noticing for the first time that it was all white except for gold fringing on the curtains and painted silver stars on the ceiling. It was modern, disappointingly lacking in opulence according to her taste, not like Mayfair films at all. The grand piano was white: that at least was theatrical.

Suddenly Ida stood outside herself, and saw how she must appear, waiting. She had spent hours in front of her mirror recently practising her posture. But the false hopes of those private moments fell away, leaving her with an honest vision. Honey coloured skin, what Jack called her cat's eyes, dark hair pulled back from a round forehead, giving unattractive emphasis to well-defined eyebrows. Plump, young girl's arms swelling out of fussy sleeves. She looked too forward, possibly pretty, and very common.

One discovery, though: race meant new things now. She felt at ease in this colourful company. Some guests were much darker skinned than she was — other men had luminous white faces, fine almost feminine features, raffish handsomeness she could not place. They were all foreigners, much more alien to England than she was. Ida was stimulated by these new presences, hands that flicked and gestured in expansive, expressive European ways.

It came to her, as she sang, that Mr Summers had arranged a deliberately English programme. Between songs and polite applause, she could hear the guests murmuring in French, Yiddish, and Polish, languages that the streets of Bayswater had taught her to recognise. During one round of applause, Mrs Summers appeared and offered her a glass of water, but Ida never took cold drinks while singing.

'Perfectly charming,' Mrs Summers praised, but Ida could see in her eyes that what she and her husband wanted was confirmation of raw talent, to display a prize possession in the 'before' and hopefully 'after' stages of development.

When she had moved away, Ida whispered across the piano to her accompanist: 'Veronica! Scrap the encore! I'll sing by myself if you don't mind!'

'Gosh, don't do anything silly . . .'

'I won't! I promise!'

It was not such a mistaken judgement. She sang 'Bei Mir Bist du Schoen', a popular, often cornily rendered Yiddish song that had become a commercial big-band success. Ida sang slowly, with seductive rhythm, imbuing the words with sincerity so that all motion in the room was arrested. She forgot a few lines, and hummed appealingly instead. When she finished, the applause was over-loud, a mixture of annoyance at her cheek, amusement, and in some quarters, indulgent sentiment.

'Honestly Ida, you've got some nerve!' Veronica said, clapping and running over to kiss her on the cheek. 'Whatever possessed you!'

Mr Summers found her. 'Well, young lady! Fancy giving me a surprise like that! Shall I forgive you . . . ?'

'Nonsense, Max.' Mrs Summers as always, chose to be positively charming. 'It was an inspired idea, quite brave, and I'm sure we all took it as intended . . .'

Ida's anxious eyes compelled Mrs Summers to explain.

'Well, I'm sure you wanted to show us how broad your musical tastes are, to give us a bit of fun . . . I dare say we do get a bit stuffy and over-serious sometimes, don't you agree Simone? Look, my cousin wants to say hallo . . . my cousin Simone, she lives in Paris . . . and that's her husband Paul, the one by the fireplace . . .' (So, the beautiful woman with the cigarette holder was Veronica's French aunt.)

Ida was almost in tears: it was so affecting to have someone interpret her actions for the best. Fancy having Mrs Summers for a mother! Veronica noticed her brimming eyes and lent her a handkerchief.

Presently Mr Summers claimed her. 'There's something I want to show Ida. Can I borrow her for a moment or two, darling?'

Mrs Summers still held her hand. 'Now, don't spoil her evening with too many serious ideas, Max. I think I understand this young lady. We'll get along fine, won't we?'

'Yes Mrs Summers!' Ida was entranced, for this woman offered all the comfort and praise she had longed for in a mother.

'You did excellently tonight. Whatever he says.'

Ida thought she could see in those polite, bright eyes the same hint of appeal that Veronica had once shown her, and wondered at it. Mrs Summers could not possibly be afraid of her husband too.

Mr Summers led her back to the billiard room. As they went in, the butler was setting down a tray of brandy and a newly cut cigar.

'Now Ida, this is what I propose,' he said, filling a large glass for himself. 'I've written a letter, here, for your father, since he could not be here for a little chat. I'll have it sent round in the morning, but I want you to read it first, make sure you approve.'

Ida tried to focus on the print, but nervousness made it difficult to absorb whole sentences. The drift was clear: they wanted to adopt her professionally, pay her expenses, find her another teacher, in London first but afterwards in Paris, and have her live with them for the weekdays.

Why only the weekdays? Ida wanted to say, hungry to begin, but decided it would be unwise to ask. Her second thought was that Veronica would be hers — a sister, almost.

Mr Summers enfolded her in one large, dark arm. He was taller and bigger than any man she knew. She liked dinner jackets; white shirt-fronts, the smell of male skin, splashed with unusually female perfume for evenings, and the gleam of hair-oil, taming that otherwise too obvious hairy appeal.

'We mean only the very best for you, my dear,' he murmured. 'I don't think you have the voice for opera. You're too small and slight for the operatic stage. I don't know what Harvey Johns has been telling you, but you won't do in those quarters. People in this country have an aversion to home-grown talent, I can tell you . . . no. Recitals, concert work, possibly oratorio when you're older. You haven't got a very big voice, but it is beautiful, smooth through the registers. I'll say this much for Johns, he hasn't ruined you, and you have an incredibly lovely, wonderful tone.'

All through this speech, he pulled her closer to his side, so that Ida felt she could hardly breathe. She kept nodding, hoping her agreement would satisfy him, and he might let her go.

But he held her even closer for an emphasis. 'I tell you a secret.'

She closed her eyes. Perhaps he would kiss her.

'It's in the recording industry you could make a fortune!' he said, abruptly letting go. Ida found a chair behind her and sat down.

'Records, Mr Summers?' she asked faintly.

'Yes! Records! It's a world that is only just opening up! And you have perfect pitch — I know several singers who have had a big career on the stage, and in a recording studio, they suddenly find out they have been singing flat for years! You will not have this problem!'

Hypnotically, he stabbed his cigar in the air in front of her and Ida watched him, round-eyed, taking in everything he said. She saw the cigar tip glow as he inhaled again.

Ida was not in a trance, she was thinking fast. Being highly stimulated, whether by alcohol or sex, seemed to make her feverishly perceptive. She saw all these fine words as a prelude to deception. Perhaps she was being ungrateful and suspicious — only going ahead would prove her wrong. Either Mr Summers expected to take her to bed, in his own good time, or he meant to use her to make a fortune. Perhaps he suggested a recording career as a means of avoiding the obstacle of her 'tarbrushed' looks. But Mrs Summers led her to think that she could present herself better, and overcome that difficulty. Could Mrs Summers be part of this plan, relying on Ida to amuse her husband discreetly in return for all their help? At least that way he would be philandering close to home.

Worse things happened at the pictures. Her Pa said she created dramas, but Ida was sure she was not being too imaginative. She felt a surge of wildness, desperate to be embroiled in any of these situations. It was all very adult and so wonderfully *complicated*! She wanted to have a life full of dramas, emotions, mistakes and victories. In short, to find out who she was, and how far she could reach.

'Thank you very much, Mr Summers. I'm very, very grateful for all your interest in me. I'll have to wait and see what my Pa says, first.'

'Of course, my child! No need to hurry! Now, here's a little thank you from me too.' He pushed a large white banknote into her hand. Ten pounds! 'Buy yourself something pretty.'

'Perhaps Mrs Summers could take me shopping . . .' Ida ventured, hoping to be mistaken in her fears.

Mr Summers did not bat an eyelid.

'What a good idea. Barbara knows all the best places. Good-night, my dear.' He kissed her forehead and Ida was suddenly sorry that this first, all-important interview was over. She admired Mr Summers' energy, his talent for creating exciting situations of all kinds. Just at this moment she did not give one thought to Harvey Johns.

Ida went home in the Summerses' car, insisting that she was quite happy to travel alone with the driver for such a short distance. Her Pa had given her a key on this occasion, and she let herself in quietly. Of course they had gone to bed. Why should they wait up?

As Ida undressed, she was sure she heard a noise in the garden between her bedroom window and Gran's house. Looking out, she saw a dark figure huddled under a buddleia. As she moved the curtain, the shape lurched upright. Fright lasted only a second. She was wide awake with excitement and quickly recognised Jack. Ida padded down the stairs to the scullery door and let him in. She could not wait to tell him all about her night, but the sight of him finished that hope.

'What on earth's happened to you!' she whispered, horrified, seeing the streak of blood on the side of his head.

'Bastard.'

'It's not Ottley, is it? Not again?' She half wanted to cry for him, but a flash of anger that Jack was spoiling this important night with ugliness, hardened her.

'Sit down. I'll get the iodine and clean you up. Oh Christ, where'm I going to find anything sensible in this mess!' She felt sick, part over-reaction, in part because Jack's head was bleeding profusely and she hated the smell of blood.

'Never mind. Salt water will do. Anything. I just had to talk to you.' He grabbed her hand, his was grimy with dried blood and Ida pulled away.

'Oh Jack, will it ever stop?'

'Yeah. I told you, I'm not going to go on like this for the rest of my life. You'll see. I'll run away.'

'No! You can't do that!' Things were happening too fast. Ida did not want him to go anywhere. All of them to stay exactly as they were, so that she had a backdrop against which to act. She clutched Jack by the collar and forced him into a seat. 'I don't want you to go. I'd miss you. Don't be silly!'

Jack looked at her with a thick, blurry expression, and Ida's heart went out to him. He was such a bright youth, with no one to help him. He was much handsomer than Felix Summers, the prig. But he did not help himself much, being ineducable, being brash and wild.

'You stink of drink! I thought you were playing tonight!'

'I was, honest! I was standing in for someone at the Essoldo in Croydon, first night with a proper band. Nice sort of do. A film, dancing chorus, you know. Had a bit too much, but nothing special — only after the end of the gig. I'm a good gigster I am.' Jack began to sound tearful, his bravado harder to keep up with a throbbing head. Ida dabbed at his head violently, wishing it was all different.

'Not so hard!' he complained.

'What happened then?'

'Tried to get home. Lost Bageshaw, he was meant to pick me up, mix-up with some girl he was giving a ride. No buses, got lost. Big area, Croydon is. Started to walk, met a mate of mine on the way, and had a quick one at a club he knew . . . Left the bass fiddle at his place after a bit — it's heavy, I'll tell you, walking all that way with a case . . . breaks your arm.'

'You're only fourteen, trying to act eighteen, and you can't even get home from Croydon in one piece! You've got to stop this, oh dear, where will it all end!' Ida began to cry in a quiet mess, her tears dripping off the end of her nose on to the top of Jack's jammy black head. The cut was in his hair-line, not too deep, but had bled for a long time. She cleaned it and managed to find a roll of plaster to cut for him. Blinking to clear her eyes, she noticed, and it pained her, Jack's still boyish thick eyelashes made a shadow on his pallid cheek-bone. Perhaps she was the only person who cared for him, no matter what he did.

'Well to cut a long story short, when I got home, Ottley wouldn't let me in. So I threw a stone up at the window — I didn't mean to break the glass, honest, and next thing I know he's at the door, going berserk. Hit me with the coal shovel, he did. Lucky my mother wasn't in.'

He wiped his hand across his lips hopefully. Ida doubted if Josephine would have prevented anything.

Jack turned clumsily, and threw his arms round her waist. 'Sit still for God's sake,' she ordered. But he buried his face in her warmth, and she found herself patting his back, caring for him as she always did.

'Good girl, Ida. Girl in a million. I'll let you in on a secret.' He lifted his face up to her, but she broke free of him, disgusted by whiffs of cheap Woodbine cigarettes and beer.

'I really have had enough. I've got to think of something. Maybe I really should go off.'

Ida cried in earnest. 'I wish you'd be normal! I hate you, I really do!'

'No you don't.' Jack stood up unsteadily, and came closer to her. He towered above her — how funny that she had not noticed how lank and thin he was. In a ham-fisted way, he pulled her hair. 'You like me, Ida. We're mates, we are.'

He kissed her like a sister. Ida felt it was a goodbye, because he was right — she was going on to great new things, and he would have to sort himself out. She kissed him back. 'Poor old Jack,' she wept, clinging round his neck. It was so lovely to hold someone, and not to feel disgust, or shame.

She did not feel any pain when he slapped her. One minute she was standing close to him, the next flattened into a chair, and her head was spinning round, round, round, round.

'I got your number! You've been with a man, you have! I can tell! Who is it? I'll kill the bleeder!' Jack roared at her.

She flinched at his vehemence, then lost her temper. 'You hit me! You hit me!' she hissed.

'Well? What do you expect?' Jack bellowed, swaying on his feet. 'Letting yourself be tampered with!'

'You hurt me! I never thought you'd hurt me!'

Jack scowled, then gave a snort of scorn while he tried to think of the right insult. His hands worked in and out. Ida saw his face, he was appalled by what he had done. She was appalled too, because for an instant she had felt a bond of tenderness with her cousin. And the moment before he hit her, she had been deeply ashamed of what she had done with Mr Johns.

She saw him square his shoulders, set his mouth grim, and knew he was wondering whether to apologise. In his eyes was panic that he had lost her affection because of what he had done. But somewhere too he did not regret it. In the end, he had to swagger.

'Be a whore then. I don't give a damn. Wait till I tell Earl!'

In a panic she grabbed at anything to make him stop mouthing off. 'If you tell on me, Jack Garland, I'll never, ever speak to you again! Mind your own sodding business, do you hear!'

He swayed a bit, blinking. No shock in his eyes, no shame, or sympathy, or secret understanding now. He knew how to make himself void of feeling.

''S your funeral,' he said thickly. 'Put them down. You don't half look stupid.'

He staggered out of the kitchen back towards Gran's house. Ida looked down at her hands. She had threatened him with a pair of scissors. On the table was a bowl of pink water, coloured with his blood, and the room smelt sickly of her fear and his drunken odour. Jack's violence had finally made her respond on the same low level to him.

Next morning Earl took Max Summers' letter to Gran for a consultation. He read it slowly out loud to her, in the parlour.

'What do you think?' he said, uncertainly.

'It's a very generous offer, they're sort of adopting her. Must think an awful lot of her voice.' Gran was satisfied.

'Is it the only way for her to go, do you think?' Earl frowned. 'Maybe we should leave Harvey Johns to decide. He's done all the work with her. It doesn't seem right, not consulting him. After all, we don't know this Summers man.'

'He's not a white slaver! They've got lots of money,' Gran volunteered. 'Ida says it's in banking. Investments, I shouldn't wonder. Sounds razor-sharp, doesn't he? Mr Summers. Of course he's Jewish. They're always good with money.'

'Ida's really keen then.' Earl fingered the letter. 'They're top of everything, the Jews. Show business, it's the same. They're not my kind of people . . .'

'Don't be wicked! Take everyone as you'd like to be taken—on their own!' Gran was vehement. Then a suspicion rose in her. 'You're going to lose her, Earl, you never thought of that when you started on all this, did you?'

'She wouldn't forget her family. Ida's proud of the Garlands.'

'Some of 'em. Not all.'

He grew pale with the insult. 'I hope you're not talking about Denise.'

Gran was not to be diverted. 'You're worrying about the business . . . supposing there's money.'

'She's got to have my agreement, legally. I'm her father. She's underage.'

'I often wondered why you were so keen on all this concert work. I never knew there was big money in it.' Gran rubbed her face, but only succeeded in emphasising her lines of fatigue.

8

'Pa, have you answered Mr Summers' letter?' Ida asked, a week or so later.

'Yes. I'm discussing terms with him. I'll let you know the minute anything is decided. Look here, Ida . . .'

'Yes?'

'I don't want you going round there, seeing that girl Veronica.'

'Why not? She's my friend . . .'

'Because it makes us look too keen. I won't have you looking like some waif and stray, just begging to be taken in.'

'Oh Pa, Veronica's not like that. I'm old enough to have a friend, surely.'

'You do as I say. I pay the bills. I call the tune. I'll handle the business. You know I only want the best . . .'

Ida was kept in suspense for weeks. Her days were monotonous, without even the diversion of school to keep her occupied. She did not go back to Dawson Court that autumn, so that she could concentrate on her singing, and new plans. But why was it all taking so long to arrange?

In the afternoons, she helped out sometimes in the boarding-house with Gran. Jack did not call to see her any more, not since the night of their fight. His excuse, to Gran, was that he had too many rehearsals now, for gigs.

Uncle Ted was out East, but due back in a month or two, for Christmas. Uncle Jim was rehearsing in the pit orchestra of a seasonal musical, and Aunt Josephine had already landed a good part in a spectacular under Albert de Courville, one of the best show managers in London.

'Everyone but me, Gran. When's my chance going to come?' Ida complained.

'Soon enough. Your Pa knows what he's doing. He's got your

best interests at heart, I'm sure of that. Now, come on. Sing for me. It'll pass the time. I'll play piano if you like.'

'Oh no. I don't feel like it. Let's listen to some of Uncle Billy's records.'

Ida could see all her family suspected Max Summers had ulterior motives. How ironic that it was the long-trusted Mr Johns who had made a mistress of her. If her Pa thought there was safety in the familiar, he was making a big mistake.

A month passed, without even a word from Veronica, let alone Mr Summers. Not a word to say when he might introduce her to a new teacher, or invite her to stay at their house. Meanwhile, she had to continue her lessons with Harvey Johns.

One afternoon she went to his flat as usual, resenting the autumnal splendour of the Park as she walked past. Something about the season's softness, the cinema films, even the songs on the radio (especially Al Bowlly crooning on Tuesday evenings), reminded her of young love and romance. She could not understand why she was being held back from her great adventure. It wasn't all Pa's fault, either, Harvey Johns had changed too. He certainly liked the bed thing, more and more. But Ida was less certain about his plans for her voice, whether he meant to keep his promises about Paris, or let her go to Max Summers.

She pressed the bell, waited for the key to be thrown down. Harvey Johns hurried to the window and dropped it barely pausing to smile or wave in greeting. As she drew near the top of the stairs, she heard another soprano voice coming out of the door. She would recognise that thin, light sound anywhere — Janet Sheldon. The door was slightly ajar, Ida went in and saw her standing in the middle of the room, hard at work on a Harvey Johns composition, one that she herself had practised on only a week before. Janet stopped when she came in.

'No no, continue!' Harvey said impatiently, 'from the D, bar 44, Azure blue . . . You don't mind waiting for a moment, Ida dear?' he asked, expecting no answer.

Ida sat by the window. How many times she had looked out over those battered, neglected gardens, the tall creaking trees, dreaming of other views, blue roof-tops, the sound of foreign voices on the stairs . . . Paris.

Janet stopped singing, Ida rather pointedly went on gazing out of the window as if to remind her rival that a paid lesson time was being interrupted. A hurried, whispered conversation went on behind her back.

The door closed. She saw Janet emerge below in the street, and Harvey returning. His voice was stern: 'You were rather rude just then. I've told you often enough you have no cause at all to be jealous.'

'Then why is she singing your new song? I thought I was going to do that at the Baker Street concert next week.'

He coughed, a sure sign he was about to lie. 'Oh. I just wanted to hear it with a slightly different effect,' he shrugged. 'But she only convinced me you sing it much much better.'

Ida supposed that a creative artist was entitled to be selfish about his work. Perhaps he meant nothing by it.

'Artistes in books are always being insensitive,' she said, trying to sound unconcerned and sophisticated.

'Yes, but my darling doesn't read novels like that . . .' Harvey put his arms round her and started kissing her ear. 'Don't be so cross with me. Please. I love you so much . . .' he pressed his hips against her as if she should be pleased that he was stimulated.

Ida wanted to say: No! You like making love to me, that's all! but she could not be so crude. Harvey Johns was older and cleverer than she was, and she had never seen him turn nasty. She wondered what he would be like if he were thwarted.

'Please Harvey, don't do that. We have to talk.' She sat by the window again, staring at her hands. There was a broken nail and a cut on one finger from peeling vegetables for the lodgers.

He sighed. 'What is it now? I tell you every week how wonderful you are, and I did get a booking for you at the Baker Street Rooms. For an outsider, that's rather rare.'

'Have you called my Pa about us going to Paris?' she blurted. 'Is that why I haven't heard anything about Mr Summers?'

'Well, actually Ida, I think your father has seen off Max Summers. Quite right too. You must make your start in the right quarters. We agreed that when he came to see me.' He let this information drop far too casually.

'Who? Who came to see you? My *Pa*?' Ida was amazed. They

only ever talked on the telephone or by letters. 'When? Why didn't you tell me about it?'

'Oh, a couple of weeks ago, quite soon after your début at the Summerses' house. I didn't mention it because I knew you'd think we were in a plot against you,' he added, with a little false laugh that made her apprehensive. 'So he hasn't told you Summers is off. I see . . .'

'You didn't talk about Paris. Otherwise Pa would have said . . . Why hasn't anyone told me any of this? What's going on? I don't understand . . .' Ida's brain was working very fast over this new development. She could see that Harvey Johns was watching her surreptitiously, almost as if he were eager to have her draw conclusions.

'Well, one thing at a time . . .' he joked. 'I've got rather a lot of commitments this autumn. We may try again later. In the spring, darling. How about that?' He bent over her and began unbuttoning her collar.

'Have you had a reply from your old teacher, what's his name? Bon something.' Ida's pulse was thumping, her mouth dry.

'Boinvilly.' He looked amused at her mispronunciation, sexually stirred all the more. He licked her neck as he lowered her dress over her shoulder. Quite suddenly, she was repelled.

'Don't do that. Harvey, listen to me.'

'I will if you come into the bedroom. I love conversations in bed in the afternoon . . .'

'No.'

'What?' He straightened, rigid with anger.

'I said no.'

He did not believe her, and tried to joke. 'Oh come on, Ida, I could hardly tell your father I was going to take you to Paris *now*, when he was full of suspicions about Max Summers . . .'

'It's all gone wrong . . . You don't want to take me to Paris, ever! What did Pa say that made you change your mind?' Ida was trembling, fighting back tears of disappointment.

'Well. I realised how — how particular he was about you. It made me see we'd have to bide our time. I can't possibly proceed against your father's wishes, or submit to his conditions over everything. Perhaps I have been over-enthusiastic. You're quite young to go abroad . . .'

'I see! Too young to take to Paris, but not too young to take to bed!' She began to feel deep anger, but instead of being filled with strength from it, she felt as if she were crumbling into little bits.

'That's a coarse remark. I don't think there's anything to be gained by losing control or becoming abusive,' he said in a light voice. 'You were very willing. I wasn't the first . . .'

Ida was taken aback. 'What do you mean?'

'You told me about Jack so many times I naturally assumed . . .'

'But Mr Johns, he's my cousin!'

'It happens, I'm told.'

Ida was utterly shocked by the lewdness of this notion. Jack's rage suddenly looked like a wild attempt at protection. He was right — she'd been deceived. Jack was *true* from childhood, her blood, her kindred spirit. And Harvey Johns, her idol, had crashed before her eyes, saying such despicable things.

Ida stared at him, and then, as she knew she must, for the sake of the Garlands, she held her ground.

'I wasn't brought up in a slum, Mr Johns. I may be part-coloured, but I'm not a primitive.'

'Heavens, Ida, there's no need to over-react. You always spoke so particularly . . . naturally I assumed . . . and you were so complying . . .'

What an education this man was giving her: in sexual matters and in the lowness of thought of which adults were capable, to justify their actions. Mr Johns only wanted her for sex, but somehow he made this seem entirely her doing. She took a deep breath, for what she wanted to say took courage, and could only be said once.

'I do love Jack. He's like a brother to me. I don't want you to speak about him, not another word. You're not to talk about him like that. Now I'm leaving. There's no future for me with you.'

'Oh you dear, silly girl! Just because you haven't got entirely your own way. Sometimes adults do know better . . .'

Ida had never imagined speaking to any adult, let alone her tutor, with such force: 'You mean, I should go on with my lessons and go on going to bed with you? Go on with it? But I can't bear it any more. I don't like what you do to me. I did try not to be ashamed. Mostly I wasn't but now — I couldn't bear you to touch . . .' She ran out of breath, startled by her honesty.

'I see. No Paris, no favours. The truth. Well, shall I tell *you* the truth?' That slight unpleasantness she had seen in him once before, came over him again.

Ida wished she could say no, but pride and anger got in the way. 'It won't make any difference.'

He blew smoke rings into the air, while he measured out his insults, so that they too floated perfectly, sounding good to his ears. 'I thought, perhaps, sexual experience would give you depth. I hoped that our affair would give you the spirituality your voice lacks . . . a subtlety. I can't quite explain it. I get hints of it in you, sometimes, I have to admit. I think you should lower your sights. Musically speaking, of course.'

'Don't go on. Please.' Ida put her hands to her face. All Madame Amate's warnings were returning, distorted and cruel in his words. 'I think I'd better go now, Mr Johns.'

'You're just doing this out of pride,' he retorted. That stung her to defend herself. By the door, she turned and accused him, with her most desperate thoughts.

'Well, you may think so. What I think is, you've finally decided that I haven't got the right background to be mixed up with your music. Ever since I told you about my family being coloured. No — ever since you met my Pa face to face, saw he was a darkie, and realised he is still perfectly serious about me. You don't like it. All that matters more than my voice, in the end. Perhaps I've got it all wrong, but that's what I think. Am I wrong, Mr Johns?'

Harvey Johns turned a most decided profile on her, thinking. She had a quick brain, that was certain. What he had concluded was that Earl Garland was an interfering, awkward kind of fellow, with his claws well dug into his daughter's career. He, Harvey Johns, was not going to stand for conditions being set by a man he considered his inferior. Harvey had imagined he had a clear run with Ida, in every sense of the word.

'I don't like to be cross-examined,' he said.

He looked vicious and angry: then Ida saw that she had presumed too far. Mr Johns did not like hearing himself explained in such banal words. People like him did not have the motives of ordinary mortals.

'Well then. That's the end, Mr Johns. I shan't be coming to lessons any more. Won't you say goodbye?'

He did not move. His silence upset her very much. She had admired him for so long, and now her idol was behaving in such a petty, shabby way. Finally he stooped, like some great exotic bird on a perch, craning down over her.

'You'll regret this,' he said stiffly, and pecked at her cheek. 'Such a silly girl. I could have helped you to have a perfectly decent career, if you'd been willing to learn . . .'

'I'll learn.' Bitterness filled her words. She knew why Harvey Johns had found her irresistible. For a long time she had tried very hard not to be uncouth but it had not changed his response to her. Coloured was an exotic idea in Harvey's mind, not a condition in her. Ida's adolescent romance with the fantasy of her past had come to an end. The reality lay with her Pa.

She could not go straight home. She sat for a while in the Park. She relived the pain of that last conversation, trying to understand what Harvey Johns had really meant.

Such a short time ago, she had visions of a brilliant future. She had inspired passion: she remembered the way Harvey looked at her on the night of the concert, transfixed with admiration. Because she had suddenly looked beautiful, and sung for him with grace.

Doubt filled her with misery. Harvey Johns had developed her voice. It was his. Perhaps he had a right to her future — even to her body. Ida began to cry. The truth was, however much she disliked his touch, his swellings and protuberances, his sweat, his *liquidness* — the fact that he wanted sex with her had always been enthralling. There was no use denying that each time they came together, his desire moved her. Distaste always dissolved into tenderness. There were moments when, afterwards, she had felt happy to lie still and hold him.

Ida wailed aloud. No one heard her. She was only a shabby

girl on a bench in the park, crying. It happened all the time. She had seen other people, weeping. How frightening it was, to be one of the great crowd of the lost and hopeless, with their broken dreams, all those sad people who shuffled, anonymous, in all public places.

Feeling more and more like a tramp, Ida went home.

'What are you doing here?' Denise said, sensing a crisis in Ida at once. 'Shouldn't you be at your singing lessons?'

'Mr Johns said I should go. We're not having lessons any more.' Ida tried to bluff.

'Oh? Since when pray?' Denise's thin little nostrils worked in and out with curiosity, like a rabbit on the scent of a tasty morsel.

Ida tossed her head to cover a lie: 'Because I'm going to go over to Mr Summers, to start lessons with someone new.'

'Oh no you're not. I know all about that. Your Pa put his foot down on that. You'll never be a real singer, you know,' Denise added comfortably, examining her glistening nail varnish for a flaw.

Like a fool, Ida retaliated. 'Of course I will! Whatever do you mean, Ma!' She knew with a sinking heart, that whatever Denise said now would be ingrained on her memory for ever. She was too depressed, too low from her battle with Harvey Johns, to be able to withstand the attack.

'Because you're not really *decent*. The sort of girl who lives for art, the way famous artists do, you know, *pure*. I've seen you my girl. Looking in mirrors. Prinking. Day-dreaming. The way you eat.'

'Eat?' Ida's lip quivered.

'Making little piles. Saving the best bit till the end. *Appetite* I'm talking about. Even with a ham-fat sandwich. You see, I know all about you . . .'

'Don't say it!' Ida suddenly shrieked. 'Seeds of filth! Seeds of filth! I'm *yours* Ma! I could be just like you! And if I was, I promise you, I'd *die*.'

'Speaking to your mother like that.' Denise was positively delighted with this outburst. 'You see? No self-control. And I was only telling you for your own good — so you don't get your hopes up. So you settle down, to some more modest, proper kind of life.'

They both heard the key in the door, and stood quiet, as if caught in the act of committing a crime.

Earl called out: 'Denise?'

Victorious, Denise yielded the ground to her husband, murmuring something casual about young girls and flaming tempers.

Ida sank down at the kitchen table, sobbing over her folded arms.

'Ida? What is all this?' He shot his shirt-cuffs, irritated at walking into a domestic scene.

'What have you said to Mr Summers? It's all off, isn't it? Tell me the truth.'

Caught off-guard, Earl fumbled for words. 'It was Harvey Johns. He persuaded me it was a bad idea.'

'No, no! I just came from Mr Johns and . . .' but now Ida was in a bind, because telling her Pa about the conversation with Harvey involved blurting out the truth.

'And?' Earl looked aggressive, suspicious.

'If you won't let me go to Mr Summers, then I won't sing for Mr Johns or anyone!' she shouted, desperately trying to find a way out of this impasse.

'Rubbish! You'll do as you're told!'

Click-clack, Denise's heels on the hall floor . . .

'What she needs is a good hiding.' The usual Garland answer to any problem. Her Ma stood in the doorway, blowing smoke into the room.

Earl rounded on Ida. 'You can't go to the Summerses. We had a row. It's all over for you there. I know what I'm doing. But I insist you stick with Harvey Johns. I'm negotiating good terms with him, for all these new concerts . . .'

Ida was stunned. She could not go back. Behind her Pa, she heard Denise's mocking laughter. 'Not so clever, are you my girl? That Yid was going to make a mint out of you. And cut your poor Pa right out of the picture . . . after all he's done for you.'

'Shut up! Shut up!' Ida ran from the room. It couldn't be true — all her hopes ending in this nightmare of confusions, broken promises, furtive liaisons . . . She locked her bedroom door and stood behind it, banging her forehead, howling in rage and despair. When she heard her Pa's steps on the stair, she curled herself away from him at the top of her bed. He tried the door and found it bolted from inside.

'Open up. Open up, Ida. I want to talk to you.'

'No!' Ida shrieked at him, hating him for betraying her.

'Look, I've just telephoned Harvey Johns. He's prepared to forgive your rudeness today. Go on giving you lessons. He says he's very fond of you Ida. I've said . . . I've said I'll give him a free hand to plan your career. No conditions. You've got to go on. D'you hear me?'

A silence. Her Pa hesitated, expecting this huge sacrifice of control over her would be the Open Sesame. Knocking down doors was not his style, unlike Sidney Ottley. But there was no movement, only silence.

'All right. If that's your attitude you can stay there until you make up your mind to do as you're told,' he snapped.

His footsteps faded. Ida sat dully on the bed. Her entire world was in pieces. All her bright hopes tarnished by lies and deceptions. A desperate pain spread in her chest. To want so much to do well, and to end up a disaster. Rage and misery beat on her, gusts in a storm. Ida screamed aloud. 'I never want to see him again . . .' Harvey Johns. She would never be trapped by him. To be physically used and diminished, to go on enduring his beastly, dry, tuneless little musical fancies, his furtive, struggling sexual antics.

Ida hugged her knees, stunned that so many promises of adventure could disappear in one fateful day. They all wanted bits of her: Pa, Mr Johns, Mr Summers. Her voice made her nothing more than a piece of property. She had flown too high. Her wings had not been singed, they had been clipped. As her mother kept yelling at her: Who *do* you think you are?

She hadn't a clue. The light faded. Her head hurt, so she sat in darkness, snivelling, shivering in misery. Eventually, she heard the others come up to bed. Earl paused at her door once more.

'Are you ready to come out and behave?'

No answer.

'Then you stay there. You're to stay in your room until you see sense.'

Next morning, Ida waited until the house was empty. She knew all the knockings and bangings and shufflings; her Pa leaving for work, her Ma, teetering about the kitchen having a cup of tea and a cigarette before her morning promenade through the Bayswater streets.

'Ida!' she called up. 'There's food in the kitchen. You come down and take it while I'm out. I don't want to see you around when I get back.' Denise exulted in Ida's fall. She really was invisible now, in disgrace. Then the house was silent.

They meant business. Ida unlocked herself, crept downstairs and rang Uncle Billy's shop.

'Bush records.'

'Jack. It's me.'

'Oh. You is it.'

'Could you come round tonight?'

'What? So you can finish me off? Got an axe behind the door? Or your fancy man, straining at the leash?'

Ida started to cry.

'That's right. Blub. So you should. Spoiling yourself.'

'Look. I'm in real trouble. All that's over. I'm so — ashamed. I've stopped lessons with Mr Johns — and . . .'

'It was him! Well I never! I thought it was this wotsisname. Summers.'

''Course not! It's no one! I'll never do it again. I swear. I've got to get out of this mess.'

'Jesus, you're not in trouble are you?'

'Listen to me! I'm locked in my room. I can't talk for long.'

'I'll be in the back yard. At ten.'

Ida went upstairs slowly. She sat in front of her triptych of glass, but this time all she saw were the repeated mocking vistas of her miserable face — tears, tears, from every angle. She kept on looking, punishing herself for her vanity and her stupid, mistaken ambitions. Girls like her were fit only for one thing: for the half-world where no one asked questions about family, class, or race.

Night-time, a week later. Ida was still confined to her room for defying her Pa. The house settled into darkness, creaking as its old bones of beams cooled down. Ida looked out of her bedroom window and judged the drop to the kitchen roof. She had already pushed open the window, in the afternoon, so that it would not make a grating noise in the dead of night. She peered anxiously into the yard. There was Jack, as planned, waiting for her signal. When he saw her begin to climb down, he stood below, ready to catch her should she lose her grip and fall. She slipped on the drainpipe the last few yards and landed heavily on his toes.

'Jesus!' he groaned.

'Shut up!' she hissed back, uncaring.

'I'll get killed for this,' he said. 'Come on. We should walk in case we get seen by any neighbours or the lodgers, waiting for a bus.'

She yanked down the blue crêpe dress tucked into her knickers, and pulled a scarf over her head. They passed all the way down Bayswater, and Oxford Street, with Ida holding Jack's arm tight.

She was going back to Soho. For once in her life, she would strike out, enter the world that her Pa had always kept separate. She'd sing her lungs out in some dive, and then they'd all leave her alone. She'd be a Garland, but better than all the others. That was where she belonged.

It did not take them long to find the area where Uncle Ted had shown her the bottle party premises, the day she wore her first best dress. She had forgotten the club's name, but thought she might remember the street, the general location. How different the place looked at night-time: not so friendly, more ominous. Tarts lined the pavements. Glowing neon signs blinked above their heads. All the cosy little shops were shut, and in their place, shady doorways leading to dark stairs gaped, like mouths waiting to assuage appetites. That was how it looked to Ida, in her nervousness.

'OK. Archer Street. Take me there, Jack, and from there I'll remember the way we went.'

'Er . . .'

'For God's sake. You do know where it is?' she said impatiently.

'I do, I do. Calm down Ida. Left. No. Right. We should be

doing this in the daytime. No one's going to have time for you at night.'

'I can't risk that. Denise checks up on me too often.'

'OK. Down here. Mind the kerb. It's broken.'

'Never you mind about my feet. Just find Archer Street.'

'Here we are!' he said too triumphant — Ida realised it was more luck than judgement that had led them to the right place.

She retraced her steps, taking several more wrong turns, but sensing she was getting close. She knew only the name of the club owner, Mrs Cavendish. But when she found the place, the old club doorway had wooden boards nailed to it, and a To Let sign pasted on the window above.

'I told you,' said Jack, exasperated. 'These places come up and disappear overnight.'

'Let's ask someone,' Ida persisted.

A drunken man lurched out of a dark doorway at them. Terrified, Ida ran quickly through the nearest lighted door: a milk bar, run by a Maltese family, like half of Soho.

''Allo signorina. 'Allo young man. Cuppa tea?' asked a pale-skinned man with jet black hair. A beggar and a frowsy woman were the only other customers.

'No. No thank you. I wondered — you don't happen to know what happened to the — the club next door do you?' she spoke in a whisper, in case any one present would be shocked.

He grinned. 'Shut up when Madame was put in jail. P'lice a finale, raided her. Las' year, no, Maria?' he called to someone in the back store. 'Musta bin July.'

'Oh dear.'

'No you worry! Out and roun' the corner. New place. Glass Slipper. Very fancy, one a them wot you say 'ot spots. Naughty!' He winked at her. 'Don't let in little boys.'

Jack was about to swear but Ida pulled him away.

'Thank you.' Ida left the shop in great embarrassment, and they continued their wanderings. Finally they found the right place, in a small lane off Regent Street.

'You wait here. Don't come in,' she said.

'Ida . . .' Jack was genuinely concerned for her, but also pretty scared of standing alone in a backstreet of Soho in the middle of the night. 'It's not just girls they go for,' he mumbled, jerking a thumb at a passing group of drunken men, who were eyeing him up, giving him pathetic grins.

'You! Being picked up! Oh Jack, that's very funny!'

His wild look made her feel sorry. 'No. You're right. You'd better stand in the doorway. Don't be cross with me — I'll come back as soon as I can.'

Ida took a firm grip on herself and went forward, down an identical flight of narrow stairs. It all came back to her.

The place was coming alive, like a not yet successful party. A small band played resonantly at the back of the room. The tables were half-empty as it was only around nine o'clock, early for clubs in Soho. A few elegant couples danced with each other as if they were in someone's country house. An incongruous row of painted china plates on a high shelf suggested manorial hand-me-downs. *Trompe-l'oeil* paintings of fountains and French gardens gave a chic, continental air. The club did not look in the least evil and decadent, but welcoming, cosily exclusive. Ida began to feel less timid.

'Hallo?' the hat-check girl said.

'I've got an appointment with Mrs Cavendish,' Ida lied.

'In there,' she said, nodding.

Ida pushed open a small door and found Mrs Cavendish, looking more fragile than she remembered. She sat by a tiny electric fire, sipping tea and stroking a bush of a cat. The kimono (doubtless to avoid pet hairs on her neat wool suit) was the same, limper than before. Mrs Cavendish peered shortsightedly through spectacles, looped chains hanging beside her ears, and reminding Ida suddenly of her horrible prison sentence for serving liquor outside licence hours. In Holloway, probably. Her hair had gone very grey, revealing an old woman's pale scalp under a fierce black dye.

'Who are you? I'm not expecting anyone.' Mrs Cavendish spoke in clipped tones, and moved as if to call for help.

'Please! We've met, though it was a long time ago. I'm Miss Garland. Josephine's niece, Earl Garland's daughter — and I'm looking for work.'

'Make an appointment.'

'Please! My Pa doesn't know I'm here, I'm trying to make my way by myself you see . . .'

'Then why mention his name to me?'

'Because you'd throw me out if I didn't.'

Approval glimmered on Mrs Cavendish's face. Then she said, 'I like people who make their own way, so to speak, using every advantage. Well, I'm always short of a waitress.'

'Gosh no! I'm a singer!' Ida protested.

'A singer! Fancy that! Starting as we mean to go on, I see. Your Pa's a reliable sort of fellow, usually comes up with good types.'

Ida made an effort to ignore the derogatory tone of her voice.

'Why aren't you on his books?' Mrs Cavendish asked. 'Maybe he doesn't think you're good enough!'

'It isn't like that! I want to surprise him, that's all. Get a job.'

Mrs Cavendish was silent, wondering if she felt in the mood to do someone beneath her a favour.

'How old are you?'

'Eighteen.' Ida lied again, this time with even more conviction.

'Next birthday? Or the one after? I'll believe you. This isn't the kind of place where people ask questions . . .' Mrs Cavendish's laughter was not very appealing. 'You can't sing here. We've got professionals. But you're pretty. Very pretty. Take off your coat.'

Ida did so, feeling as exposed as if she were naked on Harvey Johns' bed. Mrs Cavendish noted the Chanel with a raised eyebrow.

'Mmm. Classy. I like that. I'm short of a dance hostess tonight. Can you dance?'

Ida nodded. Jack showed off all the new steps from the Hammersmith Palais in Gran's parlour. If all upper-class types danced like those Arab sheikhs at the Palmer party, she'd have no trouble at all.

'I'll give you one trial night. No pay. You're Number Three. No drugs, no hanky-panky. You sit out there and dance with one of the young men. I employ them to make the place look filled up. People won't come in if there isn't a crowd. When the members arrive you mind your manners, understand?'

'Oh yes, Mrs Cavendish. I know how to behave myself. My cousin's upstairs. Can he come in and wait to take me home?'

'No. Send him round to the kitchens. There's the staff entrance. Boyfriends aren't allowed on the premises.'

Ida ran up to tell Jack the news. He was leaning on the wall outside, his thin jacket turned up vainly against the cold, a cigarette cupped in his hand for warmth. 'I got told to move away,' he said, sniffing.

'I've got a trial night! You can go round to the kitchens! You'll stay, won't you? Please?'

'It's not good enough for you. I don't like this joint. It's all right for an old pro like my Ma, but not for you.'

'Oh shut up. I've got to start somewhere.'

He shrugged and turned towards the alley, hunched up. Ida ran after him and held his arm.

'Thanks for bringing me. I wouldn't have the nerve all on my own. I'll be good, you'll see, and I'll never forget you stood by me.'

He gave a sad, reluctant grin, and pecked her cheek. His blue lips were cold. Ida ran back inside the club.

She slipped into a seat at a small table near the bandstand, enraptured. The band was swinging into the coda of a quickstep, trumpets wailing and a banjo adding some novelty texture to the sound. A fragile-featured young man came over from another table and introduced himself.

'Hallo. You're in for Number Three, right? Name's Rupert. I'm Number Two. Even numbers boys, odd ones, girls . . . Look, this one's a tango. Let's have a go. We're meant to dance all the time till the floor fills up.'

Ida rose, and nervously clutched the young man's hands. 'Tilt your head more,' he said. 'That's better. A nice line. I'm a ballet student, so I hope you don't mind my saying . . .'

'Not at all!' Ida relaxed a little as they glided neatly across the dance floor.

'She'll keep you. You look good and you dance rather well.' Rupert gave his verdict after a few more turns.

'I do hope so! But I'm a singer, really . . .' Ida wanted him to know, she had her excellencies too.

'Well, we all have our dreams.' Rupert's laugh was casual and not unkind but Ida was smitten with fear that not only did he not believe her, but that she would never, never progress.

A silvery-haired, whiskered man interrupted them. 'May I have the pleasure?' he said, an arm circling Ida's waist as if he knew the answer already.

'Oh Mr Firth. Good-evening.' Rupert disappeared, waving good luck to Ida.

Mr Firth's wife was too arthritic to dance, but she enjoyed the music and liked to see her husband take a turn . . . Mr Firth himself danced well, and was politely grateful for Ida's time. But after that mild introduction to her duties came an extremely drunken Guards officer, who had somehow lost his party and imagined a few thrashes round the floor might sober him sufficiently to remember where he ought to be for the rest of the evening . . . then she was commandeered by a desperate-looking young man, smelling of Macassar oil, and clutching a hip-flask. He watched the door over Ida's head between taking swigs and spinning her round and round. He did not speak a word, but would not let her go; until suddenly a girl in a monkey-fur stole appeared in the door, shot him a venomous glance and left at once. 'Good!' Ida's partner said, and fled; Ida could see that life as Number Three was going to be a series of unfinished dramas, let alone dances. Next a portly gentleman pressed her extra-close to his enormous belly, but fortunately this enabled her to avoid the pressure of something harder, lower down . . .

Someone tapped her on the shoulder. Ida's face was aching with false smiles, but she turned eagerly — into the hard chest of Mrs Cavendish.

'Eleven-thirty. We're full enough. You can go. Come back tomorrow if you want to be paid . . .'

'Oh, thank you! Thank you very much!'

Exhausted more from tension than physical effort, Ida slipped out to the kitchen. Her shoes were irreparably scuffed, and her body seemed to give off male odours, the imprint of all the well-groomed men who had held her: warm sweat, mingled with whisky, brandy, cigar smoke, hair-oil, toilet waters of an enticing astringency. Ida found Jack in a corner of the kitchen, lolling next to a pile of smelly pheasants. His chagrin at being found asleep almost put him in a bad mood: But the long walk home together, laughing and full of her great new plans, was fun and they parted friends.

Mrs Cavendish never asked why Ida only turned up between nine and midnight. It didn't much matter. By then the dance floor was packed, and her customers had found their own partners. One dance hostess less did not matter. At the vital time, in the early evening, Ida was willing, charming, and more than able to keep her guests amused. She did not talk a great deal but what she said was clearly not too crude or stupid to turn people away.

In between dances, she noticed Ida sat on the edge of the bandstand, listening to Tommy Trevino and the resident players, as if her whole future depended on it. Poor child. Tommy Trevino was a great pianist — but so fat he had to go to a prostitute for his pleasures, and then only took them *à la Française*.

After a few nights, Ida had the confidence to climb down from her bolted room and to walk into town alone. Jack rigged up a nail for a handhold on a difficult bit of the wall, when no one was about to see him up a ladder, hammering at the brickwork.

One night a young man asked her to dance; Ida prepared herself for the usual toe-mashing, but he was quite neat, for a change.

'I say. Haven't I seen you somewhere before?' he asked.

Ida looked down, hiding her face. Supposing he had seen her at the music school!

'I remember! Old Palmer's wedding. You sang. Gosh, you were terrific. Do you sing here?'

'No. Not tonight, that is. The other singer has the spot tonight,' she lied bravely.

'What a pity. Oh look, my party's arrived. Perhaps I'll hear you another night. Thanks for the dance. Bye.'

Depressed, Ida made an excuse of a headache and went home early. It was as well to get back and wander about the bathroom in the dead of night, just in case her Pa thought her long, lone nights too quiet.

Another time, Ida was sitting about in her blue crêpe dress which was now looking sadly the worse for wear, when one of the regulars came up to her. The young and beautiful artist, Miss Madeleine Hopp.

'Hi, Number Three, how are you?' Her voice had an unreal lilt to it.

'I'm fine, Miss Hopp.'

'"I'm fine, Miss Hopp." You're a girl with a dark secret. So-oo-o refined, my dear. I bet you're the daughter of an African chief. Or something like that.'

'Something like that, Miss Hopp. Where's your boyfriend tonight? Held up?'

'Oh, I guess so. Had to pop along to his Papa, funds, all that . . . I say, Number Three . . .' Madeleine Hopp laid her tightly-bound brunette head along a pallid arm, and smiled up at Ida, a red mouth quivering in an effort not to look too desperate. 'Will you help me?'

'Me? How?' Ida was polite but careful.

'There's a little parcel I'd like you to pick up for me. From a friend across the street. Go on, say you'll do it. I'm just dead beat. I've been painting all day, and I don't want to miss Mr MacIntyre when he turns up. Go on, I'll give you a fiver if you agree . . .'

'Just this once. The place is pretty busy . . .'

'Flat number six. Say Hopp sent you. It'll be all right.'

Ida ran out into the cold air of the Soho street. She'd been at the club about three weeks. If she did not get a chance soon, she'd have to give up. Sooner or later her Pa was going to put a stop to her locked-in protest.

Soon it would be Christmas. In the distance she could hear a drunk droning a carol. She bit her lip against the cold, but when the wind whistled tears into her eyes, it was only the season, not her mood.

She found the staircase. The usual dingy Soho doorway, with a number of nameplates outside, like her Pa's office. Up she went, fumbling in the dark. She found number six, and hesitated. Getting involved in other people's drug problems was not her aim. A solid fiver was, on the other hand, very much part of the plan. When she had enough money, she would run away from home. Perhaps one of the dance hostesses might let her share a room.

She lifted her hand and knocked timidly. Just then a heavy thud on the staircase made her turn, apprehensive.

'You go in that door and I'll call the police.'

'Who's there?'

A rotund figure moved out of the shadows into the light. It was Mr Trevino, the bandleader from the Glass Slipper. Embarrassed, he fixed his braces and adjusted his coat.

'Number Three . . . What are you doing here?'

'I'm running an errand for Miss Madeleine Hopp.'

'Fuck the errand, pardon my French. You'll do nothing of the sort. Get back inside the club.'

He put a firm hand under her elbow, and led her back across the street. 'I've been watching you. Fetching coffee for the lads, sitting there on the edge of the bandstand. What's your name? Who did you say you were?'

'I never did. I'm Number Three. But my real name is Ida Garland.'

'Garland? Some young man came up and told me about you. He says he heard you sing once. Any relation to Ted?' he asked a little more familiarly.

'He's my uncle.'

'Josephine? A daughter?' Tommy looked incredulous.

'No, my Pa's the elder brother. Earl.'

'Don't know him so well. Great lad, Ted is. Only problem he's got, doesn't like to read arrangements. Otherwise I'd have had him in my band a long time ago. Give him my regards. Say Tommy Trevino sends his regards. What are you hanging around for, young lady?'

'I want to sing with the band.'

'Ha ha. I've heard that before. I tell you what I'll do. Wait till after three, when the regular girl goes home. I'll give her an early night.'

'What about Miss Hopp?'

'I'll deal with her too. Off you go.'

Tommy Trevino smoothed back his hair and went to the bandstand, frowning. He did not like the idea of a properly brought up girl hanging around the Glass Slipper. Ted Garland was a lad, but he would hate to see his own niece end up like all the rest. It would be better if he gave her an audition, and told her once and for all she was no good. Send her home, away from trouble. The door she'd been knocking at was a Chinese dope-dealer's, of a murderous disposition.

All night Ida circulated, foxtrotting, tangoing, quickstepping with the customers. She had never stayed so late, when the club started to draw a big crowd.

To Ida's great wonder, at midnight the entire floor of the basement club was illuminated, a golden glow. The glass tiles were lit from below, transforming the room into a sophisticated fairyland. The noise grew deafening as the regulars filled up the room. Fast chatter, hard laughter, and the glitter of not so real gems among some subdued (no doubt more valuable) family jewels . . . fur stoles, lacy boleros, tail coats and wing collars, a flower in a buttonhole; in a corner, knotted on a bare back, a single strand of perfect pearls.

All the members table-hopped, as if they were passengers on some endless ocean voyage. They were of course: this was London society, floating through the murky waters of the Depression. It was the first time that Ida had seen at close quarters such a public display of casual wealth. This was where she would make her money!

Gradually the club thinned. The resident vocal artiste, a Jewish blonde who sang blues songs rather well, left early, delighted to have a break near Christmas. Mr Trevino called Ida to the stand.

'That was the wife. Now, what will it be?'

'"Someone to Watch Over Me". But can I do it jazzy, I heard it sung that way once? Double time,' she whispered eagerly.

'We'll do it once hot, and once slow. What key?'

'D.'

'See how we go.'

'I do know the verse, Mr Trevino.'

'OK. Four bars intro.'

When Ida got to the end of the verse, 'Tell me, where is the shepherd for this lost lamb?' she found herself smiling at its truth. That gave a nice irony to her singing of the refrain, and her voice darkened with sexual innuendo.

When she finished, the girl behind the bar clapped. An audience of one. Ida liked that. A few dancers still crawled drunkenly round the floor, not even feeling each other, dreaming of sleep but incapable of leaving. Tommy Trevino rubbed his hands together, because his fingers were a bit stiff from accompanying. Ida Garland needed some really good piano playing.

Mrs Cavendish came forward holding her cat, its claws pinned brooch-like in her flat chest. A cigarette dangled in the corner of her tight red mouth.

'So! You got your chance!' she said. 'What do you think?' she asked Tommy.

'Classy. Overproduced, but I think she'll mend. She looks good all right. Unusual. They like that.'

His bulging brown eyes told Mrs Cavendish another story. Tommy Trevino was signalling that they had tripped over a real gem.

'Relief for Mrs Trevino? Christmas shopping?' she suggested.

Tommy Trevino beamed. What a perfect excuse for a few Christmas bonuses for his ladies of the night . . . 'She'll like that, Gloria. I'll give her some extra money, so she doesn't feel put out.'

'Two weeks,' Mrs Cavendish offered Ida. 'Three pounds. But you'll have to be here longer hours: there's a supper show at ten, another at midnight, and then how you feel till we close.'

'Yes Mrs Cavendish.' Ida could hardly suppress her excitement. She had something to tell her Pa at last.

'Don't think this changes the rules. No drink, no gambling, no affairs. No scruffy young men loitering outside. The people who come here know what's what.' She walked away, slightly annoyed to discover that Ida had a talent.

'She shouldn't talk to a nice girl like that. She means they sleep with each other, not the servants,' said Tommy, through his teeth, still smiling.

Mrs Cavendish called out an afterthought: 'Wear something cleaner than that rag! Smart!'

'What does she mean by smart?' Ida asked, anxiously.

'As long as there's nothing to it you'll be all right,' he winked. 'Get your Aunt Josephine to give you some of her cast-offs. Though you're half the size of her, these days . . . give her my regards. Say Tommy Trevino sends his regards.'

These were no idle words; the way Tommy spoke Ida felt she carried away a small white visiting card. His private tastes were well known, but with people he respected, his behaviour was all dignity. He had the kindly old world manners of the East End, a mixture of European immigrant custom and Cockney solidarity. Ida thought he had probably started out in life as Thomas Trevor or Tomas Trevinski. It wasn't only divas who went for the romance of the Latin name.

It had happened so fast, it was a fantasy. Ida woke up in her room one morning, remembering the night before, and realised it was true. She had dived into life, dived into the stream, and come up breathing.

She took Tommy Trevino's advice and ran round to Josephine as soon as the house was empty. Midday: Josephine was cooking a late breakfast for herself and Sidney, bacon, eggs, fried bread, and yeast-spread toast. Josephine had put on weight since her second marriage.

'Jack's gone hours ago, at Billy's shop, dear, you'll have to find him there,' she said.

'No Auntie, it's you I've come to see.'

'Well, that's a nice surprise. Sit down, do.'

Sidney murmured a falsely welcoming greeting then went back to mounding up neat forkfuls of food, toast then bacon then soft egg, while studying his racing page. The fork would poise in mid air, but he managed to engulf his food just at the moment that the pile threatened to disintegrate. Timing risks was an essential part of his way of life as a gambling man.

Josephine was pleased to see Ida, lifting the vast quilted cottage off the teapot to pour her out a cup. Ida always liked her aunt's house, it was army-neat, not really out of character; Josephine was a much-travelled professional and when she came home liked to enjoy her domesticity.

'How's my favourite niece, then? I hear you've got a spot of bother. Confined to barracks by your Pa. Is that right? I always expect Jack to be in trouble, but not you.'

'Well, it's more complicated than that. Would you do me a favour, Aunt Josephine? It's a secret.'

'Well, that's what Christmas is for. Hurry up and finish that Sidney, I've got to have a private word.'

'Oh no, don't disturb Sidney — it's about a dress, perhaps we could go to another room . . .'

'Good Lord Josephine, nothing of yours will fit her,' Sidney said with a snigger. 'Not that I mind — I always liked an armful.'

'Mind your own business.' Josephine swatted at some imagined bluebottle, but she smiled as well.

'A party, I bet, and you've not got anything fancy . . .' she said to Ida.

'Sort of.'

'Oh, I see, still not sure Earl's going to let you out. Who's the lucky young man? One of your high-class connections, no doubt.'

Ida was happy to leave her with that wrong impression. Josephine liked to be appealed to on love matters.

'I've got some beautiful things, all handmade. I can't get into them now mind you, so it'll be nice to think they're enjoying themselves. All in a good cause, eh?'

She took her upstairs to her boxroom, stuffed with trunks, hat-boxes, the walls plastered with theatrical posters and bills. It was a good place for a gossip. 'Who's the lucky chap? Go on, I won't tell . . .'

Ida hesitated over the truth. As Aunt Josephine knew the night-club scene, perhaps it would be more sensible to get the benefit of her advice.

'I've taken a job at the Glass Slipper. Just for a while, see if I like it.'

'Ooh my God, what'll Earl say? He'll go mad!' Josephine sat heavily on the bed to a chord of anxious springs.

'Look here, Aunt Josephine, I'm old enough to make my own decisions. Pa won't let me go to the Summerses and I won't stay with Harvey Johns for the rest of my life . . .'

'Why not? He's respected, he's done well by you . . .' in a second Josephine was going to land heavily on the truth.

'He's a good man, but Gran's right. This business with the Summerses has shown me what's what. I'm not really cut out for that world. I'd rather be a Garland, like the rest of the family.'

She succeeded in diverting Josephine, who sighed, 'I always thought Earl was pushing you too hard. But you have a great future ahead of you. You should be grateful, not undo all his plans.'

'Well, perhaps Pa's right, and I won't like it. It's only two weeks, and Tommy Trevino is going to keep an eye on me — he sends his regards by the way — and supposing I don't get on, then at least I can go back to the concert work with a clear mind. No harm done, eh?'

'Mmm.' Josephine fingered a black satin dress with no back and diamond shoulder straps. 'You're a smart one. Always have been. Try this on, and that red velvet thing. I'll be back in a minute.'

While Ida tried on her dresses, Josephine went downstairs for some pins.

'I shan't need to alter this one, look, it's perfect!' Ida exclaimed when she returned. 'I've been losing weight recently . . .'

'It was only puppy fat, I told you. Gawd, was I ever that thin?' Josephine added with dismay. Then she sat on the bed again. 'The other one's the same size. I remember buying them together. Keep 'em, they only remind me. Just right for Mrs Cavendish. Ooh she is a Tartar, that one.'

'Thank you ever so much Auntie!' Ida kissed her.

'Now sit down young lady.'

'What is it? If you're worried, I'm not going to tell Pa, I am . . . I have to face him sooner or later.'

'That's your department. No. I want a word. Take this telephone number. It's my doctor. I should have given you this before. Now I hope you'll be a good girl. But, if you ever have any trouble, you know what I mean, he's a good man.' Josephine's expression darkened. It was like being in a familiar room, and seeing it fill up with fearful shapes when the light goes out.

'Thank you.' Ida avoided her eyes.

'I don't want to know anything more about it — Earl would kill me if he knew, egging you on. You have to look out for yourself. It's none of my business. Understand?'

'Yes Auntie.' Ida was more saddened than shocked. Josephine obviously suspected there was a man involved. Just like Gran, she did not offer useless opinions. Harvey Johns was always very careful, and Ida had no intention of getting into more complications. She decided to take comfort in the idea that Josephine accepted her as a young woman, no longer a child.

'You can't be serious. After all I've done for you!' Earl was trying to be angry, but Ida's behaviour was so perfidious, so typically female, that he began to crumble and look pathetic as if she were his wife.

'Pa! You were the one who messed up Mr Summers taking me on!'

'Thought you'd pay me back, did you? I'm not standing for this. Summers was a shark. I thought so, your Gran thought so, and so did Harvey Johns.'

Ida would have protested, but she was terrified of letting slip anything that would reveal her affair with Harvey Johns. She had no idea how her Pa would react to that. It might provoke him to violence, or much worse, it might finish her with him.

'Please Pa. Please don't be cross. Let me at least try.'

'I'll put a stop to this. Go straight to Mrs Cavendish! Report her for employing underage girls! My daughter's not singing in a Soho bottle party!'

Ida was prepared. 'You wouldn't. She's one of your best clients. You wouldn't want to offend her or Mr Trevino. It's only for two weeks. Just so I can see for myself. Mr Trevino's going to help me with some songs . . .'

Earl was incredulous. 'What's Mr Johns going to say? Throwing away your voice! After his years of work!'

'He's got other students,' she retorted, thinking of Janet Sheldon. 'He's always saying that if we aren't totally dedicated, then there's no point in going on.'

'Well, why aren't you dedicated? I'll get him on to you, I'll not stand for this . . .'

'Pa, don't go and see him. I'm not going back. I'm not going back Pa, whatever you say.'

Ida's voice had a bitterness that made him afraid. 'You were so pleased,' he went on, defeated, perplexed. 'Look, if it's because of the Summerses, perhaps I could reconsider my decision . . .' Earl looked so full of conflict Ida had to take the burden from him.

'Look Pa,' she said persuasively, 'you want me to be a big success. Make money. I'm telling you, I'll do it for you. But it has to be my way.'

'What will your Ma say? Singing in a night-club!' He spoke the words with a disgust that suggested Denise most accurately. It was his last bullet, and it misfired.

Ida laughed. 'She'll say I'm running true to type.'

Earl turned away sharply, unwilling to confess she was right. She could feel him giving up. 'But you could have been legitimate! *I'm* right behind you, even if she isn't . . . I always have been. Why are you doing this to me?' A dark thought came to him. 'Don't tell me it's because of . . .'

'No Pa. You were right. Colour doesn't matter. In fact, sometimes being different is a help. It makes you bend and turn, bend and turn, to find another way . . .' She left the room so that he would not look upon her tears as weakness.

Ida's first night at the club was on Christmas Eve, so she decided on Josephine's red velvet, to make a suitably festive impression. Now all the Garlands were helping London to celebrate the season. Trying to rest before her début, Ida stayed in her bedroom, lying on her bed and listening to crystal set radio with headphones that Uncle George had rigged up for her. There was a programme of dance music from the Savoy Hotel in the Strand. No doubt some of the people at the smart ball there, would come on to the Glass Slipper later, as part of their Christmas celebrations. She was proud to belong to London's high life, even if she was only at its service.

The house was quiet; Earl and Denise had made a point of going out elsewhere, ignoring her night-club début. Ida dressed carefully, profiting from her Ma's absence by borrowing an expensive fur-trimmed cloak.

It was a clear, starry night sky, and she looked forward to the walk all the way to the club to give her energy for singing. As she went up Bayswater, opposite Hyde Park, clouds of frosty mist billowed out through the railings, where the cold air from the Serpentine, the lake and the grass, met the warmth generated by London's life.

Now she responded to the celebratory mood of the streets, the passers-by carrying presents for friends, the lighted displays of gifts in shop windows. Ida hurried forward until she reached the heart of the night city again. The neon light of the Glass Slipper had broken, only 'ass' and 'ipper' were illuminated, but that seemed in keeping with Mrs Cavendish's raffish success and her defiance of the laws.

Ida went through the kitchen entrance, feeling at last that she belonged. She pushed through the crowd, her cloak pulled from her shoulders and hastily bundled over her arm. Tommy pointed to a baize door close to the bandstand. He held up his fingers, crossed to wish her luck. Ida ran for the door, happy to leave the din, and her usual small seat near the edge of the dance floor. She was a performer!

A ballerina was having a cigarette before her turn. There was a great vogue for 'arty' turns in revues and cabaret, but the woman looked incongruous in the shabby surroundings, with her blocked shoes and spangled tutu like a Christmas fairy come to life in the wrong room.

''Allo,' she said in husky tones. 'Two teas, and a brandy darling.'

'I'm not the waitress!' Ida bridled.

'Oh, I am so sorry. You're one of the dance hostesses.' Her eyes travelled decisively over the red velvet dress.

'No. Not tonight. I'm a singer. I'm going to sing after the cabaret.'

'My poor baby . . .' The ballerina eyed her with pity, as if she would only have the remnants of an audience left. With a cigarette in her lips, making one side of her face distort as if from a seizure, the woman retied her ribbons, and put her feet up on a chair.

'Bitch,' murmured Ida to herself. But her nerves began to frazzle in her. Ida left the room and bounced her way back through the dancing couples like a rugger ball through a scrum. She asked for two sherries at the bar. (Both for herself, one for now, one for later.) 'Gran's mellower' would lift her.

On her way back to the performers' room, she fell into the stony bosom of Mrs Cavendish, who stared at the offending glass.

'It's for the ballerina,' Ida said quickly.

'That old soak. I told the bar not to serve her, but she's sending others for it I see. Clever, but not clever enough.' She took the drink from Ida and sniffed it, looking puzzled. 'This is sherry, not brandy! Good Lord, no one drinks sherry at this time of night. She's worse than I thought, poor dear. I'd better have a word with her partner. I don't want any injuries on my hands.'

'Oh, I'm sure that's my mistake,' Ida said innocently, 'I must have said the wrong thing . . . I don't know anything about drinks. I'll take it back, shall I?'

'Yes . . .' Mrs Cavendish watched her doubtfully. When the crowd closed between them Ida downed the second sherry in a gulp and left the glass on a nearby table. Lack of height had some benefits.

Some chorus girls went on stage first, rat-tatting and shouting through two popular songs. Then a stand-up comedian did a routine on being drunk: he hurled insults at the band and mauled his party-piece song. It was a highly suggestive comic act. The ballerina and her partner danced in a manner vaguely artistic and only mildly erotic; as the stage was tiny the woman lay in her partner's arms swooning for much of the time.

Ida's turn. Tommy Trevino introduced her, not that anyone was listening. They were busily pushing back their chairs, ready to dance again.

'Now ladies and gentlemen, we've got a sweet young lady here with a very pretty voice, a very pretty dress, and a very pretty face. So I hope you're all going to be very kind to her, because she's also very new and very nervous.'

A few titters, a round of applause, and then everyone turned back to their conversations. Several couples, restless after the ballet, took to the floor. Most people were too drunk to notice more than an increase in well-being: Ida's voice blended sweetly with the swell of pleasure around them. But Tommy Trevino glowed with encouragement. They had worked on three numbers for a suitable programme, Ida had learnt them perfectly, and apart from a few misunderstandings about tempo, she sang fine.

After her first song she stopped. She looked at the vacuous faces before her, and for an instant was transported to the room in the country where a caring audience once hung on her every note. Her throat constricted; she tried not to cry. She looked across at the piano, but there was no Harvey Johns to fill her with dreams, with inspiration. Only Mr Trevino, squinting over a cigarette stub in the corner of his mouth.

But Tommy did understand. He caught her mood, and played it back to her on the keyboard. 'Go on love. Tell me all about it,' he said. Ida began to sing: 'If I Could Be with You One Hour Tonight', and Tommy, captivated, performed a piano solo that Ida judged a match for anything Uncle Ted could do. In return, Ida heard her own voice fill out with warmth. The louder she sang, the sweeter, more exciting she became. Now her voice did not sound accomplished, but was a cry of youth, eagerness and a hunger for good times. Ida lifted her arms from her sides and held them out to the audience, like a welcoming embrace to someone familiar. Tommy did not take his eyes from her. That was her moment of realisation. She was in the right place, not by choice, or chance, but by decree: her own very special inheritance. She wanted to be a musician's singer, and create such moods of contact all the time. Tommy was a generation from her, and the music from another world, America, and yet she and the man playing with her understood each other in it to perfection.

9

The morning after she received her first singer's wages, Ida put
half aside for her Pa. Then she went out and bought a hat, had
her hair cut and waved into a neat V at the nape of her neck, and
succumbed to a coloured lipsalve.

It was the first time she had painted her mouth to be seen in
public. She had been studying the female patrons of the Glass
Slipper, carefully noting hair-styles and dress, with an ambition
to look as good as they did. What her Ma had said was untrue.
The smartest women wore gold, furs, had bright red lips and
painted nails, but they were saved from looking cheap by their
behaviour: they acted as if they owned the world.

Today was a special day: Uncle Ted was returning from the
East, and she wanted to look a 'stunner' for him.

Josephine picked her up in town with Jack, in Ted's vintage
AC. When Jack got out to open the door for Ida, her new finery
made him stare.

'You look lovely, Ida!' Josephine shouted. 'About ten years
older! Doesn't she, Jack!'

Although impressed, Jack folded his arms defensively. 'It's all
that night-life. Makes a girl pasty. No wonder she needs to paint
her face.'

Josephine cuffed him about the head. 'She's beautiful, and
you know it.'

Jack shrugged, but as they drove along Ida could sense his
eyes upon her new sophistication, worrying that she was
growing away from him for ever this time. She tried to give him a
smile, but that was a mistake. Jack felt patronised, and hunched
himself into the front seat, ignoring her.

Josephine drove down to Tilbury where they were to meet
Ted off his liner. Josephine enjoyed making men stare as she
speeded past. The car itself was worthy of attention, with
white-walled tyres and chrome fittings. Josephine's feathered

hat and gauntlet gloves gave her a cavalier style well-suited to her reckless driving.

Jack kept his attention firmly fixed on the boring landscape of Essex as they approached the docks — the flat and smoked scenery, not improved by the dullness of a wet January. Small villages looked out of place, with the docks looming grey and smoke-laden over them. His studied concentration on nothing of interest was very trying. Josephine filled the silence by singing as she sped along or swearing when she was forced to slow down. Ida cuddled herself in her blanket and tried not to become carsick.

When they arrived at the dock area, Ida was alienated by the multitude of foreign faces shuffling into work on the quays. Slightly oriental, olive-skinned, or even blacker than coloured. These last were the Lascars, the navvies on the ships from India. Their aquiline, ebony faces, and thin fine bodies, were darker than any she had seen before. On the quayside, there were whole groups of West Indian labourers laughing and joking with a resigned sense of value — they were beasts of labour, for money that was barely reasonable. Even at this level, there was no acceptance of a common lot. Ida could see that whites worked alongside white, black next to black. And white casual workers, hanging about for lack of a regular job, looked distinctly bitter about their humiliation.

Josephine caught her looking as they drove slowly through the dirty streets towards the right dock.

'Another world, isn't it love?' she said. 'In my young, wild days, I used to come down here to the West Caribbean sailors' "Homeward bounders". Parties for the lucky ones going back. Calypso music, all night long — and some good local jazz. We must have been crazy to come into a tough neighbourhood. It was Ted — him and Jim, they wanted to have a look.'

'You mean, for the people or the music?'

Josephine laughed. Like her brothers, she never discussed the race issue. 'Only showed us how different we were. The only thing that makes you different is not having money in your pocket. Don't we all do nicely? And no one's ever been offensive to me. You've got to live your life above all that.'

'Didn't Pa come with you too?' Ida asked.

'Only once. Got stopped by the police after a brawl. Scared him to death. Always too good to be true, your Pa was.'

'So that was when he nearly got put on a list...' Ida remembered.

'Mind you, once or twice we saw toffs,' Josephine went on. 'Trying to act natural, having an adventure. One of them used to write poems in a corner. I suppose they were pretending it was like Paris — like those clubs they have up in Mon Marter.'

Jack interrupted: 'Ma, concentrate, will you? You nearly drove into that van.' He had been studying the ships, avoiding the conversation. 'Over there. I can see it — the one with the blue star on the funnel.'

The smells of foreign parts penetrated everyone's nostrils: rancid, spicy, rotting, pungent.

It was easy to find the right dock because the big liner, the *Orient Queen*, sat high in the water above cranes and warehouses. Besides, a growing number of welcoming families were moving through the dock offices and along the quaysides, so they just followed the stream.

'Timed it just right,' said Aunt Josephine, parking somewhere unofficial and convenient. 'I do wish Sidney had come. It's quite a show when a liner comes in.'

The *Orient Queen* was berthing, and Ida watched with interest as the seamen uncoiled the ropes, apparently at random, but no doubt according to a plan.

Ida stood beside Jack at the water's edge, where he was throwing pellets of paper from his pocket into the oily water. A stream of cabbage leaves and other bilge was being poured out of the ship on the offshore-side of its hull.

'What a thing to do. Like a Bank Holiday crowd in a charabanc.' Ida joked, looking up at him hopefully.

His lips tightened, as he ignored this remark.

'Come on Jack, we're friends, aren't we? After all we've done together?'

'You don't need me to be your friend any more. Fancy job. Fancy clothes, lots of money. New feller? Upper crust, is he? I shouldn't wonder.' His face darkened with the urge to be mean to her. Like his mother Josephine, Jack's opinions were always undiluted: either a bottle was full or it only had a drop in the bottom.

'Stop spying! You're always picking on me!'

A small Salvation Army band was playing jovial hymns for the gathering crowd. Some of the passengers had thrown streamers down at the bustling throng. Finally the gangplank was lowered and the arrivals hurried out straight into waiting arms. To the optimistic strains of the band, blaring 'This Little Heart of Mine, I'm Going to Let it Shine', the three Garlands caught sight of Ted disembarking.

A terrible shock: he was wearing a white suit, a black-banded panama hat and dark glasses — something Ida had never seen in the streets of London. His skin was khaki-stained with illness and he picked his way down the planks as if he might fall at any moment. 'Is he drunk do you think?' said Jack.

''Course not!' Josephine was indignant. She ran forward to meet her brother. 'My God Ted, what on earth's the matter with you!' Josephine practically lifted him off his feet in her embrace.

'Some bug or other. Not as bad as it looks,' he muttered. 'I'll be fine. You drive Josephine old girl. Haven't got my landlegs . . . Nice to see my old 'girl-trap' again. Running well, my motor, is she?' He hobbled to the car and climbed in the back with Ida. The journey home was most subdued. At one point Ted felt for Ida's hand under the blanket, and went on holding it as they approached London.

'Heard all about you,' Ted murmured. 'Tommy Trevino sent me a cable. Quite a turn up for the books, eh, young lady? Glad you bumped into Tommy. He'll look after you.'

'Pa's still livid,' Ida said, smiling. 'In fact, nearly everyone's livid with me at the moment,' she said, with a meaningful tilt of her head towards Jack.

'Don't you take any notice. I'll stick up for you.' He squeezed her hand, and nudged it under the cover towards Jack's back.

'What's up with him?' he mouthed.

'He thinks I'm being a loose woman, now I'm in Soho,' she whispered, trying to make light of it. Then she turned pink. Ted's face went hard and sad. He could read her like a book, he was an expert in this subject. He knew she was no longer a virgin.

'I see. Who's the lucky feller?' he whispered, with that same brutish sneer that Jack had given her. The two in the front could not hear over the noise of the car.

'It's over, Uncle Ted. I learnt my lesson.'

'Sure. So have I,' he said, looking very old and tired. His head lolled back against the leather seat and before very long, he drifted into sleep.

When they got to the boarding-house, it was already dark and Jack and Josephine had to help Ted out of the car. Gran stood on the doorstep with her hands folded in front of her. She seemed to squeeze her body up between her arms, judging the situation, as the group stumbled into the house and headed towards the stairs and a bed.

'Hallo Ma. Sorry about this. Seasick.' Ted stretched out a long, thin arm, wrapped it round Gran's neck and gave her a big kiss. The other arm he kept limply slung round Jack's shoulder, or he would have fallen to the floor.

'Hallo Ted. What've you been up to?' Gran watched, impassive as her son was wielded up the stairs, then turned to Ida.

'Right. Ida, get on the blower to the doctor. I want him round here this minute. And then go next door for Earl. I need him to talk to Ted.'

Ida did as she was told, but then she had to leave Bayswater to make her way to the Glass Slipper. As her confidence increased Ida looked forward to her evening more each night. Her repertoire was growing, and she tailored her songs to two different audiences. The first, at ten and at twelve, was comparatively peaceful; an after-supper crowd, who did not listen attentively, but made less noise than the late-nighters, the three o'clock patrons. They were tough to please.

She was now quite used to members asking for their favourites from her, and with Tommy's expert improvising was making a speciality out of singing request numbers. So she smiled expectantly that night as she saw the shadow of a dark-haired girl coming towards her pool of light on the stage. It was Veronica.

'Ida! What a sensation! How could you!'

'What are you doing here?' Ida was equally amazed to see her.

'My brothers have brought me. Didn't you get my invitation? Or my Christmas card?'

'I'll come to your table later. I must do my next number.'

Ida ran through the rest of her set with acute self-consciousness and hopped off the stage without bothering to prolong the applause she had won.

'Mr Trevino, I've been invited to sit at a customer's table. May I go?'

'Just this once. We don't make a habit of it, you know.' He smiled kindly at her. 'You're coming along nicely. Your voice is loosening up. You're not a soprano you know. Mezzo; it'll settle down, with a bit of luck.'

Ida hurried away with her confidence a little restored.

Veronica introduced her companions. 'This is Felix and Simon. My brothers, you remember! And this is Simon's girlfriend Celia. She was at school with me. We're going to do the season this year, frightful prospect honestly! Felix and Simon got nagged by Daddy to give us a taste of things to come.'

'Will you have some champagne Miss Garland? Super singing.' Felix, a dark-haired, soft-complexioned young man of about twenty poured out a glass. He was not as good looking as his photograph, being more florid in reality, with stupidly long eyelashes, and his eyes were smaller than his sister's. His looks did not justify his self-assurance. In Ida's opinion he was not so *very* handsome. Simon, obviously the middle Summers child, was plump and the devoted type. As a result, she found him likeable, but less interesting.

'Fancy!' Veronica went on, still adjusting to her discovery. 'Just wait till I tell Daddy. Now boys, go and dance, Ida and I have to have a little chat.'

Simon and Celia wrapped themselves together and disappeared into the crowd. Felix headed for the best-looking girl in the room and asked her to dance.

'Why didn't you answer my letters, or come to my party?' Veronica demanded.

'Letters? I didn't get any of them. Must have been Ma or Pa. Why they wouldn't let me keep in touch . . . Why didn't you call?'

'Heavens, how was I to know? I thought perhaps you'd gone off me for good. I was pretty angry you know. So was Daddy.' Veronica tossed her head. 'We're not in the habit of having our motives *suspected*.'

Ida took no notice of this grand manner. Her sensible good feelings for Veronica made her see through the act.

'Veronica, you've forgotten our promise,' she said bending forward with an appeal to her first friend. 'We said we'd stay friends whatever happened.'

'Well, *you* could have written!' Veronica said stiffly.

Ida was ashamed of herself. 'I had a lot of things to do. I was upset too.' One day perhaps, she might confess the truth to Veronica. When they were really friends again. 'It was a terrible time. I broke with Mr Johns. I had to get a job. But I always hoped I'd see you again. I was going to write, but . . .'

'In other words, you intended to, in your own good time. You are awful.'

'What does your Pa think of me now?' Ida asked.

'Well. He was livid. But he never dwells on these things for long. There's bound to be someone else before long . . . it's his hobby.'

Now Ida was annoyed to think that she was merely one in a long line of 'enthusiasms'. Veronica saw this and laughed.

'Why should you mind? This is much more fun! You are a scream, Ida!'

Felix came back to their table, expecting to charm.

'Are the employees allowed to dance?' he said, with a devastating smile.

'Of course,' said Ida, rising quickly. Veronica grabbed her arm.

'Be warned. Felix has just discovered his S.A. Rather late in the day — he was a frightful swot all through school . . .'

Felix's 'sexual attraction' was considerable, and he danced much better than most of his type. Ida had had enough of the rugger-trained boyfriends who took to the floor at the Glass Slipper, stuck out their bottoms and danced with empty faces, either counting the beat or trying not to tread on their own shoe laces, which invariably worked undone. Or there were the Guardsmen, peering haughtily over their partners' heads, dancing stiff-backed and on the beat, whatever the tune.

'Garland,' he said. 'We had a boy of that name in my house at school. You couldn't be a relation of his, I'm sure. He was incredibly tall and had a face like a potato.'

Ida laughed. 'Mashed, peeled, or full of eyes?' she said.

'All of those things. He wore spectacles.'

'Poor thing!' she laughed heartlessly, because Felix made her feel part of the enchanting circle of the talented and beautiful by belittling someone else he knew.

Twirling round with a personable young man intent on flirtation, and with no thought of tomorrow, was exactly what Ida had been dreaming about for a long time. To find herself dancing in the Glass Slipper was too close to her wish to be quite, quite, enjoyable.

Ida's late sleep next day was cut short. Earl shook her hard to get her to wake up.

'It's Jack. He's got news for you. I've got to get into town. He'll explain.'

'Is it Uncle Ted?' she asked, suddenly alert.

'He'll tell you. But there's something I have to say too. I went to see your Mrs Cavendish yesterday, while you were out.'

'Pa! You haven't stopped it all again. I'll never . . .'

'No. But as you're staying on regular, she should pay you right. I got your salary raised to six pounds. If you're in this business, you have to let me handle the money side. I know all about it, more's the pity. And I'm going to come to the club every night from now on to see you safe home.'

He looked pleased with himself and cross with her for making him do it, at the same time.

Ida put her arms round him, wordless, almost in tears with gratitude.

'Oh Pa. I hate it when you're cross with me. I really do. I'll make it up to you. I promise.'

'Now, now. Pull yourself together,' Earl said, patting her back awkwardly. 'Jack's waiting. Hurry up.'

Ida dressed alone and Jack waited in the parlour until she came down. Before this recent coolness between them, he would have come up and sat on her bed while she did so.

He looked unusually defeated this morning. 'Will you come with me to the hospital?' he said abruptly. 'Ted's gone in.'

'What's the matter with him?'

'Some germ he got out East, they say. Ma thinks it's a sex disease, but she's got a vivid imagination. The doctor didn't say anything like that.'

Ida was appalled. 'The stories this family makes up! It's shocking!'

He smiled wryly. 'All lies is it Ida?'

'Shut up about sex. I bet you've done it too. I don't go round blaming you. I mind my own business.'

'It's not the same. I'm a boy. For girls it's different. For decent girls, anyway. Any road, I didn't come here to argue with you. Poor old Ted's sick and I thought you'd like to pay your respects. What d'you say?'

'Of course I'll come with you. Where is he?'

'The North Paddington. We're allowed to go in any time. He's on his own.'

'Does that mean he's serious?' Ida asked anxiously.

'I don't know. The doctor took one look at him and whipped him straight in. Gran's putting a suitcase together with some extra things. I thought we'd go about two. Uncle Billy's shop is quiet in the afternoons.'

'I'll be ready then.'

Ida carefully put on her new hat, and called in on Gran for further details. The old lady was rocking quietly in her parlour, watching the street as she liked to.

'I don't know any more than what Jack's told you,' she said. 'The doctor said they'd have to do tests on him.'

'Well, Jack and I will go today. Do you want to come Gran?'

'No. He'll think it's too serious if we all go at once. He's a terrible man to nurse, Ted, he always was, not like Earl . . . He thinks he's dying when he's got a tickle in his throat.'

'Maybe Pa's more patient because he was sick when he was small,' Ida suggested.

Gran dismissed the idea. 'It's his temperament. Earl goes down like ninepins. Like Joseph used to. Ted's a fighter. He'll be all right.' Gran's face was mountainous, all crags and grim lines, and her flat voice like a stiff wind blowing round it, filling Ida with the chill of unhappiness. Gran did not mean a word of what she said, it was all for appearances. She knew that Ted was seriously ill.

Later, seated with Jack either side of her uncle's bed, Ida realised how very much she loved Ted, not for things he had done, but for what he was. He had protected her and Jack a few times, true, but most important he had shown them the warmth to be had in living life to the full, without too many self-questionings.

'Well, this is a turn-up,' Ted whispered. 'I was looking forward to hearing you at the Glass Slipper, Ida love, seeing my old mate Tommy Trevino and the boys . . . give him my regards, won't you? Say Ted Garland sends . . .' he had to stop speaking while his breathing went into strange convolutions.

'What's she like, Jack old man? Ida, when she sings hot these days?' Ted raised a hand as if he might crack a joke, but it fell limp on the bed cover.

'I haven't heard her,' Jack said, with a quick glance across the bed. 'I'm not too keen on society dives.'

'Ah, but you must, sonny Jim. You must. So you can tell me all about it . . .' Ted's eyes closed, and he drifted for a while again.

'You must, Jack,' Ida repeated. 'I really want you to come.' She was close to tears.

Jack sat back with his arms folded, in the depth of sadness. If Uncle Ted were to die, he would lose his best uncle. The only one who stood between him and the disregard of the family. Except Ida, and he felt so distant from her now.

As weeks went by the family began to doubt if Ted would ever be himself again. He was transferred to a convalescent home in the suburbs of London, and on Sundays different family groups would trail out to visit him.

On one occasion Ida went down with Jack and Tommy Trevino, who had expressed a desire to see his old friend. Jack drove: he had made an effort to learn so that he could keep Ted's car running.

Seeing Tommy, a man his own age, had a profoundly good effect on Ted. They told jokes about the good nights they had spent in each other's company in the little clubs of London, where band musicians played jazz in ways they could not in their regular jobs. Ted rallied wonderfully, sat up in bed, and asked for news of several other 'Archer Street men' known to both of them.

'Old Fred's with Lew Stone's band now. Having a good time I think. Been on tour.'

'Old Fred. What do you know . . .'

'And Bill Gerhardi's back at Grosvenor House. Maybe you knew that, did you? Reinstated he was.'

These were just big names to Ida, beyond her acquaintance.

'Go on, Tommy, please tell Uncle Ted the best news.'

'This young lady's going to come with me to the Ambassador Hotel to do the "vocal refrains". I'm forming a new band. Me and the wife Gloria can't take this five in the morning stuff much longer, and Mrs Cav is as tight as a camel's arse. Oh! Excuse me Ida, I forgot I was in the presence of a lady. With the Ambassador I'll be home in bed by three.'

'Gloria was very nice to me, Uncle Ted. Said she was glad to hand over to someone she could trust. Wasn't that kind? Made me feel like a real professional.'

Tommy coughed in a funny fashion, and Ida discovered foolishly what the old blonde singer had meant. Tommy, for some reason, did not want to seduce her.

'Pa's worked out a really good contract for me,' Ida said, keeping the conversation to business.

'I thought he'd come round,' Jack commented drily. 'You're going to make him a lot of money.'

'With three pounds a record session, if the band ever gets noticed,' Tommy reminded her.

'Oh? Pa didn't mention that, or I forgot,' Ida said, even more pleased with herself.

'Not bad,' Jack said, standing, arms folded, at the end of the bed. He was looking at Ted's medical notes surreptitiously.

'Tell you a great number you should nick from Bert Ambrose's band, pass those spoons Jack.' Ted roused himself on his pillows, and began to vibrate two soup spoons together in the way all the brothers had learned. 'Jim's the one for this,' he said. 'What's the name of the ruddy number — oh yes, "Horses Dovers" — "Hors d'Oeuvres" to you of course . . .' He picked out the piano solo running the spoons up and down his bony thighs, and along his forearms, while Tommy came in with a hummed clarinet line once he recognised the tune.

It exhausted Ted of course. He lay back on his pillows with a silent laugh, waiting till his body caught up with his desire to entertain.

'Oh Uncle Ted, maybe you'll be better in time to come to our opening. Wouldn't you like that?'

''Course I would duckie.' He winked at her.

Ida looked across at Jack for his opinion. Imperceptibly Jack shook his head. 'We'll all be there,' he lied, looking her fully in the face. 'You'd better book a table, Mr Trevino, for guests of the band. 'Scuse me Ted, I've got to pop outside for a gasper.' He shook his cigarette packet. 'Empty. I left a packet in the car.'

A few minutes later Ida found Jack on the steps of the hospital.

'Thought I'd let them have a chat, man's talk, all that,' she said.

Jack trod on his cigarette butt — grinding it unnecessarily into the gravel. 'He's never coming out you know.'

'Don't say that.'

'It's not me, it's the doctor. Gran told me herself. There's nothing they can do. He didn't get the right treatment in those oriental places.'

'But it can't be so serious, so quick!'

'No Ida, it's something he picked up years ago, in Shanghai. It's just coming home to roost.'

'I never want to travel. Never ever,' Ida said, inconsequentially.

'I don't suppose the world will suffer if you don't,' Jack replied with uncalled for sarcasm.

'Jack. Don't. I know you're cross with me, but you've no need. I'm being good. I promise you that. Don't you think, just for Uncle Ted's sake, we should bury the hatchet?'

'You're right I s'pose.' He had a strong, intelligent sense of fairness, and made his mind up quickly. But he looked the other way, across the untrodden lawns at the dark cedar trees, narrowing his eyes as he always used to. But now it was not a boyish pretence at a tough face. He was filling out, nearly six feet, and looked far older than his years. Handsome, and tough. Ida recalled Harvey Johns' words about him, and shivered.

'What's up?' Jack as ever was alive to her thoughts.

'You're awfully good-looking Jack. I don't think I'd like to be any girlfriend of yours. I hate it when you're angry with me, and I'm only your cousin.'

'You're so thick,' he shook his head, as if he despaired of her ability to survive in the world. 'Don't start being stupid when we've just made up. Tell you what.'

'What?'

'Terence Bageshaw and me, we've joined a gym. In Hammersmith. Meet some right villains down there, I can tell you. But it's all part of my plan, see.' He was bursting to tell her all the news he had stored up while they were not on good terms with each other, and he thought he had lost her to her smart, jazzy new set. Soho life. He started bobbing around on the hospital steps, ducking and feinting like a champion boxer.

'What plan?'

'I told you!' he straightened up, indignant that she had forgotten. 'I'm going to leave home! I'm going to get fit, get trained at something, for a proper job. The future lies with technology. I've been reading about it. I'm not spending the rest of my life behind some counter, or strumming some bass fiddle and drinking myself stupid. I can do it. You see if I don't. Not like . . .'

'Ssh! Don't!' It was unkind to speak badly of Ted, but she had to admit there was some sense in what Jack said.

'I thought that was all just a passing mood . . .' she replied, dismayed. There was so much violence in Jack, she could not see him settling down to discipline and study. The band world was not so bad — with so few jobs about, hundreds of young men would be glad of his chances.

'Well. I think it all sounds very sensible, and I hope you do it. Whatever it is. Machinery.'

'Girls! *Technology*. It's no joke. And I'll tell you another. Before I go away, I'm going to land one on Sidney Ottley and damage him for life.'

'Oh Jack.' Nothing had changed. Jack began to duck and feint with his own shadow across the lawn, giving her a running commentary on his imaginary foe until he landed a left hook to the jaw and stood triumphant over his own silhouette on the green canvas.

10

A clock struck, telling her to hurry. Looking up at the gilt face above a store, Ida saw that it was two, and walked a little quicker. She was lunching with Veronica.

The Ambassador Hotel was almost a second home to her now. It was not very grand, tucked away behind Knightsbridge, near the Piccadilly end. Its restaurant was justifiably famous, but the ballroom was new, redecorated just before Trevino's new house band was formed. The wall behind the orchestra dais was draped in oyster satin, and there were arches down both sides, under which the guests' tables were arranged among the privacy of palms. Glass-windowed walls separated the ballroom from the formal restaurant on one side, and on the other, a lounge bar where women were allowed to meet and drink unescorted. She and Veronica met there regularly to gossip.

Ida had to wait for her — Veronica was always late. She felt quite at home; the barman gave her a familiar nod, and Ida sat quietly as he polished glasses with a mechanical rhythm that pleased her eye.

Two years had altered Veronica considerably. She had spent a year socialising in London; taken an art course in Paris; passed the previous winter skiing with relatives in Zurich, and now had an 'interest' in an art gallery in Sutton Street. A job was out of the question. If Felix had found his S.A. late in life, Veronica was coming into her stride early by contrast, at nineteen.

'Here I am at last! Sorry darling!' Veronica swooped exotically on to Ida, shoving a smart dead animal from her shoulders, like an urban hunter, and casting down various parcels, her catch of the day, all over the floor and the bar counter. She and Ida sat at two high stools. 'Two gin slings,' she ordered, and then proceeded to rummage in her bags. Other customers in the bar watched with frozen interest as Veronica pulled out a pair of silken hose, unpinned her suspenders, and changed her laddered stockings where she sat. The barman turned his back. Ruined silk dropped in a pile on the floor, like the shed skin of an exotic snake.

Ida was always a great audience for such extremes. She was neither embarrassed nor irritated, but merely sat smiling, with a fond expression on her face. Secretly, she admired Veronica's effort to rebel, to break with her background conventions. They were just as stifling as her own, however different.

'I want to know why you didn't want Felix to come tonight,' Veronica demanded.

'Because he makes me nervous,' Ida said.

'Oh my. The men in my family really have a way with women!' Veronica sounded exasperated. 'I still want you to marry him, then we'd be sisters!'

'I've no intention of marrying him! Felix is very good company, but I'm not in love with him, I couldn't ever be in love with him, and I told you all this last week. The reason's obvious. I hope I don't offend, but as you won't take no for an answer . . .'

'What? Do tell. You've got a lover!' Veronica's dark eyes opened wide, the pupils dilating instantly.

'Your family's Jewish. I don't think your parents would approve of a mixed marriage. Particularly not as mixed as I would make it! You've never even told me if your father knows we're still friends.'

Veronica shrugged. 'My dear. With Hitler doing just what he wants to do now, I think my father would be very happy not to be Jewish. Sometimes.'

'And does he know about me?'

'Is this why you won't consider Felix? Because of Daddy?'

'No. That's not the only reason. I just don't love him.'

'You don't have to love someone to marry them. Good heavens, what a romantic idea.' Ida's face signalled the stirrings of boredom, so Veronica gave up for the moment. 'Waiter, two more gin slings . . . Are you excited about tonight? I am.'

Ida's band was to make its first radio broadcast from the hotel, live, at ten-thirty.

'Of course I am!'

'Poor Felix. I don't think he realises what a star you're going to be.'

215

'That's just it. I'd like tons of people to be in love with me, not just one! Besides, the boys in the band take very good care of their little band singer. It's fun!' Ida thought of playing cards, when the hotel was shut; sneaking a few drinks too many with the boys until Tommy caught her at it. Or going to all the Louis Armstrong concerts on his epoch-making tour that summer, and listening to the band boys' heated arguments on the trumpeter's genius and showmanship.

'Between Pa's possessiveness and Tommy's fatherly concern, I don't get much chance to be really wicked,' she added. Ida was pleased that the band boys treated her like a sister. Perhaps her long friendship with Jack helped her to know how to be a friend, not a love interest, to young men. For her own part, she felt it was a relief to rest for a while in an assumed sexual innocence.

'Thank goodness darling, dance-band players are hardly serious propositions!'

'Oh, that doesn't stop them making a few of the other kind. They're joking, I don't take any notice. I'm not *that way* about any of them. Guess what, I suggested to Tommy we call the band the Diplomats. He's going to introduce the new name tonight.'

Veronica's shrieking laugh made an arc of sound as if a jungle parrot had swooped through the room. Her hair fell back from her face, her big teeth flashed against the red of her lips. She was extravagantly physical, in a way that made Ida feel colourless.

'Speaking of diplomats, guess what I saw last night,' Veronica said, leaning forward for a stage whisper. 'I was in Prunier's. Dinner. The Prince of Wales came in with a smart dark-haired girl — I don't remember her name.'

'My Gran could tell you all of them.' Ida shook her head, unable to suggest anyone.

'Well. They had a tiff. He looked very cross and came right over to the table next to ours. There was someone frightfully good-looking, his type, you know, dark and dominant, sitting right behind my left elbow.'

'What happened then?' Ida asked. 'You did hear, I hope!'

'Yes. He actually asked her to dance — in front of everyone! While his poor partner sat watching!'

'What a stinker.' Ida was sure this was the proper response, even if he was going to be the king.

'The girl curtseyed very beautifully and said she was very sorry but her party was just leaving. And they did. They all got up and walked out.'

'Well, good for them!' said Ida.

'Terrific *savoir-faire*,' Veronica concluded.

Ida thought quickly of the coming night: Veronica might meet the rest of the Garland family. That would prove her ineligibility for all time. *Sanny fairyann* . . .

When Ida returned to Bayswater, she found Jack lying under Ted's car in Salamanca Street, fixing a rattle. Ida sat on the garden wall, which was warm after a day of sun, and she waited for the last waves of gin-pleasure to ebb from her brain.

Jack's ambition to get away was obviously gathering reality: now he was taking engineering classes at an evening school, and practising what he was learning on Ted's AC.

'Do you know what you're doing under there?' she said. 'We could just get taxis tonight, you know.'

'Don't you worry. I want to take Gran in style. Besides, I've just done engines at school. It's important Ida. The next war's not going to be like the last one,' he shouted from under the wheels.

'Been reading the papers again?' Ida said. Sometimes she did not feel two years older than Jack, the amount of news information he stuffed into his head.

'It's going to be vehicles. Air power. Not armies of poor buggers swimming around in mud. You'll see. Maybe I'll be a pilot. Or maybe I'll be a tank-driver. Armoured vehicles. There's a career.'

'Well, I don't think there ought to be another war. It's just all you hotheads spoiling for a fight again. Death lust. I heard someone say so at the hotel the other night. That's all they talk about. Chaos and catastrophe.'

'One of your Right Hon. nobs, I bet,' he said.

'You behave tonight, Jack Garland, or I'll never speak to you again.'

''Course I will. This is Gran's night out, this is. Pop and have a look at her, will you?'

Gran was in the snuggy, having a nap in preparation for her

late night. She spent more of her days in bed than by the window, as if the streets of London were beginning to tell her things she did not wish to hear. Her little room, bare as ever, was at least warm this afternoon, and the clock ticked louder in the still air. Ida could hear her Gran's heavy breathing, the odd delay in its release as a troubled thought in her dreams made her pause, looking for an answer. Ida was conscious of her intrusion, her stolen view, the queerness of Gran's supine body and fallen face, nothing like her usual appearance with upright, boned back, stern face and encompassing sense of things. She closed the door quietly and went home to dress. She wanted to get to the hotel early, to rehearse just a little more with Tommy Trevino and the boys.

Ida was anxious to see which crowd would come to the hotel tonight. Every evening, the atmosphere was different, depending on the clientele. Sometimes fabulous actresses, Tallulah Bankhead or Jessie Matthews would arrive with an entourage that acted as if it were famous too, bathed in the glow of reflected fame. On other nights, there might be a crowd of parliamentary figures, politicians, diplomats, the odd favoured journalist. They would only stay for an hour, their women cajoling them to leave their opinionated conversations and just dance. Always they talked about rearming, Socialism, Fascism, things Ida knew little about, but which Jack bored her with at times too, so she knew it was important. Or once in a while, some smart Society set would decree the Ambassador Hotel to be 'an amusing little place', and descend on it for nights in a row, this or that Lady with her boxer-lover or drug-taking son; this or that couple wedded for the third time, and already bored with each other.

The one thing all these people had in common was a pleasure in the music, the insistent, pulsating sound of commercial band music. It was 'hot', but hardly jazz. For a start the music was carefully played from written arrangements. But there were jazz influences, great harmonies in the saxes, rough-toned trombones, clarinets whistling lightly over the melody lines, and all the time an insistent, syncopated drumming that defied the customers not to take to the floor. A muted trumpet snuffled its way through a sentimental ballad; a tuba growled in sympathy with a flighty reed solo, all in variations on simple lines that teased the ear to follow. Once in a while a Jewish 'Mother' song was thrown to the lions of the audience, to compliment the few rich who were Jewish, or to amuse those who were not with a sentimental Europeanism. Many of London's dance-band leaders and players were Jewish in origin, Ida had found.

She loved her audiences, they were enthusiastic, and often came back for an evening, just to hear her sing. She was building up quite a reputation. Ida thought her smart, influential public were actually quite like children, drawn by the music's innocence, its appeal to their energies. They frolicked and tumbled like infants at a party never admitting tiredness, and waiting to be told it was time to go home . . .

'Direct from the Ambassador, Tommy Trevino's band, the Diplomats, and his regular little lady singer, Miss Ida Garland . . .'

Ida sang a new composition, a mildly blues song called 'One More Romance Gone Wrong'. Then the band played a driving instrumental piece, 'Orange Bitters', with an upbeat piano solo, that showed Tommy at his best, crisp-fingered, making single notes sparkle and laugh. To honour Duke Ellington's recently acclaimed shows in London (the entire Trevino band had attended every one), Ida returned to sing 'The Chocolate Shake':

> 'Venus de Milo had charms,
> She gave the boys quite a break,
> Now that girl is minus her arms,
> For doing the Chocolate Shake . . . !'

By now everyone in the room was dancing, and in her eagerness, Ida moved in rhythm from the microphone off her spot. Fortunately an engineer scrambled in front of the band-stand and shooed her back.

Then it was all over for her; Tommy and the boys played a couple more dance numbers, while Ida searched for her family at their table. They had been discreetly placed by the *maître d'hôtel* at the back of the room. Ida, over-sensitive, saw people directing curious glances at them all, largely because of Denise's near-nude figure, her chemical blondeness made more startling by her position between dusky Earl and Uncle Billy.

'Waiter.' Earl lifted a hand, too commanding. No one came.

Ida slipped into a seat next to Gran. Her face was a study in self-control, joy lighting the tears in her eyes.

'You sang beautifully, dear. Brought back memories.'

She looked so sad. Perhaps the scene evoked her youth, a reminder of grand times with Grandpa Joseph. Perhaps it was present troubles . . . Ida took her hand.

'Are you worrying about Uncle Ted? You know Mr Trevino got Star Sound to make a recording of the broadcast?'

'Why don't you go and telephone Ted, dearie? Have a word, he'd like that, I'm sure.'

'I will, what a nice idea.'

A waiter appeared with a bucket of champagne.

'Compliments of the management for Miss Garland's family,' he recited. Ida, looking round in surprise, glimpsed Jack shooting the boy an evil look. 'And Mr Trevino asked to be remembered, madam.' He bowed low to Gran and backed away.

'Well I never,' said Gran. 'That's elegant. Just like the old days . . .'

Jack relaxed. Ida slipped close to him. 'That was kind of you. Must have set you back.'

'Did a gig. Makes a change from evening classes once in a while. Shut up Ida, or the old girl will catch on.'

He poured a liberal splash for Gran, and gave her a big kiss. 'There you are Gran. Vintage, too.'

Surrounded by thoughtfulness, Gran began to mellow.

Ida turned to her father happily. 'Was I all right?'

Earl never liked to admit how good she was. 'I liked the first number. Confident sound.'

'I don't know I'm sure,' said Denise, mainly because no one had asked for her opinion, and she was anxious to detain Ida so that she would hear it. 'There's a lot of good girl singers . . . still, Ida, you've held down a job, and not got into trouble.'

'Well, how could I, with Pa standing over me for months and months, like some great policeman?' Ida laughed. 'At least he trusts me now to get home by myself. *You* didn't want him waiting up for me every night, I'm sure.'

Denise was staggered by the sexual insult in this remark. 'You should be grateful!' she spat.

The whole family turned to stare at this remark. 'To whom?' someone wanted to know. 'Who to?' demanded the more belligerent, including Jack.

'Why, to Earl, of course, for getting her a good contract in the first place. You don't suppose Mrs Cavendish took her on for her talent, did you? Earl launched her, let's face it.' Denise presented her powdered features to the room at large, confident she was being admired. 'It's a nice place, this. I always liked the Ambassador.'

Ida retreated to the telephone without bothering to reply. It was left to Jack to say what everyone else wanted said.

'You're sitting there dripping in jewellery your daughter paid for. Uncle Earl's doing very well out of Ida. It's you and him should be grateful, not her!' he declared.

'Earl! Are you going to let him . . .'

'Shut up.' Earl rose slowly to his feet. 'Come on Gran, here's a slow one. Let's take a turn on the floor.'

Denise's face flamed. Uncle Billy, who was nodding in a corner listening wordlessly to the band, was surprised to find himself accosted by his sister-in-law. 'Billy, I must dance this one,' Denise ordered.

Like most jazz musicians and many fans, Billy had no physical pleasure in dancing, only in listening to the real thing. But he obliged, being terrified of Denise. Both Earl and Billy danced stiffly, which curious English eyes in the crowd noted with approval. At least these 'natives' were not making a show of themselves . . .

Jack, whom Denise intended to snub, was left at the table, watching with pleasure every time Denise winced, and her satin shoes were scuffed by Billy's big feet.

'Hallo. You're Jack Garland, aren't you?' An imperious, dark-haired girl accosted him.

Jack stood up. 'I am.' He knew he should not bridle, but it was natural to him.

'Gosh, you're so big! I mean, in comparison to Ida, and every bit as good-looking as I'd imagined you'd be. I'm Veronica Summers. How do you do.'

'Oh! Miss Summers.' Jack was instantly fascinated. 'I've heard a lot about you.'

'All quite true, I'm sure. I'd love to dance.'

'Can I have the pleasure, Miss Summers?'

'Do call me Veronica, for goodness' sake. After all, I feel almost like one of the family, truly I do.'

Ida came back from phoning Ted to see Jack expertly handling Veronica round the crowded floor in demonstration quickstep. She was livid: disgusted to see Veronica's enthusiasm for Jack's sexily stylish dancing. He was the most infuriating youth — one minute a sanctimonious relative, the next a positive creep, making eyes at her best friend! Barely seventeen, and Veronica two years older than him! He had promised not to make an exhibition of himself — now everyone in the room was wondering who was this *déclassé* 'pretty boy' that Veronica Summers had taken up with. Such a lot of gossips, the Ambassador crowd — and Jack was revelling in their curiosity.

When the number finished, Veronica's laughter could be heard echoing across the dance floor. She planted a carmine kiss on Jack's cheek and skipped back to her escort in a far corner, blowing a kiss at Ida from a very safe distance.

Jack came back to the table, inordinately pleased with himself. 'She's a cracker. Why've you been keeping quiet about her, Ida?'

She scowled at him. 'Waiting till you learnt enough manners to be introduced. Wipe that muck off your face.'

'That was Miss Summers,' Gran said with decision, as she returned to her seat.

'Yes, how did you guess?' Ida was surprised at her memory. 'We met again. At the Glass Slipper.'

'You two were very close, right from the start. You don't talk about your friendships to me these days. You're happy now, Ida, aren't you love? Or does it still rankle, what your Pa did?'

Ida shook her head. 'No. Not now. I've got lots of friends now.' She looked at the smart crowds circling the floor, hoping she really did belong with them.

'I've got lots of friends,' she repeated, with pride. Then she turned leonine eyes on Jack. 'Don't be deceived,' she said, cold advice: 'Veronica's only slumming for a tease. You're not in her league.'

For some maddening reason, Jack's smile broadened.

Regular radio spots followed, and then Mrs Cavendish telephoned to suggest that Tommy Trevino should come back to the Glass Slipper for a week's special appearance, every month or so after their hotel stint had finished.

'Oh Gawd, late nights again,' said Tommy. 'I'll do three nights, Friday, Saturday and Sunday,' he counter-offered.

Ida overheard this conversation as she came into the band room. 'Mr Trevino! You're the only bandleader in London who wants to be in bed by midnight!' she laughed.

'Got to keep in the public eye,' he admitted. 'But I need to do a few tours, band spots out of town. Can't stick in the West End all the time.'

'Mr Trevino. I've had an idea. Can I tell you?'

He sighed. 'You're going to be like Gloria. My wife. I can tell. She always says I won't be a front-liner without a woman shoving me up the — now, what is it this time?'

'Let's dress up. National costumes, League of Nations, you know. Fezzes, coolie hats, turbans. For the Glass Slipper.'

'Not bad . . .'

'The Diplomats, you see?' she added.

'Good God, girl, I'm not stupid! OK, as long as I can be the Sultan of Baghdad . . .'

Ida meant it quite innocently, but given the current weak state of the real League of Nations, unable to prevent Japan from withdrawing membership to rearm, the clientele at the Glass Slipper found their get-ups 'killing'. Most particularly, a large, genuine Egyptian gentleman, reputed to be one of the most astute international arms dealers in Europe. His 'cover' was a company importing turkish delight, aniseed balls and halva. He sat smoking sweet Eastern cigarettes at a specially reserved table where he could watch Ida sing, and admire nubile girls on the dance floor. But he never touched a drink or asked anyone to dance.

'Who is that man?' Ida asked Mrs Cavendish.

'Eric Bey, he calls himself.'

'Oh. So he's half-English . . .'

'Only just. I know because my parents ran the hotel in Cairo where his father got his mother pregnant. He was an attaché at our embassy; she was from a very good Egyptian family. Needless to say, they never married.'

Ida sighed. The world seemed full of brilliantly talented people like Mrs Cavendish and Eric Bey who had been everywhere and done everything. A steady income and two years in a hotel as a 'useful' band singer hardly seemed to rate in comparison. Her ambitions were growing.

Cool fingers covered her eyes, a smell of Mitsouko perfume.

'Veronica!'

'Yes, me.'

Instinctively Ida looked behind her friend.

'No one's with me. Who were you expecting?' Veronica teased. 'Not young Jack, by any remote chance?'

'You're to leave him alone.'

'My dear girl! Your little cousin's more than capable of looking after himself. Guess where he took me yesterday.'

'I've no idea.'

'Dog racing at White City! It was simply ripping fun!'

'I suppose proletarian pastimes are the latest thing. Or am I being bourgeois?' Ida threw back the word so often bandied about.

'No. Just possessive. It's only *fun* Ida. I might just write an article on dog tracks for *Night and Day* magazine. Oh, don't look so sour. Let's have a stiff one, before your next set.'

'You've got to get up. You've got the recording date at Decca this morning, remember?'

Earl stood over her with a steaming cup of tea.

'Oh Pa, I've only been in bed four hours. Just a few minutes longer.'

'It wouldn't do to be late for your first session. I told Tommy last night we'd be sure to be there in time. You've never worked in a studio before. You should get used to the setting before you start singing. Besides, no Garland shows up late, I told you before.'

'You're an awful slave-driver Pa.' But Ida was up and wriggling into her clothes as soon as he left the room. A first record was worth the trouble even if she was half-dead with tiredness.

'It'll be funny if Uncle George is on this session,' she called out as she ran downstairs.

'I doubt it,' Earl said drily. Uncle George had been boasting recently about his mechanical engineering skills, and how lucky the Decca company was to get him in at the start of the industry.

'Don't you believe him?' Ida asked. It would be nice if George was lying and she could take him down a peg or two.

'Not lying exactly. Bending the truth, you know how good he is at doing that,' Earl said, pushing toast across the table.

'No breakfast. I don't eat when I'm singing.'

'You're getting too thin on this rule. Have some.' He shoved the plate more squarely at her.

'Oh Pa.' But Ida liked the way that Earl made a fuss over her. Compared to his cold disapproval, Pa's driving her too hard was easy to bear.

In the studio, Ida blessed those years of rigour studying with Harvey Johns. More and more these days she saw their value coming through in her work. She did not mind singing the same phrase, over and over again until they got the balance right, or having to sit inside screens, with a glass window in front of her, so that her voice would stand out against the volume of the band. The drum kit had to be screened too, otherwise it crashed and drowned out every other instrument. The double bass, even when padded, thudded on the low notes and disappeared at the top.

Tommy spent a lot of time setting up various devices so that he could achieve a 'tight' sound, not the cavernous 'horn recording' effect advertised by the company but wrong for his kind of music. He wanted a raw immediacy, as if his piano had been standing in the corner of a bar for a decade. 'When I was a lad we used to put newspaper inside the piano. Perhaps I should try it again,' he joked.

'Anything,' said Bobby Smythe, the saxman, none too fresh from a night's drinking in an after-hours club.

'I never knew it was such hard work.'

225

But Ida, like a young athlete, sang firmly and clearly, over and over again. They recorded 'One More Romance Gone Wrong' on the A side, and Tommy Trevino's 'Orange Bitters' to back it up. It was exhausting to have to repeat the entire number so many times, each one better in one respect, and falling short in another. The players persevered, and learnt the knack of standing forward for solos and back for ensemble sections, to get the right effect.

After the tenth try, the boys were ready to pack up.

'Come on,' Tommy urged, 'one more time.'

'No,' the sound engineer interrupted. 'Leave it. You won't get any better,' he added dourly.

'Funny,' said Bobby, too hungover to be tactful, 'Tommy's played that solo on "Orange Bitters" a million times better at the club than he has once today.'

'Seen it before,' the soundman agreed, 'some of you jazz types lose the spirit when you come in here. Not the same is it? Not enough smoke. Maybe it'll be better after a pint . . .'

'Now that's a good idea,' Bobby said, brightening visibly and taking Tommy firmly in tow.

'Is George Garland about?' Ida asked, for a diversion. 'I'm sure he works in this building somewhere.'

'Don't know him love,' the soundman said. 'He's not on the sales side is he?'

She pretended ignorance. 'Perhaps that's it. I don't know much about how the business works,' she said.

''Course, he could be classical. That's another department.' The man wandered off for a bacon sandwich across the road.

'Classical, that's it!' Ida called after him cheerfully. Uncle George was obviously too lowly to be known, or not working at Decca Studios at all. More likely he was selling truly 'hot' records in the street markets of Hackney and Shoreditch — his own rather special way of entering the business.

Felix and Veronica took their seats just as Ida began her second set at the Glass Slipper. They had wangled a specially-reserved table in full view of the orchestra. Suddenly Ida noticed Jack slip into a seat between them. She felt herself stiffen, her smile to the audience become too bright and her gestures inexpressive. It was the first time she had seen Veronica and Jack together in public since the night of the radio session. Now they were flaunting their friendship in front of her.

She sang as she had rehearsed, relying on familiarity to see her through the repertoire, because she was not happy with this particular audience. Or one member of it anyway. One, two, three, 'In the Still of the Night'. Nearly over.

'By popular request, Miss Ida Garland will now finish with 'One More Romance Gone Wrong' — remember, ladies and gentlemen, our new Decca release. The Diplomats, and Miss Ida Garland.'

Tommy added a rippling keyboard flourish to her introduction, helping Ida to find a mood. It was not too easy to deliver a song twice nightly for as many months. Ida smiled gratefully at Tommy's musicianly way of telling her how pleased he was for what she had achieved with his band.

She needed his support. The idea of Veronica carrying on with Jack did not please her in the least. But Jack, holding forth to Felix with no appearance of inferiority, seemed maddeningly unaware that he was being patronised. Perhaps he wasn't, and it was all in her fancy. Perhaps the Summerses genuinely enjoyed Jack's company. Veronica was always telling her off for her complexes and insecurities.

She closed her eyes and sang again, remembering Harvey Johns' description of her voice, like a clarinet, sweet and clear. Once more she heard in her head that reed-like intonation, the surety of sound that made even the humblest of lyrics seem to have sprung from her thoughts as she gave them sound. Waiting to sing was misery, but in performance she forgot herself and lived in the song — any song.

A different ripple of sound caught her half-way through the refrain. At the back of the Glass Slipper, a large crowd of girls had arrived, doing their best not to disturb the show but by sheer force of number, causing flurries of distraction among the audience. Ida was momentarily unsettled; since her early days at the club, she had grown accustomed to a more indulgent quiet when she sang.

She sang with a little more emphasis, causing the arrivals to turn and watch her. Beautiful faces; twenty-four beautiful faces peering over each other's bare shoulders, trying to squeeze their thin gauze-draped bodies into all available spaces at the edge of the floor. Peering into the gloom beyond the lights, Ida could see waiters scurrying to the front with extra tables. A tribe of women — surely Eric Bey had turned up with a harem!

It wasn't the Egyptian arms dealer. When the band had finished, Ida stepped off her platform and joined Felix and Veronica, pointedly ignoring Jack.

'What's all the fuss?' she asked. 'Does anyone know who's come?'

'Oh yes, I do,' said Felix. 'I saw that man's picture in *The Playbill* last week. Isn't that Ainslie Curtis, Veronica?'

'Why, yes, so it is. Golly, puts this hole on the map, doesn't it?'

Ida considered the Glass Slipper to be the epitome of West End sophistication, and could never understand why regulars were so derogatory. She hoped it was a sign of affection.

'Who's Ainslie Curtis? I'm sure I know the name . . .'

'My poor Ida,' crooned Veronica, 'you've been working too hard. He's directing the new revue at the Charlbury — he's very young to be so successful. Not even thirty. What's it called, Felix? We saw the last one. Wasn't it called *Dress Informal*?'

'Yes, that was it. And this one's *RSVP*. And that, if I'm not mistaken, is the show's entire chorus line. Come on Jack, shouldn't we take a closer look?'

'Chorines! They'll only be interested in men over forty,' Jack said authoritatively.

Ida was forced to acknowledge his presence. 'You'd know all about it,' she replied, also annoyed that her 'hit' number had been interrupted.

'Waiter, champagne for the ladies,' Felix ordered, rising to his feet, unable to resist spreading his charm a little further afield.

'You are crass, Felix,' Veronica said pleasantly as he walked off. 'Fancy abandoning Ida. He doesn't mean it, he feels challenged, that's all. He's wondering, who will resist?' Veronica watched her brother's advance with admiration, brown eyes bright. 'Have some champagne,' she offered.

'Not for me,' Ida was feeling hard to please.

Jack leant back in his seat, sensing her annoyance at his presence and not wishing to cause more trouble. 'It's all for the publicity. Good-looking, aren't they?' he said, casting a professional eye at the crowd. All spare men in the room, including Felix, had swooped on the girls' tables, dark-suited night-time predators drawn to exotic creatures like a flock migrating to the tropics . . .

Mrs Cavendish patrolled through the chattering crowds, ensuring everyone had service and that none was inconvenienced by the unexpected arrival of such a large party. She passed Ida's table.

'Mr Curtis wants to be introduced.' She gave Ida one of her managerial, warning looks, a reminder that she was employee, not a guest who could choose her company all hours of the night. 'He likes your voice,' she said reluctantly. It was not part of her plan to lose a rising star, a growing attraction like Ida.

'Excuse me, Miss Summers.' Ida left with elaborate politeness, wanting Mrs Cavendish to know that she had friends who needed cultivating too.

Mrs Cavendish led the way to the bar, and rapped a tail-coated figure on the shoulder. 'Here she is, Ainslie.' Mrs Cavendish waved her cigarette holder in the general direction of her 'little supper singer'.

'Ida Garland, may I present Mr Ainslie Curtis.'

'Well! If it isn't my young miss in her best frock!' He threw back his head in exaggerated mirth and roared aloud at the joke.

Although seven years had passed, she recognised him at once, as the baggy-flannel-trousered chap in Mrs Cavendish's old club: he had been rehearsing the chorus line on her very first visit. She had sat on a bar stool, and sung 'Melancholy Baby' for him while Uncle Ted played and Pa had been angry.

The man was tall and fair, his shoulders broad above the direct line of her eyes. His frame had thickened as he matured, so that he had less effeminacy in his theatrical manner. That was obviously an act, a studied exuberance. Ainslie Curtis had eyes with a kindly, blue-green expression that looked fairly capable of hardness. But a smile never left his mobile face; it only widened or became more subdued.

Children's memory-images usually diminish when they see people or places again in their adult years. To Ida, now a young woman, Ainslie Curtis seemed even larger than life. He might be only in his late twenties, as Veronica seemed to think, but he cultivated the manners of a much older man.

'I always thought we'd meet again,' he said with pleasure, 'but I didn't think I'd find you on my doorstep! Should have known better. You were a real little trouper.'

'I've made a record too,' Ida said, embarrassed as soon as she spoke that she was pushing herself too far, too fast.

'So I'm told. Marvellous!' For some unaccountable reason this set him off again, and he bayed with delight at her.

Ainslie Curtis was thinking of a small, beautiful girl, with arresting eyes and an enchanting smile, who had once said, 'I got a new dress today' in exactly that timid yet proud voice. Here she was, obviously the belle of the bandstand, with a voice more distinctive than any other in London. She was stunningly beautiful, but it wasn't her figure: she was too small to be considered physically flawless. It wasn't even her face, though it was fine-featured, dusky, like a tropical moon, an oval of honesty and vitality. Those eyes! Ida communicated with an audience: when she sang, she did not cause that slightly aggressive envy that other stars did. She gave too much of herself for that. Men were moved, and women were on her side.

'Look, I think I could use you. Why not come and see me at the Charlbury tomorrow morning? Not too early, my dear, we all need our beauty sleep. Now I must get back to my naughty girls, before they get into mischief.' He gave a theatrical bow, and shouldered his way through the crowd.

'What a performance!' Ida murmured, edging her way back round the dancing couples to her table. Unusually, Veronica and Felix had taken to the floor together.

'Well!' Jack, waiting for her, arms folded, was smiling fatuously. 'He looks full of himself, Ainslie Curtis.'

'What are you laughing about now, Jack Garland?' she flared. 'Coming here, bold as brass, with a girl old enough . . .'

'You may not have noticed, Ida, but I'm out of short pants. And don't I remember someone telling me to mind my own business? Do me a favour.'

'She'll use you. She only wants to shock people.'

Jack's eyes gleamed. 'I thought you two were friends.'

'Shut up!' she snapped.

'Honest, Ida, I don't get you. Why should you mind what I do?' He spoke playfully, but did she hear hope in his voice? He'd certainly chosen the wrong way to impress her, if that's what he wanted to do!

'Me? Mind? *You're* the one who wants to get on and get out! I don't care what you do!'

He shrugged. Now he would have to retaliate, of course, she knew that.

He spoke carelessly as she expected. 'There's a lot of girls in Shepherd's Bush who say that to me, most nights of the week.' He drained his glass with a beer-drinker's gulp.

Ainslie Curtis' office was above the doorway of the Charlbury theatre, a small, rococo-style building in a street behind Piccadilly Circus. The theatre front doors were shut; a cleaning woman with her head in a turbaned scarf was busy washing down the marble floor and signalled to Ida to find her way up through the stage door entrance.

'Oh yes,' said the doorman, squeezed inside his small cubicle, sipping a meat-extract drink and sorting the mail. 'You're on his list. Go on up: turn right at the top of the stairs, you'll know the right room by the noise coming out.' He raised his eyes to heaven and his chin bobbed up expressing his contempt for the company's inability to proceed without high tension.

The office door was open; inevitable, since at least a dozen people were inside it, though the composition of the group kept changing as people charged in and out. A meeting was just breaking up. In the middle of a desk layered in paperwork, a maquette of the stage in balsa wood looked as perfect and unreal as the hopes of all the individuals gathered round it. A designer was trying to lower some miniscule flats into position inside it, except that someone behind him persistently jogged his elbow. The offender was rolling a bolt of fabric with energy roused by fury not enthusiasm. Someone else's assistant gathered up sketches and shoved them headfirst into a folder, snivelling with flu or emotion. A composer and his assistant were warbling at each other, and beating time on the dirty panes of a small bay window. Another business assistant bellowed down the telephone for a long-distance number, while above the general air of indecision and hostility, Ainslie Curtis' voice boomed across the room.

'Sylvia! Don't be peevish! The second act is coming along splendidly, I only want a rethink for the end of the first. And here's the girl I think will solve all our problems. Ida, good-morning! What do you think Sylvia?'

'How do you do. I'm Miss Knox. Stand on that chair Miss Garland.' Sylvia Knox, presumably the designer, stood in front of her, one crimson-varnished nail jabbed into her soft cheek signifying thought. Ruffled in mood and in dress (two habitual states with Sylvia), she scrutinised Ida's body from her feet to her chin. She did not look into Ida's eyes, however. Ida could sense that would be too personal a view of someone she was busily transforming.

'I do see, Ainslie. I see just what you mean.'

'Good-o. Splendid. I'll just take her down to the stage and have a little chat. Get Miss Jordan on the piano, will you dear? Thank you.'

Ainslie shut the door, giving Ida a conspirator's grin. 'Let's leave them all to it. You'd think it was grand opera, not a little revue.'

He took her hand, his vast, warm palm closing in friendly fashion round her gloved fingers.

'Tommy Trevino told me it was your idea, calling the band the Diplomats.' His voice boomed even more richly on the stone stairway leading to the stage. Ida noted the sparkle in the steps, just like the ones backstage at the Shepherd's Bush Empire. As a girl she had thought them precious, like the marcasite of Denise's brooches.

'Well, lots of bands have fancy names, and I thought it suited the hotel,' she explained.

'Mmm. Very smart!' he laughed. Everything seemed to amuse Ainslie Curtis.

'Now dear, here we are. I don't really need to ask you to sing, we all know you do that splendidly, unless of course you can sight-read. I was naughty not giving you time to prepare anything for me, wasn't I?' His light eyes cooled slightly, and Ida accepted the challenge.

'I can try,' she said modestly, knowing full well that sight-reading was one of her better accomplishments. He handed her a pencil-written scrawl, notes wandering across the page like a secretary's shorthand practice. But Harvey Johns' manuscripts had been much worse. Ida felt a pang of nostalgia for those demands, and decided to be mischievous.

'I'll do my best,' she said, frowning as prettily as she could. If

233

Ainslie Curtis thought she was a voice and nothing else, she would give him a memorable performance.

'I — I don't dance, Mr Curtis.' She blushed. 'I do play the piano just a little bit, if that helps.'

'No, not at all. Not necessary. I just want to see how you'd look. Put this on, will you?' He gave her a blue velvet cape that rested on the back of the piano, and sat her on a footstool in the middle of the stage. Miss Jordan the pianist took her place adjusting her spectacles, waiting in adoration for Mr Curtis' nod.

'Bob, are you up there?' he called to the lighting gallery. 'Give me lots of five, half of two and a touch of three.' He turned to Ida. 'I'll just walk up the back.'

Ida waited until he was out of earshot.

'Miss Jordan,' she whispered, holding up the sheet music. 'Could you transpose this to B flat?'

Miss Jordan looked surprised. 'I don't know what Mr Curtis would say . . .'

'Please. Just for the first run-through. I'll do it as written if he doesn't like it. It's just I'd feel more comfortable.'

Miss Jordan fingered the first few chords. It was the most difficult key to move into from written music, but she was a proficient player and felt challenged. 'You could be right dear. Just this once.'

'Are you ready darling? Take your time.' This was Ainslie's way of asking her to start immediately. Ida liked his rich voice, full of nuances that she felt she understood. 'Give me four bars intro,' she nodded at Miss Jordan.

It was a very funny song, 'Singapore Swing':

'What a bore, Singapore,
Give me the peace of Nice,
But I'll swing along in Hong Kong,
Until you take me back to Menton,
Singapore Swing, Singapore Swing,
What's a girl to do but sip another gin sling . . .'

'Don't wave your arms about!' Ainslie shouted at her. 'You're not on the bandstand now. This is theatre, they'll all be watching.' Ida sang again, trying to look bored in the smart way that Glass Slipper *habituées* affected. Ainslie stopped her again.

'That's enough Miss Jordan. I don't know what you did to it, but you did something, you naughty girls, and it was quite, quite wonderful. Rodney will have a fit of course, but he's only the composer.'

Miss Jordan did not own up to the source of her brilliance and hurried off-stage, simpering.

'Now, lie back and look languid, can you?' Ida did her best. 'Languid' was not one of her natural states.

Stretched full-length on the floor, wrapped in blue velvet, Ida began to have her doubts about this audition. Ainslie ordered different lights, and changed her blue robe for a red one. Sylvia appeared at his side, and entered into a lengthy consultation while Ida lay still and worried — a much more natural frame of mind for her.

Her Pa had left early that morning, so that she had no chance to tell him she had been summoned to the Charlbury. She wanted the job for his sake, more than for her own. Revues were for the intelligentsia, the smart set, offering her some stylish publicity and a foot in West End theatrical circles. But if she had to speak, she would be a disaster. Her speaking voice was low and had a catch in it, surprisingly muffled in contrast to her clarity when she sang.

Ainslie came forward. 'I'll have to talk to your agent.' He looked very pleased with himself. 'I understand from Mrs Cavendish your father represents you. Is that so?'

Ida nodded. Could this mean he wanted her?

'Is there a script, Mr Curtis?'

'A script?' His voice rose in mock disbelief. 'The sweetheart wants a script! Darling — believe me, so do I!'

He lifted her to her feet, and stamped a warm kiss on her forehead. 'I want you, I definitely want you. Such optimism will revive me. All I can tell you is, it's about the Empire, the far-flung, lunatic fringes of it, and you're going to appear in a series of tableaux. You're to be my "Soul of the Empire" if you take my meaning, and for the finale you'll sing this reprise of Maud

French's song — she's the lead, the darling. I'll give you absolutely stunning things to wear, and by the end of it all, no one will remember anything else but how funny I was and how gorgeous you were too. That is, if I ever get a decent running order. That's where you come in. I've got some appalling costume changes, and I think you'll give us the extra minutes.'

'I see. So I don't have to speak, then,' Ida said hopefully. 'I don't want to do it if I have to speak . . .'

Ainslie took a step back and shoved his hands in his pockets. He bent forward like a prep-school headmaster.

'I can make you look like a Burmese Princess, an African Sultana, a Hindu Goddess, and a Jamaican Carnival Queen! You have the best number in the show and you're my latest inspiration to hold the whole colonial edifice together. Will that do?'

'Well, there's no need to swear Mr Curtis,' she said, pretending indignation at the tone of the word 'colonial'. 'I never said I wanted to be Sybil Thorndike, did I?'

She loved to see him throw back his head and laugh, as if the pretensions of the world were there to be enjoyed, and never to be taken seriously.

'I like you Ida Garland. We see eye to eye.'

'Whaddya know!' Jack shouted loudly over the telephone. 'I'm in! Joined up! Took the King's shilling!'

'Oh Jack!' Her recent irritation disappeared in consternation. 'Where are you going?'

'Not so far. Training camp at Aldershot. Come with me on Sunday? I want to see Uncle Ted, give him the news . . . Besides, he's not so hot.'

Ida sighed. 'I've been dreading this. OK, see you Sunday.'

They drove down in the AC, Ida bubbling with news of her audition, and Jack with all his plans for an army career. When they arrived, they were shocked to see the deterioration in their uncle, much more pronounced than their worst fears.

Fast fading health produced an ethereal light in Ted's face; the laconic darkness of his eyes was livened by a doubting, enquiring quality, as for the first time in his life, he had begun to wonder 'what it was all about,' as he put it.

His room was full of flowers. The nurses did not take them out at night, unable to resist Ted's joke that he was busy rehearsing for his funeral, and could not get to sleep without them beside his bed. He was experiencing a lot of pain that kept him awake and there was little they could do for it.

'Well, what have you two been up to?' he whispered.

'I joined up, Ted. I'm in. Took the King's shilling. Only me though — my old friend, Terence Bageshaw's got turned down. Dicky ticker.'

'Lucky for him,' said Ted. 'A weak heart's just the thing to have at this juncture . . . And you, Ida?'

'I've been offered a part in an Ainslie Curtis revue,' she replied, proudly. 'I'm going to have a record made privately of my song, just for you Uncle Ted. I can afford it now — Pa tells me it will be a mountain of money!'

'That's what I like to hear. The Garlands are certainly going places in the world. Good girl, Ida.' His hand felt for hers across the bed. 'And who's the lucky feller these days?'

'Oh Uncle Ted. I'm too busy. I'm going to cut another record with Tommy and the boys next week. Tommy's getting a new pianist so that he can stand in front and be a leader full time. I think he's coming out of his shell at last! Maybe you know him. Ivor Clarke's the name. And Bobby Smythe the alto sax, he's very sweet.' She was inventing quickly; Ted liked to hear of liaisons and possibilities, it tickled his fancy.

'I know Ivor. He's a good man. Not your type though. Bobby Smythe's one of the few who isn't married. You're in with a chance there, girl.' Ted tried to squeeze her hand, but a sudden internal discomfort removed him from her.

'Ted, what about the car?' Jack blurted. 'Shall I garage it?' His eyes were brilliant, his words harsh, for he had to be direct and not shy away from the finality of this leave-taking. It was his way, with no intention of upsetting anyone. Uncle Ted understood, although Ida was in turmoil at the question.

'I don't want Josephine to have it. She'll smash the thing, and I don't want Ottley let loose in it either. Sell it, Jack. Put the money in the bank, and when you come back on leave sometime, when you make Sergeant, after I'm — take this girl out for a night on the town. On me, I'd like that.'

'Something to aim for,' Jack smiled with an aggressive determination. 'Only I'll make that Captain.'

Uncle Ted gave a sleepy, sideways glance at Ida. 'That's right,' he whispered. 'That's what I meant. Captain.'

A nurse came in. 'You'll have to leave now,' she said briskly. 'I'm sorry.'

'Goodbye Uncle Ted. I'll send you the record soon,' Ida said, trying to sound as if they had months to fill with plans.

'Fine. But I hear your voice Ida girl, any time I like, I hear you in my head. Singing from *Chu Chin Chow*, by Ma's old piano. Don't go to any expense on my account. No need. See you soon duckie . . .'

Ida nodded sadly and moved to the door so that the two men could say their farewell in private.

'Bye Ted.' Jack stood by the bed uncertainly.

'Good luck old chap. Come here.' He gestured as if he had something naughty to whisper in Jack's ear. Jack bent low to catch what he said. All Ted wanted was to raise a thin arm round the young man's shoulders, intent on a hug. After a long moment Jack straightened up, thunderous with feeling, and left the room.

The cousins drove back to town in silence, their last ride together in Ted's 'girl-trap'.

'I suppose you're busy tonight. Your last night,' Ida managed to say finally.

'Yep. Terence and me have ringside seats for the big fight at Olympia. Then we've got a double date. I'm going to make the most of it.'

'Not Veronica then.'

'Stuff it Ida.'

'She says you're only friends . . .'

'Good.'

This was awful. They could not part without some sense of their old closeness — or was that a thing of childhood, to be put aside?

'Don't forget to write to Gran when you're away, will you Jack. She's been looking lonely lately. And if Ted . . .'

'I'll ring her up.'

'That's not the same and you know it. She'd like to get a letter. Make an effort.'

'All right, all right. Keep your shirt on.'

'You can drop me at the bridge and I'll take the bus along the Embankment,' she said stiffly.

'No, I don't mind. I'll drive you all the way. Last time and everything. In Ted's car, I mean.'

'Is Josephine going to see you off?'

'No. She's in a show on the south coast. Damn good thing. Don't want any fuss.'

'What did they say about the double bass? Can you take it with you?'

'Certainly. I've put it on the train. Can't turn up the first day without it under my arm.'

'Has Uncle Billy got someone else for the shop?'

'Terence is helping him out.'

'My God.'

'He's all right. Not a bad fellow at heart.'

'Hardly reliable, though, is he Jack.'

'You have to learn, Ida, there's a lot more to life than toeing the line. Sometimes you have to break rules to get where you want.'

'Oh yes, I can see that. Like fooling with Veronica. Where will that get you?'

'You don't know what you're saying.' He began to laugh in a falsely amused way. 'D'you know how I got into the army? I can pass for white. Ease through the system. See?'

'So you *do* think about it!'

''Course I do. Oh yeah, I think about it all right. D'you know what happened to Uncle Ted and his twin? They weren't allowed to fight in the last war, because they were coloured. Had to do the carting, the carrying, digging the trenches, non-combat work. Poor old Charlie. Got blown to bits, and never fired a shot. I'm going to be the first soldier this family's had. You can get on all right, Ida, trading on it in these fancy shows, but I need to get out. It's different for a fella.'

Ida did not answer him. He was right. This was a topic she preferred not to dwell on. It seemed to her that as long as no one spoke about it directly, everything would be all right. Better to cope with unspoken prejudices, exploit the 'exotic' silently, than draw attention to her difference, whether it was perceived or just the subject of fancy. Like Josephine said: Don't look for trouble.

'Nearly there. Charing Cross,' Jack said, to change the topic.

'Drop me here. I'll walk the rest,' Ida suggested. Jack swooped to the kerb with too much aplomb.

'Bye then.'

'Goodbye Jack. Good luck.' Ida jumped out quickly. Far too many goodbyes for one day.

He kept pressing the accelerator, showing off, anxious to be gone. She ran round the car and bent down to give him a kiss.

'They'll cut your hair!' she shouted in his ear above the roar of the engine.

'Yeah, but imagine me in a uniform. Can't fail can I?'

He surged away, and Ida wondered how much of his spirit would survive regimentation. Hers would not, but there was a steeliness in Jack, and more recently, a surprising capacity for work which he had not shown as a boy. So little approval had come Jack's way, yet somehow he had learnt to push himself without it. She wondered how much that coolness in him would be exploited. It only masked a loneliness, which she alone had understood and shared. Ida wished she could follow his example, be strong, be assertive. She was on the way to even greater success, and yet there were still certain things that held her back. She would never believe somehow, that the world was her oyster.

A week later, the Garlands heard that Ted had died in the night. Jack could not or would not come home for the funeral, but Josephine hired a car and came up to London for the day.

The church was not very full; Ted had been ill for such a long time that he had dropped out of sight among the casual world of the musicians, whose friendships depended upon chance meetings in a street, a club, or at a gig. But Tommy Trevino and some of the band boys came, and just towards the end of the service, a row of pretty girls, chorines in crisp black hats, turned up. None was known to Ida, and when two of them began to cry noisily she lost control too, because of all the good times they were remembering — harmless good times filled with music and flirting.

Earl, George and Billy carried the coffin from the church to the graveyard. Uncle Jim tried to shoulder the fourth corner, but he was too short.

'Go on Sidney, step in.' Josephine, resplendent in black ostrich feathers, pushed her ratty husband forward. Ida hated that moment. Uncle Jim fell into step behind the coffin between Ida and Gran. Ida squeezed his hand when she saw tears running down his cheeks and was very relieved when the coffin was lowered into the ground in the cemetery of St Luke's, where Jack used to sing.

'Haven't been here for years,' Jim sniffed, making quiet conversation in an effort to recover.

'Me neither,' Ida replied uselessly.

'On that corner, that was where we used to pick up our winnings from the street bookmakers, now and then,' he said, for a moment forgetting why he was there, reminiscing. 'Illegal of course, but that was half the fun.'

'That's what you did . . .' Ida too felt her spirits lift, her mind filling with images of sunny days, pubs, ice-creams, boats on the river, roast dinners, and laughter. And the strongest of such recollections was the vision of Uncle Ted, one foot tucked behind the piano-stool, making up naughty songs for her and Jack, on all the black notes.

Ida went back to singing with the Diplomats, but after her audition with Ainslie Curtis, she found her enthusiasm waning a little. The thought of her new challenge was unsettling. There was also the small problem of Felix Summers. He did not chase her: that would be too predictable for him, and besides, her looks were no more appealing to him than girls like Veronica. She was certainly not an English Rose. No. He used her, like some sort of mascot, to make himself look dashing to others.

One evening Tommy Trevino handed her a note in the band room. Charlie the drummer, a cosily married man who reminded her of her uncle Jim, was instantly at her side. 'Got a love letter, Ida? Let's see, who's it from?'

'Oh, you know, Charlie, Mr Summers again. He's got a whole party in tonight. I suppose I'll have to join his table. He loves to parade his show-biz connections.'

'That dark-haired, clever-looking feller?'

'That's the one.'

'You can do better than him, dearie. Too pleased with himself, that one. Want me to go across and sort him out for you?'

'I'll come with you!' shouted the new pianist, Ivor Clarke, a dapper Cockney. 'Let me ring my big brother!' said another. A chorus from the rest of the band made it plain they would all love a chance to 'have a go' at Felix, and in a very different way, at Ida.

'Shut up!' Ida laughed. 'I'll paint my nails crooked.' Life with the Diplomats might be too familiar, but it was very comfortable. She was going to miss the boys. No one except Tommy knew that she was in the process of leaving. Tommy, generous as ever with her, was sorry to hear that she was resigning, but realised it was time for her to move on.

'Hurry up fellers, should be on the stand soon.' Tommy was the most amiable of bandleaders, unlike some of the others Ida heard the boys gossip about. Men who docked pay if a player came late to rehearsals, and paid out the union minimum when the band was earning hundreds.

'One more hand,' said Charlie. Tommy was out of earshot, so it did not matter that such a kind man was disobeyed.

Ten minutes later the band filed on stage in tails and wing collars, and took their places behind the sequined music-stands, monogrammed with a patent D for the Diplomats. Ivor Clarke was also deputy bandleader. He and Trevino were at school together, old friends.

Ivor was good at the straight commercial stuff, and led the band through the first hour of light dance music which the band boys could read in their sleep. Suppers were served; Ida sat primly on the bandstand in her new net dress. Bored. Then some of the tables were cleared to make the dancing space bigger, and Tommy Trevino, self-conscious in a vast new tuxedo, made his first appearance. Only now did the players move on to Trevino's own compositions or original arrangements of standards, as if the whole 'tone' had lifted with his arrival. Ivor 'hammed it up' on the keyboard. The band boys did not mind — now the music was more interesting, more jazz-oriented, and they swung along happily. Like any good jazz band they did not need a conductor: Trevino was a showman now, beating time for the audience: in fact, Ida laughed because for a trick he stopped to blow his nose, and the Diplomats did not miss a beat. Panicked, Tommy grabbed his baton again, as if he had just 'saved the rhythm' in the nick of time.

Felix was well placed as usual, and nodded at Ida, as if demanding acknowledgement. The two male guests were wearing conical party hats, and blowing rolled-up paper whistles at each other. Felix's fair-haired date was all arms across the table, pale elbows, cigarette smoke and cocktails. Ida, a little irritated, sang her numbers.

Then she spotted Ainslie Curtis sitting alone at an inconspicuous table. The effect was magical. Ida's whole personality lit up double voltage and she heard Tommy murmur behind her, 'Who's in tonight dear? The Prince of Wales?'

Poor Felix was beaming under the illusion that she was making a special effort for his party. But when Ida finished, she scurried past his crowded table.

'Sorry Felix! I'll see you in a little while!' She could feel his dark, angry eyes watching where she ended up. Ainslie Curtis rose with a look of amusement.

'Your boyfriend is offended,' he said, kissing her hand.

'Oh, he's always here. It's all right. Besides, we're not encouraged to sit with customers.'

'I won't keep you. I just wanted a little chat.'

Ida heard the shading in his voice. 'Is something the matter Mr Curtis? Don't say the show is in trouble! I couldn't bear that, before I've even started!'

'Good Lord no. No, I'm afraid I shall have to be fearfully frank with you. It's your contract.'

Ida was alarmed. 'But Tommy Trevino has already said I can leave when you need me full time! And I'm free to rehearse in the mornings. He hasn't changed his mind, has he?'

'No dear. Look, I'm going to say something horribly embarrassing but I think you should know before we go any further. How much do you think you get paid here at the Ambassador?' He spoke in a low voice, no theatricality in his manner at all.

Ida began to feel pale. 'Pa handles all that. I don't quite remember. Yes I do. Tommy pays me a tenner a week.'

'Did you know he has a private arrangement with your father?'

'What do you mean?'

'Well dear, your father suggested to me that I declare one figure to you, and agree a much higher one with him in confidence. He said you were simply hopeless with money and would spend it all if you knew how much you had. It's for your old age, he says.'

Ainslie's face was serious, much handsomer than when he was animated. He did her the kindness of looking away at the dance floor as he spoke, avoiding her shamed face.

'I'm sure it's some misunderstanding,' he said gently. 'It makes no difference at all to my belief in you, Miss Garland. You're a remarkable young lady, with a splendid future.'

Ida tried to smile; words were beyond her, she was so confused. Ainslie kept murmuring, while she grasped the real significance of his news.

'Perhaps this was all agreed when you were starting out, but I don't like to have little secrets from my ladies. I thought I'd just have a word. In case you wanted to renegotiate. You are beyond what I think they call the age of discretion . . . I believe.'

Ida became horribly calm, strangely aware of her physical reaction to shock. Her hand on the edge of her glass, did not feel the curve of it. She concentrated hard on the smoothness of the surface, for some sort of sensual response. When she spoke her voice seemed to come from another person: herself at a distance. She made a supreme effort to lie with conviction.

'Thank you Mr Curtis. You're very kind to mention all this. But I've known for some time. Dear Pa. He was only thinking of my security. Pa knows what he's doing.'

'Oh I know, dear. He brought me a couple of very good girls for the chorus, in my last show. Completely reliable chap, knows his business very well. It's just that — well, some managers do become overprotective where their own flesh and blood are concerned. Actually, mothers usually are the worst. They can be so very grasping . . .'

'What are you offering, Mr Curtis?' Ida was thinking very fast. 'I mean, Pa did tell me, but as he said to you, I'm hopeless with figures.'

'Thirty pounds a week.' He looked at her steadily, her face registering the disbelief she could not conceal. He had said quite enough. They both knew that. 'Oh look, here's your boyfriend. I've kept you far too long already. Here she is, old man . . .' Ainslie stood up, giving Felix a steady handshake. 'So sorry, talking shop at this time of night!'

He kissed Ida's cheek in farewell. 'Have a lovely evening dear. You sing like an angel. Remember, I can't wait to have you in my show.'

Ida was close to tears as he moved away. Thirty pounds was precisely double the figure her Pa had mentioned. A working man's weekly wage was less than a quarter of it. Ida could have screamed with anger at her stupidity, all the little tell-tale signs she had avoided. Earl's secret visits to Harvey Johns and Max Summers; those misplaced letters from Veronica; Denise's insistence on Earl's role in her success . . .

'I say old girl, don't keep us waiting too long, will you?' Felix said, bringing her back to reality.

'Felix,' she said, suddenly spurred to suspicions. 'I've never seen your father since that time when he made me an offer. Veronica told you all about that, didn't she? Did your father ever say anything to you about it?'

He shrugged. 'No. Not a thing. What is all this? You look upset. Come on, I'll soon fix that. Come and meet some friends of mine.'

She could see he wanted to help, but not now: just at this moment he wanted to show her off, act proprietorial about his 'exotic' band singer. His sort of friends found her a real novelty. But as he walked her across the ballroom, he whispered, 'Call me tomorrow at my chambers. I'll help you if I can. How's that?' He was a decent fellow, really.

How was she to sit tight, act polite, when what she really wanted to do was to run home and beat her father into telling the truth? She could not do it: it could not be true . . . after all the years of work, trying to please him. Please don't let it be true . . . Desolation filled her. She badly wanted a drink.

Felix's girlfriend was practically asleep.

'Not much chance of my making an impression with her, is there, Felix?' she laughed harshly — Felix looked surprised at her. Some rebellious spirit in her began to fight off the depression induced by Ainslie Curtis' news. After all, *he* still wanted her, and her new salary had doubled in the last five minutes.

'Let me present Miss Ida Garland. This is an old schoolfriend of mine, Jubilee Hargreaves, and this is Johnny Tiverton.'

'Hallo!' The men half-rose with tipsy jerkiness as she sat between them.

'Hallo boys!' Ida sat on Felix's knee, blowing kisses at the two of them. Felix was most alarmed.

'Come on Felix! More cocktails! I'll have a Bloody Mary!'

'I say,' said Johnny, a pleasant-faced young man with soft, straight hair. 'Rather splendid, meeting you at last.'

Jubilee had more presence of mind. 'Take that stupid hat off Johnny. In front of a lady.' He was slightly plump, had a cheerful, very English face, full lips and a rich voice. Ida took to him at once, and perhaps because of her worries, flung herself at him for a diversion. After all, that was what Felix wanted, wasn't it?

'Jubilee? That's an interesting name,' she said brightly, wrapping her arms round his shoulders.

Felix laughed nervously, explained more than he would have otherwise. 'Not a nickname from school. His mother called him that because he was conceived in the year of Queen Victoria's Diamond Jubilee.'

'She was a great favourite of the Prince's, by all accounts,' Jubilee added, obviously used to dining out on his family history, and taking Ida's interest at face value.

Ida was fascinated. 'I say, have you got a title?' If Felix ever blushed, this was his moment.

'Oh, there's no suggestion I was born on the wrong side of any royal blanket,' Jubilee chattered on. 'Family resemblance very strong. I take after my grandfather.'

'You and Felix were at school together?' Ida asked. 'But Felix is *much* younger than you.'

She enjoyed Felix's confusion. He had expected to show her off, not to be the topic of conversation, as always very reserved, ungiving about himself in company.

'Yes, junior in the same house. We both liked to dodge games and the only way for me to get out of it officially was to run a club for the little squirts who were keen on military tactics. Felix was one of my best members,' Jubilee said affectionately. Felix squirmed.

'That should land you a desk job when the balloon goes up,' Johnny spun his paper hat on its elastic, like a propeller, and gave a brash laugh.

Jubilee's mild brown eyes (a little too soulful for him to be handsome, in Ida's opinion) registered offence.

'Gosh no,' he said stiffly. 'Long line of fighters, the Hargreaveses. I'd do my stuff.'

'Oh God!' the girl at the table lifted her head dramatically. 'Talk about something else! It's always war talk! Chaos and catastrophe! You're all so boring!' and promptly fell back to sleep. Felix stroked her head, determined to look sanguine about her condition. Ida guessed he was seething.

'Would you like to dance, Miss Garland?' Jubilee offered. Without looking at Felix she agreed.

'This is a great pleasure to me, Miss Garland,' he said firmly. Ida supposed that he always said what he thought in plain speech, not caring that others might laugh at him. She wasn't sure if he was a fool or odd and brilliant. The polish of education made it difficult for her to judge.

'Oh, I'm sure you and Felix could go dancing every night. He seems to know hundreds of girls,' Ida said. She was imagining the years of débutante parties that men like Felix Summers and Jubilee Hargreaves would have attended.

'Well, speaking for myself, I get bored rather quickly. Felix is the one who wants to cut a figure in society.'

Ida had never thought of this: now she suddenly saw that Felix was desperate to become a real English gentleman, as un-Jewish as possible. How silly she had been not to see it, and how unkind to embarrass him!

'You're so — different from those girls. You have a talent,' Jubilee declared.

'Thank you,' Ida said, contrite.

'No, I mean it.' He persisted, building up to his point like a child placing bricks one on top of another. He really was endearing, quite different from Felix. S.A did not come into it. 'I've never met a performer before. It's very strange. One minute you're singing about love most passionately, and the next minute you're in my arms. Rather disconcerting, Miss Garland.' He was obliged to acknowledge another couple dancing by and forgo her reaction to his words.

'I never thought of it like that,' Ida laughed. Jubilee's whole mentality seemed so remote from hers, a mixture of genuine curiosity and a quiet sort of self-confidence. Perhaps it was his background, or exclusively male company in his formative years that made him seem a little eccentric. But then Felix had been through the same system, and ended up brilliant, ambitious and predatory.

Their dance ended.

'That was very nice, Mr Hargreaves,' Ida said, her silly act falling flat, her worries crowding in on her again. 'I must go. I have to sing again in a little while.'

'Will you have lunch with me tomorrow?' he said abruptly. 'But perhaps you already have an engagement, with Felix . . .'

'No, I don't,' Ida dismissed any suggestion of a claim. 'I wish I could, but I have to see my agent tomorrow. I think that will take most of the morning,' she said in a grim undertone.

'Well. Another time perhaps.' Jubilee was on the retreat at once.

'Yes. What about Thursday?' She had no idea why she said it. Yes: to be kind, to have someone uncomplicated and admiring to look forward to seeing again. If she had offered a boy a new catapult he would not have shown more pleasure than Jubilee did.

'Thursday!' he agreed.

'I'm rehearsing all morning at the Charlbury. I'm not sure how long I'll be,' Ida apologised.

'That's not far from one of my clubs. Give me a ring when you're free.' He gave her a card and wrote a telephone number on the back of it.

Ida woke up early the next morning, and lay in bed for a while thinking out how she could confront her Pa with Ainslie Curtis' story. She listened for movement in the house. Downstairs her

Pa coughed lightly on his first cigarette of the day and she heard him tinkle with a cup or a plate for his breakfast. Such familiar noises. She started to cry.

She simply could not face him — it would be too humiliating for both of them. The only person left she could talk to was Gran. Jack was away, Ted gone. Auntie Josephine and Uncle Jim were also Pa's clients. Was he doing the same to everyone? Somehow she thought not, that this was a special arrangement he operated only for her. Ida did not want him to lose face before the whole family. If it was only her money he was taking, then no one else need ever know — if it were true at all. She closed her eyes, praying hopelessly that he would explain, and set it all to rights.

She heard the door shut. The house grew quiet. Denise was still fast asleep. Ida's room was cold, for it faced away from the sun and even in summer had an air of damp.

How many times she had lain alone in this room, gated, locked in, anxious, frustrated! Treated like a wilful pet in need of stern training. Her Pa was wrong: she *was* good about money. She gave her upkeep regularly to Denise, bought her own clothes and got about London on her own, paying for taxis, meals, hairdressers, and never got into debt. She was a Garland now: she knew how to be a professional, truly.

A Garland! Ida did not cry now — she just felt a pain welling up inside, hurting in every limb. She was bound to her family: to the domestic claustrophobia, the hypnotic, despising lectures from Denise, the pathetic mastery of her Pa. But there was much, much more that held her there. An overwhelming spirit, a wonderful classlessness about the best of them. Josephine had it, so did Ted — so in his still confused, blustering kind of way, did Jack. A power to take on the world, to engage in life. To perform. They were such originals, and Ida still defined herself by their lights. How could she be brave enough to take on the world without them? Everyone had a place in the Garland family order; the rules were binding and anyone who tried to wriggle found the knots pulled tighter.

She got up, dressed carefully in her best day suit, a smart navy-blue dress and long coat. Every action, every decision of the day seemed new, differently taken. In her little triple mirror, she checked her hat, a close-fitting navy straw with a bunch of daisies at the side. She studied herself gravely, put on a little make-up. Big dark eyes, a pretty good skin, her hair now tamed into a smooth loop behind her ears. Her forehead was too broad and her lips far too generous, but she was not plump any more. Rather she was too thin, and her face too big, like an underweight child's. Perhaps it was that old, sad thought that made her head seem as if it did not belong to her body.

Gran was busy checking the lodgers for the week. Summer was a quiet time; a lot of her regulars were in shows on the coast and the ones in residence, resting, were allowed to hold over their rent payments till the autumn when they had a better chance of finding work. The only one who paid regularly was the young African student in the Bay Front. These were the lean weeks in her boarding-house business.

'Can I come in?' Ida said.

'Ida! How lovely you look. You haven't had any breakfast, I'll be bound. Sit down. Dot, bring her in a plate of toast.'

'Gran, this is serious.' Ida found she was trembling: this would hit Gran very hard. Earl was the most respected son, the eldest, the conscientious one. Gran might be so shocked by the accusations that she could reject them out of hand.

'Fire away. I'm listening.'

'Did Pa ever tell you he was — saving money for me?' Ida plunged in. She would try to say it carefully, like Mr Curtis. Avoid the cruelty of ugly words, like embezzling or thievery.

'Earl? No. I never thought he had a penny to spare with Denise to keep, and then all those singing lessons . . . Neither of you has been cheap.' Ida could see that Gran was already alive to the possibilities. Money caused trouble, and she was beginning to make quite a lot of it. 'Surely you don't need more money from him. What for? You're doing nicely.'

'No Gran. It was just something Mr Curtis said . . .'

'Stop messing about. Out with it.'

Dot came in with the toast and tea and bustled away, leaving the door open. Gran frowned and barked out, 'Shocking draught. Do me a favour Dot.' The door slammed shut.

Then Ida told her Gran the substance of Ainslie Curtis' discovery. Gran's body seemed to deflate, with each sign her whole body sagged lower in her chair. In the silence that followed, Ida wondered if she had dealt her Gran the final disappointment of her life. For months she had been looking so tired, wrapped in memories, slipping from the present.

Ida flung herself round her Gran's broad shoulders, and burst into tears on a resisting boniness. After a moment Gran pushed her off.

'Pull yourself together,' Gran said. 'I've told you before, you have to get on with it, a big girl like you. There's no use crying over spilt milk. I'll talk to him. It wouldn't be right, coming from you, would it.'

'No Gran. But . . .'

'What now!' Gran was so hard; in that instant Ida realised that the bringer of bad news is always hated. Earl had never been strong, but Gran had believed in his decency.

'I won't go on with him,' Ida whispered, 'unless he says it's all a mistake . . .'

'What?'

'I won't have him be my agent any more.'

Gran rubbed at her thighs, trying to work some energy into her limbs. 'You'll break his heart.'

Ida brushed tears away with the back of her hand. Her rouge was smudged, and her fine city hat sat askew on her head. She turned to the mirror above the fireplace to straighten herself. 'I mean it Gran,' she said, speaking to her own face, willing herself to look determined. 'I want proper accounting.'

'He's not a bad man. Maybe he had a quiet season. Maybe Denise was pushing him for money — you can see all that, can't you? She's never been any good for him.'

'Well. That's Pa's choice.' Ida spoke bitterly; her dislike of Denise was so evident that Gran drew back from the unseemliness of it.

'You shouldn't be like that about your own mother,' she said. 'She gave you life.'

Ida shrugged. 'It wasn't deliberate,' she said. The thought of Denise had given her the anger she needed to stand firm. 'And you of all people should hate the way she puts herself above him. Above me. Just because she's white. Pure white, and pure hatred.'

'Ida!' Now Gran was deeply shocked.

'You tell him from me, he's got to settle up. I'll pay him back whatever he thinks I owe him, but above board. I'll agree my own contracts from now on, and I'll be the judge of what I can afford to hand over. It's my money. *My* money!' She was losing control with a fury that scared her.

'You'll need someone.' Gran's lack of argument was a measure of her conflict. 'Why don't you move in with me for a bit? Till the dust settles. You won't be able to go back home.'

Ida blinked. 'Oh God! Where am I to go! I've only got a few pounds on me! Thank you Gran. I will come back here tonight, just until I can sort something out.' She thought desperately. 'Veronica will help me. She'll lend me money . . . Thank goodness, I've got friends . . . I'll be all right . . .'

Gran sank lower in her chair, trying to avoid the worry by tossing a few household bills from one pile to another. 'I've heard girls say that before,' she said. 'There's only one way to be all right. Keep your self-respect.' She gave Ida a very hard look.

'I will Gran!' Ida kissed her goodbye and hurried away. She did not need that kind of advice, from anyone!

Ida set off for her first morning's rehearsal in the Curtis revue. As she walked down Bayswater, she felt as if her identity was emptying out of her. Today, for the first time, she felt as if she was no one's daughter, no one's mistress, and thank God, no one's fool. Ainslie Curtis had promised to give her a new personality. It might be exciting if she were not so terrified of standing on her own two feet, without help, without support. There was Felix: could she trust him to help her, as a favour, without obligations? Why was help always a question of becoming someone's property? Because that was what she had, foolishly, grown up seeing and believing.

On a corner of Marble Arch Ida passed a flower stall. She bought a large bunch of daisies just for the pleasure of holding summer flowers as she walked into town. Besides, they matched her hat and people looked at her, as she hurried by.

Maybe her Pa would follow her to the theatre, and tell her it was all a mistake, and they would be happy again, like before.

*

'Good morning, ladies and gentlemen. In case you don't know or have forgotten, I'm Ainslie Curtis, and this is the star of our show, Maud French. Now, I know you've been working very hard on your little sections. I have to tell you there've been a few changes . . .'

An indignant groan ran round the assembled group on the stage of the Charlbury. Unused to the extrovert temperaments of show people, Ida found this response exceptionally rude to Mr Curtis. Musicians only muttered mutinously against band-leaders, in public bars or when the music was loudest on the bandstand.

'So, it's back to the drawing board. Darling! Stand up!' He pointed at Ida, and her kneecaps shook. Her worries about Earl and the money had not left her with much nerve for this wholly new scene. 'Taller!' he said casually, making everyone laugh. Ida thought that was too cruel. He seemed to have forgotten all about his kindly conversation with her. The entire company, Sylvia Knox the designer, Maud French, other notables and chorines, stared at her with an almost malicious good humour.

'This is Miss Ida Garland. From the Diplomats. She's going to make her stage début with us. Be kind to her, all you hardened troupers. She might just save our bacon, but she doesn't know the difference between a green-room and a greenhouse. So. Be helpful. Not that you always aren't.'

Some of the chorus girls smiled benignly at Ida, but she also saw a couple of male dancers exchange a nudge and wink. She blushed furiously. They obviously thought she was Ainslie's latest piece of couch-casting. What a minefield! No wonder Ainslie had been obliged to disparage her publicly. Ida stuck out her chin in an effort to look as if she could never be seduced.

'Fine. Your new rehearsal schedules are pinned up here. See you all again in two weeks.'

Everyone huddled forward round a blackboard to see their postings. Ainslie roared 'Goodbye! Good luck!' over everyone's heads, and disappeared with Maud French and several other lead figures. No one spoke a word to Ida, and she slipped out of the theatre, insignificant, but put on her mettle by the company's suspicions. Sex was one route to success she was never ever going to take again.

*

253

After telephoning Felix, there was no time to go home; just half an hour to mull over his advice. Maybe Gran had spoken to her Pa by now — perhaps the conversation was happening this very moment, as she walked across town to the Ambassador Hotel. She half expected to see her Pa standing in the staff doorway — there was someone! But it was only Bobby the sax player.

'There you are at last!' he said agitated. 'Burst my shirt-front button. Hurry up — sew it on, there's a pet.'

He stood with his chin in the air, hands in his pockets, while Ida fished in her bag for emergency supplies and set to it.

'Undo your trousers,' she said, brandishing a pair of scissors.

'Jesus! What for?' Bobby looked alarmed.

'So I can cut off the button from the bottom hole, stupid, and put it on the top.'

'Oh!' Relieved, he leant against the wall while she completed the transfer.

'Done.'

'Thanks. You're a sport.'

All that only left minutes for her to change into her own outfit. No time to think of Pa . . .

Ida sat by the side of the bandstand in her favourite silver dress, watching the dancers whirling past. As often happened, girls on the floor gave her loaded looks. Some expressed: I wish I were free to be you; others said: What makes you think you're so clever? What none of them knew was that Ida was oblivious to their thoughts. Soon she would leave all this. Stop being merely the girl singer with the Diplomats. It was the *band* that got top billing outside the hotel, and she had helped to make it famous. And all the time she was a Daddy's girl. A fool.

Ida sang that night on pure experience: her heart was not in her voice. She relied on imitating herself on a good night. Ivor Clarke, a brilliant accompanist, seemed to understand, and made the texture of his playing all the richer, to support her, to make her notes have something to work against. After her set she went over to him.

'Thank you Ivor. If it weren't for you I'd have had to drink a quart of alcohol. I can't do that now.'

'Daytime job?' he asked, interested. 'If you ever need a pianist . . .'

'I don't suppose I ever will, but then, you never know . . . don't say anything to the boys. Not yet. Will you?'

Ivor shook his head. 'You're leaving. I guessed as much when I saw Ainslie Curtis chatting to you. I'm sorry to hear that. Very sorry.'

It was nice to be valued, to be missed . . . Ida went home late to Gran's boarding-house to spend the night in Ted's old room. When she opened the door she gasped. In a fit of pique someone had carried over all Ida's belongings in pillowcases and dumped them on the bedroom floor. It had to be her Ma — the only person spiteful enough to do it. It must have taken her several trips — a lot of energy, for one slow-moving. And on top of the heap, all Ida's film star postcards from under the glass of her dressing table had been ripped up and scattered, like ashes on a pyre. There was a note: 'True colours will out.'

Ida kicked the jumble in a fury, then fell into bed trying to rest. At times she startled awake, remembered where she was and cried. At times she screwed her eyes up savagely, desperate to sleep because she was nervous of not performing well at Curtis' first rehearsal. In the end she gave up the attempt, and paced the floor, thinking about her Pa on the best days of her life. When they'd sat by the river, or he had taken her for walks, and she felt like his favourite little girl. The night was too long, made longer and unendurable by memories.

She was brought to day by a tap on the door: Dot wakening her with tea. Rehearsals began at nine sharp.

'No message for me? From Pa?' she asked. Dot, fully apprised of the latest family drama, shook her head. Every moment that Earl did not come to speak to Ida was confirmation of his guilt.

She dressed as best she could in the least-creased outfit from the heap.

Then she heard footsteps, not one person but two, climbing up the stairs and heading towards her room. Ida swung open the door just as Earl was about to grasp the handle.

'I want an explanation,' he said, coolly.

'Gran spoke to you, didn't she?' Ida was trembling and held on to the door for steadiness.

'You've got it all wrong, honey,' Earl said, leaning against the banister. Ida watched his face, the lines round his mouth as he lit a cigarette and blew smoke out slowly. He was playing for time, and as he drew breath to explain himself she saw his lips twitch, and she knew he was about to lie.

'Sure I put money aside. Sure I did it on the quiet. You've been making big money, and you're only a girl. I thought it would go to your head.'

'Pa. You could try all the private deals you wanted with Mr Summers. No wonder he threw you out. I was younger then. I'm nineteen now. In any court of law you wouldn't stand a chance. I've taken legal advice!'

Denise took a step forward. 'Are you threatening him? You've got a nerve . . .' She laughed too raucously. 'I always said the worm would turn! Despicable! Self-seeking! I had your number, right from the start!'

Earl's slim fingers trailed across his jawline. 'Look, this is all a misunderstanding . . . we can work something out.'

'I'm not going to work anything out, Pa. And I'm not going to fight you for what you've taken. I just want to be left alone, from now on.' Ida's eyes filled with tears. 'I have to go. I'm going to be late, my very first day of rehearsals . . .'

Ida instantly regretted mentioning her new part — the thought of Ainslie Curtis and the revue only reminded her Ma of the profits she and her Pa would miss.

'Lady Muck!' Denise shouted, and swung a palm wildly at Ida's face. 'Ungrateful bitch!'

Ida defended herself. Earl grabbed at Denise, trying to pull her off. Too late: Denise left a trail of scratch marks on the side of Ida's face. But the heel of her Ma's high shoes gave way under the force of her unusual violence. Denise tottered and fell back down the stairs. Ida covered her face, screaming, and a crowd of lodgers ran out of their rooms. The young African lodger on the ground floor happened to come into the hall: he ran up and saved Denise from tumbling the whole length of the stairs.

That was the end of the incident. Naturally everyone ran to help Denise, and her Pa tried to lift her up, groaning with nothing more than a bruised backside. Ida slipped back unnoticed into her room, patched up her make-up, whimpering when the scratches stung.

By the time she emerged, more or less tidy, the hallway was deserted. Denise lay in state on one of Gran's battered sofas, and the nice young African law student was taking her a cup of tea from the scullery. No one had seen the assault, or cared to think that it had actually happened. Earl shifted about in the hall, himself looking mortally wounded.

'You've got to give me a chance,' he said.

'I did, Pa. Lots of times. And you took every one.'

Gran hovered behind them in the parlour. 'Take a pound note from me, Ida,' she said. 'You'll be late. You'll have to go by cab.'

Ida had to cancel her lunch with Jubilee Hargreaves because she was sent miles out of town, to rehearse in a draughty church hall, somewhere in Walworth. The stripes on her face made her specially glad not to be seen by him, and made the first day of the chorus work a particular trial. Until she was wanted, she sat in a corner, as inconspicuous as possible.

Sylvia Knox, the frilled designer, called in mid-morning at Walworth taking measurements for new costumes. When Ida's turn came, she looked closely at her cheek.

'That's a nasty scrape. You're all right, are you, Miss Garland?'

'Oh yes. Thank you. It was my cat.'

'Temperamental . . . ?'

'Very. It's a Persian. Pedigrees are the worst, aren't they?'

'I don't know . . . I've got three blues and they're always gentle.' Ida's look of alarm told her that the wild cat was an invention. 'I'll get one of the chorus girls to give you wych-hazel. It's good for skin cuts, bruises . . . dancers always keep some about when they're rehearsing.'

'Oh, please don't bother, Miss Knox.'

A few moments later a dark girl came over to her. 'Miss Knox said you'd — why, if it isn't Ted Garland's little girl!'

'Mona?' Inexplicably, the sight of a friendly, familiar face made Ida burst into tears.

'Goodness! It's only a scratch! No one's going to mind, ducks, and it'll be gone in a day or two! Come in the vestry.'

Mona set to work on Ida's cheek, dabbing and patching,

257

creating camouflage much more proficiently than Ida had managed to.

'When you get to my age, dear, you need a trick or two. Still, Mr Curtis has always been good and remembered me. I'm not in the chorus line-up now mind you. I do comic sketch routines. He says I'm the best novelty dancer in the show. How's that for you?'

The two girls admired Mona's handiwork in the church mirror, which was pitted with black freckles and kind to reflections.

'Oh Mona, it hardly shows. Thank you!'

'I thought it must be you when Mr Curtis called out your name. What a turn-up! Pity about old Ted, wasn't it? Lovely man . . . I say, is it true?'

'What?' Ida feared she was going to ask about the cause of her uncle's death.

'About you and Mr Curtis . . .'

Ida shook her head. 'No. I'm not that kind of girl. Honestly Mona.'

'I didn't think you were.' Mona surveyed Ida's pale face, whose large light-coloured eyes were dulled by some sadness.

'You'll be all right. But you've got to take the knocks and get on with it.' She shook Ida by the shoulders. 'I mean to say, if you get plum parts without a bit of how's your father, then you ain't got much to worry about! I wish I had the luck!'

Rehearsals seemed less frightening after that exchange, and when Ida's first number had to be blocked out, the knowledge that one professional in the room was on her side, made her respond to orders with some credit.

To her astonishment, when she stepped out of the dank church hall that evening at seven, Jubilee was waiting for her in a chauffeur-driven car.

'Thought I'd give you a ride,' he beamed. 'Hop in.'

'How did you find me?' she asked.

'Oh, easy. I rang the Charlbury and gave your name. The office was most helpful. A woman told me you'd had a small accident and might be glad of the ride. I see you scratched your cheek. It's not too bad.'

'The trial of rehearsals,' Ida said, airily. She was not going to risk cats this time.

'It was jolly thoughtful of her to tell me. Miss Knox, it was. People are kind. People usually are.' He talked freely, not out of nervousness, but as if he knew her well.

Ida guessed people would be good to someone who was as inoffensively pleasant as he was all the time. 'How long have you been waiting?' she asked, lacking any sort of finesse in these matters.

'Roberts and I had a rather profitable time in that betting shop across the road. He did well in the four-thirty at Epsom and I did spectacularly badly at every other course that had horses running. I hope they had horses running. I do wonder.'

Ida laughed, and continued to be entertained as the car drove them into town, back to Jubilee's favourite stamping ground, the area round the back of the British Museum, known as Fitzrovia.

'You see, I like to pop in to the Chinese galleries, look at old prints,' he explained, with that air of earnestness she still could not judge perfectly. 'Here we are. It's the favourite of my clubs. The Flitch. It's very famous. Lots of brilliant members — all the intellectuals of Bloomsbury and Soho. H.G. Wells, Howard Spring, Gilbert Frankau, that sort. Then there's the journalists, they come for a late dinner, after Fleet Street's put the papers to bed. And politicians, Sir Oswald Mosley . . .'

'The Blackshirt leader, you mean?' Ida's face showed her alarm. 'It's not a Fascist hang-out?'

'Good Lord, of course not. He's not a *regular*. The regulars are a jolly fine bunch, Fascists, Communists, Socialists, Conservatives — we don't make a distinction on that front. It wouldn't be civilised, would it? Although I'm afraid there is a bogus element creeping in. It used to be much more distinguished in the old days.'

Ida realised that Jubilee was probably a little older than Ainslie Curtis but his naïve faith in people made him seem more her own age.

The club was merely a series of lofts over some old stables. There were even iron hay-baskets, rustily not budging from their corners downstairs. Wooden stairs led up past a steamy, none-too-savoury kitchen that fed the members at tables covered in check cloths, under original barn-like beams. Space was left at one end for a miniscule dance floor, and a small dais for the combo. It was the kind of place that made the hour of the day meaningless; people ate breakfast alongside others who were ordering pre-theatre suppers. Ham, of one sort or another, figured largely on the menu: salad teas or in robust sandwiches. 'Drinks can only be served with food, you see,' Jubilee explained. All-day alcohol was fast becoming a feature of Ida's London life.

Ida overheard a heated conversation on the state of West End theatre from one table. 'That man writes reviews for *Playbill*,' Jubilee told her . . . Ida stopped to listen:

'I've come to the conclusion that this post-war public is barely aware of the four years' agony, are ruthless in their judgement, and merciless to all that makes no appeal to them.' The spectacled man with a faultless, didactic voice pronounced long words effortlessly, with no gestures for emphasis. His head produced thoughts as if it were a disembodied brain, an opinion-machine in perpetual motion.

'Since 1920 we've been living in an age of false values. Everybody lives falsely, lives gloriously, lives blindly. Talk of wage reduction is unthinkable . . . !' At this point Ida lost the flow and allowed Jubilee to lead her to a quiet table.

'Do you agree with what that man was saying?' she asked.

'Are we going to be serious?' Jubilee replied, a little surprised.

'Well, I'd like to have your opinion. I don't get much chance to talk properly,' she said, a little plaintively. She was thinking of the rehearsal. So many of the chorus girls were painfully thin, euphoric to be in work after months of inactivity and near-starvation. If the revue were not successful . . .

'I'll tell you a funny story. We had a Down and Out Gala here a few years ago. It was in the newspapers. Well, two days later, one of the frivollers made a killing on the Stock Exchange, while another chum of mine was actually having to earn a living off tips, minding cars in Belgrave Square.'

'I don't understand . . .' Ida said.

'No one does. It's a topsy-turvy universe. Most people's response is *carpe diem*. Have a good time. You're right to believe that dictators don't have the answer, I agree with you there. But I'm not sympathetic to collective solutions, communism, socialism, either. Unfortunately that leaves us with a rather silly sort of jam in the middle. Lots of theories, no solutions. Doing nothing at all is rapidly becoming pretty political. Now my dear, that's enough philosophy for one evening. Let's have a couple of cocktails, and then when you've soaked up enough Bohemian atmosphere or gin — whichever you prefer — I'll take you somewhere respectable for dinner. How about the Carlton? Or the Gardenia? It's a lovely evening, we could dance outdoors.'

He signalled out of the window to the chauffeur who was enjoying a beer in the yard below, at a mundane establishment opposite the club — the locals' pub.

'My mother's on holiday, so I'm keeping her man Roberts happy with a few nights on the town.'

Ida was glad that Roberts did not belong to him. It did not seem quite in character, too conspicuous.

'I have to be at the Ambassador by ten.'

'Then the Gardenia is the best choice — it's on the way, Park Lane.'

The idea of a very exclusive restaurant in Park Lane being 'on the way' made Ida laugh out loud — a few heads turned, and Jubilee, who was quite used to people finding him funny when humour had not been his aim, lit her cigarette with a look of devotion.

12

'What do you think?' Felix said, strolling round the apartment with his hands in his pockets. 'Lady Pringle's an old client of mine. She'll let you have it for three pounds a week. That's not bad. And it's free right away. She said I could give you the key if you want to move in.'

'I know this charming little decorator,' Veronica said, beginning to plan great things, and far removed from her exclusive school days of sleeping on bare floors, 'Enid whatever-her-name-is, used to be Fanshawe but she divorced him.'

'Fanshawe, Rickshaw, honestly Veronica, I've got to get back to chambers,' Felix scoffed. 'Do make up your mind . . . Ida would be glad of that.' Discreetly, he did not add that his advice to Ida had been to move out immediately. Under her family roof, she laid herself open to lawsuits; money could be claimed for her 'services', if she remained dependent domestically. She would only reach the age of majority at twenty-one. Ida did not think her father would go to law to win back control of her, but Felix said guardedly it was best to be scrupulous.

'Ida? Jack? Shall we do it?' Veronica thought the situation was pure melodrama. Ida could see she saw the need to find a flat only in terms of her own rebellion — just a chance to join in the fun of living freely. Did she understand what a wrench this was going to be? 'I need completely white walls of course,' Veronica went on, 'or cream. I could borrow pictures from my little gallery. Could be jolly good for business, actually.' Veronica was already installed, in her imagination.

Jack had rushed home on leave, as soon as Ida called him; he only had a twenty-four-hour pass, but that was long enough to cheer her up, give her a little courage. Now he peered out of the window at the smart sports car parked in the street. 'Looks fine to me. The whole place needs rewiring, though. You could get Uncle George to do that on the cheap.'

'What will your parents say, Veronica?' Ida said, still worried. 'They can't possibly approve of your moving in with me.' She smoothed the torn and wrinkled satin bed cover on the divan, ran her fingers over the faded blue paintwork on the bay-window shutters, obviously put in by some other 'little' interior decorator to give a little French style to this *pied-à-terre*, just behind Harrods. This was the nearest she would get to France for a very long time . . .

'Oh God Ida, Mummy and Daddy are far too busy with their own problems. They've got rather a lot of friends coming out of Europe — the house is bulging with them. Mummy's always complaining about my late hours, and quite honestly, I should think they'd be glad of my bedroom.' Veronica laughed a little too easily. Felix pretended not to hear; the situation in Europe was ominous, not a subject he found easy. He was too moral a man not to be distressed by events, but he never discussed the Jewish issue, not admitting to his ancestry even in front of his sister and her oldest friend. The Red Cross were giving people air-raid lessons . . . the Air Force was getting more planes . . . Jack was learning all about his latest thing, tanks, for a new kind of fighting . . . the Nazi party had come to power. They all knew these facts, but no one spoke a word aloud.

'So. I take it you accept,' Felix said at last. 'I'll draw up the lease, and as a favour to you, Vron, I'll pay the first quarter's lease.'

'That's very decent of you! What a nice big brother.'

'I had a little flutter on the Stock Exchange. And knowing you, decorating this place will knock a sizeable hole in your allowance.'

Ida offered just as quickly: 'I'll pay the second quarter. We'll take it in turns after that, shall we?' She would save all her wages from the tour of *RSVP*. It just had to be a hit show.

Veronica and her brother went down in the little lift; as it only took two, Ida and Jack ran down the stairs. 'Hey,' said Jack, before they rejoined the others, 'I didn't like to say anything in front of Felix — acting the big shot. But I'll help you out, if you ever get stuck.'

'Oh no Jack. I couldn't. I'll be fine. And don't mind Felix. He's just being conscientious. I think he rather likes having to be responsible . . . You really like it? I've got to find somewhere quick . . .'

'Sure! Smart address. Only — watch Veronica will you? She's an awful goer — even by my standards.'

'Well! Coming from you that's quite an admission! Don't worry. I'll hardly be here anyway. The tour starts in a few weeks.'

They joined the others just as Veronica flagged down a taxi. 'Can I give you a lift, Jack?'

'No. I'll leg it back through the park. Thanks, all the same.'

Veronica shuddered theatrically. 'So fit! *Exhausting*. Hop in Felix, you can take the cab on. Bye you two!' She drove off shouting: 'It's going to be such fun!'

Jack breathed in evident relief. 'She's a good sport . . . Tell you the truth, though. I'm well out of that one.'

Any other day Ida might have found this cheering, but her problems weighed her down.

'Where are you going now? Off to visit Gran?' Ida frowned. 'Tell her I'll be back later, to pick up my things . . . There's only the one suitcase, I left it all packed . . .'

'And you'll be seeing this Right On fellow tonight . . .'

'Jubilee? Oh no. I'm rehearsing.'

'Tell you what, I'll pick up your stuff and bring it over to the theatre. No need for any more aggravation . . .'

'Oh Jack, you're a brick.'

Edinburgh, Glasgow, Manchester, Liverpool and Birmingham . . . For Ida, the trip to the provinces brought her a widening view of poverty and harsh attitudes she had been protected from in London. Flipping through a newspaper in Liverpool, she came across a picture of two little black children, probably from the long-standing black population of the dock area: *Dark horses in the egg and spoon race*, ran the caption . . . Happy kids, labelled as animals, without feelings, as she once was.

She stuck close to the revue team, did not venture very far from their digs. Luckily she did not sense any hostility from theatrical landladies; as in Gran's boarding-house, artistes and entertainers were spared the general ignorance.

Ainslie had arranged the tour to 'try it on the dog', as he put it, and to recover his expenses to date: ten thousand pounds. But *RSVP* did not seem to go down well in the provinces, and the backers were worried. Ida was sure it was because all this mockery of the British Empire did not catch the current mood: a slowly-building belligerence.

'Noël's *Cavalcade* was more the thing, although he hated it being considered jingoistic.' Ainslie was fussing over bacon and eggs in the station platform tea-rooms at Crewe.

Maud French (who Ida had discovered was not a bit intimidating after all) pulled off her black felt hat and peeled a piece of paper from inside the hatband. She twinkled at Ida: 'Positive thought waves, you see? I'm a tiny bit psychic . . .' Maud unfolded the slip — a review. 'This is the *Manchester Guardian*. Remember? *RSVP has all the hallmarks of a Curtis revue. A chorus very much undressed, some stylish dance numbers, and a clever thread running through. Maud French is witty and polished, and Miss Ida Garland is the show's little surprise bonus, an exotic young lady who sings the hit reprise with great vitality.*'

Ida, embarrassed, looked down at her plate, speckled with the remains of far too many currant buns. It was after Manchester that Maud French had adopted her, a decent response when she could have been viciously competitive.

'We're a great team, Ainslie!' Maud went on. 'And by the time we get to London, the pacing will be perfect. I still think we should cut the tom-tom sketch, in Act Two . . .'

The pair of them were indefatigable. Ida left them to it. Feeling slightly queasy from eating bad food at the wrong time of day, she went back to their train compartment, alone, and fell asleep, sitting upright.

At Birmingham, she woke; stiff, in a daze, she struggled into her suit jacket. Maud was fully made up, even though it was seven in the morning. 'Here. Have some of this.' She handed Ida a cocktail shaker full of something smelling vile. 'Take a little nip. And put some lipstick on. You never know who might be out there waiting.'

Ida did as she was told, knowing that Maud French was one of those troupers, on a classier level than Aunt Josephine, from whom she was learning the techniques of survival.

The cocktail certainly helped. She stepped out on to a smoke-laden platform, the shot of alcohol making all her senses vibrate. Sharp air, an acrid odour from industrial waste, the whining, unfamiliar nasal accent of a passing newspaper boy. At the end of the platform a huddle of tramps lay wrapped in newspapers. Pigeons pecked round the men's empty bottles. There were even blackbirds and sparrows sidling on the platforms, but no big boys; none of the boisterous London seagulls elbow-winging their way to the best of the scraps. She was very homesick for London, for the smart Knightsbridge flat she was paying for but had barely lived in. She missed Veronica, Jack, and (difficult to admit) Jubilee Hargreaves more than anyone.

It was too early for porters; Ainslie and the stage-manager were struggling at the end of the train with the unloading of the scenery and costumes. A freelance hack — Ida was beginning to recognise degrees of importance with the Press — ran up and took a photograph of her and Maud as she lit the star's first morning cigarette.

'Maud French, isn't it?'

'Lovely to see dear old Brummagem!' she exclaimed with mechanical brightness. 'My favourite, faithful audience!'

'What's your name dearie?' the man said familiarly to Ida. 'Garland? Oh, that's right, the darkie singer. How d'you like to tour, then?'

'Well, I don't know the north,' she replied coldly, hating his description of her. Maud gave a warning glance. Ida tried harder. 'I know Suffolk,' she offered, airily, thinking of Harvey Johns' music school. 'But I'm a Londoner. This is my first tour and it's tiring . . . in town I stay in bed till noon — you know how lazy people like us always are!' Her smile had a glittering menace.

'Er, yes . . . Ta ladies. Good luck for tonight then. Any chance of a free ticket or anything?'

'There's always two for the *Post* and *Mail*,' Maud said. 'But I'll see what I can do . . . give me your card, darling.'

She turned to Ida with a laugh. 'My dear, what a tease you are! He'll jolly well have to give you a good write-up after such a *faux pas*; he'll probably say that you're on the best country weekend circuit, when you're not swanning about the London clubs with your young man! You see if I'm not right . . .'

She was, and Ainslie was delighted. 'They love a story — even to the point of inventing one,' he said next day, admiring the photograph of the two women, profiled against billowing smoke, under the Victorian iron arches of Snow Hill Station. 'In desperate times, people like to escape, to dream that anything is possible. Look, you're a fantasy . . . *Maud French shares a joke with her new rising co-star . . . the lovely café au lait singer, Miss Ida Garland . . . she's often seen in the best night spots of the capital, squired by Mr Jubilee Hargreaves . . .*'

'Oh my God, how did he find that out?' Ida exclaimed. '*Café au lait* — I suppose that's a step up from chocolate anyway . . .'

'Listen, there's more.' Ainslie went on reading: '*Contrary to other reports, the exotic Miss Ida Garland is London born and bred, and her success is an example of this country's civilised attitudes in these intolerant times . . .*'

'That's a fantasy, all right,' said Ida, thinking not only of herself, but of Felix, barred by his origins from joining most of the better London clubs.

Ida had time to read on the tour, between her numbers, when the green-room was quiet and other acts on stage. Not books, not newspapers — at least not often, in case she found things that upset her. She took to buying the *Melody Maker*, the musicians' newspaper that all the band boys used to pore over. It made her quite nostalgic for the good old days, playing cards, painting her fingernails, hanging out in pubs with the Diplomats, or eating Soho snacks.

Tonight on stage the regular thundering of the chorus line, the loose rat-tat of their tap shoes made a comfortable rhythm to her thinking, as she flipped through her music rag. Someone in this issue had analysed a Louis Armstrong trumpet solo, to prove that the notes of it were those used by a Jewish cantor. She did not like that: no one had the exclusive use of the sad notes of any scale, in her opinion. Tommy Dorsey once said the best dance music could only be played by Negroes, Jews, and Irishmen. 'Jig tempo,' she remembered: that was the band boys' term for the commercial beat of the dance floor — jig tempo, in more senses than one, jig being another word for nigger.

This was no good — being too aware of these racial fascinations. Ida, restless, skipped up to her dressing room, to put on her Burmese head-dress. As usual, a greetings telegram from Jubilee was pinned to her mirror: 'Nearly home stop I miss you stop good luck stop marry me stop love q.v. stop'.

Q.v. Ainslie had been able to explain to her. 'Quantum vis, as much as you wish . . . Nice fellow. Does he always propose by telegram?'

'Oh, at least once a week. Most particularly on first nights,' Ida laughed.

'Don't run off and get married will you? Not when you're going to be a star!'

'Oh, it's not serious. We have fun, that's all. You know my career comes first, Mr Curtis.' No time for love.

Ainslie was right: she was benefiting from the great vogue that other much more talented and authentic coloured stars were creating before her. She was his answer to Elizabeth Welch, who sang in Noël Coward's revues . . . A whole article in her *Melody Maker*, charmingly headlined *Highlights on Dark Subjects*, listed all the best black entertainers now working in London. There was handsome Buddy Bradley, who used to dance at Connie's Inn Harlem, and did all the choreography for C.B. Cochran's shows . . . Jack London, a bandleader and athlete who represented England in the Olympic Games, and whose father had been a surgeon alongside Lord Lister . . . Ellis Jackson, who had come to England with his father in 1907 as a song and dance team, and now played trombone with Billy Cotton's band . . . Rudolph Dubar, who played the clarinet and ran a music college in London . . .

Perhaps Ainslie was aware of all this when he dressed her up in these tropical-hot colours, and persuaded her to use make-up far too dark for her natural skintone. He even talked of hiring a voice coach for her, to strengthen and deepen her speaking pitch. Ida saw that she was being groomed into a new personality; she just hoped that it was her *rightful* one.

'Miss Garland please, three minutes,' the ASM called her. She flew down the stairs, hurried to the wings, and just like her Aunt Josephine used to do, forgot about everything else as the energy of performing built up in her. In an instant she was on stage, as if she had arrived there by magic: a dynamic presence, vibrant with life, giving her heart and soul to that sombre, unemployed, Midlands audience. She wanted to bring love and laughter to them, fill their hearts with the lightness of hope. Once more the orchestra gave her note, and once more Ida dazzled, in song.

London: the first night. At Ainslie's cosy theatre, the Charlbury, Ida was promoted to her own shoe-box of a room alongside Maud French, her travelling companion, instead of being squeezed in with the chorus line, as on tour. How welcome they all made her: Jubilee, still amusing her with his devotion, sent dozens of pink roses, Felix and Veronica carnations and lilies; Jack, for a joke, a large display of gladioli, because they were her secret, shameful favourites. Such vulgar, gloriously showy flowers! But he could not be there — posted up north with his regiment, just as she moved south.

In his ignorance, Jubilee arrived with a bottle of champagne. 'Shall I open it now?' he asked.

'Good Lord no! Have you seen the rake on the stage out there? I can't take any chances!' Ida sat at her mirror, dabbing furiously at her nose.

'Sorry. I thought it might calm your nerves.'

'Oh Jubilee, I'm sorry I snapped. I'm terrified, you see.'

'Do London audiences differ so very much from the provinces?'

'They do.'

Ainslie appeared — it was almost curtain up. 'Full house. What a relief.' Typically, he started retouching her make-up himself, studying her reflection, towering behind her.

'What's the matter?' she asked, sensing his nervousness.

He stood back to admire the darkening of her eyeshadow. 'Why did you send your family complimentaries? Your father's out front. In the middle of the stalls. Will you be all right?'

'Is Ma with him too?'

'A small blonde woman?'

Ida began to tremble with the idea of her estranged parents sitting in front of her, half-wanting her to fail . . . She had grown too sure of herself, being separated from the family, on tour. It was only a few months since she had left them, and now, back in London, they seemed powerful again.

'I did it on impulse. I must have been feeling braver then.'

Somehow Ainslie realised the struggle she was going through, to get away from the pair of them. He laid big hands on her arms, to reassure her. 'You'll be fine. Chin up.'

Seated in a corner by her mirror, Jubilee sipped his champagne. She had not told him very much about the Garlands. Not yet anyway. He would wait — he was a patient man.

'Do you want me to step outside?' Jubilee asked, kindly and quietly aware that she needed help from her professional mentor at this moment more than from anyone else.

'Oh no Jubilee!' Impulsively she grabbed his glass and swallowed the remains.

'I could ask them to leave . . .' Ainslie suggested.

Ida shook her head. 'No. That wouldn't be right. I've got to show them I'm standing on my own two feet.'

'Good.' Ainslie gave her a little shake, to make her concentrate on what he said. She felt a great energy of sympathy running from his hands into her shoulders, making her draw herself up in her seat. 'I want you to remember, right from the start, how you always liked an audience of one — do you remember, you once told me so? Just pick one. Sing to one, Ida, someone who loves you — forget all about the rest.'

'Mr Curtis, will you help me? Tell the porter at the stage door not to let *anybody* come up afterwards. I'm dining with Jubilee and I'd rather have time to change in peace.'

'Fine. Consider it done.'

Jubilee stood up, overcome with this small sign that Ida might actually need him. He was winning.

'Ida, darling,' he said encouragingly. 'Here's a little something. It brings happiness, the orientals believe . . .'

It was a tiny netsuke, a fat roly-poly man of jade, called Hotei, the god of Contentment, smiling in the palm of her hand.

'How sweet! He looks suitably wicked.' She kissed Jubilee with real affection, on the lips. For a moment, he held her close.

'Lucky man, Hargreaves — join me in my box for the show?' Ainslie said gruffly. 'And bring that damn bottle with you.'

'Thanks — I'd value your professional opinion; I have a lot to learn . . .' Jubilee looked genuinely pleased, even though he had seen the revue in every town along the road.

They left her alone. Ida closed her eyes on the image in the mirror: herself as an African tribal queen, staring, terrified.

For out there, in the audience, there would be two faces, staring at her too: Pa, resisting, angry, trying to make her guilty for casting him off, his hurtful dark eyes willing her not to do well without his word of approval. And Ma, cooler, sneering, making her ashamed to trade on her high colouring, 'looking as if you'd just climbed out of the trees, my girl.' Ida could just conjure them up before her now.

She put the little netsuke in a small box on her dressing table. Inside was the photograph of her Grandpa Joseph, at the end of the pier, the one Gran had given her. There too was Jack's poodle brooch, and Aunt Josephine's doctor's telephone number, and an old bottle of nail varnish, stolen from her Ma's dressing table. Talismanic objects, quite right for a jungle voodoo woman. She willed herself into another state of being — a trance.

Later, on stage, she suddenly felt the presence of love. The audience were giving their hearts to her, with a fulsome roar of praise. She could not see anyone out there at all: Ma and Pa were lost, submerged, impotent, in the inky blackness beyond the lights. Looking up at the balcony, at Jubilee's triumphant smile and wildly clapping hands, Ida knew she had triumphed.

Ainslie, very tight, watched the birth of his brightest star.

'Don't leave the party, have a little fling with me,
Don't leave the party, have a real wild time with me;
I'm yours for tonight, and I'm dancing without gloves . . .'

Ida hummed her latest song, smiling to herself. *Dancing Without Gloves* was the title of Ainslie's latest show. He got the idea from the current fashion among society women to give up formal dress when swanning about town. Nowadays no one minded being seen hatless for lunch — or as Ainslie rudely commented, 'leaving the table witless with gin slings'.

She slipped a gold lamé dress over her head and pinned a paste clip on the coils of her hair. Considering her face in the mirror, she added lipstick the colour of grapes to her full mouth. Around her jawline there was still the mat bloom, a slight fur like peach; she sighed at this obvious sign of youth. Fatigue never seemed to ruin her looks. How could it, when the world rushed at her, with open arms of adulation? In two years she still had not grown used to it — the thrill of winning people's praise, earning money, and being in the limelight. Who could ever tire of being wanted?

She had been rehearsing all day, and now it was party time with Jubilee. Midnight: he'd be calling for her at any moment. Poor Jubilee! His nickname, once a useful joke when meeting strangers, had suddenly become an embarrassment wherever he went. Even an ape at the zoo had been christened his namesake, because today marked a week of celebration for the *King's* Jubilee. May, 1935. The whole of London was out on the streets tonight, and his friends were giving an anti-monarchist ball as a smart way of passing comment. Just last month, the Italian Fascists had begun threatening Abyssinia, and no one seemed able to do anything to stop them. Jubilee said the threat of war was coming nearer. It did not really seem the time to start waving flags in the street.

Veronica rushed in, clad only in a silk slip and suspenders. 'Powder my back, will you?' Ida asked. Veronica obliged expertly, with a velvet puff.

'Can I borrow the black silk thing for tonight?' She rummaged in Ida's cupboard.

'Of course, as long as you don't return it in tatters like the last one.'

Veronica's look of hopeless charm softened her. The girls exchanged a smile in the mirror. Veronica came forward and leant down over Ida. She opened a small metal pillbox filled with a white powder, licked a finger, dipped it in and rubbed the powder over the gum above her even top teeth. 'Just a little celebration . . .' she murmured with a shake of pleasure as the drug entered her system. 'Take some. Just this once.'

Too tempting. Ida succumbed and took the cocaine. Her eyes became enormous with remembrances as the drug produced a chord in her head, like an accordion squeezed in and out, a chime of compressed notes . . .

She suddenly had a vision of how she would look in this new revue: like a coon. She was to be suspended on a silver crescent moon, in a pierrot costume with her face whited out, except for a small black star on her cheekbone. Her clown costume was to be made of fine gauze, almost transparent gold, so that her thin limbs would show through in the spotlight. This time she had persuaded Ainslie to get a wonderful blues written for her — of course, not the blues as it is properly sung by Ethel Waters or Bessie Smith, but a West End blues, a show blues, for a soulful English girl who hoped to give it a tone of her own. Was she being stupid? To use her true passion for singing in this light vein? It was making her rich — seventy pounds a week — but something was still missing.

Veronica, now fully clothed, reappeared for approval. 'Do I look chic?' She twirled round; she looked lovely, but just too fast for comfort. If only Veronica would settle to something; she too was dancing without gloves. The doorbell rang. 'That's Jubilee. I'll let him in,' she said, kissing Ida goodbye.

Too bad their maid had left at ten. The lounge was littered with Veronica's cast-offs, which Ida hastily balled up and threw into her friend's bedroom. Swirls of Veronica's chypre perfume eddied round her, making her nose twitch in involuntary spasms. The only problem with their very smart address was the smallness of all the rooms.

'Darling, you look stunning.' Jubilee touched her cheek. Not for the first time, Ida felt herself respond. He kept to the rules she had set, sometimes a little too well. 'Your flowers,' he said casually. They were beautiful, orchids the colour of sand, sprinkled with spices.

'You're so good to me. I'll wear them with my dress. Pin them in the back, will you?'

'How will you sit in the car if I do that?'

'On my hip, by your side.' She patted his hand lightly as he draped the new beaver coat across her bare shoulders.

The roads were fairly quiet until they got to the Embankment, where they met enormous traffic jams in both directions; those going into town to see the royal illuminations and those racing off to Chelsea parties. Eventually they pushed on to the south, to a place on a forested hill above Putney, south of the city.

Jubilee opened a studded garden door, but Ida could hardly see the way. Putting out her hand she found a metal bar, like a ship's deck rail, and walked a little way forward through trees. She gasped: there was the house, like some vast ocean liner, moored in a sea of rolling lawns. Round windows in the style of portholes blazed above her head. Virginia creeper twined up white walls like so many cables on a straining hull . . . In a sudden twist of remembrance, Ida pictured Uncle Ted's ship returning from the East, regurgitating its bilge into the harbour.

'Whose house is this?' she asked, curious and impressed.

'A fellow at the Traveller's Club; Martin Fernie. Been everywhere. Interesting man. Knows tons of people. Should be a good evening.'

She felt slightly crazy on entering, for her notion of a ship came alive: men swayed about with sagging knees as if seaborne. 'Oh dear. Blotto. Fernie's do's are always awash with drink,' Jubilee said cheerfully.

'That kind of party!' Ida braced herself for it.

Jubilee was taken up at once by a fat old man whom Ida had met a few times before — at the Flitch. He ran a decorative arts magazine, and wanted Jubilee to write a series on Chinese porcelain, one of his passions. (The Hargreaveses' paterfamilias was not a Lord; he had been a landowner till his death and left a crumbling house stuffed full of Peking relics. Jubilee had a very small income and a sort of job in the city, something to do with a family trust. Circumstances were boring and faded, but Ida liked him better even without a rich and titled background.)

'Go ahead Jubilee, I'll circulate. You know how much I like to plunge in.' The fat man led Jubilee to the bar.

It never took long before something happened to her. She was often recognised and felt nerveless when it came to making entrances — off-stage, that is, at parties.

A small band echoed in a long, glass-sided room. It sounded familiar — then she spied Tommy Trevino and a scratch group from the Diplomats. How wonderful — he had been hired privately for the dance! She ran across the room, and flung herself into his arms.

274

'Well, well!' he said, delighted. 'If it isn't my favourite little band singer! Here, you'll have to let go, Ida. Until the set's over. You're a guest now, remember? Go on, Number Three, let's see you dance . . .'

Tearfully nostalgic at this reminder of her past, and her grand new social status, Ida stepped back to the dance floor, for an instant unwilling to join in. Was the drug having a strange effect on her? She suddenly wanted more than anything to spend the whole night with the band boys, and give up smart circles, for ever.

Next moment, Charlie the drummer crashed a cymbal just for her. The insistent hot beat of the band made her fingers itch; if it were the done thing, she would have grabbed the nearest good-looking man and whirled him around the room. Do what the prudes in the papers called — what was it? those frenzied rhythmical gyrations of jazz.

'*RSVP!*' A promising specimen offered himself. 'I say, you're the girl from *RSVP!*'

'How clever of you to notice,' Ida sparkled so much the young man did not see she was teasing; he found it easier to lead her into the dance than to risk talking, which was exactly what she wanted.

A little later, Tommy finished his session, and was led off the bandstand by a gorgeous ingénue, unresisting. 'I'll be with you in a minute, Ida . . .'

'Come on, Ida old girl, give us a number!' Charlie and the pianist, Ivor Clarke, called her over, and a crowd gathered for an impromptu cabaret. Ida found herself hoisted on to the piano, to sing without a microphone, which she much preferred anyway. Not the clever, bitter songs from Ainslie Curtis' show, but all the popular radio and record favourites of the day. Tommy's new reed man swapped his alto sax for his clarinet, Ida gave her key and slapped her thigh to get them all to take her time. 'I want to be happy'; 'Blue Moon'; 'Lullaby of Broadway'; 'Lady Be Good' . . . a prophetic last song, as it turned out. A Mariachi band came up to the stand to take over for the next hour.

'Can I go now? I'm thirsty!' she exclaimed, though a circle of pretty young men had been refilling her glass as quickly as she emptied it.

'Do stay Miss Garland. Won't you dance with me?' another flushed young man begged. 'I used to listen to your broadcasts from the Ambassador, with the Diplomats. Ripping tunes!'

'Thank you! But I must find my partner. He'll think I've forgotten him!'

'Oh, come on, this is a samba . . .' and so she danced on.

Her head was spinning; she was at the stage of drunkenness she liked best, when nothing mattered, she could still hear and speak near-perfectly, and everything offered itself as new and fun — a sort of childlike loss of time, place and self. She sipped her drink more slowly, hoping not to go beyond the pleasure state into loss of control and the sudden pounce of paranoia.

'What's the time? Where's Tommy? Where's Jubilee? Do let me go, you're very sweet but I simply must find my partner.'

Ida wandered into the dining room — or would have except that her way was barred by an extremely drunken Indian. Not a 'wog', but a full-blooded Red Indian complete with moccasins and feathers. He was old, prune-wrinkled, ferociously odoured and shot out his hand quite involuntarily to get a handful of one breast, obviously loose under her thin dress. Ida saw from a wild glance at the room that a fascinated audience had gathered to watch, to be entertained by his 'reactions' to London society. The hand squeezed appreciatively.

'Sorry!' A bearded man with omniscient eyes loosened the old man's grip, and steered him away, like a warden in a lunatic asylum. 'He's had a terribly heavy day,' he apologised for his 'specimen'. 'Spoke to the Folk Society at lunch, and tea at the House of Commons. Overwhelming reception.'

'You must be . . .'

'Martin Fernie. Delighted. Jubilee's friend . . . Jubilee? He went upstairs, that way . . .'

The Indian growled geronimously.

'I must get the old boy a Scotch.'

'He drinks whisky!' Drunk and embarrassed, Ida began to giggle, but Martin Fernie did not see the joke, and drifted off.

'I *am* tight,' Ida said to herself with mock severity, walking carefully to the stairs in search of Jubilee. She had noticed a balcony overlooking the garden, and thought he might have gone up there for a breath of air. Downstairs the Indian started a war dance, and the guests stomped round him, copying his whoops and grunts. All over the house, the noise level rose to a fevered pitch, wilder, almost inhuman to her buzzing ears.

At a turn on the landing, Ida heard laughter from one of the portholed balcony rooms and opened the door.

A sweating mound of a man lay sprawled on the bed, stark naked, with a thin girl riding on his organ. She was so pretty — like a boy on a dolphin. But that was the only beauty in the room. The man on the bed was really a beached whale, naked, tumescent, his feet sticking out over the satin eiderdown, absurd fat toes curling with each new sensation. All round him, a nude audience, were guests she had never seen downstairs dancing, for they were moving to another kind of rhythm . . . pushed up against each other on the walls, bog-eyed, shoving in concert with the thin girl's arching and thrusting hips. Couples scrabbled after each other on the floor, like crabs locked together in the sand, shunting, grunting. The man on the bed turned his head, opened his mouth, a great hole, as if gasping for air, but his lips engulfed a young man's member, for another kind of oral satisfaction. His eyes closed, and his hungry mouth locked, sucking. It was Tommy Trevino.

No one saw her. Ida shut the door, trembling, stunned, and fled down the stairs. She had to get outside, into clear air. She had loved and respected that man. He had taught her, protected her. He was her 'king of jazz' — her very own big-bandleader. Just when she was feeling sentimental for the simple happiness of those Diplomat days, she was faced with the other dark side of his nature: in need of vice, and weak, like all the others. Wasn't *anyone* good these days? Or was everybody getting jammed in that silliness that Jubilee talked of, more and more?

In a corridor the door of a large Spanish armoire to one side swung open and she was hauled inside. Ida felt herself pinioned between two bare bodies, a woman behind her and a man holding her to his chest. One large hand found hers and thrust her fingers downwards at a set of genitals. Ida's hand encountered a bulging penis, still damp and sticky from sex. The party was turning into a nightmare.

'Fuck *off*!' she hissed, and spat as hard as she could in the

277

direction of the heavy, breathing face. The woman behind her, intent on pulling down her dress, stopped giggling when Ida jabbed her hard in the ribs.

'Oh! You bitch!'

As quickly as she had been yanked in, Ida found herself thrown out again on the hall floor.

She got up, desperately sobered. Not a trace of drug or drink dulled her senses any more. She ran outside, fit to kill the next person who assaulted her.

Looking up at the balcony, she shouted with all the force of her lungs: 'Jubilee!'

'Hooray!' some idiot roared in response.

Tears of anger whipped from her eyes. The air had suddenly turned cold.

'Jubilee!' she screamed again, and this time, amidst the hubbub of cheers and whistles that greeted her cry, a deep voice answered. 'I'm coming, stand still . . .' and there he was.

'Ida! I'm sorry. If I'd known . . .' He too had suddenly realised what was happening. 'Come on, it's time to go home.' He spoke unusually sharply, surprising her. Then she saw that Jubilee was no one's fool. He could put aside gentleness in an instant, when he had to.

He drove for a while in silence. Ida cried gently, and gradually calmed down. As they crossed the river, barges full of party-makers were floating upstream, lights bouncing with the rhythm of the dancing. All of a sudden Ida began to giggle. 'I wish Uncle Jim had been there. It was just his line.'

With a swerve, a screech of brakes, Jubilee stopped the car. Roughly, passionately, he pulled her into his arms.

'Come home with me tonight. I can't stand to leave you alone. Not a second longer.' He kissed her with an urgency that only sex could answer.

Ida kissed him back — hard, longingly. She had been shocked — but she also knew that the licence of the night had rather crudely unlocked her sexuality too. For a very long time she had traded on glamour, erotic looks, romantic words, and kept herself in a neutral state. It was important, to be a success, to be — in control.

But Jubilee would not hurt her. He, surely, was good, at

heart. He had asked her to marry him so many times she believed he meant it. In spite of being from another class, far above her. Now, when he kissed her thrillingly on her neck and held on to her hair, unpinning it, stroking her, she decided it was time to find out. Were they man and woman, properly, for each other? They'd have to be, to marry, and break all those other rules.

'All right. Drive me home,' she said, in tones of rich huskiness that Ainslie's voice coach would have wept to hear.

Jubilee let her go, taken aback by her sudden agreement. 'You mean it? Why?'

'Because you've been wanting to for months and I've decided it's all right.'

He drove fast, occasionally turning to stare at her in the lamplight. Ida snuggled into her coat, resisting an urge to giggle again, at his gravity, her passion, and the silliness of the evening that had finally broken her resistance, when many soft conversations, corsages, and courtesies had failed to do it.

Jubilee's flat was in Albany, Piccadilly. A stone hallway, then a spiral staircase led off the street into the old quiet of its apartments. His study, stacked with journals, a rack of pipes, a pile of letters (Jubilee was a reliable and generous correspondent with absent friends), was cosily familiar. Yet suddenly, because of her new feelings, the room presented her with a different image. For a long time she had laughed at Jubilee, considered him a 'chinless wonder' who was just someone socially acceptable, a reliable and devoted escort. Now she saw that he was a sensitive, clever, loving man with a depth of feeling that she had never allowed him to express.

'I'll change and bring you a robe,' he said, becoming serious. He did not intend her to wake up in the morning, disliking him for taking her to bed in a moment of weakness.

Ida knelt down to light the gas fire.

'Don't go, Jubilee. Let's do it here. It will be cold in your bedroom, come here.'

The torn dress fell from her shoulders. She stood completely naked, holding out her arms to him.

He stared, but he could not help blinking rapidly as a practical matter dawned on him. 'No underpinnings?'

'Of course not. Veronica said they ruined the lines of my dress.'

'You shouldn't listen to Veronica. She's a bad influence.' Jubilee laughed and pulled her close into his big, loving arms. Ida felt very nude pressed up to his suit buttons.

'Take off this awful jacket and stuffed shirt,' she ordered, flirting.

They lay on the old carpet in front of the popping fire. Ida could smell generations of Hargreaves dogs in the rug and even the musty, goaty smell from its origins, before that, in a tent somewhere on the plains of Persia.

'Sinning on a tiger skin . . .' he smiled at her.

'This isn't sin. We're making love on an old rug. It's much, *much* nicer.'

'Tell me what you'd like me to do . . .' he said, running a warm hand along the side of her ribs, tenderly exploring the softness just at the side of her breasts.

'Oh hell, Jubilee. You think I've done all this before.' Ida blushed for a moment, dismayed, discovered.

'Well, *I* have. Fair's fair. You don't have to be old-fashioned for my sake, you know. Too bourgeois.'

'Do you mean that? It was — a long time ago. I . . .'

'I'm not interested in your past. Only in your future. No, that's not true either. Just now I'm deeply, deeply interested in your body. Let's stop talking.'

Ida kissed him, filled with a wonderful sense of relief and certainty.

'You do whatever you like, and that will give me ideas . . .' she whispered, wriggling herself under him. He was just too honest and in love with her for any pretences. She pulled his head down to her face, kissed him full on the mouth. When Jubilee groaned, rolled over and struggled out of his trousers, she kissed him all down his back, and pressed her bare breasts to his broad shoulders. He held her and they made love hastily, far too overcome by details: a glimpse of her face, distant, eyes closed, dispassionate in passion, caused Jubilee to come without hope of holding on. But that was all right, because it was only the first time and Ida wanted to make love to him for days, weeks, years. In a little while she made him start all over again, because she had not held on long enough to his warm, solid body and smelt his skin, exuding its foreign saltiness to her tongue.

13

Some weeks later Gran telephoned Ida. They kept in touch, by phone, by letter, with very occasional surreptitious visits. She spoke loudly, distrusting modern technology and convinced that physical effort was necessary to make the equipment work.

'Is that you Ida?' she bawled. 'Dreadful line. I'll bang it, hold on. I was wondering if you would like a bite of tea with me tonight.'

'They're out, are they?'

'Yes, theatre do, shouldn't be back till late.'

'Fine. I'll come about five and leave early. I have to be up at seven for rehearsals . . . how nice of you to ring.'

It would be a quiet evening, with no chance of accidentally bumping into her Ma and Pa. It was a sad but necessary subterfuge as they still did not speak to one another, even after two years.

But Ida wanted very much to talk to Gran. Since her affair with Jubilee was developing into a serious attachment, she had to think hard about her future. Ida had certain fears which had begun to float into her dreams, no matter how hard she tried to avoid dwelling on them consciously.

She took a taxi but left it further down Bayswater, as she always did, so that Gran could not criticise her for extravagance in the way she managed her money. She'd be behind the bay-window curtain, waiting.

'Saw your picture in the papers,' Gran said with satisfaction. She looked fitter than she had for some time. Ida wondered if Gran kept a scrapbook of her activities. She had never admitted to it. She hardly had time for such a hobby, and she tended to avoid actions that spoke too much of grandmotherly sentiment. A professional just did the job, got on with it; Ida should keep press-cuttings for herself.

'Was it the one of me sitting on the crescent moon?' Ida asked her. 'Ainslie always gets such good pre-opening publicity.'

'Yes. I hope you're getting danger money. Stuck up there on a wire like that.'

'It's ever so safe. After my number they'll lower me to the floor, and all these girls dressed as moonbeams dance round me. It's very pretty.'

'What will they think of next.' But Gran was amused, and then Ida saw the silly side of the scene too and laughed with her. She was at heart a singer, not a 'performer', and the fal de rol of theatre was even now a source of amusement to her.

'Did you know Jack's home on leave?' Gran announced.

'Is he? He hasn't given me a call.' Ida was surprised.

'Well he wouldn't, would he? He's got half of Shepherd's Bush to see to first.'

'Of course. Silly me.'

'And how are you in that department? If I may enquire?'

Ida got up quickly and shut the door. The steaming odours of the lodgers' suppers were becoming oppressive.

'You shouldn't let Dot cook cabbage. The smell lingers. None of the hotels and restaurants serve it for just that reason.'

'You haven't answered my question. There's something up. Who is it? Still got Mr Hargreaves dangling? Or is it that Curtis man. You wouldn't stoop to that would you?'

'I don't need to. I'm good enough for Mr Curtis without those sort of favours.' Ida tossed her head. Her director had a large emotional entanglement with a temperamental Viennese actress for the moment, the comedy star of his new revue. Besides, the thought had never crossed her mind. Ainslie Curtis had never been anything more than a benevolent, professional influence on her life, and she respected him.

'Gran,' she began. 'I want to ask you a serious question . . . it may sound silly to you but I have to ask it.'

'All right dear. Sit down then. You give me a headache walking about all the time.'

'If I were to marry someone — well, you know, completely English, could I have a . . .'

'No you couldn't. Look at Jack. It's like barley water. The more you dilute it, the paler it looks.'

Ida thought the comparison very odd but did not pass comment. Her heart was thumping; Gran had understood, and released her from worry, as if heavy chains had been holding her down. 'It's just that — one of my girlfriends in the chorus, Mona, was talking and I wondered . . .'

'Rubbish. People have very strange notions. Once I was told, if you have a — a *connection* with one, you could have a — well, I won't use the words they used. A black child. Even years later.' Gran's words were accompanied by significant nods where the vital words were left out. It was not an easy topic for her to discuss with anyone.

'A connection? You mean just once?' Ida was so embarrassed that she bent to dust imaginary specks from her suede shoes to hide the flush in her face. She appreciated Gran's honesty; it was more admirable than her own feeble worryings.

'I was told it when I first met Joseph,' Gran went on. 'Pure East End of course. Old wives' stories, Ida. Are you telling me something serious? It's that Hargreaves man, is it? Are you getting engaged?' Gran would not refer to anything less legitimate in her granddaughter's life.

'No. Not yet at least. I just wanted to know. I've never been able to think of — marriage. I was frightened. I had to know.'

'Put it all behind you, like Jack.'

'Yes, but it's different for me. There's Jubilee's family . . . I might have children. I have to think of these things. And anyway Gran, why should we put it all behind us? I know how sad it's made you, not being able to be proud of it . . .'

'I am proud! I am proud! Whoever said I wasn't! He was a fine man, my Joseph. "I've got to be the best," he used to say. I don't think it was just his background made him that way. He was an artiste, and he set himself the highest standard. He wanted recognition, and he got it. He had a lot of good friends who respected him as more than equal — as superior, not just for the way he played, but because he was such a good person.'

'But it's still difficult. People say such stupid things . . .'

'You don't have to flaunt it. This Mr Curtis . . . all this publicity . . .'

'He likes me to get in the papers. He thinks it's a novelty.'

'Well it might be a novelty for him, but you'll be left with the consequences when he's finished with you and moved on.'

Ida moved listlessly around the room again. Some of the dance hostesses in night-clubs married the sons of peers. Such weddings were always in the papers. If she accepted Jubilee, she would be secure for ever. It was a way to acquire impeccable status; no one would comment on her background then. But in her heart, she did not want to marry anyone. She wanted to be able to come and go as she pleased — the way Uncle Ted used to, the way Veronica and Jack did. She did not like the idea of giving in. Her Ma felt that way about her life. Aunt Josephine succumbed to Ottley. On the other hand, Jubilee was a fine man, not a violent creep, and she loved him. She had the money, the taste, and the talent for freedom, but her feelings wanted easier things.

'You look after yourself,' Gran unwittingly answered her thoughts. 'Don't say yes in haste. I know I shouldn't speak, since I gave up everything for my husband. But the world's not the same place these days. You need to be able to stand on your own two feet.'

'How's Pa?' Ida asked suddenly.

'Flourishing.' Gran was not to be drawn again. 'Denise is having trouble with her back,' she sniffed. 'She says she's never been right since she fell down the stairs.'

'Oh Gran! That's nonsense! The lodger, he caught her, he broke her fall — I saw it happen from upstairs.'

'Poor Mr Alula wants to go back to Africa you know. To fight the Italians. I've told him, you get your law degree first.' Gran as usual was involved in her lodgers' lives.

'Ma's still playing her games. That's all it is.' Ida felt the claustrophobia, the old rules, pressing in on her again.

'You deprived her of a lot of money. You bested the pair of them. What do you expect: an apology? You're too proud — where's your forgiveness, for your own family.' A sudden anger lit Gran's eyes.

'I never expected Pa to say sorry,' Ida was irritated, because she had in fact wanted him to do just that. 'No one in this family ever admits a fault,' she tried to make light of it. 'They just cover their tracks.'

'We survive,' Gran said. 'And we should stick together.' Her great broad face returned to passivity again. 'That's the proper way for a family to get on. You can't cut yourself off for ever.'

Somehow Gran managed to make her feel in the wrong. Ida went back to her flat with muddled thoughts; moral scruples were very difficult to define when codes of behaviour varied so much from one end of town to the other.

West End theatres went into a decline after all the excitement of the Royal Jubilee celebrations. Ida continued rehearsing for the revue, *Dancing Without Gloves*, and one day recorded some of the show numbers with Ivor Clarke and the boys. Fortunately Tommy was not involved in the recording. Ida did not think she could face him — not just yet, anyway.

Jubilee met her for a quick break between rehearsals at the Six Bells pub in Chelsea, practically next door to Decca's studios. Ida rather liked having someone as handsome and distinguished as her lover, drawing her away from the beer and chat to have a quiet word in a corner. There were times when being 'publicly owned' by someone meant a lot to her — especially as the Diplomats always treated her like an honorary boy.

'It's going very well,' she told him. 'I should be finished by six. Shall I meet you at the Flitch then? There's a new Bette Davis flick I'd like to see, if you would too of course . . .'

'Ida!' He looked dismayed. 'Don't you remember? We're dining with my mother this evening.'

'Oh! It's tonight! Oh Jubilee. I couldn't possibly. Not after being cooped up in the studio all day. I won't have the nerve to face her.'

He looked very quiet, and Ida realised that it was impossible not to attend. In her circle, tiredness from overwork would be understood. Not to appear when summoned by Mrs Hargreaves was a sin close to murder in Jubilee's other milieu.

'Sorry darling. I'll come, if it means so much to you,' she said in a tired voice.

'You know it does. I'm amazed that you forgot. I reminded you twice on Sunday.' He looked a little stiff, the worst humour he ever displayed, and she felt ashamed of herself.

'Did you?'

'Yes. *Before* we went to bed. But I see even that was no guarantee of your concentration. You do understand, don't you Ida, that it would be far far simpler, for a number of reasons, if you and Mother hit it off?'

Ida was beginning to feel trapped. 'Why does it have to be so complicated? I'm not a waif and stray, and I'm not marrying blue blood.'

Jubilee chuckled. 'Probably be easier if you were.'

'Look, I have to go.'

'I'll pick you up at seven.' He stood up, shielding her from the band boys at the bar, who were watching their exchange with interest. He knew she would be teased about him. Bending to pick up his hat, he brushed a discreet kiss at her cheek.

'I'm going to a sale at Christie's. Perhaps I'll find you something.'

When Jubilee left, Ida hurried back to the bar. The musicians were downing their last pints before returning to the studio. Bobby Smythe the alto sax looked worried. 'He's still very keen, isn't he Ida? You like them tone-deaf, do you? I thought girl singers always fell for horn players.' He laughed and dug her in the ribs. Charlie the drummer tucked an arm in hers and metaphorically brushed the other boys out of her sight.

'Take no notice,' he said protectively. 'Looks like a catch to me. Titled is he?'

'Don't be silly,' she snapped. 'You sound like someone with their nose pressed up against a sweet-shop window.'

'And you're the one with a stolen penny and a hand inside the jar. Girls always are crafty.'

Charlie winked but left Ida surprised at the speed of his retort. It was out of character, with more than a note of ruefulness.

Dinner was as difficult as she had expected it to be. Mrs Hargreaves lived a limited widow's existence in a small flat somewhere in Belgravia, for the house in the country was too draughty and run-down for her. She met Jubilee and Ida at the Savoy, not at home; Ida wondered if this was significant but decided to be sensible, not sensitive. In the distance she could hear the music of the house orchestra, some sentimentally

286

rendered swing number, the familiarity of which gave her a little encouragement. But Mrs Hargreaves was formidable. She had been a beautiful woman. Her eyes were still lively, a clear hazel-green, her clothes flattering without aiming for unsuitable youthfulness. Her skin had the flawlessness of old age, with an opacity like silk crêpe. She knew it, and had arranged her grey hair swept back under a close-fitting hat to reveal its perfection.

Jubilee's mother had the breeding of a true Englishwoman, which largely consisted in being able to pinpoint to a minute degree the class position of any living thing with whom she came into contact. This included animals, for she had with her a Pekinese dog.

'Now angel,' she said, crooning to her pet, 'sit still won't you while Mummy has her cocktail.' One hand rested for a fraction of time on Jubilee's arm: 'Thank you darling.' Her tone changed from gentle intimacy for the dog to indulgent frailty for her son. Ida's nerves were so finely tuned that listening to Mrs Hargreaves became a game, like identifying the soloists in an orchestra. There was a voice for Jubilee, a voice for the Pekinese, a voice for the waiter (quite different in pitch from that offered to a *maître d'hôtel*), and doubtless, a voice just for Ida.

'Jubilee tells me you're a singer,' Mrs Hargreaves said. Listening hard, Ida judged the tone placed her somewhere between a Pekinese and a sheepdog: she was not wholly decorative like the first, had some use like the second, but suffered the basic flaw of not being pure bred. Ida was sure that pedigree was everything to Mrs Hargreaves. Colour did not come into it. A maharaja would have been perfectly acceptable in her presence.

'Yes. I used to sing with a band. I once worked in a hotel rather like this one. The Ambassador. Do you ever go there, Mrs Hargreaves?'

'Oh no. I'm not a gadabout at all. I lead a very simple life.' Mrs Hargreaves' faint smile was intended to suggest certain deep sadnesses in her life. Ida knew from Jubilee that her husband, a rather gentle, academic soul, had been terrorised by the social pretensions of his wife. Since his death, she found she had no money to enjoy herself, just a position to keep up.

'How do you manage to keep such late hours, Miss Garland? It does so ruin one's looks.'

'At the moment I'm rehearsing for a new revue. With Ainslie Curtis. So I try to get to bed early some nights.'

'Of course. How silly of me to forget. Jubilee did tell me. Clever young man, isn't he, Mr Curtis? I met him several years ago at Lady Tree's house. You remember, Jubilee.'

Jubilee flinched perceptibly at this name-dropping which covered titles and distinguished theatre people in one stroke. 'I can't say I do, Mother.'

'Well, she said to me, I remember it as clearly as yesterday, that she only hoped he wouldn't become successful too quickly because it would turn his head. Not quite steady, apparently. And he has done well. I wonder. Is he a *nice* man, Miss Garland?'

'Very nice. He's not a bit grand and he treats everyone considerately.'

'Well, that *is* nice.' Mrs Hargreaves barely concealed her disbelief — or was it disapproval?

Ida could not eat. That one word, 'nice' had been used three times between them in as many different ways. She was afraid that something would lodge in her throat and she would cause a scene. She picked at her fish and drank far too much wine. Jubilee plunged in with some complex information about holiday arrangements he had made for himself and his mother. It was the first time he had mentioned going away.

'You've done awfully well, Miss Garland.' Ida had not been concentrating: while Jubilee chattered she had slipped into a flat state of mind. It was all quite impossible, to think of marrying this woman's son.

'Awfully well?' she repeated, not prepared to accept the patronising voice any longer. 'But I have a good voice, and my whole family is professional. My father's a theatrical agent, didn't Jubilee tell you?'

'No he didn't. How fascinating. Most unusual. I do think certain things run in families, don't you? Background has the most tremendous effect on one's life. Your talent is in your blood my dear, just as public service is in mine. We all run true to type. No, I simply meant you've done awfully well with the *fish*. Don't force yourself to finish it. I do understand about small appetites. Especially when your figure will be *on show* to an audience.'

Ida glanced in mute appeal at Jubilee. He dabbed at his lips with a napkin. 'Would you like to dance, Ida? Go through. I'll join you in a moment.' Ida did not need more prompting.

'Mother. That was unforgivable.'

'Well Jubilee! You're not possibly serious about her are you? She's pretty enough — but a show girl! And she's not even — British!'

'She's a wonderful, talented woman.'

'My God! Do you want the whole world to turn khaki? What about brains? The Empire? Aren't you proud of your heritage?'

'Yes I am. But I want a future. Nothing you can say will change my mind.'

'Nothing you can say will ever change mine either. I will never accept her.'

In her dressing room next day, Ida contemplated the disaster of that evening. No matter how rich or successful she became, certain doors would always be closed to her. It made her rebellious, not wanting to care, to live by other rules, and not strive to join the rotten system.

Someone knocked lightly, a woman's touch. Ida flung aside her magazine, expecting Veronica for lunch. Someone to confide in.

Of all people, it was Janet Sheldon.

'Good God! What on earth are you doing here!' The girl looked deathly pale, but remote as ever. 'I'm sorry,' Ida stammered. 'That was rude of me — I was expecting someone. A friend. How did you get past the doorman?'

'I told him I had an appointment with you, and that you'd forgotten to give him my name. I told him who I was. I knew if he called you, you'd let me come up. Out of curiosity . . .'

Calculating but correct.

'Such a long time. Almost three years . . . How are you? Singing?' This was an oblique wasy of asking after Harvey Johns.

'A little. We went to Paris . . .'

That made her hostile. 'Boinvilly? Lessons?' Ida said, unpleasantly.

'Who? No. Harvey gave a recital. His work is getting much

more attention on the Continent now. I sing sometimes, but he is at work on instrumental compositions too . . .'

Ida watched Janet coldly as she sat nervously twisting her fingers. There was clearly a specific purpose in this visit. What did she want — some ghastly confession, some settling of old scores? Why now, after all this time?

'Is something the matter? You look faint. Shall I open the door? The window's stuck I'm afraid.'

'No! I'm pregnant.'

'Oh?' Ida felt disgust, a hardening of her heart.

'It's Harvey's of course. I mean, we're married.'

'I didn't know. Congratulations.'

'Look. He's at work on a large-scale project. We're terribly hard up. I can't have this baby. Harvey doesn't know about it and I don't want to have a child. I never did. I only want Harvey.' The girl's thin face was dull with wanting, deeply possessive.

Did Janet have to do all those things that Harvey made her do? Ida longed to hear the truth. It seemed incredible that she would.

'You, of all people,' Janet hurried on, 'know how intense he is, dedicated to his work. He needs — release. Relief. I understand that.' Her hands twisted, like separate life forms, fingers twining, in and out.

'I don't care about the others,' she went on in a monotone. 'I never did.' Her cold grey eyes belied her words. She regarded Ida with reptilian, basilisk dislike.

'I don't understand . . .'

'Oh, but it's simple.' Even now, when desperate, her voice was dry and arrogant. 'I need an abortion. You could tell me someone good. People in the theatre must know such things. I can't risk asking the people I know — there's a soprano I'm sure had one — but the word would get about. Mother's so frail. You wouldn't tell . . . Why would you? Our paths aren't likely to cross again.'

'No. I suppose you want money too.'

Janet sprang from her seat. 'Are you suggesting this is — some sort of blackmail?' She began to tremble, to shake with nervous laughter. 'Good God, it would do more harm to Harvey than it ever would to you, if word got out!'

'An affair with a coloured entertainer,' Ida spat it out.

'I hate asking as much as you hate knowing that I married him,' Janet said.

'Oh no, *Mrs Johns*, I think you're perfectly matched.'

Janet did not understand how these words could be spoken as an insult.

The porter arrived at the door, accompanying Veronica.

'Miss Garland? This young lady says — oh, there's the other one!'

'It's all right. She's just leaving. Wait, Janet.' Ida wrote an address on a piece of paper, from the card Aunt Josephine had given her. She also wrote a cheque for fifty pounds. Janet took both, and without a word, left the room.

'Wasn't that —' Veronica asked, 'the *Sheldon* creature?'

'Yes it was.'

'Why are you giving her money?'

'She's in trouble. The usual kind.'

'My God! How do you know she's not lying? Stealing? Getting you involved in some scandal?'

'Oh Veronica, shut up do. I'd want someone to help me, in such circumstances. Wouldn't you?'

'You amaze me.' Veronica shrugged and gathered up her furs. 'I just hope you're right. Come on. Lunch. I'm thirsty.'

'So am I.' Ida followed her down the stairs. What Veronica did not see was that Janet Sheldon was wearing a cheap, tin ring, that did not fit her fourth finger. Ida guessed she put it on only to deceive concierges in French hotels, or very old rivals, like her.

Perhaps it was just the timing that made Ida accept her Gran's offer, an olive branch. Jack was home, and Gran wanted everyone to come to lunch — including her granddaughter. Ida thought she had done more than well enough in two years without her Pa to be able to face him at last. Her new revue was about to be launched. It was sure to be even more successful than the first. Pride perhaps tempted her to return, but there was a more potent force working in her.

Her unnerving encounters with Mrs Hargreaves and Janet Sheldon had made her think again about the split in the Garland family. She wanted no more secret pasts; no more unfinished arguments. In a way, she needed to link the parts of her life, and not be a stranger to herself. After all, if she were to marry, Jubilee would have to know all about her.

Pa had tried to be a good father, in his own way, for a long time. Denise had led him on of course — and Ida had to face the fact that he was not a strong man.

Mrs Hargreaves' blatant racism made Ida understand what a conflict her father had suffered, all his life. The honour of a white woman, giving herself to him ... the knowledge of her endless despising of him at the same time. No wonder Earl had tried so hard to win his wife's regard with money, managing Ida's success, since he could not win it otherwise.

When Ida reached the door of the boarding-house, Jack opened it wearing his uniform, with a couple of important looking pips on the shoulder. Sheepish, but very proud.

'Stupid, isn't it, wearing all this on leave. Gran wanted me to put it on. Only for lunch, I told her.' He squared his shoulders, so that she could admire him. Time away from the family had made him mature rapidly, and Ida looked at him with the appreciation of a stranger.

'You always were good-looking. Now you're positively dangerous,' she teased him.

'I say Ida, what about a night out with me after all this. Will tomorrow do you? Some old haunts. Can you spare me a night from the smart set?'

'Of course I can. I was wondering when you'd fit me in ...' she said equably.

Jack was pleased. 'I've got a lot of catching up to do with you. Not now though. Ma's upstairs in Ted's room. Gran asked her to take away a few things so she can make way for lodgers. She's looking forward to seeing you.'

'Ooh, that's nice! Auntie! Josephine!' Ida ran upstairs, anticipating show-business gossip. The nicest part of growing older herself was that Josephine stayed more or less the same in spirit and she could catch up.

'Ida! Well I never. Ooh, I am glad you decided to come. I was beginning to think you'd given us all up for good.' Josephine gave her a big hug. Then on the landing, Earl came out of Ted's room. He looked thinner, much older, and did not smile when he saw her.

'Hallo Ida.'

'Hallo Pa.'

Josephine was either too involved in her task to notice the tension, or determined to avoid a scene.

'Now come here, girl. Earl, give me a hand with this trunk. You're going to have some of this lot, isn't she Earl? It's Ted's sheet music. Look, piles and piles of it, and his own arrangements too.' Josephine ignored the fact that Ida and her Pa were standing quite still, side by side, emanating a consciousness of each other that was embarrassing and painful. 'Grab the other handle,' she said, without looking up. 'Move it nearer the window.'

Ida guessed that no one had ever told Josephine what her Pa had done. Families were amazing, she thought, the deceptions, evasions, secrets that could be kept up between so few people, without question, for years.

Downstairs, Ida could hear someone, probably Uncle Billy, putting on a new pile of 78s, and those familiar strains of the best American bands, Ellington, Basie, Chick Webb, McKinney's Cotton Pickers floated up through the floorboards. She stood by the trunk, looking at the bright coloured sheet-music covers and the handwritten alterations on the pages of Ted's life. Earl did not speak or look at her at all. He kept himself occupied, lifting up handfuls, and she sorted them out.

'Uncle Jim should have them, not me,' she ventured.

'Well, we'll have a share-out,' Josephine said briskly. 'We just never got round to looking before now.'

Earl looked up at Ida. 'Uncle Billy and Jim are in the kitchen. And your mother's in the parlour with Gran. Go and pay your respects.'

The old severity reasserted itself. Nothing had changed in his way with her, but now she reacted differently to his manner. Pity, disenchantment, and an anger that she could not look up to him any more vied in her to be the defining mood.

'I'll go in a minute,' she said firmly. 'I haven't seen Josephine for ages, what with her touring and my rehearsals.' She turned in quiet defiance to her aunt. 'Did it go well, Josephine? Wasn't it the Birmingham Hippodrome last stop? Aren't they tough?'

'Nothing like Harwood's at Hoxton. Play there and you can play anywhere.'

'I think the Scotia in Glasgow's much worse,' Earl volunteered in a low voice.

Ida had made her point, a sad moment for them both. He could not order her as a daughter anymore. He had forfeited the right.

'I think so too Pa. That's what I heard Ainslie Curtis say once,' Ida agreed gently.

'The best in London is the Pavilion. The audience is good, critical, but the stage is tiny.' Josephine added, 'So I've been told. Never had the fortune myself.'

'Oh yes,' Ida nodded, anxious to make everything ordinary again. 'We have it easy at the Charlbury. Nowhere near as tough, but very classy.'

'Too many celebrities on the first night — they do distract the paying public.' Josephine sighed.

'Oh, Ainslie gives them all fair warning not to show off. He's very bossy you know, even to his friends.'

'They love it. People like confidence,' Earl said.

How easy it was to pick up the rhythms of old conversations, as if nothing had happened in between. The stage was not the only arena for artifice. Her family life was an elaborate, non-stop performance.

'Dinner!' yelled Jack, as if to a regiment. Ida let Pa go down first, and then Josephine, hoping that the spontaneous goodwill of her aunt's welcome would sustain her through this first meeting with her Ma.

In the hall, Josephine held Ida back.

'Look. One word.'

'What? What is it?'

'I saw you in *RSVP*. You outshone the entire cast. Will you remember Ida — whatever your Ma said, or ever will say to you — just remember. She's only jealous.'

'Oh Aunt Josephine! Never! She's ashamed of me!'

'All right. Don't believe me then. You'll learn, all in your own good time . . .'

'Here she is!' Josephine pushed open the parlour door and pulled Ida to her side, tucking her arm through her elbow.

'Thought she'd got away but something brought her back, I always said it would. Doesn't she look a picture?'

'Ida! Bless my socks!' Uncle Jim pinched her cheeks and shook both her hands. 'Too thin,' he murmured, 'you've gone much too thin . . .'

George, screwdriver in hand, was adjusting the gramophone. 'Fuse gone. Hallo Ida. How's the flat? The electrics? Still on the national grid?'

There was Denise, propped on cushions (this being, inevitably, a good day for her back). And Sidney Ottley, aware of their shared status as the least-liked people in the family, was sitting next to her. His face was blighted by a vast black eye. Ida glanced quickly at Jack, and he grinned with satisfaction. Josephine sat next to Ottley and took his hand.

'Poor Sidney had an accident with the ladder. In the back garden,' she explained. 'I can't trust him to do jobs on his own . . .'

'I came home and found him. Flat on his back. Didn't I Ottley?' Jack asked for confirmation, in a deadly casual way.

One watery eye registered alarm, and Ottley nodded violently in agreement.

'Well. We *are* honoured, Ida. To what do we owe the pleasure?' Denise said, edgy from lack of attention.

'Me,' Jack said. 'I asked Gran if she'd invite her.' He turned to Ida. 'One good turn deserves another . . .'

'What did I ever do for you?' Ida laughed, although she could not help admiring Jack's visceral approach to settling unfinished business. (Supposing, just supposing, Aunt Josephine was right . . .)

'Well if you don't know I ain't telling.' He pulled out a chair for her between him and Gran. Uncles Jim and Billy served the meal: water-blasted vegetables, overcooked meat, but the most delicious roast potatoes in the universe, almond-sweet insides, puffy white, rimmed with crunchy fat-soaked crusts.

'A toast,' said Jack. 'To us.'

'And to Uncle Ted,' Ida joined in.

Denise stared at Ida over her empty plate. The two years since she had last seen Ida had altered her daughter's presence beyond recognition. Ida was beautiful, radiating eagerness for life. Her big eyes shone, her hair, simply parted, was drawn back from her face, revealing high cheekbones, a ready smile, and a new warmth in her speech, as if she had grown used to friendly conversations. Her charm had unfolded entirely out of her own experience — nothing about her was false or assumed, but altogether natural. Denise sat facing this adventurer, and was all too aware of her own shallowness, her lack of engagement with anything beyond her own petulant, momentary whims.

Earl watched the two women, Denise scrutinising Ida with envy, while the girl tried not to notice her mother's hostile gaze and to enjoy the family gathering. He had been a fool to listen to Denise, to take back from Ida something that had never been his in the first place. Her talent was unique, and she owed him nothing. For different reasons, he felt as much of a failure as his wife.

Monday night began with fish and chips from the shop in Edgware Road that Coleman Hawkins liked best. Jack had a friend who had met the famous tenor saxophonist during his brief stay in London, at the Rhythm Club, a regular meeting-place for jazzophiles. Desultory conversation with the master had established his amazing preference. Adoring fans, Jack and Ida paid homage as best they could, then headed for the centre of London, burping slightly from the pickles. Past Greek restaurants, Belgian patisseries, Czech coffee lounges filled with new refugees looking lost and yet found . . . pin-table saloons, milk bars, pubs, and last, their Uncle Jim's favourite pie and mash stall. Local trollops tottered by all painted up, for a night on the job. Ida and Jack endured besides the temptations of the street the continuous thundering of traffic heading north of London, for this was the main route out. Market handcarts, mundane and local, were pushed between lorries with Edinburgh addresses written on their boards, and the swearing, wolf-whistling drivers hurled abuse from their cabs at the street traders blocking their path.

'Let's start at the Flitch,' Ida said. Tonight was going to be the pub crawl to end all pub crawls. She felt restless, elated, fit to do wicked things. They hailed a cab and headed for Fitzrovia.

'Not going to bump into any of your la-di-da friends, I hope,' Jack looked uncompromising.

'Jubilee's in the South of France with his mother, God blast her eyes,' she said, suddenly aggressive. She minded about his absence, minded about his efforts to keep his mother sweet.

'And Veronica?' he said casually.

'Somewhere else hot. That's why you didn't call to see me at the flat! No attraction there any more!'

'Course not. Just testing.' He could still tease her, effortlessly. She loved it — tonight was going to be fun.

'Here we are. The Flitch. Now behave. Look, there's that theatre critic man again. He's always here. From *Playbill* magazine. I can never remember his name.'

'Don't worry. It'd be lost on me anyway,' said Jack.

The Flitch was perhaps a mistake. The other regulars at the bar eyed Jack's smart blazer with inauthentic crest too closely. His crisp white shirt was definitely out of keeping with the *louche* bohemianism of the correct attire: holed check shirts, corduroy jackets with leather patches, very well cut Savile Row suits that had to look 'worn in'. Jack and Ida downed a couple of gins while Ida pointed out a Fleet Street columnist, a minor West End actor, and a man cited in a current Mayfair divorce. He was the only person from the newspapers with whom Jack was familiar.

'You can tell the new members,' Ida whispered. 'They're the ones in the boiled shirts. The club needed the money to keep the place open,' she added. 'The businessmen are called The Untouchables. They pay double the subscription of the artists.'

The fat man from the antiques magazine was there, eyeing her suspiciously. 'Miss Garland? How de do! Where's Jubilee?' He made it clear he did not expect to be introduced to Jack.

'Biarritz,' she said, terse.

'At this time of year?' he looked surprised.

'Yes, well it is a bit vulgar in the summer but his mother *loves* the sun.' She enjoyed that remark.

'You of course, don't need it,' he replied, thinking he was being outrageous, daring, and witty all at once. Jack's expression turned wooden.

'Take no notice,' Ida said, gripping his arm.

'Come on. Let's go somewhere else.' He was, quite rightly, unimpressed.

As they left, Ida heard someone say to a friend: 'Good Lord Scotty, you're not going suburban!' Jack raised an eyebrow, wordless comment on the Flitch's gallery of types. Ida was glad he was dismissive — it made her feel herself, and happy again.

'Right. Next stop Evie's.'

Evie ran a daytime drinking club in Sackville Street, in two upstairs rooms, where she spent most of her time sitting by a window passing comment on the expensive whores who paraded in the street below. Ainslie Curtis favoured her spot, because when pressed she would disappear into a tiny hole of a kitchen behind the bar and make perfect ham and eggs. Her tongue was vicious about absent friends, a feature in her that Ainslie relished: this one was 'a great nut', the other 'a shocking cad', a third 'a regular dope artist'.

All this Ida explained as they made their way along Piccadilly, past the Monseigneur Grill where Lew Stone's band made a great name broadcasting before moving on to the Hollywood restaurant. Jack wanted to go in to the Grill, but on reflection decided the night was definitely for floating.

Evie's was quiet; she acknowledged Ida with a stiff nod, for she had only been brought in other company before and was not yet a regular. A couple were having a tiff sat in one corner, and in another, an aged woman with a black-net head cap lit a cigarette and in an instant spewed noisomely into her shopping bag.

'Evie! I feel odd! Give me another gin!' she squawked.

Ida started to giggle. 'D'you know who she sounds like Jack? D'you remember those old crones who used to fight outside your church on Sundays? Her. She's just like them.'

'Yeah, except for the diamonds on her fingers . . .'

They had to stop by the Glass Slipper. Mrs Cavendish was momentarily pleased to see Ida, but less impressed by her escort — that same cheap young man who always used to hang around.

'We haven't got a spare table tonight dear. Frightful crush. Will you have a drink with me at the bar? I'll be with you in a moment.'

They ordered yet more gins and waited.

Mrs Cavendish came over, unusually confidential with Ida due to stress. 'Last night, sweetie. Near disaster. We had the Princess Marina in here with a party. Two minutes later Gracie Fields came in wearing the same dress! I had to have a word with her. The poor darling was able to sneak out through the kitchens. I nearly died. Imagine the embarrassment.'

'Gosh. Her couturier should be shot,' Ida said, knocking back her glass. Jack, visibly amazed by this daft exchange excused himself and asked a flimsily-clad young woman to dance.

'Your young man — cousin — dear excuse me, has a dancing style that is un-English to a quite *unnecessary* degree,' Mrs Cavendish said. She walked off, leaving Ida laughing so much she slipped off her bar stool. Jack was practically inside the girl's thighs in some form of tango. This night on the town was turning into a revelatory experience.

Jack called her over to join the table at which he had made a conquest.

'This is Kay Petrie, this is Billy Buchan, this is Jean Richmond, and this is Toby Polwith. This is my cousin, Ida Garland.'

'The *RSVP* girl! How simply ripping!'

'We want to hear some really, really good hot music. Your cousin Jack says he knows just the spot. Do take us, won't you?'

'Later,' said Jack masterfully, dragging Kay Petrie back to the floor and dancing with his hands inserted well down the small of her back.

Two hours later they called in at the Rookery — an after-hours club in Soho where bandmen, stifled by the cornfed music they played in hotels, came to 'tear it up' after hours.

'This is more like it,' Jack said, abandoning Ida and their newly acquired entourage at the bar while he played billiards, attaching himself to some locals' game as if he had been there every night of the previous week. Poor Kay and Jean, utterly amazed by this display of male nonchalance sat blinking into their drinks, and tried to show interest in the limp young escorts who had trailed behind them. Ida made sure they were all well supplied with alcohol; it was the only solace she could offer, for conversation was impossible with the band performing.

A small combo, one of the newly fashionable 'black and white bands' was playing; three West Indians on drums, bass and tenor saxes, and white musicians on trumpet, alto saxes and guitar. It was a terrific sound: the recent first visits of American performers like Armstrong and Ellington had stirred up even greater feeling for the real thing among those of London's musicians lucky enough to hear them. The Rookery players were inspired now, the music light-textured, swinging, and had at its centre still a full sad heart. Jazz was no good without a rawness of feeling, as if the instrumental phrases had just sprung into being.

It had a predictable effect on the girls. Suddenly their heads lolled into their boyfriends' shoulders and their looks became vacant. Fingers searched for fingers, as the insistent beat began to stir repressed feelings. Jean and whoever was next to her, Polwith, Ida thought, started nibbling each other's necks with a strange kind of hunger. Ida had seen all this before: people making exhibitions of themselves because of a beat.

With a pang, Ida thought of Jubilee. His love for her was so much greater than that, a strong flow of genuine loving warmth, that made sex a confirmation of great intensity. The band started to play a blues, which made her miss him too much — but even that was a kind of pleasure . . .

Ida's lonely mood flowed on through 'When Your Lover Has Gone', a solo from the tenor sax, until she overheard an aspiring youngster sitting near her being torn apart by an older player. The man was so angry his words carried clear to her down the bar.

'Your tone is poor, much too much vibrato, especially up above. You play flat at the top and sharp at the bottom. Your phrasing is bad, meaningless, and the way you broke up that middle eight in 'Dinah' last night was nobody's business. Nobody's business, sonny Jim.'

Ida laughed to herself, brought back to the present. Poor little chap, he looked so crushed . . . In jazz the effect was of no effect, and the audience responded as if to basic emotions. But inside every successful player was a long-worked-for technique. Jack's stirred-up girlfriends did not have a clue about that.

Jack came back to her. 'You know what's missing, don't you?' he said. 'I just got a whiff of 'charge' and it put me in the mood . . .'

Ida gave him a steady look, trying to look disapproving, but thinking a little oblivion would be good. 'I don't indulge in that kind of thing,' she lied. She tried to keep drugs under control, but Veronica was fascinated by it, and a supply was nearly always on hand.

'I'll let you into a big, *big* secret,' Jack said as he nudged her. 'Let's pour this lot into a taxi, and find a dive I know about.'

He turned to the girls, wrapping his arms round each one. 'How about a special treat? A real hum? Are you interested?'

Bleary-keen faces nodded dumbly, and they all fell into yet another cab.

They headed west out of London. Half-way down Bayswater, Ida began to panic.

'Jack, you wouldn't dream of taking them to Gran's house would you? Think of the lodgers. She'd be livid.'

'No no. Keep your shirt on. What sort of fool d'you think I am?' He glared at her, and Ida realised that he had reached the stage of inebriation where arguing with him would do no good. She sat back, the fun of the evening waning just a little as he got the upper hand and started showing off to the girls again. He was telling them one of his favourite north-west frontier yarns. What she needed was another drink.

'Tough life. I tell you. I heard the last chap went out there, went to the mess, first night out. He was warned mind you. Step through doorways quickly. That's rule number one. Well he didn't. He stood right there, for a breath of air, right in the light of this beaded curtain and ping! He got picked off by a sniper. An Afghan in the hills.'

'You sure it wasn't Gary Cooper in *The Bengal Lancers*?' Ida giggled, but no one took any notice. The taxi pulled up outside Uncle Billy's record shop.

'What are we doing here?' she asked, surprised. Jean, Kay, Billy and Toby began to shiver in the icy blast circling off Shepherd's Bush Green. The girls pulled their furs closer, and the men began to sober slightly into responsible behaviour.

'I say, old chap, you do know where we're going?' They looked to Ida for confirmation; someone as well known as she was surely could not be involved in anything criminal or dangerous?

Above the shop, Ida could hear laughter and loud music. How odd: Uncle Billy was the mildest of people and she had no idea that he held parties till three in the morning.

'Come on up,' Jack invited, looking unbelievably pleased with himself. 'The music's great. You wanted good music, didn't you?'

Uncle Billy was not in — no doubt he was sound asleep in his little attic room at the boarding-house. It was Uncle George who acted as host. The flat above the shop was bulging with assorted individuals, mostly well-to-do town types, but with a thrilling mixture of bottle-party 'hostesses', of the kind identified by numbers, one or two authentic working class beautiful boys, and even a Jamaican. The music pulsated from the back of the flat, and over all hung the strangely incongruous smells of marijuana reefers, perfume and cigars.

'George has a little sideline selling dope to people in high places. Didn't you know?' Jack whispered. He was exultant: Ida had shown off her top spots, but he had one of his own.

'No I didn't,' she said, truly amazed. 'I say. Is that why you got him on to our flat? Rewiring indeed! On the national grid! He supplies Veronica, doesn't he?'

'What d'you take me for! I didn't plan anything of the sort! Don't look at me like that Ida, I've got nothing to do with her habits. I had no idea . . .' A thought dawned on him. 'You're no innocent yourself! So don't go all stiff on me now. It's only a bit of fun.'

'It's only a bit of fun . . .' He was right. Absolutely *right*. This was her kind of life, her kind of night — full of fun, freedom, and great jazz. It was the kind of night that Uncle Ted had wanted them to share. Ida drew heavily on the weed he passed her, draped herself over a sofa as alcohol and drug combined to paralyse her from head to toe. Across the room she recognised young Palmer, at whose wedding she had once sung . . . older, thinning-haired, still mad about the music, oblivious or untouched by the goings-on. Earnest and irresponsible; like everyone else still awake in London at three in the morning. How wonderful it was, to lie there immobilised, neither happy nor sad, but taken over, listening to Bunny Berigan's superb tone in every register, and not to give a damn.

14

As dawn broke Jack delivered Ida home, comatose.

'I'll give you a ring later, see how you are. Great time, Ida, thanks.'

He disappeared with his drugged troop. Ida was not in the least surprised when he did not telephone her for days. After all, she was only his cousin, and probably Jean or Kay, or both, were giving him a good time.

Two weeks later, he rang in different mood, excited and distant, his news overtaking any interest in her affairs.

'Hallo old girl. Just a quick word — I'm off. Wish me luck. I've been posted to India.'

'Oh Jack! What you always wanted!'

'Yeah. No time to talk — got to get back, new kit, injections, all that. I won't see you for quite a while old girl. Shall I call in — to say goodbye, all that?' He was trying to sound casual, although both of them were conscious that this was his biggest challenge — his chance, like hers, to get away for ever, from the Garlands.

'Well Jubilee's just back from France. Look, perhaps I'll pop round this evening. I must say goodbye to you, in person. And I suppose, if you're going away, you ought to meet him. If he'll come.'

'Whatever you like. I'll be pretty busy, so you'll have to be quick.'

Was this a good idea — should she really launch Jubilee at the Garlands, all at once? Yet restlessness, a sense of being trapped by the inevitable, made her want to test him out. After all, she'd been subjected to his mother. This was her chance to show him her background, with a sense of occasion — before Jack went off for his adventures in the world. Jack was on her side: he would understand her reluctance to commit herself, her conflicting feelings of needing love, and yet hating to tie the knot. She might be too wild, too unknowing about herself to behave as she should. She might want to cut the ropes and escape.

Jubilee of course agreed to come with her, knowing how important this first meeting was.

Jack met them at the door swathed in a mosquito net.

'Oh. It's you. I was just testing . . .' he said, gathering the thing up in his arms, trying to look embarrassed, though Ida knew at once he had acted silly just to undermine Jubilee's entrance.

'In here. I'm Jack. You must be Jubilee,' he said, needlessly, leading them into the parlour.

The floor was covered in stacks of records. A huge crate was half stuffed with straw and shredded papers.

'What's this?' Ida asked, curious.

'It's the double bass. I'm going to run a combo on the north-west frontier.'

Jubilee, whose father had spent his years in diplomatic service out East, more sedately collecting porcelain, tried to show no amazement at this idea.

'So!' Jack said, putting on his bullish air again. 'You're the Right On. We've heard a lot about you, over the years.'

'Yes. I'm afraid I've become something of a habit . . . I'm hoping to make it legal,' Jubilee added, trying to be honest, and to be a friend.

'Habit! Legal! Not all of Ida's habits are like that!' Jack coughed theatrically, and Ida could not help a small titter.

Gran came in, looking majestic.

'You'll have to come and sit in the lodgers' dining-room. Jack's stuff is making a wreck of my parlour. The sooner he goes the better. You're Mr Hargreaves. I'm very pleased to meet you.'

'And you — Mrs Garland.' They shook hands, very pleased with each other. Ida could tell. This was an instant alliance. She was not sure how she felt about that.

Denise and Earl called in, as if they had been counting the seconds till their entrance. 'Why, Ida!' Denise said, pretending surprise. 'We just had to say a word to your Gran . . .' Both were dressed in full evening dress, and Ida saw, without prejudice, how handsome her Pa was, even now, growing older, and how diminished Denise was, in beauty, by the years.

'My parents,' she said, almost inaudibly, fiddling with Gran's tray of drinks. 'Whisky, Jubilee?' she poured him a sympathetically large tumbler, aware that this was quite an ordeal.

'None of that,' said Jack. 'We always used to have champagne when there was new suitor sniffing about, for Ma — remember? My Ma's in a show, so she can't see me off. But I've got the important people. Especially my Ida. You know I think the world of her, don't you, Hargreaves?'

'I do, indeed. Childhood friends. No one replaces them. She'll miss you very much.'

'She's the only one who will!' Jack laughed, without emotion, because it was a fact. No one in the room contradicted him, least of all Gran. Try as hard as she might, she could not understand why Jack should want to *volunteer* for the army. Not after what had happened to her twin son Charles. To be taken up, discriminated against, not allowed to fight, and then to die . . . She could hardly be proud of the family's first soldier, passing for white. Jack and Ida understood.

He poured out the champagne, fixing Jubilee with a steady look. 'You look after her. She needs looking after. I expect you know that.'

'Oh stop it! Anyone would think I was a five-year-old!' Ida interrupted. 'Anyway it's only fathers make that speech: it doesn't sound right coming from you!'

'Fancy you observing the decencies . . .' Denise could not resist.

Earl pulled her by the arm, sharply. 'Come along now, Denise. We're due at the theatre. Delighted to make your acquaintance, Mr Hargreaves. We won't interrupt your evening. Ida and Jack have to say their goodbyes . . . Goodnight Ida. God Bless.'

Earl backed out of the room, with as much dignity as he could muster. Denise followed him, too angry to do more than nod. Earl knew it was not his place, to expect to approve any part of Ida's life. She felt sad; in a small, illogical corner of herself, she still wanted her Pa to examine Jubilee, and tell her he was a good match . . .

'You'll be going to Delhi,' Jubilee said, cutting across this awkward moment, addressing Jack. 'Would you do something for me?'

He pulled a photograph from his wallet and wrote an address on the back of it. 'This is a friend. I was at school with him. If ever you have time, on leave, look him up for me.'

Jack looked at the picture with curiosity; so did Ida, leaning over his shoulder. The man was obviously a very wealthy person, in a silk turban, with a large diamond on his finger.

'Loves the English. He'll give you a good time. Show you the sights.' A bare flicker of an eyelid suggested the kind. Ida was livid. Jubilee was demonstrating the most extraordinary resourcefulness, in his bid to win the family's affections.

'Right. Thanks old man.' Ida could tell by the way the two of them shook hands, that Jack had been disarmed.

He now turned to her, too abrupt in his manners. Such leave-takings were not easy, between people who had been left by others, in childhood, far too many times.

'I'll have to get back to my packing,' he said.

'Look after yourself.' Ida hugged him. 'Have lots of adventures — just like the films!'

All those days in childhood rushed back, when she had cleaned him up, shared secrets about the lodgers, patched his wounds, and fed him chocolate from a cracked cup. No doubt Jack remembered them all too, because he pulled back and stared at her for a moment, frowning, as if puzzled by the feelings she induced in him, that no one else could do. The way he always used to, when she stood by the piano, and sang for everyone at the Garlands' Friday night *musicales*.

Ida's sadness at Jack's departure wore off quickly, like a hangover, leaving only the memory of the good times they had had. Work also offered increasing rewards. For the autumn and winter, Ida had some dates on the radio, travelling up to Crystal Palace for the sessions. She was building up a select list of people on whom she could rely for the right kind of sound. Ivor Clarke was a much better pianist for her than he could be for the Diplomats, and with Charlie the drummer and Bobby Smythe the alto saxman formed the basis of her recording group. They were all familiar with her style, and other soloists were grafted on to this solid foundation as needed.

Over Christmas, in what was becoming an annual ritual, she

sang at the Ambassador with the Diplomats. Tommy behaved regally as always and obviously had no idea what she had seen him do. Ida was relieved to find that a few months' gap made her less embarrassed to be with him — she was only too keen to let the image of that night be supplanted by others. As the chimes of the New Year struck, she and Jubilee circled round the ballroom floor, and he kissed her tenderly. Tommy leant down from the bandstand, waving his baton, like some wicked, pagan spirit of Christmases past.

'This year!' he decreed. 'You marry that nice young man this year, Ida!'

But 1936 promised to be her busiest ever. Radio and records were followed by a small part on film, a cheap 'crook drama' in which Tommy's band appeared in a night-club set. The sequence only lasted three minutes but took two days to shoot, which amazed Ida. In comparison with recording time, such a long session seemed like folly to her.

Ida was tempted to call in on the family and boast, for the film was being made at small studios in Lime Grove, Hammersmith, not far from the boarding-house. Somehow, since coming to a truce with her parents, going home had lost a little appeal. Jack's absence discouraged her, for there were too many reminders of their past times and lack of a shared present. She thought of Gran and nearly changed her mind, but decided to wait until she was properly invited.

Then in spring, Ainslie's latest revue, *Vernissage*, went into production. The same dreary rehearsal days; first out at Walworth and then in a set of rooms in Stalk Street, Soho. Tall mirrors and bare floorboards made the accumulating debris of each day more tawdry: if you looked at the walls, the mess was multiplied in images on all sides. Crumpled woollens, cast-off ties, torn dance shoes piled up on rickety chairs. Sandwich wrappings and tea-streaked cups with cigarette butts floating at the brim added their familiar, depressing odours.

Ainslie's supply of theatrical jokes was inexhaustible and his company so well acquainted with his style that progress was fairly rapid in the early days. They all knew that troubles showed up in the final stages.

The worst day of all was the dress rehearsal. The company

could not get into the Charlbury theatre until midnight on Saturday, after the previous week's show had been 'struck' — the sets dismantled. The *Vernissage* set was erected magically in the small hours. Such was the pressure for revenue that the show had to open the very next week, on Monday. That meant the cast working non-stop, reruns all through Sunday, day and night, and Monday morning if necessary.

'I can't get ready for the Lollipops number, Ainslie, it takes me three minutes to get out of this stupid dress!' An hysterical Mona was terrified that through no fault of her own, she would lose her comedy spot in the following number.

'Thinking time! Silence!' Ainslie roared. He had the kind of temperament that thrived on crisis. Much to everyone's annoyance, he often got his best ideas when his original plan was frustrated.

He spoke firmly to the dancer, with no sign of real irritation. 'Don't worry Mona sweetie. Please don't snivel. Firstly, you remind me of my mother when you cry, which is not a pleasant experience for a man as callous as I have been, and secondly, I can't possibly afford to lose a stunner like you from the Lollipops. If I'm short of a girl in the dance number, I can always stick Arthur on the end of the chorus line in drag. All right Arthur? You're not on again until the dogs-in-the-park number, eleven minutes later. Got that? Everybody happy? Right. Where's Sylvia!'

'Where is Sylvia, Who is She . . .' the chorus line sang, a tired company joke.

Ainslie's permanent and long-suffering designer was the same woman who had inspected Ida on that first audition. She hurried on stage, nodding agreement before she even received formal instructions on Arthur's costume. Her ruffles were beginning to flatten like the petals of a dying tulip with the effort of a solid night's work, but nevertheless, the new chorus outfit, orange satin and gold spangles, was being run up in the wardrobe within the hour.

Ainslie looked around at the rest of the cast who were waiting in boredom for the end of this interruption. They relied on him to know their breaking-point, but on the other hand, if he were to be unreasonable tonight, no one would blame him.

'Ida Garland,' he said abruptly. 'Go and get a coat. I won't get to the gallery scene now for fifteen minutes. Do come prepared darling. If you catch cold we're in the soup.'

Ida did not bother to remind him she had been called five minutes before and that he had shouted at her for being slow to appear. He was only concerned for her well-being — even if it did come out as self-interest! She knew him closely enough not to be offended. She left the stage as Arthur was being incorporated into the chorus routine.

With uncanny timing, Jubilee arrived, slightly mellow from a night out with his chums. He carried an ice-cold cocktail in a shaker and a hamper of sandwiches and pies. Ida's capacity for starch on these occasions was gargantuan, and she was very pleased to see him.

As had become the custom, he launched at once into his main topic of conversation.

'I've had a brilliant idea. Putting aside the issue of Mother, which I'm not prepared to discuss anymore, how d'you feel about Bali? Just met a chap at the Flitch who was raving about the temples. After this revue, Ida, will you do it? This summer? Forget Mother. We could honeymoon in Bali.'

Ida was irritated by his persistence. Fancy talking to her of honeymooning in Bali! At three in the morning, in the middle of a dress rehearsal, in the green-room of the Charlbury! She knew why he made the suggestion. The rich were moving on. France was familiar. Italy had become unpopular because of Il Duce and his intentions to invade Abyssinia. In fact the whole of Europe was becoming a little too accessible and fraught for the smart tourists of England, and for some reason Bali had become the smart place to be.

'I don't like travelling,' she repeated. 'I once swore never to leave England. I'm not keen on holidays.'

'All right, forget about Bali,' Jubilee agreed. 'But don't forget, this year you're marrying me. I'll wait as long as you like. I'm the type.' He grinned without a trace of complacency. 'What's to stop us?'

'The trouble is,' she confessed, 'I can only do one thing at a time. At the moment it's the revue, and I can't think beyond it.'

'Ainslie is outdoing himself again, I imagine?' Jubilee could not help a note of disdain in his voice.

Ida did not answer him, for she was warming up inside a blanket, eating in a daze of tiredness, and her thoughts were wandering. When they got married, she would have to give up desperation. Being desperately drunk for instance. Jubilee's wife could not do that, at least, not out of his company. A night spent with twenty band boys, playing cards and fending off tired, familiar advances was also pretty desperate. Especially if they were all sitting in some draughty railway station, waiting for the milk-train home. Tommy Trevino tried to avoid tours, but lucrative one-night engagements a fast ride from London were more manageable, except when the train schedule went wrong.

Being desperate about a collapsing revue was also an enjoyable experience, because every time, the despair pulled out more talent and inventiveness.

'Tell me about it,' Jubilee reminded her of his presence in his mild way. His patience with her was limitless.

'What, the revue?' she said, suddenly making an effort.

'No, the virtues of matrimony,' he joked. 'Your favourite subject.'

Ida ignored this remark. 'Well. This revue's the best one for me so far,' she said more positively than she felt. 'I've got a new bit as of yesterday. I think it will work.'

'Is it still all a spoof on the Surrealist exhibition? You quite liked that.' Jubilee smiled. He had finally persuaded her to look at art because it had become part of her work.

'I'm a picture, I come alive, like a dream.'

'Comic sketches . . .' he suggested, smiling.

'Oh very good!' Ida laughed and kissed him.

'So. You're inside a picture frame . . .'

'How did you guess?'

Jubilee saw that with the egocentricity of her profession, Ida was surprised that an outsider like himself might have the wit to guess how Ainslie's show could be staged.

'I'm learning,' he said calmly. It did not dawn on Ida that he had been sitting around listening to show-biz chatter for over two years. He would have to be a moron not to have a few ideas by now.

311

'Yes, I do, as a matter of fact,' she sailed on. 'I'm a sort of portrait, just a face surrounded by six feet. They're really dancers who are blacked out, only their feet are illuminated, all around my head. It's funny. They're pink and bulbous-toed, like in one of those modern paintings. Then I start to sing 'Happy Feet'. The band really jazzes it up, my 'feet' escape and go mad to the music, and then these two wonderful American tap-dancers, Babbs and Brewin come on and chase them all into a box.'

She omitted to mention that the two tap-dancers had whited faces and black sequined suits, in contrast to her brown face and spangled white ruff. Snapshot ghosts, Gran's end-of-the-pier world came back to her, and her words trailed away.

'And where do you go then?' Jubilee asked brightly.

'Well that's the best part. I step inside my picture again, and the painter comes along and decides to give me a bicycle wheel and a rose instead of a nose.'

'Ainslie is excelling himself again!' Jubilee's laugh was too boisterous.

'Don't you think it sounds funny?' Ida was alive to his lack of enthusiasm, instantly worried.

'These things are always more amusing in the performance than in the telling . . .' Jubilee was anxious not to make her nervous. He sighed. Ida could be so single-minded, yet if he ever showed signs of tiring of her, or disapproving, she became angry and possessive.

'I'm sure it will be terribly good,' he repeated. 'And when it's over, you'll name the day? Seriously this time?'

'Beginners, Act Two please.' The stage-manager on the tannoy, bored and exhausted, might have been announcing rush-hour cancellations at Waterloo Station.

'I promise. Thanks for the supper.' Ida was fortified, gave Jubilee a fond hug, and hurried to the stage.

Vernissage sold out, a tremendous twelve-week run. There had been no try-out in the provinces, and no tour was offered afterwards. Ainslie had learnt from experience: the show was too metropolitan in taste to survive beyond the West End, and profits were respectable enough without going further afield.

Ida got good reviews, and her recorded version of 'Happy Feet' did very well while the revue lasted.

Afterwards Ida felt flat, with a sense of inevitability. It seemed to her that she had two predictable alternatives: to appear in Ainslie revues, scoring mild witty jokes at her own expense, exaggerating her tarbrushed looks, or to go back to commercial big-band singing and the limitations of the little fence that separated the orchestra stand from the world twirling past it every night. Now that she had succeeded at both, neither prospect excited her. If she had to get married, she wanted to do it feeling pleased with her own life, as a reassurance. Just in case . . .

One summery day she was in the Six Bells pub in Chelsea with the band boys when the idea of a spin to Le Touquet was put to her.

'We're going to play golf. Why don't you come along?' Charlie suggested. 'Me, Bobby and maybe old Ivor and a couple of others will join in.'

'Your wife's going, is she?' Ida teased him.

Bobby Smythe, who was still a little smitten with her, laughed aloud. 'Got you there, Charlie, hasn't she?'

'She hates golf, the wife,' Charlie said defensively.

'I'll come. I'll be your mascot,' Ida agreed on impulse. 'I'm not very good in a boat,' she added, having never set foot off-shore in her life.

'Jesus, we ain't going by boat!' Charlie laughed at her. 'We're hiring a plane, aren't we boys? From Croydon Airport. We all club together, twenty quid apiece, and you're there in less than an hour. We get in a couple of rounds of golf, a good French meal, and we're back in London in time for the evening's gig.'

The extravagance of it appealed to her. Besides, next time Jack came back she would have news for him: she too would have been abroad! And perhaps the adventure would give her another perspective, help her to see her future.

Jubilee was surprised at the news. 'I thought you hated travelling.' They were walking along Knightsbridge one honey-coloured evening.

'I do. I just feel like a change — oh Jubilee, it's just a lark with the boys, try to think of it as a — a dress rehearsal! I'll have to fly if we go on a honeymoon, won't I?'

313

He was not in the least mollified, but quite insulted that she should offer such a specious argument. Ida was ashamed of herself for underestimating him.

'Look,' she explained more honestly. 'I just want a little time to think before I give you my answer. You know how hard I've been working. It's only a day trip — don't you see, I've travelled a lot with Tommy and the boys. It makes me feel comfortable, going with them.'

'Of course I understand.' He took her hand as they neared a crossroad. 'I was rather looking forward to taking you first myself, that's all.'

He left Ida at the Ambassador. 'Ring me tomorrow,' he said. His mild expression tried to suggest he understood her, but as he walked away, the slight slump of his shoulders made her feel guilty.

The flight was a nightmare. The small charter plane juddered continually and blasted her eardrums with a frightening series of noise changes, each one of which suggested the engines were failing or the propellers falling off. She wished she had worn thicker clothing, for she had not realised that it would be cold in the air even when the land was hot. The band boys, impervious, sat together on wicker chairs drinking whisky and playing cards. However, the thought of smart French shops cheered her a little, and presently the aeroplane started its descent.

The boys hired a taxi, stuffed all their golf-clubs in the back, and headed off directly for the links in the pine woods covering the dunes just outside Le Touquet itself. Ida was disappointed. At first sight the bungalows lining the Avenue du Golf looked a little like the thatched mansions of Berkshire and Surrey. Sprawling and expensive, of course, but too English to be of interest. However, the terrace of the golf club was an impressive sight.

'The money!' she whispered to Charlie. Resting golfers and their lazy companions sat drinking cocktails, wearing the most beautiful summery things Ida had ever seen, soft chiffons, white blazers, picture hats with brims wide enough for Hollywood films. 'If you think I'm going to sit here while you play, you're wrong. I'll take the taxi back into town.' She was thinking of chic French boutiques . . .

'OK Ida. We'll meet you at the Casino at six.' Charlie turned away to organise a caddy for the game.

'Buy yourself a swimsuit, and head for the beach!' Bobby called over his shoulder, trotting from the taxi to the clubhouse with a large bag on his shoulder. Ivor Clarke, always trim and appropriate, had managed to change into flannels and golf shoes already somewhere and was waving from the clubhouse for them all to hurry up. She was forgotten; Ida realised that Charlie and Bobby were passionately fond of golf, and the others had caught the mood. The sight of two resplendent nine-hole courses, one through the woods, and one lake-strewn between the dunes, made them all short on manners and keen to set off.

Le Touquet was more of an adventure than she could ever have imagined. She drove through the pine forests and smart holiday villas, to the town centre, dominated by the Westminster Hotel on one side and the Casino de la Forêt on the other. The hotel was a vast edifice that would not have been out of place in Belgravia except for a row of bright-striped rounded blinds, bulging like crinolines. Too gay, too frivolous for a truly English establishment. The dining-room beneath them was deserted, but already set for lunch and filled with flowers.

Ida left the taxi, and followed the lightness and air that suggested where she might find the sea. Narrow streets, laid out at right angles to the coast, led her to La Digue, the sea-wall and promenade, and a magnificent, pale-sanded, crowded beach. A busy roadway stretched beside it, separating the shore from a long row of holiday villas, facing the sea: tall gabled houses, strange combinations of Swiss chalet, English cottage and Moorish palace.

There was something curiously feminine about them, all pastel painted and lined up as in a beauty parade, their rounded windows shining like eager eyes. Ceramic-tiled arches, Tudorish timbers, or barley-twist stone pillars, gave each house a distinctive personality. Ida walked along trying to pick out the one she liked best, as probably every holiday-maker did while taking a stroll by the sea.

The side-streets tucked between these expensive homes were filled with tempting sights: exquisite clothes, over-priced *objets d'art*, trivial water-colours of seaside views, 'English' tea-shops, far too chic to be anything but French, and restaurants unashamedly redolent with garlic and herbs. Ida soon discovered that everyone understood her limited, operatic French, so that it was easy to buy a swimsuit, a wrap and a floppy hat for the beach. As she did not have time to rent a bathing hut for changing, she walked from the shop to the shore in her new clothes, having observed that others did so with impunity.

As she walked across the sand, she recalled her Gran saying about smart clothes: I'm relying on you to set a tone . . . don't buy cheap frills. The words brought relief: an excuse for her extravagance. The black satin costume gave her limbs an athletic sleekness; on the brim of her hat she had pinned a red flower, the colour one of the Allaines would have called 'young': rose-pink.

An hour of hot sun was more than enough. Ida had not swum since all those years before when she had first met Veronica. The memory made her girlish once more; she paddled in the sea, splashed her face with salty water, and lay down until her skin dried. Then she licked off the salt in the crook of her elbows, noting the stiffness of the fine hairs on her forearms. After a while she wandered through the boutiques again, recklessly buying a new dress and a large canvas bag for all her cast-off things. Lunch was a late and picturesque refreshment, taken beneath an umbrella at a small restaurant in the pine trees. All at once it was time to meet the fellows, and to head back towards the Casino.

They were late too; no one was gambling yet, so she drifted into the bar to wait.

It was the first time Ida had spent a day alone, entirely alone in a strange place, and the ease of the adventure, the fullness of its pleasures were vivid to her. Perhaps it was quite inevitable, in the circumstances, that on entering the room, she fell in love with the piano-player.

He was black, obviously an American: there was something stylish in his gestures emanating a self-consciousness West Indians in London did not have to show. But most of all, his piano playing reminded her of Uncle Ted, particularly the way he sat with one foot tucked back, and his long-fingered hands with a magnificent stretch almost stroked the keyboard, finding the notes like a series of caresses. He played a lot in octaves, in the style of Earl Hines — not a bad idol for anyone. Freed from the 'stride' style, the laying down rhythms with a percussive left hand, he produced a complete, rounded sound, as if the piano were an entire orchestra.

Ida sat quietly, not too embarrassed after years of hotels and bars at being alone in such a place. Engrossed in the music (he had a double bass and drummer to back him up), she did not notice Charlie, Bobby, Ivor and the others sneak up. At that moment the pianist looked up and waved at her group.

'Do you know him?' Ida asked Ivor quickly.

'Oh my, oh my. Boys, she's fallen for him.' Bobby overhearing the question, caught the tone of her voice in an instant.

'You're in deep trouble Ida. I'm not sure I shall introduce you,' Ivor said.

'Don't be silly!' she tried to sound cool. 'He's the best pianist I've heard in a long time. Listen to him! What's his name? How do you know him?'

'He came over to London last autumn. Played in a showband, broadcast a few times, did some arranging for a few other orchestras — Jack Payne, mostly I think. He used to turn up a lot at the Rookery after hours and sit in. Comes from New York. Played with the greatest in his time. Name's Ray Merritt, though we always called him Sunny. He makes me think I should take up woodwork.' Ivor pushed his spectacles up the bridge of his nose, an adjustment that signalled to all the sincerity of his compliment.

'What's he doing here? He's far too good for this place.'

Ivor laughed. 'It's the height of the season in Le Touquet! That's good money. I expect he had labour permit problems and had to leave the country for a spell. Here, Ida, you can ask him all your questions directly!'

Ray Merritt stood before her, and it was obvious to everyone in the group that the attraction between them was mutual. So conscious were they of each other, that when formal introductions were made in a prim style by Ivor, they both found some small physical distraction — a dropped matchbox, a handbag that suddenly slipped — to avoid shaking hands. Actual contact would have been an embarrassment; they wanted that to happen only when they were alone.

'Let's drift boys,' Charlie said heavy-handedly. 'If you need us, Ida, we'll be at the roulette table. Remember, the plane leaves at seven and you don't have a passport, so be on the airstrip.'

'But I do have my passport,' Ida said, half to herself. In her ignorance, she did not know about the day-trip relaxations, and had turned up armed with everything — brand-new passport, birth certificate, one of the newly-issued driving licences, recently acquired, a list of emergency telephone numbers . . . her lack of experience had proved to be a benefit.

'So.' Ray spoke first when they were alone. 'You're free for the evening. Ida Garland . . . nice name. I saw you several nights runnin' around on Piccadilly.' His beautiful, mobile features broke into the biggest, slowest smile she had ever seen.

'D'you mean in my act at the Charlbury, or my act on the town?' She laughed, but her nervousness was not in the least diminishing.

'Both,' he laughed. 'Happy Feet. That's you all right.' His deep voice and brief words attracted her even more to him.

'Did you like London? It must seem quiet after New York.'

'Yeah. It sure is *quiet*.' The word was meant to suggest advantages she could know nothing of. 'I like the galleries. The Tate. The National. Concerts at the Wigmore.'

She smiled at his misnomer; he noticed at once and corrected himself. 'The Wigmore Hall.'

'I don't suppose you've ever heard of it, but I once had a billing in the Baker Street Concert Room. That was a long time ago.' She said too much out of nervousness. 'In the days when I sang Giordano, Purcell, that kind of thing. And some moderns.' Ida hesitated. She had nearly mentioned Harvey Johns' name, but stopped just in time for him to turn the conversation to another line.

'You gave it all up? So did I. My family gave me a classical education too. It broke them up when I flunked my studies and joined a band. Jesus, a boy from *my* kind of family, playing jazz in a dive!'

'What kind of family?' she asked with innocent interest.

'The kind that live up in Harlem and ignore white New York. The kind that prefer Pavlova to Florence Mills, Walter Hampden to Paul Robeson. The kind that just hates jazz because they're trying so hard to be high-cultured. That's their way for the nights: the days they spend fighting for equality.'

Ida was silenced. A small personal arena had suddenly widened into a vast battlefield, and in that moment she felt pretty white, English, and sorry.

'Florence Mills came to London — C.B. Cochran brought her over in the Blackbirds revue. I was only a girl, but I remember my Pa saying she was a great star.'

'Yeah. When she died, a hundred thousand people in Harlem went to the church for the funeral. But not my folks' kind of people.'

There were things that made the links between people indissoluble. She was not part of this struggle. It wasn't colour, it was memories, experiences, and expectations that linked people. Their pasts, their presents, and their futures . . .

'Hey. Don't go away.' He reached out a hand and slid it gently along the young, pretty line of her jaw, until his fingertips brushed the lobe of her ear.

'I won't.' She smiled and looked directly into his face. It was a shocking, thrilling moment. He was a stranger, and yet Ida was looking into the eyes of desire, and answering a man's need with her own.

'I better be getting back. I'm only the relief; the main band gets here at eight. Then we can blow.'

'I'll wait.'

For Ida, the next hour was perversely a pleasure in its inordinate length, a time in which to savour exactly what she was doing; exactly what she knew she would gain, and what she was risking. No drink or drug had ever induced the sustained elation of that interval of time.

At some moment in the hour she called the airport and left a message that the boys would receive on their departure: 'Have passport: staying over. Ida.' She sent exactly the same message by telegram to Jubilee too, but added one word: 'Love.'

When Ray had finished his early evening session, they left the Casino, dined at a small restaurant in a side-street, then walked along the front, where Ida pointed out to him all the details she had observed for her own amusement earlier in the morning.

'Can I call you Ray? I don't like the idea of Sunny.'

'Anything you want honey. I ain't particular about names. Except yours. Ida. You can't mess around with that.'

'Where'm I going to stay? Your place?' she asked, quite certain that she had no need to pretend to be coy.

'No. I'm sharing with the bass fiddle. I fixed you up real nice.' He laughed, a rumbling sexy sound that made Ida cling even closer to his side. His body was slim, his movements alternating between a gracefulness and nervy tension.

'I'm going to get you settled because I have another set at the Casino. Then I'll come to the hotel and see how you've been passing the time without me.'

He had booked her a room at the Westminster; he must have arranged it in the afternoon, sure for his part too of what would happen. It did not cross her mind to ask if he made this reservation for a string of willing young women. She did not care, really. As long as she had his undivided attention for the present.

He waited while she signed in and the porter took her beach-bag — Ida had to concentrate on dignity, not to be embarrassed by her paltry luggage: a beach-bag.

'Bye honey. I hope you have a comfortable night.' He shook her hand formally. As Ida stood in the glass-windowed lift, she noticed with relief that no one paid the slightest attention to Ray Merritt, standing in the foyer watching her rise up the wrought-iron lift-shaft like an apotheosis, till she was out of sight.

He certainly knew how to make her yearn for him. By the time he reappeared, two hours, not one hour later, she was in a mindless state of wanting. He saw it in her face as she sat on the bed. Under her bathing wrap she was naked.

'Hey, you didn't think I wasn't coming?' He smiled, looking wicked and yet somehow reassuring in his tone.

'No. I knew you would. But I wanted you to come soon.'

'We've got time. Plenty of time.'

She could understand how wound up he still was after playing. He kissed her, many times; she could have gone on savouring his sweet mouth without words, for hours. But he broke away, poured drinks, took off his jacket and tie, then opened the window so they could smell the flowers and hear voices, laughter, even this late, on the streets.

'White girls like it,' he said quickly, only half in jest.

'That's not why I'm here. If you think that I'd rather leave. I know all about that,' Ida said bitterly.

Something in her voice made him look at her more closely.

'Oh honey, it means nothing to me. You, passing? That's something else my folks don't approve of. I can't see it that way. It's a state of mind. To me, you is *English*.' He put on a mock jive-talk voice and opened his hands to her, palms upwards, a caricature of a show-biz type.

'I wish you could play for me.' The issue of colour seemed irrelevant more than awkward. She pulled the silk cover off the bed, wrapped it round herself, and stood close to him by the window.

'You sing instead,' he replied.

So she gave him everything, funny songs from Ainslie Curtis shows, 'Singapore Swing'; 'One More Romance Gone Wrong'; 'The Chocolate Shake'. The last one amused him, as he had played at the Apollo in Harlem and seen Duke Ellington's orchestra there on many an occasion.

'Sing me the other stuff, the songs you learnt with your classical teacher.' Ray walked round the room, alternately filling their glasses with Dom Perignon, and chain-smoking. In between he drank shorts of whisky. None of this seemed to alter his state of tense expectation.

Ida had not forgotten a single note; in a soft, pure voice she recalled a few songs by Giordano, one or two of Harvey Johns' own compositions, some snatches of Mozart.

'I can't do it!' she said suddenly. 'My voice won't do it!' It had changed from a pure high sound to a richer, shaded timbre.

Then she sat next to him on the bed, and slapped out the rhythm she wanted on the satin of her thighs. 'This is my favourite, "Honeysuckle Rose".' He hummed, he clicked his fingers, he beat out chords they both heard perfectly on the edge of the bedside table. When she finished, he shook his head smiling in disbelief.

'You're a winner, baby. Real class.'

With that, he gathered her in his arms, and they rolled back on the bed and made love. It was easy; they found each other so swiftly. He knew about the side of her breasts that she liked to have caressed; he understood her grip on the back of his neck, a signal that he responded to at once, sensing her urgency to be one with him, from head to toe. She was won by the sweet affection of his gesture, worrying his foot against the softness of her instep, as they lay panting when it was all over. Ida and Ray fell asleep instantly, nervous exhaustion overtaking passion.

In the dawn Ida woke up to his love-making. Curled round her back, he was almost inside her, and she stayed asleep, mentally at least, letting him rouse her for as long as she could hold away from him. They went on making love until there were no more climaxes between them, and then they went on making love for the sheer fascination of tangling with each other — until it became a joke, and their bodies were too numb for sensation.

'OK, so now what do we do?' He spoke with lethargy, as if not too many suggestions would interest him.

'You stay here and sleep. You have to play tonight. I'll go and buy some more clothes,' Ida said. Unlike Ray, she was energised by sex.

'Take some money. In my jacket.' He was already drifting into oblivion. Ida rustled in his pocket and found two fifty-pound notes. He was either making a fortune, or he was hopeless with money.

On reaching the hotel desk she wrote a more considerate express letter to Jubilee, telling him not to worry, that she had met up with a girlfriend and was going to stay on and rest for a few days. Certainly she felt bad about deceiving him, but only for a few moments. When she had explained her absence, so that he would not be left anxious, she had no difficulty in putting him out of her mind. This lack of guilt surprised her and she noted her reactions objectively, as if she were someone new, outside herself, someone she was meeting for the first time.

She returned to the Westminster Hotel later after a visit to a beauty salon and the purchase of several chic outfits (more overtly flirtatious than her usual clothes). Ray was out. He had left a large bunch of roses for her, and a huge box delivered from Au Chat Bleu, Le Touquet's most noted chocolatier, and a note: 'I'll play for *you*, sweetheart. Come to the Casino when you're through spending money.' How sweet — it was *his* money she had been extravagantly shedding — and he liked it.

Ida's appearance, in a spotted voile dress, with a new softer make-up, cherry-red on her lips, made him leave the bar and the man he was talking with to embrace her in front of whoever was present. She was astonished. In the following instant she realised she was thrilled that he kissed her in public, secondly no one was shocked, for France was not like England, and thirdly, he behaved as if he were sixteen, and in love for the first time. Three good reasons to order champagne, and feel bubbles of excitement rising in her, again and again.

They lunched on the terrace at the back of the Casino, strung with lights, while a jolly 'jig tempo' band trotted through the season's favourites. For a while the piano bar was empty, curtains drawn, and they passed a shady, peaceful hour, talking of music, of the famous singers and players Ray had known and accompanied . . . all legends in Ida's book. Ray shook his head disbelieving her knowledge and admiration.

'I heard Ellington say the same thing about his visit in '33. It's kind of moving to come here and find all you people know more about our records than the folks do back home. But sometimes, it gets kind of heavy, too, the interest, you know . . .'

'All this stuff about authentic coloured sound?' Ida had heard these long discussions too, among the band boys, at the after-hours sessions in the Rookery and other bottle parties. Much of the best jazz had been published under 'Race Record' labels.

'Yeah. No one plays jazz like coloured people do . . . that's a Jim Crow concept about jazz. Sure no one can sound like Louis Armstrong, but no one sounds like Benny Goodman either. There's a lot of good white guys. What the hell is jazz anyway? I don't know.'

'Then there's the opposite problem, like Reggie Foresythe,' she ventured.

'Who's he?'

'He was born in London too, he's a pianist at the Café de la Paix in Regent Street. He tries to play more modern things, his own compositions, and people say they want him to play 'the true music of his race'. He's not allowed to experiment, get clever, you know, he's stuck with what they expect from a coloured man.' She glanced quickly at him. He took the word with that same dispassion she had seen the night before. As if being angry about it all the time was something he had learned long ago would destroy anything good he had to offer. Or perhaps his stillness was self-protection — even boredom, or worse, a long, long suppressed hatred of her kind. She did not know. All these feelings were possible, and justified.

'Uh uh,' he replied.

'Jazz means something different in America.' Ida became tentative, because her thoughts were being formed in the instant, through the richness of her encounter with Ray, and her trust that he would not laugh at her. 'Your music may be about colour, but I can't hear colour in it. I hear feelings. I grew up with that. It was something special to me. But in the end, perhaps that's just my history.'

'Back home it *is* to do with colour honey. It's a minority interest. That's why we like it over here, the big audiences. But in England, maybe it's more to do with class.'

'Like everything else . . .'

'Ever heard of a young writer, George Orwell? He wrote a good book about Paris and London. Try it.'

He played some more, beautifully rendered jazz classics, some Ellington pieces she knew very well, 'Mood Indigo'; 'Solitude'; 'Creole Love Call'. She hummed the last, perfectly unselfconscious and happy to be with him.

Soon it was time for his afternoon stint, so Ida wandered to the beach, enjoying the warm long shadows of the sun across the deep-heated sand. She sat quite still, hugging her knees, studying the details of family life as nannies and mothers gathered up sunhats, shawls, spare shoes, buckets, and shepherded their flocks back to their homes.

After that, all her days were the same . . . in the gaps when Ray played, she preened herself, bought new clothes, observed life at a distance unfolding with its seaside rituals. When she could not make love, she thought about making love, all the time.

Then the telegram came. Ainslie Curtis had sent it: 'Special request. Return at once.' Five days of euphoria, and now the world was closing in. She wanted to ignore the summons.

'I'll say I'm ill. I won't go back!' She buried her face in Ray's shoulder.

'You can't do that, honey. From what you've told me this Ainslie's a big shot and he's been good to you. You'll have to go. You'll never know what could have happened . . . if you don't go.' Ida sent a message that she would return, then notified Veronica of the time when she would arrive home.

That last night Ida and Ray lay in bed apart from each other, because it was so hot that their skins stuck together in sweat. Ray flung one hand across her belly, and she held on to him, one hand curled on his shoulder. Tears streamed silently down from the corners of her eyes, tears so vast that he heard them plop on to the stiff linen sheets.

'Hey.' He rolled over and kissed her.

'I don't want to leave you.'

'I'll be back in London in a couple of weeks. I'll see you then. I haven't finished with you yet, believe me . . .' He smiled so engagingly that she could not be hurt by his lightness, his verging on flippancy. They spent all night making love and talking. He was a whole world of knowledge to her, but she had no sense of being improved by him, more of being shown how to explore for herself.

Her plane was scheduled to leave early in the morning. She dressed quickly while he was still sleeping, keeping to their familiar, loving routine.

'Take some money for the journey,' he murmured. She did so, marvelling as always at the wads of notes he kept casually stuffed in his pockets. She bent down to say goodbye, and he caught her wrist hard, rolling her over him on the bed again.

'This is it,' he said, kissing her all over her face, her nose, her eyes, her earlobes. 'I'll see you in thirteen days. I'll ring your apartment as soon as I get in. And you can take me to that fish shop on Edgware Road, like you promised.'

She nodded, unwilling to risk speaking because she knew she would start crying again. When she got back to London it would all become complicated, and she did not want to face up to anything.

Flying back in a larger plane was not as terrifying as the journey out had been. Ida was in a strange state where the physical pleasures of the past few days made her feel remote, one of a different species of living thing from everyone else around her. Someone bumped into her casually while bending to retrieve his baggage. The unexpected roughness of this physical contact shocked her, as if she had been sleepwalking and unkindly woken.

As soon as she reached her flat, Veronica was upon her. She had made a great effort: the maid had tidied the rooms and Veronica had restrained herself from undoing the girl's work for several hours. Denied the diversions of bathing, changing her clothes, eating chocolates or rifling through magazines and records, she was desperate for entertainment.

'What have you been up to? Poor Jubilee! He's been so worried for you. Who were you with? It wasn't a girlfriend, you haven't got any girlfriends except me. Was it a person from the show? Sylvia? That chorus girl creature, Mona, or someone new?'

'I fell in love,' Ida said simply.

'Oh Lord. Should we celebrate?'

The two girls looked at one another with frank uncertainty.

'I don't know yet,' Ida said, smiling thinly. 'I think I should telephone Jubilee.' She was beginning to feel the enormity of what she had done: she had broken trust, deceived the man who wanted to share her entire life.

'No need. He's gone to his family's place in Kent for a few days. I got Felix to go with him. You didn't say when you'd be back, and honestly, I couldn't bear to see him hanging around the clubs waiting.'

'That was very good of you Veronica. Thank you.'

'And Mr Curtis has rung twice. Honestly, I might as well be your secretary!'

Ida ignored this remark: Veronica was hardly ever at home except for moments of high drama. 'I think I'll go to bed. I have to meet the others at the Charlbury at four.'

'Mmm. I'll give you tea.'

She reappeared quickly, sitting on the edge of Ida's bed in the hope of more details.

'Are you going to tell me about it?'

'No. I don't think so. Do you mind?'

'Of course not. Turn over. I'll rub your back. You're as white as a sheet.'

Veronica's firm small hands massaged Ida's shoulders and neck. The warmth of her hands, their familiar friendliness began to coax Ida back to reality. Then she suddenly felt the imprint of those other hands loving her the night before and burst into tears.

'You sound very strange. Perhaps it's this line.' Jubilee had called her. She felt sick, just hearing his loving, warm voice, innocent of what she had done to him.

'Where are you?' she said, trembling.

'In the village post office. It's the only place for miles with a telephone. I'm ringing to say I can't ring, really.'

'Are you coming back to London?' She dreaded his answer: she simply could not face him.

'No. I've just put Felix on the train but I'm staying down. I've got things to do down here. The old place is a wreck. One of these days I'll have to get builders in.'

'Don't be long, will you?' she lied, feeling that old, horrid feeling of worthlessness that her affair with Harvey Johns had induced.

'Why? Are you missing me?' Was it her imagination, or did Jubilee sound odd — positively ironic?

'Of . . . of course I am.'

'If you have anything to tell me — anything at all — I'll leave you this number. Hartmere 216. As I said, I can't call you very easily. So don't expect me to.'

'Jubilee . . .'

'Yes?'

'Oh, nothing . . . have a nice time . . .'

'Goodbye.'

This conversation unnerved her completely. She was risking losing the most faithful man of her life . . . but there was nothing at all she could do about it. Everything hung on Ray's return to London, and whether they could go on being good together, here in her own world. Ida watched herself, watched the progress of this madness as if she were outside herself, and thoroughly dismayed at the sight.

She flung herself at her work. Ainslie's hush-hush show was a cabaret at some exclusive Royal ball. It was meant to be exciting because the King and Mrs Simpson were to be present. Ida was unimpressed, not in the mood to be amused by this chance of a glimpse at a popular scandal when she was being utterly two-faced herself.

Thirteen days. Time was up: any moment now she would get Ray's call. Jubilee had not phoned again, and she could not bring herself to contact him. She had absolutely nothing to say.

Fifteen days passed. Surely Ray would ring today. She arrived home late after rehearsing with Ainslie to find the flat was empty. No note from the maid, no calls. A letter from Jack, with a photograph showing him riding on an elephant, in some far-flung spot. 'Dear Ida. You should travel. Broadens the mind . . . How's the Right On? Seemed a decent chap, if you have to marry anyone.' Ida laughed bitterly at that. Veronica had deserted her in favour of dinner at the Café de Paris. Ida could not endure the suspense any longer, and Jack's card made her irritated to be waiting, passive. *He* would not stand for it, and would tell her to get on with what she wanted. This thought made her bold, almost indignant at the silence. Ray had given her a London number where she could ask after him, in an emergency.

'Hallo?' A soft-spoken woman answered the line.

'Oh. Do you have any news of Mr Merritt please? I'm calling from a Mr Curtis' office. The impresario.' Her lie sounded lame even to her own strained hearing.

'I'll have to see. Leave me the number Miss . . . ?' The woman spoke so calmly that Ida was reassured; she must be a friend's wife, or his agent, or someone who took messages . . .

'Just say Mr Curtis' office called. Sloane 3125. Thank you. Goodbye.'

At three in the morning the phone rang again.

'Is this Sloane 3125?'

'Ray? Is that you? You're back?'

'Hi! Ida! What's wrong?'

'You're back, and you didn't call me? I — I was worried about you . . .'

'I said I'd be in touch. I had things to do . . . you worried *me*,

328

calling like that, in the middle of the night! I shouldn't like anything to happen to you.'

'I'm sorry. Perhaps it would have been better if I'd left it — I'm sorry, I — I,' Ida heard herself begin to stammer, at a loss for words for the first time ever with this man.

He chuckled, and her heart banged about in her chest, as if it had been released from a spring. It was all going to be all right. Even now.

'Yes, especially as your call gave me a bad time with my woman. Boy, was she mad at me. But that's OK, I've smoothed her feathers.'

'Your — your woman?'

'She's *very* suspicious. Is it true, what I read in the papers, you're going to be in this gala thing? In front of the King? Do you have your song?'

'No. It's being written for me . . . Ray, you said, I thought, oh God . . .' Tears streamed down her face.

'Hey. Don't cry. We had a good time . . . I'm your friend, remember? Things never last, honey. Whatever the songs may say.'

'You didn't tell me everything.'

'It wouldn't have made any difference . . . 'cept you wouldn't have had such a good time. When am I gonna see you again? I've just got this booking, a real nice club in Denmark Street. Come tomorrow. I'd like to see your pretty little face . . .'

'Oh Ray!' Now she was stifling sobs. But he was right. It would not have made the slightest difference. She was astonished at how quickly she had thrown morality aside. What was hurting was his honesty, and the loss of a most particular adventure in her life.

'Listen honey. Listen to me. You haven't learnt one thing. You're very beautiful. You don't know how irresistible that is. OK, beauty's only a thing on the surface, but it disturbs people. I didn't do anything you didn't want me to do. You're playing with loaded dice and you have to know the rules.'

Making a huge effort, she found her voice. 'You always make me see things another way . . .'

He laughed, but realising that would make her cry again, he made an effort to restrain his pleasure in her words. 'Don't be too impressed. I'm only a bit player in your life. I'm sorry you're sad. Maybe my philosophy isn't right for you.'

'Goodbye.'

'No goodbyes. I'll be seeing you. Sometime.'

There was not much of the night left after that. Ida drank a bottle of whisky, waiting for Veronica to come back. When she did, she was very tight-lipped. 'Good Lord. Blotto. You got a phone call, I take it.'

'There's no need to take that tone with me. Why're you mean to me?' Ida began to rise in temper, hysterically.

'Because you've been a bloody fool, and you never listen.' Veronica lit a cigarette and paced the room (as best she could between bed and dressing table, kicking discarded silks out of her way).

'Look. Send a telegram. Get Jubilee back up here and for God's sake don't tell him anything. Or at least, tell him as little as you need. Don't hurt him. He doesn't deserve it . . .'

'But what about me?' Ida fell back on the bed, awash with pain, an agonising sexual hurt.

Veronica grabbed her shoulders and gave her a fierce shake. 'You ought to know better. You've got no excuse to go lurking about in illicit relationships for the rest of your life. I know why you paid up for Janet Sheldon. I must have been a fool not to guess about Harvey Johns . . . but now, you're *someone*. Your own person! Jubilee's your lover, I do realise, but he's offering you marriage. This French gigolo is quite, *quite* another matter.'

'Don't you dare say that! He's American, he's a jazz man, a brilliant piano-player!'

'Yes, well. Brilliant maybe. I see the attraction. He's coloured, isn't he? But he doesn't want to go on caring for you, all the same. You're in love with the mere idea of him.'

'Oh God, Veronica.' Ida wept again.

'Think about it. I'm going to bed.' She left the room and Ida felt cheated of her friend's sympathy, her shoulder to cry on. But then she realised Veronica had abandoned her on purpose, so that she could feel her loneliness, her disappointment, more acutely. That way, she might come to her senses all the sooner.

*

In a frightening, harsh way, Veronica succeeded. It was the mention of 'illicit relationships' that did it. Ida, at dawn, felt a desperate need to struggle into the light once and for all, and shake off the secrets, the doubts of the past. She watched the sun rise, feeling washed out by her tears, hoping it was not too late to wake up to another existence. Later she sent a telegram to Jubilee, asking him to come up to London, if he could possibly manage it, soon. Then she walked all the way to the Charlbury to lessen the thudding of her head: there had been far too many tears in the night. Before she spoke to Jubilee she wanted to sort things out with Ainslie.

Some crises are so intense that they are spectacularly short-lived. Ida felt this affair was like that: a dish breaks, a soup gets burnt, a soloist hits a bum note. The porcelain may look even more beautiful, mended and imperfect; the cook produce a superb meal from the ruins of the first; the musician play better than he has ever played before, in recompense for his mistake. Ida did not feel sorry for herself; she hurt too much for such a trivial response. She just wanted to pick up the pieces of her life and set them all straight.

Ainslie Curtis was comparatively quiet — only six people around his desk — but he sensed she had something important to tell him, and led her away to the little Italian restaurant opposite the theatre; it was his second office.

All this happened with a minimum of direction from Ida, who was still having some difficulty finding words for her thoughts.

'My dear girl. You have a look on your face that spells trouble for me. I can always tell. It's either a pregnancy or an engagement. Which is it to be?'

'I — I don't think it's either,' she grasped the table, wondering if she would lose Ainslie's favour with her news.

'I've never had an agent, Mr Curtis. Not since my Pa. Between you and Mr Trevino, I felt myself to be well placed, and I trusted you both.'

Ainslie studied the moulding round the ceiling. He knew every crack in the cornice work of this cheerfully shabby interior.

'It's more money,' he pronounced. 'You want a rise. I'm hurt. Just when we're preparing a gala.'

Ida was scared. Ainslie had never been anything but good to

her, except for a few moments' snappiness, in mid-rehearsal. She knew he had to be capable of ruthlessness to get financial backing for his shows. Perhaps his harsher side would now be revealed to her. Everyone had a bad side . . .

'No. I don't want more money. I need to be let out of the show. I don't want to do any more revue work. It's not right for me.'

Ainslie's powerful features squared up to her, his eyes penetrating and his mouth set firm. It was a fairly intimidating experience. 'Why not?' he demanded.

'Because I'm being turned into something I'm not. I'm not a novelty performer. I'm tired of being exotic and wearing tropical costumes and golliwog frills. I don't want to be your symbol of all things primitive and daring, tarbrushed, titillating a smart white audience . . .' In spite of herself, she was getting worked up.

'I see.' He stared away, and Ida was suddenly reminded of Harvey Johns, in the full flight of his rejection and vanity. 'You were happy once, to be moulded . . .' Light dawned. 'It's a man. You're trying to decide whether to marry that rather good catch. Hargreaves,' he said, possessively. 'I understand. You want to leave the company.'

'That's got nothing to do with it!' Ida blazed in return. 'And I don't want to leave the company! I know how much it all means to you — the Charlbury, the revues — I know I went along with it, but people change . . . I do want to go on working with you, but you've got to let me be myself! I'm more white than I am black, but in this world that always makes you a darkie! Let me find out how to be unique. Me: a *somebody*!'

Ainslie laid a very large hand on her arm. Pink, firm flesh, with bronzy hairs curling over dark-freckled skin. He was instantly apologetic.

'I'm sorry. I spoke in haste. You're absolutely right. I've been guilty of falling for easy formulas — how crass.'

Her respect for him grew boundless. She had never imagined he had the humility to confess a mistake, he was always so grand and sure of himself . . .

'I should have seen this coming,' he said, thinking out loud. 'Principally you need a rest. I suspected you were flinging yourself at entirely the wrong kind of people, in an effort to define things for yourself. That's why I sent you the telegram.'

'You mean — it wasn't just the gala?'

'No. I had a sixth sense . . .'

Ida blushed, and tears began to fall down her cheeks. He had dragged her away from Ray, when she was so happy . . . But then, the end would have come. Sooner or later.

'I'm sorry that you've been made to suffer. You're far too talented to get into trouble. Now, how long do you want off? Forget the gala, but can I count on you for the autumn?'

'You're going too fast. I haven't made any plans . . . what do you mean, the autumn?'

'Well. Let's forget the revues. We have to put you in another setting. I think a small cabaret would be good for you for a while. Build up another kind of following. Your instincts are good. I'm sorry I've been rather slow to see the light. If I've caused offence . . .'

Ida stared at her unwanted lunch, marvelling at how quickly and simply the future could be reshaped, if you had the courage to take decisions. But she had not looked very far into the future — she had hardly considered any alternatives.

'I need more time.'

'I should think you need to ask that chap Hargreaves a few questions. He isn't going to be tiresome and insist that you stop singing if you marry him, is he?'

'Good God no!' Ida heard her own vehemence, and began to laugh.

'That's better.' Ainslie was pleased to see some vitality in her. 'Now I have to get back. Mario!'

He left immediately, and Mario, the restaurant's careful owner who adored his dramatic clientele, kept Ida company while she ate her lunch. He showed her photographs of his family back home in Venice, which he always kept at hand for such moments.

When Ida returned home, Jubilee was waiting for her. The maid had let him in and he had sent her to the pictures.

'Well?' Jubilee had never looked more dignified or handsome, waiting for an explanation. A final answer.

'I — I think I should explain.'

'Don't. I'd rather not know. I'm not a fool. All that concerns me is whether your — recent experiences — have led you to know if you love me or not.'

'Yes. I do.'

'Do what?'

'Want to marry you.'

'That's not the same thing at all. That simply won't do.'

Jubilee looked quite ill, his big face drained of colour and she thought he might pass out. Then it dawned on her that he was beside himself with anger.

'Oh God!' she exclaimed.

He opened the door and made for the lift.

'Jubilee!' she screamed in a panic, for she realised she had hurt him very badly, had imagined he would always be there, like a devoted boy on the end of a kite string.

'Don't go!' She held on to his coat, while Jubilee held on to the lift bars, clenching his teeth in an effort not to look back at her. Ida let go and sank to the floor almost faint herself with fear.

'I'm sorry. I'm sorry. Please forgive me. I'm sorry,' she whispered. She was too scared to cry. The lift began to rise, and Ida began to shout. 'Don't go, don't go, please don't go.'

Jubilee roughly pulled away, got in and clanged the doors shut. As the cabin descended, Ida rattled the lift-shaft bars with such violence that the mechanism stuck. She heard him between floors, thumping with rage on the buttons as if telling her to let him be. Then she heard a thud, a silence, and he did not respond when she called.

'Oh Christ, he's sick!' Ida was terrified. She rattled at the doors until the electric connection was made good. She pressed feverishly to make the lift come up again to her floor. It rose; inside she found Jubilee slumped in a heap, his hands over his face, not crying, not sick, but in utter misery.

'You mustn't leave me, I'd die. I've only just realised that I love you. Forgive me. Please. I love you.' She pushed open all the doors and sat beside him on the carpet.

Veronica returned an hour later, and found the lift out of action. She had to walk all the way up the stairs, and in breathless annoyance found them both still huddled together in the open cabin, deep in conversation.

15

'You know what they've been dug for, don't you dearie?' Gran said. She and Ida were taking an August 'constitutional' through Hyde Park and passed the gaping network of trenches that had been laid.

'What, Gran.' Ida was feeling the weight of her hot body in mid-pregnancy, and the effort of keeping cheerful.

'Mass graves. My neighbour Mrs Philips told me.' Gran had revived with the outbreak of war; it drew out all her relish for adverse circumstances.

'God, Gran, don't be so morbid! We've got air-raid shelters, and gas masks, and barrage balloons, and so far nothing's happened to London. Well, not much. I think you're getting carried away.'

'Carried away! I shall be, ducks, carted off, in a cardboard box! Not before time, I can tell you! That I should have lived to see the day!'

'Oh come on, Gran, that's no way to talk. You must be more careful: don't say things like that in front of other people. It could get you into trouble. Depressing talk is positively illegal. Besides, Jubilee told me, he has it on great authority from one of his friends at the War Office that Hitler has said London is not to be bombed. Those few we had the other night were a mistake.'

Gran snorted with disbelief. 'Very careless of Mr Goering I'm sure.'

Ida tried another approach. 'What about the baby? That's something to look forward to. A great grandchild! You can baby-sit for me. I'll have to do something useful, it wouldn't be right to stay home just because of the baby . . .'

Gran suppressed a reply to this lecture. She hoped history was not going to repeat itself — that Ida would be an absentee mother the way Josephine had been. When Jack was born

Josephine had rushed straight back to work, charging round theatres making a name for herself, and left the poor baby boy in the boarding-house to be dandled on the knees of lodgers. God knew, with a war on, Ida had every reason to stay at home.

They arrived at Salamanca Street. 'Gosh, I'm glad to get back,' Ida said. 'My feet are killing me.' Some aspects of being pregnant were not very attractive; feeling ninety years old after a walk was one.

'Took the words right out of my mouth, dear,' Gran said, easing her curves slowly into the rocking chair. Ida flopped on one of the battered parlour sofas and pulled a greyish mound of knitting from her shoulder bag. She began to wield her needles slowly, frowning a great deal, her pink tongue-tip poking in and out with every manoeuvre of the wool.

'My Gawd, Ida, it's a good thing you've got a voice. You certainly weren't blessed with many other skills. Give that to me. What's it meant to be — a dishcloth?'

Ida giggled. 'It drives Jubilee mad. He can't stand the needles clacking.'

'Well he won't have to for much longer, will he?' Gran could have bitten off her words the moment they were spoken. Ida's girlish smile faded, and she concentrated even harder on her knitting.

'Sorry duckie. I shouldn't have said that,' Gran said.

'We think he'll get his papers any day now.'

'He didn't have to volunteer. With the baby and all.'

'Well Gran, he won't be in the firing line. And they'll give him quite a bit of leave when the baby comes.'

'Hand over that shambles to me. I'll get you started and you can carry on when you get home tonight.' Gran unravelled a good part of Ida's matinée jacket, picked up several dropped stitches and sped rhythmically along several rows. 'I don't suppose this will be the only piece of knitting I do before Christmas,' she said comfortably, and Ida was glad to see her a little more benign. She began to think that Gran's doom-laden manner was only an act, and that her determination to 'hang on and face up to it' as Londoners said was slowly growing stronger. Just being with her made Ida believe that nothing too awful could happen to any of them.

'Will you pop next door to your mother on your way home?' Gran asked, spoiling the mood of hope.

'No.'

'I only asked.' She did not force the issue, and the two women sat quietly for a while, the ticking clock and the knitting needles nicely punctuating the silence.

When the air cooled in early evening, Ida made her way home by bus to Jubilee's flat in Albany. It was a pity not to be able to wander down Park Lane, as she usually did, but she got tired too easily, and the streets of London had a tense expectancy, in sharp contrast to the desultory mood when she strolled there before the war. Soon it would be dark, and that inky nothingness of the black-out would wrap everything familiar, turning buildings into lumpen silhouettes. Shapes and distances deceived the eye as if trusted landmarks had stealthily shifted. Ida hated the way that roadways she could see so clearly in her head became impassable mazes after nine o'clock. A well-known pavement seemed to shrink in width to a lethal strip, or confusingly, widened to so broad a path that you lost confidence and thought you had strayed into the wrong street.

Twilight faded while Ida sat on the bus, retracing in memory her favourite journeys. Lonely night-walks into Soho as a girl, pub crawls in Edgware with Jack, now miles away in India, and wonderful, loving dawdles with Jubilee in the city parks, during the four blissful years of their marriage. Her thoughts turned to her baby, due in a month. One day she would take her precious morsel out for its first airing in a pram. It gave Ida a great deal of pleasure to think of doing all those things for the baby that her Ma had never wanted to do for her in her childhood.

She was sorry now that she had not been kind enough to visit her Ma. Having a baby did not seem to be softening her feelings. It irritated her that Denise appeared to be heading into the war as self-assured as ever; constantly complaining about unavailable items, especially hairpins.

Earl had signed up to be an air-raid warden in Bayswater to stay near her; he was just too old, at fifty-two, to be liable for conscription. Uncle Billy was out of it on two counts, having a one-man business and weak eyesight, but nevertheless he had volunteered with his elder brother. Like many middle-aged men they both wanted to avoid the jeered, geriatric ranks of the Local Defence Volunteers who had worked themselves up into a state of exaltation after Dunkirk. The British and French troops, in full retreat, had got back to the south coast safely from France the past June. Invasion was next, the Home Guards argued; England was now to see action, the last bastion against Hitler.

Uncle George, typically, had chosen this moment to disappear into London's underworld, into the multitude of unregistered draft-dodgers, factory-work shirkers, and general profiteers who looked at the declaration of war as a justification for crime, greed or self-preservation.

Perhaps to make up for his brother's dishonourable behaviour, Uncle Jim had made a big sacrifice. He could have gone on in music, in a military band perhaps, but he decided to offer his services as a cook in a tent-making factory at White City. That way he too could be near Gran, do something useful, and get a bit of pleasure playing in his spare time. But his poor fingers were being dreadfully mauled about, peeling potatoes into dustbins.

On her way from the bus stop to Albany in Piccadilly, Ida passed the narrow street where Ainslie's chic supper club, the Au Fait was boarded up. Ainslie had kept his promise.

The last few years before the war had been borrowed time; she knew that. The club opened just after she married Jubilee. Happy days; that little side-street, close to the Royal Academy, had attracted a nice crowd of people, artists mainly, bohemian types, but also foreign diplomats from embassies nearby and the fringes of the Mayfair set. Ida had developed a sophisticated repertoire of torch songs; Jubilee said that listening to her was like lighting one candle at a lovers' table. Seduction was certain. Ida had never lost that quality of singing for one person, even if her repertoire was made up of popular, crooning songs, still not quite the individual jazz sound she still hoped one day to find.

The Au Fait was smart, romantic, with little booths along one side, and a dais at the far end. A long bar with pink mirrors behind the bottles gave a speakeasy ambience, as did Ida's highly personal way of dealing with the customers. She knew now that anyone grand loved to be treated as an anonymous person, and that anonymous people adored being spoken to familiarly as if they were celebrities. Ainslie, Maud French, and Jubilee all contributed to that style, besides her Garland background. She had built up a reliable clientele, but with the outbreak of war, people panicked and stopped coming into town. Theatres closed; Ainslie lost a lot of money in 1939. He had been forced to give up the Au Fait lease.

Now she was pregnant, the war was in earnest, and like everyone else's life, hers had to stop.

She got home to Albany heavy-bodied again, flopped down and set about her knitting for a distraction, trying not to be downcast by all that had been lost. Jubilee came home from work shortly after, and found her struggling to interpret her pattern instructions. On the pattern-cover picture a trussed-up baby in bonnet, mittens, coat and bootees grinned at him.

He laughed, thinking how glad he was Ida would not have the patience for the whole set. 'It's a good job I didn't marry you for your domesticity.'

Ida clapped her hand to her mouth. 'Supper! I completely forgot!'

'Why didn't you get Mrs Higgs to knock up something for us before she went home?'

Ida looked guilty. 'I didn't see her. I went over to Gran's. I only got back just before you did.'

Jubilee looked disappointed. 'So you didn't take a nap today? Look here, if being cooped up doesn't suit you, perhaps you should move into lodgings near me when I'm posted. In the countryside somewhere. I do think you'd be safer . . .'

'I'm not leaving London. We've been through all this before. But I can't just wait for the baby all day, wander about Piccadilly endlessly shopping. Besides, there's not much to buy, and I don't think it's fair to go hoarding . . . have you seen what Mrs Higgs is stacking up in the pantry?'

Jubilee was not prepared to be critical. 'She's thinking of you, Ida. You'll have to look after yourself properly, eat good things, at least for the baby's sake. Mrs Higgs is an old timer, she remembers the shortages in the last war and that's why she's buying in essentials. I'm willing to bet Gran Garland's doing the same thing.'

She was, but Ida did not wish to admit to it. 'Oh, I suppose you're right. You always see the good in people first . . . though I bet Mrs Higgs takes home three packets of candles for every three she leaves here. On our housekeeping money too.'

'We can afford it.' He put his arms round her. 'I can see you're tired. I'll get supper delivered here from the Papillon. Why don't you lay the table and break into those supplies? Only two candles! We'll have a romantic supper, like the old days.'

'Well, in that case, we'd better start with another gin and I'll slip into something *louche*.'

While Ida was changing the telephone rang. She thought how odd and revealing it was, since the war had started, that everyone kept in touch with each other on a much more regular basis: Gran, Veronica, Felix, even Jack, with his endless exotic postcards . . . true friends. This time it was Ainslie, with details of her next radio broadcast.

'Be there at three. I can't send a car. They've cut down on all but essential journeys to save petrol.'

'Don't worry. I need the exercise and it will calm my nerves.' She did not add that she was missing her cabaret work so badly that she would happily fly to the BBC in Langham Place for her performances.

'So you're still feeling well?' Now there was no professional motive behind his question: just a friendly concern.

'Perfectly fine. It's not an illness, you know.'

'How's Jubilee? Heard about his posting yet?'

'No. Any day I expect.'

'Lucky chap . . .'

'Oh Ainslie, you aren't going to go off and do something heroic, are you?'

He laughed a little too heartily. 'I doubt if anyone would have me . . . I'm awfully good at stage-rages, but when it comes to a real fight, I'd probably be a handicap.' (This was a rather obvious piece of self-deprecation and Ida did not believe a word of it.) 'Besides, I've been told that this broadcasting thing is really rather crucial. It's a question of morale . . . could be vital.'

Ida felt a little chill of apprehension. She and Ainslie were intimate with smart society circles where knowledge of war plans emanated from high levels. Sylvia Knox's father was in the War Ministry now. Maud French was married to someone 'top brass'. Jubilee's father had been a diplomat and he had various connections in public service. Jubilee protected her from the alarming murmurings of his government contacts because he cared for her peace of mind. Ainslie, a gossip who loved to be in the thick of things, would not be quite so careful.

'That raid on the East End of London. Things could be hotting up soon,' he said. 'But I really mustn't talk on the phone.'

'Well, that's no state secret, Ainslie, everybody knows it's going to get worse sooner or later.'

How horrible it was, to live in this state of tense impotence, almost wanting chaos and bloodshed, an end to the 'Phoney War' that everyone complained about. Ida's baby gave a turn and kick, and a visceral determination filled her. She was very glad to be pregnant. She and Jubilee must survive, Hitler must be destroyed, and her child *must* grow up in a finer world. It simply had to be willed that way.

Jubilee appeared at the door. 'Ready?' he whispered, brandishing one of his father's best bottles from the cellar. Dinner had arrived while she was on the telephone.

'I have to go now Ainslie. I'll be there, I promise.'

'Oh! I forgot to say — Ivor Clarke confirmed,' Ainslie added. 'Cheerio.'

'Wonderful!' Ivor had left the Diplomats to lead Ida's 'combo' at the Au Fait. Ainslie had been trying to reach him for days unsuccessfully because he lived in the East End where some of the very first bombs had been dropped. It was touch and go, this broadcast — a nightmare of arrangements for Ainslie. Trains and buses were subject to frequent alterations; hordes of people were leaving London in fear of invasion now that air raids had reached the city. Funny, how Ainslie treated the war as a particularly trying production problem, such was his single-minded devotion to the world of the theatre.

'Sit down,' said Jubilee, filling her glass. 'Here's to . . .'

'Oh Jubilee! You've heard something! You know when you're to be sent away.'

Jubilee held hands across the table. 'Not now darling. Let's just have supper. Reminds me of old times. Remember? We had dinner from the Papillon the night we got back from our honeymoon.'

'We never did get to Bali.' Ida was suddenly tearful. Due to preparations for the new club, the Au Fait, Ida had not been free for the long eastern trip. They married in Kensington registry office, and went to Paris on the boat train for two weeks. Little did Jubilee know how many ghosts were laid by that wonderfully romantic fortnight.

'Now now! Chin up! Paris was terrific.'

That thought only brought back the present: their beautiful honeymoon city was occupied now by the Nazis. God knows if their little hotel in Montparnasse still stood, or if German troops were billeted in it.

'You'll have to tell me. I can't bear the suspense.'

'Oh, all right. It's next week. I'm going down to Salisbury Plain on Friday for a training course. Hush-hush. Just a week to start with. I've told them the baby's due in September and they've agreed to let me come back for a month. After that I stay there for some serious stuff.'

'That's wonderful!' Ida was incredibly relieved. 'You'll be out of the action for ages yet!'

'Hardly the proper attitude for a soldier's wife, but I can't help agreeing with you. I do love you so Ida.' He stood and came round the table to kiss her.

'Hold me tight.' Ida buried her face in his shirt-front.

'That's another thing will have to go,' he said, beginning to laugh at her. He seemed different tonight, glad to have something settled, light-hearted, not a bit regretful of his choice.

'What has to go?'

'My soft belly. Too many years behind a desk, I'm afraid.'

'I like your body.' Her look added passion to that simple statement. 'And I've had quite enough supper, thank you.'

'Well unlike that other meal from the Papillon, this one had better lead straight to the bed, not the fireside. If you mean what I think you mean. You're in no condition for erotic performances. Come on now, bed.'

'Dear old rug. No one would ever guess how many times we've made love on it. Do you think it would increase its value if we let on?'

'You mean, sell our rug for its aphrodisiac qualities?' Jubilee slid into bed beside her. 'Over my dead body.'

'Good Lord Jubilee, mind your language.' Ida laughed, but like any other wife in England whose husband had received his papers, she clung to him with a fervent wish for his survival more than ever that night.

'Can sex bring on labour, nurse?' she asked, dopey with drugs and lack of sleep. 'We were pretty active before my husband went away. Is that why the baby's early?' This was the time for direct questions and simple answers: in the delivery ward, at night, wondering if there would be an air raid. The nurse who had been rubbing Ida's big belly stopped abruptly when she heard the words. Ida could see that she was shocked that a West End 'personality' could be so frank. No doubt it would be all round the canteen in a few hours, but Ida did not care.

'Stands to reason,' the nurse answered, trying to give a friendly laugh. She recovered her cool by staring at her watch, ready to time the next contraction. 'Though don't you think the bombs had anything to do with it, Miss Garland?'

'Spectacular, wasn't it?'

The day before, September 7th, a large V-shaped formation of planes had been seen heading over London, followed by a smaller similar pattern. Silver dots of aircraft, so high they left puffy white trails behind them, harmless, pretty patterns that dispersed gently in the clear autumnal sky.

But by early evening the whole of London could see a weird, magnificent, astrological phenomenon: a sunset in the east. There was an unearthly glow of such red brilliance that only the sun going down on the wrong side of the world could have been the cause. Then slowly came the realisation that the East End had been firebombed, and the entire area was going up in flames. Later, in the night, came the pounding of the German bombs, guided to their targets in the docks by those beacons of destruction.

'I could read a paper at midnight in Piccadilly,' Ida said. 'It was frightening, but I couldn't help being excited at the same time . . . I do wish Jubilee would come soon . . .' She had telephoned his billet in Salisbury when she felt the first pains, and he was trying to get a train back up to town. 'I'm really Mrs Hargreaves, you know. But please call me Ida.

Where were you?' she asked the nurse, small-talking, trying not to worry.

'On duty here. Now, get ready, here comes another one.'

A stronger contraction began: for a few seconds Ida could actually see her belly harden, before the pain reached a sharp intensity.

'I felt the pavement shudder!' she gasped.

'Nonsense, there's no raid on now!' the nurse sounded sharp. 'Don't panic, Mrs Hargreaves!'

'No! Last night! In Shaftesbury Avenue! I went-for-a-walk-and-a-bomb-fell-near-Charing-Cross . . .'

'That's right, talk and breathe, all the way through.'

The baby began to be born while Ida, breathless and struggling to keep control, gave the nurse an eye-witness account of her first experience of the Blitz. 'A tearing-sound-a-whistle-they-*rush*-down-don't-they? Gravity, pulling, oh, pulling, oh!'

The dangers of the birth process and the menace of the bombings became one to Ida. As each contraction brought its wave of pain and sudden terse order from the nurse, she felt the life and death struggle, physically in her. At times she was confident that her body knew what to do, as if she were a well-trained pilot in a night sky. Her nerves were pitched up, her responses accurate and instinctive. But time wore on and the night grew very long. Sirens sounded outside the hospital. She and the nurse were in a makeshift basement ward, and every now and then the lights flickered. Ida could hear the roar of the hospital generator down the corridor. Jubilee did not come, and her battle to keep up her spirits and her concentration began to fail. Then she heard the urgent instructions of the doctor or the anaesthetist who had just arrived, and it was as if she had lost her bearings, and the enemy, bearing death, was getting the upper hand in the battle.

'It's turned again, goddammit. We may have to operate. Try once more.' They talked as though she were unconscious.

'How's the breathing? How's the pulse, still steady? Keep listening. Watch closely. I don't like the look of this.'

Noises like the rushing of air in a tunnel confused her. Perhaps it was her blood pressure fluctuating, perhaps it was the evil swooshing sound she heard the night before from the bombs, drawn magnetically to the earth as if needing contact, but really only wanting to deal it destruction.

And worst of all, a final crisis, a sense of all cooperation being over. No one could help her now. She was without support, sensing the pressure of imminent delivery. The live thing toiled through her loins, a desperate force determined to be free of her, leaving her torn, bleeding, almost cast aside like a corpse.

Then, within seconds, came a remarkable peace. Ida was regenerated as soon as her baby was laid in her arms. The agony was forgotten, all she could focus on was the pure beauty of her daughter's tiny form, and a sense of great victory at the end of a near-fatal struggle for life.

'Is she all right?'

'Perfect. Look, lots of black hair, and your mouth.' Ida and the nurse studied the baby carefully, as if she was an artefact they had both worked on for a long time.

'She's got white bits all over.' Ida worried.

'It's to protect her skin in the water of the womb. Like a channel swimmer. Because she was a bit early there's not so much.'

'Clever system, isn't it?'

'Birth? Oh yes, that's why I like it.' The nurse looked satisfied, but just then an enormous crash sounded outside.

'Bad tonight,' Ida said, determined to stay calm. 'Her hands are like my husband's.' Ida would have added, 'And her skin is fair,' but in truth, the baby was beetroot red, and blotchy from a difficult breech birth.

'That'll settle down in a day or two. Don't worry. I wonder if she'll be a famous singer like you!' The nurse's tired face broke into a warm smile. She looked like a humanised version of Janet Sheldon, blonde, regular features, usually firm but now enlivened by friendliness. She liked Ida, and was proud to keep her company in these important first moments. Too bad her husband had not arrived . . .

'I'm not famous,' Ida laughed.

'Oh you are! I hear you on the radio, and once for a birthday treat I had cocktails at the Au Fait. One of my patients, her hubby got us in. Pity it had to close . . .'

'That must have been . . .'

'Before the war — let's see, 1938. I was twenty-two then. And you sang "Blue Moon". I love that song.'

Ida smiled. 'When I go back to work you'll have to come and see me again.'

'Be a good girl first — we have to finish this!'

The baby was taken away while Ida was 'tidied up' as the nurse euphemistically put it, and finally left comfortable. After all the stitching and swabbing she revived, euphoria bringing its special gift of energy as a reward for hard labour.

At last! Jubilee was there. He stank of the outside world, his uniform full of smoke and sweat and London's bomb-smell that made her nose prickle: a mixture of cordite and brickdust too strong to be masked by a hospital white tunic.

'Did they show you your daughter?' she asked, and put her arms round his neck for a kiss. Jubilee looked an awful mess from the journey, but his big brown eyes were full of affection and pride.

'Nurse took me for a look just now. She's quite a fan of yours.'

'Did you decide?' she said. They had agreed, if it was a boy, she would choose her favourite name. That was Edward. If it was a girl, then it would be for Jubilee to have the last word.

'Cecilia. I wasn't sure till I saw her, but she looks like a Cecilia. Dear little thing. Besides, her mother will give her music, which will no doubt make her patron saint very happy. You have to help the gods to be good.'

'Oh Jubilee, what a lovely thing to say.'

'I didn't invent it. It's Latin.'

'Yes, but you picked it out for just the right occasion.'

'Trust you to find a way to make me sound clever.' He held her very close, and kissed her fondly.

Gran Garland came to visit the following afternoon. She bought oranges, a rare treat, for citrus fruits had disappeared from the shops. She rummaged in her shopping bag, and placed the precious golden globes on Ida's bedside table.

'George popped home for a cuppa. He bought a big bag of 'em.' She went back to rummaging in her bag. 'That baby's the spitting image of you, God Bless her. Your Pa sends his love, but he had to go to bed for a bit, up all night, he was . . .'

346

'You sound different Gran, look at me, what's up?' Ida said, peering closer.

Gran's face was working with indignation. 'I can't find my hankie, and I haven't undressed for days! Last night I put my teeth in a glass. In the shelter. It's not my fault if I can sleep. You don't travel the length and breadth of England working the halls, then run a boarding-house for thirty years, without learning how to get your hours in. Herr Hitler isn't going to break my habits.'

'Do you mean someone's stolen your false teeth?' Ida laughed.

'Some ruddy bugger's hidden them for a joke. I'll have someone's guts for garters if they don't put 'em back tonight.' Gran retrieved a lace scrap from her handbag and held it to her face to hide her gums, so that she could express herself with dignity.

'Oh Gran!' Ida giggled till tears ran down her cheeks. The drugs she had taken the day before had left her weak and silly.

'You'll see. I won't take over the gramophone, and then they'll all be sorry.'

'Music?' Ida could not believe Gran's cheerfulness.

'Oh yes. When it's really loud we have a sing-song. I run a good, clean, happy shelter. And I tell you something else.'

'What Gran?'

'Earl's doing so well. Goes out from post to post, checking, all round the shelters near our streets, learning everyone's names. Brings down his 'specials', you know the old ones who need a hand, as soon as the wobblers sound — you know, the sirens. And the funny thing is . . .'

'Go on.' Gran might be in her sixties but was clearly not in the category of any warden's 'special'.

Gran leaned nearer. 'Just like with my Joseph. He's *popular*. They think a coloured man brings them good luck. All over London. It's the same. Listen to me Ida.'

'What now Gran.'

'I want you to bring that baby back home. You should be with your own kind.'

'Oh no Gran. I couldn't. I'm glad for Pa, though I think he's crazy to do such dangerous work. He didn't have to.'

'Well. It was only a suggestion.'

'It's Denise. I don't want her interfering with Cecilia.'

'She wouldn't do that — she's never been keen on babies.'

'Yes Gran. I know that.'

Ida's steely expression was shockingly at variance with the bloom of motherhood that lit her face before. Gran gave up, and turned to baby matters, so that Ida would soften and glow once more.

Contrary to Jubilee's hopes, he was not allowed a very long leave. He had only two weeks to be with her. It was obvious that Ida would need someone's help, for the birth had been difficult and she had not recovered her strength. Ida wanted to go home to Albany at once, so that she and Jubilee could be alone with Cecilia as much as possible. Anyone anxious to leave hospital was not held back, for London wards were making ready to look after air-raid casualties. So on the third day she was let out.

'I promise to be good, I have Mrs Higgs, and anyway I'll have to stay in bed with all these stitches,' she said to her nurse.

'That's not going to be easy,' the girl replied shaking her head. 'But do try, Miss Garland? Look after yourself.'

Ida was very emotional, parting from this friendly young admirer who had helped her through the birth.

'I'll send you an invitation for the Au Fait's re-opening,' she whispered, so that Jubilee would not hear and worry before he needed to.

Jubilee managed to find a rare taxi for the journey back to Albany. That afternoon Ida lay close to him on their own bed and the baby nestled between them. While Cecilia dreamed, her little fingers flexed in and out, like a swimmer's in an imaginary sea. Ida and Jubilee watched in fascination.

'Look. Her lips are moving. I bet she's saying something,' Jubilee said.

'Maybe she's singing. My little mermaid.' Ida smiled. For a moment the menacing world was forgotten.

But Jubilee was anxious about arrangements. Mrs Higgs left early to get home on foot before any of Gran's 'wobblers' sounded the warning. When he went back to Salisbury, Ida could not possibly stay in the flat all by herself. The situation was untenable. Since that first attack the German bombers had come back, night after night after night. Not just to the East End: now there was no corner of London that might not be hit. Ida had not seen the Blitz, but Jubilee had on that ghastly journey across town the night that Cecilia was born.

There were fires everywhere, craters in the roads big enough to swallow buses, gap-toothed streets with whole buildings smashed. The fires raged through the day sometimes, because there was simply not enough water to douse them. Firefighters had to tear down buildings, finish off the bomber's half-done work, to make spaces and prevent the spread of flames. Stepney, Poplar, Bermondsey, Southwark, all the friendly-sounding names of old London, lay ravaged as if a giant's boot had trodden on them. And now the nightly bombing raids came nearer, following the line of the river, westwards through Lambeth all the way across to Fulham.

Jubilee dozed, trying to put these scenes of destruction out of his mind. He woke once to see Ida sitting up beside him, feeding the baby. She looked so beautiful and rapt, watching her baby's face and murmuring soft sounds, that he stared without moving. When he went away next time he wanted to be able to recall how she looked, full-breasted, soft-featured, oblivious to all the world. It was inspiring that a woman could do that while a city was being destroyed. It gave him hope.

Ida felt him watching her, but understood that he wanted to do so undisturbed. After a while she sensed Jubilee drift back into sleep. His army training was obviously punishing. Cecilia, being an early baby, did not cry very much; she barely woke to be fed. Ida changed her, then lay down next to Jubilee to rest herself.

They both awoke to the sirens wailing.

'Come on. Down to the cellar.' Jubilee started bundling blankets together, a torch, their coats.

'Oh, must we?' Ida said, turning over and burying her head under the pillow. For a second she had forgotten about her new responsibility.

'Christ! The baby!' She scrambled out of bed, her stitches making her wince, snatched up Cecilia's basket and ran for the door ordering Jubilee about hysterically. 'The nappies! That glucose bottle! The dummies! Where did you put my suitcase when we came in!'

What seemed like hours later, they joined the other tenants going down to the basements, many of whom shuffled arthritically on the stone staircases. There were no families; children had been sent to relatives in the countryside, and their mothers were stalking round London at this minute, probably, barking orders in their upper-class authoritarian accents in civil defence services. Ida knew how intimidating these sort of women would be, how bloody-mindedly brilliantly the majority would do their duties.

The cellar below Albany was quite comfortable, but already full of querulous county ladies and some noxious Mayfair types secure in their 'reserved occupations' of one sort and another. Ida huddled in a corner on a mattress that smelt of mould, hugging her knees and leaning against Jubilee's big shoulder.

'What a way to spend your first leave,' she said.

'Never mind darling. At least we're together. Think what's going on up there.'

Ida could not conceive of it. She peeked at Cecilia, so innocent of all the evil raging above. As she did so, a pinch-faced old woman started to complain loudly:

'Who *is* that woman? I thought this shelter was for residents only. Not riff-raff. Too many of them coming over here, with this wretched war. *Colonials.* Who let her in?'

Ida went dead with anger. Most of her life she was protected from this kind of talk by the circles she moved in. She thought she could handle ignorance, but every time it came at her, the sheer, boring repetition of prejudice diminished her forgiveness.

She lay down next to the baby's basket, fighting back tears. Unaware of her agitation, Jubilee cuddled round her. The shock of the incident sapped Ida's resilience and thankfully, she fell asleep. An hour later, they were both wide awake again, listening to the roar of the anti-aircraft guns in St James's Park, and the dull thudding tremble of the ancient stone buildings in Piccadilly.

'I'm not doing this every night,' Ida whispered, growing claustrophobic, and at her wits' end what to do if Cecilia woke up and cried. 'How can I feed her in here, with all these awful people?'

'I'll come down and rig up a curtain tomorrow,' Jubilee suggested. 'But I think, when I go back to Salisbury, you should move in with Gran Garland.'

'I thought you said it was too close to the ack-ack batteries in Hyde Park.'

'Well, I did think so, but if you won't leave London you must have support. Mrs Higgs can't be relied on, she's got her own kin to think of. I'll worry, darling. Do as I say, just this once.'

'Ma and Pa . . . so close. I don't want to go back.'

'The alternative is to join my mother in the country. Or lodgings near me in Salisbury. You've got to decide.'

Jubilee's mother gave her the horrors. She never went near her, in town or at the country house, preferring not to give Mrs Hargreaves a chance to act out her disapproval. Salisbury was out of the question. Jubilee did not know it yet, but Ida was determined to find work of some sort as soon as she was fit.

'All right. I give in. I'll go to Gran's.'

At least, as Gran said, she would be among her own kind. Perhaps there was some strength to be derived from sticking close together. They could share the nightly vigil, keeping loved ones alive in their thoughts.

On September 17th Jubilee set out for Bayswater, after scouring London for some special food for Ida's supper. He was feeling particularly pleased with himself, for he had located a shop selling bacon, and paid a ransom for a tin of Bartlett's pears that Gran Garland could also eat, with or without her teeth. The lads in her shelter were still up to their tricks . . . It would be a feast. He thought he might say they were a gift from his mother, to make amends for her intransigent attitude to Ida, not softened by war, the Blitz, or the news of Cecilia's birth.

He just reached Lyons Corner House at Marble Arch when the air-raid warnings sounded. A policeman began herding pedestrians into the underground shelter, but Jubilee hurried forward to push on to the boarding-house.

'Let me through, officer. I've got my wife in Salamanca Street, just down Bayswater.'

'You won't make it guv. Sorry, you'll have to step down in here.'

351

It was not the time or place to throw his weight about, thought Jubilee, so he went down the steps, clutching the tinned pears and the bacon and cursing the Luftwaffe for arriving earlier than usual that day.

Ida sat tensely in the dark of Gran's parlour. She could not be bothered to light a candle. It was not just Jubilee's delay and the accumulating torture of the air raids that affected her nerves. Her mother Denise was snivelling, laid out on a sofa.

Usually, when Earl left the little back house on his rounds to check the black-out, Denise went straight to the shelter and bagged a good spot early for the night. But today she claimed her back had 'suddenly come on again', and she had limped round on Earl's arm to Gran's parlour for tea, in spite of an unsympathetic audience.

Denise had been laid out like some Eastern houri. She barely glanced at Cecilia, as usual. 'You're not feeding her yourself are you?' she accused Ida, shocked. 'It will ruin your figure.'

'The nurse recommended it.' Ida rose hurriedly from the rocking chair to finish nursing Cecilia in privacy. There were no lodgers, only the uncles and Gran at the boarding-house these days, and she had grown used to sitting in the afternoon sun in the parlour, cuddling her baby and listening to Uncle Billy's old blues records. But if Denise was going to amuse herself by playing games, she would rather be elsewhere.

'Too much handling is bad for a baby,' Denise's peevish words pursued Ida as she went upstairs. She decided to hide out in Ted's bedroom until Jubilee returned from the shops. He would provide some sort of buffer. Denise toned down when her smart son-in-law was around.

But Jubilee did not come. Gran took the baby to the shelter. Ida would not budge till her husband came, and Denise made out she was incapable of walking so far. So now the two of them were locked in a war of nerves in the dark, Denise prone, helpless and snivelling, Ida mechanically rocking, willing Jubilee to turn up.

What seemed hours later, Earl came by on his rounds, to check on Gran. He let himself in through the scullery at the back and felt his way along the pitch-black hall past the parlour. He intended to let himself out through the front door once he was sure the family had all gone to the shelter across the street. Denise's whimpering stopped him in his tracks.

'My God what are you lot doing here? Get across the road!' he snapped at his wife and daughter.

His bossiness infuriated Ida, driven to breaking point by her Ma's noise. 'No!' she screamed. 'I'm waiting till Jubilee turns up, and Ma won't move 'cos of her stupid back! Gran's taken the baby, but I'm staying put!' The sickly smell of fear and sweat in the shelter revolted her. The ratcheting coughs, the spitting and the slop-bucket . . . Too many nights of that . . . and now Jubilee had got caught up on his way home.

Just then they heard an almighty shudder somewhere near. The three of them listened intently to the sounds of the batteries in Hyde Park trying vainly to smash the bombers as they veered upwards after dropping their load.

'That was too close,' Earl said, his voice suddenly low and flat with real urgency. 'Get up Denise,' he hissed.

'I can't! I'm in agony,' she whined.

'Get up you bitch!' he roared. 'I've got five sick old grannies need my help this minute and I'm not putting up with your fucking nonsense any longer! Get up before I tan your hide!'

It was lucky the room was dark. In the midst of her anxiety about Jubilee Ida could not help stretching her arms wide, unseen, and a big shout of joy almost broke from her lips. She threw back her head and covered her ears, trying to make do with a silent scream. But the temptation was too strong. Her hands dropped. She could not see Denise's humiliation, but she could listen to it. Denise whimpered just once before Earl grabbed hold of her. He slapped her face really hard. Ida could hear the snap of muscles in her Ma's neck and the baubles on her ears ricocheting off the floorboards. Ida flattened herself against a wall while Earl dragged Denise, screaming, to her feet.

'March! Goddamn you! I'll kill you if you don't!'

Ida did not want to leave with them, but she had to see with her own eyes Gran's reaction when Denise reached the shelter on her own two feet. Ida left the door of the boarding-house open wide and groped her way to the shelter, guided by the tiny blue spot of Earl's black-out torch, a mere slit of light, pointing at Denise's wobbling heels.

Gran was winding up the gramophone and had a few youngsters gathered round her knees. They watched while she mimed crudities to the music, an old comedy number, the scratched record more hiss than words: 'The Bird on Nellie's Hat'. Gran took one look at Denise's tearful face as she stumbled in, then smiled, the mirthless grimace she reserved for people she loathed. The force of her dislike was dramatically enhanced by the reinstatement of her teeth: shiny-white, and very savage.

> 'Well 'e don't know Nellie like I do
> Said the saucy little bird on Nellie's hat . . .'

In the morning, Ida found out what had happened. The raid had flattened a section of Oxford Street and the John Lewis store had been gutted. People caught unawares in Oxford Street and the top of Park Lane were herded down into the Marble Arch underground station. The impossible occurred: the nose-cap of a bomb got through the girders of the roof and exploded. Some were found dead, not a sign of blood or a mark upon them, but their bodies stripped naked by the blast. Others were killed by flying tiles, deadly shafts torn off the walls by the force of the explosion. Jubilee was one of the first to be identified, because he was wearing a wedding ring engraved with his and Ida's names.

Amongst the many friends who telephoned was Felix Summers.

'Felix!' Ida whispered. 'I can't . . .'

'Can I do anything? Can I help you?'

'The funeral . . .' She cried hopelessly down the telephone. There was a long silence.

'Ida . . . try to think how Jubilee would want you to be brave. You've got the baby . . .'

'He wanted to be a father! He was so happy!' Ida wept.

'Look, old girl. I'm not one for coping with this sort of thing. Dammit, none of us are, and all of us will have to. He was my best friend too, you know. My best friend. A bloody good man.'

354

Ida just stood holding the phone tight, feeling her tears running down her fist, streaking the black thing in her hand.

'Look,' Felix was clipped, trying to bring order to the situation. 'I'll handle the funeral. Have you spoken to his mother yet?'

'No. Gran did. After the police came. It's difficult, phoning the country.'

Felix was appalled by her lack of proper responses. There were certain formal duties that not even a war should prevent someone from observing. Ida knew that Jubilee would have been shocked too, and it only made her sob out loud.

'You must try! You know he left you everything — the house in the country, enough money to be comfortable? And he secured the lease on his mother's flat. Mrs Hargreaves is well provided for. You should be able to comfort her with that.'

'Oh! No!' Ida began to shake her head violently, not wanting to hear these details.

'I was his solicitor, so I know. I'm telling you this entirely off the record, Ida, because I want you to understand: Jubilee worked hard to leave his family well set up. Don't let him down and give in. It's not on.'

His indignation almost made her smile. Felix had succeeded in sounding terribly British, and she was behaving like some over-emotional foreigner. 'I wish I could talk to Veronica.' Ida stumbled over her words. 'I rang the flat. Where is she? She's all right, isn't she?' she asked, plaintively.

'You haven't heard? They've taken my father. He's an alien you know, born in Austria, came here when he was five. He'll be interned for the duration. There's no hope of getting him out. Veronica's gone to the Isle of Man where they've put him and mother in some sort of camp.'

Through her misery, Ida felt a welling up of sympathy, and stopped crying, surprised. 'But he's mad about absolutely everything English! He's no threat!'

Felix laughed sharply. 'I imagine they think thirty thousand people will just have to suffer, on the off chance one of them turns out to be a real spy.'

Ida took a deep breath, gripped the phone harder, trying to focus on other people's tragedies. Felix, now caught up in his own difficulties, was still explaining: 'I'll manage his finances, and meanwhile Veronica and I are getting involved in a few of his — philanthropic enterprises.'

Ida dimly remembered her last meeting with Veronica. The war had transformed her; she never did anything by halves. The social whirl was over, the gallery interest abandoned, the toying with drugs a thing of the past. She worked for a Jewish relief agency and had obviously roped her brother in. Felix's legal background would be invaluable to the refugees.

'Ida? Are you still there?'

'What? Yes Felix. I was just thinking . . .'

'Bad habit at the moment. Take things one at a time. Sorry, I shouldn't have mentioned it, all that stuff about my father. Look, can I call round in the morning?'

'No. I'll meet you at your office,' Ida said firmly.

'Good girl. That's the ticket. We'll discuss everything then. And Ida, one last word . . .'

'Yes?'

'Ring his mother. Please.'

She was afraid to do it, obscurely terrified that Mrs Hargreaves would say it was all her fault. If she had not married; if she had not followed her own selfish inclinations, staying up in London; if she had been a proper person, none of this would have happened.

While Felix's disapproval was still sufficiently strong in her mind to make her do it, Ida got the operator to put through a trunk call to the post office in the village near the Hargreaveses' house. She left a request with the local postmistress, to walk up to the house and ask Mrs Hargreaves to put in a call to her, when she could manage to get down to the village. Several hours passed before the reply came.

'Hallo?' A wavering yet indomitable voice enquired.

'Mrs Hargreaves? Felicity?' This took courage.

'Yes?' Not a hint of recognition.

'It's Ida. Are you all right? Would you like me to come down and visit you?'

'No thank you. I'm perfectly fine. I've got a good friend from the village with me.'

'Can I do anything for you?'

'I'm sure you've got your hands full with — dear me, I'm

sorry I've forgotten your baby's name. It's my memory . . .' Her cool, perfectly enunciated words cracked, in a way that was only just audible, like the sound of ice-cubes splitting in a cocktail.

'Cecilia.' Ida could suddenly hear Jubilee's voice murmuring it, and the heart went out of her.

'Cecilia. Cecilia. Jubilee did tell me. Poor little thing. There'll be a lot of fatherless children before we're through. Now listen. I expect you'll want this house, now it's yours, so that you can be safe with . . . your baby. Jubilee confided all his plans in me, you see. So I'm coming right back up to London. I know all about the Blitz, but quite honestly, I'd rather be in my own little place. I like London. Especially now that . . . Well. I'll see you at the funeral. That charming young man, Felix Summers, isn't it? He will see you through the details. I don't suppose it's very easy for him, either. With his background, poor thing.'

'You don't have to move out. I haven't made any plans — especially not about the house . . .'

'Oh, but I want to! It's the proper thing to do.'

'Well do call me if you . . .'

'Of course I will. Goodbye, Ida. It was very kind of you to ring.'

That was the last time Ida spoke to Jubilee's mother. The funeral took place a few days later, a quick, sombre affair attended by few of Jubilee's many friends because most men were away at the war, and the women working. Ida was ill with a high temperature and could not attend. She stayed in bed, blotting out the sadness of the day with sedatives and sleep. All Gran could do was hold the baby up so that Ida could still feed her.

One night, a month later, Ida heard that Mrs Hargreaves suffered a stroke when bombs fell dangerously close to her London flat. She died sitting in an armchair, clutching her dog, who stayed mute on her lap until the policemen found them together in the morning. Animals were not allowed in air-raid shelters, and Mrs Hargreaves would not be parted from her pet.

Ida was prostrated by losing Jubilee. He had been her best friend, as much as her lover; someone who consistently saw the best in her, encouraged her, and loved her for what she was, not for what she might become. Perhaps because he was a shy man, his admiration for her gift of communication in singing was always strong.

That was how he understood her nerves, Ida recalled. She cried to think what he had endured at her hands in those tense times before performances. When she was very nervous, she would have to work herself *down* to be able to sing well. If she felt too tired, too blasé or too flat, she would have to summon *up* strange energies, secret imaginings, to get her act to work. Jubilee used to know instinctively how she felt, would watch the transformation take place in her with no resentment that she was slipping from his grasp. Because he knew that at the end of it, what she most wanted was someone to be kind to her, be there for her, in a shared home. Which he was without fuss, just with friendliness, every night. And when she came back late, at dawn, and he was fast asleep, he seldom complained. He never once asked ugly questions about her affair with Ray. She had made her choice, so he let the past drop. His trust had made her good; after that, she had never been unfaithful to him again.

She had been so selfish! Ida sobbed, filled with an aching guilt to think how devoted Jubilee had been, listening to the endless sagas of stage revues, rehearsals, first nights, poor orchestras, sick accompanists, and the like. He took her to art galleries, to suggest ideas for her sketches; he put magazines under her nose, or left them by her make-up table at the club, with the page turned down, and an exclamation mark by the relevant joke.

Some people might have found his gestures too deliberate, but Ida had given in to love so late that she found his efforts very reassuring. Tears filled her eyes, remembering the way he always asked (trying to sound innocent) what she would be wearing. She knew there would be flowers then, because he liked to be sure that his token would match her clothes . . . Little marks of kindness that she had accepted without valuing them enough.

What pained her most was that they had just created a life together. Cecilia. This joy might have repaid Jubilee for all the patient loving he had given her. Now there would never be a family life. She had not told him all of these hopes, her wishes for that future, all *her* love for *him*.

358

Most of the time now she stayed in bed in Ted's old room at the boarding-house, alone with her regrets. This was the bed that Jack had often slept in, dreaming of being big and strong, and running away from his loveless life. No running now; he was under orders. He did not know Cecilia was born, or that Jubilee was dead. This was no time for love or hope, just for fighting back, dying, or grimly resisting. Even this last was more than she could do.

She curled up in the bed, nursing only her misery, shivering with cold in spite of many blankets. There were no windows left in the house, of course; bomb blasts had torn them out, and the floors of the upstairs rooms were coated with brickdust and glass. The holes were boarded, and only the middles of rooms were swept. It was pointless to waste energy cleaning up more than was necessary. The place could be reduced to rubble any night, and even as it remained standing, it got a new layer of brickdust, soot and black ash flakes again every time a bomb fell nearby.

During the day, Cecilia slept safe and sound down below in Gran's snuggy, but Ida wanted to be alone, away from the cosy cheerfulness of Gran's crisis routines. Neighbours who had previously kept themselves to themselves called in constantly for tea to share the endless chit-chat of the Bayswater 'services'. Air-raid wardens, ambulance-drivers, firewatchers, the heavy rescue service men who dug out the buried, stretcher parties — they all found their way to the Garland scullery and discussed the past night's 'incidents', as the locals termed a direct hit.

The nights were the worst times. As weeks went by, fewer people bothered going to the shelters, and the wardens gave up the struggle to force everyone to do so. They had their work cut out dealing with fire and bomb reports, and coping with the incendiaries that fell on their patches. Sandbags and stirrup-pumps were usually enough to quench the metallic tubes, pouring out a stream of brilliant flame and sparks, threatening to set aflame anything within a few yards' radius.

On a night in December, Ida got out of bed, and pulled out the cardboard blocking the bedroom window. It was the night of a full moon: something all Londoners had come to dread, for it gave the Germans their best chance of maximum damage. She shuddered with cold, watching the weaving patterns of the searchlights high over Hyde Park.

Her beautiful night city was being blown to bits. The Silver Cinema, the home of so many of her childhood dreams, had gone. So had most of Little Wapping, that evocation of a past century, down by the river in Hammersmith, where she and Jack ate face-smothering ice-creams. Martin Fernie's house on the hill in Putney would no more sail into the orgies of the night. Bombed flat. The dock area, in Tilbury, was hammered night after night. And the exclusive Glass Slipper had been turned into a shelter for bombed-out Soho residents. Mrs Cavendish would be appalled.

That was not the cruellest irony. The Baker Street Rooms, where she had once sung but never would again . . . She had memorised the item in a newspaper: *Amongst casualties in the early evening raid were the composer Harvey Johns and his leading soprano for Friday's concert, Miss Janet Sheldon. They were rehearsing with full orchestra, when the Baker Street Room received a direct hit. Mr Johns, a distinguished composer of modern songs, leaves no close relatives . . . Miss Sheldon, who had made a speciality of interpreting her tutor's works, is survived by her mother. Enquiries re casualties Welbeck 4126.* Not time, now for love, or hope, but perhaps for some pity. Who had any heart for personal enmity now?

The orange glow of fires was intense — Ida judged the night's raid to be as close as the Fleet Street and St Paul's area. The anti-aircraft blast from the batteries in the park shot up like giant fireworks, great arcs of light in the cloud-laden sky. Shrapnel from these guns fell back lethally on the pavements, as much a threat to life as the bombs. And all the time, the dull, pitiless droning of the aerial attack.

It was impossible to sleep, but she had to rest or she would have no milk to feed her child. Ida went back to bed, leaving the window bare. In spite of its menace, there was something eerily beautiful about a London sky in a raid.

Ida dragged herself through the early months of 1941, alternating between despair and anger at losing Jubilee. She lost all will to be causative. Only an animal instinct stopped her from killing herself: Cecilia must survive. Her friends telephoned, but Ida refused to speak to them, becoming immured in this one task, to the exclusion of any other reality.

In the boarding-house she returned to that status of spectator that she had grown up with. Watching the dramas of the Garland family, and more or less ignored.

Denise was so determined to spite Earl for his one act of defiance, that she got herself a job as receptionist in a hotel in Knightsbridge. Revenge was more important than the Blitz; the pains in her back miraculously never reappeared. The place was a billet for Canadian volunteers. Denise was a faded, but still accomplished flirt; she had her fill of handsome men to comfort, and when they wanted prettier, younger attractions, she was not averse to procuring for them. That way she got booze, black-market; extra clothing coupons, and specially rare, troublingly missing items, like stockings, knicker elastic, lipstick, and 'Bourjois' perfume.

'Honestly, they're so *gallant!*' she cooed at Ida, expecting her to be happy about the news. 'There's one who puts a red rose on my signing-in book, *every* Friday night . . .' Earl struggled with the news, trying not to let Denise demoralise him. Ida did not care any more. She was numb with grief, deaf to her Ma's verbal tricks.

Earl kept out of the way more and more. Sometimes he called in on the boarding-house, and stooped awkwardly over his grandchild, as if to say, 'another time, another place, I could love you sweetie'; but in general, he stayed in his uniform for two or three days at a stretch, snatched a snooze on his bed, then immersed himself once more in duties.

Uncle Billy developed a very strange expertise. He was known throughout the neighbourhood as a good 'sniffer'. Uncle Billy could smell blood. He could look at a pile of rubble and tell if the body trapped beneath it was alive or dead. This knack was immensely valuable to the Heavy Rescue Units and was discussed with detailed relish by the dears and ducks in Gran's scullery. 'Honest, I 'eard 'im! He stands right next to this Red Cross feller, shovelling away like a bleedin' lunatic, and he says, he says with his four eyes all hanging out like chapel hat-pegs: "It's no use you doing that. It's stopped running. The blood's congealing. She's dead." Fair turned my stomach . . .' Ida would start shivering involuntarily, feeling herself slipping further from self-control, further from reality.

'Have another cuppa,' Gran would suggest at the vital moment before the conversation sagged into morbidity. Hands spread on thighs, she would offer a gem of knowledge to her callers. 'They've got offal today at the butcher's in Queen's Road. Ration Books A to M. You lot haven't missed it, have you?'

Then Josephine turned up. Her neat house in Shepherd's Bush had been razed to the ground. The couple had not much more than the clothes they stood up in; one wardrobe full of Ottley's suits, plastered red with brickdust, and a trunk full of Josephine's sheet music, that resisted a ton of rubble and had been dug out of the ruins.

'I *was* going to bring my tea cosy,' Josephine added. 'I saw it, right there, just under this broken window. The frame fell in on the tea things — because Sidney of course never washes up before he goes to work. Next thing, I look, and some thieving blighter's nicked it from under my very nose.'

Earl got Josephine bookings with ramshackle ENSA shows, touring round the troop camps. In between, she and Ottley worked in a servicemen's club in the Tottenham Court Road. Ottley was unfit for any form of useful service beyond entertaining the forces in his own dubious way. But the couple were drawn closer together by the needs of the moment. Josephine roared songs, and Ottley got the lads into card games. Needless to say a lot of long-saved soldiers' pay ended up in Sidney's soft hands.

Josephine and Ottley needed Ted's double bedroom. Ida moved without protest into a smaller attic upstairs. They slept in the mornings, when the worst of the cleaning had to be done. They squabbled cheerfully through lunch, which of course Gran laid on for them, surrounded by assorted neighbours. Josephine and Sidney went to work in the city just as dusk fell, and the raids began.

It was after they came that things grew intolerable for Ida. It was bad enough, no one mentioning Jubilee, as if not speaking did away with grief. But no one mentioned Jack either, least of all Josephine and Ottley. Their attitude was, he was still 'skiving'. 'Well looked after, the British Army, while it's us at home take the brunt of the Nazis.' Their self-involvement, self-importance appalled Ida. The essence of her life had been always to doubt, and to reach out to others. No more.

Over lunch one day, Josephine related the bombing of the Café de Paris, where the most popular West Indian band-leader, Snake Hips Johnson and several of his band, had been killed.

'Broadcasting live to the West Indies, they were,' she said, 'sending wishes home. Tragic, when they were trying to show how the workers who'd come over here were bearing up under it all . . .'

Ida passed Cecilia to Gran and mechanically started piling up the dishes. 'Those musicians. Snake Hips. What a dreadful blow for the West Indians. The band was a symbol . . .'

Ida's words were a reminder of difficult differences that neither Ottley nor Josephine entered into. They glanced at each other. Why did Ida have to be so 'significant' all the time? Just when they were getting over their own bomb, enjoying the boarding-house atmosphere again, just like the old days . . . This seemed to serve as Josephine's excuse to attack Ida.

'Look, why don't you get a job somewhere? I mean, we could do a few little sing-songs together, put ourselves on the lists for ENSA together. I'll play for you, if you like, dearie. If it's your family you wouldn't be embarrassed would you?'

'It's kind of you to offer, Aunt Josephine. I don't even know if I have a voice any more. I'm tired, and I don't think I can sing.'

'Oh, come off it,' Josephine said in curt tones. 'I just don't like to see you moping about the place like this. We've all got to soldier on. Do our bit.' For some unaccountable reason, this fairly positive remark broke the floodgates of Ida's long-suppressed anger.

Ida started quietly, but her voice gradually rose to a pitch of hysteria. 'I don't want to soldier on. I don't want Jubilee to be dead. I don't want any more bombs. I hate this war! Gran's been in the same clothes for two weeks now, we didn't have water for days last week, now you and Ottley are here saying stupid things all the time, and I want to get OUT!'

363

She slammed the door and ran up to her room. She meant it: living at close quarters with the Garlands was driving her into a total breakdown. She was sucked back into feeling she was on the edge of a stage, where a mad play was being enacted.

After a while, she started packing. She would take Cecilia out of London, down to Jubilee's house in Kent. They'd be safe, away from the Blitz, away from all this vulgar stoicism, and she could think about Jubilee with no one trying to distract her. Every day, think about missing Jubilee, and who knows, sleep through a night without bombs.

She heard Gran plod up the stairs and enter her room without knocking.

'What's this? Packing?'

'What does it look like!' she retaliated, aware she was behaving badly but unable to control herself. 'I've got to get away.'

'You'll go to Jubilee's place? The country?' Gran was almost disbelieving. 'Away from home?'

Ida regretted her rudeness. 'Oh Gran. Why don't you come with me? It would be much safer . . .'

'I'm marshal of the shelter!'

'I'll only go for a bit . . . Oh dear. I know you'll miss the baby.' Ida sat down, indecisive.

'I don't want you here in this state. And there's no denying it's no place for the little mite. But speak to your Pa. Do that for me, Ida. I'll send him up when he comes round for his tea.'

'What do you take me for! I wouldn't go without saying goodbye!' Ida flared up again unjustifiably.

Gran sighed heavily and rumbled out of the room. Ida swore, and went back to her packing.

Earl appeared later, for once freshly bathed and in a well-brushed uniform. Just like his old self.

'Hallo Pa. You got a break today then?'

He nodded, and sat awkwardly on the edge of the bed.

'I've had a word with Gran. She says you're leaving us.'

'Yes. For Hartmere.' She only mentioned the house — she did not trust herself to say Jubilee's name aloud, in case she started to cry again.

'Safer there. I suppose you don't want me to come down with you?'

Ida was astonished. 'Oh no! I'll manage!'

There was a silence. 'I wish I could get Gran to go with you, but she won't,' he said. 'The old-timers, they're all like that. "This is my home!" they say. Even when they're bombed out they only move round the corner.'

Tears ran down Ida's cheeks, involuntarily. 'I can't stay here. I don't belong any more. I can't stay in Albany either. Pa, will you do something for me?'

'Anything.' Earl looked embarrassed and wary.

'Here's the keys to our flat. Piccadilly. Get — the suits sent to the Red Cross. And the blankets. Anything useful. There's supplies there too. Put them in a box for Gran.'

Earl was troubled. 'But you'll be back won't you? You might need the place then.'

'No!' Ida was vehement. 'It was his. Then it became — *ours*. I couldn't bear it.'

'Look Ida.' Earl stood up, nervously fingering his helmet strap. He contrived to look dapper even if a little suspect in a uniform. 'There'll always be a home here. Whatever happens.'

She laughed bitterly, with a note of hysteria. 'Until the bombs blow it apart!'

'I don't mean bricks and mortar,' Earl said, driven to be precise and knowing this could be his last chance. 'I mean me. With me. Whatever happens I'm here. I'm not up to much, but I am still your father.'

In the midst of wretchedness Ida was uplifted. 'Yes Pa.' Just for a moment Ida was his adoring daughter again. She kissed his cheek, and he nodded, trying not to be embarrassed by what he had said. 'Look after yourself,' she added. Forgiveness came easily when one was demoralised.

It was the middle of a war. She had nothing to lose in acknowledging there was a real link; that in spite of everything she still loved her Pa.

16

Kent, ironically, was not a bit quieter than London, for the aerial dog-fights along the coast could be plainly seen from Ida's windows. But by the end of 1942, the raids became less centralised: the London Blitz came to an end and instead came hit and run attacks, scattered all over England. For long periods, Ida heard no bombs, and the silence in the wide sky over flat fields lost its ominous echo.

Not at all as she expected, she grew to love Hartmere, a place she had never wanted to visit before the war. In olden times it had been a priory; a tower over a moat lay in picturesque ruins, and in the grounds was a fine Tudor barn, impressive bare of thatch. Once there had been a cloister; a few pillar stumps could be seen in the grass. The only remaining stone wing had been rebuilt in Tudor times by a yeoman farmer, and ever since then had been the home of various local families. The Hargreaves people had owned the place since Victorian days and Jubilee's grandfather had restored a small chapel, adding some violently-coloured stained-glass windows.

Ida had never been so quiet in her whole life. Not lonely; she had Cecilia to care for, and a number of old people from the village nearby came in most days to work on the vegetables in the front garden, supplies for the airfields nearby. If she needed help or company, she could have turned to them; but she had Jubilee to think of, so she did not.

Ida spent most of her first weeks at Hartmere sleeping, feeding Cecilia, and recovering her strength. Surprisingly quickly, the horrors of London in the Blitz receded, and she began to poke about, in a shuffling, sad fashion. Jubilee's mother had retreated to the house only for a short time when the war started and people fled from London in a panic, fearing gas attacks. Mrs Hargreaves had never liked Hartmere, and had abandoned it for London, obviously not caring if a stray bomb blew up the entire place. I suppose, thought Ida, she did not think there was any one much to save it for, with Jubilee dead.

Ida's first feeble effort was to crate up the odd beautiful thing left lying about. She knew Jubilee would expect her to do that, and she liked to do tasks that connected her to him. There was a pair of Chinese vases; a couple of pieces of fragile lacquer furniture; lots of valuable, leather-bound old books that were his father's. More rugs of the sort they had in Albany. Eyes blurry with tears, Ida rolled these up and took them down into the cellars, a widespread network of cool tunnels dating from the days of the monks. All this work exhausted her. She decided to close off the upper floor of the house — it was almost uninhabitable, with leaks in all the ceilings — and live in the kitchen and the adjoining living-room, easier to keep warm at night for Cecilia. She was content to live in a small space; she did not have the energy to do more than camp out. She did not need to bring down a bed: there was a huge, battered leather sofa that would do perfectly well for her. She fixed up a sturdy crib in a large drawer taken from a chest, and lined it with newspaper then blankets. This she placed close to the sofa, with an old screen on the other side to keep off draughts and protect Cecilia from a sudden drop in temperature in the small hours.

Night-times were the worst times. Alone, without Gran as moral support, Ida was prey to fears for her baby. The house was utterly silent; not only no bombs, but no traffic, no voices floating up from any street. Only the creaking of old trees, the shriek of a bird, or the scratching of unpruned bushes at the windowpanes.

At times she would lean forward, holding her breath, desperate to hear a small expulsion of air from the sleeping baby. Nearly every night she was so scared that she would strike one of her precious short-supply matches, just to watch Cecilia's little breast rise and fall rhythmically. Then crying with mingled relief for Cecilia's existence and pity for her fatherless state, Ida would fold herself into the rugs on the sofa, and try to sleep. Mostly she planned how to get through the next day.

There was a full-size grand piano in the room: Ida decided that if there was ever a bombing raid, she could crawl under there with the baby. If the oak beams above that gave way, then God meant for them to be killed.

In the mornings, she filled the kitchen range with wood, creating clouds of smoke, boiled Cecilia's clothes in a copper on top of it, and hung nappies, night-gowns and vests in a greying, steaming line over the heat.

Hartmere began to take on austerity. She swept the bare stone floors and boarded up the windows to protect the mullioned glass. A damp, bone-penetrating cold swept under the ill-fitting, heavy doors. Ida stuffed more newspaper or old clothes from cupboards upstairs into the cracks. The atmosphere reminded her of the life that had gone on centuries before in Hartmere, when the priests from France first came to the place, ran a hospital for the poor, kept pigeons to eat in the lean winter months, and stored grain for their bread. She thought of their snug stone cells in the original cloisters, while the wind roared through the empty upstairs rooms, and rain tip-tapped into strategically-placed buckets on the oak staircase. Hartmere might be financially secure, but Jubilee had never had time to set about major repairs, and now it was too late.

There were lean times everywhere. Food was rationed even in the country. Ida's diet consisted largely of potatoes from the store, turnips, powdered egg, and an occasional chop purchased with her coupons from the one and only village shop-cum-post office.

But there was the old piano. It was out of tune, not that Ida cared, and she spent a lot of time when Cecilia took her naps, plonking on it and thinking of other times.

There was also the wine cellar. She knew nothing about wines — Jubilee did all that — but judged that the most recent the date, the least damage she could do. Trying to be good, she restricted herself to drinking only from five o'clock onwards. A bottle or two a night was very comforting, especially on a not very full stomach.

Cecilia thrived. During the day she provided a good way to get through the hallos and goodbyes with the village people, none of whom had an inkling of Ida's past life and found her a strange choice of wife for their local young squire, Jubilee Hargreaves. Ida's hair grew wild in a big bush; her face puffy from too much sleep (or too much wine and potatoes), and from lack of company. Her features became puddingy and unresponsive as she withdrew into herself.

'That mite's the spitting image of her Dad,' said Mrs Weekes, the rubicund postmistress, leaning in at the kitchen door one day, determined to check on them. 'Terrible, never knowing your own father. Such a nice man, Mr Hargreaves. I knew him from a lad. Fancy getting cut down in the prime of life, and not even in the fight. Now his mother, old Mrs Hargreaves, was a different kettle of fish. I was never very much taken with her. But still a tragedy. Your whole family going like that.'

Funny, Ida thought, how this business of resemblances depended on family loyalties. To Mrs Weekes, Cecilia was all-white, a true Hargreaves.

'She's got his eyes. My mouth,' she offered grudgingly.

'Yes, but you'd never *know* . . .'

Mrs Weekes, bless her soul, was only trying to be friendly. Ida noted that she could endure this woman's litany of woes, meant to be sympathy, without breaking down. That meant she was getting used to the fact of Jubilee's death and she did not want that to happen. She wanted to be able to cry at will, because that kept her in contact with him. To recover from the loss was the last thing she hoped to do.

'You've got a nice lot of mail today,' Mrs Weekes persisted, handing over the letters. 'Why don't you ask some of your London friends down for a weekend? If they bring their coupons with them, you could get in quite a lot of food. If you don't mind me saying so, Mrs Hargreaves, you're looking a bit peaky.'

'I'm fine. I haven't had the time to dress yet this morning, that's all. Cecilia gets me up rather early.'

'Sure there's nothing I can get you from the village? It's not right, you being in this big old house all by yourself. There's burglars — raiders — deserters. Aren't you scared?'

'No.' Ida shrugged. 'I'm cosy. This is Jubilee's home.'

'I could ask Mrs Terry to call round,' Mrs Weekes persisted. 'They have a Mothers' Union in the church hall on Mondays. Coffee and a chat. Do you good.'

Ida managed to laugh. 'Coffee! Dandelion roots and chicory. No thanks. I'm perfectly fine Mrs Weekes — and if the vicar calls, I'll know who sent him. I'm not a believer, you may as well know now.' Aggressively, Ida lit one of old Mrs Hargreaves' cigarettes, left above the kitchen range with the matchbox. She nearly choked on it, but wanted to create a suitably depraved, citified image.

'Well! Suit yourself!'

Mrs Weekes pushed away her black bike, the noise of its whirring chain muffled by the long grasses caught against it in the back lane. None of the letters was a brown, official thing, or an unavoidable instruction from Felix. Ida recognised Ainslie Curtis' handwriting on an envelope — not the first he had sent her. She hesitated, then tore it in half. She kept only one letter from Gran, a lifeline with her family, but threw the rest into the kitchen range, and went back to the sofa for another long nap.

Her second spring at Hartmere came, and with it more pleasures to explore with Cecilia. The baby could waddle about now, so in the mornings Ida spread a mouldy blanket and set her toys out on the grass verge outside the kitchen door: a cocoa tin, a box of cotton reels, some knitted soft toys Gran sent down at Christmas. Ida sat behind her, keeping watch from the kitchen step, propping herself against the doorway and sipping tea. Cecilia would wave her arms at anything that moved, cows in the lane, an insect buzzing by, a clump of a bush stirring in a breeze. Her silky brown curls caught the sunlight, flecks of gold, just right for someone precious. When the breeze lifted wisps of her hair, Ida could still see soft pink skin underneath, the crowning dome of her brain. Such a thin skull, babies had, such palpitating, thinking life in a wobbly little globe. Now Cecilia could hold herself quite straight. It made Ida's heart tighten in an ache, imagining all the worries that would crowd into that dignified, small head as Cecilia grew up.

Ida preferred this quiet spot where an old forsythia was in full bloom, and cast-out hyacinths, no doubt planted by some servant a few years back, grew crookedly in a small patch of earth by the dogs' old, empty kennels. If she sat round at the front of the house she would be in full view of the old folk planting out vegetable seeds, and she did not want to attract conversation. Besides, it was only a step inside to fetch a cardigan, or a cup of orange for Cecilia, or to see to any other small errand that watching a young child involved.

One day, when she heard the sound of the car wheels on the

front drive, she guessed who was to blame. Mrs Weekes had been busybodying, informing on her, probably sent the 'District' round to check on her progress with her baby. Ida had already seen in London how the war had led to a general increase in interfering 'services'; your life was not your own, and mothers with small offspring were badgered with advice about diet, clothing, inoculations and the like. People were always meddling.

But this was not a Morris Minor Traveller, the beaten-up wood trimmed car belonging to the local health visitor. Anyone local would know to come up the back lane beside the kitchen. No, it was a resplendent convertible with Ainslie Curtis at the wheel, Veronica by his side, and another couple, small dark people, low in the back seat. In spite of her comfortable gloom, Ida felt her spirits rise at the sight of two such familiar faces, and she struggled to her feet to welcome them. Of course they *would* sweep up the gravel path to the front door when she had nailed it up in the winter (using a lethal sledge-hammer more suitable for stone-breaking).

There was no time to find her shoes; luckily she had on a pair of thick socks, the sort Jubilee's father wore to go out shooting. She hurried on padded feet round the corner of the old house, with the baby balanced on one hip. Cecilia unfortunately spilt her drink down her shoulder as she was bounced along, leaving a bright stain on the front of her blouse. Ida shifted Cecilia a little so that she could pull her cardigan over the damp patch. 'Hallo. If you want to come in you have to come round the back. That door's blocked off.'

'Good God! Ida!' Veronica was appalled. 'What have you been up to?'

Ida was irritated by this utterly urban preoccupation with appearances. But then, it was over a year since they had met. No, a year and a half. OK, so she had put on weight, which was why her skirt was done up with a nappy pin. Her hair, come to think of it, was a bit of a bird's nest. She had cut it a few times with kitchen scissors, but the last time must have been before Christmas. Jubilee's cardigan was not exactly fashionable, but long and warm, and she had never washed it because it smelled of his favourite tobacco. With a baby it was hard not to get stains on things . . . though now, she realised, she had been wearing the same blouse for quite a few days.

'Oh. Nothing much. Looking after Cecilia. Having a rest. You look terrific as usual. I like your hair done that way.'

Veronica was wearing smart grey slacks, an efficient white shirt and had her thick black hair tied up in a vivid headscarf. It was fixed in a sort of bag arrangement behind her ears and let a jolly cluster of curls bounce on her forehead and waves furl back from her temples. Ida had never seen her looking better — vitalised by a cause.

Ainslie, by contrast, was shocked rigid. The deterioration in Ida was worse than he had expected. For a while, he had respected her wish to be in retreat, in mourning, to stay away from his world. But he had missed her more and more, and worried now for her future. He had thought she would not be happy without an audience for long. Now he wondered if she would be that wonderful singer, Ida Garland, ever again.

Ainslie cleared his throat, and took a determined step forward to give Ida a hug. A little dodging choreography took place as he aimed for Ida's cheek, while Cecilia stuck out a filthy hand to grab his earlobe. Ida shifted the child back to her other hip, and gave Ainslie a warm kiss on the lips. 'Hallo Ainslie. I'm sorry I look such a frightful mess. You might have warned me.'

'Ha! Would you believe it?' He roared — then looked nervously at Cecilia in case his noise might make her cry. Cecilia of course knew he was only acting and chuckled. It broke the ice: Ida laughed too, and held her baby close; Veronica and Ainslie started talking simultaneously.

'Warned you! My dear girl — I've written hundreds of letters! Months of letters with no answers!'

'Finally had a brainwave,' Veronica interrupted. 'The post office number, remember Ida, before you were married, when Felix and Jubilee stayed down here that summer?'

Ida did remember. How could she forget? How selfish and faithless she had been that summer.

'Your father was worried, came to see me at the Charlbury — you haven't heard about that have you? We re-opened last month. Back in business — no one gives a damn about the black-out these days. A nice musical comedy, to cheer the troops . . .' Ainslie kept up a steady flow of news, trying to make her be human again. Alive, interested.

'All our haunts, Ida . . . Quaglino's restaurant got bombed. The Café Anglais, a great slice of Jermyn Street . . . Part of Westminster, even Buckingham Palace . .' Veronica lamented.

Ida could not believe it. Suddenly London was on top of her, inside her, choking her, the smell of the Blitz, brickdust, cordite, burnt paint flakes . . . She took a deep breath, and leant against a windowsill until the shock passed.

'Ida darling, can we sit somewhere sensible? We've brought some other visitors . . .' Veronica's voice steadied her up.

Ainslie strode back to the car, where the two small dark people were still quietly waiting to be told what to do. Something about their patience caused another constriction in Ida's chest. They were strangers, old, broken-looking people, one, a lady clutching a large cheap, plastic handbag, the other, a man, sitting quite still, his hands folded on his lap inside a brand new pair of leather gloves. Ida just knew the handbag was empty. The man's gloves were too big and made his hands look useless. With Ainslie towering blonde and handsome over them in a smart linen suit, the trio looked like an old painting of an angel defeating the shades of death.

Veronica led Ida into the kitchen to explain. 'They're refugees, from my agency. We're helping them with papers, helping them decide where to go. I thought the fresh air might do them good. Ainslie rang me, said he'd got hold of some petrol, no questions, and would I like a spin down to check up on you. I couldn't waste two car spaces on a day like this. Not before time it seems. Ida, what's happened to you?'

'I'm perfectly all right. Don't fuss. Look, the place is in a bit of a state. I hope your friends won't mind.'

'No. I don't think they'll *mind*. Not after what they've been through . . .' Veronica's flat, ironic voice took Ida back in an instant to an attic room at a music school, where Miss Janet Sheldon had packed her bags and changed rooms, because Veronica Summers was Jewish.

'Remember my aunt and uncle from Paris? At the recital you

gave, for Daddy's party? Remember Paul and Simone?' Veronica suddenly said. 'Vanished. Like most of the others at my home that night.'

Simone: the beautiful woman on the edge of a man's seat, her arm angularly elegant holding up a cigarette. A combative woman, a survivor . . . Ida looked at the wan old lady clutching her empty handbag. She could have been Simone herself.

Ida was startled by her mind's power to edit images. She realised that living alone had jumbled the immediate past and those more distant days, into random memories. Her emotions pieced them together now with no regard to dates or time. Only to the real links — the moral truths in stored-up incidents.

'What's the matter? Don't you feel well?' Veronica gripped her arm.

'No. I'll be all right in a moment. Here's Ainslie.'

He hesitated at the kitchen door, glancing at Ida for directions. She led him and the couple through to the living-room.

'Come this way.' Ida welcomed them as best she could. 'I'm sorry about the kitchen but this room's cosy — make yourselves comfortable.'

The couple did not understand a word she said, but Ainslie spoke a schoolboy's German and installed them in the big old sofa with a comforting murmur of conversation. Ida meanwhile put the kettle on the range, and set Cecilia on the edge of the kitchen table with a carrot to bite on.

'Good for her teeth,' she explained. Veronica looked at the baby for a moment with a mixture of exasperation and pity, then took a deep breath and launched herself at Ida.

'This is ridiculous. You've got to snap out of it, pull yourself together. I mean, a few months is one thing, but this could go on for years! I wish I'd checked up on you sooner . . . Come back to London. I need your help. I've got all these people in various homes dotted about London, waiting to be given papers and moved on. Why don't you give me a hand? We've got a reception centre. You could go on the tea rota. Sing them a song. Anything. I can't believe you're going to rot down here for the duration.'

'There's a fixed period for mourning?' Ida asked, not very belligerent. 'I don't think about time. It just feels right to be here.' She slouched round the kitchen, searching in cupboards for some good china in place of her favourite chipped mugs, emptying out the teapot, shutting the door on a basketful of empties, and wondering if the refugees would settle for Cecilia's rusks . . .

Ainslie interrupted. 'Don't worry about food. We brought our own supplies for a late lunch. Come and sit with us.'

'A picnic!' She brightened. 'Then I'll just go down to the cellars and bring up a couple of good bottles! Or better still, Ainslie, you know all about that sort of thing. Take the candle down and choose. There's only the best left.'

Delighted to see some animation in her, Ainslie agreed. He did not know the cause: Ida desperately wanted a drink to get her through the upheavals in her feelings at the sight of old friends.

'Tell you what, Veronica,' she said to fill the time until she had a glass in her hand, 'grab the other end of the table. Why don't we move it outside and give your people lunch on the grass? Do them good, a bit of sun.' She and Veronica wangled the table through the doors on to the front lawn. There was only a strip of grass left: rows of newly planted cabbages and early-sprouting potatoes stretched away to the beech hedges surrounding the garden.

It *was* a feast. Two bottles of vintage white Mercurey, cool and green, not overchilled in the monks' cellar. A big flask full of onion soup, a rare delicacy in the city where onions were one of the first commodities that had vanished. A leek pie, made by Ainslie's housekeeper with a crust so thick it shot off the plate when pressed with a knife. Not enough fat for a crumbly crust . . . A disgusting cake made with thick evaporated milk, carrots and cocoa — from a tin given to Veronica by a new friend.

'You have to have a friend with access to a PX now,' she said, blushing, or was it a flush from the wine?

Then kidneys, quickly fried up and served on toast (just for Ainslie who liked to keep to the grand pre-war habit of savouries at the end of a meal). Ida had a big dish of apples stewed with local honey in the larder for Cecilia; the old Austrian couple loved this best of all, and spooned up the purée slowly, imagining the tortes that once surrounded that familiar, mellow flavour. The very small effort of enjoying themselves made the couple tired, and after lunch they went back into the cool of the sitting-room, to the sofa, and soon fell asleep.

Here it comes, thought Ida, the lecture. Aloud she said: 'I haven't any coffee. But there's brandy. Ainslie, what about you? I'm having one.'

She thought she saw Veronica start to speak but Ainslie moved rather abruptly, reaching for his cigarettes, and Veronica changed her mind. 'I'd love one,' he said. Ida felt a rush of gratitude towards him, that he had at least understood, and did not push her to do something impossibly hard — start living again.

Ida shuffled away. 'Gosh, still got my socks on.' She rummaged in the kitchen for her brandy, an emergency supply from the cellar. 'It's very good,' she said. 'French. Very old. I don't suppose Jubilee would mind at all . . .' Pouring the drink she realised that she had spoken his name as if he were in the other room. Two years, eight months after his death.

'You do know London's crawling with Americans now they're in the war?' Ainslie broke in on her thoughts, distracting her from a moment's sadness.

'Oh yes. I don't ever listen to the radio but that old gossip at the post office insists on telling me all the news . . .'

'Mrs Weekes,' said Ainslie, a complete give-away. He never could resist sounding 'connected' wherever he went, even to the nodal-cruxy buxom postmistress in a Kent village.

'You've lied to me!' Ida exclaimed. 'She telephoned one of you! That's why you came down! Old barrel-hipped busybody!' But she could not help laughing. Then the realisation that she was doing so made her weepy. It was awful to laugh, with Jubilee dead. Brandy overcame resistance, and soon she was sobbing aloud.

Veronica moved round the table to mop her up with her napkin. 'Ssh! Don't go on so Ida! Please!'

Ainslie, well draped over a rickety chair, reached out for the brandy bottle, helped himself to some more and gave Ida a hefty tot. 'On the contrary. Have a good cry. Have a good wallow with all of us, Ida. I don't think you can grieve alone. It isn't right. Jubilee was a terrific chap. He had all those sterling qualities people go on about, and yet he wasn't a bore at all. In fact, he was remarkable enough to let you have your head. I liked him very much, and it must have been bloody awful for you to lose him.' Ainslie was perturbed, and swigged his drink. 'Can't say I've ever been that close to anyone. At times like this, I don't know whether to be glad, or damn sad about it.'

Veronica pulled her chair close to Ida's, provided a shoulder, and in spite of all the times she had already cried alone, Ida discovered there were deep wells, full of tears, still inside her, and howled.

Ainslie stood up. 'I'm going to let you two girls have a good session. I'll take a look at the church. Got the key, Ida?'

'It's . . . under . . . flowerpot . . .' she stammered. For some reason, this key reminded her of the red lily on the door of her parents' house, the lonely returns home she had made after so many secret adventures. A silent house and a child finding a front-door key under a milk churn, at night.

'Oh Veronica, he was the only person who really really loved me, and now he's dead!' She cried. 'He — he *liked* me!'

· Veronica patted her back and said nothing until the upheavals began to subside. Sunshine, brandy, and tears gave Ida a thudding head. Cecilia would wake up soon; she would have to take a rest before she did. 'I've got to lie down . . .' She flopped to the ground, burying her face into the cold pungent earth-smell beneath the fresh spring grass, and fell into a fainting doze.

Veronica got a blanket from the kitchen. Ida found it comforting to have her closest friend wrap her up, and sit on a spare corner, quite accepting of her state.

'I don't think Jubilee was the only person who loved you,' Veronica said in a plain voice. 'I love you. Jack loves you. Felix does too, in his distant, legal sort of way. Ainslie is positively bereft without you . . . But I do understand, my dearest old thing. For some reason, he was the only person who convinced you with his love. You're very lucky, Ida. Some people never get convinced, ever. Jubilee had the knack of loving. I wish I did. So does Ainslie, I think. One day, perhaps, you could feel a little pity for the likes of him and me.'

377

This was a difficult thought for Ida, whose only response was to fling her arm across Veronica's lap, and nestle into the curve of her thigh. Veronica stayed quite still, enjoying the peace of the countryside, the slowly softening breathing of her friend, and the greenness, the wild lush greenness of Kent in spring.

The visit unsettled her. Ida moped around the house for days after they had left, feeling less immured than before. In the back of her thoughts, she knew that Jubilee would be distressed by her opting out, and this worry began to oppress her. She had the strongest feeling that he was watching, planning all kinds of new treats to make her feel better. Then she cried, because she began to imagine things — that Mrs Weekes would bring a telegram to say he would be there for dinner, or that the pipe smoke in the garden came from his deckchair, not from an old man weeding under the window there.

A night in June: she went to bed early, because the air was sultry hot, in need of a thunderstorm. Her brain felt heavy too, with the effort of not looking beyond her grief. Ida tossed and turned, wondering what she should do next. The rain began, big globules of it, beating against the windowpanes.

Battering noises grew louder. At first Ida thought it was just branches in the garden, scratching against the glass. She could not see, of course, because now the panes were boarded. Then she thought it must be a window upstairs, somehow free of its catch. She ought to go and fix it, before it got wrenched from its hinge . . . Suddenly she knew that someone was beating at the door — the one she had nailed up in the cold weather.

Thank God Mrs Weekes had warned her about marauders; at least she was prepared. Ida reached for the sledge-hammer, close by her bed. It must be the rain — a gang of deserters, forced to find shelter. Cecilia slept on, but Ida was wide-awake, scared out of her wits.

'I know you're there. Open up. It's only me,' a voice said. A drunken, thick, man's voice, that meant nothing to her.

The scullery door shuddered. Eventually it gave. A hulk began to walk into the living-room. Ida did not scream: that would wake Cecilia.

'Your face! You'd think I was a ghost! Thought I'd surprise you . . .' The figure swayed, and came nearer. It was Jack.

'You idiot!' she hissed, and without thinking raised the hammer.

'Not again!' he parried, grabbing her wrist. 'It's only eight o'clock — you'd think it was midnight, the way you look!'

'What are you doing? Breaking in! Who the hell do you think you.are!'

'Don't be pleased to see me. That would be too much.' He fell into a chair, suddenly sober, and very tired.

'You could have rung. Sent word. You frightened me to death. Don't you ever think of anyone else . . . ?'

He didn't answer her. He tipped forward on his knees, and crawled over to the hump in the blankets where Cecilia lay sleeping.

'She's beautiful. She doesn't look like you, does she? More like him. Old Jubilee. Poor sod. Pretty, all the same.' He sat back, leaning against the old sofa. 'Oh Ida. I've had enough of London. First leave in three years — and I come back to ruins. Blitz is shocking. I'll be glad to get back to the unit.'

'Why did you come?' she said, exasperated. 'Turning up here, breaking in . . .'

'Because I'm going to North Africa, and I could get my head blown off! Thought I ought to pay my respects. Seeing as I don't get any letters. What's the matter with you, anyway?'

'How dare you ask. In the state you're in.' She sank to the sofa, exhausted with him.

'Oh for God's sake, I only had a few with the man who gave me a lift down. Nothing wrong in a soldier on leave having a few drinks, is there? Look here Ida . . .' He came closer, then changed his mind, and produced a half-bottle of gin. Several large swigs went down. He was twice the size she remembered him, big, tough, bulky, and very intent on something.

'What?'

'This won't do.' He blinked, mournful. 'You mean everything to me Ida. Other girls — women — I've had a field day, of course. But when I'm out there, it's you I think about. My cousin Ida, singing. Making everyone feel good. You were always too good for me Ida. That's why I can't have this . . .' he waved his bottle wildly, 'this *moping about*.' He was slurred and sentimental but Ida began to see he was staying very drunk so that he could say things he would otherwise never admit.

'Want a drink?' he said hopefully, raising his chin.

Then Ida saw in his eyes what she had always known but resisted seeing. Jack loved her with a passion that was beyond reason. Not even an affair would kill the feeling he carried for her — not even all the women in the world would make her mortal to him. For somewhere, in the past, he had built a vision of her as everything female, talented, spirited, he would ever love. Because she was a brighter star than his mother? No — nothing so worldly as that. Because she was the only one who had cuddled him when he was a lonely boy; the only one who kept faith with his dreams of getting away; the only one in the Garland family who looked at his white skin, and *forgave* him for it.

'Poor Jack. It's not your fault.' She put her arms around him, and rocked him. 'I'm going to be fine. Don't you worry.' As children again, they stretched themselves out on the sofa, fully clothed, in each other's arms. Jack told her all his yarns about India, about the Pathans, the punkah-wallahs, the mountains, the tiger hunts, market-places, mystics and whores. Eventually they fell asleep, dreaming only of that wonderful, innocent acceptance of each other that made them unique among the Garlands.

When she woke in the morning, Jack had been up for some time. He had fixed the door, cleaned out the range, and the kettle was rattling for tea.

'What's on the agenda today, eh?' he said, rubbing at the now shining metal rail round the range with a tea-towel.

'Well. I don't usually have an agenda,' she confessed, 'but we could walk to the village, if you like.'

Ida got Cecilia dressed, and they took turns carrying her down the lane. Jack had brought a tin of beef in his coat pocket; they bought a cabbage to go with it, and a morning paper. Ida had not read the news for months. When they came home, she cooked, while Jack fiddled about finding all kinds of jobs she had avoided. He fixed the plug on the radio — Ida was not too keen on this invasion of her enclosed world, but Jack found a music programme, picked up Cecilia, held out her pudgy arm like a real partner and smooched her round the kitchen table. Cecilia was delighted by her new 'uncle'; Ida found the music so redolent of cheerful flag-flying that her heart went out to the pair of them, alive, making friends, in a brief moment of sweetness before Jack went back to the killing.

They ate a large lunch. Jack gave Cecilia a hug and kiss before she went for a little nap, and Ida knew it was time for him to be going. The closeness between them loomed up; Ida felt a muddle of emotions swirling round them, an invisible fog.

'So. What'll you do, Ida?' Jack was trying to be brisk, to 'keep things on an even keel', as he often said.

'I don't know yet. But I tell you what . . .'

'Yes?'

'When you come back, you'll be proud of me. I promise.'

'Atta girl!' he said, giving her a smacker on the cheek, and a matey sort of hug. He walked down the lane jauntily, but then he had to look back. Ida's eyes blurred with tears. He waved slowly, as any soldier does who wonders if he will ever return.

After that, Ida had to start again. Jack became the symbol of all the others, needing to be kept going. Perhaps if she kept faith with his dreams, he would not get his head blown off . . .

She could never love Jack, be his for ever. Of course there had been times when she had felt possessive, but only because they had grown up close, and she felt he belonged to her. At first she was his little mother; then his sister, then his ally in good times. Now it seemed that the best way she could honour his respect, his devotion to her, was to be the very thing that kept her beyond his reach: the best singer he had ever heard. His classy, adored, great lady of jazz. Because in her song, he could hear the voices of his past, his grandfather, his mother, the sadness of a father he had never had. His lack of a rightful place. His blues.

One summer Sunday at Hartmere, Ida brushed her hair, and buttoned on a cotton dress she had picked up at a jumble sale in the village. She wondered who would come with Ainslie today. He had telephoned Mrs Weekes at the post office to say that as usual, he would be bringing lunch. There was no need for surprise, now that Ida had begun to hint she wanted some contact with the outside world. Still, she wondered at this strange new hobby of Ainslie's: regular Sunday picnics at a wreck of a house with a wreck of a person. It hardly seemed a suitable diversion for a grand theatrical name, even in wartime.

He came by himself. For the first time in all the years she had known Ainslie Curtis, Ida felt nervous at the prospect of spending a whole day alone with him. They had met in crowds, at rehearsals, at parties, at smart dinners in hotels or clubs, and always Ainslie had been in the thick of things, creating shows, rehearsing choruses, dealing with famous 'temperaments'. She hardly knew him as a private person, and it made her shy. Perhaps that was why she was thankful she had bothered with her hair, piled it up, with a mass of crinkly curls at the top. And the dress, which Mrs Weekes had volunteered to shorten for her, looked almost smart. At least it was fresh and clean. Bare feet had to do because she only had plimsolls or wellingtons otherwise. Cecilia looked sweet in patched clothes from the same sale, sun bonnet and dungarees so that she could totter about in the garden without hurting her knees. Cecilia would be her protection, as always . . .

Ainslie climbed out of the car and walked slowly up the lane to the kitchen entrance. His body drooped from his shoulders. Perhaps he was tired from the long drive, or the difficulties of keeping a show going every night, with random raids, electricity failures, and numerous shortages.

'What is it?' Ida asked quickly. Her heart was thumping. She was feeling stronger, but not strong enough for bad news. 'Don't say anyone's hurt. I couldn't bear it.'

'No.' He sank into a chair. 'It's the Charlbury. It got hit by a firebomb. It's burnt out. Not a stone left.' His body sagged more heavily as he spoke.

'Christ! How dreadful!' Ida covered her face with her hands. She could not look at Ainslie, at his embarrassing, untypical helplessness.

'I hope you don't mind that I came, Ida. I know I'm supposed to cheer you up. I nearly turned back . . .'

Impulsively Ida put her arms round his neck though her cheeks were wet with tears. 'Poor Ainslie. It was your life! I'd have been very hurt if you hadn't turned to me. Was anyone— I mean, were there casualties?'

'No, thank God. My God, when I think of it. We'd had a full house. The usual air-raid warning, nobody budged. They don't these days, anywhere, cinemas, theatres . . . Later, the all clear. Finished the show as usual, went to supper at the Savoy with friends: Maud French, you remember.'

'Of course I do! Go on.'

'Lucky I was there. About one o'clock there was another raid. We all went down the hotel basements, well set up they are . . . Someone came and told me what had happened. I ran back at once.'

'Ainslie! You could have been killed!' Ida grasped his shirt. He put his hand over hers, his big, blistered hand, and gripped her fingers hard.

'No such luck.' A shocking remark: he meant it. To her dismay, he brushed her off and bent forward in his seat, elbows on his knees, his hands supporting a heavy head.

Ida stood over him with nothing to say. Ainslie had always been the master, the magician with words. Now he looked shattered. His whole life had been directed outwards, to being creative with others. The Charlbury was his empire, every brick of it paid for by his brilliance, by the stars he had made. Now he was ruined and unable to take comfort. There was so much that Ida understood of these feelings, but it was not the moment to offer him sympathy. She left him, went to rescue Cecilia from among the vegetables. 'Nap?' the child said, plaintively, not wanting to go to bed.

Cecilia now had a mattress of her own, next to Ida's sofa; luckily the summer was good, and she was not bothered by draughts. Next winter would be more difficult, Ida thought; she would need a proper bed. She laid her daughter down, tucked her favourite blanket under one fat arm. Cecilia gave the bundle a squeeze, all the while keeping her thumb firmly lodged in her mouth. Ida sat back on her heels, waiting. There was still no sound from the garden. She hoped Ainslie was pulling himself together. She smoothed Cecilia's brow and watched her, unwilling to sleep, her eyes swimming, her eyelids drooping, once, twice, a third time . . . Poor Ainslie, not to have anyone to help him. To know hundreds of famous people, and when the crisis came, to have to face it alone. If only there was something she could do, but she was still in awe of him. Then suddenly inspired, Ida stood up. Ainslie needed a new project — something to get him going again.

'Go to sleep,' she commanded. Ida walked out into the garden, where Ainslie still sat hunched in his seat, grimly trying to cope with the collapse of all his life's work. With a timid step, she crept up behind him and put her arms round his neck.

'Dear Ainslie,' she said, awkwardly kissing him somewhere in the region of his ear. 'Dear Ainslie. Can I help you? Do you want me to — come back to London with you?'

He twisted round, and gave her a long, tired look. He sighed, as if he regretted something, which disappointed Ida. She had hoped her 'gift' of herself would cheer him up more than it had. Then it occurred to her — perhaps he had thought she was suggesting an affair! The idea had never entered her mind.

'I mean, work,' she said. 'I should do something to contribute. I'm not a stalwart type like my Gran. At first I couldn't think how to be useful. Now I do. I've got capital. And I own Hartmere. I can raise a loan. Why don't we re-open the Au Fait? Not as an exclusive place, officers only, like the rest of Mayfair. I'd like to have a place where regular soldiers could come, WAAFS, WVS, nurses, people like that, but it must be smart, to give them a treat. Smart and romantic. Let's make the dance floor bigger, no need for lots of dinner tables because there's no food to serve anyone. And I'll get a good band together, like swing numbers, get old Ivor Clarke to play some solid boogie rhythms in between . . .'

Ida stood in front of him, swaying her hips and clapping her hands lightly, this way and that.

'Go on, what do you say?' She made herself smile — because she could not bear to see Ainslie miserable.

He watched her, his face tiredly affectionate, then shook his head at the prospect of starting all over again.

'Oh please!' she said. 'I really want to do it!'

Then he mustered the response he imagined Ida wanted. 'I'll go fifty-fifty. Raise some sort of loan. I still have a name. When you move your hips like that, my dear, you look a little too much the red hot momma. You're going to have to lose a helluva lot of weight before the opening night.'

When she ran the Au Fait before the war, Ida discovered she had a real talent for club work. She had grown more sure of herself, with her marriage to Jubilee, and seized the chance to display a classless sort of friendliness, which was just what she felt a club doyenne needed to have. In *her* night-spot, anyway.

'You run things exactly as you want,' Ainslie had told her. 'It's your clientele. Build it up. Throw out anyone you don't like, and sing the songs you love. I think you'll be fine.' He was right to be confident.

Between her sets on stage, Ida liked to join various tables, listen to conversations, tell people what was best on the menu. She would crack jokes and help guests get drunk if that was their mood. Everyone was treated the same: from a diplomat to an unemployed musician. Yet she could put a distance between herself and the clientele with a touch of authority when it was necessary. She called it 'Bayswater balls' — she had plenty.

The lease on the Au Fait was easily revived, for there were few takers. Not many people were willing to take the risk on a property in the city centre these days. Especially anyone crazy enough to want to bring in the general public — the lower ranks, not the usual officers and Mayfair crowd.

For Ida, deciding where to live was more of a problem. She did not want to go back to Bayswater, although it seemed the obvious answer. Life went on there just the same: Gran stoic and tired, Billy and Jim at their wartime tasks, Earl still on duty as the local warden. Denise still embroiled in her heroic crusade lifting soldiers' spirits.

Bayswater held too many memories, and Ida could not be business-like and creative amidst the turmoil of the Garlands. She booked in temporarily at the Ambassador Hotel. It was cheap because no one wanted to live on the top floors and hotels had a bad record when it came to direct hits. Miraculously, the windows in her room were intact; for that reason alone Ida decided the place had a charmed existence. The *maître d'hôtel* remembered Ida well and found a babysitter for

Cecilia in the evenings; in the days she toddled along behind Ida, because they were used to being together.

Everyone in London seemed to have adopted an incredible fatalism. Sirens were a nuisance; the only people who dropped face to the earth if a bomb swooped anywhere nearby were the newly-arrived American troops. Londoners ignored them. They also avoided looking at shattered landmarks, familiar old buildings, the way people avoid looking at a vigorous aged relative, suddenly paralysed.

This was living on the short fuse. The seething mass of humanity on the streets every night had an insatiable need for a good time. Poles, Belgians, Scandinavians, French jostled after dark, clustered in their chosen hang-outs. All round them swam shoals of girls, some from camps for a night out in the hot spots, some who had run away from the tedium of factory work; some had left behind babies and husbands, and come to London to see the sights, and in case they died tomorrow, have a romance. In the black-out, men could not see faces, distinguish a beauty from a raddled hag. The pin-light of a torch revealed only a stockinged ankle, a willing, lipsticked smile. No one got too particular if there was a chance of a 'roger' in an alley.

But there were plenty of decent people, working girls in their uniforms who risked their lives nightly, soldiers off-duty who did not always want the trash, but to go away with the memory of a nice girl's conversation and a wholesome body. Big, well-fed Yanks who hung around the pavement by Rainbow Corner in Piccadilly Circus, the Red Cross social centre for the GIs. Walking through Piccadilly was an uplifting experience for any girl — the whistles, the admiring looks, the harmless, enticing remarks uttered in captivating Hollywood-inspired drawls. And the black GIs, less boisterous, more charming, courteous, reminding Ida of an old romance, and her origins . . .

It was human. Ida wanted to give as many of them as she could the night of their lives. It suddenly seemed the right, the only thing for her to do: to celebrate survival as lustily and publicly as she knew how. Because her London, Jack's London, was disappearing, being torn down by fires and bombs. These people in Soho, black, white and beige, were still the pulse in the heart of the night city, and they had to keep the beat, to be able to go on.

386

She and Ainslie had cocktails at the Ambassador to celebrate signing the lease. For lack of anything smarter Ida disguised a silk wrap as an evening dress: she wore it backwards and gathered a drape at the neck with a nappy pin and some fake flowers. Ainslie drew her attention to the fact that he was one of the few men in the room in a dinner jacket; the rest were in uniforms. 'Do you mind?' he asked her, and she realised that it was a sensitive issue to him.

Ida dismissed the idea. 'You raised the money to put on a show in the middle of the Blitz, and stood in that theatre every night for over a year! It took courage, and then you lost everything. I hardly call that shirking.'

'The band's hopeless,' he said, suddenly diverted, 'but perhaps you'd like to dance . . .'

'Not the same since Tommy retired,' Ida agreed, and was sad for the passing of the old days. Not too sad that she would not dance, however.

Ainslie towered over her, but as she had often found in very big men, he was very light on his feet. It only came to her afterwards, as they returned to their table among the potted palms, that this was the room where she had first met Jubilee, and first danced with him too. Nostalgia increased into a wave of sorrow, sucking her out of the present, as if she were being swept out from a sunlit beach into a cold sea.

She made an enormous effort not to be submerged. As she lifted her head, she caught Ainslie staring at her with clear eyes and firm, emphatic features, an expression of intuitive understanding.

'You're a brave girl, Ida. You'll pull through. Furthermore, I want you to know, you're pulling *me* through . . .'

He laid his hand on hers and ordered a wildly overpriced bottle of mock champagne. They held hands very tightly for a moment, both thinking of their lost lives, his in his theatre, hers with Jubilee. Ainslie kissed her fingers, trying to make light of his genuine feelings. 'I don't know how to say this, but . . .'

'Oh Ainslie, you needn't . . .'

He leant forward. 'Thank you,' he said. 'Thank you for standing by me. I've always done everything my own way. When the Charlbury collapsed, that was the end, for me.'

'Only the end of one chapter,' she said, quickly. 'We've got to go on, because we're the lucky ones. We're alive.'

'Yes,' he said. 'I'm alive. But you don't understand.' His feelings bore into her. Ida could not mistake what he was trying to say. Before he was half-dead, a solitary man. He was alive with a sense of discovery: what intimacy could bring him. Perhaps because they had seen each other in crisis, she had managed to reach the private man. The strength of his unspoken feelings was so overpowering that she had to accept, he had never expressed them to anyone before.

Next day they made a tour of inspection of their old-and-new premises. It looked exactly as it had been left, even down to the furnishings: a low-ceilinged room with a long bar down one side and alcoves along the other. Cecilia sat primly in her pushchair.

'Dirty,' the child said, disapprovingly.

'Yes, filthy,' Ainslie agreed, patting her hand. 'Don't worry. It's nothing that a good swabbing out won't cure.'

'You always speak to her as if she's your age, Ainslie,' Ida commented, amused.

'I know. I was brought up alone with a widowed mother who packed me off to school as soon as she remarried. I don't know the first thing about babies, family life. However, I'm always a great hit with children. Strange, isn't it?'

Ida sat on a bar stool. 'I remember. The first time we met. I showed you my new dress. You were very nice then.'

'My God! Don't remind me! That was '26!' As usual, he turned the conversation away from himself, as if he had said too much already. Not for the first time, Ida was tantalised by this glimpse behind the public face.

He strolled around the club. A small stage had a curved proscenium around it, covered in silver stars to match the alcoves. There were even paper streamers under the tables from the last night's final thrash, although the tops were filmed with brickdust. A couple of the pink mirrors behind the bar had shattered when a bomb fell nearby. Not much serious renovation was necessary: just a visit from the rat catchers. The Blitz had thrown up a plague of beetles and rodents from exposed, long-forgotten cellars, which even the new, wild army of abandoned household cats could not remedy.

'Just a clean-up. Nothing more. We'd never find the paint, anyway,' Ainslie commented drily.

'New furniture? Could we manage it?'

'That's a possibility. There are bomb sales all over the place.'

Their visit to a depository next day was an awesome experience. The warehouse was in a suburb. Even here, great gaps appeared in the terraces of houses. The streets were deserted, shops shut, only frail old couples and solitary housewives walked about, pinch-lipped, their faces lined with tiredness. Dust everywhere; great punch-holes in standing walls, evidence of shell damage. A handscrawled pub sign said: Beer today.

'Let's have one,' Ainslie invited, tucking his arm through hers. It was tempting: Cecilia had been left behind at the hotel, and Ida had time to herself. They managed several, and on the euphoria produced by an unusual quantity of daytime alcohol went to the warehouse and bought wildly. Particularly some astounding purple velvet chairs.

'Good Lord! These must have come from a bombed-out brothel in the docks!' Ainslie said, making Ida laugh. He looked so relaxed and happy, for the first time in several weeks.

Maybe it was sentiment from the drink, maybe it was the surroundings, piles of furniture, waiting to begin new lives: Ida had a sudden yearning to share more than the club with Ainslie. He was an old friend; he knew Jubilee well; the past would not be forgotten. That attracted her. Also, she loved having this extraordinary effect on him. She could feel him expanding, relaxing into trusting her; she felt in some ways stronger than he was. Supposing it was just a mood — until he was back on top of the world? She almost did not want him to be successful, brilliant, public, alone, all surface again.

Tommy Trevino had disbanded, and was quietly retired, though Ida doubted if he was getting many early nights in the East End. Putting the word out in Archer Street soon proved that Ivor Clarke was still around. He was glad to start up Ida's new combo, and swiftly set to the task of finding the rest of the personnel required. A little quieter and less dapper than in the old days, Ivor could still play a mean piano. In fact, a meaner piano, because Ivor had been hanging around clubs in London where the GIs were now calling the tunes, and had begun to hear new things, musically speaking. He had come across a few black musicians drafted into the American forces. They sat in after hours in a handful of Soho jazz dens. Ivor picked up a sense of the new music, the strange, nervy sounds from New York, especially a place called Mintons.

He was always open to musical ideas, and not a fervent 'trad' player like many jazzmen in London. Now he worked on some fragmented, edgy little solos, stripped-down tunes with a jagged percussive quality, where the gaps and the beat created as much tension as the played chords. Ida liked his experimental style: it wasn't swing, which was still the big attraction, because everyone wanted to dance. If Ray Merritt was back in New York, that was the music he would be playing. Late at night, when the crowds thinned and were prepared to listen, it might be the right sound for the Au Fait.

Rehearsing with Ivor and the band was easy. He understood her so well that they shorthanded the steps.

'I'll give you the tempo,' Ida would say.

'OK. This time, Fred does the intro on sax.'

'OK Trevor, then we'll diddle through the middle . . .' at this Ivor would spread big chords in unusual sequences, giving a sketch of the song and Ida would hum approximately what she would try to sing over them.

'Now the end . . .' the drummer would somersault into the final eight bars, and someone, either the piano or the sax would feed her ideas as she climbed vocally into the finale.

They worked out about thirty numbers on that basis; enough for a polished first night, some in reserve that needed more thinking but might work well on an inspired evening, and a few standards in case Ida got in the mood to keep going till morning.

She was apprehensive at first, not having sung for nearly two years. But the rest had done her voice some good, if nothing for her stage confidence. The sound she made was still pure, but a little more veiled and mellow, and her pitch had dropped only a shade further, to its truly natural level.

Ida thought it was a cliché that singers told of their lives, their sufferings in their music. Work was never that simple. It seemed that experience changed her feelings about words she had sung a thousand times. She approached them with altered emphasis, a little more irony, at times, a shade of regret. Hopefully, her audience would hear new meanings for themselves.

Opening night was to be on Ida's birthday, her twenty-ninth. She wished she was going to be thirty, serene and sophisticated, a more appropriate age for a young widow. She wondered if Ainslie would remember the date. He was very professional about birthdays. He had seen internationally famous stars dissolve in tears in their dressing room, in spite of a theatre waiting packed to the gods with adoring fans, just because no one had 'thought to send flowers'. Ida knew that in the days of the Charlbury theatre, Ainslie's secretary kept a book with the dates of all his favourites. It had probably been lost in the ruins among a million other invaluable details.

Ida was growing tense and excited, but there was another important date to celebrate before the reopening of the Au Fait. One afternoon after rehearsals she took Cecilia for a walk. It was September 8th — Cecilia's birthday. They crossed Ida's favourite park, along the path she had taken so many times before, from the Ambassador Hotel to Bayswater. The gun batteries were silent; all through the war, it was wonderful that people could still stroll through Hyde Park. It was particularly moving to do so on this day with her child, so close to the anniversary of Jubilee's death. Ida did not cry for Jubilee; she just held on to Cecilia's hand and concentrated hard on her pleasure in collecting beautiful autumnal leaves. Ida was alive with love for this moment, a sunlit day in the middle of a war-torn city, in which she and Cecilia could be simple and unthreatened.

Uncles Billy and Jim opened the door of the boarding-house, singing 'Happy Birthday'. Cecilia was not yet familiar with her relatives and hid her face in Ida's shoulder.

'Don't crowd round her!' Gran shouted. 'Bring her in to me.'

She did not rise from her rocking chair; Ida hurried over and placed the baby on her knee. 'Three today,' Gran murmured. The child felt at home with her, and did not pull away.

'We haven't got a cake,' Gran apologised.

'I bought her a banana.' Ida fished it out of her bag. 'Look, Cecilia,' she said.

They stuck a candle on a plate, and brought it over to Cecilia with the lone banana curled ceremoniously around it. Billy and Jim gathered round the rocking chair helping Cecilia to blow out the flame. But faced with the banana, Cecilia looked puzzled.

'Blimey,' said Uncle Jim. 'She's never seen a banana before. She doesn't know how to peel it, poor mite.' Gently he revealed the ritual, holding the base, and removing the skin like sections of gold leaf.

George was absent; Ida had heard he was making a mint on the black market. But her Pa was there, marooned on the sofa. 'My day off,' he said wryly. 'Sprained my ankle falling into a bomb crater.' He tried to get up, but she hurriedly settled him and sat on the edge, warily testing her weight on the pile of books beneath.

Denise, done up to the nines in a black suit, seamed nylons, tight kid gloves, could only pause for a moment. 'Sorry, can't stop. I'm on my way to work. You look better today, Ida. Not so bloated, like the last time you visited . . .'

Gran's eyes narrowed. 'Yes, you are! How can you need to diet when there's a war on, my girl?'

Ida laughed. She laughed so much she felt the sofa wobble. Suddenly the excesses of her time at Hartmere struck her anew. Yes, those days had been full of pain, but she had been dramatic and stupid to eat nothing but potatoes and wine.

'I'm making a big effort, Gran. You'll see, I'll lose it all again.' (She made a decision to stop drinking beer and champagne with Ainslie whenever they got the chance.)

'Right, I'm flying on my way girls. Happy birthday Jemima!' This was her Ma's tiresome little joke at what she had always considered a pretentious Christian name for a Garland baby. Denise adopted a birdlike cheerfulness and flitted from the room. Ida did not mention that her Ma's tight-skirted suit and expensive accessories were the recognised uniform of the prostitutes in Burlington Arcade. She noted the fact, but rejected the idea that Denise's outfit signified actual sin. The woman was nearing fifty . . . it was probably the fantasy of her one-track, vain little brain.

Opening night: the Au Fait was crowded, the band finding its stride, and Ida stepped to the front of the tiny stage. Ainslie had given her a beautiful blue lace dress, borrowed from some theatre wardrobe by his old colleague, Sylvia Knox. Ida wore long black gloves over her elbows and crystal earrings Jubilee had given her long ago. She had arranged for a spotlight to shine so brightly into her face that she could not see the bobbing faces beyond it, a wide sea of curious faces, wondering if she could make a come-back. Everyone loves a drama, and the music papers had made good publicity out of her tragedy, her absence, Ainslie's loss of the Charlbury, and their joint venture.

Ivor Clarke smiled encouragement over his tortoiseshell spectacles. For a moment Ida could have sworn he was Tommy Trevino ten years before, this another bandstand at the Glass Slipper, and that she was just beginning, a young girl wearing a borrowed red velvet dress . . . She missed her cue.

Ivor played over the gap. Ida turned her back to the audience and mimed a vast scream at her band. Then she turned to the microphone with a beatific smile and let rip. They had picked a big bouncy favourite to open the set: 'All of Me'. Somewhere in the bridge, the third eight bars, Ida 'moved out', the way musicians do to improvise. She heard something Ivor played, and a complementary sound, not the written melody, just occurred from her lips. It was such a freeing experience, her own little arrangement, that Ida's spirit floated above herself. 'All of Me!' she soared, like an angel singing. 'All of Me!' There was nothing between her hopes and the aspirations of all those happy, swaying young people in the audience. All they wanted was the chance to be good to each other, to rediscover the simplest joys of peace, and to forget that death was just around the corner.

At dawn the club closed, and Ivor staggered to his borrowed billet in a friend's flat. Ainslie and Ida were too thrilled with the Au Fait to leave it empty and go home. They sat together in an alcove. Ainslie for once looked almost middle-aged, with a few grey hairs at his temples, and pouches under his eyes. It was not a glamorous moment, but they both felt blissfully happy.

'You looked beautiful tonight,' he said. 'Transformed. Lit up from inside.'

'Thank you.' She blushed.

'I've got something for you. A birthday present.'

'I knew you wouldn't forget!' she exclaimed, still finding the energy to bounce like a child.

'Close your eyes.'

Ida did as she was told.

'Put out your hands.'

With a beating heart, she stretched her fingers forward. She felt him slip a ring on to her right hand. Ida opened her eyes and saw a fiery diamond set in a ring of pearls. Ainslie kissed her fingertips across the table.

'It's huge,' she said, confounded.

'Who cares! I've never incurred a debt more willingly.' He pointed to her wedding ring. 'I imagined you'd always want to keep it on. And mine can't be an engagement ring because pearls mean tears. The man in the shop told me so. But I liked it anyway. I suppose people are superstitious about things just now . . .'

'Ainslie, what are you saying?' The tears in her eyes made the ring sparkle, the colours shimmered, red of flames, blue of a clear sky, yellow rays of sunlight. All the colours that make up white.

'I mean that in time, if you ever thought you'd let me try, I would cherish you. Try to make a marriage. You've been there, under my nose, all these years. How did I never realise what you meant to me?'

'Don't, Ainslie — maybe it's just tonight, you know, us working together, all that . . .'

He looked very downcast. 'I'm sorry. If I've said something incredibly stupid, forgive me. You'll have the ring as a symbol of my constant affection and friendship.'

Ida shook her head, unable to sort out her feelings, but she held tightly to Ainslie's hand. She did not know if love could happen more than once, if it could be different. She thought of Veronica's words, about the gift of loving. Perhaps it was her turn to persuade someone that communion between two people could be achieved. She had a fine example to follow, and a very good man to teach.

17

Gran sat under a cherry tree at Hartmere watching Ida circulate among her guests. Cecilia followed her mother closely, offering up a dish of anchovy straws to the drinkers. Gran smiled, watching the child attempt her first-ever duties as a hostess. The bowl wobbled precariously because Cecilia would only hold it with one hand; the other hovered over the frills of her mother's skirt, ready to grab at her if she moved away too quickly.

Ainslie's cocktail cup was what Gran would describe as vicious. No wonder raucous laughter burst out amongst the guests. Everyone's nerves were stretched to breaking point and it took very little stimulation for their mood to swing from apathy into spurts of fevered gaiety. Spring 1945, and still the war was not at an end. Gran's heart gave a nasty little flutter. The Second Front, last summer, then the Germans driven out of France. It had to be done with soon. The Allies were crossing the Rhine, and here they all were, celebrating no more bombs . . . 'The Battle of London is over,' they had been told by one of those ninny-hammer Tories.

Too late for her. Too late, the end of the 'Farting Furies', Gran thought: the V-1s, and those low-flying coffins of death, the V-2s. None of her neighbours gave those a nickname. The V-2s had done her in. They made no sound: the black cigar-shaped objects moved fast and silently. Survivors heard a sonic double-crack, but the victims had not a second to prepare for death. Too late. Just as well that her poor Billy, always an innocent, did not die with terror as his last emotion. There he was, walking home from the shop in Shepherd's Bush, the next minute, he vanished, exploded to death. When they brought her the news, she felt her heart falter, and knew without need of a doctor that from now on her body would be unreliable. Too late, just when she had thought they would all make it to the grand finale.

Gran felt coldness seep up her legs, a discomfort she knew intimately. She did not shiver, her old limbs were too exhausted for such activity. She too would need another drink or two to withstand the odd sharp breeze that accompanied a cloud passing over the sun. It was a typical English garden party, all those society girls determinedly wearing flowered, thin cottons, flopping straw hats, relaxed and languid when the sun warmed their flesh, and suddenly shivering, borrowing a lover's jacket, when a patch of cool air tightened their skins. Immobilised, Gran let her eyes adventure for her, and her imagination recreate lively scenes from her own past, when she had shared such fun. Such was the happiness of memory that physical pleasure revived in her, she felt the delicious touch of sun and shade on a beach on the Isle of Wight. Wading through the shallow water under cotton-puff clouds, the sea lukewarm then icy drifting over her feet. The cool lining of a man's blazer, put round her, silky on her bare back. When she was a young girl, when she and Joseph held hands in the waves, the two young stars from the end of the pier show . . .

A shadow fell across Gran's face.

'Having a doze? Can I get you anything?' Ainslie touched her hand. He was a great favourite with her, because of his rich, theatrical voice, reminding her of Edwardian stage-folk she had loved.

'Move me, the sun,' Gran said thickly.

'Too chilly for you here. Hold tight.' He trundled her wheelchair away from the tree, whose blossomed branches, thick and pink as blancmange, had cast her into shade. He tucked the blanket tighter round her cold, still legs.

'Guests . . . guests . . .' Gran's eyes grew stony, belligerent. Ainslie understood and obediently left her in peace. She was a difficult woman to comfort, impossible to pity, yet quite unable to see there was a difference. Reluctantly, he let the chatter of the party replace her in his thoughts. He stopped for a word with a young writer whose latest play he was hoping to stage in the summer. They argued idealistically about great theatrical duos who might do for the piece: Laurence Olivier and Vivien Leigh, John Clements and Kay Hammond, Lynn Fontanne and Alfred Lunt.

Then Ainslie moved on to find Ida conversing happily with Maud French, their long-standing actress friend, and Sylvia Knox, once his revue designer. Maud French was touring the troops' camps while trying out a new musical in the provinces. Sylvia was staging a historical drama at the Phoenix. Both Ida and Ainslie had invested in her play, entirely out of profits from the Au Fait, and Ida's recent records. Ida had had a scandalous hit with one of her best club numbers, 'My Place':

> 'Why not come back to my place;
> There's a whole lot of booze at my place;
> There'll be you and me and the baby makes three;
> You get a real good time at my place . . .'

The BBC would not allow it to be played, considering it was immoral, too cynical a comment on the kind of offer any soldier on leave had heard more than once. The radio people did not see the way Ida sang it in the club, contempt and sympathy mingled in her words. Her audience understood, its popularity spread, and soon it was a notorious success.

She looked so gorgeous beside the other two women: Maud French was wearing a ludicrous picture hat that made her hard face look old. Sylvia was pretty enough with her lace and bows . . . but Ida was all woman, small, dynamic, and enchanting. The big vibrant petals splash-printed on her dress made her glamorous, but it was the warmth shining in her eyes, and the generosity of her smile that made Ida incredibly alluring. She had a glow, as if there was a hidden fire within, permanently smouldering. Ainslie had a fleeting fantasy of entering a silver wood, smelling a sweet mixture of beechnuts and brilliant-coloured leaves, catching alight . . . and the place all teeming with small pulsating creatures, secret-eyed like Ida. She was an adorable, unpredictable individual, with sensuous, moist lips now blowing him a kiss . . .

Ida left her guests, and went after Cecilia, who had wandered off. The kitchen was empty, but Ida heard music from the room beyond, the room where she and her baby had slept side by side in a bleak winter not so long ago. Now it was full of flowers and a bar loaded with liquor courtesy of numerous uniformed friends, associates of Ainslie's, and some old colleagues from Jubilee's regiment. Her Ma and Pa sat either side of the fireplace, listening to *Music While You Work* on the radio. Cecilia was tucked on to Earl's lap, her white-socked feet hanging lax, doll-like, between his well-pressed trousered legs. Earl's new precious baby . . . Ida did not mind his fancy for the child. She felt sure enough of herself not to be jealous. Her Pa had worked hard all through the war until he was stood down last September. There had been a parade before the King in Hyde Park. With the lifting of the black-out to a dim-out he deserved a few quiet family moments. They had all come to hope that the end was in sight until Billy died. The war was not over. Not yet. Besides, Ida was waiting for news of Jack.

'Don't Fence Me In' the brass band on the radio tried to swing, and Ida out of habit hummed a little. She had sung for the programme many times, until they stopped voices because girls in the munitions factories downed tools too often, to copy down the words.

'Aren't you going to join the others?' she asked, not surprised at her Pa, but curious at her Ma's reluctance. After all, a garden party full of West End celebrities, writers, socialites, handsome officers, was the kind of setting her mother had always aspired to.

'Laddered my nylons . . .' Denise yanked up her skirt to reveal a long white sliver of skin beside the black seam.

'I'll lend you another pair . . .' Ida suggested.

'Don't bother. I've had a good look. I'm cosy now.' Denise sighed, threw a red-stained cigarette butt at the pine cones in the grate, then walked unsteadily to the bar for a refill. Her grey hairs were getting harder to conceal, the bottle blonde more violently yellow and stained at the front from the constant spiralling of cigarette smoke.

'What's yours, Earl. Same again?' Denise expertly filled two glasses with gin and black-market olives without waiting for his answer, not even bothering to give him a glance.

'OK,' he said, watching his wife warily. Ida leant over him to kiss the top of Cecilia's head: 'Comfortable too, sweetheart?' she said.

Her Pa crooked a finger to whisper in her ear. 'Your Ma had this Canadian guy. Killed. Last week.' The long dark look Earl gave her made Ida recoil. He was glad, yet he had the strangest affection for Denise that enabled him to stand by her even in this fraudulent grief. A gleam in Earl's eyes suggested that this had been the last opportunity for Denise to hurt him. She was too old, too tired, and too burnt by her flirtation to do more than live with regrets from now on. The war would soon be over; her final fling. He did not want her soul — she could be unfaithful to him in her thoughts a million times. All he wanted was her body, her fair, ageing body, to be his, alone.

Ida went back into the garden, disturbed by this revelation, searching for Ainslie as a reminder of more wholesome feelings. He sensed her looking, and drew himself out of a conversation to be near her.

'Come over here. I don't want any photographer getting the two of us, and "confirming rumours" again,' she said.

Ida led him to a quiet corner behind the forsythia, now a thick screen of green.

'Kiss me,' she said.

'What's the matter?'

'I just wanted a kiss, that's all.' He obliged at length.

'You don't regret opening the house?' He held her close, reassuring her.

'No. Jubilee would have had a lovely time — the end of the tyrant. He'd have talked about it all day, phoned up his friends for the latest news from the Rhine . . . You know how he liked parties, club life.'

'I think he'd be even more pleased if you'd mend the roof.' Ainslie pointed up at the guttering, where a clump of corydalis was growing thick.

Ida laughed. 'I'm not tempting fate. Only when the war's really over . . .' She tried to sound bright, but she was not very convincing. Ida still had not named their wedding-day.

'Only when the war's over. God, I'll be glad when nobody ever has to say that again.' Ainslie sighed. Without thinking he put his arms round her shoulders and started to lead her back to the guests.

'Don't Ainslie. Not in front of everyone. Not yet.' Ida slipped out of his grasp, and ran ahead. Of course, Uncle Billy's death had not helped, Ainslie reminded himself. And there was the young cousin, Jack — she was always fretting about him. She did not want to make an announcement, and tempt fate: yet Ainslie wondered why Ida thought the Furies were not looking when they kissed round the back of the kitchen hedge.

Later that day the visitors all took the train back to London, continuing the party on board, and arriving at Victoria warm and inebriated. Only a few lucky ones like Maud French and her top-brass husband had driven to Kent in an official car. But yet again Ainslie had managed to fiddle petrol for his own vehicle. 'This *is* essential business,' he said, as he and Earl gently lifted Gran into the back seat. 'Shelter-marshals' recuperation programme . . .'

Ida hurriedly locked all the doors of Hartmere and boarded the windows, this last out of the habit of security, rather than need. It was hard to believe that what was left standing would definitely be there next week.

It was such a warm, gentle day; they did not drive fast in order to economise on the fuel, and to give Gran a smooth ride. With the hood down there was not much need for speech. Ida sat in front, Earl, Gran and Cecilia on the back seat. Denise, in a sudden revival of defiance, had elected to go on the train with the rest of the revellers.

Ida glanced back, and saw that Cecilia was holding Gran's hand and stroking it absently while she looked out at cows and sheep in the fields. Ida caught her Gran's eye, and they smiled at each other fondly.

'Had a good day Gran?'

'Lovely.' Gran nodded, and closed her eyes for a nap. Her big bun was awry, a pin dangled down on a loose hair at one side. Ida leant back and removed it in case it fell insect-like into the collar of Gran's black dress and startled her awake.

At Bayswater, it took Earl and Ainslie all their strength to lift Gran out of the car and carry her to the snuggy. She did not stir as they laid her on the bed, and Ida became anxious.

'I can't undress her,' she said. 'She's very heavy, and I don't want to disturb her. I'll cover her with the blankets, she feels a bit cold. Do you think she's all right, Ainslie, should I call the doctor just in case?'

'Her skin colour is fine, and she's not in pain. I think she's just very sleepy after a lot of sun and the car ride. Why not check on her in the morning, and if she's at all uncomfortable, call the doctor then?'

'OK. We'll just say goodbye.' She and Cecilia crept into the snuggy, and as Ida put out her hand she realised she was still clutching the fallen hairpin, something to play with. While Cecilia clambered up next to Gran's inert body and planted a clinging, wet kiss on her cheek, Ida put the hairpin back in the old china pot on the chest of drawers. It was the same little flowered pot Gran had kept for years, the one Uncle Ted used when he first plaited Ida's hair to match her smart new dress: probably the one Gran used when she put up her pale brown locks, to go out courting with her Joseph.

'Gran?' Ida spun round, suddenly scared that they had been very foolish to give the old lady such a tumultuous day, surrounded by smart people idly chattering, and far too much noise.

Gran was fast asleep, peaceful, and Cecilia lay quiet by her side, with her arm laid cosily on the old woman's mountainous, spreading breast. Ida kissed her Gran's pearly forehead, lifted the child in her arms and went out to find Ainslie.

Her Pa was waiting by the door. 'I'll sit with Gran until Uncle Jim gets back,' he offered. 'He usually looks in on her during the night . . . And Josephine's here in the mornings. There's someone around all the time. Don't you worry. I'll make a cuppa first, in case she wakes up thirsty.'

'Goodbye Pa.'

He kissed her farewell, placed six precious sugar cubes in Cecilia's lap, and went back to the scullery to brew up the inevitable life-saver, a pot of strong, sweet tea.

Gran caught a chill, and deteriorated rapidly. She could not speak clearly in those last few days, but made her needs felt by a frown, a nod, or an unmistakeable signal from her broad fingers. She refused to go to hospital, and when the doctor examined her, the exhaustion in her eyes moved him to follow her wishes.

The surviving Garlands closed ranks with the approaching death of their mother. Earl, Josephine, Jim. Even George occasionally turned up with some expensive, futile offering; light bulbs, clothing coupons, American vitamins. The others organised their days so that someone could be with Gran at all times. Ida felt almost redundant, such was the instant co-operation amongst the older relatives. Grudgingly, they let her have half an hour or so each evening, before her duties at the Au Fait began.

Ida sat beside Gran, who had been freshly sponged and changed by Josephine that afternoon. Sidney was not too keen on the lingering presence of her illness in the house, and made himself scarce; a cinema double bill steadied his nerves before a night's work with the playing cards.

Josephine in her neat way had buttoned Gran's nightdress to the throat, and folded a shawl precisely over her chest. It made the old lady look curiously innocent. As a child Ida had disliked seeing Gran lie in bed, strangely inert, threatening even in stillness. But now Gran had shrunk, her whole body seemed thinner and light. Her hair was spread out on the pillow, brushed silvery and thin, but with kinks in it from being kept up in a bun. Ida had a fancy that Gran looked almost youthful, the lines of her face smoothed out in sleep so that she lost the craggy grimness of her widowhood.

A thin sigh escaped Gran's lips, such a soft, airy sound that it could have been the wish of a girl hoping for her lover to appear. Gran was fading fast. Ida began to cry not in sadness, but with joy, for Gran was so clearly waiting on the threshold of death for her beloved Joseph to welcome her into that void that Gran always liked to call, 'the great majority'. A place that was very full these days, not only with lost lovers, but the blasted pieces of millions of despised souls. 'The great majority', where no minorities exist, where all souls come to unite, casting aside cruel, unjust, earthly distinctions.

'Goodbye, Gran,' Ida whispered. 'All my love.'

Ida heard the back door click and left the snuggy. Her Pa had come for his turn; Ida was glad he should be the one to take her place, the eldest Garland boy.

'I'm going to the club,' she said simply. 'I don't think Gran's going to be here by morning. I'm sure she'd want me to do my job. Don't you think so? Do you mind?'

'No Ida, don't you worry. It's my place to be here. I'll give you a ring if anything should happen.' Earl straightened his tie, perhaps out of nervousness, perhaps out of respect for his Ma, anxious to keep her company in the best way he could. Ida left him sitting bolt upright beside his mother in the snuggy, nervously lacing his long, thin fingers on his knees, and watching Gran's face with his sad dark eyes, tearless.

On the night of VE day, Ida and Ainslie walked in Hyde Park. It had been a blazing hot day; after Churchill's broadcast there were torrential thunderstorms, but later the skies cleared and a huge bonfire was lit. Dampness from the rain lifted up in the warm air, as if the earth itself was breathing. The atmosphere exhaled hope. They walked past the fire, in the direction of Westminster, where the huge crowd stood silent for the midnight chimes of Big Ben.

'So.' Ainslie kissed her longingly. 'Do you believe it's all over now?'

'Oh yes.' All she wanted to do was cry, for Gran, for Jubilee, for dear sweet Uncle Billy. Ainslie picked her up off her feet and held her long and hard. She knew he understood and would not intrude on the past.

'Let's go back, wake up Cecilia,' he suggested. 'Little poppet — it's an important night for her.' They walked slowly through the crowds to the Ambassador where the music and dancing was in full swing, but did not join in. Upstairs, Ida woke up Cecilia and held her up to the window, for her first view of London at peace. Ainslie took Cecilia on his lap, then hugged mother and child close to him. Silently they watched the searchlights patterning the sky, thinking of all the good people in their world who were not there to share the day.

'Two things she'll remember,' Ida whispered sadly. 'Her Grandma's funeral, and getting up in the night, when the war ended.'

Weeks passed. At the Au Fait Ida was going through her set with Ivor Clarke, when a barmaid brought a message: a soldier was asking for her most particularly. With a premonition, Ida hurried from the bandstand.

'Hallo old girl,' he said, leaning on the bar.

She hugged him close, tears of relief filling her eyes. Crossly, she brushed a hand across her face.

403

'Jack! Fancy coming here when I have to be on! You'll have to wait so we can talk later . . . Ooh, it's so good to see you!'

Jack gave a long whistle. 'Time hasn't done you any damage, that's for sure. You look terrific, Ida.'

'Well thank you!' But she could not say the same for him. He looked years older; tanned, fit, lean of course, but different. Hardened. Jack's eyes did not light up and he lost his face in his beer glass as soon as the words were spoken.

'Go ahead now. Don't mind me. I've been wanting to hear you . . . Soak up the atmosphere . . .' He was not eyeing the talent on the dance floor the way he used to. If he had bothered to look, there were game-looking girls, still in their uniforms, or one or two sophisticates in black he might have fancied. Instead, he sat hunched on a bar stool hardly aware of the noisy, highly-charged atmosphere of the club packed with its regulars. All types of uniforms: 'other ranks' as the Americans were known, the French, the Dutch, Canadians, Australians, everyone prolonging the victory mood as long as they possibly could.

'Here, sit here. I keep this booth for honoured guests.' Ida dragged him into one of the curved alcoves, ordered him a beer and whisky chaser. 'Will you be all right?'

'Sure. I've got plenty to keep me busy, I've got plans . . .' he said, drawing letters from his pocket. Presumably they were his demob papers.

Naturally she rearranged her programme and sang old favourites just to please him: 'Sunny Side of the Street'; 'Honeysuckle Rose'; 'Melancholy Baby'. But then she segued into a more recent hit, 'Is You Is or Is You Ain't My Baby?', and for a finale, 'I'm Beginning to See the Light'. She got them to play a spotlight on his table. Jack did not take his gaze off her. But he had that resisting, hard-eyed look she had forgotten about, and which his last years in the Middle East had obviously developed. Not callousness exactly, but a burning, resentful desire not to be moved. Ida felt apprehensive; it was as if their last meeting had never happened.

'I hear you're going to get married again,' he announced as she joined him afterwards. 'Ainslie Curtis. Isn't he a bit long in the tooth for you? Loaded I suppose. Not that I've got anything against business marriages . . .' He laughed at her, a horrid, harsh sound.

'It's not like that and you know it Jack Garland.' All at once she found again the even, imperturbable voice she always had to adopt for him, in all those ancient, rankling conversations. 'Ainslie's only eight years older than I am, not even forty! I've known him all my working life, and he's been good to me. We love each other and we're going to be happy.' She heard herself and was glad: it took her cousin, her fool of a Jack, to get the truth out of her. Emboldened by her statement, Ida out-stared him, wondering how long it was going to take before they could be friends again.

'We'll have the wedding as soon as everything's calmed down and we have time to organise one,' she added. 'Oh God, Jack, why couldn't Gran hang on just a little bit longer?'

He hissed on his cigarette and shrugged: the old Jack, acting tough. 'That's life. No one said it was fair. Did you know the old girl put the boarding-house in my name? Josephine's livid. So's Ottley. What a turn-up, eh?'

'Oh Jack — that's wonderful! Gives you a start! Will you sell it?' Ida said, thinking that his casual tone suggested it.

'Sell it?' he roared at her belligerently. 'Prime property in central London, overlooking the Park? With the war just ended? What d'you take me for, a bleeding idiot?'

'Ssh Jack. Keep your voice down!' Ida found herself reacting as she would to any pushy serviceman, and was sad that Jack could not or would not drop his front.

'I'm going to convert it. Turn it into a high-class hotel. London's going to need new places. I'll probably get redevelopment money. Then there's Billy's shop. The goodwill and stock in that should fetch a bob or two.'

'Who owns it?'

'It's a lease. But the business came to Gran as next of kin. I expect Josephine and Earl will want a piece of the action. They'd be fools not to come in with me, if they've got any spare cash.'

Then Ida saw that Jack was terrified of being sucked back into the fecklessness of his old life, before the army, and needed to start out as he meant to go on. He had the desperation of a man veering to avoid a corner ahead of him on the road.

'Thing is . . .' Jack stubbed out a cigarette with his old fierceness. 'I might be getting married. There's this girl I met. Last time I was home on leave. I think she might be pregnant. There's going to be a load of babies nine months after VE night. Not that I mind. It's time I settled down anyway.'

Ida was appalled at this news. He was too confused, too angry, to take up these responsibilities.

'And what's her name? Your — fiancée?'

'Annette,' he said stiffly.

He would do his duty and marry, but Ida knew he did not love this girl. Maybe she was his insurance in case of failure. Someone to be there, someone to blame. Ida was so worried for him.

Just then a coloured American soldier came into the club. Timidly at first, he eased himself on to a bar stool. The girl behind the counter served him with a big smile, and before long, another girl had sidled into a seat beside him. At first the soldier looked self-conscious, quietly grateful, but when he spotted a couple of other black Americans at a table by the bandstand, he straightened, raised his glass, and his back began to broaden.

Jack looked on with interest. 'Get many of them in here, do you?' he asked.

'Quite a few. There's lots of them around, waiting to get sent home.' She laughed, remembering a frequent joke of the establishment. 'They think the name's funny. Au Fait, if you say it the American way means the opposite of nigger. A whitey. Ofays. It's French of course, for *in the know*.'

Jack registered offence. 'You don't have to tell me. You always think everyone else is pig-ignorant.'

Ida decided to ignore his aggression, and chat on, hoping to mellow him. 'They like Ivor's music. Late at night I get a lot of Archer Street men in. I put a bottle of whisky on a table if I recognise anyone, and we have good sessions. You should stay late sometime.' Jack did not respond.

'So they're popular?' he asked, persisting with his topic, pushing a thumb at the black men.

'My girls don't like the way the white GIs treat them. Pure racism. It's a pretty general feeling.' In spite of herself she went on. 'British love of the underdog . . . or hypocrisy? What do you think?'

'I don't believe in mixed marriages. I saw too many problems in India.'

'How can you say that! You sound like a . . .'

'You wait. Wait till we get boatloads of ex-servicemen from Jamaica flooding in. Jobs will be scarce. It'll be a different story then. Then there'll be no sympathy. Can't say I blame them.'

'What do you mean?' Ida's face flamed.

Jack laughed. 'You always fall for it, Ida. I love to put the wind up you. But I mean it. That's the difference between you and me. I'm a pragmatist. What d'you think it's going to be like for that feller when he gets back home, after he's been well-treated here? They won't be able to keep him down . . . and the same thing's going to happen here. They're going to want a proper place, and it won't be given to them. You know that as well as I do.'

Perhaps it was his own insecurity, his desperate ambition to make good that drove him to say such things. Suddenly Jack relented, as if he knew he had gone too far. He leant forward, and chucked her under the chin.

'Tell you what, though, Ida. The music's great. And you sing better than I've ever heard you.' He gave an emphatic nod, as if the oracle had spoken, then turned to the band with an easy bounce of rhythm in one knee. But Ida saw how his fist tightened, and she felt desperately sorry.

Ida wanted to get married quietly, but Ainslie was outraged at the idea. It was his first wedding, and he wanted the whole world to witness his commitment. The honeymoon was easier. They were going to spend several months at Hartmere. Ainslie loved the place because it was where he had fallen in love with her.

So a string of black cars, white-ribboned, lined the street of the Kensington registry office, and crowds jammed the pavements, not so much well-wishers as star-gazers. Peering at the guests who hurried up under the striped awning that covered the steps, they spotted revue performers, actresses, journalists and writers. A couple of bandleaders' faces were better known than those of several distinguished jazzmen who slipped in unnoticed. Josephine Garland, dressed to kill in borrowed white fox, was delighted to get a cheer from the onlookers. ENSA shows had given her career an unforeseen revival and much appreciated praise in her declining years.

Ida wore a lace dress from Norman Hartnell, covered in silver moon and star embroidery. Tommy Trevino came out of retirement to lead a band of the original Diplomats at the Ambassador Hotel where the reception was held.

Veronica danced with Jack, and they glided as stylishly as ever they had, before the war. His fiancée, Annette, a pretty, fair girl, watched them from her seat at the edge of the floor. Shy, admiring, impressed by the ambience.

'Maid of honour.' Jack gave Veronica's sharply-tailored satin suit a cool once-over. 'When's it going to be your turn? You're the same age as Ida, aren't you?' His hand pulled a little more urgently into the small of her back.

Veronica laughed. 'Just the wrong side of thirty. I know what you mean. I haven't had time to think about it.'

'I know. Ida told me you've been a bit of a heroine, getting Jews out of Europe. Good for you. Now. I've got a proposition,' he launched in, never one for small talk.

'I bet you have. Weddings are the place for old scores to be settled, isn't that right? Especially before you tie your own knot.' She gave him a downright wicked leer and pressed herself against him.

Jack blushed. If there was one thing he could not handle, it was a woman being crude. 'Jesus, Veronica. It's Ida's day. I don't know what you're . . .'

Veronica's laugh was irrepressibly vulgar. It was a long time since she had had the heart or spirit to be wickedly embarrassing. 'Just testing . . .' She could see he had something else on his mind and stopped dancing. 'Want a smoke? You're talking business, apparently . . .'

'Yes, you see, I have this property . . .' He tucked a confidential hand under her elbow, and led her to the bar. He did not bother to introduce Annette.

Ida meanwhile climbed on to the bandstand amidst loud cheers, and sang one last song before slipping away with Ainslie.

'Come on back to my place,
There's a whole lot of booze at my place,

There'll be you and me and the baby makes three,
We'll have a real good time at my place . . .'

Only this time she had asked Tommy to arrange the piece as a slow, blues-tinged ballad, and she directed her words with a loving, mischievous smile, at Ainslie. By the time she finished singing there was hardly a dry eye in the place.

Ainslie and Ida took a long summer off from work that year, putting substitute acts in at the Au Fait. It was not strictly a honeymoon, but reconstruction time at Hartmere. They had made grand plans for the house, for it was to be their retreat from London, where new plays, new shows, and Ida's development of her recording career would take shape. They wanted to hold starry weekend gatherings and have inspired ideas in late-night conversations. The old Tudor barn was rethatched and turned into a music room for Ida. The acoustics inside the wood-beamed space were imperfect, but the knowledge that no one would hear the racket of rehearsals more than made up for that.

The front lawn was returfed (no one was remotely interested in growing vegetables anywhere on the property, in reaction to the war), and a pony for Cecilia installed in a meadow just the other side of the old moat.

'I'm not touching the chapel,' Ainslie said. 'It's my thinking place.'

'And the leather sofa in the living-room stays.' Ida was definite.

When building work was partly finished, Ida began to unpack a few things in the living-room. Ainslie leant against the door, observing her; she could feel him admiring. She turned a Chinese blue and white vase in her small, dark hands, trying to decide whether to put it on the high shelf above the fireplace.

'Will you lift it up for me?' she said.

Ainslie came nearer and kissed her. She had a whim to make love to him, there and then . . . Ainslie always loved her beautifully, with nothing but a wonder that sex could become so much more than pleasure. But sometimes, she wished she could let go, have fun, and shed herself of an unbearable intensity, as if she could not quite believe she was allowed to love again.

'What about this screen, Ainslie? By the door, or behind the sofa?'

'Behind the sofa.' He helped her unfold the lacquered coromandel. 'Valuable. I should think. It looks ancient.'

'Don't you like it?' she asked quickly, suddenly conscious of her attachment to Jubilee's things. 'I'm quite prepared to put things away if you can't live with them . . .' Ida was embarrassed to find herself blushing, not wishing to hurt his feelings.

'Not at all. You want this room exactly as it was. I think that's right. It's a room to retire to after a heavy meal, to take up an old leather book, and fall asleep, side by side. I hope you and I do that when we're old.' He risked making a joke of his dearest wish.

Ida saw what he meant, and answered lightly too. 'You'll never grow old. You're not the type.'

'Is that a criticism or a compliment?'

'Today it's a compliment, because I love you rather more than usual. Let's go and look at the painters.' She went ahead of him, deciding she had said quite enough.

When the rooms upstairs had been unlocked, they were discovered to be in a terrible condition. Loose slates all over the roof meant that rainwater had rotted floorboards and stained plaster with verdigris. Ida let Ainslie have his way, and each bedroom was now being decorated with a dramatic theme. Velvet for the *Gone With the Wind Room*; brocade and glass in appreciation of Noël Coward salons; cream satin and maple furniture, for Astaire's Hollywood musicals, and for Ida, the ebony, blue and black of jazz.

'When people come we can put them up with Fred or Vivien . . . or Noël . . .' Ainslie was good at poking fun at himself.

'Certainly catering for all tastes,' Ida murmured, suggestively. But it felt right that he put his own stamp on the place too.

While work was being finished, they were staying in a small pub on the other side of Hartmere. The publican was only too glad to have customers with all the airmen packing up and going home. Ainslie and Ida shared a picnic supper with Cecilia at a wooden table outside the bar, before her bedtime.

'Ainslie read me a story,' she demanded. This was one of his most brilliant accomplishments, as far as she could see.

'Right. See you later Mum,' he said, and the two of them disappeared.

Ida sat sipping her beer. Down the lane she recognised the unmistakable hips of Mrs Weekes, trundling home with a string bag strung on her handlebars. It seemed impossible that a bike could stay vertical when someone pedalled so slow. Faster! Ida wanted to say — faster! Then she realised that the urgency came from within her. A tension, a certainty that happiness lay in her own hands.

She went upstairs, and found Ainslie and Cecilia rapt in imagination, peering into the depths of an empty waste-paper basket.

'Ssh!' said Ainslie. 'It's the Heffalump pit.'

'Fallen in!' said Cecilia solemnly. 'Poor Pooh!'

'Well, you get him out, and Ainslie, come to bed . . .' Ida laughed. 'Ainslie's tired Cecilia — too much working . . .'

'Poor Ainslie,' Cecilia said, woeful, patting his hand.

'Now, cheer up, my dear, you can't feel sorry for the whole world . . .' Ainslie went on with his story as Ida closed the door.

Ida went to bed, and waited for him. The mattress was lumpy, and the frame made a fantastic noise with the slightest movement.

'This bed has seen some action,' Ainslie joked, moments later, turning to Ida as he always did to fold her into his arms.

'Do you think anyone can hear us?' she whispered.

'Cecilia was fast asleep when I left her. Besides, she's across the corridor. We'd hear her if she had a dream, but she won't be disturbed by us, I'm sure.'

'No. I mean, in the bar downstairs.'

Ainslie bounced a little.

'Ooh, ssh!' Ida hissed in alarm.

'Great Scott we're married. Why do we have to keep sex a secret?'

'I don't want my entire life in a glare of publicity. I know you love it, of course.'

'Publicity?' Ainslie swiped at his forehead and roared with laughter. 'We're in a pub bed in a Kent village surrounded by cabbages with a couple of old men supping on their pints downstairs and you're complaining about the publicity!' His laughter made the bed rattle even more.

411

Then he pretended to be serious. 'OK. I'll make a rule. Until closing time, we'll just lie here side by side. You're not to move, whatever I do. I'll just . . . warm you up . . .'

He held his body away from her, bending forward teasingly to cover her face with kisses and run his big hands, full of suggestions, over the outline of her figure. Ainslie's athletic, fair body flushed with ease and sexual pleasure. He was a tanned, golden-russet colouring, with a deep V of dark skin where he wore his shirt open-necked. Fair hairs, mixed a little with grey ones now, curled on his freckled chest. Ida brushed her fingertips on them, as he stirred her into a fair old frenzy for sex.

'What the hell,' she laughed, and the bed groaned violently as she climbed on top of him. Downstairs someone obligingly struck up a medley of wartime favourites on an out of tune upright, but Ida and Ainslie were lost to each other, and did not hear a single note.

The following Christmas saw the grand opening of Jack's hotel. He had begged and borrowed money from everyone, including Ida and Ainslie, raised a large bank loan through Felix with prompting from Veronica, and a sizeable mortgage against the existing boarding-house. He bought out the owners of number Two Salamanca Street, a tired couple who had stuck out the entire war of attrition on the spot, but when peace came, found that they were strangely unsettled in their home. The proceeds of sale were just what they wanted to retire to somewhere smaller near the coast.

Ida heard reports of his progress from her Pa or Uncle Jim; Jack himself was far too busy to come and see her. Ida did not mind, accepting that he had the young girl, Annette, to look after. She hoped he was spending his free time getting to know her. At least he allowed her and Ainslie to help, financially.

Jack knocked the two buildings into one with a series of corridors between. He had in mind all those luxurious establishments he had seen out East, swanky hotels in Egypt with aeroplane fans in palm tree courts, lively bars in the Lebanon with French chefs and succulent buffet tables. Of course in the dull climate of Bayswater, the effect he achieved was somewhat subdued, but confident and exciting nonetheless.

412

For the first night he hired an unremittingly professional swing dance band. None of the convolutions of rebop or bebop for Jack.

Uncle Jim had offered his services for the kitchens. No one could persuade him to play again, when the war ended.

'Nah, not the same,' he said, smiling cheerfully. 'I buggered my hands for music years ago. Besides, I like my food. It's a chance to be a sous-chef for someone good.'

'OK Uncle.' Jack drew heavily on a cigarette, determined not to be trapped by family favours. 'On condition you make the grade. I can't afford deadbeats.'

It was to Uncle Jim's credit that he took this piece of insolence from the family's military hero without rancour, not so much as an expressive roll of the eyeballs. But when he told Ida all about Jack's doings, he did so with a frightful barrage of expletives.

For the opening night, Ida drove up from Kent with Ainslie.

'I see what Uncle Jim means about exotic,' Ida said. The house was unrecognisable, which made her pleased, not sad. The old world had been bombed out of existence anyway, and there was no point in looking back. Why else had Gran left the place to Jack, if not to ensure that he had a serious chance of a new life? The old lady was a pragmatist, as he was.

The hotel façade gleamed white, double fronted, with glistening plate-glass windows. The privet had gone, replaced by discreetly swishing gravel and looped chains between pillars. Two palm trees flanked the portico of the entrance, and a pink neon sign above it scrawlingly glowed: The Salamanca Hotel.

'He's got a lot of style, your cousin,' Ainslie said. 'I hope it doesn't descend into a clip-joint. You never can tell with this neighbourhood.'

Ida laughed. 'Bayswater grew up out of brothels, Gran told me that.'

Jack came to greet them at the door. He stood proudly on a large coconut mat inserted inside a brass trim, with the cipher, SH, woven in green against the brown.

'Hallo Ida! Hallo Ainslie! What do you think?'

Ida was pleased to see him cheerful, too full of his new venture to be difficult with her tonight.

'Show me round. I want to see everything,' she said.

'See? Brass rails on the stairs. Matching doorplates. A lift for the luggage. Attention to detail. Like the army taught me. Uncle George was very handy about supplies . . . I reserved you a room upstairs to change. It's Ted's old room actually. Thought you'd like the view of the park. Oh. By the way, you remember Annette? My wife, as of last week.'

Annette stretched a hand out towards Ida, while the other clutched nervously at her new husband. She had put her hair up — looked older than she had when Ida first met her, at her own wedding. Her pregnancy was well advanced. Oh God, thought Ida — I never liked small blondes.

'A secret! Why did you . . . ? Congratulations, anyway!' Ida had to be kind, for the girl's sake.

'Isn't he awful?' Annette said, in a girlish, attractive voice, with a Somerset lilt in it. 'First he can't make his mind up, then he rushes me off, and it's done in a minute.'

Ida felt sorry for her. She was a country girl, adrift in a big city and no match at all for Jack.

'See you downstairs, then.' Jack left them, worrying about his other duties, with Annette trotting behind.

Ida and Ainslie went up the widened staircase, admiring the handwoven carpeting and the restored dado rail. 'We never had that before. He must have copied it from number Two next door,' Ida commented.

She bathed, and slipped into a velvet dress, a tight black sheath: her thinness was hard-won and she intended to reveal every supple curve of it. Ainslie had given her a sparkling necklace, to match his first ring.

'How do I look?' she said, parading in front of him when he emerged pink and steaming from the bath.

'Take it off,' he ordered, unwrapping the towel from his hips.

'Oh Ainslie.' She pretended reluctance, sighing. 'Then I'll have to do my make-up all over again.' She stepped out of her dress and lay on the bed ready for him. His body smelled almost too clean, until he exerted himself and the warm, arousing aura of sex mingled with the perfume she had just been dabbing on her wrists.

Later, they went downstairs. The hotel bar was filling up with guests. Ainslie had helped with publicity and sent an invitation list for Jack, so Ida recognised the usual London free-loaders, actresses, rentable aristocrats, all indispensable for the opening of anything fashionable in town. A gaggle of the Press hung around the bar, hoping to spot or invent new connections among the gossip column favourites.

But there were others that she did not know.

'Who are all these people?' she asked Jack.

'He's a property dealer. Those two are local MPs. That man was Colonel in my regiment. I tell you, some of these army types are pretty keen to get on the heading of some notepaper, now the war's over. It's not going to be easy in civvy street.'

'I didn't know you were so well connected,' she teased.

'You don't think Ida. I left the army a Major. Not many boys with my background did that.'

No wonder rivalry shone in those hard blue eyes. She had failed to acknowledge that he had finally grown up. When he came back from the war, she had thought he would be her lonely soldier, her problematical, charming but wild old Jack. No more. This realisation was confusing, difficult — she had believed that her success alone was enough for them both to feel good.

'I'm sorry,' she said, impulsively. 'I should have thought. You've been very brave to do all this.'

'It's got to be different . . . I've got to make a go of it,' he said.

The band started up. 'Where's Josephine tonight?' Ida asked, beginning to see what he truly intended.

'Busy. In a club. This isn't her scene, anyway.'

Ida began to tremble with sadness. He had broken away, broken the spell. He was completely a white man. In this new world he feared race would be an issue. He did not want to live in the shadow of their secret understanding.

'Want a dance Ida?'

'What about your wife? Where's Annette?'

'Having a rest.' He smiled with a grim sort of satisfaction. 'She'll be down in a minute. She loves a good dance . . .'

'Are you sure you want to be seen with me?' Ida could not resist an inflammatory remark. 'Touch of the tarbrush . . .'

'Ida. That's enough.' She could see he was serious. It was so sad that their affinity was at an end. 'You do understand, don't you Ida? I have to . . .'

415

'Oh yes. I understand.' She wished he was wrong, but this was the way of the world.

Then he squeezed her hand. 'Come on. After all, you're a celebrity. It'll be good for the publicity.'

To a little spatter of applause, Ida and Jack took the floor first of all the guests, while the drummer tisked away at the standard, wartime American dancing pace. And the song Jack had chosen for the band's opening number? 'When Dreams Come True'. Ida hummed it, feeling sad, because there was nothing more to be said.

Irresistibly, the music took over. The band began to play a current hit, 'Blue Skies', driving it into a compelling, swinging beat. Ida could feel Jack relaxing into it.

'Come on,' she said, 'let's show them how to do it . . .' and Jack could not help smiling as she swayed into her jivey, fancy footwork. They danced together as one, memories of joyous sounds, happy songs, jazz days, shared in every step they took.

Ainslie watched the scene. He saw the photographers line up in the best corner, and ordered the head waiter to dim the lights while cameras clicked for the papers and magazines.

When the floor filled up, Ida pulled away from Jack. 'Look, there's Annette. You should dance the next one with her. I'll be off. Goodbye Jack.'

'You aren't leaving?'

'No. You know what I mean. Good luck.'

'Luck doesn't come in to it . . .' he said, letting her go as the music ended.

Ida walked through the crowd until she found Ainslie. Awareness of their recent love-making made them soft with each other, enjoying the smallest touch.

'Hallo, my Lady Jazz.'

'I need a drink,' she said. 'Band's good, isn't it?'

'I like watching you dance with Jack.' Ainslie kissed her bare shoulder. 'You fit together like brother and sister; you do the steps as if you've practised for years on the parlour carpet, getting ready for all those others who'll fall for your charms . . . Comfortable. Not the way lovers dance, but loving all the same. It made a very good picture.'

'Yes,' said Ida, lightly, 'it was very sweet.'

416